PATHETIC LITERATURE

Also by Eileen Myles

For Now

Evolution

Afterglow (a dog memoir)

I Must Be Living Twice / New and Selected Poems, 1975–2014

Snowflake / different streets

Inferno (a poet's novel)

The Importance of Being Iceland / travel essays in art

Sorry, Tree

Tow (with drawings by artist Larry R. Collins)

Skies

on my way

Cool for You

School of Fish

Maxfield Parrish / Early & New Poems

The New Fuck You / Adventures in Lesbian Reading (with Liz Kotz)

Chelsea Girls

Not Me

1969

Bread and Water

Sappho's Boat

A Fresh Young Voice from the Plains

Polar Ode (with Anne Waldman)

The Irony of the Leash

PATHETIC LITERATURE

AN ANTHOLOGY

EDITED BY

EILEEN MYLES

Grove Press
New York

FIRST EDITION

Published simultaneously in Canada
Printed in the United States of America

First Grove Atlantic hardcover edition: November 2022

Library of Congress Cataloging-in-Publication data
is available for this title.

ISBN 978-0-8021-5715-7
eISBN 978-0-8021-5717-1

Grove Press
an imprint of Grove Atlantic
154 West 14th Street
New York, NY 10011

Distributed by Publishers Group West

groveatlantic.com

22 23 24 25 10 9 8 7 6 5 4 3 2 1

for East River Park
and everyone who played
there, who lived and landed and
leapt through the branches
of its trees, its trees
and the activists
who sat there too
on the coldest
morning ever

Contents

Introduction

In general poems are pathetic and diaries are pathetic. Really Literature is pathetic. Ask anyone who doesn't care about literature. They would agree. If they bothered at all.

Perhaps the only accomplishment here is I'm saying that as an insider. This book is a kind of hollow. All these pieces of the rock (meaning Literature) long and short are just what I like. The invention of pathetic literature surely is Sei Shōnagon's The Pillow Book. More than a thousand years ago she kept her diaries, her interminable and adorable lists, her sovereignty to herself. Being discovered, she admits, kind of ruined things.

In light of our different pace I'd say we're ready for ruin.

I need to start this book at the beginning which is to say how I landed on pathetic as a badge of distinction. In the late twentieth century there was a movement in visual arts known briefly as Pathetic Masculinity that has since vanished as a genre and simply became part of what we know. What exemplified pathetic art then was an orientation to crafts, to feeling, to the handmade and diaristic. It was kind of dykey. Using cuddly and abject stuff like stuffed animals rather than producing work that was determinedly abstract. There was a readymade aspect to a lot of it. And it wasn't just any stuffed rabbit, it was the one you carried with you for all twenty-eight years of your childhood and now even to look at it produces trauma so the objects had secondary meaning too. Which is how it got to be art. And I have to say that pathetic art really pissed me off. Right out of the gate it resembled feminism. I mean give credit where credit is due! Feminist artists had long been appropriating crafts—not to be "natural" as the late Mike Kelley once said in an interview (as opposed to his own "'ironic'" use of similar materials) but to deliberately hijack the production of doilies and hand-sewn cushions and knowhow *away* from the den of the patriarchal family in order to pump up the pleasure in collective women's spaces and community activism.

Other feminists, Eleanor Antin and Mary Kelly, seized on the ubiquitous graphs and diagrams of sixties and seventies conceptual art to chart the veracities of domesticity like being descended upon by in-laws when you had a new kid. I heard one tale of a giant abstract painting on women's land that basically was a giant menstrual chart of everyone living there. Feminists were pretty funny and also were using the materials of art to make a statement, to undo something, there was a utopian purpose as opposed to Mike's being sad or Paul McCarthy bad. Their art was boyishly satanic cause they had suffered too. Nobody in the art world of the 90s "enjoyed" patriarchy (punk was against it) but good men and bad men and especially sad men made a terrific living in there whereas women more likely reaped the pathetic jouissance of community and later academic jobs. The story about seventies feminism is that it was dominated by white women which is not really true but what feminist artists and activists did share was a desire to undo white male dominance and the system itself. The work had a message or was definitely floating in one.

Which gets me to literature in that there are parts of the literary world where one can readily make political meaning with the messily colloquial, the hand-writ, the felt. I mean who gave Judy Grahn the authority to enclose an entire world, all its institutions, in a single poem, "A Woman Is Talking to Death." Having been tossed from the military for being a lesbian in the early sixties she then turns out to be uniquely prepared to know everything. In 18 pages, so I've included the whole thing here. I'm eager for everyone to know this poem, a moment in time and a political folk art masterpiece. The tone shifts at will from vulnerability to pompousness. Lawrence Braithwaite in a chapter from *Wigger* slides a peephole open onto a druggy vortex where by means of a bit of graffiti scrawled on an office door an abused kid sends a valentine <u>and</u> rats on his teacher at once. It's pithy horror syncopated by a poet (in prose). The variegated pieces of the rock in this collection make a whirling system of difference, young, established, yes Beckett's in here, that old weirdo. But Gertrude Stein isn't. I actually don't think of her as pathetic. Burroughs is not pathetic. Ginsberg is. I had to stop myself while this volume is only immense.

I am definitely interested in the surprising edges or the forced march of a riveting pattern. And there's something indeterminately true about each and every one. Sometimes it's in the writer's very willingness to make *that* gesture at all. To make *this* of that.

Like Robert Musil said of Robert Walser, he was "sui generis, inimitable," his work being "not a suitable foundation for a literary genre." Is that praise? Like you couldn't start anything *here*. But what if that lack was the organizing force?

Samuel Delany tells us that in the gay porno theaters of Times Square (circa 1970–1989) men were not only getting blow jobs but were very often making friends. He essays for the dirty fealty of contact over networks. He met his own life partner in such a way. Each of these writers has a discomfort or a restlessness that exceeds their category somehow. Work that acknowledges a boundary then passes it. "It" being the hovering monolith, that bigger thing that confirms. There's no institution, or subculture, where any of this all belongs. This gathering is not so much queer as adamantly, eloquently strange, and touching, as if language itself had to pause. Less an avant-garde than something really beside the point. Until it begins to steamroll. In literature there are so many little empires. If you begin in the state of poetry and I guess a great percentage of the writing here is that or is poetry-influenced so what we're really talking about is a teeming hive of mini-fiefdoms. They don't make an arc—unless it's toward devastation like Victor Hugo.

I've collected whoever's in here for their dedication to a moment that bends, not in a "gay" way but you know how when you're walking towards the horizon it seemingly dips.* And you feel something. That's pathetic. It's an empathetic thing. The light shifts and biologically we turn too. People get different. Take the word *crepuscular*. The blue moment. Some creatures only come out right then. A lot of the world is

---

* I got this idea from the poet Brian Teare.

trained to think of that part of existence as vacation or what happens during drinks but I'm saying that no I think it feels like a life. As a citizen of the United States I'm always surprised by where I live and how I live. Looking back on 2003 when George Bush was bombing the hell out of Iraq (and Joe Proulx shows us in "An Obituary" what that looked like "on the ground") it's clear the destruction of the world trade center handed George an opportunity.

Same way Hurricane Sandy is creating one right now here in New York (after doing nothing for nine years), turning East River Park, the most human playground where little league kids play and families barbecue on the poor side of the river into a vivid real estate opportunity. Rather than "freedom and democracy" they are calling it "flood control." Because natural disasters yield development.

When I talk about the bigger world, bigger literature, bigger things that's what I mean. Something with enormous resources and a singleness of purpose. Something that puts women's names on storms. Is it just white supremacy and patriarchy and capitalism rolled into one. Does it have another name? Gwendolyn Brooks reporting the mundanity of being the only Black people in a movie theater and her 1950s narrator Maude Martha, lovingly noting the apricot stain on her partner's shirt bring on the embodiment of being Black in this country more than a Hollywood account of Fred Hampton being shot in his bed.

Trayvon Martin got shot in a gated community because there were no Black people "in there" though there were. Racism is a language in the minds of white people that gets read onto the bodies of Black people (undoubtedly occupying their minds too) so that just being with his skittles in the wrong place is reason enough for a kid to be killed. The skittles are pathetic. Everyone knows about them. When Frank Wilderson describes (in Afropessimism) going as a teenager to Fred Hampton's bullet-ridden apartment (which the Chicago Police Department kept open like a cautionary amusement park for ninety days) on a date, his story authenticates the horror. It inhabits it.

Cindy Sheehan's 25-year-old son, U.S. Army Specialist Casey Sheehan was killed in action in Iraq and so she met several months later with other military families and Bush who then pretty much kept bombing and destroying Iraq in the name of freedom. So Cindy Sheehan wanted to talk to him again. She sat at the end of George Bush's street in Crawford, Texas, and waited. They called it Camp Casey. 1,500 people joined her. Sheehan said "if he even *starts* to say freedom and democracy, I'm gonna say, bullshit. You tell me the truth. You tell me that my son died for oil. You tell me that my son died to make your friends rich. . . . You tell me that, you don't tell me my son died for freedom and democracy." She also vowed not to pay her federal income tax for 2004. I mention Cindy Sheehan because I recall a conservative commentator called her *that pathetic woman*. Her sitting there, her famous act, meant that as a woman Cindy Sheehan was taking more space than she deserved. And that aspect of pathetic is what I am truly interested in here. The act of taking a little less or a little more. It's the essence of a political meaning. A pathetic man is chatty, effusive, sort of *gay-ish* in the high school sense of the word but what does gay mean other than nonconforming. The space he is taking is a woman's. You can't take the wrong space, a woman's space and be masculine.

Because gender is a counterweight to keep everything and every body in line. It's a military formation. It's our national poetics. We are free to be feminist here (and I remember going to Germany in the 90s on a literary tour and we were floored by how retro and patriarchal the German literary community was. *Look at us*, we crowed) but contempt flung at any woman who dares to approach the seat of power reveals how flammable, how violently reactive the slimy surface of our freedom and democracy is to anyone even nominally opposed to patriarchy. You can't even say patriarchy exists. You can barely say in textbooks now that slavery existed. Or jails. Why *are* people opposed to wearing masks during a pandemic. Has the right to bear arms ever included Black men. We have a language of suppression and it keeps everyone in line and you can't be too fat or too sick or too ambivalent or joyous or resistant or poor or hungry or loud or unstable (because outside of porn any deviation makes us feel the weight of your body = too heavy for democracy) so show us your *type*, then we will commodify you into another form of silence. Does Oprah talk or not.

It took about a hundred years for pathetic to mean mean. It went from "pathetical" to "pathetic" in the 19th century and it still meant something touching or pithy, "felt," but then pathetic went negative real fast. Whatever brings up feeling in here must get squashed. The word didn't do it by itself, but something closes in on us like a vice and all unlikely approaches will get slapped down. So what you're stepping into here is a tiny monument for witnessing change, not of any one sort but of many sorts like a sex club of thought. A bar that serves only time in different and peculiar-sized doses.

When I saw how good Porochista Khakpour was at talking about being sick, what lengths she went to, how many plateaus of suffering she endured, I was delightedly aghast. She could just go and go. It's so bold. It reminded me of what I once heard a male critic say at a party about a female artist. She's *an endless woman*. The room got quiet. He had named his fear.

I'm not sure I can ever truly stay inside of the mind of Robert Walser. It makes me so uncomfortable. I first learned about him one day in the 80s on a drunken visit to poet and book dealer Gerrit Lansing in Gloucester, Mass., who regaled myself and David Rattray with a description of this Swiss writer from the turn of the century who wrote in bits and pieces changing directions at will depositing an entire novel on the corner of a napkin, doing everything at the absolutely wrong scale. Almost topographically, if you know what I mean. And in his almost manic directionlessness he created this extra space. He was sent to review a play and he reviewed the audience. It's like ADHD taken to a pitch where it becomes useful if not spiritual. It was infectious. I didn't read Walser for another ten years but even hearing about him gave me permission to write prose for the first time—<u>if</u> I could be volumetric. Take that pill and grow larger and then scrunch myself up if I wanted to be small.

The *act* of writing as we know is pathetic. I want to go out but I want to stay in. What torture it is to do *this*. I'm thinking about the enormity that Lucille Clifton conveys in simply *looking* at the bench that held the ass of a woman who was enslaved her whole life (Aunt Nanny) who could spell her own name and did it right here.

There's no monument anywhere in America just like that because it's pure apprehension. Ivan Dixon's 1973 *The Spook Who Sat by the Door* actually showed Black militants holding guns and shooting white soldiers so of course our government would not let <u>that</u> be screened anywhere in the world for at least twenty years. And shouldn't art make an action outside itself. That's what I mean by feeling. Qiu Miaojin's writing tugs inexorably toward her death, first Bunny (the pet rabbit) dies in the book's dedication and now Zoë (Qiu) will die. And Angie is dying and Ed is dying and Nate's mother died. And each death happens in a solution, in a differently constituted percentage of love or lovelessness. AIDS is a lot of the reason for this pathetic book. Some of us knew all about dying in the 80s while others were still whispering about who their one gay friend may've gotten it from. Just like now with covid where the people who die are often not my friends and entire zip codes in New York City have been decimated. The selectivity of the virus explains the resistance to the mask. What's been politicized is a feeling that the disease *knows who we are*. It's almost sung. I remember everyone's horror when Dennis Cooper said AIDS ruined death. What we did learn is that everyone dies different. The horror of life is that everyone is dying, not now but eventually. It's a horrible pact we make with existence and we became connoisseurs of how differently people *get at it*.

Looking at death, imagining it. Literature, this scraping sound, is a way we deal with that one unknowable space. I'm afraid of death, of my friends who are dying. I was afraid to go see Allen Ginsberg when he was dying. I was welcome (I think he even called me) but I was afraid to be *that* close to him at the moment (like Allen had to do all the loving) so Rosebud's document gathering every pointillist detail of Allen's dying still feeds my sense of loss at not having the courage to walk in. Each shred of story in here is a little machine of feeling that bends like this and that. Charline, my European friend, smiles at the difference between *our* pathetic and the one embedded in any romance language. It got ugly here. It should be our motto. You could say we invented slavery because we made it be our economy. We became modern. We made it everything and now we don't know where to hide it. In our guns. We bail out banks but reparations for generations of damage is just not "a real thing." I know that language changes by use, mostly in the mouth of the underclass, but I wonder if a book can be a new mouth and lips to re-make a word's intention on this day in a culture.

If you deliberately go through the door the wrong way, many of us at once, I hear a whoosh, there's this profound redundancy meaning we *go* to literature to describe states of being, of mind producing sudden and inexplicable feeling. Can a feeling go both ways. Can we hate and love. I would never argue why anyone needs *poetry*, but everyone *can* find a poem that elaborates a model responsible to their own way of thinking not so much for consolation as confirmation—it bestows on you a gestational feeling like *it* birthed you *and* you feel like you did it. It's your double. What author has not had that feeling when they meet a reader and they smile at you like you are them. Yikes. It is so violating. And yet aesthetics will not protect you. You are not alone when someone thinks they can see your mind. Reading is a collaborative act. It takes away the once-ness of the world and gives it back repeatedly. And language is the loss that repairs.

Sallie gave me her old battered copy of Sei Shōnagon. It felt precious. I had heard of The Pillow Book for years. I figured it was too feminine for me. Turns out Warhol is a copy of her. Her lists beautiful redolent lists are so unlike her flip side Huysmans, who isn't saying what he likes (or dislikes) or notices so much as what he's covetously *explored*. It's a masculine tack & it's just not pathetic at all.

Masculinity being a cage that feels just great about itself.

And because that's true, Bob Flanagan crawls in one literally and spends a weekend in there trying to eat shit.

Laurence Sterne's Tristram Shandy is in here since he's going back and forth through the door of gender perpetually. He's formally pathetic—the famous black page sentimentalizes his friend Yorick's death but then he does a little shimmy on the ole masculine contempt for women in lieu of what would more likely be a gray page, his absolute disinterest. He likes men.

I taught a Pathetic Literature seminar at UCSD in 2006 and we read Kevin Killian and Dodie Bellamy, Can Xue and Delany among others. Walser of course. We even had a pathetic conference. It was a late-night event, scantily attended. Chris Kraus came and I screened a wretched print of Warhol's "I, a Man" with Valerie Solanas and it was so dark we really couldn't see it at all. The sound was bad too. We had a pathetic panel and I'm sure I talked about foam. It would be my obsession for the next ten years because every book we read in the pathetic seminar had some left over froth in it. Like the action in all these novels and poems exceeded their own frame—some sludge sat right there on the water, there was spit on the corner of the boy's mouth—you know how anxious kids used to produce spittle in grade school.

Every act had this extra dose of froth. Like the stories were bobbing in a vast and inexplicable solution, like the squeaking sounds I just heard coming out of the pasta I was cooking tonight. I got closer with my phone to record it but then the sounds stopped. What the hell was that. It wasn't just pasta, or literature, but something tiny, mysterious, unjustly alive.

Eileen Myles
October 2021

PATHETIC LITERATURE

ALICE NOTLEY

All my life,
since I was ten,
I’ve been waiting
to be in
this hell here
with you;
all I’ve ever
wanted, and
still do.

we're the only colored people here

GWENDOLYN BROOKS

When they went out to the car there were just the very finest bits of white powder coming down with an almost comical little ethereal hauteur, to add themselves to the really important, piled-up masses of their kind.

And it wasn't cold.

Maud Martha laughed happily to herself. It was pleasant out, and tonight she and Paul were very close to each other.

He held the door open for her—instead of going on around to the driving side, getting in, and leaving her to get in at her side as best she might. When he took this way of calling her "lady" and informing her of his love she felt precious, protected, delicious. She gave him an excited look of gratitude. He smiled indulgently.

"Want it to be the Owl again?"

"Oh, no no, Paul. Let's not go there tonight. I feel too good inside for that. Let's go downtown?"

She had to suggest that with a question mark at the end, always. He usually had three protests. Too hard to park. Too much money. Too many white folks. And tonight she could almost certainly expect a no, she feared, because he had come out in his blue work shirt. There was a spot of apricot juice on the collar, too. His shoes were not shined. . . . But he nodded!

"We've never been to the World Playhouse," she said cautiously. "They have a good picture. I'd feel rich in there."

"You really wanta?"

"Please?"

"Sure."

It wasn't like other movie houses. People from the Studebaker Theatre which, as Maud Martha whispered to Paul, was "all-locked-arms" with the World Playhouse, were strolling up and down the lobby, laughing softly, smoking with gentle grace.

"There must be a play going on in there and this is probably an intermission," Maud Martha whispered again.

"I don't know why you feel you got to whisper," whispered Paul. "Nobody else is whispering in here." He looked around, resentfully, wanting to see a few, just a few, colored faces. There were only their own.

Maud Martha laughed a nervous defiant little laugh; and spoke loudly. "There certainly isn't any reason to whisper. Silly, huh."

The strolling women were cleverly gowned. Some of them had flowers or flashers in their hair. They looked—cooked. Well cared-for. And as though they had never seen a roach or a rat in their lives. Or gone without heat for a week. And the men had even edges. They were men, Maud Martha thought, who wouldn't stoop to fret over less than a thousand dollars.

"We're the only colored people here," said Paul.

She hated him a little. "Oh, hell. Who in hell cares."

"Well, what I want to know is, where do you pay the damn fares."

"There's the box office. Go on up."

He went on up. It was closed.

"Well," sighed Maud Martha, "I guess the picture has started already. But we can't have missed much. Go on up to that girl at the candy counter and ask her where we should pay our money."

He didn't want to do that. The girl was lovely and blonde and cold-eyed, and her arms were akimbo, and the set of her head was eloquent. No one else was at the counter.

"Well. We'll wait a minute. And see—"

Maud Martha hated him again. Coward. She ought to flounce over to the girl herself—show him up. . . .

The people in the lobby tried to avoid looking curiously at two shy Negroes wanting desperately not to seem shy. The white women looked at the Negro woman in her outfit with which no special fault could be found, but which made them think, somehow, of close rooms, and wee, close lives. They looked at her hair. They liked to see a dark colored girl with long, long hair. They were always slightly surprised, but agreeably so, when they did. They supposed it was the hair that had got her that yellowish, good-looking Negro man.

The white men tried not to look at the Negro man in the blue work shirt, the Negro man without a tie.

An usher opened a door of the World Playhouse part and ran quickly down the few steps that led from it to the lobby. Paul opened his mouth.

"Say, fella. Where do we get the tickets for the movie?"

The usher glanced at Paul's feet before answering. Then he said coolly, but not unpleasantly, "I'll take the money."

They were able to go in.

And the picture! Maud Martha was so glad that they had not gone to the Owl! Here was technicolor, and the love story was sweet. And there was classical music that silvered its way into you and made your back cold. And the theater itself! It was no palace, no such Great Shakes as the Tivoli out south, for instance (where many colored people went every night). But you felt good sitting there, yes, good, and as if, when you left it, you would be going home to a sweet-smelling apartment with flowers on little gleaming tables; and wonderful silver on night-blue velvet, in chests; and crackly sheets; and lace spreads on such beds as you saw at Marshall Field's. Instead of back to your kit'n't apt., with the garbage of your floor's families in a big can just outside your door, and the gray sound of little gray feet scratching away from it as you drag up those flights of narrow complaining stairs.

Paul pressed her hand. Paul said, "We oughta do this more often."

And again. "We'll have to do this more often. And go to plays, too. I mean at that Blackstone, and Studebaker."

She pressed back, smiling beautifully to herself in the darkness. Though she knew that once the spell was over it would be a year, two years, more, before he would return to the World Playhouse. And he might never go to a real play. But she was learning to love moments. To love moments for themselves.

When the picture was over, and the lights revealed them for what they were, the Negroes stood up among the furs and good cloth and faint perfume, looked about them eagerly. They hoped they would meet no cruel eyes. They hoped no one would look intruded upon. They had enjoyed the picture so, they were so happy, they wanted to laugh, to say warmly to the other outgoers, "Good, huh? Wasn't it swell?"

This, of course, they could not do. But if only no one would look intruded upon. . . .

People Without Names

THE FRIEND

My therapist says you are unavailable.
She means “emotionally unavailable,” of course.
A phrase that is like a death sentence
among the salty hills of Los Angeles,
pabulum of gurus, isotopes and glue.
And I know, like a second breath,
where I secretly breathe always,
with hidden lungs and emissary logic,
that you have always been unavailable—
and this is your immense appeal to me,
not as torture device,
the mills of catholic monasteries englassed,
but as inner truth, preferred and true.
You will have future lovers,
and you will be glad and bored,
alike indifferent, converted or annealed,
like a band of trifling steel clippings
magnetized by the obstinacy of a door stop.
Shaved pubes of the peach or a snarling
dog lip put in the wrong painting:
they are neither here nor there. Truly.
I prefer the glass of my phone to crack,
and be taken away;
for the miserable inscrutable odor of saints,
to arrive at the harness of the window,

drunk like a kettle, fearless,
and gradually amused, like an ugly plant
that refuses to grow or die,
but sticks with the needles of invisible light,
dignified to irrelevance.
To want nothing from you is what
we already have; the theater of these muscles;
muted vestments, eyes (blighted) passed
around; my unobtrusive ghost
thumping like cattle on the sill.
What is specifically new about anyone?
My body has been used and disposed of;
the crimped sleeve of a fresh collared shirt
looms like a patrician's house
tucked into ancient prairies,
where back pain is veneer, vermillion sky;
a thistle stuck in the toe of January.
The agreement is always this, unavailable one,
you will circle, all mental crucible,
expending and taking energy, lav-
ishly—honey for the hive, world without bees;
some sweet-fire near the splashing intersection of
conversations clotted on a crosswalk
by a crudely over lit gas station. As long
as I do not look into your eyes when I speak to you—
I know I say anything. And though
I travel through desert statuary, escaping
even the memory of my own failed desires,
redundant pungency, memoirs of the eel,
I will find you, be found; onboard a bus,
in the early light of too many centuries ago,
you board. Rattling with compartments;
shuffling stiff on mildew seats after dawn; now
sharpen the claws of our indifference.
No one cackles in the beige pocketbook languidly.
No one erects a squinting parakeet. But they

could for you, and you'd take it—coldly—
as you hover through the naked aisles.
And you will sit down next to me, in the thousand
rows of this bus, that indeterminably change
and empty while the agreement, issued,
is repeated. As long as I look, I cannot speak;
as long as I can't see what I do see, I might as well
say anything. When I falter like furniture,
you evaporate like a headache. The
punching clock is drunk with more than prayers.
I am leafing through the venial sins of elders;
their hairy tomes and brittle pearls.
To this salutary urn, I also bow. But
you would remind me of the agreement;
the astuteness of your posture; the
fact that you are exact and final—
the flowers, not liquid, are flesh.
Inconstancy stammers too whitely.
I imagine in your infinite backpack
there is a woman persona, whose name
is like the prefecture of emeralds;
in a world beyond and before gender,
where you are spoken of in totality
that has nothing to do with the undisclosed
violence of all households. The letter M.
Magic is not your name; or the real one.
Marring the opportunity, I find a new way
to break the commandment of fathers
and dead fathers. I write you into this poem;
gambling on too-recent rigidity.
Tucked around the corner from or exiting
out the café of an indecent futuristic movie,
it is impossible to plan how guarded
and vacant your hold on generosity may yet be.
The missing persons of the library clap

shut when we ask if the letters swim against
each other in the empty, static night.
When did you not love the unavailable one?
How can there be this real something,
more perfect than refusal,
in which the suffering of our mothers,
our trans childless souls, speak without language
in the seesaw utility belt drawbridge west of all heres.
Siroccos are somersaults; winding oscillations
of the gutter harp trill; these
are proximate symbols;
whereas you are approximate and never flinch.
I avow the old enemy returns.
Penicillin heaters chug and chatter.
The unavailable one through a river of bruises;
utility bills; post-political upheavals;
an adversary fog twilled with chewable vitamins.
Lint shrapnel reminds that wars are
inside/across bodies of gendered stamps;
crudely botched by names and accents;
harkened to with gaudy travail.
When everyone goes home from their favorite
paragraph, and I am set to put the seals
on certain periods and chubby syllables,
I slump down in the gusty oratory of stacks,
in lop-sided winters in city offices.
The argument isolates itself backwardsly.
No one believes that I have seen you
folded in the rectangle of tissue paper;
watched you cry at deprivation tanks.
"He" conceals this lanky shoe of "she";
and I am not allowed to utter her name.
But one time, while rowing across the lobby,
with a kitchen thrown down inside it,
like a mystic wooden knee cap,

I clutched the sides of that name
in neon distribution and unqualified praise.
I am looking at you and saying it.
And because you are not here, nor would be,
I know now, you are readying to receive
this familiar queer-adjacent violence we share.
There is time for silence. There is still time.

Loveland

KEVIN KILLIAN

I grew up in Smithtown, a suburb of New York, a town so invidious that still I speak of it in Proustian terms—or Miltonic terms, a kind of paradise I feel evicted from. Smithtown, Long Island, kind of an MGM Norman Rockwell hometown, a place so boring they gave it a boring name . . . When I was 14 I began to go to New York on a regular basis, sometimes on the train, sometimes hitchhiking there, looking for a jungly eroticism I supposed Smithtown, with its manicured lawns and its country club airs, couldn't afford me. I was right and wrong at the same time.

By day or night New York's a seedy Burroughs kind of place, and hurrying down the street I could hardly catch my breath, there were so many affecting things to watch and so much architecture. At Gristede's all the food's so expensive I felt I knew why everyone in Manhattan's so thin, but it seemed worth it, and thus I found myself buying things I never wanted before—simple things like: apple. Doughnut. Cup of coffee. I took a job clerking there for a month and famous people, like Jackie Kennedy, would come in off the street and buy these very same things. These would be my dinner; a fellow I knew in school had a cigarette, a cup of coffee and the *Daily News* when he woke up every morning, and he called it the chorus girls' breakfast. I knew another guy who always carried the same book in his back pocket, like Bruce Springsteen that red bandanna. A book of poetry: Bob Kaufman's *Solitudes Crowded with Loneliness*. I loved him for that: I used to touch the book in his pocket and feel direct connection to the ancient rain of San Francisco, now my home then only a mysterious flavor like guava, succulent, almost too rich. I used to tell him, "You are so cute with that book," and he would smile, unwillingly, as though he'd pledged never to reveal his connection to poetry.

The subway ride to his house seemed endless. Sealed in with the dismal frightened figures of subway America, I couldn't help but feel different and special, in that I was heading towards a love life that, I imagined, would have frightened them more, would have made them more dismal. "Loveland" I called it, as though it were an address like Rockefeller Center. It's when you look into someone's sunglasses and try to see his eyes, or the space you feel rolling over a cliff or a ramble. From these two fellows I took the sense that being a New Yorker involved high style, one was so camp with his "chorus girls' breakfast" and his operatic airs, the other so serious, a walking dictionary of soulful poetry like Kaufman. "Camp" and "Seriousness" themselves became characters I could cruise first, then nuzzle, then accept or decline.

Life's so much simpler here in San Francisco.

Then I was 20, still convinced New York's the most dangerous place in the world. I came out of the subway once, for example, and Francis Coppola was filming *The Godfather*. The cameras whirled as I made my entrance. I blinked and smiled, and lingered till I heard the word "Cut." One of the little people asked me to step aside so that Richard Conte, who was waiting inside the car, could get his face on screen. "If you want me to I will," I said. "You guys making a movie? Can I be in it more than I am already?" He explained that it was a period piece and that was why everyone was dressed in forties suits and hats. "I love those suits," I told him. "I love those hats men used to wear."

"Sorry," he said.

Out on the street it was four o'clock in the afternoon and girls were wearing summer dresses and acting soignée. My favorite time of day. A large cloud, pumped full of black gases, loomed overhead. I felt goosebumps, perhaps because I was tripping. In my pocket a handful of red crystals, wrapped in pliofilm, gave me a kind of sexual energy I haven't felt since, and plus I made money this way, and plus I felt powerful, ambitious, and also I had lots of friends (and what they say about New York is true: eight million people, each with a different story to tell and a different drug habit); plus I was a homosexual primitive like a Frida Kahlo mural the Feds tear down.

In winter up on Carey's fire escape at East End Avenue and 86th Street I wrapped myself in a bearskin and sat there telling my diary the story of the novel I hoped one day to write. "This will make me famous," I thought. And what was fame, I felt, but an extension of my present being? I was seeing a man who had picked me up hitchhiking when I was in junior high, out on Long Island where I grew up. We'd known each other for six years—I'd grown a foot taller and my hair had changed color and I used to wonder, "If I grow any taller will I still be loved?" His name was Carter, but I called him Carey.

The night we met I noticed how warm his car was. A piece of toast. I'd sat shivering in it, in a black jacket and white buckskin shoes. "Where are you headed?" he said.

"Take me to New York," I said.

"Show me where it is on the map," Carey said, producing a large roadmap from his glove compartment and unfolding it like an accordion across the width of the car. His right hand fell unerringly to my lap. The names of the roads on the map blurred before my eyes like sudden tears. "Show me where it is," he said once or twice, all the while playing with my prick. That's how I fell in love.

In many ways a cold fish, Carey was capable of surprising me with extravagant gestures I thought showed some emotion. He gave me a hundred dollars once. Another time he came out of a taxi filled with balloons to cheer me up after a depressing exam in Linguistics. Still I used to wonder, "Now that I'm blond no longer how much longer will we be tied together?" Even at 18, or should I say especially at 18, I knew balloons were corny and I squirmed and hoped to God none of my friends were watching. But as the taxi sped north up Third Avenue, the colors, the warm rubber suffocation, had the power to send fleets of taxicabs over the pier and into the blue and gray Hudson.

His wife I never cared for. She had a critical eye on me from the time I was 14. They lived in an apartment designed by *Architectural Digest*. Once I woke up there and only she was home. Anita gave me a steely look but fixed me a boloney sandwich, though she kept rattling the knife around in the mustard jar like she was having a nervous breakdown or something. I sat at her kitchen table, nervous myself, twiddling my thumbs and rapping the underside sharply like a seance. "Quit fidgeting," Anita told me.

It was eight in the morning, and outside the sky was full of orange light, white clouds scuttling across the horizon towards Brooklyn Harbor. Under her cool black-eyed gaze, the white jockey shorts Carey insisted I wear seemed a little *de trop* at breakfast. I crossed my legs. Then spread them wide. "I'm reading a really good book," I said at a stab. "*One Hundred Years of Solitude*." I thought this was a clever touch because Anita came from some Central American country or another, probably the same one Bianca Jagger did.

But she merely turned her head impassively and dropped the sandwich onto a plate, thrusting it my way. "Eat," she said. "Eat and don't talk." How much of my love life she knew about I'm not sure. It was as taboo as anything in Levi-Strauss. Carey had a respectable life and liked it like that. He was capable of affection, although not in public, usually in a car.

Even when it was happening to me, I thought, "This will make a good story someday," but now that I think of it, its story's not that good at all. More important than its plots, it's the quality of feeling that strikes me now—something out of this world, "outlandish" in its literal sense. I had a pair of white shoes and a black jacket I used to regard in the same way, draping them atop chairs and talking to them in the stylish, sophisticated accents of David Niven or Peter Lawford. "I love those shoes," I would say to an imaginary visitor. "I love that jacket."

At my high school graduation I saw his face in the crowd. Afterwards I tried to find him, though I don't know what I would have done with him if I had. But anyhow I couldn't. Later he denied having been there, but with one of those roguish twinkles that can pass for truth or a joke. "I was not hallucinating," I said. "I saw you there."

"I think you've been smoking too many bananas." I never found his drug humor amusing, the way some people are turned off by bathroom humor.

"You were wearing your gray suit with a green tie."

"The luck of the Irish."

"You must have just gotten your hair cut."

"Oh sure," he said, "could you smell the talcum powder?"

"Bay rum I smelled," I said. "And you had a hard-on."

"Oh well then, that couldn't have been I," he said.

We drove somewhere in Westchester and entered an antique water-mill preserved from Colonial times for its shock value. There, on its dusty wooden floor, he asked me what I wanted out of life. "Not to be like you," I said, first to annoy him, then also because it was true, plus he had a hard-on. I really liked being desired. And I liked money and kept hoping he would give me another hundred dollars. He kept peering around afraid that the caretaker would spot us. I liked the dangerous aspects of our affair, I liked even the fact that he did not. I thought that otherwise he would long since have tired of me and sought out someone else, someone younger, someone 12 or 13. He seemed old to me then, but working out our birth dates I realized sometime later that he must have been 35 when we met, and since that's my age now I get goosebumps. Here in San Francisco in October the sky is a pale and delicate blue, like a robin's egg in a child's picture book.

It's four o'clock in the afternoon as I write this: my favorite time of day. A car is moving slowly down the street, pushed from behind by two sweating workmen in grayish overalls. I want it to roll down the hill. I want its trunk to leave their hands. I want them to stumble a bit in surprise, then begin chasing the car, as it picks up speed and strips its gears, then they fall back out of breath and grow fatalistic. Then the car plunges off the cliff and you see the faces of the lovers rising from the back seat, steamed in a kiss, the kiss they can't feel, and you see the car hit a rocky mesa way down below. From vertiginous heights I watch and smoke a cigarette, humming a little tune and acting very debonair. I am reminded of a misspent youth—someone's misspent youth, not necessarily mine.

Once Anita was knitting me a sweater and waxing sarcastic: how kind Carey was, taking a disadvantaged child out of the suburbs, bringing him to Manhattan! "Fresh Air Fund except in reverse," she snorted.

"Well I need to get streetwise," I said, "brush some of the country cobwebs off me."

"Carey's not the man to teach street smarts. We were mugged by three Guatemalan borrachos on Lexington and Carey told them to take the Lady Seiko that they didn't even know I had."

"He helps me with my school work," I said.

She said nothing, kept rocking and knitting. Presently she spoke again. "*Espera*," she said, her voice and face deadpan. "*Espera* Kevin."

"Esperanto you mean," I cried. "Talk English to me, you know I don't understand that loco lingo of yours."

"When you grow up I will talk to you, not now. If you want a sandwich you know how to make one, so go."

"I do want a sandwich," I said. "I'm so awfully hungry."

"How are your parents and your brothers and sisters and boys' school?"

"I guess everything's fine," I said, suddenly frightened. "Tell Carey I'll wait for him in the car, okay? I'll skip the sandwich, all right?"

She shrugged. "If I see him I'll tell him." The needles began to flash in the light. "In English," she added. "In the language you and he have."

When it came time for me to go to college I picked one in New York, actually three, but that's a different story. In my cheap room, all grays and whites and pinks, he and I met one night so I could tell him it was over. Carey washed his face in the bathroom and came out with water cupped in his hands. He threw the water on my face, meaning to wake me up. "My classes are all very interesting this semester," I said, ignoring him. "Sometimes I feel like an ashtray—like you're a cigarette and you put yourself out in me. Ever wish you had passed me by on that highway? I bet you do, cause I've caused you grief." I didn't really believe this. "But I got to like you, Carey, your candy breath, your mouth stuffed with cotton, your pleasant gray eyes. O baby don't come."

He wasn't about to come; coming was far from his mind. He stood up and pulled off his pants. What is the trick of description, that writers must use? How do I make him more clear, vivid, real—or even imaginary? You know the film actress Rosanna Arquette? He had the sulky pouting look of a male Rosanna Arquette. But what happens if you don't know her? I could say: Pia Zadora; Brigette Bardot: but at each remove the similarity fades a bit more, so you don't get my picture.

Shall I stick to Rosanna? But then I'll seem obscure, oblique. He had the sulky pouting look of a male Rosanna Arquette, while I, who knew I could never pull that off, thought it politic to ape the vacuous, slightly zombie drug stare of the 50's singer Johnnie Ray.

Carey told me so many stories about growing up in Wilkes-Barre, Pennsylvania, that I came to feel I knew as much about that city as he did. One of the stories was of a little boy who worked a paper route, all summer long, to earn enough money to buy a suit for the first day of school. The paper he sold published his picture on their front page. So Carey and some other boys pushed this boy in a ditch and laughed at him and pissed all over his neck and throat and chest. Sometimes I felt like that paper boy, that all my love did for him was to give him a big laugh.

"You want ice cream, Kevin?" he said. He put his pants back on and zipped up the fly. "I'll go down to the store."

"Sometimes I feel like a piece of paper," I said. "That you wrote your name on then pissed on."

"What flavor?" said Carey. "I know your favorite."

"I don't want any ice cream," I said. "Why don't you take off your pants and listen to me?" I loved him so much I couldn't let him out of the room. He had had everything and I had only been able to give him just a little. "Remember that old woman who lived at the end of the block and you were never allowed to step on her lawn?"

"I remember," he said gravely, his pants round his knees.

"She'd come running out of her house to chase you away if you stepped in her yard, a lawn so shabby and unkempt you never understood why she got into such a dither about it. After you broke her mailbox with your fists, she came calling on your mother in moth-eaten black widow's weeds with a calling card and a reticule. I feel like that old eccentric widow woman—that you're the meanest boy on the block. Under my windows I crouch and wait till you've stopped vandalizing my house. Then I straighten up and breathe again. She smelled like mothballs and sour cheese and her house was unpainted and one day she was dead. She had turned up the gas to light the stove and she fell forward, asleep, while her face burned away. It burnt completely away like strips of bacon leaving only grease and fat behind. Sometimes I feel

I'd like to burn in Hell with no face if it meant you wouldn't be looking into my eyes with your Devil's look. Your mother worried about your bad temper. At night while you slept she'd watch over you and cry, thinking of you. She wanted your happiness and could see none for you in the future. She couldn't even talk it over with your father because it seemed to her that he'd lost all interest in his family. He, your mother knew, was dicking that little girl in Philadelphia—the one he'd told her he'd given up. When she touched him it was like he or she wasn't there but never both at the same time. Sometimes I feel like your mother, that when I turn to you, you're not there, that you're somewhere else and never were in my bed. Sometimes I feel like your father and I feel you touching me and I wish I wasn't in bed with you and I dream or daydream of someone else. She needed your love so much then but you were embarrassed by her affection: weren't you, Carey?"

"She tried too hard," Carey answered.

"John Lennon said, 'Mother, you needed me but I didn't need you.' Or, 'I needed you but you didn't need me.'"

"The latter I think," Carey said, a towel made of an expensive material knotted around his waist.

I wish I had that towel right now. Whatever happened to it? Anita probably has it along with everything else.

"And I say, 'Kevin, you're going out of your mind!'"

"If you love me why do you have to go out tricking with those tricks not to mention your wife . . . O baby don't come. Prove to me, Carey, I haven't wasted my time."

"What do you want me to do?" He was exasperated with me and my constant demands and I knew it; yet I couldn't stop going on and ruining it all. I didn't ruin what counted but I ruined whatever I could. He got up and went out in the rain to get me my ice cream but I didn't like ice cream.

"I don't want you to do anything," I said. He was walking in the rain and probably picking someone up in the bargain as well as the ice cream neither of us wanted. "My name is Kevin Killian," I said. "I come from Smithtown, Long Island. I'm going to send away for a gun I saw in a magazine."

I never did send away for that gun, probably because I didn't have enough money for it. Instead I wrote more of my novel. In grad school, years later, I decided to write my dissertation on child pornography but I had yet to connect my decision with my own experience.

That night Carey got into his big warm car and drove out fifty miles to Smithtown, the town where we'd met. I'd said something to him he couldn't forget. He took his razor and opened a little vein in his cock, trying to expiate for the awful way he'd treated me. The car was warm as a piece of toast. Yet once, I'd sat shivering in it, in a black jacket and white buckskin shoes. "Take me to New York," I said.

"Show me where it is on the map," Carey said. His right hand touched my cock. The names of the roads on the map blurred before my eyes like a turning kaleidoscope. That's the night I fell in love for the very first time.

Now he was somewhere in Manhattan's oily dark streets getting drenched to the skin for the sake of my love. A boy passed him on the street. He had no conscience. That's what was so remarkable about him. Two boys passed him on the street. He was like nothing in the world I had been brought up in. A double life was exactly suited to my consciousness, so I went along with him and got excited. His voice was so much deeper than those of my teenaged friends that when he called my house asking for me I told my parents he was one of my teachers. Then I told them he was a writer in New York. They said, "But I thought he was one of your teachers."

"I never said that," I told them, full of scorn and counting the days till I could get away from them. "No, he's a writer in New York." Later on I made him a piano salesman I had fooled into thinking I had enough money to buy a piano. Who knows what Mom and Dad made out of my lies. They probably thought I was a drug dealer. After writing hundreds of pages of it, I gave up my dissertation not too long ago. I remember thinking that to lie and deceive, to lead a secret sexual life, was to me the greatest of all pleasures and by far the most natural. Maybe I should have been a spy for a foreign power, or a better Catholic.

In Loveland, only a few colors stain the crystal radiance of the skies, gray, pink, white, black; someone holds you for a few minutes, then lets you fall to the rocks, and nothing hurts, and you're never betrayed. All your allegiances are to the holy. All the phones are tapped. If there's someone younger than you in the nightclub he or she's an enemy agent to whom you must show the marked roadmap and speak the secret words. Once you've made your way there, you never, never grow old. First he frightened me, then he made me come, then he amused me, then he left me, then he made me recall him.

I went to the window, shivering in jockey shorts, holes in the seams in required places, and drew back the cheesecloth curtain. I looked out onto windows and chimneys. I saw shabby storefronts and New York rain of the pearly white and gray. I looked over my shoulder to quick-trip on our unmade bed, a sprawl of similarly pearl and gray mattress and stained sheets. Then to the glass again. Once I kissed his face in a mirror. Another time I kissed a glass ashtray. Out on the street a car was lurking, its motor running. The car seemed sinister and it hummed danger.

The noise was incredible.

The walls were thin there. Glossy magazine covers hung from the walls to increase their thickness. Once he said he wished we had no windows, since glass is too thin and lets in and out too much heat and noise. I remember arguing with him. I asked him how else if not for windows would we be able to see out onto the city streets. I reminded him that they, the streets, were what provided him with almost all his excitement and inspiration. "But I don't need any windows now," he said, "since I fell for you." You can imagine how that made me feel. I looked out into the rain and I was glad to be indoors. I began to spit on myself because, if he was getting wet out there, I wanted to feel wet too. The night is long. I didn't have much self-protection. I opened my pants and maneuvered my cock and pissed all over my chest and throat and face.

Years later I read a poem, by Eileen Myles, that exactly answered my need to express what I felt about that time in my life, during which I grew from a little boy into a young man, so that I felt then that I'd never have to write about it myself, only relax and wait and then someday be wrapped in swaddling clothes.

THE HONEY BEAR

Billie Holiday was on the radio
I was standing in the kitchen
smoking my cigarette of this
pack I plan to finish tonight
last night of smoking youth.
I made a cup of this funny
kind of tea I've had hanging
around. A little too sweet
and odd mix. My only impulse
was to make it sweeter.
Ivy Anderson was singing
pretty late tonight
in my very bright kitchen.
I'm standing by the tub
feeling a little older
nearly thirty in my very
bright kitchen tonight.
I'm not a bad looking woman
I suppose   O it's very quiet
in my kitchen tonight   I'm squeezing
this plastic honey bear   a noodle
of honey dripping into the odd sweet
tea. It's pretty late
Honey bear's cover was loose
and somehow honey   dripping down
the bear's eyes   catching
in the crevices beneath
the bear's eyes   O very sad and sweet
I'm standing in my kitchen   Oh honey
I'm staring at the honey bear's face.

Yesterday I Was

AMA BIRCH

Counting
Caterpillars with Pun.
We were reciting lines
"Boys Don't Cry."

"Are you a boy or a girl?"

Do caterpillars ever get asked
such questions?

Pun was interested in death
And burial in New Orleans. I
Tried to explain it to her.
Language can be so futile.
The barrier of knowing and not
knowing.
Don't all butterflies look
The same yet male
monarchs have spots.

Do butterflies have second-line
funerals?

A parade of butterflies
Carrying their ancestors spirit
Home as they travel from
South to north?

I wrote Eileen today.
They are in Greece.
I asked them if
they had been to Lefkada?
I wondered if there is a
marker on the spot that
Sappho jumped from.

I am sure you have heard
About Steve Cannon by now.

AFTERWORD

The Great Punctuation Typography Struggle

ANDREA DWORKIN

this text has been altered in one very serious way. I wanted it to be printed the way it was written—lower case letters, no apostrophes, contractions.

I like my text to be as empty as possible, only necessary punctuation is necessary, when one knows ones purposes one knows what is necessary.

my publisher, in his corporate wisdom, filled the pages with garbage: standard punctuation, he knew his purposes; he knew what was necessary, our purposes differed: mine, to achieve clarity; his, to sell books.

my publisher changed my punctuation because book reviewers (Mammon) do not like lower case letters,

fuck (in the old sense) book reviewers (Mammon).

> When I say god and mammon concerning the writer writing, I mean that any one can use words to say something. And in using these words to say what he has to say he may use those words directly or indirectly. If he uses these words indirectly he says what he intends to have heard by somebody who is to hear and in so doing inevitably he has to serve mammon. . . . Now serving god for a writer who is writing is writing anything directly, it makes no difference what it is but it must be direct, the relation between the thing done and the doer must be direct. In this way there is completion and the essence of the completed thing is completion.
>
> —Gertrude Stein

in a letter to me, Grace Paley wrote, "once everyone tells the truth artists will be unnecessary—meanwhile there's work for us."

telling the truth, we know what it is when we do it and when we learn not to do it we forget what it is.

form, shape, structure, spatial relation, how the printed word appears on the page, where to breathe, where to rest, punctuation is marking time, indicating rhythms, even in my original text I used too much of it—I overorchestrated. I forced you to breathe where I do, instead of letting you discover your own natural breath.

I begin by presuming that I am free.

I begin with nothing, no form, no content, and I ask: what do I want to do and how do I want to do it.

I begin by presuming that what I write belongs to me.

I begin by presuming that I determine the form I use—in all its particulars. I work at my craft—in all its particulars.

in fact, everything is already determined,

in fact, all the particulars have been determined and are enforced.

in fact, where I violate what has already been determined I will be stopped.

in fact, the enforcers will enforce.

> "Whatever he may seem to us, he is yet a servant of the Law; that is, he belongs to the Law and as such is set beyond human judgment. In that case one dare not believe that the doorkeeper is subordinate to the man. Bound as he is by his service, even at the door of the Law, he is incomparably freer than anyone at large in the world. The man is only seeking the Law, the doorkeeper is already attached to it. It is the Law that has placed him at his post; to doubt his integrity is to doubt the Law itself."
>
> "I don't agree with that point of view," said K., shaking his head, "for if one accepts it, one must accept as true everything the doorkeeper says. But you yourself have sufficiently proved how impossible it is to do that."
>
> "No," said the priest, "it is not necessary to accept everything as true, one must only accept it as necessary."

> "A melancholy conclusion," said K. "It turns lying into universal principle."
>
> —Franz Kafka

I presume that I am free. I act. the enforcers enforce. I discover that I am not free, then: either I lie (it is necessary to lie) or I struggle (if I do not lie, I must struggle), if I struggle, I ask, why am I not free and what can I do to become free? I wrote this book to find out why I am not free and what I can do to become free.

> Though the social structure begins by framing the noblest laws and the loftiest ordinances that "the great of the earth" have devised, in the end it comes to this: breach that lofty law and they take you to a prison cell and shut your human body off from human warmth. Ultimately the law is enforced by the unfeeling guard punching his fellow man hard in the belly.
>
> —Judith Malina

without the presumption of freedom, there is no freedom. I am free, how, then, do I want to live my life, do my work, use my body? how, then, do I want to be, in all my particulars?

standard forms are imposed in dress, behavior, sexual relation, punctuation. standard forms are imposed on consciousness and behavior—on knowing and expressing—so that we will not presume freedom, so that freedom will appear—in all its particulars—impossible and unworkable, so that we will not know what telling the truth is, so that we will not feel compelled to tell it, so that we will spend our time and our holy human energy telling the necessary lies.

standard forms are sometimes called conventions, conventions are mightier than armies, police, and prisons. each citizen becomes the enforcer, the doorkeeper, an instrument of the Law, an unfeeling guard punching his fellow man hard in the belly.

> I am an anarchist. I dont sue, I dont get injunctions, I advocate revolution, and when people ask me what can we do that's practical, I say, weakly, weaken the fabric of the system wherever you can, make

possible the increase of freedom, all kinds. When I write I try to extend the possibilities of expression.

. . . I had tried to speak to you honestly, in my own way, undisguised, trying to get rid, it's part of my obligation to the muse, of the ancien regime of grammar.

. . . the revisions in typography and punctuation have taken from the voice the difference that distinguishes passion from affection and me speaking to you from me writing an essay.

—Julian Beck, 1965, in a foreword to an edition of *The Brig*

BELIEVE THE PUNCTUATION.

—Muriel Rukeyser

there is a great deal at stake here, many writers fight this battle and most lose it. what is at stake for the writer? freedom of invention, freedom to tell the truth, in all its particulars, freedom to imagine new structures.

(the burden of proof is not on those who presume freedom, the burden of proof is on those who would in any way diminish it.)

what is at stake for the enforcers, the doorkeepers, the guardians of the Law—the publishing corporations, the book reviewers who do not like lower case letters, the librarians who will not stack books without standard punctuation (that was the reason given Muriel Rukeyser when her work was violated)—what is at stake for them? why do they continue to enforce?

while this book may meet much resistance—anger, fear, dislike—law? police? courts?—at this moment I must write: Ive attacked the fundaments of culture, thats ok. Ive attacked male dominance, thats ok. Ive attacked every heterosexual notion of relation, thats ok. Ive in effect advocated the use of drugs, thats ok. Ive in effect advocated fucking animals. thats ok. here and now, New York City, spring 1974, among a handful of people, publisher and editor included, thats ok. lower case letters are not. it does make one wonder.

so Ive wondered and this is what I think right now. there are well-developed, effective mechanisms for dealing with ideas, no matter how powerful the ideas are. very few ideas are more powerful than the mechanisms for defusing them, standard form—punctuation, typography, then on to academic organization, the rigid ritualistic formulation of ideas, etc.—is the actual distance between the individual (certainly the intellectual individual) and the ideas in a book.

standard form is the distance.

one can be excited *about* ideas without changing at all. one can think *about* ideas, talk *about* ideas, without changing at all. people are willing to think about many things, what people refuse to do, or are not permitted to do, or resist doing, is to change the way they think.

reading a text which violates standard form forces one to change mental sets in order to read. there is no distance. the new form, which is in some ways unfamiliar, forces one to read differently—not to read about different things, but to read in different ways.

to permit writers to use forms which violate convention just might permit writers to develop forms which would teach people to think differently: not to think about different things, but to think in different ways. that work is not permitted.

> If it had been possible to build the Tower of Babel without ascending it, the work would have been permitted.
>
> —Franz Kafka

> The Immovable Structure is the villain. Whether that structure calls itself a prison or a school or a factory or a family or a government or The World As It Is. That structure asks each man what he can do for it, not what it can do for him, and for those who do not do for it, there is the pain of death or imprisonment, or social degradation, or the loss of animal rights.
>
> —Judith Malina

this book is about the Immovable Sexual Structure, in the process of having it published, Ive encountered the Immovable Punctuation Typography Structure, and I now testify, as so many have before me, that the Immovable Structure aborts freedom, prohibits invention, and does us verifiable harm: it uses our holy human energy to sustain itself; it turns us into enforcers, or outlaws; to survive, we must learn to lie.

The Revolution, as we live it and as we imagine it, means destroying the Immovable Structure to create a world in which we can use our holy human energy to sustain our holy human lives;

to create a world without enforcers, doorkeepers, guards, and arbitrary Law;

to create a world—a community on this planet—where instead of lying to survive, we can tell the truth and flourish.

Truth or Consequences

ARIANA REINES

One day a woman took me down
To a stream to smoke
Then up a hill
To a plain
Where we walked an old road
German tourists were soft in the distance
We reached a city built into cliffs

Beside the sun an eagle
Unfurled and stayed
And I stared at it for an hour beside the woman
Not knowing her yet or myself

Another day she took me to a town
Called T
Or C where pools
Of water stand along the road

She stood me
In warm water there

I in her speedo and she
In somebody's shorts
The square trough
Dark with minerals
Was dark with them for us

The sun was up
The people were quiet along the road
Giving me the panicking feeling the sight
Of people patiently having fun
Always gives me. Then
All of a sudden

I saw jerky

A curtain
Of jerky spread
Over the world

I blinked and blinked into it
It was jerky veined with white fat
No matter where or how I looked it was the center
Of all I could see

Why do visions of beef keep on
Being given to me was my way of saying
Fine then, lord of my heart, even though
I am not a bovine woman
But rather a chipmunk or rat
A raccoon on a good day

My lord god said nothing. The jerky continued to spread
In my eye. We have to get out of the water now I said
My friend, a seer and wise woman, agreed

We got in her car

The sun started to talk to me
I was in such a state of submission

Jerky makes a cross, Ariana, he said,
Between fire and water

Air and earth
As the middle of the animal
Is both a medium and a center
An X of substances and methods belovèd by me

He said that cattle
Belong to him and that when they're dead he loves
To touch them with his heat
As he loves to touch all that lives
And dies

Inside the cow it is a place
A cave red with light
As where men and women lit their early fires
To draw pictures of herself
At the center of this place is an invisible X
That marks the nothing out of which real things occur
To put this another way
The wooden post at the center
Of the peristyle may well hold up the ceiling
But really it is the staff of Mercury
Down which spirits slide like firemen
To mount thee

The secret of dried meat
Is my love for it, said the sun, above
And beyond your own

Cattle are pulled by the sun, he explained,
Who is himself pulled by the cattle of heaven
Thus the human is meant to follow the clatter

Of cattle over the earth
It is simple he
Said, as anyone could know who

Knows how to read the book before
Her eyes. The people follow

The cattle. The cattle follow
Me. The dog forsook
The wolves to be with thee
Which is a mystery
Of love

At this there was a pause

All water follows the moon
Who is a woman who follows
The earth who is also
A woman with fire in her belly like you

Ariana. I felt it, the fire
And the water in me and the salt
Of my longing and didn't deny it

Of course you know, he went on
That the wood is beloved
Of the fire that bends its back in ecstasy

And the air even when pale
And cool in mild cascades
And ionic colonnades
Of ascending negation

Keeps you and keeps you as best
As it can

You and your firewater in mild
Poses as information panics morosely and jocosely through you
Are the lodge into which I have put my black stone

And I love you
To keep it hot where you are
Ariana,
And by your nature
As best you can

What do I have to do I said
You don't have to do anything he said
Why do you always think you have to do something

I don't know I said maybe
Because I'm a girl. That's
No excuse said the sun
Just have fun. Yeah sure
I said suddenly feeling envious and macho
I do have fun I said
Not enough he said
Fine I said I'll have more fun.
Have more he said
Fine I said, *Dad*,
I'll have more fun

If my tone annoyed him he didn't
Show it.

I love
To touch the cow
The sun said (again). I even love to touch her bones
I whiten them in my perfect heat
I sweat the last milk from her dead tit
And make a sacred saddle of her skull

Which when you take it up is an instrument
By which you can know me and love me if you like
To whenever you want. So you do
Want me to worship you I said

Only if you want to he said
If you ever feel sad or confused.

I want you to know the sun went on
That the earth's back is lonesome
And sore for the massage
Of the hooves of cattle

And when you get money
Here is what I want you to do with it.

I said, When I get money?
I thought I didn't have to do anything.
How am I going to get money?
You said to have more fun.
I know what I said said the sun.
Have more fun. When you get money—
But how will I get money I said

Ariana he said you are starting to sound very common
When you get money, treat yourself right and then
Buy cattle and go in the night
To the plains with them and leave them there to go
Whichever way they want to go, and then get
More money and return with more cattle in the night
To that place and to other places
With accomplices
Who love you and know my light by you
And combine your money with theirs
For increase of purchase
And put the cattle out in the nights where the moon shines my light
Enough to silver their horns and shimmer
Their coats again and again as they walk
The muscle and hides on their shoulders and hips

As Johnny Appleseed planted trees Ariana
I want you to plant cattle for me
And for Earth who is a lonely
Woman always complaining in a shrill voice up to me
Though I admit with good reason. I hate the way she whines.
She yearns desperately to be touched in this way

And in any case if she does not get what she wants
I will miss you, all of you
Never to kiss you again.

Do you know what I'm talking about he said
Yeah I know what you're talking about I said
The end of the world bla bla bla

Well not quite but it's too complicated to go into he said
Don't worry I'll kill all the assholes
I can't tell if you're joking or serious I said
Ariana sometimes you pretend to be stupid he said
I know I said I'm sorry

The flesh and the bones of these animals
Has always been mine as the milk and water of these animals
Was thine for a long time and of course by their water I mean their
Sweat and the brine
And dew on their eyes.

The weight, rhythm and blood of these hinds
Is meant for Earth who as I said longs
For them and deserves them.

I get it I get it I said.
Good he said.

As I write you my eyes are round
As gold coins, the left one still goggling

Up at the moon, the right one like the bursting belly
Button on a happy baby though not happy at all
But glad. My secular life
If I ever had one is over

Excerpt from *The Pain Journal*

BOB FLANAGAN

April, 1995

4/1/95 Hotel performance done. People watching me from one hotel room while I performed supposedly auto-erotic activities in my own room, all alone. Don't know who saw what, or what anyone thought, or what it all meant. I'm just glad it's over. Wine enema, butt plug, alligator clips, ball whacking, piss drinking, masturbating, bondage—they wanted a show, I gave them a show. Felt disoriented and depressed through most of it, as I feel disoriented and depressed through most everything these days. No more commitments! Sheree doesn't seem to give a shit about me anymore. I'm mad at her about it.

4/2/95 You—whoever you are—must be sick to death of me in front of the TV in bed, every night, describing Sheree's snoring and whining about how awful I feel. Sometimes I don't feel so bad—but then I have to do something, like go from point A to point B. Didn't get to sleep till 3 AM last night—4 AM daylight savings. Here I am tonight, 12:30. Her snoring. Still plugging away at the punching bag design. Don't know what I'm doing. Hearing more good reports about last night's show. Was feeling kind of depressed about it. Thought maybe it was stupid—maybe it still is, but no one's telling me. Ear plugs.

4/3/95 Bills paid. Saw Obler. Doubled my Zoloft. Our work returned from Boston. Hope it's all there. Storage space full. Depression lifting—maybe—a little.

4/4/95 About ready to check into the hospital. Maybe Thursday or Friday. Not breathing well. Pain in left chest. Weight loss. Tired. Time to go. I'm more and more afraid each time that this time I'll get admitted and won't come out. So I hold back, try to finish up what I can around here. Worked on the computer today. Confetti casket. Scanned in a bunch of photos. Watched TV with Sheree. Women who suddenly remember in therapy that they were sexually abused as children. Another show about John Lee Hooker. I didn't want to watch it cause I thought I didn't like his music, but I was wrong—I was thinking of Dr. John—it's Dr. John I don't like. But John Lee Hooker was good, at least in his early days. Weren't we all good in our early days?

4/5/95 Hardly slept at all last night and I'm up late again. Most likely going into the hospital tomorrow morning. Just can't hack it. So short of breath sometimes it gets really scary. Heart pounding. Headache. Buying a new Powerbook computer tomorrow. Maybe I'll get some writing done. But now I'll stop.

4/6/95 The hospital—finally. Seems like I've been talking about coming here ever since the last time I left here. Haven't been breathing or feeling well the whole time and will probably never breathe well or feel well again. I'm not being pessimistic when I say it's only going to get worse. That's the reality. My blood gasses are much worse: PO2 81, PCO2 57. Don't know if that's forever, but it's fucked. Really tired. Done for the day.

4/7/95 Hospital. Wake up at 3:30 in time to make a note here about something, anything. Headache. How about something else, something good. Sheree picked up and brought me the new Powerbook today. Feel guilty and uncomfortable about the expense, but ideally I can use it to write when I'm here—but so far all I've done is play games.

so what does it mean to be here in the hospital again, not breathing?

SWEAT HEAD

keep sweating nit wit nothing to write oj oj oj all day coughing and not writing now not now such a drag when does it happen when does it begin

So now that I have this computer here what do I do with it besides play computer games? Where did all that writing come from. Why won't my fingers or my mind work. I can't even type.

4/8/95 I have to write about being collected. Sort of like being a slave. Art slave. Sheree's slave, her pet. We have a cage and all that. I threw up in it on St. Patrick's day, last year. This year I was not feeling well enough to do anything on St. Patrick's day, or any day. But I still want to be in the cage for an extended period of time. 3 days feels right. After 3 weeks in the hospital, what's 3 days in a cage? What's that movie/book, *The Collector*? There wasn't a cage in that movie, though. I'm thinking of *Lady in a Cage*. And it wasn't a cage, it was an old elevator.

4/9/95 I'm in the hospital. So what else is new? Illuminated by my computer screen. I've been bringing computers to the hospital with me for more than ten years. I'm back here for the sixth or seventh time in a year. I'm averaging every two months. I was in here last Valentine's Day, as well as Thanksgiving. Next week will be Easter, and I'll probably still be here.

4/10/95 Still hospitalized. Didn't feel like writing the past two days. Not much happening. Feeling somewhat better. Headaches still. "Pain Management" doctor concerned about all the Vicodin. Knows nothing about CF. Asshole. I just got done yelling at a respiratory therapist for leaving me here with no O^2 for 15 minutes while he was out of the room doing whatever. This same guy has done the same thing to me several times before. How would they like to sit here for 15 minutes with a plastic bag over their heads? Feel guilty for blowing up, but they can't keep doing that. Ah, what the hell, I feel good blowing up. Sheree and Kirby were here today. Yesterday, Phil and L.R.—Bill Sine and his "Bob Fest" idea. Please don't make me the center of attention just because I'm sick. It's ok if I do it, but not from the outside in. What?

4/11/95 So what not much. In the hospital. The sun's too bright. We don't need a cloud. Investigate. Testimony. Illness.

4/12/95 So the doctor says I'll be around awhile. Not dying yet, even though I might feel like it. Even though I might wish for it. Even though I've got all these credit card bills filled to the max.

I'm taking a new pill that's supposed to help me sleep, so of course here I am, 3:30 AM, writing and sweating and thinking and peeing. I use the urinal at night cause I'm too lazy to go to the bathroom. Nothing wrong with me. Going home Friday. Even Dr. Riker says he thinks I'll be around till next year at least. But they want me to cut down on the Vicodin. Afraid I'm getting addicted.

4/13/95 Before I die. just let me say one thing. What do I do now? "It makes for a very unproductive day." Well that's the way they wanted it. They lied over and over and over. A brand new box of rubber gloves. Protection for everybody. Phlegm. Bob Phlegmagain.

Last night here (hospitalized.) 2 AM. Drenched in sweat. Had to change my gown and have the nurse change the sheets cause they were soaked. Something to do with the pills they're giving me. Zipamine, or something, an anti-depressant, but low dose. It's supposed to bring back endorphins that have supposedly been knocked off by all the Vicodin I've been taking. That couldn't be bad. Wouldn't hurt to get some endorphins back. But meanwhile, a side effect is I'm drenched in sweat. Talked to Deborah Drier today. She met Ira Silverberg, and Amy Gerstler was there, and somehow my name came up and Amy gave her my number here. Sheree's picking me up tomorrow. She says she misses me, but she sounds depressed. Karmen's spending the weekend. What set off Sheree's depression, I wonder? She says she doesn't know, but I'm sure I'll find out.

4/14/95 Home from the hospital. 2 AM. Crazy drug schedule. Sheree upstairs with Karmen, house guest for the weekend. Watched video's at Mike Kelley's with him, Anita, Jim and Marnie, Rita and Kirby, Jake and Karmen. Eyes tired. Home.

4/15/95 Late again (2:30.) SM party for crazy Sharon. I didn't want to go because I never want to go anywhere. But it was ok. Nice people. I don't care much for watching people play SM at parties. I either feel bored, left out, or intrusive. Sheree zoning out again. She seems to interpret "stress leave" as time to not go to work so she can stay home and dwell on things to be stressed and depressed about. So after a week of her moaning about my being away from her—I'm home—and she's as distant as hell. Shit. I would rather have stayed in the hospital. I don't need the stress.

4/16/95 End of Easter. Late again. Drugs. Saw *Portishead* with Scott, Sheree and Karmen. Sheree's upstairs with Karmen. Sounds like she's whipping her. Just got done cutting her. Wanted to cut me, but I said no. Over and over again cause she's stoned and won't take no for an answer. I feel guilty and unfulfilled saying no. But I'm tired. That's a good excuse. I'm stupid—that's a better one.

4/17/95 I don't get many visitors when I'm in the hospital, and most of the time that's fine with me. It's an awkward situation all around and on both sides of the bed nobody feels good.

More late night drugs. No going out tonight—good. Sexy women, scantily clad, some horror movie on TV. Sheree's snoresville. Karmen back home. Besides doing drugs most of the day I've been playing/working on the computer—the punching bag design, blackjack, and a little writing. Writing about the hospital. I seem to have more energy than I've had in a while. Just need to focus somehow.

4/20/95 Haven't written in the journal for the past three nights because I haven't been downstairs for three days because I keep falling asleep on the couch while running my antibiotics. Since I don't finish up until 2 am and have to start all over again four hours later, there's not much sense in going down stairs. But I might tonight. Drove Sheree down to Irvine, to school, even though that was the last thing I wanted to do, but she was sick all day and wasn't going to go, and then she got stoned and started feeling guilty about not going but too stoned to drive, so I drove her, after much bitching and whining cause she was driving me crazy in her stoned state, but I drove her, and waited for her, still residual slave stuff inside there somewhere.

4/21/95 Four nights and I still haven't been downstairs—wait—last night after writing here, and after running the three antibiotics, I did go downstairs to bed, forgot. After all these years, I still miss it when I don't sleep with Sheree, even with her snoring. But right now I'm still up here, upstairs, computer on the coffee table, and the pile of usual shit, and the constant tv, bombing news, tragedy, nuts, psychopaths, can't tear myself away. And of course, OJ. Went to dinner with Sheree, Molly, Murray, Richard and Ted. Met Donna and Jeff at the Nuart afterwards to see Michael Powell's *Stairway to Heaven*. Dated but brilliant, like me. Let the drugs flow. I have to go.

4/22/95 Another night of drugs on the couch after a Saturday of laziness. I finally took a shower, but that was about it. Just drugs. But tonight Sheree's sleeping on the couch—and snoring! Ahhhh. She won't go to bed. Ahhhh.

4/23/95 Here again. Drugs. Computer. TV. Couch. Naked. Alligator clip on my dick. Fantasize about putting dozens and dozens of clips on my dick, but I can barely stand one. Trying to get this writing thing going. My fingers don't work on these keys. Maybe I'm just a lousy typist? Maybe I'm just a lousy writer. How would I know when I hardly ever write? Headaches headaches headaches. Sheree in bed. She handcuffed me today while she went out with Rita. We both liked that. Can we get our mistress/slave thing back? How can it work with me barely able to stand anything or do anything?

4/24/95 Here I am tippydetyping on the couch cause I'm still on the drugs, nothing interesting, just antibiotics. Lately I've been longing for Demerol. Reminiscing about those days of post surgery when I got it when I wanted it and liked it—a little too much. But, ho hum, nothing but Tobramycin, Piperacillin and Ceftazidime in my veins. A couple of Vicodin in my mouth, but that doesn't do much anymore beyond dulling the headache, which is fine I suppose. Sheree's here on the couch too. Not sleeping cause she slept till noon today. She's out on stress leave so she has no schedule. She's waving her naked legs in the air.

She's reading about gardening, her new hobby. I want her to put dozens of alligator clips on my dick and balls, but I don't know if I'd freak out or not. I can put a couple on myself. It hurts like hell but most of the time I can hold on until the pain subsides and I get kind of a rush. But can I take it when she's in control? The ultimate question.

4/25/95 Letterman. Couch. Drugs. How we do drag on. Getting hard to breathe again. Thought I was doing much better. It never lasts. My mood has been better, though. And I've got a renewed interest in sex, mostly fantasizing about this alligator clip thing, and trying it out a little bit with a couple of clips here and there, those jagged little teeth biting into my tender spots as I grab hold of something like the bed rail and squeeze until the pain floats off a little, turns sweet almost, and then it's time for another. It's almost like eating hot chili peppers, except these taste buds are in my balls.

4/26/95 Itchy eyes. Can't focus. Tired . . . again. On the couch . . . again. Drugs . . . again. And I'm still into this alligator clip thing. Last night, after I finally went down to bed, I put seven of them on my dick—along the shaft, on the corona and the tip of the head—and I kept them there—and I came (well, it's a pathetic form of coming, but I came). Now I'm ready for Sheree to go at me with even more clips for a longer period of time, and then hot wax afterwards. We would have done it tonight but she had to go to school and I had to go to Debbie's, then there's these stupid drugs to do—we're exhausted, as usual. I'll probably dabble with a few of them again tonight, just to stay in shape: alligator clip training.

4/27/95 Last night for antibiotics. This time around. Last call for Demerol (I wish). Don't need pain killers now. I'm a masochist again! Thirteen alligator clips after last nights entry. Wasn't as turned on as I was the previous night, but the discipline is still there. The obsessiveness, which I've missed. Tomorrow Sheree leaves for Oregon for a few days. I have it in my head to do a few things to myself, if I don't chicken out or tire out or crap out. The world is blowing up around me, but I shall be entertained.

4/28/95 No more drugs. But I'm still here on the couch, naked, tv on, coffee table full of junk, headache. Sheree in Oregon. She just called, stoned, talking about art again, mad at me again cause I didn't like whatever idea she was going on about. Trapped. I went for the cheese once again. Rats. All's well otherwise. Still in the mood for torture. I always get it into my head to eat shit when Sheree is out of town and I'm here alone left to my own devices. I never have been able to go through with it. I haven't even tried it in years. But I've got some energy now, and I'm in a mood, and it's still a cherry I haven't plucked. But it's so disgusting. Auto-humiliation. The plan is to handcuff myself with my hands behind my back in a cage with a plate full of my own shit in front of me. Embedded throughout the shit is a string of five candy Lifesavers tied together with fishing line and fed through a hole in the plate, down and out of the cage, up and over and back down again suspended over my back. On the end of the line is the handcuff key and the cage key. When I finally get my nerve up and eat through the shit I find the Lifesavers and suck them until they melt, one by one, freeing the fishing line so it pulls through the hole in the plate, allowing the handcuff key to drop down behind my back to my waiting hands where I then unlock myself and let myself out of the cage, feeling thoroughly disgusted with myself, but at the same time turned on and strangely filled with an overwhelming sense of accomplishment. But talk is cheap.

4/29/95 Can hardly keep my eyes open. It's not real late, but I'm still tired. No shit eating tonight. Lots to do. Video to set up. Have to take my time and not get too tired. Can't even write I'm so tired.

4/30/95 Let the shit eating begin. I'm downstairs, in bed, watching tv. Tv keeps me grounded and keeps my mood up. Setting up these elaborate auto-erotic sm scenarios is by nature isolating and lonely. Tv, and its window on the "normal" helps keep the depression at bay. Shit is disgusting. It's supposed to be. That's why the need for all the padlocks, keys, handcuffs, fishing line, rope, etc. Once I cross that line and snap those locks, there's no way out but to eat shit. Literally "eat shit or die." No matter how much I fantasize about this ultimate degradation, no matter how much the thought of it gets me hard, I always chicken out at the moment of truth. The couple of times in the past when I've done the hidden keys and padlock thing, I very Houdini-like, managed to escape without a bite, feeling very stupid, very humiliated—as humiliated by what I almost did as I was for not having the guts to do it. But tonight is different. I think I've completely outsmarted myself. I'll be in bondage from head to toe, no way out until I eat through this big pile of my own shit, find the hidden Lifesavers which are tied to fishing line, suck the Lifesavers until they melt, freeing the line and allowing the keys to drop down behind my back, where I can then unlock my handcuffs, ankle restraints and nose pierce. Assuming I don't chicken out. I've been assembling this coprophеliac contraption for three days. I can't back out now. That would make me a failure. It's hard enough being such a weirdo, I don't want to be a failed weirdo.

All that for one lousy little bite. I'm only a partial failure. The best laid plans of perverts . . . First of all the bondage was a little too much. I was afraid that once I tied my nose down and locked my hands behind my back that I wouldn't be able to breathe. Very uncomfortable. But that was the idea, right? But the biggest flaw was the Lifesavers. They dissolved in the shit before I ever got to them. Why the keys didn't drop right away, I don't know. I had to push the shit away with my face and nudge the line with my tongue. And that's another design problem. That's what tying my nose down was supposed to circumvent, but even after I tied it it came loose right away. I didn't have to eat the shit at all. All I had to do was push it away with my face. Back to the drawing board. But I did get two good bites out of it. Tastes like mud. Bitter mud. Felt stupid at the sight of my shit covered faced in the mirror. But I'll try it again. Keep doing it until I get it right.

A Description of the Camp

BAHA' EBDEIR

It is a place where there are few neighborhoods, so many windows overlooking each other, and so many doors left open. There are numerous small groceries next to each other. There is one bakery that supplies the whole neighborhood with bread. In the morning, people bump into each other to buy a loaf of bread. If you don't bump into people, there is no way you can get your bread for that morning. Flowers dangle from the window frames. The window boxes are made from milk and yogurt boxes. Clothes hang from lines, drying in the wind.

Everyone knows each other. Women gather together and gossip about who got married and who got divorced. Fatima, who picked a fight with her husband, is the talk of the whole street. The houses are so close to each other, you can see a house built at the top of another house. You can see the black water tanks that are barely filled with water at the top of each house. Unnecessary objects litter the roofs of houses: broken bicycles and worn-out shoes. The waste container that is always full, but barely emptied. To empty the waste container would mean to burn the waste. The smoke will start spreading all over the street. The sewage water flows excessively all over the streets. There are broken speed bumps in the street. These speed bumps are treated like a game rather than an obstacle. Cars speed up in anticipation as they approach the speed bumps.

When it rains, the water leaks everywhere. A family could be sitting peacefully at home while the drops of water fall on their heads. Every corner of the house leaks water. They place buckets under each corner of the house. There you can see the indifference of the people. They turn on five heaters at one time and they wonder why the electricity keeps going off. Then again, why should they care, they are refugees.

A TOUGH NIGHT

It was 2:00 am, everyone was peacefully sleeping, except those who have been making a call for peacemaking, but never make peace. There was a knock on the door, young Sarah heard the knock, but she was afraid to open the door. She looked through the window and saw a tan-faced soldier, holding his gun and pointing it towards her house. The whole neighborhood was surrounded by military jeeps. There were so many soldiers waiting in anticipation to throw a gas bomb. Their gun fire sounds, the smell of their tear gas, and their broken Arabic words are part and parcel of the night ambience of the camp. That night, I opened the window of my room, I started looking at the sky; a thing that both me and my enemy can see. It was the first time that I had a sense of justice and freedom. This time my beloved occupier couldn't occupy the blue sky, besiege the sparkling stars, or cut the moon in half. This was the only assurance for me that there is still an inalienable part of my freedom that no one can take.

A COLD MORNING WITH WARM PEOPLE

I woke up in the morning and the weather was so cold and dreary, but the people and their possessions were as warm as a cup of tea. The window of my room overlooks the window of my neighbor's room, I saw Uncle Mahmoud sharing a loaf of bread with his four young sons. They were all sitting by the fire in their cramped basement. Smoke was coming from Uncle Mahmoud's house. For a moment, I thought their house was on fire, but I soon realized that it was just the usual habit of Aunt Fatima's daughter, who burnt the Taboon bread while she was busy looking at her boyfriend through the window.

THE KEY OF RETURN

As I entered the gate of Ayda Camp, there was a large statue of a key at the top of a gate. They call it the key of return. It is so huge and is a metallic grey color. Every time I see someone entering the gate, I start thinking of the possibility that this key of return might fall down on one of those many people coming in and out. It is so unfair and annoying when your freedom is hung up at the top of a gate. It is so high that you cannot reach it, touch it, or even know what it smells like.

I have always seen the children in the camp climbing the steel pillars and the walls, but I have never seen any of them climbing the gate in order to reach out to the huge key of return. At that time, it crossed my mind that if we cannot touch a piece of metal representing the right of freedom and return, then how can we still hope to have our right of freedom and return signed on an official paper. Young Basil climbed up the gate and embraced the huge key of return so tightly. It was not until he touched and embraced the key of return that I started believing again in freedom. Basil hung up the Palestinian flag at the top of the gate. The Palestinian flag was dancing to the sound of the wind. It was not just waving, but singing to those who were standing below the gate. The people of the camp were cheering for Basil, calling him fearless and free.

CHILDHOOD MEMORIES

Please don't call me Mr. Ayda camp because I am not only a place for people to camp. I am a place where the street becomes a playground. Where children can't afford going to a fancy gym, so they climb the metal pillars and jump over the high walls instead. You can see the children playing football with their slippers. Boots and sneakers aren't actually their type. A child carelessly plays in his underwear. Another one walks through the streets barefoot. He falls to the ground, looks like he wants to cry, but holds back his tears and smiles instead. Children play with rocks instead of a Nike ball.

I am a circus where you can see children spinning broken tires. Where kites are made from plastic bags. No matter how high the kite flies, it always ends up getting stuck in the barbed wire fence. But still, that doesn't stop them from flying more and more kites. I am an adventurous experience and a risky life. Young Basil was bored, so he escaped from school. He threw a rock at a group of soldiers and ran away. He was as fast as the spread of their tear gas, so they couldn't catch him.

Basil and Sarah were young children playing hide and seek together. You could hear their laughter and screaming in every corner of the street. Sarah is all grown up now, she wears Hijab, she doesn't talk to guys. She walked by Basil's grocery the other day, but couldn't look him in the eye. He wanted to become a young child again, so he would grab her by the arm and be her superman. He wanted her to smile back at him when he smiled. Now, the camp is no longer their playground, but a prison that imprisons their emotions. Neither the camp nor the people can tolerate their spontaneous smiles and loud screams anymore.

THE APARTHEID WALL

My mother calls me the apartheid wall, but my stepmother calls me the separation wall. I am a wall that dehumanizes the humans living in the camp. I categorize them as criminals. I am an ugly wall with a metallic grey color, a whistle-blower if you will. One of my eyes is an observation bridge and the other is a surveillance camera. My head is so sharp, it is a barbed wire that no one can climb.

Yesterday, I decided that it is time for a change. I couldn't stand the sight of my grey face anymore. I wanted to try some makeup. A group of graffiti artists came to visit me. My whole body has become a masterpiece! It is plastered with paintings of doves and olive trees. I am not just a wall, but a place where dead bodies are still alive on my walls. Here is a painting of last week's martyr and another of last month's. My eyes are fixated on a painting of the martyr *Thawra*. I see courage and resistance in her dark black eyes. She guards the apartheid wall with an olive branch she holds so tightly. She stands still like a mountain waiting in anticipation for a soldier to pass by.

Every day I have new guests. Those who come and visit me never come back. I am a portrait studio where posers come to pose. When their conscience pricks, they come and take pictures of me. This is all they can do. I have the most creative background to take a photogenic picture. My background could be a settlement or any painting on my wall. You don't need a filter to make your picture blurry. Just wait for the soldiers to throw a gas bomb and you'll have a natural one.

THE APARTHEID WALL AS A PLAYGROUND

The other day Laith and his friends were bored to death. They were sick and tired of playing hide and seek and running through the streets. They decided to invent a new game that combined these two games. All they had to do was just to throw a rock at the observation bridge and then the fun began. They hid behind the waste containers when they wanted to throw a rock. The waste containers served as a shield to protect them from the gas bombs and bullets. The more children that gathered together, the more exciting the game became.

The children challenged each other to approach the soldiers. It was not until they heard the sound of the gunfire, that the children started running away. It was a game that put their lives in jeopardy, but they still wanted to play. An Israeli soldier was wearing his military uniform with a combat helmet on his head. He pointed an F-16 weapon at one of the children. His combat bag was stuffed with gas bombs, knives, and binoculars. Laith was only wearing his pajamas. He covered his face with the Kuffeya. He pointed his slingshot at the soldiers. His hands and legs are his F-16. His black big eyes are his binoculars. His Kufeya is his combat helmet.

Laith went home after a tiring day. He and his family sat cross-legged on the floor. They had Manakeesh for dinner. He talked a lot that night. He ate a piece of Manakeesh in a hurry. Suddenly, a group of Israeli soldiers barged into their living room. They didn't even wait for him to finish the last bite of his Manakeesh. They blindfolded him and took him to the military jeep.

Would You Wear My Eyes?

BOB KAUFMAN

My body is a torn mattress,
Disheveled throbbing place
For the comings and goings
Of loveless transients.
The whole of me
Is an unfurnished room
Filled with dank breath
Escaping in gasps to nowhere.
Before completely objective mirrors
I have shot myself with my eyes,
But death refused my advances.
I have walked on my walls each night
Through strange landscapes in my head.
I have brushed my teeth with orange peel,
Iced with cold blood from the dripping faucets.
My face is covered with maps of dead nations;
My hair is littered with drying ragweed.
Bitter raisins drip haphazardly from my nostrils
While schools of glowing minnows swim from my mouth.
The nipples of my breasts are sun-browned cockleburrs;
Long-forgotten Indian tribes fight battles on my chest
Unaware of the sunken ships rotting in my stomach.
My legs are charred remains of burned cypress trees;
My feet are covered with moss from bayous, flowing
across my floor.
I can't go out anymore.
I shall sit on my ceiling.
Would you wear my eyes?

August 6, 2011

Excerpt from *The Grave on the Wall*

BRANDON SHIMODA

Every story, every testimonial, begins with it having been a day like any other. Blue sky, clear. But it was also a day like any other because it was a day in an endless series of days in which the sun rose, and the people with it, to war. Blue sky, clear, not because these are details of a day like any other, but because they were the final details.

At 8:15 and 15 seconds on the morning of August 6, 1945, a United States B-29 Superfortress dropped a uranium bomb on the city of Hiroshima on the island of Honshu. Little Boy exploded 1,903 feet above Shima Hospital, on the east bank of the Motoyasu River, incinerating, in less than a second, 80,000 people.

At 8:15 on the morning of August 6, 2011, a bell was struck in the Peace Park. The bell's reverberations were heavy and thick. 60,000 people in the park were spellbound, could not move. At 8:20, the mayor recited testimony from a woman who was sixteen at the time of the bombing:

In that soundless world, I thought I was the only one left . . .

Suddenly I heard lots of voices crying and screaming . . .

I did manage to move enough to save one young child . . .

Then Masahiro Fukuhara and Nanoka Fujita mounted the stage. They were sixth graders—Masahiro at Misasa Elementary, Nanoka at Koi Elementary—and had been chosen to be the children's representatives of the memorial ceremony. Their task was to deliver the Commitment to Peace. They stood side-by-side and fixed their eyes on the sky beyond the museum:

On March 11, countless lives were lost in the Tohoku earthquake and tsunami. Even now, many people are still missing.

Their voices were plangent, definitive. They sounded like they were delivering soliloquies at the edge of a cliff. I thought of the young boy standing up to the spirits of the peach orchard in Kurosawa's dream (*I can buy peaches at the store! But where can you buy a whole orchard in bloom?*). Masahiro and Nanoka's message was of sorrow and hope, but they were speaking to the ruins. Adults, what can adults provide? What can adults instill in the faithful and faithless alike that the thousands of disappeared and disappearing witnesses cannot? The morning was a ritual, but Masahiro and Nanoka, their voices pitched into the sky beyond the museum, reinforced the fact, by way of the sun and heat—eyes closed, sweating, clenching their fists—that we were gathered in a burial ground. It was as if they were saying: if *we* understand, if *we* are courageous enough to raise our voices above the bodies of the dead . . .

The basement auditorium of the Memorial Museum was full, but during the intermission between Japanese and English, it emptied, and only a small number of people remained. Ten westerners, Americans mostly, moved to the front to listen to five hibakusha—two women, three men—share their stories. I opened my notebook and wrote down as much as I could, because I knew I wanted—that I would continue to want—to return, every year, to their stories, to what they had come such an extraordinary distance to share.

Keiko was eight at the time of the bomb. She spoke the longest. Her story began with a refusal. People were dying all around her—burning, thirsty, in need of water. She gave them water from the family well. They drank the water, vomited, died. She knew she did not kill them but felt, *it was me!* It was easier for Keiko to take responsibility for their deaths than to try to explain what she could not. Her story began when she decided she was never going to tell anyone. She called it her *invisible scar*.

Isao was thirteen at the time of the bomb. Shoso and Keijiro were sixteen. Sumiko was seventeen. Shoso said he hated America. He took our hands in his and thanked us for being there. I felt in his hands the burden of his hatred yet saw on his face the complexity of his hatred being unresolved, solicitous, open.

Shoso Hirai (16)
My father and younger brother were killed instantly . . . My older brothers were in China as soldiers . . . But the air raid alarm was soon cancelled . . . As soon as I touched the door, I was hit by a strong blast . . . It became dark all around me . . . Every path that led to my house was engulfed in flames . . . I thought, There must have been a big disaster in Hiroshima . . . We spent the night at the farmer's house . . . It seemed as if we had just walked through the Gate of Hell . . . We carried my father's bones back home.

Sumiko Hirosawa (17)
But at this moment, everybody is happy now . . . But, everything had to go away anyway . . . But, what did you want to know? . . . But, everything is okay now . . . It was a long time, but it was okay . . . It took a long time to make the rice and the vegetables, and they came to pick them up . . . It was the farmers that took care of everybody . . . We had to help ourselves, but it was okay, we had the farmers.

Keijiro Matsushima (16)
That springtime, my father died . . . Beautiful, shining in the morning sun, white-silver planes . . . The whole world turned to something like an orange world, a sunset world . . . I felt like I had just been thrown into an oven . . . Hundreds, hundreds of thunders at the same moment . . . No one screamed, no voice, no sound . . . I was just crawling around on the floor . . . Everyone felt one bomb was dropped here beside me . . . Their hair had stood up straight, charcoal-gray skin, and their clothes were torn and singey . . . I could see red muscles under the peeled skin . . . Their faces were like baked pumpkins . . . Exactly a procession of ghosts . . . They were still able to walk, that's good . . . For many days these bodies were floating in the river, up and down, with the movement of the tides . . . Real hell . . . Real hell . . . I decided to leave Hiroshima, and I wanted to go to my mommy's home . . . My whole city of Hiroshima is dying,

maybe I was a little sentimental at the moment . . . I began walking to my mommy's home in the farm country . . . So, you can tell a man's fate . . . And even today, there are many old women who couldn't get married, they are living very lonely lives . . . Well, that's almost all I experienced, so I say that's all . . . I had read an article in Boys Magazine about A-bomb, and as I was crossing the bridge, I thought about that article . . . I was a smart kid, but it didn't help . . . I will also have to disappear soon.

Isao Aratani (13)
Sweet potatoes were planted there, and we went to pull weeds . . . We heard an unusually loud propeller sound . . . Two or three parachutes . . . Heard the sound of full-speed engine . . . At the same time we were blown off the ground . . . We didn't have any idea what had happened . . . Sky-scraping mushroom-shaped cloud . . . Walked like ghost . . . Skin had slipped . . . One of my classmates gave water to several victims, all of them died soon after saying Thank you . . . We tried to escape deadly exposure to the sunshine, which increased our pain . . . They tried to cool themselves by the rain, they drank the rain . . . Immediately after the bombing, 8:15 a.m., it was high tide, and the water was deep . . . They supplied food such as crackers and rice balls . . . The city was burned and reduced to ash in one night . . . And couldn't even tell if the bodies belonged to man or woman . . . They died while standing . . . I remember the smell of cremation . . . We had a complicated feeling about the defeat, and also relief . . . We didn't want to talk about our memories for many years . . . The Poplar Tree Will Transfer the Story from Generation to Generation.

Keiko Ogura (8)
I am the youngest who still remembers that day . . . Every year I stand on the riverbank . . . There were a bunch of bananas and oranges . . . My mother sold her wedding ring to the army . . . Americans had a tall nose . . . Shiny . . . Children had to bite [edible grasses] *100 times . . . They heard a kind of rumor that near Hiroshima City there had been a big fire . . . At midnight they tried to*

escape from the temple . . . That was the time the teacher decided to tell the children about the atomic bomb . . . Look at the Buddha—can you see all the faces behind the Buddha? Your parents are already in heaven . . . Only this year did I ask my brother how he spent his days in the temple . . . I want you to understand the invisible scars of the survivors, the invisible sorrows . . . I would like to tell my invisible scars from now on . . . On August the 7th I climbed up the hill near my house and saw the city . . . Behind the city I saw Ujina Port and the Seto Inland Sea . . . Everybody will be the victim soon . . . I want to say, I am sorry, we have the same destiny . . . I feel we are all connected by the sea . . . We couldn't have time to sleep . . . We stayed up all night . . . All Hiroshima people were so sleepy that morning . . . Finally, my mother said, I want to die at home, not in a shelter . . . Father had lucky inspiration . . . I was hit on the road . . . I woke up in darkness, pitch darkness . . . So quiet . . . The thatched farmer's house started to burn . . . Oily, gray, charcoal-colored rain . . . It was so sticky . . . There were so many traces of black rain everywhere in my house . . . It goes together for a while, and then there was a curve . . . He wanted to follow the plane . . . He could see from the top of the hill, the top of the cloud, and its color was pink . . . It aches a lot to touch your body, so not to touch your body . . . I could smell the smell of burnt hair . . . The other side the victims there could barely move, they were moving so slowly . . . They died, squatting in a line on the road, on the stone steps . . . That was the beginning of my invisible scars . . . And that moment I decided not to tell my story to anyone . . . Everywhere there were hundreds of big flies . . . In the afternoon, they stopped moving their hands, and they were covered in black flies . . . And then I could see the Inland Sea, and it seemed so near, because there was nothing . . . We have a strong fear about our genetic problems . . . As soon as I saw the shiny wings of the Enola Gay, I was frozen, I started to cry . . .

We sat on the stone embankment above the Motoyasu, our legs hanging over the water, the Genbaku Dome behind us. Thousands of people sat along the embankment. The water was dark, except for where it was illuminated by paper lanterns. There were thousands of lanterns. The volume of love was concentrated in their colors. Prayers were written on each lantern: the names of loved ones, ancestors. Then the lanterns were sent into the river. Each held a small flame. The lanterns, in their slow, tentative movements, became a community. Pink, tangerine, lavender, light blue, watermelon. They gathered and slid against each other. The sea pulled.

Pumpkin-yellow lanterns floated beneath our feet. Silent, bound together with the countenance of a family making its evening rounds, each member decorated with hearts, red suns, birds, stripes of color. The family of lanterns, moving in one long streak, and gathering beneath the bridge, resembled a hive, each family member guttering out, until fully extinguished, the souls of the dead taking leave of their performance in the ceremony. Would the fires burn through the night?

Excerpt from *The Romanian: Story of an Obsession*

BRUCE BENDERSON

We make another attempt to find Mioriţa, and our cab driver gets lost again. The ride ends in a mud path, where eerie light from an art nouveau window in the unlit street illuminates the uniform of a soldier, working in this city in conjunction with the police. I want to ask directions, but Romulus grabs my sleeve and keeps me from crossing the street. It seems no one asks the police for help.

We cross to the other side farther down, through mud. Why do I feel that I'm becoming lost in a marsh? I'll eventually discover that Bucharest was built on forested wetlands and a tangle of roots. Once across the mud, we end up in front of a large, red Victorian house that could have belonged to *Psycho*'s Mrs. Bates. There's a sign in front of it that says "Opium." We enter out of curiosity, and a woman in a revealing red cocktail dress asks whether we prefer the smoking room (we aren't sure what substance she's referring to), the "bath lounge" or Purgatorio, a room in the basement with chairs decorated alternately with red devil horns and white angel haloes. The establishment is owned by the Romanian actress Ioana Crăciunescu, whose much younger partner, the director Bogdan Voicu, is working with her to create theater entertainments for the special few.

There are, says the manager—who has appeared to give us a tour—weekly performances in the bath lounge, a bordello-red room featuring an immense golden bathtub. And in Purgatorio, a new trend of stand-up comedy in English has begun, because, she says, Romanian stand-up is just a bunch of potty jokes. Next door, in the yellow smoking room, spooky pantomimes are going on among the Oriental cushions. But there's no food here. Someone calls us a taxi, and we turn to the hotel, defeated and hungry.

Too tired to keep looking for food, we switch on the television. In front of it and an endless soccer match, we learn a series of passional attitudes designed to fit his smaller, steelier body into my padded bulk. I'm stretched out on my back with him using my stomach as a cushion, or we lie entangled like two tarantulas, a perfect balance of lighter on heavier limbs that avoids bone pressure. Or I'll be lying belly-down with my head by his waist, so that my hands can wander over his body like tortoises inspecting every blade of grass on a beach.

Because he doesn't complain, I've decided we're in paradise. Visions of him change, but they're always highly sexual, with elements of the predatory. I feel like a falconer with his hawk, that beady-eyed, sharp-beaked and alert but dependent creature that pecks ever so carefully at its master. At other times, his sinuous muscles enlace me in the fantasy of a python, our corkscrew intertwinings thrilling me into believing myself some circus performer who's ready to chance being strangled for the right to be caressed. But then, every so often, he suddenly diminishes to a poor wren, for what is the real difference, except in the sense of motive versus action, between vulnerability and predation? Isn't each part of the same formula?

It's his emotional hunger, often presenting itself as stoical machismo, that keeps promising a trapdoor into his heart. And as we lie here, the unreal atmosphere of the room is as disorienting as the description of some powdery scent in a decadent novel, while snippets of his fairy-tale past float into the air.

"And then what happened?"

"Why you want to know? You will write a book about? The story of my life, such a book that will make."

"How you ended up in Budapest. You were telling me."

"I got to go to the toilet. Toss me those cigarettes."

"Can you hear me?"

"Say?"

"You were telling me."

"They threw me out at eighteen . . ."

"Who, who?"

"Say?"

"Can't you hear me?"

"My parents, when is no more money from state for me, even though they keep money they get for me when I still live with my grandmother. Toss those matches in here at me, please, will you?"

"Your parents threw you out?"

"Surely. They fabricate this fight in Vîlcea to make me exit when I was eighteen," he claims. "Say I steal from them. Which is how I end up on Corso in Budapest where you find me. But you know, my stepfather wastes what little they have for drinking, and soon as I am to coming back, it is money all the time, they take it from us all, me, Bogdan."

"But tell me again about Macedonia. Come on, come back on the bed."

"All right, give me the remote, you know they have this erotic evening on TV every Friday, they showing one of the *Emmanuelles*."

"I saw them in the seventies. What'd you say happened in Macedonia?"

"I am crossing Macedonia two or three times, with two other guys, mostly walking, you know? They throw us out of train at every stop because they don't like our passports, but we just keeping walking and get on at next station. But then they throw us out again."

"And that's how you made it to Greece?"

"Hm, hmm, three weeks there, my Greek becoming very functional, but I not write it, not write any of the languages I speak except Romanian."

"Did you ever get caught in Greece?"

"Yes, yes. First time they send me back in closed train with other illegal Romanians. But I climb through window at station. Two days later they catching me again. 'Let's see you jump from this window,' they say. They put me on a plane. Bring me to plane handcuffed."

"A regular plane?"

"Of course. I get the meal, the drinks. But is November, still warm in Greece, and we land in Bucharest and freezing. I wearing only T-shirt. Have to hitchhike back to Sibiu."

"But what about the time you got shot crossing from Macedonia into Greece?"

"Which time? I went over so many times, I start to make money that way, border guide, you know? I prefer bullets to staying home. Listen, this Mexican border. I read in a Romanian paper that plenty of people cross over to U.S."

"Come on, Romulus, there are easier ways."

"You do it your way, I mine."

What did history do to him? The question sounds absurd, for we're all to some extent victims of history; but I'm convinced that, as my friend Ursule Molinaro suspected, Romulus is ancient. His half-finished projects and sudden departures, his enslavements and sullen betrayals are micro-recapitulations of the fate of his land.

Like my beloved Times Square, Romania was a crossroads of cultures and clashes—Byzantine glories, wily Levantine schemes for survival, the nexus of three empires: the Ottoman, the Austro-Hungarian and the Soviet. Romanians are, they themselves believe, Latins lost among the barbarians, the Roman victims of Turks.

It's midnight and we're finally eating dinner, the only customers in the hotel restaurant. The mottled marble and enormous mirrors are exquisite, baroque and unreal, the room cavernous. The way the waiters and whores who walk through look at us says that we, too, are lost, isolated. Romulus's eyes, I can tell, see doom and are perpetually disgusted by it. But such a stance is overruled by courageous passivity, which the Romanian poet Lucian Blaga called the "Mioritic space."

According to the great Romanian myth of Mioriţa, three shepherds from different regions came down with their flocks from the Carpathian Mountains. Two of them began to plot to murder the Moldovan shepherd, who was warned of the scheme by Mioriţa, a magical ewe. The shepherd didn't flee. With a vast and perplexing sense of spiritual acceptance, he planned his own funeral, which took on the character of a wedding with Nature, a return to Eden.

Critics have debated the ancient myth's meaning since it was first published by the Romantic poet Vasile Alecsandri. There are those who have associated it with pessimism and passivity, going so far as to call Romania a "suicidal" culture. But Mircea Eliade, the controversial Romanian historian and mythologist (who was accused of being a

Fascist early in his career), saw the myth of Mioriţa as being about an active transformation of fate, the will to change the meaning of destiny into something self-empowering.

In light of this, Romulus's surrender of his body to me takes on a morbid and transfigured aura. It may be an arrangement of circumstance, but to him it's part of a timeless cycle. I can see it in his eyes. His prostitution has a sacrificial, portentous significance. And so it is that the fixed expression of his eyes, the angry, almost pious gentleness of his touch are signs of sacrifice that can't be possessed by me. But in any case, the buyer can never control the ritual of prostitution.

His face is getting paler during dinner as I flounder to stake a claim, shamelessly offering him long-term financial schemes as if they were car insurance. The obsessive-compulsive nature of my feelings for him makes me spit out vulgar maintenance plans whose function is to take away the guesswork of our relationship. I want marriage instead of doom. Each of my offers is an insult to his ritualistic approach to transgression. He's getting increasingly furious at my attempts to buy him.

Eventually, my attack temporarily obliterates his machismo. Back in our room, he strikes me as a little boy, an effeminate one, as he angrily tosses his few possessions into a bag. Now I must beg him to stay yet again, which subjects me to the domain of ritual. And so we're back in our trance once more. He puts down his bag.

It's 2 a.m., and we've decided to have a drink at a tony club we noticed in our wanderings. It's called Byblos, and it features a fancy restaurant with live entertainment and nearly New York prices. How can I explain the despairing rage that fills Romulus at the sight of its Armani-clad clientele? This isn't simple resentment of the bourgeoisie on the part of an outsider, an underclass person, but something even more inherently political. His rage is, in part, Communist. It could even be interpreted as prudishness. But Romulus is himself in many ways a crass materialist who dreams of killer sound systems and flashy cars. Even so, the discipline and conservatism of real wealth, such as those exhibited by the privileged young people in this bar, crush his spirit. What repulses him most is the lack of Mioritic sacrifice in the comfortable life style of the young people around him. He's looking at the faces of children of politicians or publishers, and he knows what strategies their parents have employed to achieve such security in this impoverished country. He wants to put out the eyes of their children, whose blandness negates all the wisdom of his suffering. Once again, his rage leaves me feeling helplessly inferior. There's nothing I can do but slavishly admire this odd man out of global capitalism.

Back at the hotel, he strips for bed and I gobble two of my fortuitous codeine tablets. I know what my duty is. Within an hour, I'm in that sparkling night gallery made of little explosions of codeine. They blot out most of the sociological details surrounding our situation, leave only his hard, shadowy body mysteriously laid out for me, dappled by the streetlight piercing the gaps in the heavy curtains. This is a funereal, or should I say vampiric, scene. I fall to my knees in the darkness because I know that to worship his abjection is to drink at the fount of cultural doom and play at entangling my fate with his. He's a door out of the repetitive banalities of North American capitalism. His penis plunges into my throat like an eel into inky water.

My Faggot Kansas Blood Confessions to the Earth

CACONRAD

for Anne Boyer

In a Kansas field I spent several hours burying my feet in the soil while listening to the insects, birds and cars on the highway beyond the trees. I was born January 1, 1966 at the 838th Tactical Hospital, Forbes Air Force Base of Topeka, Kansas. My mother said the doctor held me by my ankles and announced, "ANOTHER FINE SOLDIER FOR JESUS!" And I say FUCK YOU to those first words said to me! My mother ate food grown on this land when I was inside her, we drank from the same aquifer; the sky was as big as it is today. I took notes for the poem. I dug a hole and deposited shit, piss, vomit, blood, phlegm, hair, skin, fingernails, semen, and tears, and in that order. I apologized for being alive.

I apologized for having no answers on how to stop the hyper-militarized racist police on the streets of America while the racist US military is on the streets of Arab nations. I apologized for paying taxes that purchase the bullets, bombs, and drones. I apologized for not convincing my queer sisters and brothers that repealing Don't Ask, Don't Tell was only putting a sympathetic face on a multitrillion-dollar military-industrial complex. I apologized for not finding a way to protect Chelsea Manning. I apologized for many things for a long while then covered the hole holding my offerings and took more notes for my poem.

My Faggot Blood on His Fist

the first time
someone sent
Homer through
the internet
dot
dot dot
we are all
falling in
love while
standing in
line for death
fuck this way we
slowly adjust to suffering
an ant finding her way home in
the downpour
lovers are weapons subjugating your
heart if you smell them years after they die
if you feel
destroyed
let us talk
do not
turn it
off yet
we dreamed
our obliteration for
centuries then
Hollywood said
This is what it will look like
Or maybe this Or maybe this
you think it's everyone's job to

make you feel good which
is why we all hate you
the disgraced hairdresser
pours us another shot
we will figure
it out my friend
the ocean is
never far
when you feel
your pulse

Reading My Catastrophe

CAMILLE ROY

The mind ends in a sort of swamp. We are swamp creatures, paddling around in the mud and mangroves of our neural landscape. I also imagine there is a horizon with a fringe of reeds and little lights, maybe fireflies. That is the boundary, where mind turns into nature. You can wait there for a gust of spirit. That is where I dream, the cat curled next to me, the one who used to curl next to you.

I knew you would come with a word for me. A tender flutter, a wing, syllables. The medium opened her palm and there I saw it.

"When things feel unbearable . . ."

That's not it exactly. It was the sudden rise up of incomprehension. Have you ever had those moments where you know you don't have the resources or capacity to deal with what is coming next, or even understand it? I don't know about you, and that is partly because my state of unknowing has become so large. I know this about myself: I'm not porous enough, big enough, small enough, to fit through the hole of the next hour. It's the rollercrasher.

The weird thing about the steep decline and death is that it doesn't feel real. It feels like a life blasted open until it reaches the nooks and crannies of superstition, coincidence, pitiful moments, sorrows, vast stores of tenderness.

July 1, 2017

She is in a hospital bed in the dining room. I am in the next room, looking at her in a baby monitor . . . The light reflects in her slit of an eye, it gleams. She nods an answer to one question and then no response.

It's a ghostly little image. Grainy, black and white. Shot in the dark. My companion, my dying lover.

The future is a mental cramp. Tonight, I had the intense frustration of yearning for her companionship, her thoughts, her humor, her taste. I thought, it is stopping now, our lived relationship. She is still here but she is slipping away.

When will the future stop being a hostile force?

Her sister Candy told me this story, about Angie's last text. It was garbled and misspelled but it was something about 'it would happen tomorrow.' Candy called her and they talked on the phone. Angie explained that she was dead. She was already dead. This was soon after her mother, Peggy, died. Candy just asked questions. How were Megan and Reese dealing with this? Oh, I'm helping them, she said. You know I was a counselor. Have you seen mom, Candy asked. No but I'm working on it, she replied.

We have these bodies. We drag them around, they exist beside and through us. But what do they mean, really? When Angie told me that she thought she was dead, she said that there, in that after life place, there was no gender. What was that like, I asked. It was a relief, she said.

July 2, 2017
(12:15 am)

Today Angie was very quiet and not eating. I went on a walk in the evening and brought back a blackberry (juicy and sweet) and a rose I picked from a hedge in front of the house with the French garden and fountain, across from McKinley Park. When I came home I rubbed the blackberry across Angie's teeth and that seemed to wake her. Then she ate half a banana and drank milk. I put the rose on her pillow.

Reese fell asleep next to her. He said, I love you mom. I was on the other side, cuddled up. She ran her hand up and down my arm.

She murmured something about animal spirits and I said, Yes, I have always loved your animal spirits. You have such animal spirits. She said, She is roused by her animal spirits. She has strong animal spirits. She talked about herself as 'she,' as if she is beginning to separate from herself.

July 6, 2017

Night 1, without my love in the world.

First, she was warm, then as the hours passed she became cool. I was frightened when I kissed her cheek. It looked so familiar but felt, and was, other. Her deep chill, the blood pooling in her back, her stiffening fingers: She had gone! Flown! Where???

Just now I woke up with anguish and walked around the house, dazed with sleep. I looked in on dining room with the empty hospital bed. I felt her absence keenly and mysteriously. I went to the window because I thought I heard birds and there was glimmer of light on the horizon. I realized it was dawn. And there were birds. Their songs floated in a lovely mass, cool cooing and burbles and sharp calls. A soft breeze seemed to lean against me. I recognized all this as the place where Angie had gone; that thought flowed over me like a gentle wind.

Charlotte Joko Beck says, joy is exactly what is happening, minus our opinion of it.

Tonight I remembered with something like pleasure, the final bathing of her. Her beautiful white-haired pussy, the lips, which hang down, which she wondered at. She thought that they either hung down or . . . what? I don't remember. She thought there were two types. I bathed her, perhaps with Reese, or Pince, and it felt fine somehow. I felt a joy in her body, now relaxed in death, but it was still warm, and so it felt like my lover. I dressed her in a dark cobalt blue shirt I had just bought her and some dark grey-black pants. I put her beret on and the witches cord decorating her neck. The bones in her face seemed more prominent and her bones were lovely.

From July 10, 2017

People say a relationship is work. Ours was like a thrown pot that had been smoothed by both our hands. It was a pleasure to continually open to her, to turn to each other, to untie the knots, to return with confidence to the peace and comfort of our connection.

I have a t-shirt hanging in my closet, I snatched it away from the washing, I wanted to keep it with her smell. Yes, her smell. She always loved my smell and I didn't know what she was talking about. I didn't think I loved her smell. But of course I did, I do. I would put my head on her shoulder by her neck and smell her. A dusty sweetish smell, very mild, delicate in that it could be distant and yet it was not, it was intimate. It was the closest thing to me in the world.

Angie declined for months. She couldn't see, lost her balance, lost her muscles (wasted), then she lost memories, short and long term, skills (tooth brushing, using the fork), then the ability to think and speak, then to swallow . . . God, endless. So of course, she had to die.

I kept arguing with death. I kept saying, this far and no farther. But it kept coming, relentless. I felt her love as this great massive thing, no matter what else faded away, it seemed even stronger and more beautiful. It was only at the very end that I didn't see those love lights in her eyes. And I think they were still there, submerged. In the final moments she kept gasping for breath until I was there, until Reese entered the room.

July 11, 2017

Today, a witnessed cremation at Pacific Interment in Emeryville. At 11 am we went into the chapel and, there she was. Does a person own their corpse? "Angie's corpse." She looked peaceful but unlike herself. Her once plump face looked drained. It appeared narrower and more sculpted. Her body wasn't personal. It seemed much like a casing, or a shed skin. We stayed there 15 minutes and then moved into the crematorium room.

The man pointed to the button on the oven and I pushed it. A grinding sound of wheels as the box moved towards the opening, a source of heat and noise.

Dawa chanted her prayers with her friend. She held a book with Sanskrit and translation, syllabic sounds and English. I stood behind her, and Reese and I held hands. I felt very stable. The ceremony was to support the spirit in travelling through bardo to their next destination. During the whole thing I felt her near me, a spirit coiling in my lap, around my torso. Affectionate and playful. Dawa also felt she didn't want to leave.

Afterwards I commented to Larry that there was a conflict between wanting to stay and a soul that travels to rebirth. And he said something surprising and interesting. He said that if there are spirits and souls, that we can't know what they are like, they won't be modeled on us. So Angela's spirits may be multiple, and may follow different paths.

Bob told Reese, "That was a take-no-prisoners funeral."

July 13, 2017

I have developed a skill through all this, an ability to go into a trance with a question and come back with some sort of answer. The answers often have a satisfying if mysterious quality.

This one came to me in the throes of Angie's decline. I can't remember exactly which awful thing had me terrified. But I did one of these trances because of my fear and the message I got was bracing: *Angie is okay, you are okay, and this is normal.* This helped me relax, for some reason.

Today I did another trance, because I felt stricken with the prospect of the loss of Angie's love. It hurt like hell and it seemed it would hurt like that for my whole life. The trance wisdom was simply that her love is still here. It hasn't disappeared. That shook me out of my mood and also made me look at this situation a little differently. I have been with her so long, and so deeply, that her love has entered the structure of my being. I am a host! Reese also, I think. We are her material expression.

My mind is prone to mistakes. I believe in the forms I experience (see). But they are misleading. The Buddhists believe nothing disappears, and if you look deeply, you see its transformation.

August 2, 2017

Today, Reese's 24th birthday. I gave him a Viking amulet from 900 AD, a duck's foot. It's strange but perfect. He picked it out. Now he is out doing karaoke.

But I woke up feeling twisted and this morning I had a meltdown. Some disappointment related to this birthday. Reese had to tell me to stop.

He called Bob and fixed it and we had our nice party. Although through it all, I felt the raw sewage of grief, under my surface.

August 3, 2017

I have been thinking about what I wrote yesterday . . .

He called Bob and fixed it and we had our nice party. All through it I felt the raw sewage of grief, under my surface.

Grief as sewage. Why did that feel so right. As in, accurate. Today, when the grief stirred, it felt like a sickness, even a sickness of the bowels. Tightness across the face, unrest in the gut, breathlessness. Today, before I left work, I had to shit. And it made me feel sick, repulsed, like something out of control and wrong was about to happen, I was about to throw something out of me. I had a moment of worry as if I was about to shit my pants. At the moment of worry, I realized this worry is not uncommon for me. It's a reason I prefer to shit before I go to work. Defecation has an edge of nausea, desperation, and violence.

I thought about that in relation to my grief. It's shocking to think that the purpose of grief is to turn our love to shit. And that's not it, but it's a part of it. Eating and shitting turns food into muscle, bone, blood, heart, love, sleep, life. Shitting is the excrement. It's not the point of eating, just the consequence. Grief, this deep grief, the sickness that comes over me, it makes me cry and cry. And after a bout of tears, I feel clear and not happy, but calm. I wonder if this shitty grief will turn our great love and our decades together into a kind of nourishment. It will be transformed into memory. It will be entering my life forever, but through memory.

One thing this does is persuade me that I should try to allow the grief to roll through me, roll with its thunder and cramping, its slippery dive into helplessness and agony, just to let that happen, let it take me. I am shitting something, I am not losing anything I need.

My Father in Dementia

(My father was hard of hearing so that I wrote what I wanted to communicate in large letters on white paper menus from the cafeteria. After he responded I also wrote that down. These are his words from one of our conversations (except where I indicate my response). I transcribed this from a pile of menus which I brought back from a visit after he had been moved to a memory care unit.)

I'm afraid I live in a world of spectacle.

I can't escape the conclusion that the world is not on our side.

I can't escape the conclusion that skepticism is the prudent position, though I'd like to think otherwise.

It's so thrilling to have something that breaks through fear and leaves room for hope and something more than hope.

I don't know what to say.

What is it that we feed upon that creates hope? I don't know.

Hope is always there . . . but how much is it beyond justice, the sense of hope. I don't know. At a moment like this I don't see anything beyond hope.

"At a moment like this hope is all we have," (say I).

At a fleeting moment like this you just don't know how to find grounds for hope. It is not visible on the horizon.

Listen sweetheart this was just a wonderful surprise. Wonderful. To have your voice appearing out of the ether.

I'd like to pick up the phone sometime and just find that you are there. But the truth is that is not something I can detect.

The truth is sometimes I wake up in the middle of the night and find myself feeling that there are grounds for hope I can't even articulate.

Maybe that is the least we can do: hope that we are right. The fact that you made this call says to me that I can call and surprise you sometime.

I love you sweetheart, just as much as ever.

Soap Bubbles in the Dirty Water

CAN XUE

Translated by Ronald R. Janssen and Jian Zhang

My mother has melted into a basin of soap bubbles. Nobody knows what happened. I would be called a beast, a contemptible, sinister murderer, if anyone knew.

Early this morning she started calling from the kitchen. Her shouting caused fits of bursting pain in my temples.

For the past year, she has slept in the kitchen. In fact, the house does not lack space. But she never stopped complaining that her room was as cold as an icehouse, her nose running and saliva dripping as soon as she started in. She called me "an unfilial son, torturing his old mother like this." The whole show could end with a loud wail. One day, God knows how, she found the old worn-out camp bed in the attic, where nobody had been for years. Her face lit up with delight at finding this "treasure." Immediately she set up the bed opposite the gas range in the kitchen.

"Mother, please don't. Be careful you don't gas yourself."

"Good God, son!" She patted my shoulder and said, "Isn't that just what you've been hoping for? You dream of it every night. I understand very well. Just wait patiently. You might get your wish someday."

My face flushed, and I mumbled something meaningless.

As if to demonstrate, she shut the windows in the kitchen noisily and propped the door shut with a stick every night before going to bed. Strangely enough she never got gassed. Sometimes when a headache attacked me at midnight, I would become suspicious that Mother might be dead from the gas. Throwing on a jacket, I would rush out. But the sow-like snoring I would hear even before reaching the kitchen told me she slept soundly.

However, when she used to sleep in the bedroom she would complain about a lizard stinging her. Half of her head would be numb. Then she would get up to ransack boxes and chests, and I would spend the whole night without sleep. Whenever I hinted cautiously about my suffering, she would fly into a rage, shouting, "What's this? Your faithful mother has to be deprived of even such a tiny distraction? Oh, my good heavens!" Then, howling and slobbering, she would shove her body against me.

In the kitchen, I saw her poking her pasty little face from under the black quilt. Spitting filth from her teeth, she said, "Send the gift to Wang Qi-you today. I bought it yesterday. It's in the closet." She smiled treacherously, as if she had cooked up some plot and was waiting for me to eat it.

Wang Qi-you is an assistant section chief in my mother's workplace. He has a daughter, a thirty-three-year-old spinster whose face is exactly like her father's, with a tiny mole on one cheek. My mother adored him and took every chance to fawn over him. Unfortunately, the chief assumed grand airs, looking cold and indifferent, disliking her, perhaps, because of her age and ugly face. After failures on several social occasions, she had a brainstorm and found a good solution: to give me to him as a live-in son-in-law. I had been to the chief's house once. Of course, all his family knew the reason I was there. They murmured in each other's ears, laughing grimly. The section chief was picking his ears with a special little spoon. His earwax filled a whole watchbox. The thirty-three-year-old spinster was sitting beside a huge fireplace snorting out a strange noise that resembled a collection of animals roaring in a cave. As soon as she opened her mouth, cold sweat soaked my body.

"What damned business do you have here? Hmm? Scram! My piles are acting up!"

My mother is indeed an iron woman. She stayed there about a quarter of an hour, talking and laughing, not turning a hair. She took out a packet of dried bamboo shoots and said, "My little son presents this to the chief." Then she walked out the door, keeping her head high in the public gaze. In the following days, she couldn't resist boasting and hinting in a suggestive tone that she had a "special relationship" with the section chief.

"I have sore feet, Mother."

"What?" She jumped from the bed, breaking a web newly woven during the night. The spider clambered away somewhere into the bed.

"Whenever I hear you calling me, I feel as if my feet were being sawed through to the bone, and my stomach gets upset. I might vomit at their house."

"Stop that trick with me!" she shouted, waving her arms. The two veins in her thin neck danced like fish. "I have expected this. You're simply running against me! You put the spittoon on the threshold so that I'd step in it and fall down . . . Good Lord, what's happening here!"

Pausing, she ordered me to bow my head low before her. She poked my head left and right, searching up and down, even jabbing the back of my head with her filth-blackened nails. Finally, she spit a mouthful of water in my face and declared, "Your scheme can never work!" After that she started drumming her chest and boxing her ears until she was out of breath. And just then, something happened.

The instant she raised her hand to beat herself, she overturned a cup of tea she had left on the windowsill yesterday. The tea splashed in her face. She tried to dry it with her sleeves, but rubbing only produced white bubbles on her skin. And where she rubbed, the flesh became hollow.

"Mother, why don't you have a bath. Let me prepare some water for you," I said as if commanded by a ghost.

After pouring boiling water into the wooden basin, I hid outside the door. I could hear Mother mixing in cold water and cursing me, saying I intended to burn her to death. Then she fell silent, taking off her clothes, perhaps. My face turned pale from nervousness, and I was shivering all over. I heard a stifled scream, as though somebody were calling for help before dawn. After that everything was quiet.

I jumped from the stairs. My clothes were soaking wet, my nails blue, my eyes bulging. After at least an hour, I forced open the kitchen door with a hammer and dashed inside.

The room was empty. My mother's clothes were at the bedside along with a pair of slippers. I stared at the water in the wooden basin, a basin of black, dirty, soapy water, on top of which floated a row of shining soap bubbles, spreading the smell of rotten wood.

I let myself sink down onto a small stool. I cried for her dirty, thin neck and her ulcerated feet watering all the year round.

I didn't call the others until noon.

So people came, swarmed in, their stomping feet breaking one of the floorboards. They looked left and right, observing my swollen eyes suspiciously. Finally, they came to the kitchen. One bent down to study the water in the basin and even broke a bubble with his finger. He was a short man with long hair who looked like a thief.

"She disappeared after her bath," I managed to speak up, something surging up from my stomach. The spider wove a new net on my head. The crowd grinned at one another.

"The water is smelly," the long-haired, short man said affectedly. "Maybe something has melted there? Just now I gave it a jab and felt I had jabbed the backbone of a woman."

"You might have jabbed the thigh," the crowd replied excitedly. Opening their blood-red mouths, they burst into laughter. The tiles on the roof jumped, and the walls gave out pitiful cracking sounds.

They flew out like a swarm of bees, dancing for joy, reveling in the short man's unexpected discovery. Some couldn't restrain themselves from pissing under the eaves.

After they had left, I sat for a long time, keeping my head low. Some cold leftover rice was in the pot. I had two mouthfuls, which tasted of soap.

"San Mao, San Mao,* have you sent the gifts?" Mother's voice came from the bottom of the basin. The rows of soap bubbles seemed to stare at me in the ghastly light.

I staggered out. It was pitch-dark everywhere. Several street lamps shattered like thieves' eyes.

"San Mao! San Mao!" the shouting from the kitchen continued in a rising pitch as if getting angry.

Suddenly, I felt an itching in my throat. After a forceful cough, my mouth gave out a bark and then another and another. People encircled me as I jumped up and down barking ferociously. I discovered a particularly disgusting old fellow who pushed here and there in the crowd with an idiotic smile on his face, his crotch all wet with urine. I charged and bit his shoulder. Tearing hard, I ripped off a piece of flesh. He crashed down, bleeding, like a pile of firewood . . .

Excerpt from *Texas: The Great Theft*

CARMEN BOULLOSA

Translated by Samantha Schnee

On James Street, just before Charles, a small group of his men are chewing the fat, gathered around Doña Estefanía's shopping: sacks of unripe oranges, onions, and garlic, tied to the back of a mule.

Ludovico—a gunman and an excellent *vaquero*—has stopped in this spot next to the window where the smiling face of Moonbeam, the pretty Asinai Indian, sometimes appears. She's so pretty. If the Smiths would sell her, he'd buy her in a heartbeat. And if they won't sell her, he might just steal her from them, or else he's not a man. He eyes the window, searching for Moonbeam's face.

From her bedroom balcony, hidden behind lace curtains, Caroline, the youngest Smith, spies on them, hoping to catch a glimpse of Nepomuceno, whom she's completely infatuated with.

Ludovico is daydreaming, blinking at the window; Fulgencio and Silvestre are busting a gut laughing at him, who knows why; they don't spot their men until they're right in front of them. They toss the sacks of oranges across their saddles, mount their horses, and hurry after them.

In their haste, one of the sacks of oranges turns upside down. No sooner have they passed the corner of Charles and James than—wouldn't you know it!—the fruit begins to fall out, bouncing on the cobblestones.

The pack heads toward Elizabeth Street, Nepomuceno in the lead. The mule carrying the onions and garlic follows fast on their tails out of sheer instinct—who knows where it gets the energy from—its short legs look like they're flying.

On the outskirts of Bruneville, further inland, another small band of Nepomuceno's men waits. When they see where the group is headed, they mount their horses and follow.

They're creating one big cloud of dust. They take the turnoff to the dock, and as the earth becomes damper the telltale cloud of dust settles down. They arrive at the muddy riverbank.

They stop several feet from the barge, which is already loaded with livestock.

Pedro and Pablo, who help old Arnoldo on the boat and have been well-trained (both boys are barefoot; and since their combined age is sixteen their nickname is "Two Eights"), have just loaded the last of the herd onto the boat and are about to close the gate. The barge is balanced. When Nepomuceno and his men appear, the boys are just closing the gates, walking along the edge of the deck. The coal has been moved to the tugboat to keep the barge balanced, the motor is running hot, they're about to release the moorings, two thick chains which keep the barge moored to the dock at its bow and its stern. They both have rope wrapped around their torsos, they'll tighten it if the barge begins to list. Pedro will travel on deck with his German shepherd; Pablo will sit with old Arnoldo at the tugboat's stern, in the cabin.

Old Arnoldo, who is deaf as a doorknob, is already at the tug's tiller. He doesn't like transporting livestock one bit; in addition to the whims of the river, you have to contend with the whims of the herd. He's got the bullhorn at his feet, in case he needs it.

The livestock aren't restless but they rock the boat and roll the tug. Pablo and Pedro work with steady hands. One mistake could make the barge lose its balance and tip them over. If the animals become agitated, it's not enough to be on the alert. The herd is traveling unattended; the wranglers are depending on the barge's rails and the animals' fear of water. They wait on the opposite riverbank.

On the dock, without saying a word, Nepomuceno motions his orders. Ismael, a *vaquero,* leaps off his horse and jumps across the gap between the dock and the barge. All aboard!

Patronio takes the reins of Ismael's horse.

Pablo and Pedro watch and weigh up the situation. Pablo thinks, *Nepomuceno is crazy*, but there's nothing he can do against fourteen men, or thirteen, if we don't count drunken Lázaro. Plus, who in their right mind would take on Don Nepomuceno?

Ismael opens the barge's main gate; the herd senses this immediately; Ismael keeps them back with his riding whip, cracking it and shouting "Back!" in a stern voice.

Pablo's dog barks at Ismael, baring his teeth. From land, Fausto throws a stone to scare him off, and the dog retreats between the legs of the cattle, who also shy away.

Patronio passes the reins of Ismael's horse to Fausto. He pulls his horse back, causing it to whinny, and takes a running jump onto the barge—landing so softly (as if he's polishing a gem) there's hardly a sound; the animals shy away from the impact of his landing, rushing against the railings of the barge. After Patronio, Fausto follows immediately, shadowed by Ismael's horse and the others.

Once aboard the barge, Ludovico, Fulgencio, Silvestre (who's no longer laughing), Patronio, Ismael, and Fausto (all good *vaqueros*) attend to the Herculean task of controlling the animals. Once the cattle are subdued, they must ensure they don't bunch together on one side of the barge, which would capsize it. Nepomuceno's remaining horsemen board one by one.

What horses! They're like one with their riders; full of vigor, they are momentum incarnate, and handsome devils. The same can't be said of the cattle—focused on the unpredictable waters, who knows how they can be controlled? But they respond to the whip, shoves, and the dog nipping at their ankles (Two Eights' dog understands who's in charge now and joins in to help Nepomuceno's men). In short, the herd fears the *vaqueros* and obeys them out of fright, not because they understand.

As soon as the herd is under control, El Güero jumps aboard, followed by their riderless, fresh horses (six in total, one horse for each rider). Then Nepomuceno, with Lázaro Rueda, who has passed out. It's the last jump and the most graceful, a beautiful arc, the highest of all; their bodies trace a miraculous triangle through the air (the three points of the triangle are their three heads: Nepomuceno's, Lázaro's, and Pinta's).

(You might ask, why did he go last? Isn't he the only one they're protecting? But if you think about it, the answer is clear: they don't want to take any unnecessary risks and he might have capsized the boat, plus on land there's not a soul who could catch him.)

The mule with the sack of garlic and onions stays behind on land. She ran after the horses through the streets of Bruneville, following them like a faithful dog, but jumping such a wide gap over the water, old and heavily loaded as she is, that's out of the question. She's an ass but she's not an idiot.

With the assistance of Two Eights, who understand who's calling the shots, Ismael closes the gate he opened to let Nepomuceno and his men aboard.

The repositioning of the herd continues, the very picture of wrangling skill.

Now the barge is really full. To ensure they aren't crushed by the cattle, they must keep the herd calm.

Nepomuceno doesn't need to speak his orders. Fausto points at Pedro and Pablo, "Go tell old Arnoldo that we're ready to go, now! Release the moorings!"

Pedro asks, "Where are you in such a hurry to get to?"

"Where were you headed?"

"To Matasánchez, to pick up some feed and some pots; from there we're headed to Bagdad."

Fausto and Nepomuceno exchange looks and make a few signs; Fausto understands and shouts the orders at the top of his lungs, "To Matasánchez, to the Old Dock, the herd disembarks with us. Let's move it!"

Pablo heads to the tugboat's cabin, working his way along the side of the barge, outside the railings; with swift agility he places his bare feet on the ropes and chains that moor it to the barge. He's already aboard the tug when he feels a jerk: Pedro has just released the first mooring, and the motor is pushing the vessel, though it hasn't started forward yet.

"Let's go, Don Arnoldo!" he shouts in the old man's ear. "To the Old Dock in Matasánchez!"

"The Old Dock? But no one uses it any more! Did you say the Old Dock? And what the hell was all that rocking? What was going on back there?"

"I'm telling you, Don Arnoldo, the old one! The Old Dock! Old like you are! Let's go!" Pablo tells him.

"Off we go to the Old Dock," the old man says, as merrily as he can, "old like me!"

"And make it snappy!"

"I can step it up . . . if you want us to capsize, you wacky kid! I can waltz but I can't fly!"

He feels another jerk, stronger than the first: Pedro has just released the second and final mooring.

Moonbeam, the pretty Asinai Indian, has appeared on one of the Smiths' balconies (not on account of the Lipans' quarrel—which she didn't see—or because of the sound of the shot—which she didn't hear because she was in the patio fetching water—or because of Nat; it's because of Nepomuceno's horsemen galloping past, although she arrives too late to see who was in such a hurry); she saw the oranges rolling around, opened the balcony windows and jumped down into the street to pick them up. On another balcony, Caroline Smith—she knows whose fruit it is because she's been standing at attention by the window—opens her windows too, but Moonbeam doesn't hear, absorbed as she is in gathering the oranges into her skirt.

Mrs. Smith is wondering why her daughter is shouting. When she sees her hanging out the window into the street shouting nonsense, culminating in "I love you, Nepomuceno!" and sees Moonbeam, "that exasperating Indian girl, picking up oranges" off the cobblestones "with her legs fully exposed," she faints, unable to bear either of these indignities.

Santiago watched Nepomuceno and his men board the barge. The other fishermen, who were mending their nets, had left to investigate the ruckus in the Market Square and hadn't returned. Several of them got lost. Santiago, on the other hand, knows what has happened as if he has seen it with his own eyes, the same ones that witnessed Nepomuceno's escape.

"Now that's a real man!" he says aloud. "That's what you call balls, big ones!"

* * *

As soon as they have finished tying up the last crab, Melón, Dolores, and Dimas get down off Hector's cart; Mr. Wheel will only transport what's for sale. Without talking it over, they all run to Mesnur, halfway between the center of Bruneville and the place where the fishermen mend their nets. Mesnur is where the children always gather at the end of the afternoon, and sometimes when their work is interrupted. Most of the kids work, and most of them are Mexicans or immigrants. They fly kites, sail toy boats they build themselves, catch dragonflies and tie them up on leashes, play ball (if there's one around), jump rope, and share secrets. Sometimes they're mean to each other, but mostly they share the goodies that might have come their way.

Melón, Dolores, and Dimas want to share the news about John Tanner, the White Indian, and about the sheriff and Don Nepomuceno.

Luis arrives at the same time holding his little sister's hand and with empty pockets; he's worried about that, it won't go down well at home. Along comes Steven—hanging his head because he hasn't made any money either—and Nat, with his hidden treasure.

But Melón, Dolores, and Dimas don't talk about John Tanner and no one stops to discuss what happened with Shears and Nepomuceno, no one even thinks about swimming or playing freeze tag, because Nat removes the Lipan's knife, the one he picked up on Charles Street, from his pants. They all agree they should hide it.

It takes the gringos a little while to mount their horses and begin pursuing the "*banditos*." Their horses are in the stables, on the city's outskirts, and the minutes drag by as they wait for their servants to bring their horses (on the way they were distracted by the oranges Ludovico carelessly dropped—the Asinai had gathered what she could, but many remained—and after they gathered what was left of the oranges it took a while to hide them in Judge Gold's stables).

Once mounted on their horses, the gringos lose more time stopping at each intersection and corner to ask everyone in the vicinity if they've seen the fugitives and where they went. "They headed inland."

"I think they went that-a-way." Folks' directions are no quicker than their explanations. There's no one on the road to the river to tell them whether "the fugitives" went toward the river or inland; the kids who usually gather to play there are nowhere to be found (they've already gone to hide the knife). Just in case, Ranger Phil, Ranger Ralph, and Ranger Bob head down to the dock. The rest of them head inland, continuing to question folks along the way.

Beside Mrs. Big's Hotel, Ranger Phil, Ranger Ralph, and Ranger Bob catch sight of the barge loaded with cattle, floating slowly down the river (no matter how much the boy hassles him, old Arnoldo wisely maintains a snail's pace, he takes good care of his cargo), and they hear the herd lowing at a distance. The vessel rocks a wobbly dance. There's no way it could be brought back to dock.

"So much rocking!"

"It looks like there's a ruckus on board, there must be an angry bull."

"Nah! He's not angry, he's in heat!" As usual, Ranger Ralph has a one-track mind (you can hardly call what his brain does "thinking").

"A bull in heat, you say? Ain't no bull, it's a steer like you!" Ranger Bob says in bad Spanish, which Ranger Phil understands, but not Ranger Ralph.

All three laugh, two because they get the joke, the other because he's so stupid.

Watching the barge float along like it's fighting the waves is both humorous and soothing, like watching sheep being rounded up into one big flock with mastery and skill; they don't know the real reason for the boat's swaying.

The barge turns upriver toward the Old Dock.

"I thought from here they went down-river to Point Isabel and then to New Orleans to sell cattle, but look, it seems like they're heading upriver," says Ranger Bob.

"They'll be picking up feed, no doubt, they don't want to deliver 'em hungry," says Ranger Phil.

"Or maybe they're trying to catch the current," says Ranger Bob.

"Don't make no sense to me," says Ranger Ralph.

They turn their backs and enter the swinging doors of Mrs. Big's Hotel.

Inside, it's business as usual: a few whores are waiting for customers, folks are drinking liquor, four musicians begin to torture their instruments, competing for attention, and at her table Mrs. Big presides over her never-ending card game. To one side of the swinging doors—which don't cover his face or the lower half of his legs—Santiago the fisherman hangs back, barefoot, by the entrance.

Jim Smiley is the only one who gets up when the Rangers come in. But not to shake hands or show respect. Smiley bends over to pick up the cardboard box where he keeps his frog, and says clearly for all to hear, as if he's rehearsed it, "I betcha two bucks my frog can jump farther than any other."

"And where am I gonna find a frog to bet you with? I don't ride around with a frog in my pocket!" Ranger Phil says.

"What else you got in your pockets? What's more important than a frog?" Smiley smiles.

Ranger Phil holds up his revolver. He smiles too, showing his gold teeth.

"You wanna take my bet or not?" Smiley dares him, still smiling.

"I'm askin' you where am I gonna get a frog?"

Santiago the fisherman mutters, "Down by the riverbank, I'll bring you one, Ranger. Wait here."

Santiago is itching to get out of the saloon.

Ranger Phil turns and looks at him with admiration. If this backwater fisherman dares to speak to a gunslinger like him, there must be good reason. Santiago heads outside, the doors swing behind him.

A few seconds later, Ranger Phil follows Santiago, and the two other Rangers follow reluctantly—they wanted to grab a drink. Irritatingly, they can still hear the music, which makes them even thirstier. But when they see the fisherman looking so helpless, jumping around like a child, they turn around and head back into Mrs. Big's.

Santiago continues leaping around on the muddy riverbank, without realizing the Ranger is nearby. He catches sight of a frog at the edge of the river. He follows it, leaps to the right, and then to the left. He squats to capture his prey. Ranger Phil follows him stealthily, so as not to scare the frog—now he understands what Santiago is up to—until he arrives at the edge of the dock. He stops and watches the fisherman. Then he notices the hoof-prints in the mud.

Santiago captures the frog.

By this time the barge appears to be fading away and you can no longer hear the cattle lowing.

Pointing to the horseshoe prints in the mud, Ranger Phil asks Santiago, "What's this?"

Santiago, who has the frog in his hand, doesn't say a word for a few long seconds.

You can still hear the music of the four fools in the saloon (each of them wandering around with own their instrument, gathering only to look for handouts), scratching strings, their music lacking all melody.

What happens next takes place in the blink of an eye. Santiago, who is a good man and doesn't know how to lie, realizes what trouble he's in and begins to cry in Spanish, "I don't know anything, I saw them jump on the barge but didn't understand what was going on." He drops the frog he caught.

Unfortunately, Ranger Phil understands Spanish.

In Mrs. Big's Hotel the musicians' torturous song ends. Ranger Phil whistles to his men; they appear through Mrs. Big's swinging doors.

The musicians start a new song. Ranger Phil grabs Santiago by the arm and drags him over to his partners, the fisherman bawling like an animal on the way to slaughter. Ranger Phil translates the fisherman's confession for his partners, pointing to where he found the prints in the mud.

From the barge, Fulgencio (who has an eagle's eye) observes the three gunmen approaching Mrs. Big's Hotel. He whistles to Nepomuceno (softly, not to disturb the herd), who dismounts and hides behind his horse. His men copy him, using the horses as shields to keep them from sight of anyone on the riverbank, in case they have a spyglass, despite the fact this leaves them exposed to the herd.

The herd reacts to their movements. They nearly capsize with the commotion. Old Arnoldo curses the herd and steers the tug, yanking its tiller. Fulgencio cracks his whip. Just the sound of it is enough;

the herd recognizes his authority—luckily all Nepomuceno's men are *vaqueros*—and settles back down.

Nepomuceno wants to go to Matasánchez. He would have preferred to go to his own ranch, but he knows the gringos' vengeful nature; it's better to hide out somewhere that doesn't endanger his own people. For the time being he knows he can't go near the place, or any of his mother's ranches either (where the food is much better than anywhere else, there's no contest). He must cross the border and prepare to face the Rangers there. If not, they'll crush him. Once again, it occurs to Nepomuceno, as it has on many occasions, *We should have allied ourselves with the warrior tribes; it's a shame it didn't work out, but they're like wasps' nests, even among themselves. Together*, Nepomuceno thinks, *Indians and Mexicans would fry the gringos up with a little chipotle, some garlic, and a pinch of* . . . You can tell he's the son of Doña Estefanía, the best cook in the whole region. Her desserts are without compare, as are her marinades and her stews. You're fortunate to dine at her table.

Chipotle, frying, garlic: this is no way to talk about gringos, who don't even know how to hold a frying pan. Even the Karankawa were more civilized, may they rest in peace.

While all this is passing through his head, Nepomuceno has an idea. Traveling with the herd puts him in good spirits, there's a lot of *vaquero* in him . . . Since they're hiding behind their horses, they don't see what's happening on the dock in Bruneville.

Those awful musicians have begun yet another tune back at Mrs. Big's. One of them squeezes an accordion. Santiago the fisherman is on his knees, crying silently like a child, clasping his hands and begging for mercy. Ranger Ralph takes out his pistol. He points it at Santiago. The shot hits him in the forehead. (The bullet that has come to rest in Santiago's head comes to life. It knows it wasn't meant to end up there. The fisherman's noble, sweet brains, washed with the sea air and the silence of high tide, soothe it. His brains pour out in luminous silence, the bullet has rendered them insensate. No fear, no fatigue, no longing, no children, no wife, no nets, no Nepomuceno; not even the river remains.)

The Rangers stick a fishhook into Santiago's ass—one that might have belonged to him. Then they tie a rope around his neck and hang him from the icaco tree, "Mrs. Big's stick."

"Leave him there to teach 'em a lesson."

The three Rangers mount their horses. The animals seem oblivious to them. It's not that they don't obey them, it's like they don't recognize them.

Before yanking the reins, Ranger Bob notices a frog leaping in the mud. He dismounts and follows it; his boots get muddy; he traps the frog without chasing it, as if the frog has surrendered.

"I'll catch up with you," he says to his partners. "I'll see you in the Market Square, or at the Town Hall, somewhere around there!"

Ranger Phil and Ranger Ralph pull their reins and gallop back to the center of Bruneville, straight to the Town Hall to share their discovery.

Excerpt from *My Mother Laughs*

CHANTAL AKERMAN
Translated by Daniella Shreir

One morning she talked to me for a long time. And I replied, though I don't remember what. Sometimes the words she says don't matter. The only thing that matters is the response to the thing that isn't expressed. So I tell her what she wants to hear.

I told her that I wouldn't stay in New York, that I would return to Paris, that way I could be nearer to her and I could come and see her in Brussels regularly. Not every week, but often. Yes, I'd like that, she said. And then I remembered that I don't know how to protect myself.

Immediately I think that I shouldn't have said that to my mother and that maybe I would be better off staying in New York, that way I could call her from time to time on Skype and that would be all. Anyway, we'll see.

My mother says it one more time, I'm not coming back here again.

No. Probably not. I tell her, they'll come and see you instead, my sister and her husband, her niece and her husband, and her grandson whom she fusses over when he lets her.

He's so handsome, she says. Yes, it's true, I reply. And so gentle for a boy, it's surprising. Yes, I say to her, that's true. Sometimes he takes me by the arm and we walk around the block together for a few minutes because I can't manage more than that. And I feel proud and my heart feels full. Yes, I know, maman.

She also adores her granddaughter who has just got married.

Her granddaughter will probably have a child soon, but nobody knows when and no one dares ask her if she plans to. My sister says,

I think they're going to wait a little longer, her and her husband. But why wait, there's no time like the present, says my mother, she's not so young anymore, of course she's young but not that young.

Everyone sighs and everyone wishes that my mother would stop bringing up this subject, especially in front of her granddaughter who is very touchy and quick-tempered like her mother. Luckily, she and her husband have just gone off to Asia on their honeymoon. It will be a lovely trip and everyone is happy for them.

You know, your father and me, we went to Paris for our honeymoon, says my mother, and there were bedbugs in the mattress and the toilet was out in the corridor, and we spent the whole night scratching. Then we came home. But it was still a honeymoon. And the next day we went back to work, we had to work, you know. Yes, maman, I know.

We worked hard all our lives. Yes, maman, I know that, I was there. And you work too. Yes, but not as much. Well, in any case you still work. At the moment I'm not doing much at all. I have nothing in mind, no new ideas. Or too many, I've sometimes thought.

They'll come, my mother replies. That's what you always say. What if this time they don't?

Maman, the nurse is going to dress you now. You put some make-up on, you put some lipstick on even though you can see that it doesn't go with your dressing gown. Oh it's good to have a chat, isn't it. Yes.

My mother says, I'm hungry. They'll be here soon and we'll all eat together. But it's already three o'clock and I'm hungry. In Belgium I eat at half past twelve. Here things are different. Well, why don't you have a bowl of soup while you wait.

The nurse already gave me some soup but it was so watery that I can't feel it. I want them to get back from work, I can't stand all this waiting. Eat some bread then. I can't with this in my mouth, it'll hurt my gums.

Yes, I know. I never should have told her to eat some bread while she was waiting.

Well what about a piece of fruit in the meantime. What, before the meal?

Yes, it's actually better to eat fruit before a meal than after it. I read an article about it.

I don't fancy it.

Well you can't be that hungry then.

She sighs.

The nurse starts to worry.

My mother tries to get up from her armchair.

You see, I still need someone to help me.

Yes, I can see that. But you're already doing better than before. Take a few steps. That'll help you to forget your hunger.

I have no desire to eat even though I'm hungry.

Take a few steps, that'll give you an appetite.

She takes a few steps with the nurse and says a few words to her in French. The nurse smiles and nods though she hasn't understood a word.

My mother leads the nurse towards the dining room, the nurse helps her sit down in her seat.

My sister enters the room and says, ah you're already sitting down. Yes, I was waiting for you all.

Everyone sits down. The food is on the table.

The nurse cuts her meat and vegetables into tiny pieces. My mother can't do it by herself because of her broken shoulder.

Everyone eats enthusiastically except for my mother.

And out of the blue she makes a comment about the way I eat.

My nephew laughs and says, You treat her like a four-year-old child, and everyone laughs.

I don't want to laugh but I do it anyway, to be like everyone else.

My mother says, why are you laughing like that, like an idiot. My child will always be my child. My nephew says, yes of course that's true but you treat her like a child who has never grown up so of course we laugh.

Go on then, laugh at me, says my mother. Laugh, I don't care. Yes, laughing is good, especially because we haven't laughed much since the wedding and especially not about the photo where my mother is smiling during the service. None of us liked that smile.

* * *

Anyway laughing does me good and in Harlem I had almost stopped laughing except for sometimes. I had brought her to live in this apartment, in this city she hardly knew. I'd left her first for a wedding then for a dying mother. As for the dying mother, she'd offered to come with me.

I'd said no.

She'd left her apartment, a girlfriend, her job, but every week, sometimes twice a week, I'd tell her, I don't think this is working, we're not getting on. I'd ended up telling her proudly, I don't love you anymore. And she'd said, that's not possible. I know that's not true.

I was proud because I'd finally been able to say something I'd never been able to say before. So I'd said to myself, for once I'm being strong, I'm saying something. I'm saying what I really feel.

I felt spied on, analysed, scrutinised, she had such a keen ear that even when I spoke on the phone and said, you too, she could hear it, she knew that I was saying, I miss you too.

She would come into the bedroom with her eyes black with rage and make me listen for hours on end saying that she couldn't put up with it anymore. She was screaming. The dog looked at us one at a time. I stroked her paw and said to her, don't worry, nothing's wrong. But she was worried. The dog was worried. C. was worried and I was terribly worried, and I was suffocating. I was suffocating more and more every day except when I gave in, when I stopped phoning L., when I stopped finding excuses to leave the house, when I stopped running away from her. No, I was giving in. And the first few days of that were good. And then it became awful again. No, I didn't want to give in, I wanted phone calls and laughter with friends and strangers about everything and nothing. At the wedding, a friend of my sister had come up to my mother and kissed her with such warmth, with such affection even, that my mother had finally smiled.

Then this friend had gone to stand behind my mother and called the photographer over to take a photo of them together. My mother said, I'm not very photogenic anymore, not at all photogenic anymore, even.

Don't be silly, the friend said, of course you are. She'd draped her arms over my mother's scrawny body. The noise of the room was maddening, a mixture of music, shouts, laughs, they were even dancing the hora. You had to shout to be heard.

My mother half opened her mouth for the photo. Immediately I felt sick. A smile held with such effort. Don't smile maman, it's not worth it. But she insisted. Her mouth was held open for a smile and the photographer took her time. My mother waited there, holding herself as upright as she could, her mouth fixed into what might be considered a smile, her face a shade of green, her lips red with too much lipstick. From afar, you might think they were bleeding.

Finally the photo was taken. I was relieved, and she was too. I'll send it to you, the woman told my mother, with her arms still around her.

That's nice but you don't have to, said my mother. You probably already have a lot more important things to be getting on with. Don't be silly, said my sister's friend.

Maman, it's late, why don't we start heading back.

Yes, it's late, I don't know why but I feel tired. I never used to get tired at weddings.

I know, but it's been a long day. She gives me a look that's almost hostile. That's not a reason. Yes, it is.

But I can't take it anymore. The day started at seven and the photographers arrived at eight and the hairdressers and make-up artists just after that. Luckily you had your hair and make-up done. At least I don't feel ashamed.

I take a sip of wine. Mind you don't spill that. I won't.

Because the stains are impossible to get out. I know. Though sometimes you can.

She waits a bit longer. For a while, she seems less drowsy.

Then she says, but how are we supposed to get home. There's a minibus and a driver over there. That's what they're there for.

Do you think? The anxiety has returned. Yes, I'm sure, but if you want I can go and check. Yes, go and check. She wrings her hands again. I unravel them gently. So she grasps at her clutch bag instead.

And suddenly she asks, what about your dog, where is she. In Paris.

Is someone looking after her? Yes.

When I returned to her side after checking with the minibus driver it was even worse. She couldn't get up. Clara and I helped her up and navigated her across the dance floor and its noises, through groups of dancers and between tables and thundering screams of joy.

My mother struggled with each step, each time she was more out of breath.

We practically carried her into the minibus and up the stairs of the house and into her room before undressing her in silence.

Clara and I looked at one another. We knew that this was serious. We said to each other very quietly, this isn't good.

She looked like the living dead, her eyes were transparent, almost lifeless. But they still had a bit of gleam.

I held her hand as she closed her eyes. I wasn't sure whether she was sleeping but her eyes were closed. She was breathing and gurgling.

The next day she went back to hospital, to A&E.

I was meant to leave that day, to return to my life in New York.

My sister said, go on, there's nothing you can do for her here anyway.

But what if. No, she'll be here when you come back, I'm sure of it. I'm not. Of course she will. She'll be here. Go on, the driver will take you to the airport.

Go back to New York. Go and focus on your work. Go on. Go back.

In New York I couldn't sleep again, night after night.

We'd chosen the apartment for the alcove which separated the two main rooms.

But we'd done it all by email, at a distance, the tenancy agreement, the deposit.

We weren't able to tell that the windows looked out onto the facing wall.

Just a tiny bit of sky.

Sometimes it was blue.

It snowed only once, on a day in November.

C. was delighted.

She felt a bit cold but was delighted.

I got on the plane. And already I felt guilty, I never should have left.

I tried to read but I couldn't. Then I thought, I should prepare myself. But how. I should try and imagine myself without her. But I didn't have any imagination. So I looked out of the window, at the sky, at the clouds. It took so long to get to New York. I thought, we'll never get there. I started to kick the seat in front of mine without realising I was doing it. A woman turned around aggressively and asked me to stop. She couldn't have known, of course. She thought that I was doing it deliberately, that I had no respect for her or her back. I didn't eat or drink. I got up, sat back down. We still hadn't arrived. Nothing to be done. I tried to breathe using the method I'd been taught to use when anxious. But I wasn't even anxious. No. I was just trying to prepare myself for my mother's death.

Then they told us in Spanish and in English that we should fasten our seatbelts. We were about to land. But I didn't want to land anymore. I wanted to spend the rest of my life on the plane.

But we landed and people started rushing towards the exit, I waited. When everyone had got off I managed to get up. I couldn't feel my legs but I was walking.

The suitcases made their way around the belt. I wasn't paying attention. I waited there like everyone else but I'd forgotten why.

Then suddenly I remembered that I had a suitcase and that I had to take it off the conveyor belt.

But I got mixed up. I took a suitcase that wasn't mine.

Someone came up to me and grabbed the suitcase from my hands, shouting something in Spanish.

I said sorry, graçias. Mucho graçias. I knew that wasn't the right thing to say so I didn't say anything.

I stayed in front of the belt for a while and ended up with my suitcase. It was the only one left so it had to be mine.

Before You Go

CHARLES BERNSTEIN

Thoughts inanimate, stumbled, spare, before you go.
Folded memories, tinctured with despair, before you go.
Two lakes inside a jar, before you go.
Flame illumines fitful lie, before you go.
Furtive then morrow, nevering now, before you go.
Lacerating gap, stippled rain, before you go.
Anger rubs, raw 'n' sweet, before you go.
Never seen the other side of sleep, before you go.
Nothing left for, not yet, grief, before you go.
A slope, a map, insistent heave, before you go.
Stone & stem, nocturne, leap, before you go.
Compass made of bones & teeth, before you go.
The wind up acts, delirium's beast, before you go.
Spilt quell, impatient, speaks, before you go.
Rippling laughter, radiance leaks, before you go.
No place, no sound, nor up, or down, before you go.
Smokey, swollen seeps, before you go.
Tossing in tune, just like last night, before you go.
I'm nowhere near the fight, before you go.
Nothing to make it right, before you go.
It won't congeal, no more deals, before you go.
Hope a fence, well's on fire, before you go.
Slammed when you don't, damned if not, before you go.
A hound, a bay, a hurtled dove, before you go.
Coriander & lace, stickly grace, before you go.

Englobing trace, fading quakes, before you go.
Devil's grail, face or fate, before you go.
Suspended deanimation, recalcitrant fright, before you g
Everything so goddamn slow, before you
Take me now, I'm feelin' low, before yo
Just let me unhitch this tow, before y
One more stitch still to sew, before
Calculus hidden deep in snow, befor
Can't hear, don't say, befo
Lie still, who sings this song, bef
A token, a throw, a truculent pen, be
Don't know much, but that I do, b
Two lane blacktop, undulating light

Excerpt from *If He Hollers, Let Him Go*

CHESTER HIMES

I went to Mac's office and asked Marguerite for a sick pass to go home. She gave it to me in her cold business manner without saying a word. But I felt she was all right, she was a fine person, she didn't have anything against me. I smiled at her and said, 'Thank you,' and went out.

That was what it did for me. 'Unchain 'em in the big corral,' the boys used to say in Hot Stuff's crap game back in Cleveland. That was what did it for me; it unchained me, made me free. I felt like running and jumping, shouting and laughing; I felt something I'd felt the time Joe Louis knocked out Max Schmeling—only better.

When I checked out Gate No. 2 the gatekeeper looked at me and said, 'What, you going home already? You just got here a few minutes ago.'

I wagged a finger at him. 'You don't know how tempus fugits.'

He didn't like that. 'You coloured boys better lay off that gin,' he said, winking at the guard.

I laughed, 'The only way you can make me mad now,' I told him, 'is to get a mouthful of horse manure and blow it through your teeth at me.'

He turned red and started to say something else, but I didn't stop. I backed out my car, circled in the parking lot, crossed the Pacific Electric tracks, and turned into the harbour road, just idling along. I didn't feel like speeding. The car drove easy all of a sudden, I thought. Not a jerk in it, not a squeak; it took the bumps like a box-spring mattress. It was a pleasure just sitting there, my fingers resting lightly on the steering wheel, just idling along.

I was going to kill him if they hung me for it, I thought pleasantly. A white man, a supreme being. Just the thought of it did something for me; just contemplating it. All the tightness that had been in my body, making my motions jerky, keeping my muscles taut, left me and I felt relaxed, confident, strong. I felt just like I thought a white boy oughta feel; I had never felt so strong in all my life.

A warm glow went all over me as if I had just stepped out of a Turkish bath and had had a good massage. My mind was light, relieved, without a care in the world. As I idled along past the long line of industries I felt a sudden compelling friendliness toward the white people I passed. I felt like waving to them and saying, 'It's all right now. It's fine, solid, it's a great deal.'

A well-dressed, slenderly built middle-aged white woman stepped from the curb in the path of my car. I eased to a stop and waited for her to pass. She looked up; surprise was first in her eyes, then she gave a tentative, half-decided smile. I smiled in return, warm and friendly. It made all the difference in the world; the weights had gone out of my head.

Now I felt the heat of the day, saw the hard, bright California sunshine. It lay in the road like a white, frozen brilliance, hot but unshimmering, cutting the vision of my eyes into unwavering curves and stark unbroken angles. The shipyards had an impressive look, three-dimensional but infinite. Colours seemed brighter. Cranes were silhouetted against the grey-blue distance of sky.

I felt the size of it, the immensity of the productions. I felt the importance of it, the importance of the whole war. I'd never given a damn one way or the other about the war excepting wanting to keep out of it; and at first when I wanted the Japanese to win. And now I did; I was stirred as I had been when I was a little boy watching a parade, seeing the flag go by. That filled-up feeling of my country. I felt included in it all; I had never felt included before. It was a wonderful feeling.

Glancing up, I saw a dine-dance café across from the Consolidated. I pulled into the parking lot and coasted to a stop, got out, and went inside. It was cool inside and so dark I had to pause just inside the doorway for my sight to pick out objects. The bar was flat across one side, and the dining-room circled out in front of it.

There were a number of men at the bar, a few women. A group of loud-voiced shipyard workers sat at a table playing Indian dice. They were all white. I found a seat at the bar between a woman and a man and made myself comfortable. The fear of being refused service might have come into my mind, but I didn't notice it. After a while the bar-tender stopped in front of me. He was a thin, indifferent-faced man with thinning black hair and a winged moustache. I ordered a double scotch and he grinned. The white woman next to me stopped talking and looked around. I could feel her gaze on me.

'You would take gin though, wouldn't you?' the bar-tender said.

I let my eyes rove over the stock. All I saw was gin, rum, tequila, vodka, and wine. I grinned back at the bar-tender. 'Gin's fine,' I said. 'I was nursed on gin.'

He picked up the bottle, poised it. 'Double?'

'That's right,' I said. I turned to look at the white woman at my side. Our eyes met. She had brown eyes, frankly curious; and blonde hair, dark at the roots, piled on top of her head. In the dim orange light her lipstick didn't show and her mouth looked too thin for the size of her other features. She had taken off her brassiere on account of the heat and the outline of her breasts showed distinctly through her white rayon blouse.

She looked away after a moment and when I looked into the mirror I met the eyes of the man on the other side of her. I smiled slightly, looked away before seeing whether he returned it or not.

The bar-tender replaced the gin bottle. 'Chaser?'

'Water,' I said.

He set up the water. 'We don't have no more whisky, only once or twice a week,' he said. 'I ain't seen no Scotch since I don't know when.'

'Scotch? What's that?' the blonde girl said. She had a man's heavy voice.

'Speaking of Scotch reminds me of a joke,' the man on the other side of her began. 'Two Scotchmen went to a Jew store to buy a suit of clothes . . .'

I got interested in watching a guy down the bar balance a half-filled glass on its edge and didn't listen. When I finished my gin I went over and sat down at a table. A young dark-haired girl in a blue, white-trimmed uniform came over to take my order. She had two imitation daises pinned on each side of her hair. Her face was impersonal.

I ordered the biggest steak they had, then a double martini as an afterthought. A big rawboned old-timer came in and looked about for a place to sit. Finally he sat at the table with me. I thought to myself, I must be turning white really and truly, and grinned at him.

'If it's one thing I don't like, it's sitting at a goddamned empty table,' he greeted.

'It is kinda bad,' I said.

'You married?' he asked.

I shook my head. 'Still in the field.'

'I been married thirty-two goddamned years,' he said. 'Got the best goddamned finest woman in the world. Got three boys in the Marines. And goddamnit, every time I come into this goddamned joint I don't find nothing but empty tables.' I thought for a moment he was going to bang on the table and complain to the management.

'You work at Consolidated?' he asked suddenly.

I shook my head. 'I work at Atlas.'

'That goddamned stinking joint!' he said. 'The Navy had to take over that goddamned yard before they could get any work done. That is the goddamnest, laziest, prissiest, undermanned, prejudiced shipyard—' He cursed out Atlas until my steak came, then he looked at it and said, 'That looks pretty good. They must be getting some better beef out this way now.' Until his steak came he cursed out the West Coast beef.

We ate silently. I'd never eaten steak that tasted so good. When I'd finished I got up, paid my bill, said, 'See you,' and left. He didn't say anything; but I felt all right about it.

I decided to go back to Figueroa, and when I turned into it a couple of white sailors thumbed me and I stopped to give them a lift. They were very young boys, still in their teens, scrubbed-faced and lightly tanned. The three of us sat in the front seat; the one in the middle put his arm behind me to make room. For a time we went along without talking, then I asked, 'What's you guy's names?'

'Lester,' the one in the middle said, and the other one said, 'Carl.'

'What's yours?' Lester asked, and I told him, 'Bob.'

'You work in a shipyard?' Carl asked.

'Atlas,' I told him. 'I'm a sheet-metal worker.'

'I worked a while up at Richmond—Richmond No. 1, Kaiser's yard,' he said. 'I'm from San Francisco.'

'I was up there once,' I said. 'I like Frisco, it's a good city.'

The boy in the middle hadn't said anything, so I asked him, 'Where you from, Lester?'

'Memphis,' he said. 'You ever been there?'

I gave him a quick side glance; then I chuckled. 'No, I never been to Memphis,' I said. 'I'm from Ohio—Cleveland.'

'I bet you'd like Memphis,' he said as if he really believed it.

'Maybe,' I said. 'But I'll never know.'

He grinned. 'You like Los Angeles, eh?'

'Just between you and me,' I said, 'Los Angeles is the most overrated, lousiest, countriest, phoniest city I've ever been in.'

That was one thing we all agreed on. They liked my car and we talked about cars for a time as we skimmed along the wide straight roadway. The boy from Frisco said, 'Of course if I had my way I'd take a Kitty.'

I said, 'Who wouldn't?'

We passed a couple of girls jiggling along in thin summer dresses and the boy from Memphis whistled.

I said, 'I bet you wouldn't take it if she gave it to you.'

'What you bet?' he said, and they both blushed slightly.

I got a funny thought then; I began wondering when white people started getting white—or rather, when they started losing it. And how it was you could take two white guys from the same place—one would carry his whiteness like a loaded stick, ready to bop everybody else in the head with it; and the other would just simply be white as if he didn't have anything to do with it and let it go at that. I liked those two white kids; they were white, but as my aunt Fanny used to say they couldn't help that.

When we got closer to town and saw more women on the street we started a guessing game about every one we passed, whether they were married or single, how many kids they had, whether their husbands were in the Army, if they played around at all. All the elderly women they called 'Mom.' We had a lot of fun until we came to a dark brown woman in a dark red dress and a light green hat carrying a shoebox tied with a string, falling along in that knee-buckling, leaning-forward, housemaid's lope, and frowning so hard her face was all knotted up. They didn't say anything at all. I wanted to say something to keep it going, but all I could have said about her was that she was an ugly, evil-looking old lady. If we had all been coloured we'd have laughed like hell because she was really a comical sister. But with the white boys present, I couldn't say anything. I looked straight ahead and we all became embarrassed and remained silent for a time. When we began talking again we were all a little cautious. We didn't talk about women any more.

When we neared Vernon Avenue I asked them where they were going and they said down to Warner's at Seventh and Hill. I took them down and dropped them in front of the box office. They thanked me and went off. I kept over to San Pedro and turned south. It was two-thirty when I got home. Henry had already left for work and Ella Mae had taken the baby out for a sunning.

I took a shower, shaved, put on slacks, sport shirt, and sandals; got my .38 Special out of the bottom bureau drawer, and checked to see that it was loaded, went out, and got in my car and drove over to Central to get some gas. I put the gun in the glove compartment and left the car in the station for Buddy to check over while I strolled down past Dunbar Hotel.

I felt tall, handsome, keen. I was bareheaded and my hair felt good in the sun. A little black girl in a pink draped slack suit with a thick red mouth and kinky curled hair switched by. I smelled her dime-store perfume and got a live-wire edge.

Everything was sharper. Even Central Avenue smelled better. I strolled among the loungers in front of Skippy's, leaned against the wall, and watched the babes go by. A white woman in a Ford roadster with the top down slowed for the traffic and a black boy called, 'Hello, blondy!' She didn't look around.

Tia Juana pulled up in his long green Cat and parked in a No Parking zone. He got out, a short, squat, black, harelipped Negro with a fine banana-skin chick on his arm, and went into the hotel, and some stud said, 'Light, bright, and damn near white: how does that nigger do it?'

A bunch of weed-heads were seeing how dirty they could talk; and a couple of prosperous-looking pimps were standing near by ignoring them. Some raggedy chum came from the barber shop across the street where they had a crap game in the rear and said that Seattle had won two grand. The coloured cop grabbed him for jay-walking and started writing out a ticket; and he was there trying to talk him out of it: 'You know me, man, I'm ol' Joe; everybody know ol' Joe—' Everybody but that cop, that is.

It was a slick, niggerish block—hustlers and pimps, gamblers and stooges. But it didn't ruffle me. Even the solid cats in their pancho conks didn't ruffle me. It wasn't as if I was locked up down there as I'd been just yesterday. I was free to go now; but I liked it with my folks.

A couple of my boys came up. 'You still on rubber, man?' one wanted to know.

'That's right,' I said.

'Say, run me out to Hollywood, man.' It was twelve miles to Hollywood. I laughed.

'Don't pay no 'tention to that nigger, man,' the other one said. 'That nigger's mad. Lemme take a sawbuck, man. I got a lain hooked down here and all he needs is digging.'

'That's right,' I said. 'Try a fool.'

They grinned. 'You got it, Papa.' They went off to find another one.

My people, I thought. I started to get a drink, then glanced at my watch. It was a quarter to four. I hurried over to the parking lot, got my car, circled into Central, and began digging. It was just four-thirty when I pulled up before the entrance to the parking lot at Atlas Ship.

I got out, walked over to the gate where the copper shop let out. My boy was one of the first ones through. I was thinking of him as 'my boy' now. I followed him, wondering how I could work it if he caught a P.E. train. But I got a break; he waited on one side of the street until a grey Ford sedan slowed for him and climbed in. I sprinted back across the street, got in my car, and dug off just as one of the yard cops was coming over to me. I muscled in ahead of a woman driver three cars behind the grey Ford; kept the position until we came to Anaheim Road in Wilmington, then pulled up to one car behind and stayed there. I thought about my riders; they were burning, I knew.

The next instant I'd forgotten them. It felt good following the guy, knowing I was going to kill him. I wasn't at all nervous or apprehensive. I thought about it like you think about a date with a beautiful chick you've always wanted to make; I just had that feeling that it was going to be great.

The grey Ford had five riders besides the driver. At Alameda Street it turned north into Compton, and two of the riders in back got out, leaving my boy alone. When it stopped before a house in Huntington Park I rolled up and parked right behind it. My boy got out, said something to the fellows in the front seat, and the car moved off. He glanced idly at my car, took two steps towards the house, then wheeled about and stared into my eyes. His eyes stretched with a stark incredulity and his face went stiff white, like wrinkled paper. He stood rigid, half turned, as if frozen to the spot.

I reached into the glove compartment and got my gun, then I opened the door and got out into the street. I wasn't in any hurry. They'd probably hang me, I knew, but I'd already accepted that, already gotten past it. He turned quickly and started up the walk toward the house, walking stiff-jointed, his shoulders high and braced and his back flattened like a board. When he got to the steps a homely blonde woman opened the door from the inside and two small towheaded kids squeezed past her legs and ran toward him.

He pushed the children back through the door with a rough, savage motion, then whispered something sharply to the woman. She snapped a quick frightened look toward me and her mouth opened as if to scream. She let him in and slammed shut the door and I could hear it being bolted from the inside.

I stopped. I didn't have to kill him now, I thought. I could kill him any time; I could save him up for killing like the white folks have been saving me up for all these years.

Out of the corner of my eye I saw two old ladies coming down the sidewalk with loaded shopping bags, giving me frosty looks. It didn't occur to me that my boy might stick a gun out the front window and blow off the back of my head. I felt cool, untouchable, indifferent. I thought perhaps he might be calling the police, but it didn't worry me.

When the two old ladies came opposite me I gave them a wide, bright smile and said in my best manner, 'It's a beautiful day, isn't it?'

I left them standing dead still on the sidewalk, twisting their scrawny necks about to stare at me with outraged indignation as I climbed into my car and dug off.

I could even go back to the shipyard and work as a mechanic, I thought. As long as I knew I was going to kill him, nothing could bother me. They could beat my head to a bloody pulp and kick my guts through my spine. But they couldn't hurt me, no matter what they did. I had a peckerwood's life in the palm of my hand and that made all the difference.

Excerpt from *I Love Dick*

CHRIS KRAUS

"He took me by the shoulders and shook me out." That's how Jennifer Harbury described meeting Efraim Bamaca.

Jennifer was interviewing rebel fighters in the Tajumulco combat zone in 1990. She felt so pale and large. "Compared to everyone else I'm huge, I'm 5'3. A giant." Bamaca was a Mayan peasant educated by the rebel army. At 35 he was notorious, a leader. Meeting him surprised her. "He looked almost like a fawn," she said. "He was so quiet and discreet. He never gave orders but somehow everything got done." And when she interviewed him for her oral history book, that most self-erasing lefty genre, he turned the questions back on her and listened.

They fell in love. When Jennifer left Tajumulco, Bamaca promised not to write. "There's no such thing as a fantasy relationship." But then he did, notes smuggled from the highlands to a safehouse, mailed from Mexico. A year later they met again and married. "It was a side of Jennifer I'd never seen," another law school friend told the *New York Times*. "She seemed so happy."

After dinner, then, you leaned back in your chair and fixed me with your gaze and asked: "What do you want?" A direct question tinged with irony. Your mouth was twisted, wry, like you already knew the answer. "What did you expect by coming here?"

Well I'd come this far, I was ready for all kinds of trials. So I said, out loud, the obvious: "I want to stay here tonight with you." And you just kept staring at me, quizzically, wanting more. (Even though I hadn't slept with anyone but my husband for 12 years, I couldn't remember sexual negotiations ever being this humiliatingly explicit. But maybe this was good? A jumpcut from the cryptic to the literal?) So finally I said: "I want to sleep with you." And then: "I want us to have sex together."

You asked me: "Why?"

(The psychiatrist H. F. Searles lists six ways to drive another person crazy in *The Etiology of Schizophrenia*. Method Number Four: Control the conversation, then abruptly shift its modes.)

The night Sylvère and I slept over at your house I'd dreamt vividly about having different kinds of sex with you. While Sylvère and I slept on the sofabed I dreamt I'd slipped into your bedroom through the wall. What struck me most about the sex we had was, it was so intentional and deliberate. The dream occurred in two separate scenes. In Scene One we're naked on your bed, viewed frontal-horizontally, foreshortened like Egyptian hieroglyphics. I'm squatting, neck and shoulders curved to reach your cock. Tendrils of my hair brush back and forth across your groin and thighs. It was the most subtle, psycho-scientific kind of blowjob. The perspective changes in Scene Two to vertical. I sit on top of you, you're lying flat, head slightly arched, I'm sinking up and down your cock, each time I'm learning something new, we gasp at different times.

"What do you want?" you asked again. "I want to sleep with you." Two weeks ago I'd written you that note saying the idea of spending time alone with you was a vision of pure happiness and pleasure. On the phone you'd said, "I won't say no" when I asked you what you thought, but all the reasons, factors, desire splintered in a hundred hues like sunlight through a psychedelic prism came crashing with a thud when you asked me: "Why?"

I just said, "I think we could have a good time together."

"We were in love," Jennifer Harbury told the *New York Times* about her life with Efraim Bamaca.

"We hardly ever fought—"

And then you said, "But you don't even know me."

Route 126 runs west along the base of the San Padre mountains. The landscape changes when it hits the Antelope Valley from rounded rolling hills to something craggier, more Biblical. The night (December 3) Sylvère and I stayed at your house because, as you said in a letter to him later, "weather reports had indicated that you might not be able to make it back to San Bernardino," we were amazed by where you lived. It was an existential dream, a Zen metaphor for everything you'd said about yourself . . . living, "all alone," you kept repeating, at the end of a dead-end road on the edge of town opposite a cemetery. A roadsign outside your place said, No Exit. And all night long as the three of us got drunker you found so many ways to talk about yourself, so many ways of making loneliness seem like a direct line to all the sadness in the world. If seduction is a highball, unhappiness has got to be the booze.

You said, "There's no such thing as a good time. It always ends in tears and disappointment." And when I blundered on about blind love, infatuation, you said, "It's not that simple." We had totally reversed positions. I was the Cowboy, you were the Kike. But still I rode it.

"Can't things just be fabulous?" I said, staring out the window. Things were getting dreamy, elongated, metaphysical. Moments passed. "Well then," you asked, "have you got any drugs?"

I was prepared for this. I was carrying a vial of liquid opium, two hits of acid, 30 Percoset and a lid of killer pot. "Relax, you've got a date!" Ann Rower'd said when she counted out her gift of Burmese flowerheads. Somehow this wasn't going how either of us had planned. But I rolled a joint and we toasted Ann.

The record ended and you got up to make some coffee. In the kitchen we stood fumbling accidentally-on-purpose brushing hands but this was so embarrassing and clunky we both withdrew. Then we talked some more about the desert, books and movies. Finally I said: "Look, it's getting late. What do you want to do?"

"I'm a gentleman," you answered coyly. "I would hate to be inhospitable. If you don't feel you can drive . . ."

"It's not about that," I said brusquely.

"Ah then . . . Do you want to share my bed? I won't say no."

Oh come on, had mores changed this much while I'd been married?

"Do you want us to have sex or don't you?"

You said: "I'm not uncomfortable with that idea."

This neutrality was not erotic. I asked you for enthusiasm but you said you couldn't give it. I made one final stab within this register: "Look, if you're not into this, it'd be more—gentlemanly—just to say so and I'll go."

But you repeated, "I'm not . . . uncomfortable . . . with the . . . idea."

Well. We were electrons swimming round and round inside of a closed circuit. No exit. *Huis clos*. I'd thought and dreamt about you daily since December. Loving you had made it possible to admit the failure of my film and marriage and ambitions. Route 126, the Highway to Damascus. Like Saint Paul and Buddha who'd experienced their great conversions as they hit 40, I was Born Again in Dick. But was this good for you?

This is how I understood the rules:

If you want something very badly it's okay to keep pursuing it until the other person tells you No.

You said: *I won't say no*.

So when you got up to change the record I bent down and started to untie my bootlace. And then things changed. The room stood still.

You came back, sat on the floor and took my boots off. I reached for you, we started dancing to the record. You picked me up and now we're standing in the living room, my legs are braced around your waist. You tell me "you're so light" and now we're swaying, hair and faces brushing. Who'll be the first to kiss? And then we do . . .

Here are some uses of ellipses:

• ...fade to black after ten seconds of a kiss in a Hayes Commission censored film.

• ...Celine separates his phrases in *Journey to the End of Night* to blast the metaphor out of language. Ellipses shoot across the page like bullets. Automatic language as a weapon, total war. If the coyote is the last surviving animal, hatred's got to be the last emotion in the world.

You put me down and gesture to the bedroom. And then the record changes to *Pat Garrett and Billy the Kid* by Bob Dylan. How perfect. How many times have each of us had sex in the foreground of this record? Six or seven tracks of banjo strum and whine that culminate around Minute 25 (a Kinsey national average) in *Knocking At Heaven's Door*. A heterosexual anthem.

And then you're laid out on the bed, head propped on pillows and we take our shirts off. The blue lamp beside the bed is on. I'm still wearing the black Guess jeans, a bra. I watch you feel my tits and we both watch my nipples as they get hard. Later on you run your index finger across the outside of my cunt, not into it. It's very wet, a Thing Observed, and later still I think about the act of witnessing and the Kierkegaardian third remove. Sex with you is so phenomenally . . . sexual, and I haven't had sex with anyone for about two years. And I'm scared to talk and I'm wanting to sink down on you and then words come out, the way they do.

"I want to be your lapdog."

You're floating like you haven't really heard so I repeat it: "Will you let me be your lapdog?"

"Okay," you say. "C'mere."

And then you ease me, small and Pekinese, 'til my hands are braced above your shoulders. My hair's all over.

"If you want to be my lapdog let me tell you what to do. Don't move," you say. "Be very quiet."

I nod and maybe whimper and then your cock, which until now'd been very still, comes rushing up, waves pulsing outward through my fingers. Sound comes out. You put your fingers on my lips.

"Come on little lapdog. You have to be real quiet. Stay right here."

And I do, and this goes on for maybe hours. We have sex 'til breathing feels like fucking. And I sleep fitfully in your turquoise room.

I wake up around six and you're still sleeping.

Rain's made the weeds outside your window very green. I find a book and settle on the living room sofa. I'm scared about the morning part, don't want to make my presence too invasive or demanding. But soon enough you're leaning in the doorway.

"What're you doing out there?"

"Resting."

"Well rest in here."

So we had fuzzy halting morning sex, the sheets, bright daylight, everything more real, but still that flood, the rushing of endorphins and for a long time after it was over neither of us said a word.

And this's when things get pretty weird.

"*Get* weird?" Scott B. said on the phone tonight when I was telling him the story. "What did you expect? The whole thing was completely weird."

Well yeah, I see his point. But still—

"So," I said as we sort of shifted out of sex, "what's the program?"

"What program do you mean? *The Brady Bunch*?"

"Noooo . . . I mean, I'll be in town 'til Tuesday and I was wondering if you think we should see each other again."

You turned and said, "Do you want to?"

"Yes," I said. "Definitely. Absolutely."

"Definitely . . . absolutely" you repeated with an ironic curl.

"Yes. I do."

"Well, actually I have a Friend (you somehow feminized the word) arriving for the weekend."

"Oh" I said, this information dropping like a stone.

"What's the matter?" you asked, seizing an idea. "Did I burst your balloon—destroy the fantasy?"

I struggled for a way to answer this without my clothes.

"I guess you were right about the disappointment. Probably if I'd known I wouldn't've stayed."

"What?" you laughed. "You think I'm *cheating* on you?"

Well this was very cruel, but loving you'd become a full-time job and I wasn't ready to be unemployed. "No," I said. "I don't. You just have to help me find a way to make this more acceptable."

"Acceptable?" you mimicked. "I don't have to do anything for you."

You were assuming a position, mockery heightening your face into a mask. Ultra-violence. Attack and kill.

"I don't owe you anything. You barged in here, this was your game, your agenda, now it's yours to deal with."

I wasn't anything at that moment except shock and disappointment.

Changing gears, you added archly: "I guess now you'll start sending me hate letters. You'll add me to your Demonology of Men."

"No," I said. "No more letters."

I had no right to be angry and I didn't want to cry. "You don't have to be so militantly callous."

You shrugged and made a point of looking at your hands.

"So militantly mean?" And then, appealing to your Marxist past, "So militantly against mystification?"

This brought a smile.

"Look," I said, "I'll admit that eighty percent of this was fantasy, projection. But it had to start with something real. Don't you believe in empathy, in intuition?"

"What?" you said. "Are you telling me you're schizophrenic?"

"No . . . , I just—" and then I lapsed into the pathetic. "I just—felt something for you. This strange connection. I felt it in your work, but before that too. That dinner we had three years ago with you and Jane, you flirted with me, you must've felt it—"

"But you don't know me! We've had two or three evenings! Talked on the phone once or twice! And you project this shit all over me, you kidnap me, you stalk me, invade me with your games, and I don't want it! I never asked for it! I think you're evil and psychotic!"

"But what about my letter? When I left Sylvère I wrote it trying to break through this thing with you. No matter what I do you think it's just a game but I was trying to be honest."

("Honesty of this order threatens order," David Rattray'd written once about René Crevel and I was trying then to reach that point.)

I continued: "Do you have any idea how hard it was for me to call you? It was the hardest thing I've ever done. Harder than calling William Morris. You said to come. You must've known then what I wanted."

"I didn't need the sex," you barked. And then a gentlemanly afterthought: "Though it was nice."

By now the sun was very bright. We were still naked on the bed.

I said, "I'm sorry."

But how could I explain? "It's just—" I started, foraging through fifteen years of living in New York, the arbitrariness of art careers, or were they really arbitrary? Who gets to speak and why? David Rattray's book sold only about 500 copies and now he's dead. Penny Arcade's original and real and Karen Finley's fake and who's more famous? Ted Berrigan died of poverty and Jim Brodey was evicted, started living in the park before he died of AIDS. Artists without medical insurance who'd killed themselves at the beginning of the onset so they wouldn't be a burden to their friends . . . the ones who moved me most mostly lived and died like dogs unless like me they compromised.

"I hate ninety percent of everything around me!" I told you. "But then, the rest I really love. Perhaps too strongly."

"I'd rethink that, if I were you," you said. You were leaning up against a dusky wall. "I like 90 percent of everything I see, the rest I leave alone." And I listened. You seemed so wise and radiant, and all the systems that I used to understand the world dissolved.

Of course the truth was messier. It was only Friday morning. The drive to Lake Casitas, the motel room, the percoset, the scotch were still to come. I lost my wallet, drove 50 miles to find it on 1/8 a tank of gas. There was still the phone call Sunday, meeting you for dinner and then the bar together Monday night. A production number medley of all the highlights of the show. It wasn't 'til I reached Ann Rower on Saturday on the phone that I stopped crying long enough to start shifting things around. Ann said: "Maybe Dick was right." This seemed so radically profound. Could I accept your cruelty as a gift of truth? Could I even learn to thank you for it? (Though when I showed Ann the outline of this story, she said she never said that. Not even close.)

On Saturday I spent the night on Daniel Marlos' couch. José made beans and carne asada. Daniel was working three jobs seven days a week to make money for an experimental film and not complaining. Sunday morning I walked through Eagle Rock down Lincoln Avenue to Occidental College. "Even here," I sat writing in my notebook, "in this bunched together neighborhood, people are taking Sunday morning walks. The air smells like flowers."

At the library I looked up *Gravity & Grace* by Simone Weil: "It is impossible," she wrote, "to forgive whoever has done us harm if that harm has lowered us. We have to think that it has not lowered us but revealed to us our true level."

Excerpt from "Some Other Deaths of Bas Jan Ader"

DANA WARD

Then the only thing I see is light on water.

It's the kind of water you could maybe drown tyrants in? This sort of baptismal of need Bas Jan Ader disappeared beneath searching for miracles over the near-death-experience shimmer the open sea shines on its liminal pilgrims. His grail hunt results in the dreamiest picture: nothing there but ocean, open surf, the suggestion of sea-life, of leisure at its edges, work painted over in fairy-tale tints, empty cupcake colored houses, allegorical post-snipe Olympus that's written in liquid by peaceable gods.

Still the purity of Ader's disappearance can't survive the general (capturing) audits of life. Even Mutt Lange, though mysterious, survives in a fetishized stock photo they always show anytime they have to talk about Shania. His Switzerland is like a shallow ocean, & "You're Still the One I Love" contains a measure of his face as the short, benign plunge from a tree contains 'Major Tom' longing for Zero-G floating away, outfoxing all habeas corpus. The scene of Ader's death is so smudged for me today by such time as I interpolate the whole of it to mine my callow innocence & blessings for a wormhole in the represented world.

Is that what I think of as dreaminess then? "Jesse's Girl", covetous & urgent comes on, 800 pounds of marijuana are found off the coast of Orange County in the morning & I flourish--in their molten convergence of largesse & need there is a fixture of interludes believed to be respites from history somehow inside me like a disappearing act. In the meadows festooned with the precious calamities inherent to my class, this one, unassuagable & durative keeps calling back then I blink at the patterns of dust on my copy of Loveless, or flash my eyes over the differential snowflake (ontology) that orders my belief. That dreaminess makes time seem personal & neat, a flag of one color folded perfectly & buried with its casualty, alone, in the sea. Then that song goes off. Then its friendliness departs. My only desire is to love the music, hard, & to unlearn its world without drowning. At the edge of this desire there's a phantom TBD, endless trailers play in faint black & white flickering patterns I can't seem to process in time, to be carried from their distillate figure to where, as if mated to Howl's Moving Castle, the health center moves on my Fortress of Solitude, breathing public fire, & melts my isolation chamber down into puddles of contact solution, a rinse conceived to make me more clear eyed.

Because my own sight is of no consequence alone. Nearly anything I see is like a Bethlehem to me, giving birth to the most divine irruption then the advent adapts & its violence is blunted. Everyday is like Training Day; little red school, vibrant blue sky strobed together, the cherries & berries of its light effects & sweetened vegetation. But I would wage war on everything I've ever written to produce a form of gratitude surpassing what, permitted to return to, I acquire. Still I am so thankful for life. Yet this gratitude, brutally partial, unsettles. I want the commons of its radical suggestion yet only end up with my signature Dubai. *Still I am so thankful for life*. It's an odd thing to say, to repeat, because it departs for no site of reception. The math is sound but the soul takes it on as a joke like the water on the knee in "Hymn to Life". Its raiments are offered up in total supplication, but to whom? The styles go limp on the absence of a frame. They puddle in silk, in stiff denim, a pink cotton shirt on which someone's printed YOLO. I wait for the ghost to stand true in these clothes & deliver affirmative hugs. But there won't be commensurate floods of receipt, no circulating joy, & for me that means there is no absolution.

When we lived near Eden Park I was green & now I think in saying that I might be even more so. I would drink Folger's espresso near a citronella candle reading Mandelstam & then I'd go & visit Mirror Lake. Under the glare of the water was a wonderful pattern, curvaceous & made of spring colors, these children had painted one summer as part of a public arts project, now defunct. But the horror was the way in which the lake was all for me—existence seemed the emblem of a hurt, romantic man exteriority had processed & rendered as material no thought would ever eclipse. The wind styled over the surface of the water, freely, with easy intensity, enough to cause commotion although never any panic. The currents were mild, patterns brief from wave to wave, so I never felt obliged to organize them in my mind as more than sated victims of an uncoordinated surging. The sun was just a paper moon, its warmth an effect of its need for some beloved to believe in it & authorize the venue of its beaming. Slow swarms of dandelion spoors would migrate north from the riverbank & settle on an aimlessness the airflow agreed to. Shamelessly happy I sailed into a parallel universe dreaminess blew into this one's unbearable completeness.

"As sweet as pain to the saint" as Notley wrote, "is the door to the actuality of those events." I am pushing it open with my nose like a cat, & going blind as the dazzle from its surface hits my eyes I wince & shudder making vague figures out in a room overcoming or eluding crude representations through maneuvers which appear to me, like dancing to a child, as the movement of the real world in rehearsal.

There's a flickering black & white pattern moving over the air & their forms are bleeding endlessly & freely flowing into it, out of it, streams, & sprays untraceable & lost to destination like the most evasive sentiment seeming to come to a critical truth. My eyes loose the thread of this movement in a moment of being bound into it, care like distortion through being enforced or bound inside these audits to the forms of certain persons whose abandonment describes the very limits of existence. Then one of them, another svelte & hurt romantic man, emerges from the overwhelming motion to seek the miraculous, alone, in the dreamiest fashion, as then he went down to his ship, which was already poised, tiny argosy of sacrificial love, where the Venus deer he would become found its headlights, the sea, reached via the streets of a city at night.

The last thing he would see is light on water.

Then Micah stops by & I smoke while he nurses a nicotine lozenge & helps me better understand Laurelle.

Then Kathy moves her shoulder in just such a way so that I can sneak around her through the door.

Then Nancy is working my shift.

Then I shit my pants & a friend of my mother's comes to pick me up from school so I can change.

Then Blake sits beside me on the waterbed talking me down from some harrowing trip.

Then Anne brings me ice in a washcloth to see to the finger I've busted in Overland Park.

Then Jen hangs out with Vivian while I track down my car.

Then Charlie drives me back from the impoundment lot on Sunday.

Then Randy is taking me home.

Then Joey comes to take me to the openings, & dinner.

Then Joe picks me up for the show.

Then Maria gets me home before midnight.

Then Pastor finds some money in the budget.

Then cris hooks me up with a gig.

Then Paul stands me drinks at the Comet.

Then Kasey has me out to Ashland I see all my friends.

Then Brandon is lifting my head with an amulet he's typing up for me against my meltdown.

Then Karen reassures me that she knows it's going to happen.

Then Patricia tells me that the basement's not on fire.

Then Bill recommends this sci-fi book the Starlight Fraction.

Then Jesse holds the baby while I'm smoking at the protest.

Then Thom buys me coffee & a bagel.

Then Jordan gets me high in his terrarium during the noise show that's raging downstairs.

Then John lets me play the piano.

Then Cynthia brings Vicodin, cheese cubes & beer

Then David sends a line-inducing rainbow in the mail.

Then Chris reminds me shit like this is really no big deal.

Then Rob is introducing me to several of my heroes.

Then Emily's making me laugh on the porch.

Then Stephanie's taking me to buy some stomach pill.

Then Norman is fixing the hole in our floor.

Then Geoff helps me out of the bar to my yard where he leaves me outside to sleep it off.

Then Caroline gives me a drawing.

Then Nat gives me magazines I'd never find.

Then Brandon escorts to some tiny grocery & buys me a vitamin water, granola bar, C-Pak & bottle of Dasani.

Then Charles helps me navigate the trains.

Then Les helps me clear the fallen tree limbs from our porch.

Then Anselm is walking me home on his arm.

Then Kathy is lending us money.

Then my brother takes me to the Greyhound station late Thanksgiving evening where a friend has been stranded for hours.

Being Close to Data

DARA BARROIS/DIXON

You can't see the forest, the pandemic
for the trees, our everyday lives
and thank god for that as it is as it is
I'm never in the mood for a pandemic
to take up residence in my brain
it is not in me to take up thinking
of people as nothing but numbers
to be counted for the story to grow ever
more and more awful and for the public story
to be gotten under whose control
If this were a data love poem
I'd be tearing out my hair and ranting
against just who thinks they can take this
from us with so little visible at our peril
without our permission as if in this case
now is not sufficiently present and we
who are here now will acquiesce in silence

Excerpt from *God Jr.*

DENNIS COOPER

"Well, what have you got?"

* * *

"Besides the mega-jump, I've got three nice cheats," says the snowman. "First, if you push the joystick forward and hold down R and L, you get to be invisible, but only in this level. That one's fun for sneak attacks, but considering the state of things, I wouldn't recommend it. Second, if you pull the joystick back and do a zoom on my face, then push B, I melt. But I regrow, so don't get greedy. That cheat's just silly. But if you hold down every button at the same time, you'll see a ladder on my back. It's there right now, but it's intangible. You'll have three minutes to make it to my head. You probably can't see it, but I'm wearing a funny old top hat. It's just a crushed tin can to you. There's a coiled spring inside it, don't ask me how. If you reach the brim in time, the spring will send you flying. You can land almost anywhere you want, if you're not too picky. Just aim with the joystick as usual. Now, from what I can see going on in levels four and five, I recommend you use this third cheat and aim for level three, because paganism is running rampant, and you're a marked bear. But level three looks pretty mellow."

* * *

"That sounds good. Speaking of level three, can you see a building there? It's—"

* * *

"Of course," says the snowman. "It's famously and inexplicably your favorite."

* * *

"Since you're so wise, can you tell me what's inside it, or make an educated guess?"

* * *

"Okay, why are you doing this?" says the snowman. His big head starts to rotate very noisily. When the grinding stops, it's dangerously balanced on his second-smallest ball. Then he smiles at us a little too enthusiastically, like a preschooler's mural of the moon. "You're God. It's your call. The game's your fixer-upper. But it just seems kind of hostile."

* * *

"You're changing the subject."

* * *

"It's a puzzle," says the snowman. "I mean, what isn't? I mean, nickname it what you want. I'm not trying to be rude. It's just that when you see everything, you realize that nothing means anything."

* * *

"You mean it's not a glitch?"

* * *

"You're the glitch," says the snowman. "I'm not referring to the bear. He fits in. He likes solving puzzles. He likes winning fights and getting gifts. We like being solved and getting killed and giving bears our gifts. I'm talking about you inside there. You and Tommy in particular. How long have you been working on that puzzle? For us, it's been centuries. This isn't the Giza Plateau, sir. Or should I say, I guess it is now, thanks to you. So you tell me. What does God think he's going to find in there, assuming you could solve it? And before you get your hopes up, the mega-jump won't help. Good try, though. You'll smash the bear to smithereens. You'll drizzle down that puzzle. No, it takes something else. You're not even warm."

* * *

"Look, you guys are great. You give gifts the way clouds give raindrops. You're generosity incarnate. Still, your gifts are kind of shitty, to be honest. But imagine some serious, unbelievable gift. Imagine if, say, you could move, walk, drag yourself around the game, or whatever mobility means here. I'm talking go anywhere at any time."

* * *

"Wow," says the snowman. "That's such a great gift, I'll feel depressed for the rest of my eternal winter knowing I can't get it."

* * *

"I just know whatever's in there, it's important. Maybe something so great my son will ollie in his grave. Or maybe just some charming, empty house where I could live. This'll sound pathetic, but I kind of don't have anywhere to go. And before you remind me bears sleep in the woods or bring up drugs, I'm well aware I'm out of it. I know what wouldn't work. I'm too big and corporeal, et cetera. Just call it a weird combination of desperation and faith."

* * *

"It's a honeycomb," says the snowman. "It's an extraspecial, super-duper honeycomb, if that makes you feel better. It gives the bear infinite life. Kind of ironic, isn't it?"

* * *

"You're just saying that so I'll erase you. I know that's all you creatures want."

* * *

"If only wisdom were that messy," says the snowman. "I miss my devious past. No, I tell the ugly truth. But if I might interject a little sanity, please do. And if I might be so bold, you did promise you would, if you remember. And if I might lift a page from your book, if you don't, I'm going to jump yay high and do the job myself. That's not devious, that's just called doing my thing. So take a minute. Consider that my prayer."

* * *

We've won our standoffs in the past. Or enough of them to know our biggest draw is doing nothing. So I ignore the bear until he's just an itchy, yawning bore. But when the snowman's base starts smoking like a pad at Cape Canaveral, I panic. I wring and yank on the controller, but I might as well be a guy with a fishing pole trying to haul in Atlantis.

* * *

"Look, here's the deal. Tommy was my son. He liked that puzzle. I don't know why. He did a lot of drugs. So do I. Maybe that's the only reason. Now Tommy's dead. I loved Tommy. I think that's safe to assume. But he's gone, and that puzzle's still there. Whatever's in it meant a lot to him. Or it didn't. Probably it didn't. He was probably just stoned and bored and had nothing else to do. I'm probably just stoned and hiding out here in your game because my life is even more unsolvable than you. Imagine if every puzzle here, including you, was too difficult. Then imagine that miserable, boring bear you'd have to live with. That's what my life is like. My wife, my job, my friends, my house . . . you name it. Everything and everyone I know is either broken or locked so tight I can't break in. It's my fault. I accidentally killed my son, and I'm too scared or egotistical to face it. But you want to talk about a puzzle? Try making up a world where having killed someone you love isn't important."

* * *

"Love sounds familiar," says the snowman.

* * *

"Love's this thing you'd call the biggest prize in life. It's like that building or you, not to make your big head even bigger. You want to be inside that love, even if it's empty, and even if the ones who hide it are divorcing you or dead."

* * *

"I was being sarcastic," says the snowman. "Don't worry. I get that all the time. It's my face. I've outgrown it. Point is, I know love, or let's say I've read your mind. We all have, ad infinitum. How do you suppose we got our values? But we're a game, and you're the bear. Big difference. We think, Enough already. You think, I'll win. It happens all the time. The last time we met, I let you walk. I let you turn a puzzle any child could solve into a Sphinx. I let you turn my majestic view into your blighted neighborhood. You want to know about guilt? Still, the one good thing about us ivory towers is we're smart enough to learn from your mistakes. How can I phrase this so you'll understand? Oh, I know. Your son's dead."

* * *

"Yeah, I know that."

Excerpt from "Fat Chance"

DODIE BELLAMY

for Casey McKinney

Ed-thoughts keep banging around inside my skull *Ed and I step out of the black and white of e-mail and into the Fairmont's floral mauves and teals* I close my mouthhole, hoping the Ed-thoughts will suffocate, but they frizzle and hiss, whoosh out through noseholes *I can't believe he would stop loving me* I snort like a moose *my absolute belief in our fused magic* so now I'm typing, hoping to lock the Ed-thoughts in a file, maybe I could print it out and burn it, maybe that would rid me of them *his body felt solid yet puffy, like a water balloon, I loved the way clean cotton slid so easily across his massive flesh* my keystrokes are the click of heels on a mausoleum floor—the vowels are all the same, it's the consonants that change *mrbl mrbl* I make puddles to stay alive. Rejection is such a prickly emotion, you breathe it in as something transparent, but inside you it condenses, hardens, takes on pointed geometric shapes between your organs. A cock can gouge the soul right out of your pussy, but I've heard the soul grows back, slowly, like a lizard's tail, I'm counting on that. He told me I was "fantastic." Fantastic—a word which darts about braying and sputtering like a jackass, a fucking jackass. Oh, I'm such a bitter girl *hollow mush of mouth and tongue* what are words without an audience, what is a woman without an audience *bitter herbs relieve constipation* I dream I'm a stone skittering across a cold marble floor. This happens in a corridor so I must still believe in linearity.

Back to 1996: After months of email and dirty talk on my turquoise Princess phone, I'm finally going to set eyes on him. I'm at SFO, sitting on a ledge to the side of the security check station, nervous, chatting with two midwestern women about weather and airports, ladies in crisp white skirts and sandals. "It's cooler here than in Nebraska." From down the hallway, a stream of rumpled people gushes towards us, lugging carry-ons, none of them Ed, then finally he walks past the metal detectors, large and squishy, swelling about the middle in black pants and a dark brown shirt, tucked in, I recognize him from his photo but I'm shocked at how round he is. The dark clothes make him look like an eggplant, an excitedly smirking eggplant, his mouth a slit splitting his big pale face in two, soft fringe of black curls *kind of femmy* what to do about the issue of touch—fluorescent airport air, colorless indoor/outdoor carpeting, Ed in his dark brown shirt scanning the area, an eggplant lost in a wasteland—I stand and wave. No sign of recognition, so I run up, "Hi, it's me." He laughs. "Sweetie, I can't believe I couldn't find you." He reaches out and I give him a quick hug, no kiss, so that maybe the Nebraskan women will think he's just a friend. "Let's get your luggage," I say.

When we get down to the baggage claim he hugs me again, his body's soft with lumps at unexpected places, like I'm embracing a rag doll whose stuffing has shifted. He hunches down and kisses me, gently, but I remain stiff, unresponsive. He looks much younger than 33, he could be a boy. We lean against a chrome railing and stare at the oval baggage carousel, a series of triangular metal plates shifting at weird angles, endlessly standing there in public, tentatively rubbing pinky fingers against one another, then sliding closer, arm pressing against arm, his soft dense heat, the dissonance of so much information, so much emotion, so many orgasms projected upon this foreign body whose fingers are now stroking my hand, harder and faster, chrome railing indenting our asses. The baggage carousel's jerky revolutions. Many of our fantasies have centered on fucking in a rental car, as soon as we get in the mid-sized Honda he leans over and really kisses me. Twenty minutes later we're still making out around the gear shift. I pull back and say, "Don't you think we should like, leave the parking lot?" He drives with his left hand, with his right he reaches over and tweaks my nipple, then he moves his hand between my legs, rubs my cunt through my black dress, wet spot of pre-cum on the front of his Dockers. My clit gets hard as I write this, not because he was so good, but because he was so strange. I wasn't attracted to him one iota, yet I submitted to him, it was thrilling, so Story of O. I did not know the hulk beside me. "Play with my cock," he barked and I reached over, green rectangular exit signs whooshing by. We didn't talk much.

I know I liked kissing his lips, soft, pillow-like.

It's mid-afternoon when we arrive in San Jose, Ed's hand still wriggling in my crotch. I marvel at the clean and manicured downtown, its broad pavements creamy as mother of pearl. We check in at the Fairmont then ride the elevator to the fourth floor. It takes forever for the bellman to deposit our luggage. We hover awkwardly around the two huge beds in the center of the room. Ed pulls back a stiff quilted cover. "Ready?" We lie down beneath its vaguely biomorphic design and sex until it's dark out. I rub my face against his breasts, reach my arms around his fat belly, he feels like a tribal fertility figure, both tits and a cock—I suck on him until my cheeks collapse. He tweaks and turns my nipples, saying let's turn up the volume, let's balance the channels. To our right a wall of windows, heavy light-blocking drapes glide open, beneath them a layer of sheer white gauzes the skyline. Free from all context beyond our charged, leaking bodies, we tumble slowly through the Fairmont's muted color scheme, teal, apricot, rose. I have to put a pillow under my ass to endure his breadth, his initial slow heaves shifting to rhythmic slamming, thighs spread achingly wide my whole body lunges with each thrust, and then he bellows and collapses on me THUD I am a pancake with bulging eyes, red tongue dangling to one side. Ed kisses me and with our lips still touching, whispers, "I love you." A barely audible whisper *I love you* his lips pooching and parting against my lips, it's as if he's feeding me the words.

Around nine that evening we get up, woozy, and walk to the Italian cafe around the corner. The streetlights sparkle like crystal. Both of us are too nervous, too amniotic to eat much of our pizza margherita. Ed hunches over the white-clothed table, mutely clinging to my hand, inert, smooth, his back rounded as a Henry Moore sculpture,

I want to climb on top of him, sprawl there, child-limp, unleashing the full weight of my body, warmed by the warmth of sun-warmed stone. Still I'm embarrassed to be seen in public with him *the fat man with the mooning eyes*. "Ed, you're so quiet!" He says he doesn't know what to say, that he was used to silence due to his deaf parents. "Were they born that way?" "Spinal meningitis. My father was three and had already learned to speak. Said he could remember what sound was like." "And what was it like?" "I don't know, he was such an asshole. My mother was only a year old when she got sick. Silence, or whatever it is that goes on inside her head—you know, John Cage—is all she's ever known." "You mean like silence as noise?" "Yeah, Sweetie, you got it." He squeezes my hand and hypergrins, silky skin stretched over his hefty cheeks. My clit is so excited it glows in the dark *sex uranium*. "My mother was frightened of hearing people, she was like this little mouse huddled in our living room, everything covered with plastic, and so am I, a mouse. I need to be inside you."

I loved our hotel room—small flat bottles of Neutrogena soap in the shower, pale amber, the glass door, the sink lined with pill bottles, burnt orange, bathtub, built-in vanity in the dressing room, Hollywood globe lights lining a huge mirror, me sitting on the wide padded stool putting on make-up, the hush of wall-to-wall carpeting, my movements are so slow they're almost imperceptible, a series of stop frames dissolving into one another, his loose shit exploding into the toilet and then the air, my impulse is to retch, I suppress it, kiss his guilty face. His suitcase open on the floor, cotton shirts spilling over the sides. In the mornings Ed went down to the database convention DownWorld had sent him to and I'd lay in bed dreaming and reading, this messy left-over from the day before. The maids must have hated me. At lunch he'd climb back in bed with sandwiches, and we'd kiss and belly-rub, his cock snaking through the folds of his Dockers, breadcrumbs and mayonnaise gunking the sheets. Then I'd spend the afternoon sauntering through San Jose's mall-like downtown, writing in my diary *arousal mixed with pangs of What Am I Doing Here,* drinking white wine while listening to the grand piano in the Fairmont's cavernous lounge, lots of gold and foliage.

* * *

San Jose Fairmont Lounge, 7-9-96—Everyone's wearing suits and high heels and I feel like a frump. A giant ficus is looming over me, a pony-tailed pianist is playing "My Funny Valentine." So here I am, finally, with Ed—words, hair, semen, blood. We ordered room service this morning, and as we were eating I thought of our intimate emails, how writing abstracts life into words, but this is the opposite of writing, this is writing made flesh. I wonder how the writing feels about this turnabout, if it resents it. In movies characters are always leaping off the page into the material world, solid, breathing, wreaking havoc—like Freddy Krueger or even in that drecky Woody Allen comedy where Mia Farrow is the small town fan. Perhaps all return-from-the-grave/haunting plots are really about writing incarnating, moving from the safe realm of fantasy into treacherous life. Suddenly to be involved in all this fucking, love, romance. It reminds me of those android movies where the creature is born full-grown with memories and feelings implanted in its circuitry. I sat on the toilet and wiped myself and there on the toilet paper was a long black hair. He has the longest pubic hair I've ever seen. Fingering it I call him, "Rapunzel." He's not being dirty with me at all like we've been in letters and on the phone. In life he's sweet, considerate, rather quiet. God, is my cunt sore. And my inner thigh muscles so stretched I feel bow-legged. I wish he would talk more during sex. I feel little physically when he fucks me, none of that intense connection that makes you want to kill to get it. He doesn't really know how to connect sexually, body to body. The kissing is better, lying together, this incredible loving energy bouncing back and forth between us like a ping pong ball. Lots of shyness and awkwardness at first—now I feel as if I could stay with him forever.

San Jose, 7-11-96—Yesterday he snuck me into the computer conference lunch buffet. A zillion computer programmers in polo shirts, the collars and sleeves of the polo shirts trimmed with contrasting colors, all these men dedicated to interactive databases—we were standing in line and Ed said to me, "I'm not used to not being able to touch you." It was a whimper—so primal. He likes to be held the way my cats like to be held when they're freaked out—submitting completely like I'm the

Virgin Mary of safety. He's so stunningly beautiful and interesting. I watch fat men now, this secret ostracized world of ridicule and invisibility. I feel scorn for the mainstream, the hip, the cool. I can't believe he's going home tomorrow.

San Francisco, 7-19-96—A week since San Jose. This is the first morning since we got involved that I've woken and there wasn't an email from Ed, and this is the first morning I can remember since I "went under" in March where I am struck with the simple beauty of my life, my pale green dotted Swiss comforter, my geometrically-etched drinking glasses. Things have been strained between us since he went back to Chicago. Clearly he's distancing from me, which hurts, but it's for the best—I need to separate from him. His total impotence the last couple of days was intolerable—and makes any continued long-distance sexual involvement ludicrous. I need to start reclaiming my life, to be productive. I need a more meditative state, to read, to think, to take notes. All my systems, my schedules have fallen apart since March. I stopped brushing my teeth and flossing like I should. I stopped misting the plants. I never unpacked my suitcase from my February trip to Los Angeles. This romance has been wonderful but cancerous, eating all my energy. It's hard to let go of. I've been in mourning ever since we left San Jose. It's not the same as what we had before—our innocent onrush of desire and excitement has degenerated into this grudging, guarded thing. My sweet pure baby that I trusted with my soul is becoming a straight male, pulling out that bag of tricks. No wonder I've been teary-eyed. I think my days of being a sexual amazon are over. Any wonderful connection we did have happened when we were lying together, or when we were out experiencing The World together, holding hands, perhaps quietly talking. Last night I left an urgent message, "I've got to talk to you!" I called and called and when I finally got through, around 9:30, he said he didn't call me back because he had to pay his bills, do the laundry. The washing machine's in the basement of his building. He says he's totally out of touch with his libido, that he tried masturbating yesterday and failed.

Who'd believe that in less than two months I'd hurl myself back into his roly-poly arms. Six weeks in Chicago. What was I thinking? I tossed my body about as if it were a dress, the skin mere fabric wrapped around pulp. No brains. The woman Ed was in love with is inaccessible to me—a sex goddess he called her, this raw ethereal creature. His silence during phone sex, I'd beg him to speak, but the line would remain dead save for his rapid exhalations and the slapping of fist against cock—he was with *her* then, a space bitch with three tits and fangs. Ed and She didn't need words—thought waves, breath waves were their units of transmission, impulses shooting directly from her cunt into his bloodstream. When I arrived on his doorstep, my flesh a thick, sloppy shield, he lost her, his true alien mate. I unbutton my blouse a bit and lean over but Ed averts his eyes from my cleavage. It is then I know he's an alien—like the man who suddenly stops smoking, like the lame man who can suddenly walk without a cane. Or any man unwilling to take off his shirt and show me his back. During a manic episode an evolved being from another dimension entered Ed's body, and that's why he got fat—to protect it. Aliens puff up right before our eyes, mature in a matter of days or even minutes. Under a microscope their cells reproduce wildly, hysterically, jigging around. Aliens have an obscene passion for life, they are so lowclass in that regard.

Hong Kong, 6-11-98—I'm in the back, waiting for my wine, surrounded by fatties, working class blacks whites Latinos, leather daddies, nerds, crazies. The Hong Kong is my salvation from trendy San Francisco, a pocket where "it" simply doesn't matter. Two humongous fat guys behind me, one white, one black, eating two orders of potstickers. I've had those potstickers, they're a bit bland but *so* creamy. Third time this week I'm sitting at this same table, my palms leaning on the pale veneer, my journal angled on the dark brown trim, restroom door just a few feet behind me. A middle-aged Chinese guy sets down my white wine, filled to the brim, icy, too sweet too cheap for my friends, I want it more than anything in the world. All the waiters wear boxy Hawaiian shirts, the same shirts they were wearing in 1977 when I first came here with a bisexual vet (psych discharge) who I would fuck, unsatisfactorily, the following New Years Eve while listening to a Grateful Dead concert on the radio. A square of sky is pasted on the cover of my small black notebook. Over the pale lavender and white cloud pattern is printed a lavishly smiling globe, meridian lines along the outer edges, on either side of its mouth-curve half moons suggest jolly corpulent cheeks. Energy lines emanating from his circle-head arch into space *centrifugal swirl of Jesus' thought waves* Ed's fat face beams cosmic glee *no body no Carla.* Walking over here I saw this 300 pound guy, not that tall, waddling towards me with two matching little fluffy dogs on blue leashes—blond and given the dogs and the neighborhood, most likely gay. I thought of Ed. He was nothing like Ed. It's been two years, but my eyes still suck at fat men, their skin taut and smooth as helium balloons, balloons with cocks bouncing down the street, wrinklefree, so irreducibly Other, I wish for X-ray vision that could bare their souls—with a shimmer the greasy world of grit and concrete dissolves to the Shangri-La that lies within the caverns of every fat man's belly—waterfalls, monkeys swinging from vines, squawk of bright yellow beaks, the air scented with green herbs and gardenias. I want assurance that the world is, in fact, a bauble, me lying on my back, kicking and pawing, the world inches from my face dangling at the end of an elastic cord, bobbling. A couple tables over a guy I almost slept with in the 70s, Spanish, still cute, got to the point of lying on a twin bed with him taking my clothes off. "I can't do this." And then I left. I hope he doesn't remember. In front of me, dark-haired light-complexioned guy large as Ed is paying his bill, jaw more angular. He's with a thin arty blonde, he walks with his hands curled backwards, like Ed did, like I've seen so many heavy men doing. He may be a bit larger than Ed. Loss. Let's take a moment here and salute it. I bet Ed had no trouble replacing me. I feel like an invalid with my nose pressed up against the window, my eyes enormous as the rest of the world connects and copulates. A most successful vomit just now. Though I'd love to have another glass of white wine. *Your present plans are going to succeed.* 07 18 32 40 48 5 My fortune cookie is stale.

Everything is seen through the lens of Over. Ed lying on his back, his hinged arms and legs slow and graceful as a spider's. Skin pink as kleenexes, and up close just that frail. I touched him gently. Ed in the Fairmont's guest robe, hunched over as he clutches the front—he looked like a giant white single quotation mark. An opening quote. Six months later, when he curled down to kiss me at O'Hare, that was the closing quote. Color and texture took precedence over narrative progression, our moments were bathed in blue and pink and neon, a sultry ambience heightened by a bluesy sax *my paunchy Venus, my bucket of playdough, my fucking zeppelin* during sex my body felt too small, like a doll's, like I would be crushed beneath his enormous weight, my little bent-back thighs snapped off. He was disappointed I was too tall to comfortably fuck from behind like he did his last girlfriend. Sometimes he couldn't come but stayed hard, sometimes he went soft while fucking me, sometimes he couldn't get hard at all—except when we were getting ready to go someplace. Small beams of light focus on him: pale hazel eyes, the pinkness of his lips, palms and fingers gnawed bloody. I'd catch a glimpse of him sometimes, a little animal racing through this white mass of flesh, peeking out through the holes. His eyes reminded me of John Cassavetes', so much brain activity going on behind them, eyes registering with superhuman precision—like those security cameras in supermarkets and buses, stereoscopic cameras sweeping and weeping. Ed's panoramic emotions scared most people, but bottomless need has always felt natural to me.

I pull out a snapshot of Ed from his college days. Lounging in the passenger seat of a car, he exudes an air of confidence that's alien to the Ed I know. He's checking himself out in the rearview mirror, smiling in sunglasses and red bandanna, like Johnny Depp playing a gypsy. He's very thin, very handsome. Is his past an improvement? Fat chance. The oneness, the delicious harmony of a stretched round face, huge Buddha-men ambling past me on the street, my head turns towards them all, Hispanic, black, Asian, white, my eyes wet with longing. My breasts leap forward, plump nipples stiffen to rosy Buddha-heads. In front of me on the Mission bus sits a blond guy with a shaved head, fuzzy ripple of fat at the base of his neck, I imagine the tips of my fingers gently brushing across it, peach down *everything comes and goes, no continuity except these fat men who wash over me, wave after wave of being—no longer am I a solid woman, whirling bits give the impression of the form of Carla, like a surrealist painting of a female tornado* super vegetarian taco, decadently gunky—cheese, guacamole—and a

Dos Equis, a fat black guy, kind of swan backed, just walked by, I look at his belly and wonder—is that how fat Ed was? Another fat guy cruises by, a white one, his flesh is jiggly, so he doesn't count. Both of them in T-shirts. The city is so gorgeous I can barely stand it—hazy overcast sky, gust of wind, the streets are lined with Sumo wrestler silhouettes, so curvy, generous *I gawk and BANG I'm creaming* Mission Grounds, all the old timers sitting on Valencia Street in the cold chainsmoking, adapting to the 90s, some fat guy in a blue down jacket comes in, sits down two tables away from me and polishes off the potatoes left on a plate *beneath every puffy surface elation flows* on Lafayette two fat Filipino boys, 11-ish, short-cropped dark hair, peachy faces, matching baggy jeans, oversized black T-shirts, techno-tennies, gray with black racing stripes, apparently with little wheels on the soles, the boys begin gliding across the sidewalk, like telekinetic salt and pepper shakers, like Coppola's Dracula, only cute. Walking down Van Ness from Geary to Market as the sun sets, I remember walking this same half mile when I first moved here, I must have done it a hundred times these past fifteen years *snapshots of weather and concrete* I see myself, Carla, as a line of selves in multiple exposures, one self stepping into another *Nude Descending Van Ness* at Market I get on MUNI, a heavy-set guy is sitting sideways at the front of the bus, the position Ed preferred, thighs spread, hand gripping the chrome railing, he'd talk to the driver *pang of nostalgia and loss* the guy doesn't really look like Ed. Dark-haired, fat, sideways—that's enough for me.

This sack/ is ripe like fallen fruit, like the earth/ used to be.

We fucked during one lunch and Ed skipped the afternoon session on object-oriented programming. He fretted that "that prick Donald" would notice his absence, but he was glued to my cunt. After a couple of hours we unstuck ourselves and drove North on 101. It's drizzling as we walk through a park near Fort Mason. We're on a pilgrimage to revisit places Ed knew in San Francisco, for he lived here, briefly, in his early 20s. Against the overcast, shadowless afternoon the grass glows, an unearthly chartreuse, the winding path is painted a Technicolor red. Ed wraps his arm around my shoulders and I hook a finger in a belt loop on the back of his pants, melt into his fondue-hot body. Entwined, we lurch from side to side towards the Marina. We're so bubbled up into one another's heads and bodies I hardly give a fuck who's looking at us. It's like we're encased in this erotic space suit, gliding together through San Francisco's alien atmosphere. Ed points to a tree, "I ate leaves from that tree." "Ate leaves?" "Yeah, I thought I was a dinosaur. This asshole doctor refused to give me my medication because I asked his receptionist where to buy some grass. The receptionist was black, so I thought he'd understand, but then he told the doctor and the doctor said I had to go into rehab before I could have any more drugs and I said I'd go crazy without them, and sure enough, within a month, here I was in the Marina, eating leaves." I look at the emerald grass, the ruby red curving walkway and think of Oz, the black and white of email bursting forth to glorious color. "What kind of dinosaur?" "A T-Rex." "But weren't T-Rexes carnivorous?" "When I was a T-Rex I ate leaves. What are you, some kind of lizard expert or something."

Excerpts from *Nightwood*

DJUNA BARNES

Night Watch

She stayed with Nora until the mid-winter. Two spirits were working in her, love and anonymity. Yet they were so "haunted" of each other that separation was impossible.

Nora closed her house. They travelled from Munich, Vienna and Budapest into Paris. Robin told only a little of her life, but she kept repeating in one way or another her wish for a home, as if she were afraid she would be lost again, as if she were aware, without conscious knowledge, that she belonged to Nora, and that if Nora did not make it permanent by her own strength, she would forget.

Nora bought an apartment in the *rue du Cherche-Midi*. Robin had chosen it. Looking from the long windows one saw a fountain figure, a tall granite woman bending forward with lifted head; one hand was held over the pelvic round as if to warn a child who goes incautiously.

In the passage of their lives together every object in the garden, every item in the house, every word they spoke, attested to their mutual love, the combining of their humours. There were circus chairs, wooden horses bought from a ring of an old merry-go-round, venetian chandeliers from the Flea Fair, stage-drops from Munich, cherubim from Vienna, ecclesiastical hangings from Rome, a spinet from England, and a miscellaneous collection of music boxes from many countries; such was the museum of their encounter, as Felix's hearsay house had been testimony of the age when his father had lived with his mother.

When the time came that Nora was alone most of the night and part of the day, she suffered from the personality of the house, the punishment of those who collect their lives together. Unconsciously at first, she went about disturbing nothing; then she became aware that her soft and careful movements were the outcome of an unreasoning fear—if she disarranged anything Robin might become confused—might lose the scent of home.

Love becomes the deposit of the heart, analogous in all degrees to the "findings" in a tomb. As in one will be charted the taken place of the body, the raiment, the utensils necessary to its other life, so in the heart of the lover will be traced, as an indelible shadow, that which he loves. In Nora's heart lay the fossil of Robin, intaglio of her identity, and about it for its maintenance ran Nora's blood. Thus the body of Robin could never be unloved, corrupt or put away. Robin was now beyond timely changes, except in the blood that animated her. That she could be spilled of this fixed the walking image of Robin in appalling apprehension on Nora's mind—Robin alone, crossing streets, in danger. Her mind became so transfixed that, by the agency of her fear, Robin seemed enormous and polarized, all catastrophes ran toward her, the magnetized predicament; and crying out, Nora would wake from sleep, going back through the tide of dreams into which her anxiety had thrown her, taking the body of Robin down with her into it, as the ground things take the corpse, with minute persistence, down into the earth, leaving a pattern of it on the grass, as if they stitched as they descended.

Yes now, when they were alone and happy, apart from the world in their appreciation of the world, there entered with Robin a company unaware. Sometimes it rang clear in the songs she sang, sometimes Italian, sometimes French or German, songs of the people, debased and haunting, songs that Nora had never heard before, or that she had never heard in company with Robin. When the cadence changed, when it was repeated on a lower key, she knew that Robin was singing of a life that she herself had no part in; snatches of harmony as tell-tale as the possessions of a traveller from a foreign land; songs like a practised whore who turns away from no one but the one who loves her. Sometimes Nora would sing them after Robin, with the trepidation of a foreigner repeating words in an unknown tongue, uncertain of what they mean. Sometimes unable to endure the melody that told so much and so little, she would interrupt Robin with a question. Yet more distressing would be the moment when, after a pause, the song would be taken up again from an inner room where Robin, unseen, gave back an echo of her unknown life more nearly tuned to its origin. Often the song would stop altogether, until unthinking, just as she was leaving the house, Robin would break out again in anticipation, changing the sound from a reminiscence to an expectation.

Yet sometimes, going about the house, in passing each other, they would fall into an agonized embrace, looking into each other's face, their two heads in their four hands, so strained together that the space that divided them seemed to be thrusting them apart. Sometimes in these moments of insurmountable grief Robin would make some movement, use a peculiar turn of phrase not habitual to her, innocent of the betrayal, by which Nora was informed that Robin had come from a world to which she would return. To keep her (in Robin there was this tragic longing to be kept, knowing herself astray) Nora knew now that there was no way but death. In death Robin would belong to her. Death went with them, together and alone; and with the torment and catastrophe, thoughts of resurrection, the second duel.

Looking out into the fading sun of the winter sky, against which a little tower rose just outside the bedroom window, Nora would tabulate by the sounds of Robin dressing the exact progress of her toilet; chimes of cosmetic bottles and cream jars; the faint perfume of hair heated under the electric curlers; seeing in her mind the changing direction taken by the curls that hung on Robin's forehead, turning back from the low crown to fall in upward curves to the nape of the neck, the flat uncurved back head that spoke of some awful silence. Half narcoticized by the sounds and the knowledge that this was in preparation for departure, Nora spoke to herself: "In the resurrection, when we come up looking backward at each other, I shall know you only of all that company. My ear shall turn in the socket of my head; my eyeballs loosened where I am the whirlwind about that cashed expense, my foot stubborn on the cast of your grave." In the doorway Robin stood. "Don't wait for me," she said.

In the years that they lived together, the departures of Robin became slowly increasing rhythm. At first Nora went with Robin; but as time passed, realizing that a growing tension was in Robin, unable to endure the knowledge that she was in the way or forgotten, seeing Robin go from table to table, from drink to drink, from person to person, realizing that if she herself were not there Robin might return to her as the one who, out of all the turbulent night, had not been lived through, Nora stayed at home, lying awake or sleeping. Robin's absence, as the night drew on, became a physical removal, insupportable and irreparable. As an amputated hand cannot be disowned because it is experiencing a futurity, of which the victim is its forebear, so Robin was an amputation that Nora could not renounce. As the wrist longs, so her heart longed, and dressing she would go out into the night that she might be "beside herself," skirting the café in which she could catch a glimpse of Robin.

Once out in the open Robin walked in a formless meditation, her hands thrust into the sleeves of her coat, directing her steps toward that night life that was a known measure between Nora and the cafés. Her meditations, during this walk, were a part of the pleasure she expected to find when the walk came to an end. It was this exact distance that kept the two ends of her life—Nora and the cafés—from forming a monster with two heads.

Her thoughts were in themselves a form of locomotion. She walked with raised head, seeming to look at every passer-by, yet her gaze was anchored in anticipation and regret. A look of anger, intense and hurried, shadowed her face and drew her mouth down as she neared her company; yet as her eyes moved over the façades of the buildings, searching for the sculptured head that both she and Nora loved (a Greek head with shocked protruding eyeballs, for which the tragic mouth seemed to pour forth tears), a quiet joy radiated from her own eyes; for this head was remembrance of Nora and her love, making the anticipation of the people she was to meet set and melancholy. So, without knowing she would do so, she took the turn that brought her into this particular street. If she was diverted, as was sometimes the case, by the interposition of a company of soldiers, a wedding or a funeral, then by her agitation she seemed a part of the function to the persons she stumbled against, as a moth by his very entanglement with the heat that shall be his extinction is associated with flame as a component part of its function. It was this characteristic that saved her from being asked too sharply "where" she was going; pedestrians who had it on the point of their tongues, seeing her rapt and confused, turned instead to look at each other.

The doctor, seeing Nora out walking alone, said to himself, as the tall black-caped figure passed ahead of him under the lamps, "There goes the dismantled—Love has fallen off her wall. A religious woman," he thought to himself, "without the joy and safety of the Catholic faith, which at a pinch covers up the spots on the wall when the family portraits take a slide; take that safety from a woman," he said to himself, quickening his step to follow her, "and love gets loose and into the rafters. She sees her everywhere," he added, glancing at Nora as she passed into the dark. "Out looking for what she's afraid to find—Robin. There goes mother of mischief, running about, trying to get the world home."

Watchman, What of the Night?

About three in the morning, Nora knocked at the little glass door of the *concierge*'s loge, asking if the doctor was in. In the anger of broken sleep the *concierge* directed her to climb six flights, where at the top of the house, to the left, she would find him.

Nora took the stairs slowly. She had not known that the doctor was so poor. Groping her way she rapped, fumbling for the knob. Misery alone would have brought her, though she knew the late hours indulged in by her friend. Hearing his "come in" she opened the door and for one second hesitated, so incredible was the disorder that met her eyes. The room was so small that it was just possible to walk sideways up to the bed; it was as if being condemned to the grave the doctor had decided to occupy it with the utmost abandon.

A pile of medical books, and volumes of a miscellaneous order, reached almost to the ceiling, water-stained and covered with dust. Just above them was a very small barred window, the only ventilation. On a maple dresser, certainly not of European make, lay a rusty pair of forceps, a broken scalpel, half a dozen odd instruments that she could not place, a catheter, some twenty perfume bottles, almost empty, pomades, creams, rouges, powder boxes and puffs. From the half-open drawers of this chiffonier hung laces, ribands, stockings, ladies' underclothing and an abdominal brace, which gave the impression that the feminine finery had suffered venery. A swill-pail stood at the head of the bed, brimming with abominations. There was something appallingly degraded about the room, like the rooms in brothels, which give even the most innocent a sensation of having been accomplice; yet this room was also muscular, a cross between a *chambre à coucher* and a boxer's training camp. There is a certain belligerence in a room in which a woman has never set foot; every object seems to be battling its own compression—and there is a metallic odour, as of beaten iron in a smithy.

In the narrow iron bed, with its heavy and dirty linen sheets, lay the doctor in a woman's flannel nightgown.

The doctor's head, with its over-large black eyes, its full gun-metal cheeks and chin, was framed in the golden semi-circle of a wig with long pendent curls that touched his shoulders, and falling back against the pillow, turned up the shadowy interior of their cylinders. He was heavily rouged and his lashes painted. It flashed into Nora's head: "God, children know something they can't tell; they like Red Riding Hood and the wolf in bed!" But this thought, which was only the sensation of a thought, was of but a second's duration as she opened the door; in the next, the doctor had snatched the wig from his head, and sinking down in the bed drew the sheets up over his breast. Nora said, as quickly as she could recover herself: "Doctor, I have come to ask you to tell me everything you know about the night." As she spoke, she wondered why she was so dismayed to have come upon the doctor at the hour when he had evacuated custom and gone back into his dress.

The doctor said, "You see that you can ask me anything," thus laying aside both their embarrassments.

She said to herself: "Is not the gown the natural raiment of extremity? What nation, what religion, what ghost, what dream, has not worn it—infants, angels, priests, the dead; why should not the doctor, in the grave dilemma of his alchemy, wear his dress?" She thought: "He dresses to lie beside himself, who is so constructed that love, for him, can be only something special; in a room that giving back evidence of his occupancy, is as mauled as the last agony."

"Have you ever thought of the night?" the doctor inquired with a little irony; he was extremely put out, having expected someone else, though his favourite topic, and one which he talked on whenever he had a chance, was the night.

"Yes," said Nora, and sat down on the only chair. "I've thought of it, but thinking about something you know something about does not help."

"Have you," said the doctor, "ever thought of the peculiar polarity of times and times; and of sleep? Sleep the slain white bull? Well I, Dr. Matthew-Mighty-grain-of-salt-Dante-O'Connor, will tell you how the day and the night are related by their division. The very constitution of twilight is a fabulous reconstruction of fear, fear bottom-out and wrong side up. Every day is thought upon and calculated, but the night is not premeditated. The Bible lies the one way, but the night-gown the other. The night, 'Beware of that dark door!'"

"I used to think," Nora said, "that people just went to sleep, or if they did not go to sleep that they were themselves, but now"—she lit a cigarette and her hands trembled—"now I see that the night does something to a person's identity, even when asleep."

"Ah!" exclaimed the doctor. "Let a man lay himself down in the Great Bed and his 'identity' is no longer his own, his 'trust' is not with him, and his 'willingness' is turned over and is of another permission. His distress is wild and anonymous. He sleeps in a Town of Darkness, member of a secret brotherhood. He neither knows himself nor his outriders; he berserks a fearful dimension and dismounts, miraculously, in bed!

"His heart is tumbling in his chest, a dark place! Though some go into the night as a spoon breaks easy water, others go head foremost against a new connivance; their horns make a dry crying, like the wings of the locust, late come to their shedding.

"Have you thought of the night, now, in other times, in foreign countries—in Paris? When the streets were gall high with things you wouldn't have done for a dare's sake, and the way it was then; with the pheasants' necks and the goslings' beaks dangling against the hocks of the gallants, and not a pavement in the place, and everything gutters for miles and miles, and a stench to it that plucked you by the nostrils and you were twenty leagues out! The criers telling the price of wine to such effect that the dawn saw good clerks full of piss and vinegar, and blood-letting in side streets where some wild princess in a night-shift of velvet howled under a leech; not to mention the palaces of Nymphenburg echoing back to Vienna with the night trip of late kings letting water into plush cans and fine woodwork! No," he said, looking at her sharply, "I can see you have not! You should, for the night has been going on for a long time."

She said, "I've never known it before—I thought I did, but it was not knowing at all."

"Exactly," said the doctor. "You thought you knew, and you hadn't even shuffled the cards—now the nights of one period are not the nights of another. Neither are the nights of one city the nights of another. Let us take Paris for an instance, and France for a fact. *Ah, mon dieu! La nuit effroyable! La nuit, qui est une immense plaine, et le cœur qui est une petite extrémité!* Ah, good Mother mine, *Notre Dame-de-bonne-Garde*! Intercede for me now, while yet I explain what I'm coming to! French nights are those which all nations seek the world over—and have you noticed that?

Campaign Letter for President of the United States, 1991

EILEEN MYLES

Eileen Myles
86 E 3 St.
NYC 10003

Dear Citizen, September 11, 1991

Today I am announcing my candidacy for the office of President of the United States of America.

I've actually been on the campaign trail since last April when I made my first public announcement in New York City and since then in a variety of places including Chicago, New Hampshire, Vermont, Colorado, New Mexico and now New Hampshire again.

The initial impulse to run for office was spurred on by George Bush's speech at a college graduation at Ann Arbor Michigan last Spring. He stated that the "the politically correct" are the greatest threat to freedom of speech in America today. By that he means members of ACT-UP, victims of bias crimes: women, homosexuals, ethnic and racial minorities. He would like them to shut up. As President he functions as a grand employer who has a complaint box. Each of us may get our two cents in. Once. After that we're on our own because there is no special treatment for the vast majority of Americans today. There is very special treatment for white upper middle class heterosexual men and their spouses and children, there is special treatment for fundamentalist Christians and fetuses.

George Bush does not write his own speeches. The statememts he made in Ann Arbor flowed from the pen of a new speech writer, an alumni of the left-baiting Washington Times. The New York Times which covered the Ann Arbor event suggested that this was the beginning of the '92 campaign trail, for which freedom of speech would be a big issue. I thought if he's starting now, I will too.

I am a 41-year old American, a female, a lesbian, from a working class background, a poet, performer and writer making my living pretty exclusively from those activities. I am a taxpayer. I've lived the majority of my adult life under the poverty level, without health care. I have never made over $20,000 a year nor have I ever lived in a household where our combined incomes approached that amount. More Americans, far more Americans are like me than George Bush. Why is he ruling this country and our lives?

My campaign is about freedom of speech. Mine and yours. I am not a professional politician, not a CEO or a lawyer. I write all my own speeches. I believe in total disclosure. What you see is what you get. I'm turning all my upcoming art events, readings and performances until election day into political events. I regard my campaign as a gesture of activism. An opportunity for me to vote. I will be a write-in candidate in as many states as I can file my papers in by next fall.

-2-

I need help in this area. I've got contact people only in the states I've mentioned here. This is the first monthly letter on my campaign I'll be sending to all who are on my mailing list. Feel free to publish it. If you would like to xerox it and send it to 10 or 20 other people please let me know and I will send you a portion of the mailing list. I'm also enclosing a flyer each month which you should feel free to reproduce or distribute as you see fit. I have no campaign fund. If you would like to be on the mailing list it's free, though the price of 14 mailings (.29 plus xerox plus envelope = approx. $7.00) would be helpful. I also have campaign buttons ($1). But, mainly,

I WANT TO RUN, I WANT YOUR VOTE, AND I'D LIKE TO WIN.

Sincerely,

Eileen Myles

that flaming brand

ESSA MAY RANAPIRI

the light was only ever a sword
was only ever a fire to take my skin
from me

the car wrapped around a pole at the
centre of the milky way

Boulder/Meteor

please don't say it's got anything to do with
mobiles clinking in the wind breeze will
scatter sound i swear it will make a promise
let the bug down from the tree how did it
get so high made a milkbud cave made
a crumb into a kingdom with just one mouth i
stare at the austerity what a policy to give us wings
to fall from what mud slick dinosaur prays
for meteors every night the stars could be so
much bigger i know i really do please
don't stay you won't like what you see
two magnets pressed together on the wrong sides
everything of great size started out smaller than
the human eye could recognize if i glue
these two pebbles together and add dirt everyday
for a thousand years would i have the boulder
needed to crush everything we've done wrong
would i be adding to it megalomania is only
mania if you're wrong and i promise please
leave the element going with the pot empty of
water to run to hot hot please please leave

Excerpts from *Sitt Marie Rose*

ETEL ADNAN

Translated by Georgina Kleege

We're going to the window to look outside. That's always more fun than learning to read on lips things that, most of the time, we'd rather not know, and about which we don't have much to say. But we do have things to say, lots and lots of things, but no one's interested.

It's the second day . . . where did they sleep last night? We went up to our dormitory and this morning they woke us up, made us get into line, and made us come down into the classroom just as usual. Though, this year, school hasn't been what it used to be. There are interruptions, long holidays, classmates who have gone far away to France and England, while we're stuck here, waiting for the war to end. This war has changed the colors of everything we see. Men wear less and less blue. They're grayer. Sometimes they wear military uniforms. The cars have also changed. There are a lot of vans, and jeeps that go very fast. No one seems to be afraid of breaking them. The cats are also freer than before, no one hits them or chases them away. They're on balconies, roofs, walls, sidewalks, garbage cans, demolished buildings. There are a lot of rats all over too. And the cats don't eat them anymore!

There they are still, sitting before us. It's like in the movies. They're very scary. There will be no recess for us today. If it's like yesterday there won't be any recess. But why doesn't she tell them to go away? It's true that there haven't been any policemen for a very long time. Is she afraid of them, she who's never afraid? We look and look at her but her eyes never meet ours. Her eyes say nothing. They're blue like the sky. The sky. Our father the sky.

If only we could be grown-ups all of a sudden. We'd defend her. We'd beat up those guys like Mohammed Ali, the champion. We'd break their heads and twist them right off their necks. But how could we do that now?

Lately, there have been a lot of funerals. Funerals are sad but they're better than going to school. There are always a lot of flowers and it smells good. This year there have been more funerals and less flowers. There have even been people who didn't get buried. No one knows where they are. There have also been fewer weddings, fewer parties than usual. But it's as though there's been a different kind of party. People who can talk and hear must have a lot of fun in war. They look so happy. We are locked in.

We're beginning to get the feeling that something really bad is going to happen. We're tired of waiting. Something really bad is going to happen. Those men are getting more and more ferocious. Their eyes are bloodshot. They look at Sitt Marie-Rose with eyes like cats have in the dark, eyes that do more than just glow. Everything glows. Everything glows. When they were walking around in the street they wore masks cut out of their mothers' stockings, that made them look like pigs or cows. What were they doing that was so bad that they had to hide themselves? But now it's worse. They're even scarier. They quiver. They look like a stormy sky. And we feel hot and cold at the same time.

Sitt Marie-Rose trembles but, with her, everything's always different. We love her so much. More than our parents. More than cakes. More than weekends. More than the sea. If she went away, we'd go too. Where, we don't know, but we'd go away from here.

But she's not going anywhere. Where could she go? There's the war, and there are no boats. They bombed the airport and there are no planes leaving.

She never does anything bad, Sitt Marie-Rose. She's good. She always tells us not to pull dogs' tails, and not to fight in the yard, and not to catch cold when we sweat too much.

These people talk and talk. They're tiring her. They're wearing her out. They're making her suffer. And yet, she's the boss. All she has to do is tell them to go away. But who can she call to help her? And how? There are no more people in this neighborhood.

They've forgotten all about us, but we see everything. One of them has left and the others are all on her. Devils have come up from underground and they've fallen on her. There's an explosion in the air and a return of trees into this room. Everything's spinning. No human being would ever do what they're doing. Where did they come from? How did they get so wild? She's been drowned! She's been drowned! In blood. Perhaps one day speech and sound will be restored to us, we'll be able to hear and speak and say what happened. But it's not certain. Some sicknesses are incurable.

* * *

I want to talk about the light on this day. An execution always lasts a long time. I want to say forever and ever that the sea is beautiful, even more so since the blood washed down by the greedy rain opened reddening roads into the sea. It's only in it, in its immemorial blue, that the blood of all is finally mixed. They have separated the bodies, they have separated the minds, those who govern as well as those foreigners brought on a wind from the West, those from Iran and the Soviet Union, all, all have sown poison herbs in these peasant mentalities, in these uprooted brains, in these slum children, in their schizophrenic student logic. They have done this so that the population, turning a hundred ways at once, loses its way, and sees every mobile being as a target or a sure threat of death. Madness is like a hurricane, and its motion is circular. It all turns around and around, drawing circles of fire in this country, which has become nothing but a closed arena, and in this city which is nothing but a huge square of cement. They circle around each other in their hollow arguments, hollow like their ramshackle walls, their hatred, their blindness. They only address each other with cannons, machine guns, razors, knives. And the sea, receiving them in an advanced state of decomposition, reconciles them in the void.

What is the light like on a day of execution? An ordinary light. It's only in our heads that electric light bulbs spin and the heat of the day explodes. It's our heads that irradiate and change Nature. It's because they still function with the momentary independence of machines, that one asks oneself how behind their windows, behind their piece of wall, people still survive, women alone, women and men, men alone, etc. Why don't animals come and rent houses, or why isn't there a coming and going of Martians, moonmen, spacemen, a new animation on this ravaged landscape? Why is everything so ordinary?

When I'm right I know it. The temperature of my hands rises to let me know. Something quakes through my body. Everything becomes silent around me and I see it. The silence makes a sort of halo. My head becomes an empty water-skin without resonance, the inner lining clean and stretched. Everything freezes. There's a slight buzzing like the sound the earth makes turning in space. I'm right, oh, how right I am! Then I take off, believing that I'm really free of the cage. But to discover a truth is to discover a fundamental limit, a kind of inner wall to the mind, so I fall again to the ground of passing time, and discover that it's Marie-Rose who's right.

It must be said, said so that this civilization that was born in the night of time, and now finds itself dazed before the nuclear wall, brought to its knees before this new Power, hears what its masses want to tell it, so that it can scale the final mountain. Like patients maintained with transfusions of blood and food, the Arab world lies on an operating table. The equipment should be removed, the respirator unplugged. The patient should be obliged to spit out, not the mucous, but the original illness, not the blood clogging his throat but the words, the words, the swamp of words that have been waiting there for so long.

Look at them! Those four men set upon that passing bird. They bend over her case with the posture of rug merchants, and the age-long heavy gestures of connoisseurs of merchandise. She was, they admit, a worthy prey, though they don't consider her a museum piece, real booty, an exemplary catch. She was a woman, an imprudent woman, gone over to the enemy and mixing in politics, which is normally their personal hunting ground. They, the Chabab, had to bring women back to order, in this Orient, at once nomadic and immobile. On the Palestinian side, they dealt with crimes similarly. The stakes were different, but the methods were the same.

She made the mistake of venturing into their territory. She overlooked the instinct of the jackal that lies in wait for chickens, that instinct which still exists under the skins of men living from the Gulf to the Atlantic. The scouts of the clan hunt and bring the prey back to the fold. This is a common good, be it in Islamic tribes in southern Tunisia, or in Christian tribes from the Lebanese mountains: the trapped gazelle is always shared by all. In concrete houses or under black tents, they wait for the raiders' return with the eyes and claws of falcons. Every day they nonchalantly trap and take away their quarry, and add another victim's name to their already long list of acts of glory.

She was also subject to another great delusion believing that women were protected from repression, and that the leaders considered political fights to be strictly between males. In fact, with women's greater access to certain powers, they began to watch them more closely, and perhaps with even greater hostility. Every feminine act, even charitable and seemingly unpolitical ones, were regarded as a rebellion in this world where women had always played servile roles. Marie-Rose inspired scorn and hate long before the fateful day of her arrest.

However, fear of torture often crossed her mind. She had told her friends that if she refused to join certain clandestine political parties it was because of her fear of prison. But she supported the Resistance with a profound conviction, and because it seemed more a question of love than politics, a question of Life and Death for all Arabs. She believed that this cause must be sacred to all, and when she suspected hypocrisy, she silenced her mistrust.

Torture preoccupied her because she saw in it, or rather in the person who could resist it, the summit of human courage. She hated physical suffering, abhorred it, and considered it a fundamental injustice to Nature. She was persuaded that men could be cured of moral and physical ills if only, if only. . . . She sometimes managed to convince herself that torture did not exist, while she knew that it was practiced in all the capitals of the world.

One afternoon on the balcony of a friend's house overlooking the city's sole public garden, the one she called the Big Garden in childhood, she met a Belgian journalist, passing through Beirut on his way home from Viet Nam. He had been captured near Saigon by the Viet Cong, and after finally managing to prove his identity, was released after several days. She asked him if he wasn't afraid, and he said that of course he was afraid, he was constantly afraid in Viet Nam. He had decided, in order to overcome his fear, that if he were taken prisoner, or rather if he found himself on the point of being tortured, he would swallow his tongue and try to choke himself to death. He also decided, he said, that if things "got bad" and he could find no way to escape, he would throw such outrageous defiance in the face of his interrogators, that they would speed up their work.

This conversation came back to her very often over the next few years when, in Bagdad, Amman, Damascus, and Jerusalem, nightmares were accumulating. In the streets near these cities' prisons, you could hear the wails of political prisoners. At least, Marie-Rose (as many others) said to herself, people in Lebanon live under regimes that, while corrupt, are still made of "nice guys." No one seemed to want to admit that cruelty was part of a moral cancer that was spreading through the whole of the Middle East. That was how Beirut became a huge open wound. If suffering could be measured in ounces and square centimeters, then the suffering of this city was greater than any other city in the century. Berlin, Saigon, Madrid, Athens, none of them knew the murder and sadism this city did. Thus, in the smoking bath of acid, under bullets, rockets, napalm and phosphorus bombs, with assassinations and abductions, each being met his personal, definitive apocalypse. Like a bird flying alone in a seemingly untroubled sky, Marie-Rose was cut down by hunters on the look-out.

One still remembers the famous picture drawn by Gamal Abdel Nasser of concentric circles, with Egypt, the Islamic Third World, the rest of the Third World. . . . But this hero of Arab History should have denounced the concentric circles of oppression, and taken on the task of breaking them.

At the center is the individual surrounded by the circle of his family. Then comes the circle of the state, then the circle of the Brother Arab countries, the circle of the Enemy, the Super Powers, and so forth. . . . These circles of oppression are inevitably circles of betrayal. In their interior spaces, lively forces are crushed, annihilated, and apparent confusion is maintained through a mortal order.

Power is always obscene. It's only in thickening the sensibility that the human brain attains power and maintains it, and all power finally expresses itself through the death penalty. Marie-Rose was a blade of grass in the bulldozer's path. The Palestinians too. And the Syrian bulldozers come to take over from the executors of the universal Power. From the east to the Mediterranean, tanks come to continue the work of crushing Life. The circles of oppression have also become circles of repression. Marie-Rose is not alone in her death. Second by second the inhabitants of this city that were her comrades fall. Where the tanks stop, planes take over. Airplanes have become the flies of the Arab world, conceived in a frenzy of power, and the plague they carry is the vehicle of its new curse.

In the classroom, held in their bewildering simplicity, is the group of justices, Mounir, Tony, Fouad, and Bouna Lias. Before them, Marie-Rose, beneath the extinguished electric light bulb hung by a cord, and the deaf-mutes. On the wall there is a crucifix. But, in this room, Christ is a tribal prince. He leads to nothing but ruin. One is never right to invoke him in such circumstances, because the true Christ only exists when one stands up to one's own brothers to defend the Stranger. Only then does Christ embody innocence.

Whether you like it or not, an execution is always a celebration. It is the dance of Signs and their stabilization in Death. It is the swift flight of silence without pardon. It is the explosion of absolute darkness among us. What can one do in this black Feast but dance? The deaf-mutes rise, and moved by the rhythm of falling bombs their bodies receive from the trembling earth, they begin to dance.

A Child in Old Age

FANNY HOWE

Every room is still a mansion to you:
you who wants to live in an Irish hotel!

To sit in a lobby beside the fire with your feet
 in a chair.

To stare at the other children seeking asylum.

• • •

Your brain is a baby.
And all the ancients are in it still.

Your heart is a channel
and a crib for them.

They rarely come down

or out in the light
but steer you awkwardly with their cries.

Your brain is still becoming
an independent being

while your heart always needs air.

• • •

I had an infant who was an orphan who lived
    between my ears.

Its sobs could only be heard
when it circled the pump.

How it hurt!

Another infant lived like an octopus fully exposed
with a skull like a bottle cap inside its thought.

It was the arms of my heart.

A heart is a mind that's only trying
to think without an unconscious.

The tentacle is a brain too.

And its adaptable jelly's
just as intelligent as human blood.

Sometimes you look into a baby's eyes.

"Bless her," you suggest to passersby
yourself being old and unnecessary.

But no one does.

Please, you beg. The tears of an infant can be bottled
    and hidden
for special occasions.

One drop on your tongue and you won't ask for more.
You've thought this somewhere before.

A Vision

Some old people want to leave this earth and
experience another.
They don't want to commit suicide. They want to
wander out of sight
without comrades or luggage.

Once I was given such an opportunity, and what did
I find?

Mist between mountains, the monotonous buzz of
farm machinery,
cornstalks brown and flowers then furrows
preparing to receive seeds for next year's harvest.

A castle, half-ruined by a recent earthquake still
highly functional.
Computers, copying machines and cars.
It was once a monastery and home for a family
continually at war.
Cypress trees and chestnut and walnut trees. A swing
hanging long from a high bough,
where paths circle down, impeding quick escapes by
armies or thieves.

I was assigned the monastic wing that later became
a granary.
Brick-red flagstones, small windows with hinged
casements
and twelve squares of glass inside worn frames.
From the moment I entered the long strange space,
I foresaw an otherworldly light taking shape.
Scorpions lived in the cracks.

I came without a plan, empty-handed except for my
notebooks from preceding days.
This lack was a deliberate choice: to see what would
be revealed to me by circumstances.

I took long walks that multiplied my body into
companionable parts.
Down dusty roads and alongside meadows,
and pausing to look at the mountains and clouds,
I talked to myself.

Mysticism "provides a path for those who ask the way
to get lost.
It teaches how not to return," wrote Michel de Certeau.

. • .

One day I had the sense that there were two boys
accompanying me everywhere I went.
I could not identify the boy on the left,
but the one on the right was overwhelmingly himself.
Someone I knew and loved.
The other one was very powerful in his personality,
an enigma and a delight.

His spirit seemed to spread into the roads and
weather.
Silver olive trees and prim vineyards.
Now a rain has whitened the morning sky but every
single leaf holds a little water and glitter.

. • .

Mirror neurons experience the suffering that they see.
A forest thick with rust and gold that doesn't rust.

I saw a painting where the infant Jesus was lying on his back
on the floor at the feet of Mary
and his halo was still attached to his head.
And another painting where there were about forty baby cherubs
all wearing golden halos. Gold represents the sun as the sun represents God.

Outside wild boars were still roaming the hills.
Maize, sunflowers, honey, thyme, beans, stones, olives and tomatoes.
Rush hour in the two-lane highway.
Oak tree leaves curled into caramel balls.
A Franciscan monk sat on a floor reciting the rosary,
a concept borrowed from Islamic prayer beads centuries before.

Figs, bread, pasta, wine and cheese.
These are not the subconscious, but necessities.
People want to be poets for reasons that have little to do with language.
It is the life of the poet that they want, I think.
Even the glow of loneliness and humiliation.
To walk in the gutter with a bottle of wine.
Some people's lives are more poetic than a poem
and Francis is certainly one of these.

I know, because he walked beside me for that short time
whether you believe it or not. He was thirteen.

That night I drank walnut liqueur, just a sip, it tasted like Kahlua.
The inner wing of a bird is the color of a doe.

And the turned-over earth is the color of a nut, and
a bird,
but soon it will be watered for the green wheat of
spring.

Flying up the hill on the back of the motorbike in the warm Roman air was like drinking from the fountain of youth.

Umbrella trees along the Tiber.

I walked on the rooftops across Rome, including a grassy one, and one where a palm grew out of a crack in the rocks.

I was carrying an assortment of envelopes containing paintings and notes for my Mass but they could not be managed easily because their shapes were irregular. Some had juttings, some were swollen, the color red was prominent. They depicted divided cities, divided into layers not all in a line. A layer cake sagging under the weight of accumulated dust, dirt and now grass.

Each layer had been purchased at the cost of decades, even centuries of hand-hurting, back-breaking slave labor. *Caveat emptor!*
Broken columns, mashed marble friezes and faces. The
triumph of greed
was written across my storyboard. The city was a
mighty and devouring creating,
a creature with a crusted skin.

Even in the city you look for a place that welcomes you. You actually want to be found!
Being found is the polar opposite of making a vow.

You are a pot of gold and not the arc of the rainbow.
When you sit down on a stone, face up to the sun, you
can't help but think, *Mine, mine.*
And you don't have to promise anything to anyone
in time.
You may be called to a place of banality or genius,
but as long as it is your own happiness that responds
to it,
you are available to something inhuman.
Mozart sat at the piano for the better part of every day.

All over the world monks have lived in desert hovels
as scribes, prophets, mendicants.
They are the extreme realization of one aspect of
human personality
that tends towards lack of possession and solitude.

There was a hole in the roof of the Pantheon where
we were told
that the snow fell through onto the relics of Catherine
of Siena
the mystic and onto the porphyry.

A man in Rome told me that a monkey climbed down
a wall
holding an infant in his arms and in remembrance
there is a statue of the Madonna
on the very rooftop where he began his descent.

there is religious tattooing

FRED MOTEN

for a long time, the lotion stigma swirled
on the man who clothes me with a broken

world. I came when they called me. that
cotton rubbed me the wrong way all the

way inside over the course of time. way before
cotton sewn into the coat of the one
who clothes me. before I started clothing

them with paper. before cotton sewn into

their coats they curled up on flat boats
all the way back up the country. the beaded
strips of leather and cotton made me come
to myself when he called me and wrote me

on the one who clothes me. pour some water
on me. make coming matter cut and twirl

on me. the law of emulsion is always broke
on me. somebody pour some beautiful jute

on me. let her blow some horn on me. the man
who clothes me in my skin is gonna write

on me. your writing moves to stop on me.

someday they're gonna curve this on a pearl

on me but now it's time to go and I can't wait
to get up out from here. it's simple to stay furled

where you can't live. for a long, long time I've

been wearing this other planet like a scar on me.

Play It Again, S

GAIL SCOTT

Dawn. It's snowing out. The street is so quiet, I feel like I've stepped through a glass. Now I can keep the whole picture in my head walking to Bagels' for breakfast. Eggs over lightly. Paprika potatoes. Coffee. Extra bagel to keep me going. So where was I in the story?

Oh, yes.

This is the city. November 1, 1980. Five a.m. Suddenly the little girl minus her yellow raincoat emerges from behind a parked car. She's been hiding there for hours, nearly frozen. But too scared to move in case the sandwichman is lurking. Upstairs in an empty room her mother's crying. Unaware her daughter is so close. The positive note is, soon they'll be together. In the street, the snowploughs are cleaning up their first load of winter snow. And on the radio they have the press clips for early birds. What Ronald Reagan has for lunch. What scientists say about the fatal levels of chemicals in the food chain. And for gays, a warning about a new disease more fatal than any environmental poisoning. All treated in the witty language of a joke.

The heroine raises her head from the Arborite table. Half awake, she sees a dream-face still looking through her window. Strangely familiar. Vines around its neck. Glistening as though it has risen from the sea. But outside (actually at the bottom of The Main) only a large brown river runs. On the table lay the blue pages where she has copied passages from her diary. Open at the entry: *When I woke up, the Papa Moon you gave me was floating on the water.*

The window fades to dawn. The heroine stands up. Drawing her blanket close, she takes the blue sheets and puts them on a violin stand beside the television. She steps back. Now they're at a distance. She smiles, liking how those pages on which she's written pain in curved letters change the context of the room. Making Janis's *It's all the same goddamned day* so clear. She looks around at last night's storm flashing on the television screen. At her own veined, slightly swollen feet standing on the old linoleum. Elements for a novel. But first she needs to eat. In the cupboard there's a hole where the tile's off. It's a wonder a rat hasn't come through. Never mind. She's not about to become one of those former revolutionaries hanging around health food stores, stocking up on engevita, ginseng, calcium, rice, fibre, and verbena. Then finally moving into condominiums. Not yet anyway. She's got other things to do.

She searches for winter boots, finding only sneakers. Over the faded olive jumpsuit (it's a bit silly to dress so badly) she puts on the old fur jacket. Then steps out onto the front steps covered with green turf rug and a layer of snow. The rooftops are growing ever clearer in the grey dawn. High up, in an arc, a snow blower blows its charge. She walks forward on the white sidewalk (still faintly in the shadow of the night), then stops. Under the glass balcony that grey woman is waiting for Patchwork Rosanna. Mornings she always does that, waits under the balcony until Rosanna comes out and looks. Then big Rosanna in her patchwork robe goes back in and puts the kettle on to make them tea. A door swings open into Rosanna's dark courtyard. The grey woman steps in mumbling something like: '. . . *typical bailiff*.' The heroine stands behind trying to hear. '"*The money", said he,' mutters the grey woman, '"or I'm taking your Christmas tree." The dirty muggins (she's talking rapidly in a low excited voice). They were taking off the lights the turkey came out of the oven the children were hiding under the table he put his beefchopper on my button breast. He said: "Madame, the rich get rich and the poor get poorer."*' Then the grey woman throws her long grey tangled hair back and sings a little ditty: *To Schwartz's Smoky Meat / And to all the ragshop policemen on the street / Montréal International Sheets / Lyrical Linen at Prices Most Discreet / Lolly lolly jolly jolly / I know you love me / Because I'm a stuffed hen in taxidermist's shop* - - - Seeing the heroine she stops short.

The heroine keeps walking. Wondering why a woman can't get what she wants without going into business on every front. Social, political, economic, domestic. Each requiring a different way of walking, a different way of talking. She looks instinctively for her own reflection in a store window. But it's as yet too dark to see clearly. What if Marie is in Bagels'? Film crews often breakfast there after working late. Looking tired, rumpled, yet chic in their designer jeans and jackets. She grins provocatively at her own tackiness. Marie a horreur du cheap. Once the heroine said to her: 'Don't you ever watch a soap opera, turn on popular music, read the comics or the horoscope? I mean even in the interest of sociological research?' And Marie answered: 'Je n'en ai pas besoin. J'ai grandi avec le quétaine.'

Her damp sneakers continue up The Main. Moving beside her in the grey early winter light: the snow blower. And a kid coming from a pharmacy carrying a sketchbook. His pale-blue eyes trained on the sky, gull-searching. But it's not 6 a.m. so the light is still quite dim. He's headed towards the park where in the summers of the eighties, the seventies men stroll with ever younger brides. Where I saw you (my love) at the end of our reconciliation, pouring adoration over the girl with the green eyes. The birds were singing wildly. Which really shocked me, for I thought you'd left me to be with Venus. In a way I felt you'd lied.

The heroine crosses northward at Rachel Street. A block behind her the grey woman is sitting down on a cement block drinking Rosanna's tea. She keeps walking. Suddenly, up a staircase to her left, a mother screams for joy as her freezing little daughter falls against the door. The heroine takes it all in, her face a divided map of the present moment. One side savouring the sweetness of existence: the waking street, the kid's blue eyes gull-searching in the sky, Rosanna's tea. The other smarting against something vaguer. Something like what lies behind that song, popular in periods of unemployment, blasting forth as she opens the door of Bagels': "Puttin' on the Ritz."

Eating, she thinks that in the eighties a story must be all smooth and shiny. For this pretends to be the decade of appearances. Like a photo of the silhouettes of figures passing on the street outside the restaurant window. Or the beautiful faces of those women (Marie's colleagues?), lit by a small light at one of the diner's tables. She actually loves the ambiance of the period.

But walking back down The Main, just past the staircase where the mother hugged her lost girl, she thinks: 'Yet I feel this terrible violence in me.' In any story, it will break the smoothness of the surface.

Looking up she notices she's standing in the shadow of a building that broke the zoning laws when constructed, because so high. Leaving the surrounding smaller houses eternally in deep shade day and night. Once she, with another woman friend, joked about blowing it up. They talked and talked about how to do it. Obsessively at restaurant tables over cups of coffee. Each one knowing the other wasn't serious. Each one also knowing they needed something to salve their incredible frustrations with the left as well, they said, as with capitalist society. (Her friend is married to a doctor.)

Now, standing there in the shadow of the cold wall of grey, with gulls circling overhead and the mother's joyous scream still threaded through her mind, the heroine feels that old desire for a terrible explosion.

She thinks: 'Maybe I should talk to someone.'

Startled by a sudden glimpse of her reflection in a window, she thinks: 'Maybe I should get a job. Then I could buy one of those second-hand men's coats trendy women wear this year. I could probably get one cheap. Or else one of those beautiful espresso pots I saw in the window up the street.'

She walks a little farther, wondering.

She passes the grey woman sitting in her long skirt on the cement block.

She thinks: 'Maybe I should talk to her.'

She thinks: 'The question is, is it possible to create Paradise in this Strangeness?'

In the grey light, she's standing on the sidewalk (snowy, of course), her pale red curls her one sign of beauty. Looking to the left, the right.

She—

Excerpt from *Letter to His Father*

FRANZ KAFKA

Translated by Arthur S. Wensinger

I remember going for a walk one evening with you and Mother; it was on Josephsplatz near where the Länderbank is today; and I began talking about these interesting things, in a stupidly boastful, superior, proud, detached (that was spurious), cold (that was genuine), and stammering manner, as indeed I usually talked to you, reproaching the two of you with having left me uninstructed; with the fact that my schoolmates first had to take me in hand, that I had been close to great dangers (here I was brazenly lying, as was my way, in order to show myself brave, for as a consequence of my timidity I had, except for the usual sexual misdemeanors of city children, no very exact notion of these "great dangers"); but finally I hinted that now, fortunately, I knew everything was all right. I had begun talking about all this mainly because it gave me pleasure at least to talk about it, and also out of curiosity, and finally to avenge myself somehow on the two of you for something or other. In keeping with your nature you took it quite simply, only saying something to the effect that you could give me advice about how I could go in for these things without danger. Perhaps I did want to lure just such an answer out of you; it was in keeping with the pruriency of a child overfed with meat and all good things, physically inactive, everlastingly occupied with himself; but still my outward sense of shame was so hurt by this—or I believed it ought to be so hurt—that against my will I could not go on talking to you about it and, with arrogant impudence, cut the conversation short.

It is not easy to judge the answer you gave me then; on the one hand, it had something staggeringly frank, sort of primeval, about it;

on the other hand, as far as the lesson itself is concerned, it was uninhibited in a very modern way. I don't know how old I was at the time, certainly not much over sixteen. It was, nevertheless, a very remarkable answer for such a boy, and the distance between the two of us is also shown in the fact that it was actually the first direct instruction bearing on real life I ever received from you. Its real meaning, however, which sank into my mind even then, but which came partly to the surface of my consciousness only much later, was this: what you advised me to do was in your opinion and, even more, in my opinion at that time, the filthiest thing possible. That you wanted to see to it that I should not bring any of the physical filth home with me was unimportant, for you were only protecting yourself, your house. The important thing was rather that you yourself remained outside your own advice, a married man, a pure man, above such things; this was probably intensified for me at the time by the fact that even marriage seemed to me shameless; and hence it was impossible for me to apply to my parents the general information I had picked up about marriage. Thus you became still purer, rose still higher. The thought that you might have given yourself similar advice before your marriage was to me utterly unthinkable. So there was hardly any smudge of earthly filth on you at all. And it was you who pushed me down into this filth—just as though I were predestined to it—with a few frank words. And so, if the world consisted only of me and you (a notion I was much inclined to have), then this purity of the world came to an end with you and, by virtue of your advice, the filth began with me. In itself it was, of course, incomprehensible that you should thus condemn me; only old guilt, and profoundest contempt on your side, could explain it to me. And so again I was seized in my innermost being—and very hard indeed.

Here perhaps both our guiltlessness becomes most evident. A gives B a piece of advice that is frank, in keeping with his attitude to life, not very lovely but still, even today perfectly usual in the city, a piece of advice that might prevent damage to health. This piece of advice is for B morally not very invigorating—but why should he not be able to work his way out of it, and repair the damage in the course of the years? Besides, he does not even have to take the advice; and there is no reason why the advice itself should cause B's whole future world to come tumbling down. And yet something of this kind does happen, but only for the very reason that A is you and B is myself.

This guiltlessness on both sides I can judge especially well because a similar clash between us occurred some twenty years later, in quite different circumstances—horrible in itself but much less damaging—for what was there in me, the thirty-six-year-old, that could still be damaged? I am referring to a brief discussion on one of those few tumultuous days that followed the announcement of my latest marriage plans. You said to me something like this: "She probably put on a fancy blouse, something these Prague Jewesses are good at, and right away, of course, you decided to marry her. And that as fast as possible, in a week, tomorrow, today. I can't understand you: after all, you're a grown man, you live in the city, and you don't know what to do but marry the next best girl. Isn't there anything else you can do? If you're frightened, I'll go with you to see her." You put it in more detail and more plainly, but I can no longer recall the details, perhaps too things became a little vague before my eyes, I paid almost more attention to Mother who, though in complete agreement with you, took something from the table and left the room with it.

You have hardly ever humiliated me more deeply with words and shown me your contempt more clearly. When you spoke to me in a similar way twenty years earlier, one might, looking at it through your eyes, have seen in it some respect for the precocious city boy, who in your opinion could already be initiated into life without more ado. Today this consideration could only intensify the contempt, for the boy who was about to make his first start got stuck halfway and today does not seem richer by any experience, only more pitiable by twenty years. My choice of a girl meant nothing at all to you. You had (unconsciously) always kept down my power of decision and now believed (unconsciously) that you knew what it was worth. Of my attempts at escape in other directions you knew nothing, thus you could not know anything, either, of the thought process that had led me to this attempt to marry, and had to try to guess at them, and in keeping with your general opinion of me, you guessed at the most abominable, crude, and ridiculous. And you did not for a moment hesitate to tell me this in just such a manner. The shame you inflicted on me with this was nothing to you in comparison to the shame that I would, in your opinion, inflict on your name by this marriage.

Now, regarding my attempts at marriage there is much you can say in reply, and you have indeed done so: you could not have much respect for my decision since I had twice broken the engagement with F. and had twice renewed it; since I had needlessly dragged you and Mother to Berlin to celebrate the engagement, and the like. All this is true—but how did it come about?

The fundamental thought behind both attempts at marriage was quite sound: to set up house, to become independent. An idea that does appeal to you, only in reality it always turns out like the children's game in which one holds and even grips the other's hand, calling out: "Oh, go away, go away, why don't you go away?" Which in our case happens to be complicated by the fact that you have always honestly meant this "go away!" and have always unknowingly held me, or rather held me down, only by the strength of your personality.

Although both girls were chosen by chance, they were extraordinarily well chosen. Again a sign of your complete misunderstanding, that you can believe that I—timid, hesitant, suspicious—can decide to marry in a flash, out of delight over a blouse. Both marriages would rather have been common sense marriages, in so far as that means that day and night, the first time for years, the second time for months, all my power of thought was concentrated on the plan.

Neither of the girls disappointed me, only I disappointed both of them. My opinion of them is today exactly the same as when I wanted to marry them.

It is not true either that in my second marriage attempt I disregarded the experiences gained from the first attempt, that I was rash and careless. The cases were quite different; precisely the earlier experience held out a hope for the second case, which was altogether much more promising. I do not want to go into details here.

Why then did I not marry? There were certainly obstacles, as there always are, but then, life consists in taking such obstacles. The essential obstacle, however, which is, unfortunately, independent of the individual case, is that obviously I am mentally incapable of marrying. This manifests itself in the fact that from the moment I make up my mind to marry I can no longer sleep, my head burns day and night, life can no longer be called life, I stagger about in despair. It is not actually worries that bring this about; true, in keeping with my sluggishness and pedantry countless worries are involved in all this, but they are not decisive; they do, like worms, complete the work on the corpse, but the decisive blow has come from elsewhere. It is the general pressure of anxiety, of weakness, of self-contempt.

I will try to explain it in more detail. Here, in the attempt to marry, two seemingly antagonistic elements in my relations with you unite more intensely than anywhere else. Marriage certainly is the pledge of the most acute form of self-liberation and independence. I would have a family, in my opinion the highest one can achieve, and so too the highest you have achieved; I would be your equal; all old and ever new shame and tyranny would be mere history. It would be like a fairy tale, but precisely there does the questionable element lie. It is too much; so much cannot be achieved. It is as if a person were a prisoner, and he had not only the intention to escape, which would perhaps be attainable, but also, and indeed simultaneously, the intention to rebuild the prison as a pleasure dome for himself. But if he escapes, he cannot rebuild, and if he rebuilds, he cannot escape. If I, in the particular unhappy relationship in which I stand to you, want to become independent, I must do something that will have, if possible, no connection with you at all; though marrying is the greatest thing of all and provides the most honorable independence, it is also at the same time in the closest relation to you. To try to get out of all this has therefore a touch of madness about it, and every attempt is almost punished with it.

It is precisely this close relation that partly lures me toward marrying. I picture the equality which would then arise between us—and which you would be able to understand better than any other form of equality—as so beautiful because then I could be a free, grateful, guiltless, upright son, and you could be an untroubled, untyrannical, sympathetic, contented father. But to this end everything that ever happened would have to be undone, that is, we ourselves should have to be cancelled out.

But we being what we are, marrying is barred to me because it is your very own domain. Sometimes I imagine the map of the world spread out and you stretched diagonally across it. And I feel as if I could consider living in only those regions that either are not covered by you or are not within your reach. And in keeping with the conception I have of your magnitude, these are not many and not very comforting regions—and marriage is not among them.

Excerpt from *Lenz*

GEORG BÜCHNER

Translated by John Reddick

On 20th January Lenz crossed the mountains. Snow on the peaks and upper slopes, down into the valleys grey stone, green patches, rocks and pine-trees. It was cold and wet, the water trickled down the rocks and leapt across the path. The boughs of the pine-trees sagged in the damp air. Grey clouds marched across the sky, but everything so close, and then the mist came swirling up and drifted dank and heavy through the bushes, so leaden, so sluggish. He carried on, indifferent, the way meant nothing to him, now up, now down. He felt no tiredness, just the occasional regret that he couldn't walk on his head. A surge swept through his breast at first when the rock seemed to leap away, the grey wood shuddered beneath him, and the mist devoured the shape of things then half revealed their giant limbs; the surge swept through him, he sought for something, as though for lost dreams, but he found nothing. Everything was so small to him, so near, so wet, he would have liked to tuck the earth behind the stove, he couldn't understand that he needed so much time to clamber down a slope, to reach a distant point; he thought he should be able to measure out everything with a few strides. Only sometimes, when the storm cast the clouds into the valleys and they swirled up through the trees, and the voices awoke amongst the rocks, at first like distant rumbling thunder, then arriving with a roar in mighty chords as though they wished in their wild exulting to sing the praises of the earth, and the clouds galloped up like wild whinnying horses, and the sunlight pierced them and came and drew his flashing sword along the sheets of snow so that a bright, blinding light went slicing over the peaks and down into the valleys; or when the storm drove the clouds downwards and tore a hole in them, a light blue lake, and then the wind fell silent and far below a sound like lullabies and church bells rose from ravines and treetops, and a delicate red spread upwards in the dark blue sky, and tiny clouds went past on silver wings, and all the mountain peaks, sharp and solid, flashed and glowed far across the land—then his breast burst, he stood there panting, his body bent forward, his eyes and mouth wide open, he thought he should draw the storm right into himself, embrace all things within his being, he spread and lay over the entire earth, he burrowed his way into the All, it was an ecstasy that hurt; or else he stopped and laid his head in the moss and half closed his eyes, then everything receded far away, the earth beneath him shrank, grew small like a wandering star and dipped into a roaring stream whose limpid depths stretched out beneath him. But these were only moments, and then he stood up, sober, solid, calm, as though a shadow-play had passed before him, no memory remained. Towards evening he reached the crest of the mountains, the snowfields that led down again to the westward plain, he sat a while at the top. It had turned calmer towards evening; the clouds lay solid and motionless in the sky, nothing so far as the eye could see but mountain peaks from which broad slopes descended, and everything so quiet, grey, increasingly faint; he felt a terrible loneliness, he was all alone, completely alone, he wanted to talk to himself, but he couldn't, he scarcely dared breathe, his footfall rang like thunder beneath him, he had to sit down; a nameless fear took hold of him in this nothing, he was in empty space, he leapt to his feet and flew down the slope. Darkness had fallen, heaven and earth had melted into one. It was as though something were following him, as though something terrible would catch up with him, something no human can bear, as though madness were chasing him on mighty horses. At last he heard voices, saw lights, he felt a little easier, he was told it was another half-hour to Waldbach. He walked through the village, the candlelight shone through the windows, he looked in as he passed, children at the table, old women, young girls, in the faces all calm and still, it seemed to him as if they were the source of the radiant light, he was filled with ease, he was soon in the vicarage in Waldbach.* They were sitting at the table, he entered the room; his

* *the vicarage in Waldbach*: Properly speaking, 'Waldersbach'; the village is in the Steintal (Vallé de la Bruche) some twenty-five miles south-west of Strasbourg. The

blond locks hung about his ashen face, his mouth and eyes twitched, his clothes were torn. Oberlin* bade him welcome, he took him for a journeyman. 'I don't know who you are, but I bid you welcome.' 'I am a friend of Kaufmann's† and bring you his greetings.' 'Your name, if you please?' 'Lenz.' 'Ah yes, let me see, are you not in print? Have I not read a few plays that bear such a name?' 'Yes, but pray do not judge me by that.' The conversation continued, he hunted for words and then rattled them out, but as though on the rack; gradually he grew calm, the homely room and the calm faces emerging from the shadows, the radiant face of a child upon which all light appeared to rest, looking up full of trust and curiosity, glancing at its mother sitting calm, like an angel, in the shadows at the back. He began to talk, recounted where he came from; he sketched all manner of local costumes, they thronged around him full of interest, he was soon at home, his pale child's face, now full of smiles, his knack of bringing his story to life; he grew quiet, he felt as if forgotten faces, figures from long ago, were reappearing from the darkness, old songs came to life, he was away, far away. It was finally time to go, he was led across the road, the vicarage was too small, they gave him a room in the schoolhouse. He went up, it was cold upstairs, a large room, bare, a high bed right at the back, he set his candle on the table and paced up and down, he went over the day in his mind, his journey here, the place itself, the room in the vicarage with its lights and kindly faces, it was like a shadow, a dream, and emptiness overcame him, as it had on the mountain, but he could fill it with nothing any more, the candle had gone out, the darkness swallowed everything; a nameless terror seized

---

vicarage now houses the Musée Oberlin.

* *Oberlin:* Johann Friedrich (Jean Frédéric) Oberlin (1740–1826) was the (Protestant) parish priest of Waldersbach for no less than fifty-nine years, beginning in 1767. He became widely renowned and revered for the immense benign influence that he exerted on his community throughout a period of often drastic social change: he was instrumental in introducing or encouraging such things as nursery schooling; raising of the school-leaving age to sixteen; agricultural improvements; road-building; local loan schemes; development of weaving and other local craft industries. He was buried in the same graveyard at Fouday that figures in Büchner's story.

† *a friend of Kaufmann's*: Christoph Kaufmann (1753–95) was a friend of Lenz and Lavater, and was acquainted with Goethe and Herder. The term *Sturm und Drang* ('Storm and Stress') was first coined by him (in reference to a play by Klinger). It was Kaufmann who sent Lenz to stay with Oberlin.

him, he leapt up, he ran through the room, down the stairs, in front of the house; but no use, darkness everywhere, nothing, he himself but a dream, random thoughts came ghosting by, he grasped at them and held them tight, he felt as if he had to repeat 'Our Father' again and again; he could find himself no longer, an obscure instinct drove him to save himself, he banged his head against the stones, he ripped his flesh with his nails, the pain began to restore his consciousness, he hurled himself in the fountain, but the water was shallow, he could only splash about. Then people came, they had heard the noise, they called to him. Oberlin came running; Lenz was himself again, the situation was clear to him in every detail, he felt easy once more, he felt ashamed and sorry to have given the good people such a fright, he told them he was accustomed to taking cold baths, and went back upstairs; at last, exhausted, he fell asleep.

Excerpt from *My Dog Tulip*

J. R. ACKERLEY

On August 22, spots of blood appeared again on Tulip's shins and I phoned the news to Miss Canvey. When should I bring her along? Miss Canvey at once supplied the clue I had missed in the autumn:

"Bring her as soon as she starts to hold her tail sideways when you stroke her."

Wonderful Miss Canvey! No other vet, nor any dog book I had ever read, had thought fit to provide this inestimably important piece of information, a truth, like many another great truth, so obvious in its simplicity when it is pointed out that I wondered how I could have failed to notice it before and draw from it its manifest conclusions. Tulip herself supplies the answer to the question of her readiness. At the peak of her heat, from her ninth or tenth day, her long tail, as soon as she is touched anywhere near it, or even if a feint of touching her is made, coils away round one flank or the other, leaving the vaginal passage free and accessible. This pretty demonstration of her physical need goes on for several days; during all of these she is receptive.

I took her down to Miss Canvey on September 1. The arrangement was that I should leave her there on my way to work and call for her on my return. There was a stable yard attached to Miss Canvey's old-fashioned establishment, and there the two animals were to spend the intermediate hours together, under observation from the surgery windows. Tulip evinced no particular pleasure at meeting Timothy again; her desolate cries followed me as I left. When I rejoined her in the evening I was told that he had penetrated her but had not tied.* This, I gathered, had not been achieved without help. Miss Canvey was displeased and asked me to fetch her back in a couple of days for another go. On this second occasion, again with help, the animals tied for ten minutes, and Miss Canvey declared herself satisfied. After a lapse of three weeks I was to produce Tulip for examination. I did so. She was not pregnant. She was not to be a mother after all.

This was the end of my second attempt to mate her, and since it had seemed successful, it was a greater disappointment than the first. Was it a confirmation of Chick's dark suspicion? Miss Canvey thought not: Tulip was a little narrow in the pelvis but seemed otherwise perfectly normal, she said. She was deeply apologetic and offered to try again in the autumn if I had no better prospects. But my mind was in as great a muddle as ever. I did not know, of course, what had gone on in the stable yard, for I had not been present; but it seemed to me on reflection that I had come pretty close to those stud practices which Chick had deprecated and I had intended to avoid. Miss Canvey was the kindest of women and a qualified vet; she must know far more about these things than I did; yet my questioning mind remained doubtful. Doubtful and now distressed. Call it "helped," call it what one would, my virgin bitch had been ravished, it seemed to me, without spontaneity, without desire, and I could not believe that that was right.

Then I came across a book, *The Right Way to Keep Dogs*, by Major R. C. G. Hancock, which formulated and confirmed all my suspicions. The importance of wooing in a bitch's sex life, he says, cannot be over-estimated. Though she will not consent to consummate the act of mating during the first week of her heat, "she is strongly attractive during this wooing period to all the males of the pack, who follow her in a hopeful procession, fighting amongst themselves from time to time to settle the primacy of approach. The result is that by the second week, when the bitch allows mating to take place, she had gone through a process of strenuous wooing, so that the ovaries have been

* Or locked. The dog's penis only reaches full erectal size after entering the bitch. It cannot then be withdrawn until detumescence occurs. Foxes and wolves have the same coital pattern.

stimulated to shed a large number of eggs into the womb, there to await fertilization." He then repeats much of what Chick had told me. "Only those familiar with the breeding technique of the present-day pedigree breeder will know how far their methods negate this natural certainty. The bitch is kept shut up during the week when she should be the object of constant wooing and stimulus by the male. On the day she is adjudged ready for mating, she is taken and held, often muzzled, while the precious stud dog, lest he be injured, is carefully lifted into position. Under these circumstances, with no love-making precedent to the act, both sexes are indolent in performance, eggs are few in number, and the male seed poor in quality and quantity. In many cases the 'tying' of the dog to the bitch is not affected because of this sexual indolence. No wonder the resulting litter is small or non-existent . . . If possible, let them have a run out together daily during the first week. When one or other parent has never mated before, this is particularly important to allow the subconscious instincts to organize themselves, and, by trial and error, the technique of mating becomes possible. I have seen many virgin males introduced to a bitch ready for mating, and the dog, though showing every sign of desire, just does not know what is expected of him."

Since these passages described, with an accuracy so startling that I wondered for a moment whether their author had been shadowing me, everything that had happened to Tulip, I could hardly do other than accept them as truth. If she was not barren I had simply muddled two of her heats away. Yet it was all very well! Reconsidering Major Hancock's counsel of perfection, how was I to organize a large pack of pedigree Alsatians to pursue and fight for her during the first week of her heat? And where was this interesting scene to be staged? No doubt it was a splendid idea, but difficult to arrange. Failing that, the implication seemed to be that if she had seen a good deal more of Max, Chum and Timothy from the beginning they would have stood a better chance. Well, perhaps . . . But was it true to say that she had gone to any of them unwooed and unstimulated? Admittedly they had not wooed her themselves, but she had had the prior attention of quantities of Putney mongrels on all these occasions, so that if followers and their wooings fertilized the womb, hers should have been positively floating with eggs before she met any of her prospective mates.

Indeed, during this second wasted season, both before and after Timothy's failure, I had a lot of trouble with the local dogs, far more than I had had in the winter. Theoretically, Tulip was perfectly welcome, so far as I was concerned, to canine company at these times, so long as it was the right company. The right company depended upon the period. At the onset and decline of her estrus I did not mind what company she kept, for it seemed safe to assume that she was unconsenting, if not impenetrable, during the first six and last six days of her cycle at least. Even between these dates I was still willing to permit followers, so long as they were too small, or too old, or too young, to be able to give and obtain any satisfaction greater than flattery. I felt, indeed, extremely sympathetic towards Tulip's courtiers (I would have been after the pretty creature myself, I thought, if I had been a dog); she clearly enjoyed being pleasured by their little warm tongues, and I wished her to have as much fun as she could get. But theory and practice seldom accorded. The dogs were scarcely ever the requisite size and age; moreover, they constantly abused my hospitality by persecuting her and each other. And of them, it seemed to me now, the little dog, to whom hitherto I had felt especially well-disposed, was far more tiresome (at any rate, when he was plural, which he usually was) than his larger brethren, more lecherous, more persistent, and more quarrelsome.

"They are like the little men," indignantly remarked a rather *passée* lady of my acquaintance to whom I recounted my woes; "*always* the worst!"

They took no hint, as the bigger dogs sometimes did, from the symbolic use of the lead when I kept Tulip on it, but sexually assaulted her at my very heels if they thought they could do so with impunity; and since there are degrees of littleness, it was often a question of where to draw the line.

"Don't bank on physical improbabilities," someone had warned me. "Before you can say knife the blade is inserted!"

The determined hoppings and skippings of these dubious and pertinacious little creatures in particular, therefore, alarmed me when she was receptive and inconvenienced me in any case. It became quite a puzzle to know where to exercise her. Why exercise her at all at such a time? it may be asked—but only by those people who have never had my problem to contend with, the problem of confining an active, eager and importunate young bitch to a small London flat for three weeks. Difficult though it was to take her out, it was more exhausting and demoralizing to keep her in. This took on the terrible aspect of punishment, and how could I punish a creature for something she could not help and, moreover, when she herself was so awfully good? For even in heat Tulip gave me no trouble of any kind. Other bitches of my acquaintance, in a similar condition, whose owners had the resolution and the facilities—sheds, gardens, cellars—to shut them away out of sight and sound, were always on the watch for chances to escape, and sometimes found them, returning home only when they were pregnant and famished. But if I had opened my flat door to Tulip she would not have gone out of it alone; if I had taken her down into the street and put her with her friends, she would have left them to follow me back upstairs. The only fault I could find with her was that she was apt to spread the news of her condition by sprinkling the doorstep on her way in and out (a dodge I noticed at this time too late to prevent it), which naturally brought all the neighboring dogs along in a trice to hang hopefully about the building for the rest of her season. This, if she had been a rational creature, she would have seen to be shortsighted, for her walks, which she valued even now above all else, became thereafter as harassed as are the attempts of film stars and other popular celebrities to leave the Savoy Hotel undetected by reporters.

In the kindness and weakness of my nature, therefore, I took her out once or twice every day, and, in consequence, I fear, punished and upset her more than if I had kept her in. Our objective was usually the towingpath, not more than five minutes' walk away, and if only we could reach it unsmelt and unseen, or with, at most, a single acceptable companion, it offered a reasonable change of pace, for town dogs seldom roam far from human habitations by themselves and such as we might meet would probably be in the control of their owners. Stealth, therefore, was an essential preliminary to success. I would spy out the land from my terrace, and, if the doorstep and Embankment approach to the towingpath were temporarily clear of enemy patrols, sally forth with Tulip on the lead (to prevent her from urinating again), exhorting her *sotto voce* to silence. For a single bark would undo us now: the locals, alerted for news of her, would come flying helter-skelter from all points of the compass. Bursting with excitement though she was, she was usually wonderfully intelligent over this, and would trot along soundlessly beside me, gazing up into my face for guidance. Now we were on the Embankment, and only five hundred apparently dogless yards separated us from our goal. How close the prize! How seldom attained! As though some magical news agency were at work, like that which was said to spread information among savage tribes, dogs would materialize out of the very air, it seemed, and come racing after or towards us. And what a miscellaneous crew they were! Some, like Watney, were so small that by no exertion or stroke of luck could they possibly achieve their high ambition; some were so old and arthritic that they could hardly hobble along; yet all deserted hearth and home and, as bemused as the rats of Hamelin, staggered, shuffled, hopped, bounced and skirmished after us so far that I often wondered whether those who dropped out ever managed to return home. And now what did one do, with a swarm of randy creatures dodging along behind with an eye to the main chance, of which they had the clearest view, snarling and squabbling among themselves for what Major Hancock calls the "primacy of approach," and provoking Tulip to a continual retaliation which either entangled my legs in the lead or wrenched my arm out of its socket?

I usually ended by doing two things. I released her from the lead, which, since she might be said to live always on a spiritual one, was more an encumbrance than an advantage. Then I lost my temper. For it was at this moment that her intelligence failed her. I would turn upon our tormentors with threatening gestures and shouts of "Scram!", but before the effect, if any, of this could be gauged, Tulip, always ready to please, would assist me as she thought by launching herself vehemently at her escort. This, of course, defeated my purpose. It was precisely what I did not want because it was precisely what they wanted. They did not take her onslaughts at all seriously and, one might say, could scarcely believe their good fortune at finding her in their midst. Yet, command and yell at her as I did, I could not make her see that all I required of her was that she should remain passively at my side. Poor Tulip! With her bright, anxious gaze fixed perpetually on my stern face striving to read my will, many a curse and cuff did she get for being so irrepressibly helpful! And how could she be expected to understand? Most of these dogs were her friends, with whom, a few days ago, she had been permitted, even encouraged, to hobnob; now apparently they were in disgrace, yet although I seemed angry with them and to desire their riddance, I was angry with her too for implementing my wishes.

The same thing happened, when, threats failing, I took to pelting the dauntless creatures with sticks and clods. Tulip, accustomed to having things thrown for her to retrieve, instantly flew off to retrieve them, and earned another slap when she playfully returned with the stick in her mouth and sundry dogs clinging to her bottom. Whatever she did, in short, was wrong, and soon she herself was in such a state of hysterical confusion that she no longer knew what she did, but, with all the intelligence gone out of her eyes and succeeded by a flat, insensitive mad look, would jump at me to seize the missile before I threw it, and even when I had nothing to throw, tearing my clothes or my flesh with her teeth. It was in these circumstances that she inflicted upon me the only bad bite she ever inflicted on anyone, as I have related earlier.

My Struggle: Confessions of a Tall, Aryan White Man—Volume 7 or Nothing According to Karl Ove Knausgaard

JACK HALBERSTAM

"Nothing matters." So wrote anarchitect Gordon Matta-Clark as he worked out how to bring structures to the point of collapse. "Nothing really matters . . . to me," so sang Freddie Mercury as he was dying of AIDS on a global stage of rock stardom. And while I am writing a book about nothing, about having nothing, owning nothing, about empty handedness, about nothings that become something and about how to keep nothing from becoming something, this essay is sadly about something or about how white male literature keeps the threat of nothing emanating from radical, anarchist, queer, black thinkers from turning their legacies to dust.

An example of the hegemonic deployment of nothing can be found in the monumental six-volume account of "My Struggle" by Norwegian author and global literary sensation Karl Ove Knausgaard. While women have been writing about the minor, the domestic, the importance of small nothings for centuries, Knausgaard figured out how to turn nothing into something, and by resignifying one of the most notorious literary memoirs of the twentieth century, *Mein Kampf*, he deployed the charisma of Fascism to tell a supposedly small and anti-fascist story.

Indeed, I did find that rummaging through the minutiae of Knausgaard's daily life was oddly addictive—Zadie Smith has said that she got to the point with reading these mammoth tomes that she "needed the next installment like crack." Ok, I would not go that far but I was certainly able to become absorbed by the small predicaments of daily life that he draws out in such details. Like other readers, however, I found the 6th volume, where he goes on a 400-page detour into the life and times of Adolph Hitler, in order to justify calling his autobiography *My Struggle/Mein Kampf*, pretentious and disturbing. His quarrels with all the literature on Hitler boils down to a desire to offer a more mobile depiction of the man, one less sure that the dictator was always on a genocidal mission. In this way, Knausgaard imagines himself as accessing a better and more meaningful account of the Holocaust. It is this gross egotism in the face of an event that defies ego altogether that pulls Knausgaard out of the realm of nothing and places him firmly in the world of accumulation, profit, commodity and, yes, white supremacy.

Other disturbing features of the series: a preoccupation with shit and shitting that translates into long passages on creating and then birthing large and monumental pieces of shit—an analogy for his creative process, surely. This alchemical process by which Knausgaard literally turns shit into gold, demonstrates the continuing hegemonic insistence on male narratives and male genius. Shit, literature, the father, truth, women and sex, including "premature ejaculation," these are the components of "his struggle." In an era of #metoo and at a time when all kinds of gendered people would like to bring patriarchy crashing down, it is kind of amazing that Knausgaard is the literary sensation that he is. Volume 4 of *My Struggle* after all is all about his experiences as a teacher in a remote Norwegian village. And while he has some great things to say about teaching—both its tedium and its unexpected pleasures—he mostly feels exasperated by being so close to forbidden fruit (the young, adolescent girls he teaches). He struggles with hiding his erections from them and with his desires for them and his obsessions with their breasts:

"Her breasts were big, her legs long. What more could I want? Nothing, that covered everything."

* * *

"Quite often I caught myself wishing we were still in the stone age, then all I needed was to go out with a club, hit the nearest woman on the head and drag her home to do whatever I wanted."

And don't get me wrong, I am not standing in moralistic judgement at these thoughts, after all, they mostly remain in the realm of thought and fantasy, but rather, **I am interested in the anatomy of patriarchy and male desire that the novels give us and how little seems to have been written on that, and never mind on the relation between male desire, patriarchy, and fascism.** Fascism, I am willing to claim, lives on in this geometry of male desire, forbidden fruit, the desire for women and simultaneous desire to destroy them, and the celebration of the narrative forces that bring all of reality to our doorsteps in the form of white male experience.

I end by offering something as nothing—let's imagine Volume 7 of Knausgaard's novel/memoir, it goes a little something like this:

I dreamt I was in a small cabin on an island and I was writing page after page. The words poured out of me as if they had been damming up inside my head my whole life and now were free. I wanted to tell everything—what I ate, what I wore, where I went, who I loved. I wanted to record my life minute by minute, the good, the bad, the banal and the monumental, and I wanted to preserve it in a multivolume accounting. In the dream, my writing gushed forward and splattered onto the page, like a Pollock painting, and as the words took on the shape of narrative, I ascended to the pantheon of "great writers." I saw my books on the shelves alongside all the greats—Thomas Mann, James Joyce, Shakespeare, Proust, the Bible—and, like these books, my books were big—not just big in terms of their impact but physically big, blocks of words and paper, virtually impossible to carry around in a backpack. When stacked side by side, they were huge, big tomes brimming with, well, everything. Yes, my books were big and my name was on them, therefore I was big. I wanted to shout this truth to the world—I am big, these books represent me and they are better than anything else that has been written on the topic of me. They will live forever, they will be compared to the greats. They *are* great, therefore I am great. Karl Ove the Great. I was shouting my own name to the world when I woke myself up. Karl Ove! Karl Ove! Karl Ove!

Where was I? I glanced over at my companion on the other side of the bed. Who did I come home with last night? Oh yes, the lithe co-ed who caught my attention in the bar after many beers. She was blond and tall with fantastic breasts. I felt a stirring in my groin but the soft ping of a text message coming in interrupted the beginnings of an erection. I padded across the bedroom floor, fished around with my feet for my slippers, and headed downstairs to make coffee. The kitchen was cold and still dark as I felt around for the coffee jar, opened it, scooped three heaping spoons into the pot and turned on the kettle. As I lit up my first cigarette of the day, I remembered the text message and picked up my phone. It was my editor from England. Check your email, the message said.

Who was trying to sue me now I wondered? The very young girls with budding fantastic breasts whom I had ogled in my first teaching job? My brother? His wife? My former wife? The woman with small breasts who claimed I had raped her? My classmates from college, especially the woman writer I had written harshly about? Or maybe it was my best friend, Geir, angered perhaps by my constant concerns about being taken for a homosexual while hanging out with him. Oh god, oh god! No, not that! Maybe he actually was a homosexual and was truly offended, or maybe his son was homosexual and he was now offended by what he had read in *My Struggle* Book Six. This could be bad, very bad. If he charged me with homophobia, I would no longer stand in for everyman, the universal subject, the person in the street through whom the complexity of the world flowed. Instead, I would be marked as a bigot, a prejudiced and biased person, a homophobe. Or else, people may conclude that my comments served to cover up an actual simmering homoerotic desire for other men. In Book Six, I had written about the time that he and I were in a grocery store with his son and a couple in line looked at us and beamed. What had they been thinking, I had wondered at the time. Were they smiling in tolerant recognition at what they presumed was a gay male couple with their adopted child? I had freaked out and started shoving my best friend around to prove that I was normal, a real man, a heterosexual man who loved very young women with blond hair and fantastic breasts.

But it was not a lawsuit, just a mean-spirited review of the last three volumes of *My Struggle*, written by a professor in New York. Apparently, the review had circulated widely and there was much commentary in its wake about the gender and sexuality politics of my books. This person, and I say person because I honestly have no idea what gender they were, and this even after looking them up on google, this person had written a horrific parody of me and was getting some attention for it. As I began to read the review, I calmed down. It was obviously a third-rate scholar trying to score some points for an Identitarian ideology that reeked of simplistic judgment and was devoid of literary insight. Thank god I am a white man, I thought, and I don't have to engage in the tiresome jockeying for position that marks the work of homosexuals and women. No, a white man can just sit down and write and he writes his way into the whole world! The fact that this "world" also comprises mostly other white men in no way invalidates the labor, the art, the craft, the sublimity of what we write. In fact, by building on each other and on the work that came before us, we can bypass the petty squabbles of the others and just dig into the important stuff—like whether to eat cornflakes or museli for breakfast, how best to appreciate pornography and what to do about the crazy women who pursue us.

Given that I am probably the second-best living writer in the world, after Peter Handke, I do not have to worry about pathetic transsexual scholars trying to score points by imitating my style. I texted back to my editor, told her all was fine and not to worry about the review. Next I texted my girlfriend and positioning my smart phone at crotch level, pulled down my pajama bottoms and, once I had managed to get the angle just right, giving a bit of heft and length to my otherwise flaccid member, I snapped a dick pick, checked the photo quickly and then hit send, smiling to myself and hoping that my girlfriend would reciprocate quickly with a picture of her fantastic breasts.

* * *

Over the past few years, I had been engaged in a massive writing project in which I set about to create a detailed account of my life, from my first shit in the woods to my first experience of premature ejaculation, from my earliest memories of my mother to my early encounter with pornography. I had dug deep into the vast archive of Western literature from which my own writing was drawn—Joyce, Proust, Musil, Hölderlin, Goethe, Celan, Mann, Hamsun. The wretched professor from New York who was writing a parody of me had claimed that I only mentioned male writers. This is ridiculous, it is not a matter of whether the writer is male or female but only whether they are great, whether their prose rises to the level of classic, as mine does, and whether they are able, as I am, to capture the minutiae of their lives and then elevate it to the level of the universal. If women cannot perform this simple rhetorical operation, then I am not to blame. The satirist, who calls themselves a queer theorist, suggested that when women write about minutiae the work is deemed trivial but when men do it, it is literary! Nonsense! The literary requires no alibi and I will provide none for mine.

And as for this charge that I am a normative white guy insisting on putting myself and my experiences in the center of the world, well, what can I say? Far from being normal, I have always understood myself to be an outsider, a misfit, an odd and strange person living at the very edges of polite society. Look at me! I am a tall, reasonably good-looking guy, I have a wife and kids, I listen to Talking Heads, I drink beer, a lot of beer, I fall down drunk, I love and hate my father, I love and respect other men, I fear and desire women, I write, I play drums badly, I confess, I look after my children, what could be further from mainstream culture than that? Indeed, since I was a small boy shitting in the woods and recording the color of my shit, I have known myself to be different from others. I have been marked by traumas big and small—the ferocity of my father, the indignity of being called a faggot at school, my abuse of alcohol, my struggles with premature ejaculation. Indeed, when people ask why I called my books "My Struggle," I try to explain the hardship that losing my erection so quickly has caused me over the years. I have struggled and struggled to find and bed beautiful blond women with fantastic breasts, but once in bed with the woman of my dreams, my desire, like my words, comes spilling out all at once and, before my partner has even removed her coat, the main event is over. At that point, I have felt humiliated and embarrassed and I have rushed these women to the door and asked them to walk home.

My struggle has been real. I have tried wanking, tried thinking of Nordic literature, tried remembering my own short stories in order to delay the inevitable but to no avail. The only way to stave off the implications of my short and quick sexual experiences is to create a long, hard, huge set of writings that offset sexual inadequacy with literary abundance, the minimalism of my desire with the maximalism of my inner life. Look, I want to say, I am big, I am Karl Ove, I am a writer, I can have sex for longer than 2 minutes.

I remember the day that Geir told me that the title of my books, *My Struggle*, was not original. What? I said, flabbergasted. Has someone else also written about premature ejaculation at length? In a way, he answered. Have you heard of a little man called Adolf Hitler? Vaguely, I had heard of him, he was the father of Fascism and another man who struggled with his father, with his desire for women, with sex. There was a world of men out there, I realized, like me. Men who loved and hated daddy, loved and ignored mommy, men who wanted to be great and famous. I resolved then to pull my books out of the weeds, out of the mundane recording of events—what I ate, when I moved my bowels—and make them meaningful. I turned on my computer and dropped a four-hundred-page account of Hitler, fascism and the Holocaust into the middle of my book about family. There, that should do it, a big story sandwiched within a little story, a story of a son who becomes the uber-Vater in the middle of a story about a father who dies and leaves a mess. If the title *My Struggle* was taken, I needed a new one—*The Birth of a Nation* had a ring to it. That may do it! I turned on my phone to text my editor/love and tell her about the new title. But there were three text messages there already from Geir! I tapped on the first one and saw that he had sent me a photo. What was it? A turkey neck? A hairless mole? A large worm? Oh no, no no no, it was a dick pic! But why was he sending me this. I scrolled up the message thread. Oh my god, my dick pic had gone to him and not to my girlfriend, and now he was reciprocating and declaring his love for me. He was a homosexual! Maybe I am too? No, no, no. I cannot be, I love women, sort of, I hate men, sort of. Or do I love men and hate women? All the writers I read and love are heterosexual too, aren't they? Proust? Mann? Shakespeare? Wait, wait, the queer theorist had implied these writers were all homosexual. This deviant had implied I was a homosexual in denial. But, of the many shameful desires that churn inside me, homosexuality is not one. In the end, my orientation is not to man or woman but to art!

I needed yet another title. But, before I came up with one, I decided to go to the store and shop for everything I would need to sustain me while I wrote Book 7 of my magnum opus. I walked down the stairs, out into the street and headed for the convenience store that had opened recently in the neighborhood. I pushed my cart down the aisles and picked up some spaghetti and a marinara sauce, 5 ramen packets, 2 tins of coffee, a 12-pack of Pepsi, 3 bottles of good red wine, 5 packs of cigarettes, cornflakes, 2 cans of tuna, a carton of washed lettuce, some Swedish meatballs, reindeer meat from Norway, pickled herring, a carton of milk, some condoms and breath mints. Stopped next at the pharmacy and picked up my supply of Viagra. The queer theorist had accused me of making shopping lists in my book, again to prove what a good house husband I was while detailing the many faults of my many wives. But the lists are important to me. Not because, as Frederic Jameson says in an interview about my books, that I am committed to "itemization," but because this is truth, this is the real stuff of life and this is how I remain the hero of every story I tell, because once you know me, really know me, you cannot judge me for my infidelities, my arrogance, my abuse of my wives, my tendency to judge all women by their looks and their breasts. The lists help me to seem banal, vulnerable, helpless and hard-working. By my lists, you know I am good, a good man, a man who leads with his heart not his head, a man who you can love.

In the end, I have taken this risk, the risk of writing down everything I think and everything I do and of examining life down to its most trivial detail, and I have done so because this is the only way to tell the truth, the truth of who I, Karl Ove, really am. And yes, that includes loving very young women with fantastic breasts, listening to white guy bands and reading white guy novels, and patiently putting up with the women in my life while they experience self-induced meltdowns despite my best efforts to support them to support me. My story, you see, has never been told. This is the story of a young boy struggling to make a mark on the world and then a young man struggling not to have to work and then a husband struggling to get away from his wife and kids and then a man struggling to be free. It is a story that we catch glimpses of in Knut Hamsun's *Hunger* and in Ernst Jünger's *Storm of Steel* because they, like me, were young men who declined to bend their narratives to the whims of public opinion and the fluctuating orientations of popular politics, they like me dug deep into the psyche and found the truth, they like me struggled with struggle, flirted with Fascism and desired "a man in black with a meinkampf look" as a nameless female poet once wrote. Except, unlike this second-rate poet, I *am* the man in black, I *have* the meinkampf look, and like Knut Hamsun, I offer psychological complexity in order to capture "the whisper of blood and the pleading of bone marrow." In the heart of many a good, white, Aryan man lies a swastika, contempt for women, fear of death, a desire to be god and to conquer death. But we cannot conquer death nor reconcile to it and so the whole world must burn. But, as I grow older, as death beckons to me, as impotence sets in, I realize that death is not the problem, it is the solution. That was it, I had my title at last for *Book 7 – The Final Solution*. The publisher loved it, the work was over, the struggle is real.

This Dark Apartment

JAMES SCHUYLER

Coming from the deli
a block away today I
saw the UN building
shine and in all the
months and years I've
lived in this apartment
I took so you and I
would have a place to
meet I never noticed
that it was in my view.

I remember very well
the morning I walked in
and found you in bed
with X. He dressed
and left. You dressed
too. I said, "Stay
five minutes." You
did. You said, "That's
the way it is." It
was not much of a surprise.

Then X got on speed
and ripped off an
antique chest and an
air conditioner, etc.
After he was gone and
you had changed the
Segal lock, I asked
you on the phone, "Can't
you be content with
your wife and me?" "I'm
not built that way,"
you said. No surprise.

Now, without saying
why, you've let me go.
You don't return my
calls, who used to call
me almost every evening
when I lived in the coun-
try "Hasn't he told you
why?" "No, and I doubt he
ever will." Goodbye. It's
mysterious and frustrating.

How I wish you could come
back! I could tell
you how, when I lived
on East 49th, first
with Frank and then with John,
we had a lovely view of
the UN building and the
Beekman Towers. They were
not my lovers, though.
You were. You said so.

Chronicle

FRANK B. WILDERSON III

Two.
they smile tip their hats lower their
shotguns and let us
cross the mississippi line
legs dangling from the pickup in front i don't recall
the guns mom remembers dad
doing the nothing he could do
up north he'll make it
a career

Six.
for Halloween I washed my
face and wore my
school clothes   went door to
door as a nightmare.

Eight.
at night dad builds a fire feeds it with my clippings
castro on parade   why does my penis stick out more than most
he stares at the rug where embers fall
lose some weight it'll go
back in

Excerpt from *Winter in the Blood*

JAMES WELCH

I awoke the next morning with a hangover. I had slept fitfully, pursued by the ghosts of the night before and nights past. There were the wanted men with ape faces, cuffed sleeves and blue hands. They did not look directly into my eyes but at my mouth, which was dry and hollow of words. They seemed on the verge of performing an operation. Suddenly a girl loomed before my face, slit and gutted like a fat rainbow, and begged me to turn her loose, and I found my own guts spilling from my monstrous mouth. Teresa hung upside down from a wanted man's belt, now my own belt, crying out a series of strange warnings to the man who had torn up his airplane ticket and who was now rolling in the manure of the corral, from time to time washing his great pecker in a tub of water. The gutted rainbow turned into the barmaid of last night screaming under the hands of the leering wanted men. Teresa raged at me in several voices, her tongue clicking against the roof of her mouth. The men in suits were feeling her, commenting on the texture of her breasts and the width of her hips. They spread her legs wider and wider until Amos waddled out, his feathers wet and shining, one orange leg cocked at the knee, and suddenly lifted, in a flash of white stunted wing, up and through a dull sun. The wanted men fell on the gutted rainbow and second suit clicked pictures of a woman beside a reservoir in brown light.

I climbed with Teresa's voice still in my head. Although the words were not clear, they were accompanied by another image, that of a boy on horseback racing down a long hill, yelling and banging his hat against his thigh. Strung out before him, a herd of cattle, some tumbling, some flying, all laughing. The boy was bundled up against a high wind.

I didn't know whether I was asleep or awake during this last scene, but the boy changed quickly into a pale ceiling. The room was stuffy and smelled of liquor. Sun streamed through the white curtains of a tall, narrow window. The curtains were hung about a foot below the top of the window and through this space I could see sky, without depth, as though the window itself were painted a flat blue.

I swung my legs over the edge of the bed, sat up and waited for my head to ache. A quick numbing throb made my eyes water, followed by a wild pounding that seemed to drive my head down between my shoulders. I closed my eyes, opened them, then closed them again—I couldn't make up my mind whether to let the room in on my suffering or keep it to myself. I sat for what seemed like two or three nauseating hours until an overpowering thirst drove me to the sink. I drank a long sucking bellyful of water from the tap, my head pounding fiercely until I straightened up and wiped my mouth. I gripped the sink and waited. Gradually the pounding lessened and I was able to open my eyes again. I stared at my face. It didn't look too bad—a little puffy, pale but life-like. I soaked one of the towels in cold water and washed up. My pants were knotted down around my ankles. One shoe and one white sock stuck out beneath them. Above them, the vertical scars flanking my left kneecap and the larger bone-white slash running diagonally across the top. Keeping my head up, I reached down and slowly pulled up my pants.

Ah, there was the clean shirt—but then I remembered I had left my paper bag of possessions at Minough's. And I had helped roll the big red-headed cowboy. He was probably out looking for me right now. I wondered if he could recognize me or if he had been too drunk. No, he couldn't, I decided; he was passed out after all. But somebody at the bar might have described me or given him my name. I couldn't remember if anybody had been in the bar. Of course—the bartender. How could I explain that I had come to Malta only to find a girl who had stolen from me, and that it was only an odd circumstance that led me to steal from him, or at least try? No, he would not understand. The girl, the one item we had in common, would lead to my downfall sure as hell . . .

I cursed Dougie and his sister for bringing me to such a sorry pass, and I cursed the white man for being such a fool and my hotel room for being such a tiny sanctuary on a great earth of stalking white men. I cursed the loss of my possessions, for my teeth were mossy and my shirt lay wrinkled and stained across the sunlit bedspread.

A corner of the bed had been turned down. I must have tried to get into it before passing out. The sheets looked so clean and cool, so white, that I thought about taking off my clothes and slipping down between them. But it was too late, the sun too high.

I wet my hair and combed it with my fingers. Then I slipped my Levi jacket on over my T-shirt—the shirt was awful, I must have vomited—and left the room, walking down the hall first to the toilet, then to the carpeted stairs. The desk clerk didn't look up. A group of old men sat on the orange-vinyl couches in the lobby. Two of them leaned forward on their canes, while the rest repeated the sagging curves of the furniture. They were watching baseball on the television. I walked quickly by them and out into the sunshine. A woman said excuse me.

28.

JEROME SALA

The years I worked in corporate life, the air
Within the labyrinth was underscored
With a low buzz. Perhaps this was the AC
Or heat, depending on the season. Or maybe

The whisper of lights, computers, or the many tiny
Machines that ran all day and night: the breathing
Of technology. But now that I'm "packaged out,"
At home, sitting at my table, the freelance starting

To roll in, you'd think that sound would be gone.
But windows open or closed, it's here with me still.
I hear its neutral moan in back of car horns, bus growl,
The squeal of drills in the building as it's repaired:

I heard it when I was young, on the way to the factory:
Like morning anxiety, it's something that follows me.

An Obituary

JOE PROULX

Bar closed, depraved cokehead's apartment, another night, another bro desperate to finish the conversation we'd started. No problem, because he's hot and, whether it's my story or my attention he's after, I'm happy to be a good boy. My star anecdote: I was in Iraq, illegally, during the weeks leading to 9/11.

I just can't believe you were there, he says, flipping a Springsteen record.

I pull a bloody dollar from my nose. I find his eyes, look into them, and hold them while I reach down to the bulge in my jeans. Squeezing an outline of my cock like a dog toy, I playfully release his gaze, and watch his smile turn to scrutiny as he sees I'm playing with myself. Momentarily ashamed, I detour back, Iraq, I say, it's actually really hard for me to talk about it. Like the sub that even a whiff of my war story has made him, he quickly assures me we don't have to. I just—it's so crazy, he says. I can't believe you went there. Were there other Americans? He rips a line off the table, and hands the dollar back to me. His eyes say, let's do all this coke tonight, and then, at dawn, maybe I'll let you suck my cock.

In a rare occurrence, The Washington Post had published a story with a somewhat sentimental human twist on what was the typical wartime scene of carnage. In an unimportant village, with few people, few sheep, too hot, with a ground too hard and nothing of value to speak of, a mother and father seek shelter from the sun in their tiny mud hut, mourning their dead twelve-year-old boy, Omar. The way in which I'd managed to take the plight of the Iraqi People personally had me imagining them in negation to the American Master Narrative: I believed they possessed a pure virtue, a kind of magical innocence. As it turns out, the real Iraq is filled with horny teenagers wearing bootleg Titanic Tee's with Leo's face airbrushed on the front. Most Iraqi children enjoy Hollywood exports and American made pop music. The most we learn from the Post, though, is that Omar was a "happy boy," killed by a cluster bomb when two young American soldiers flew over his village, playing a game to see the effect of their weapons on sheep. Omar was skipping home from school on his last day before the summer break when a deafening explosion cracked across the silent land. Shrapnel flew in every direction. Four shepherds were wounded. And Omar, the others recalled, lay dead in the dirt, most of his head torn off, the white of his robe stained red. I had told this story to leftist churches, to activists at anti-war events, to college humanities classes, and to small local papers over the course of the spring of 2001. The tour set up by The Campaign to End Sanctions Against Iraq was being called The Remembering Omar Bus Tour. Tasked with coordinating veterans of the Iraq war, foreign policy experts, Jesuit priests, and delegates of our campaign who had witnessed the effect of sanctions firsthand, I rode in a school bus across the US, capitalizing on Omar's story in an attempt to bring the reality of war to curious American citizens.

The apparently straight stranger who's invited me back to his apartment reminds me his name is Josh. I wonder about Josh's sex—is it skinny like he is? Often, bodies like his have sacrificed all their muscle for a girthy nine-inch cock. He smells like Old Spice Sport Stick and cigarettes—like high school. I want to sniff his ass.

The result of the tour was clipped newspaper articles and testimonies I had personally collected, for posterity laminated, and archived in a black plastic binder from Office Depot. The tour was, as it turned out, all part of a vetting process I was to undergo before I was able to receive a visa by way of the Iraqi Foreign Minister, Tariq Aziz. Until this moment of my life, I was by all standards a failure. The fact that I would be part of something that required vetting at all, and that I was one degree of separation from the Foreign Minister of the world's scariest nation felt altogether presidential. At some point, it was decided by someone in our campaign that we should go to Omar's village, that I would bring that black binder from Office Depot and show his family that their son's death was not just in vain. Throughout this experiment, I had been drafting a sort of coming of age story for myself in the form of an obituary for a boy I'd never met, an obituary I could only finish by meeting the family and friends who survived him. And in the months leading up to crossing the Jordan-Iraq border, I imagined that meeting again and again, daydreaming of being a folk hero. What a gift it would be—showing them what I had done for their son, for the people of Iraq.

It had only been a few months after Omar was killed. What we were even doing in that village is now a mystery to me. I don't know whose idea it was, I say, searching Josh's ashtray for a smokable butt. I have more, he tells me, jumping up to his desk and grabbing a fresh pack of Camel Filters. I lick the film in my mouth onto my lips and ask for a glass of water. Of course, he says. He brings one, sits closer to me, and spreads his legs so that our knees are touching. I search his pants for movement, imagining the way the muscles in his legs will tighten and retract in the moonlight, as he walks from the light switch to the bed in his briefs. You asked me why I wasn't afraid? Solidarity, I say, an unfinished gulp of water running out the sides of my mouth like an invalid. We were all going through it together. Me and the others on the campaign, we were being tracked and recorded by the FBI or the CIA or whatever. Our phones were tapped, and we'd hear the wires cross and voices in the background, sometimes Arabic. I help myself to another one of Josh's cigarettes. You know what I'm just remembering? A week before we left for Iraq, we'd got a report from an ally close to someone in the British Intelligence. They said a bombing campaign was imminent. I remember, because we sat in a circle and we discussed cancelling the trip. I was twenty years old, and the others twenty-five or something, I said, let's go, and we went.

After we arrived in Baghdad and changed our dollars to dinars, we met our minder for breakfast to go over the itinerary. Saad, minder and reluctant Baathist, was less than eager to promise a trip to Omar's village. What happened in his village, he told us, has become a normal event in the Iraqi countryside. Folding and unfolding his hands, bringing his eyes down to the table, he insists without specifying, Toq al-Ghazali is not safe for you. I had barely spoken a word since I was woken in the middle of the night by our driver to travel twelve hours across the border. Instead, I watched those with more experience than me navigate my every move, from my position riding bitch in the SUV to being made to wait in the lobby of the Karameh Border Cross to watch Looney Toons on a staticky TV, while my colleagues bribed the guards. I was increasingly feeling more important than I was being treated. More responsible for and specifically invited because of my contribution to the Omar campaign, I sat up straight, re-introduced myself, pulled the binder from my bag, and slid it across the Formica table to Saad. The friendly faced minder opened it, smiled, and gave the pages a quick glance before handing it back to me.

After the initial meeting with Saad, the senior members of our delegation and I retired to our hotel rooms. I took another Valium, closed the binder, and pushed it aside, I became flush with anger—*I've been brushed off*, I began to prattle under my breath, *he doesn't speak to me with respect and candor the way he addresses the others. It's not fair. I was the one to give three months of my life to this tour. I was the one Remembering Omar.*

In Baghdad, in the days to come, I saw the aftermath of the Amiriyah Shelter bombing, where two US cruise missiles were dropped through the roof of a bomb shelter, blowing up the water heater in a basement where hundreds of children were seeking cover. The children drowned to death in boiling water, their silhouettes frozen on the walls from the heat of the initial impact, their flesh and eyeballs stuck to the cement forever. My colleagues and I toured what were once some of the world's leading hospitals, hospitals which had been transformed into hovels of hospice—not by accident, as collateral damage or due to lack of national export, but by calculated efforts on the part of the Clinton administration, whose bombs were targeting public hospitals, sewage treatment plants, and water filtration systems—policy meant, in the words of Clinton's secretary of Defense, to accelerate the effect of sanctions. As a result, children were dying of waterborne illnesses, illnesses, the doctors, who to my surprise chain smoked in the cancer ward, told us, were previously unheard of in their Iraq, that would have been easily preventable had the sanctions not prohibited life-saving medicines from entering the country. These doctors we met, trained at the best medical schools from around the world, had been reduced to the watchmen of dying children. One of the more pleasant activities scheduled for us: a trip to the souk, where celebrated academics forced into squalor sold their beloved book collections for money to feed their families. I rarely feel confident with the money I've saved for trips, but the two hundred dollars I had been given was changed to suitcases full of large banknotes. I walked away with a stack of vintage interview magazines (the perks of being a secular government), and a copy of Hegel's *Phenomenology of the Spirit* and its supplement reader. I paid the asking price and not a penny more, and at that price I can afford not to read them. I stopped at a gallery on my way back to the hotel and bought three paintings, and when I was finished, I still had enough of the pretty pink and purple dinar with Saddam's face on them left to give as souvenirs to friends back home for years to come.

I want one! Josh stands, flashing me his abs nonchalantly. My only regret, I say, is not saving any for myself, Saddam's face has got to be worth something now.

The morning of our trip to Omar's village we met Saad for breakfast, okra stewed in canned tomato juice, the tenth meal just like it since we'd arrived, apparently a delicacy when the only thing most had to eat were the dregs of America's Oil for Food Program. We sat at our regular table in the hotel's dining room. With floor to ceiling picture windows, there were great views of the child hustlers in the street. Flush alongside the table was the cage of one of the mascots of The Al Fanar: a mischievous white and brown vervet monkey called Coffee (the other house pet was a parrot that greets guests by mimicking the sound of a missile falling). Coffee was sound asleep, his eyes twitching as he dreamt, perhaps of his native land, or some real food. I was sick to my stomach, hung over from an endless amount of valium I'd bought over the counter in Amman and the "whiskey" the UNICEF employee had illegally procured for me the night before. As I pushed away my plate of red stew, Saad, our gold-watched and sympathetic character with the unfortunate prosperity of being a member of the Baathist regime, sprung on us a twist in our itinerary: *a quick stop with the Iraqi Women's Society before the meeting with Omar's family*. Kenneth, a seasoned delegate of our campaign with close to ten trips to Iraq under his belt, buried his face in his hands, mumbling, Saddam Hussein in an abaya. At that, Coffee woke up startled, leaped up from the bottom of his cage, clung to the bars, and let out an incredulous howl. The rest of us, pathologically codependent, constantly competing for the power of least confused, canvas each other's expressions for a shared ignorance. Finally, since the minders are the only ones with coordinates to Omar's village, Kenneth resigns us to taking the meeting with the Iraqi Women's Society.

The Iraqi Women's Society is a mud hut. Inside it, a room lined with a border of folding chairs. As promised, the women enter in full black abaya. I find myself looking to see what footwear a woman of the Iraqi Women's Society wears. They sit, filling all but the chairs left for our delegation, our two minders, our translator, and our drivers. Tea is served in shot glasses, as always, too sweet. I searched for Saddam in the eyes of the women—Kenneth's joke, transformed into a very real fear as we sat sandwiched between two towering portraits of Him. The Iraqi Women's Society were now insisting we travel with armed guards to the Shia village. But Kenneth insists through our translators, We are pacifists, we're fully aware of the danger, and willing to risk our safety to enter the village as friends. Eventually though, the women get their way.

A one-hundred-and-thirty-degree wind outside our speeding SUV scorched my face, as a muscle memory rolls down the tinted window for relief from the heat inside. I twist my neck to see the cavalcade following us, snaking the dirt road behind. Guns protrude from dust and black abaya as the fiery wind passed over the procession of Jeeps.

The children drowned to death in boiling water, their silhouettes frozen on the walls from the heat of the initial impact, their flesh and eyeballs stuck to the cement forever, I nod over my host's guilty pleasure, Katy Perry, playing at full volume. Masterful, from a music theory perspective, Josh explains to me. In Basra, I visited the children's unit of a bombed-out hospital where infants were born with deformities caused by Depleted Uranium. What kind of Uranium? he asks, stopping me a moment so that I can listen to the bridge of Katy's "Firework." Do you have more coke? I ask him. Of course, he says. I went to a Sufi mosque, I say.

The months leading up to the Remembering Omar Bus Tour, I lived in a basement, in a room made of sheets that hung from the water pipes along the ceiling, snorting heroin. I would leave my stupid job, rush home to my cozy chair, unfold the tinfoil, cut a few bumps, lay back, and let the oceanic blanket envelop me. The feeling of heroin is ineffable, like God. I'd only had to read the first few pages of *Civilization and its Discontents* to know Freud describes this oceanic feeling of oneness that we attribute to God as a memory of infancy, as a narcissistic expression of one's self. I'm minutes from nodding off into my oneness when the phone rings. We're looking for someone to coordinate the bus tour from the road, it's someone calling from the campaign headquarters, a three-bedroom apartment on the second floor of an old bungalow in Uptown. You'll be gone for three months at least, they tell me, and you will have a lot of responsibilities—including ensuring that people coming and going off the tour arrive safely and get to their speaking events. If you're successful, and you feel ready, we're discussing a delegation to leave in August. There is an opening. We believe in you. Come to the office tomorrow to discuss details.

Our armed caravan turned the last corner around a copse of palm trees when I realized I'd forgotten the binder. *Our proof*—our only reason for being there. The documentation of labor, culminating in pages and pages of testimonies from concerned and well-intentioned Americans, trying to grieve with the family we were moments from meeting, was sitting on the bed in my hotel room back in Baghdad. As the dust kicked up from our motorcade settled, we began to make out the stone-cold faces of the villagers waiting to receive us. I turn to Kenneth and tell him what I've done. At the hotel, I say. I thought I had it, I'm sorry. Kenneth is angry but kind, indulging me with pity as he now has the added responsibility of keeping me calm in front of our hosts. Everyone is already exiting the SUVs, rushing to see the poor Iraqis, and Kenneth is quickly corralled by our minders to begin introductions. What they had been told of our visit beforehand will forever remain a mystery to me. But it was clear by the way they waited that they'd known we were coming, lined up in a kind of formation—Omar's father in the foreground, behind him what looked like a slaughter block, possibly where they chop the sheep, behind that, the boy's brothers, his friends, and their fathers, and behind them the women, all covered but their eyes, leaning from windows of their mud huts. My hangover, the Valium, and whatever feeling of safety, along with that deeply secured sense of self-importance from being an American—something at the very core of my being that, until having traveled to the Arab World, I hadn't known I'd possessed—were being burned off right then and there by the sweltering feverish sky. Moves were made and words exchanged in Arabic. To assuage our feelings of discomfort, the villagers were being compelled to enact our fantasies of gratitude—first by the minders, then the Women's Society, and lastly by the men accompanying us with assault rifles. The minders and translators conspired, attempting an explanation of who we were, and why we were there. But any effort to explain us simply unmasked our Americanness like a villain in Scooby Doo. They have come all this way to see you, someone from the hired part of our gang asserted to Omar's father. The old man was the village patriarch, a man who had spent his life in the fields of their village cultivating tufts of vegetation from the hard desert earth, to feed his sheep, the sheep which had been torn apart by very same shrapnel of the same American made cluster bomb that had ripped the face off of Omar's body. My tight fists squeezed the sweat from my palms as it vaporized under the August sun, and I was becoming dizzy. The whole time we'd been there, Omar's father had stood silently, looking down at his feet. Finally, he looked up, stepped forward, his face twisted, and looking at each one of us directly in our eyes, he began to speak. If I—or any one of these men behind me—could fly a plane above America, and take the lives of your peoples' children, we would do it at once.

Should we lay down? I ask Josh, licking the inside of the bag. At this point in the night his pale face is full of color from the booze, faking an aliveness. Are you tired? he asks, running his fingers through the sweat that has fixed his hair back wet on his head, then over the residue on the table, then licking the table when he thinks I'm not looking. Getting there, I lie. You can stay in my room if you want, he tells me, shrugging his broad shoulders. It's too bright out here when the sun comes up, he says. I say Ok, feigning a reluctance. I walk to his room and pull my shirt over my head. Pants or no pants? I ask, dropping my jeans to my ankles and stepping out of them, climbing onto a sheetless mattress surrounded by empties. I came out in Baghdad, I tell him, in almost a whisper. His room is hot, and a box fan is grinding dead New York August air over my head. You did what? he asks, pulling his shirt over his shoulders, undoing his belt and dropping his dickies.

I came out, I say. Admitted I was gay. I roll to my side and watch the way the muscles in his legs tighten and retract in the moonlight, as he walks from the light switch to the bed in his briefs. It seemed, I guess, no big deal, considering. I said it anecdotally, to Kenneth, outside the Hotel Palestine in Baghdad. It was during a wedding ceremony. There was this big crowd. Everyone was dressed up, dancing and laughing. The women were ululating, Kenneth and I were covered in confetti. I can feel the stranger's hand hesitate as it moves across the mattress. I can smell his stale breath inches from my neck. The bombing, I say. The bombing campaign I told you they'd warned us about. It missed us. The day we arrived in Amman after leaving Iraq—the US and the UK led a joint bombing campaign and annihilated a suburb of Baghdad. I saw it on TV at a café in Amman. I can't believe you came out in Baghdad, the stranger says, smiling from the dark outer edge of the mattress.

I said, I'm gay, I tell him. It felt small. I just said it like he was supposed to know. Strangely, the shock of how similar I felt after saying it felt more shocking than having had finally said it. I don't know, I thought, I guess I thought that . . . I slide my hand over his stomach . . . I'd been promised like . . . an irrevocable change.

Stop

JOAN LARKIN

I hate it when you
fill my glass up
without asking me.

I always liked
a little
on a plate
in a cup

an egg
with space around it
an orange
with a knife
next to it

a cup
with space above
the coffee

discrete colors
orange   pewter   black

the porcelain glaze on the china
the blue napkin.

I want to keep things
separate.   I hate it
when you break my egg.
I hate when you salt things
when you assume
I want cream

The Merry Widow and The Rubber Husband (or How I Caught HIV: Version 4; Fall 1983)

JOE WESTMORELAND

That night it was just going to be Ali, Kat, and me getting high. We were celebrating Kat's recent move from New Orleans to San Francisco to try to break into the music business. She was staying on the back porch/tiny guest room. She'd cut her hair short and bleached it blonde. James and Felipe came home and wanted to join us so we had to go get more dope before we could get started. The five of us piled into Ali's VW and went out and scored.

Back home, my little cafe table next to my bed was the best place in our entire apartment to shoot dope. It was cozy and out of the way. In my dresser drawer I kept candles, a bent spoon, some cotton, and my syringe. Ali, Felipe, James, and I had to share the same needle. Ali used to be able to buy U-100 insulin syringes at the Star Pharmacy in the Castro until they started asking him to show ID proving he was diabetic. Kat brought her own syringe. My syringe had only been used once so it was still kind of sharp. And besides, we always sterilized our needles with rubbing alcohol and ran them through the candle flame to burn off any germs. The main thing we had to be concerned about was accidentally squirting blood back into the glass of water when we were doing the syringe wash. That's when we'd draw water into the syringe after we shot up and squirt it into our mouths to be sure to get every last drop. Ali always made a mystical ceremony out of fixing the drug and shooting it up. I just wanted to get high, but we let Ali do it his way. It was our family ritual with him as the high priest.

Kat had tiny veins and had to dig around a lot with her needle to find a good one. She was getting kind of messy, with blood running down her arm, so finally Ali and I took over. We were both good at shooting other people up. They called me "Dr. Joe." It's just that I would never push the plunger into myself. I didn't have a problem pushing it in for other people, but for myself I'd insert the needle in my vein and then have someone else, usually Ali, pull the plunger out slightly then push it in. I figured that way I'd never become a junky because I wasn't good at shooting myself up.

By this time, there were frightening articles about the horrors of AIDS every week in the gay newspapers. The *B.A.R.* started to run an obituary column. I saw the guy who'd poured beer down my chest in it one week. The article said he was survived by his partner of seven years and their dog. We were also beginning to hear more rumors of guys committing suicide when they found out they had it. Every time any of us caught the flu we were sure that the end had come. When I was helping Felipe do his shot we looked at each other like this was really crazy, like we both knew that this was serious business. We were playing for keeps. But the look didn't last too long and we didn't stop what we were doing.

Felipe said, "Well, I guess we really are blood brothers now. If one of us gets it then the others will, too."

Ali said, "You know what? Being blood brothers is a good thing. It's spiritual, like an American Indian tribal ritual."

James asked, "What if one of us really does get sick? Would we all get sick?"

It still seemed unfathomable. We weren't the type of guys that were getting sick. Most of them were older than us. They were the ones that sat in sex club bathtubs all night and had everyone pee on them. Or the ones that went to the baths five nights a week and lay in their cubicles on their stomach waiting for anyone and everyone to fuck them.

Ali said, "Listen, why don't we make a pact that if any of us gets sick with AIDS then the others will stockpile heroin and provide enough for the sick one to overdose if we want so we won't have to suffer a horrible death?"

That sounded like a good idea but it was hard to comprehend. No one said yes or no to him. We just got quiet. I watched as a thin trail of black smoke rose from the long flame of the small white candle in the middle of the table. I stared at the blue Star of David on the box of candles. Rokeach Sabbath candles. Sabbath. That word stuck in my head. My mind started to wander, thinking about stockpiling heroin. James wiped off the top of the cafe table with a cotton swab and rubbing alcohol. My room started to smell like a doctor's office so I got up and lit a stick of orange blossom incense.

Ali snapped me back to the conversation when I heard him say, "I've suffered enough in this life and I don't want to have a horrible painful death."

We all nodded in agreement.

"Besides, there's nothing wrong with ending your life if you know there's no hope," he added.

"There's always hope," Felipe said.

"No there isn't," Ali said. "What about the children of the Cambodian boat people who watched as their fathers were forced by pirates to jump into the boat's propellors, then saw their mothers get thrown overboard, then were left by themselves to drift in the sea without food or water?"

I said, "Hope or no hope, when I'm dying I don't want to be in pain. I want it to be over as soon as possible. I just want everyone to be sure that I'm really dying."

James mumbled thoughtfully, "Yeah, me too."

Instead of asking if we wanted to, Ali announced that from now on we had an official pact. We would help each other end it all in a peaceful way.

Kat lifted up her head from digging around in her purse and said, "You guys, quit being so morbid. Just hurry up and finish fixing the stuff."

We all got sufficiently high and were lying around on my bed, nodding out and snuggling close to each other. My red handwoven Indian blanket glowed in the soft light from the lamp on my table. It was one of those special nights where we were all psychically bonded. Warm love flowed through my bedroom. I tuned my Fifties' grey Bakelight plastic AM radio onto the easy listening station. It was silly but fit the mood exactly. Relaxing. Mellow. I stared up on my wall at the big Talking Heads in Paris poster that Michel had given me. I noticed the background grid of the poster matched my grey and white checked curtains that I'd made myself. Well, really all I did was sew a hem at the top and bottom by hand.

After a while, James and Felipe went off to their bedrooms. Ali pulled out another small bundle of dope that he'd stashed away and he, Kat, and I each did a shot. Then we had a three-way. It started when Kat wanted to show us her extra-large clitoris. It was half the size of my small finger. Ali started sucking on it, then she told me to suck on it, which I did. She told me where to lick to make her feel good and I followed directions. We all made out, rolling around on the bed while we peeled off each other's clothes. Kat had large breasts, a small waist, and wide hips, an "hour glass figure." She loved it when I'd rub her tits, not too rough though. Ali was better at that than I was. He and I both sucked on her nipples at the same time while we felt each other up and intertwined our legs. Ali took my hand and guided a finger inside her. He and I both had our index fingers up in her soft wet fleshiness at the same time while we were sucking her tits. Ali moved up and put his dick between her tits and humped back and forth. I'd try to catch the head of his dick in my mouth as it poked out between her cleavage. I mostly just got a good lick in occasionally. While she was on all fours getting it from behind by Ali, I put on her Merry Widow corset, got off the bed, and psychedelic free-danced in front of them. Kat pulled me over and sucked on me. Ali and I watched each other for a while then leaned over Kat and started kissing while I was getting sucked and he was still inside her. Kat wanted us to fuck her at the same time, me in the front and Ali in the back, but both of us kept losing our hard-ons, mostly from the heroin. I was semi- to two-thirds erect most of the time, except when Ali fucked me while I was fucking Kat. That felt good. I just wished he was bigger and she was smaller.

The three of us were lying side-by-side next to each other, jerking each other off when Ali started shaking and got the chills. We were a little worried about him but didn't know what to do. I took off the Merry Widow, sat up and felt his forehead. It was hot even though he was shivering.

Kat said, "I think he might have 'cotton fever'."

"What's that?" I asked.

Ali said through chattering teeth, "That's when your dope cotton is too dirty and you get an infection."

My dick shriveled with that bit of information.

Ali said, "I think I'd better go lie down with James since there's more room in his bed. Wow, you guys, sorry for ruining our fun time."

Kat said, "Hey listen, this is more important. You take care of yourself."

I nodded my head in agreement and gave him a loving smile.

After he left Kat started making out with me again. She said she wished she could fuck me. I said you can, kind of. She asked what I meant and I told her about the Rubber Husband. It was a dildo that we kept under the towels in the bathroom closet. Anyone in the apartment could use it as long as they cleaned it off afterwards. Kat got all excited and sent me to the bathroom for it. When I brought it back she'd put her Merry Widow back on and was ready. We lubed it up with some baby oil, I lay on my back, and then she put it part of the way in me. It felt good. I immediately got hard.

She started slowly rocking back and forth saying stuff like, "Do you like that Joe? Do you like getting fucked by a woman? Do you like me fucking you?"

Well, of course I couldn't deny it. It felt great. She rubbed baby oil on my dick and started jerking me off at the same time. She didn't have quite the right stroke for me, so I took over and soon I was coming all over my stomach. She climbed on top of me and started to rub her crotch on my stomach as she fingered herself. Then she rolled over onto the bed on her stomach with her hands in her crotch and humped for a little while. She started to shake a little, then sighed, then a deep long moan, another sigh, another shake, and then she collapsed. A few minutes later we kissed and hugged and then started laughing.

Kat smiled to herself and said softly, "I've finally had a dream come true. I got to fuck a man."

Once we'd calmed down we tip-toed into James' room to see how Ali was. They were both snoring so we figured he must be okay. In the morning James and Felipe wanted to know all the details of what exactly happened after they went to bed. They said it must of been good since we'd done Ali in like that.

The Copyists

JOCELYN SAIDENBERG

Hardship revealed the path. I entered blindly, will-lessly, treading recursively, hardly steadfast, with hesitating steps. Dead Branch to Wall Street, a shallow, middle way, while lost in perplexity and intricated with an unclear object, and in my complicated parts involuted, all bewildering all objects. Hunger was there, and so was weariness and remainder, that refuse, my not unfamiliar companions who marked my passive journey outside. My unthinkable volition accrued from where I began and where then I end.

I arrived upon answering an advertisement, motionless one morning at the open door of an attorney's chamber, at this threshold, in summer.

Pallidly I stood awaiting notice, neat, respectable, incurably forlorn, there as he found me, my summoned object as if unthought, unthinkable at first he liked me, my almost singularity, pitiably sedate, as compared with the others, flighty and fiery.

And I was hungry for copy, a silverfish gorging on glue and pulp, I craved to scrive, having deciphered, consumed, interpreted, burned what had already been written, useless and unintended for my receipt, at last, and irrevocably, I was to author, if not my own, a copy of others, if necessary. My hand steady, my ink sea ever before me, rhythmic waves of script along my ruled lines, scribing copies, doubles, triples, quadruples, the law of my letters of what law would recall, bequeathing, dictating, deeds and documents afloat and strewn with my letterings.

* * *

I wrote on industriously, cheerlessly, and within a silence the letters echoed back. No pause for digestion, a self-consumer of the law in letters in lines. Mechanically I moved my pen across the page, burning inevitable letters.

What was this law whose hand I lettered?

What law recalls the letters for whom to receive the law? Neatly and pallidly penned, my hand reaching and withdrawing, wavering over the vast pages to which I was the author, too.

At least at first.

Ravenous to express myself in a language alien to all other languages to speak the weather of strangeness under the weight of that, for my melancholy refuses naming, a dirge that feeds on lament—that endless debt.

There I was shelved, suspended in abeyance, passively docile, between the figures: first, Turkey; second, Nippers; and third, Ginger Nut. Names the likes of which are not usually found in the Directory, mutually conferred and expressive of their person or character.

Turkey was short, and English, not far from 60 in age, pursy. In the morning he was a fine florid hue, after noon ablazing, and blazing on without waning, until 6 when he left and no more was seen of Turkey. Turkey whose face gained its meridian with the sun, and seemed to set with it, to rise, culminate, and decline, with undiminished glory and continually. After the noon meridian, Turkey authored blots, a copyist altogether too energetic—a strange, inflamed, flurried, flighty recklessness.

Turkey's body so uncontrolled in its motions and reckless scattering his sand-boxes, splitting his just mended pens, flaming with augmented illuminations, being ever so rash in tongue.

In short
he was
incautious
noisy
spilling
a racket
impatient
boxing his papers about
undecorous in manner
rash and insolent
yet before noon, the quickest, steadiest creature, a style not to be matched easily, civilest, blandest, ever reverential.

Pulsating in the law office of the endangered, of bodies, of unbalanced motion, either too fast or too slow, of activities who negate their outcomes, result in unthoughts, or unwanted evidence, lawless. A pulsing circularity, revolving, into whose cross currents, I floated. I appeared as they found me among these who erased all they wrote wantonly, heedless and fiery, rash and oratic, impatient, methodically arranging the office of derangements, morning through afternoon, smudges, peevish blots, thwarting objects, unreadable and eaten raw. Save for Ginger Nut, who neither vexing nor thwarting, both the shell and its seed.

Was it madness was mad because it cannot write or because the writing itself horrifies the one writing?

Nippers, the second, a sallow, whiskered pirate, young, the victim of two evil powers: ambition and indigestion. His impatient and nervous testiness proved grinning irritation, hissing rather than speaking, and especially discontent with the height of his worktable.

Though of a very ingenious mechanical turn, Nippers could never get his table to suit him. He put chips under it, blocks of various sorts, pasteboard, and at last went so far as to attempt an exquisite adjustment by final pieces of folded blotting paper. But no invention would answer.

* * *

For if he wanted anything it was to be rid of the copyist's table altogether. Nippers and Nippers's body so blocked in circulation, sores and pains, lacking all design, delirious in his body, for his writing pains his writing body, for writing assumes its own body, only by consuming the body of the body, an erasing textual cannibal.

What love could find our bearing there, be borne? What love could think or write the relation of this, that inside to this outside, this outside to that inside, the openfield of a body whose interior sails off into an other inside. These spaces, the offices, the tombs, the dead letter branch, all opening to that dense beyond. Among the ferns, the moss, the rotting maples. In this I too see shadows, think shadows or the cloud that is the possible of weather of all shadows. What love could reach this night of bodies? When shadows are all. For it is shadow through which I speak, through which I love, among these confounding bodies, blocked erasing burning.

My office mates haunt these chambers, clad among, with their rebellion against writing. And yet, is this not why the attorney pays us? For both Nippers and Turkey, who make the words say what they can't, ingest their own bodies, destroy their tools, tables, pens, with their undigestible grief and unaccounted bodies. For this ginger is the heart of this very brain, and this heart eats as it is this brain. Ravenous. Relenting.

Addicted to what haunts. That motionless sustenance, remedy to singularity.

Word by word I went, copying titles, recondite documents, deeds, until, word by word silently, mechanically, palely, I could copy no more, nor as weather, nor as shadow, nor as cloud.

I stopped. I would not. I not.

Catullus Tells Me Not to Write the Rant Against the Poem "Good Bones" by Maggie Smith

THE CYBORG JILLIAN WEISE

You don't like the poem. So what?
Why are you clicking on her, following her?

I know, I know. The metaphor sucks. So let's
get drunk. Score some poppers. Act like horses.

Call up Alec. Who is he to deprive me
of the local geraniums? Just because

he owns a thrift store. I got thrift and I got
stored in the libraries. I am checked out.

That poem is boring. It's the same poem
ya'll been writing in your centuries. Someone

gets sad, buys a house, has children, politics
and little birdies. Throw some ableism

in and publish it. Here's a poem for you.
Ignatius had a beard and I fucked him.

Selections from *The Hotel Wentley Poems*

JOHN WIENERS

A poem for record players

The scene changes

Five hours later and
I come into a room
where a clock ticks.
I find a pillow to
muffle the sounds I make.
I am engaged in taking away
from God his sound.
The pigeons somewhere
above me, the cough
a man makes down the hall,
the flap of wings
below me, the squeak
of sparrows in the alley.
The scratches I itch
on my scalp, the landing
of birds under the bay
window out my window.
All dull details
I can only describe to you,

but which are here and
I hear and shall never
give up again, shall carry
with me over the streets
of this seacoast city,
forever; oh clack your
metal wings, god, you are
mine now in the morning.
I have you by the ears
in the exhaust pipes of
a thousand cars gunning
their motors turning over
all over town.

6.15.58

A poem for Painters

Our age bereft of nobility
How can our faces show it?
I look for love.
My lips stand out
dry and cracked with want
of it.
Oh it is well.
My poem shall show the need for it.

Again we go driven by forces
we have no control over. Only
in the poem
comes an image that we rule
the line by the pen
in the painter's hand one foot
away from me.

Drawing the face
and its torture.
That is why no one dares tackle it.
Held as they are in the hands
of forces they
cannot understand.
That despair
is on my face and shall show
in the fine lines of any man.

I had love once in the palm of my hand.
See the lines there.
How we played
its game, are playing now
in the bounds of white and heartless fields.

Fall down on my head, love,
drench my flesh in the streams
of fine sprays. Like
French perfume
so that I light up as
mountain glorys
and I am showered by the scent
of the finished line.

No circles
but that two parallels do cross
And carry our souls and bodies
together as the planets,
Showing light on the surface
of our skin, knowing
that so much of it flows through
the veins underneath.
Our cheeks puffed with it.
The pockets full.

2.

Pushed on by the incompletion
of what goes before me
I hesitate before this paper
scratching for the right words.

Paul Klee scratched for seven years
on smoked glass, to develop
his line, LaVigne says, look
at his face! he who has spent
all night drawing mine.

The sun also
rises on the rooftops, beginning
w/ violet. I begin in blue
knowing why we are cool.

3.

My middle name is Joseph and I
walk beside an ass on the way to what
Bethlehem, where a new babe is born.

Not the second hand of Yeats but
first prints on a cloudy windowpane.

America, you boil over

4.

The cauldron scalds.
Flesh is scarred.
Eyes shot.

The street aswarm with
vipers and heavy armed bandits.
There are bandages on the wounds
but blood flows unabated. The bath-
rooms are full. Oh stop up
the drains.
We are run over.

5.

Let me ramble here.
yet stay within my own yardlines.
I go out of bounds
without defense,
oh attack.

6.

At last the game is over
and the line lengthens.
Let us stay with what we know.

That love is my strength, that
I am overpowered by it:
                                        desire
                                                  that too
is on the face: gone stale.
When green was the bed my love
and I laid down upon.
Such it is, heart's complaint,
You hear upon a day in June.
And I see no end in view
when summer goes, as it will,
upon the roads, like singing
companions across the land.

Go with it man, if you must,
but leave us markers on your way.

South of Mission, Seattle,
over the Sierra Mountains,
the Middle West and Michigan,
moving east again, easy
coming into Chicago and
the cattle country, calling
to each other over canyons,
careful not to be caught
at night, they are still out,
the destroyers, and down
into the South, familiar land,
lush places, blue mountains
of Carolina, into Black Mountain
and you can sleep out, or
straight across into States

I cannot think of their names.

This nation is so large, like
our hands, our love it lives
with no lover, looking only
for the beloved, back home
into the heart, New York,
New England, Vermont green
mountains, and Massachusetts
my city, Boston and the sea.
Again to smell what this calm
ocean cannot tell us. The seasons.
Only the heart remembers
and records in the words
of works
we lay down for those men
who can come to them.

7.

At last. I come to the last defense.

My poems contain no
wilde beestes, no
lady of the lake music
of the spheres, or organ chants,

yet by these lines
I betray what little given me.

One needs no defense.

Only the score of a man's
struggle to stay with
what is his own, what
lies within him to do.

Without which is nothing,
for him or those who hear him

And I come to this,
knowing the waste, leaving

the rest up to love
and its twisted faces
my hands claw out at
only to draw back from the
blood already running there.

Oh come back, whatever heart
you have left. It is my life
you save. The poem is done.

6.18.58

A poem for early risers

I'm infused with the day
I'm out in it

even tho the day may destroy me.
Placating it. Saving myself

from the demons
who sit in blue
coats, carping
at us across the
tables. Oh they
go out the doors.
I am done with
them. I am
done with faces
I have seen before.

For me now the new.
The unturned tricks
of the trade: the Place
of the heart where man
is afraid to go.

It is not doors. It is
the ground of my soul
where dinosaurs left
their marks. Their tracks
are upon me. They
walk flatfooted.
Leave heavy heels
and turn sour the green
fields where I eat with
ease. It is good to
throw them up. Good
to have my stomach growl.

After all, I am possessed
by wild animals and
long haired men and
women who gallop
breaking over my beloved
places. Oh pull down
thy vanity man the
old man told us under
the tent. You are over-
run with ants.

2.

Man lines up for his
breakfast in the dawn
unaware of the jungle
he has left behind
in his sleep. Where
the fields flourished
with cacti, cauliflower,
all the uneatable foods
that the morning man
perishes, if he remembered.

3.

And yet, we must remember.
The old forest, the wild
screams in the backyard
or cries in the bedroom.
It is ours to nourish.
The nature to nurture.
Dark places where the
woman holds, hands
us, herself handles an
orange ball. Throwing it

up for spring. Like
the clot my grandfather
vomited / months before he
died of cancer. And
spoke of later in terror.

6.20.58

A poem for cocksuckers

Well we can go
in the queer bars w/
our long hair reaching
down to the ground and
we can sing our songs
of love like the black mama
on the juke box, after all
what have we got left.

    On our right the fairies
giggle in their lacquered
voices & blow
smoke in your eyes let them
it's a n[--]'s world
and we retain strength.
The gifts do not desert us,
fountains do not dry
up there are rivers running,
there are mountains
swelling for spring to cascade.

    It is all here between
the powdered legs &
painted eyes of the fairy
friends who do not fail us
  in our hour of
    despair. Take not
away from me the small fires
I burn in the memory of love.

6.20.58

A poem for the old man

God love you
  Dana my lover
lost in the horde
on this Friday night,
500 men are moving up
& down from the bath
room to the bar.
Remove this desire
from the man I love.
Who has opened
  the savagery
of the sea to me.

See to it that
his wants are filled
on California street.
Bestow on him lar-
gesse that allows him
peace in his loins.

Leave him not
to the moths.
Make him out a lion
so that all who see him
hero worship his
thick chest as I did
moving my mouth
over his back bringing
our hearts to heights
I never hike over
  anymore.
Let blond hair burn
on the back of his

neck, let no ache
screw his face
up in pain, his soul
   is so hooked.
Not heroin.
Rather fix these
hundred men as his
lovers & lift him
with the enormous bale
of their desire.

6.20.58

The Cult of the Phoenix

JORGE LUIS BORGES

Translated by Andrew Hurley

Those who write that the cult of the Phoenix had its origin in Heliopolis, and claim that it derives from the religious restoration that followed the death of the reformer Amenhotep IV, cite the writings of Herodotus and Tacitus and the inscriptions on Egyptian monuments, but they are unaware, perhaps willfully unaware, that the cult's designation as "the cult of the Phoenix" can be traced back no farther than to Hrabanus Maurus and that the earliest sources (the *Saturnalia*, say, or Flavius Josephus) speak only of "the People of the Practice" or "the People of the Secret." In the conventicles of Ferrara, Gregorovius observed that mention of the Phoenix was very rare in the spoken language; in Geneva, I have had conversations with artisans who did not understand me when I asked whether they were men of the Phoenix but immediately admitted to being men of the Secret. Unless I am mistaken, much the same might be said about Buddhists: The name by which the world knows them is not the name that they themselves pronounce.

On one altogether too famous page, Moklosich has equated the members of the cult of the Phoenix with the gypsies. In Chile and in Hungary, there are both gypsies and members of the sect; apart from their ubiquity, the two groups have very little in common. Gypsies are horse traders, potmakers, blacksmiths, and fortune-tellers; the members of the cult of the Phoenix are generally contented practitioners of the "liberal professions." Gypsies are of a certain physical type, and speak, or used to speak, a secret language; the members of the cult are indistinguishable from other men, and the proof of this is that they have never been persecuted. Gypsies are picturesque, and often inspire bad poets; ballads, photographs, and boleros fail to mention the members of the cult. . . . Martin Buber says that Jews are essentially sufferers; not all the members of the cult are, and some actively abhor pathos. That public and well-known truth suffices to refute the vulgar error (absurdly defended by Urmann) which sees the roots of the Phoenix lying in Israel. People's reasoning goes more or less this way: Urmann was a sensitive man; Urmann was a Jew; Urmann made a habit of visiting the members of the cult in the Jewish ghettos of Prague; the affinity that Urmann sensed proves a real relationship. In all honesty, I cannot concur with that conclusion. That members of the cult should, in a Jewish milieu, resemble Jews proves nothing; what cannot be denied is that they, like Hazlitt's infinite Shakespeare, resemble every man in the world. They are all things to all men, like the Apostle; a few days ago, Dr. Juan Francisco Amaro, of Paysandú, pondered the ease with which they assimilate, the ease with which they "naturalize" themselves.

I have said that the history of the cult records no persecutions. That is true, but since there is no group of human beings that does not include adherents of the sect of the Phoenix, it is also true that there has been no persecution or severity that the members of the cult have not suffered *and carried out*. In the wars of the Western world and in the distant wars of Asia, their blood has been spilled for centuries, under enemy flags; it is hardly worth their while to identify themselves with every nation on the globe.

Lacking a sacred book to unite them as the Scriptures unite Israel, lacking a common memory, lacking that other memory that is a common language, scattered across the face of the earth, diverse in color and in feature, there is but one thing—the Secret—that unites them, and that *will* unite them until the end of time. Once, in addition to the Secret there was a legend (and perhaps a cosmogonic myth), but the superficial men of the Phoenix have forgotten it, and today all that is left to them is the dim and obscure story of a punishment. A punishment, or a pact, or a privilege—versions differ; but what one may dimly see in all of them is the judgment of a God who promises eternity to a race of beings if its men, generation upon generation, perform a certain ritual. I have compared travelers' reports, I have spoken with patriarchs and theologians; I can attest that the performance of that ritual is the only religious practice observed by the members of the cult. The ritual is, in fact, the Secret. The Secret, as I have said, is transmitted from generation to generation, but tradition forbids a mother from teaching it to her children, as it forbids priests from doing so; initiation into the mystery is the task of the lowest individuals of the group. A slave, a leper, or a beggar plays the role of the mystagogue. A child, too, may catechize another child. The act itself is trivial, the matter of a moment's time, and it needs no description. The materials used are cork, wax, or gum arabic. (In the liturgy there is mention of "slime"; pond slime is often used as well.) There are no temples dedicated expressly to the cult's worship, but ruins, cellars, or entryways are considered appropriate sites. The Secret is sacred, but that does not prevent its being a bit ridiculous; the performance of it is furtive, even clandestine, and its adepts do not speak of it. There are no decent words by which to call it, but it is understood that all words somehow name it, or rather, that they inevitably allude to it—and so I have said some insignificant thing in conversation and have seen adepts smile or grow uncomfortable because they sensed I had touched upon the Secret. In Germanic literatures there are poems written by members of the cult whose nominal subject is the sea or twilight; more than once I have heard people say that these poems are, somehow, symbols of the Secret. *Orbis terrarum est speculum Ludi*, goes an apocryphal saying reported by du Cange in his glossary. A kind of sacred horror keeps some of the faithful from performing that simplest of rituals; they are despised by the other members of the sect, but they despise themselves even more. Those, on the other hand, who deliberately renounce the Practice and achieve direct commerce with the Deity command great respect; such men speak of that commerce using figures from the liturgy, and so we find that John of the Rood wrote as follows:

> Let the Nine Firmaments be told
> That God is delightful as the Cork and Mire.

On three continents I have merited the friendship of many worshipers of the Phoenix; I know that the Secret at first struck them as banal, shameful, vulgar, and (stranger still) unbelievable. They could not bring themselves to admit that their parents had ever stooped to such acts. It is odd that the Secret did not die out long ago; but in spite of the world's vicissitudes, in spite of wars and exoduses, it does, in its full awesomeness, come to all the faithful. Someone has even dared to claim that by now it is instinctive.

A Woman Is Talking to Death

JUDY GRAHN

Once a woman poet begins telling the truth there is no end of possibilities. This poem is as factual as I could possibly make it—literary permission which was granted to me at the time by the work of Pat Parker and Alta in some of their poetry and Sharon Isabell in her striking novel, *Yesterday's Lessons*.

The range of effects it has on other people continually astonishes me. It has made drunken women pound the table protesting having to listen, and mature men break down publicly in tears, temporarily unable to function. It has often made large groups of women feel strong and in agreement. For myself, I have grown considerably more determined by having to live up to the poem's forcefulness as well as its commitments, and other people have expressed similar reactions. Pat Parker, who used it as a model for her stunning and much more specific poem, *Womanslaughter,* understood it before I did. It is odd to think that what we make leads us, rather than the other way around.

One characteristic of workingclass writing is that we often pile up many events within a small amount of space rather than detailing the many implications of one or two events. This means both that our lives are chock full of action and also that we are bursting with stories which haven't been printed, made into novels, dictionaries, philosophies.

The particular challenges of this poem for me were how to discuss the criss-cross oppressions which people use against each other and which continually divide us—and how to define a lesbian life within the context of other people in the world. I did not realize at the time that

I was also taking up the subject of heroes in a modern life which for many people is more like a war than not, or that I would begin a redefinition for myself of the subject of love.

A Woman Is Talking to Death

One

Testimony in trials that never got heard

my lovers teeth are white geese flying above me
my lovers muscles are rope ladders under my hands

we were driving home slow
my lover and I, across the long Bay Bridge,
one February midnight, when midway
over in the far left lane, I saw a strange scene:

one small young man standing by the rail,
and in the lane itself, parked straight across
as if it could stop anything, a large young
man upon a stalled motorcycle, perfectly
relaxed as if he'd stopped at a hamburger stand;
he was wearing a peacoat and levis, and
he had his head back, roaring, you
could almost hear the laugh, it
was so real.

"Look at that fool," I said, "in the
middle of the bridge like that," a very
womanly remark.

Then we hear the meaning of the noise
of metal on a concrete bridge at 50

miles an hour, and the far left lane
filled up with a big car that had a
motorcycle jammed on its front bumper, like
the whole thing would explode, the friction
sparks shot up bright orange for many feet
into the air, and the racket still sets
my teeth on edge.

When the car stopped we stopped parallel
and Wendy headed for the callbox while I
ducked across those 6 lanes like a mouse
in the bowling alley. "Are you hurt?" I said,
the middle-aged driver had the greyest black face,
"I couldn't stop, I couldn't stop, what happened?"

Then I remembered. "Somebody," I said, "was *on*
the motorcycle." I ran back,
one block? two blocks? the space for walking
on the bridge is maybe 18 inches, whoever
engineered this arrogance. in the dark
stiff wind it seemed I would
be pushed over the rail, would fall down
screaming onto the hard surface of
the bay, but I did not, I found the tall young man
who thought he owned the bridge, now lying on
his stomach, head cradled in his broken arm.

He had glasses on, but somewhere he had lost
most of his levis, where were they?
and his shoes. Two short cuts on his buttocks,
that was the only mark except his thin white
seminal tubes were all strung out behind; no
child left *in* him; and he looked asleep.

I plucked wildly at his wrist, then put it
down; there were two long haired women

holding back traffic just behind me
with their bare hands, the machines came
down like mad bulls, I was scared, much
more than usual, I felt easily squished
like the earthworms crawling on a busy
sidewalk after the rain; *I wanted to*
leave. And met the driver, walking back.

"The guy is dead." I gripped his hand,
the wind was going to blow us off the bridge.

"Oh my God," he said, "haven't I had enough
trouble in my life?" He raised his head,
and for a second was enraged and yelling,
at the top of the bridge—"I was just driving
home!" His head fell down. "My God, and
now I've killed somebody."

I looked down at my own peacoat and levis,
then over at the dead man's friend, who
was bawling and blubbering, what they would
call hysteria in a woman. "It isn't possible"
he wailed, but it was possible, it was
indeed, accomplished and unfeeling, snoring
in its peacoat, and without its levis on.

He died laughing: that's a fact.

I had a woman waiting for me,
in her car and in the middle of the bridge,
I'm frightened, I said.
I'm afraid, he said, stay with me,
please don't go, stay with me, be
my witness—"No," I said, "I'll be your
witness—later," and I took his name
and number, "but I can't stay with you,

I'm too frightened of the bridge, besides
I have a woman waiting
and no license—
and no tail lights—"
So I left—
as I have left so many of my lovers.

we drove home
shaking, Wendy's face greyer
than any white person's I have ever seen.
maybe he beat his wife, maybe he once
drove taxi, and raped a lover
of mine—how to know these things?
we do each other in, that's a fact.

who will be my witness?
death wastes our time with drunkenness
and depression
death, who keeps us from our
lovers.
he had a woman waiting for him,
I found out when I called the number
days later

"Where is he" she said, "he's disappeared."
"He'll be all right" I said, "*we* could
have hit the guy as easy as anybody, it
wasn't anybody's fault, they'll know that,"
women so often say dumb things like that,
they teach us to be sweet and reassuring,
and say ignorant things, because we dont invent
the crime, the punishment, the bridges

that same week I looked into the mirror
and nobody was there to testify;
how clear, an unemployed queer woman

makes no witness at all,
nobody at all was there for
those two questions: what does
she do, and who is she married to?

I am the woman who stopped on the bridge
and this is the man who was there
our lovers teeth are white geese flying
above us, but we ourselves are
easily squished.

keep the women small and weak
and off the street, and off the
bridges, that's the way, brother
one day I will leave you there,
as I have left you there before,
working for death.

we found out later
what we left him to.
Six big policemen answered the call,
all white, and no child *in* them.
they put the driver up against his car
and beat the hell out of him.
What did you kill that poor kid for?
you motherfucking n[--].
that's a fact.

Death only uses violence
when there is any kind of resistance,
the rest of the time a slow
weardown will do.

They took him to 4 different hospitals
til they got a drunk test report to fit their
case, and held him five days in jail

without a phone call.
how many lovers have we left.

there are as many contradictions to the game,
as there are players.
a woman is talking to death,
though talk is cheap, and life takes a long time
to make
right. He got a cheesy lawyer
who had him cop a plea, 15 to 20
instead of life
Did I say life?

the arrogant young man who thought he
owned the bridge, and fell asleep on it
died laughing: that's a fact.
the driver sits out his time
off the street somewhere,
does he have the most vacant of
eyes, will he die laughing?

Two

They don't have to lynch the women anymore

death sits on my doorstep
cleaning his revolver

death cripples my feet and sends me out
to wait for the bus alone,
then comes by driving a taxi.

the woman on our block with 6 young children
has the most vacant of eyes
death sits in her bedroom, loading
his revolver

they don't have to lynch the women
very often anymore, although
they used to—the lord and his men
went through the villages at night, beating &
killing every woman caught
outdoors.
the European witch trials took away
the independent people; two different villages
—after the trials were through that year—
had left in them, each—
one living woman:
one

What were those other women up to? had they
run over someone? stopped on the wrong bridge?
did they have teeth like
any kind of geese, or children
in them?

Three

This woman is a lesbian be careful

In the military hospital where I worked
as a nurse's aide, the walls of the halls
were lined with howling women
waiting to deliver
or to have some parts removed.
One of the big private rooms contained
the general's wife, who needed
a wart taken off her nose.
we were instructed to give her special attention
not because of her wart or her nose
but because of her husband, the general.

as many women as men die, and that's a fact.

At work there was one friendly patient, already
claimed, a young woman burnt apart with X-ray,
she had long white tubes instead of openings;
rectum, bladder, vagina—I combed her hair, it
was my job, but she took care of me as if
nobody's touch could spoil her.

ho ho death, ho death
have you seen the twinkle in the dead woman's eye?

when you are a nurse's aide
someone suddenly notices you
and yells about the patient's bed,
and tears the sheets apart so you
can do it over, and over
while the patient waits
doubled over in her pain
for you to make the bed *again*
and no one ever looks at you,
only at what you do not do

Here, general, hold this soldier's bed pan
for a moment, hold it for a year—
then we'll promote you to making his bed.
we believe you wouldn't make such messes

if you had to clean up after them.

that's a fantasy.
this woman is a lesbian, be careful.

When I was arrested and being thrown out
of the military, the order went out: dont anybody
speak to this woman, and for those three
long months, almost nobody did;   the dayroom, when
I entered it, fell silent til I had gone; they

were afraid, they knew the wind would blow
them over the rail, the cops would come,
the water would run into their lungs.
Everything I touched
was spoiled. They were my lovers, those
women, but nobody taught us to swim.
I drowned, I took 3 or 4 others down
when I signed the confessions of what we
had done   together.

No one will ever speak to me again.

I read this somewhere; I wasn't there:
in WWII the US army had invented some floating
amphibian tanks, and took them over to
the coast of Europe to unload them,
the landing ships all drawn up in a fleet,
and everybody watching. Each tank had a
crew of 6 and there were 25 tanks.
The first went down the landing planks
and sank, the second, the third, the
fourth, the fifth, the sixth went down
and sank. They weren't supposed
to sink, the engineers had
made a mistake.   The crews looked around
wildly for the order to quit,
but none came, and in the sight of
thousands of men, each 6 crewmen
saluted his officers, battened down
his hatch in turn and drove into the
sea, and drowned, until all 25 tanks
were gone.   did they have vacant
eyes, die laughing, or what? what
did they talk about, those men,
as the water came in?

was the general their lover?

Four

A Mock Interrogation

Have you ever held hands with a woman?

Yes, many times—women about to deliver, women about to have breasts removed, wombs removed, miscarriages, women having epileptic fits, having asthma, cancer, women having breast bone marrow sucked out of them by nervous or indifferent interns, women with heart condition, who were vomiting, overdosed, depressed, drunk, lonely to the point of extinction: women who had been run over, beaten up. deserted. starved. women who had been bitten by rats; and women who were happy, who were celebrating, who were dancing with me in large circles or alone, women who were climbing mountains or up and down walls, or trucks or roofs and needed a boost up, or I did; women who simply wanted to hold my hand because they liked me, some women who wanted to hold my hand because they liked me better than anyone.

These were many women?

Yes.   many.

What about kissing? Have you kissed women?

I have kissed many women.

When was the first woman you kissed with serious feeling?

The first woman ever I kissed was Josie, who I had loved at such a distance for months. Josie was not only beautiful, she was tough and handsome too. Josie had black hair and white teeth and strong brown muscles. Then she dropped out of school unexplained. When she came back she came back for one day only, to finish the term, and there was a child in her. She was all shame, pain, and defiance. Her eyes were dark as the water under a bridge and no one would talk to her, they laughed and threw things at her. In the afternoon I walked across the front of the class and looked deep into Josie's eyes and I picked up her chin with my hand, because I loved her, because nothing like her trouble would ever happen to me, because I hated it that she was pregnant and unhappy, and an outcast. We were thirteen.

You didn't kiss her?

How does it feel to be thirteen and having a baby?

You didn't actually kiss her?

Not in fact.

You have kissed other women?

Yes, many, some of the finest women I know, I have kissed. women who were lonely, women I didn't know and didn't want to, but kissed because that was a way to say yes we are still alive and loveable, though separate, women who recognized a loneliness in me, women who were hurt, I confess to kissing the top of a 55 year old woman's head in the snow in boston, who was hurt more deeply than I have ever been hurt, and I wanted her as a very few people have wanted me—I wanted her and me to own and control and run the city we lived in, to staff the hospital I knew would mistreat her, to drive the transportation system that had betrayed her, to patrol the streets controlling the men who would murder or disfigure or disrupt us, not accidently with machines, but on purpose, because we are not allowed out on the street alone—

Have you ever committed any indecent acts with women?

Yes, many. I am guilty of allowing suicidal women to die before my eyes or in my ears or under my hands because I thought I could do nothing, I am guilty of leaving a prostitute who held a knife to my friend's throat to keep us from leaving, because we would not sleep with her, we thought she was old and fat and ugly; I am guilty of not loving her who needed me; I regret all the women I have not slept with or comforted, who pulled themselves away from me for lack of something I had not the courage to fight for, for us, our life, our planet, our city, our meat and potatoes, our love. These are indecent acts, lacking courage, lacking a certain fire behind the eyes, which is the symbol, the raised fist, the sharing of resources, the resistance that tells death he will starve for lack of the fat of us, our extra. Yes I have committed acts of indecency with women and most of them were acts of omission. I regret them bitterly.

Five

Bless this day oh cat our house

"I was allowed to go
3 places, growing up," she said—
"3 places, no more.
there was a straight line from my house
to school, a straight line from my house
to church, a straight line from my house
to the corner store."
her parents thought something might happen to her.
but nothing ever did.

my lovers teeth are white geese flying above me
my lovers muscles are rope ladders under my hands
we are the river of life and the fat of the land
death, do you tell me I cannot touch this woman?
if we use each other up
on each other
that's a little bit less for you
a little bit less for you, ho

death, ho ho death.
Bless this day oh cat our house
help   me be not such a mouse
death tells the woman to stay home
and then breaks in the window.

I read this somewhere, I wasnt there:
In feudal Europe, if a woman committed adultery
her husband would sometimes tie her
down, catch a mouse and trap it
under a cup on her bare belly, until
it gnawed itself out, now are you
afraid of mice?

Six

Dressed as I am, a young man once called
me names in Spanish

a woman who talks to death
is a dirty traitor

inside a hamburger joint and
dressed as I am, a young man once called me
names in Spanish
then he called me queer and slugged me.
first I thought the ceiling had fallen down
but there was the counterman making a ham
sandwich, and there was I spread out on his
counter.

For God's sake I said when
I could talk, this guy is beating me up
can't you call the police or something,
can't you stop him? he looked up from
working on his sandwich, which was *my*

sandwich, I had ordered it. He liked
the way I looked. "There's a pay phone
right across the street" he said.

I couldn't listen to the Spanish language
for weeks afterward, without feeling the
most murderous of urges, the simple
association of one thing to another,
so damned simple.

The next day I went to the police station
to become an outraged citizen
Six big policemen stood in the hall,
all white and dressed as they do
they were well pleased with my story, pleased
at what had gotten beat out of me, so
I left them laughing, went home fast
and locked my door.
For several nights I fantasized the scene
again, this time grabbing a chair
and smashing it over the bastard's head,
killing him. I called him a spic, and
killed him. My face healed. his didnt.
no child *in* me.

now when I remember I think:
maybe *he* was Josie's baby.
all the chickens come home to roost,
all of them.

Seven

Death and disfiguration

One Christmas eve my lovers and I
we left the bar, driving home slow
there was a woman lying in the snow

by the side of the road. She was wearing
a bathrobe and no shoes, where were
her shoes? she had turned the snow
pink, under her feet. she was an Asian
woman, didnt speak much English, but
she said the taxi driver beat her up
and raped her, throwing her out of his
care.
what on earth was she doing there
on a street she helped to pay for
but doesn't own?
doesn't she know to stay home?

I am a pervert, therefore I've learned
to keep my hands to myself in public
but I was so drunk that night,
I actually did something loving
I took her in my arms, this woman,
until she could breathe right, and
my friends who are perverts too
they touched her too
we all touched her.
"You're going to be all right"
we lied. She started to cry
"I'm 55 years old" she said
and that said everything.

Six big policemen answered the call
no child *in* them.
they seemed afraid to touch her,
then grabbed her like a corpse and heaved her
on their metal stretcher into the van,
crashing and clumsy.
She was more frightened than before.
they were cold and bored.
'don't leave me' she said.

'she'll be all right' they said.
we left, as we have left all of our lovers
as all lovers leave all lovers
much too soon to get the real loving done.

Eight

a mock interrogation

Why did you get into the cab with him, dressed as you are?

I wanted to go somewhere.

Did you know what the cab driver might do
if you got into the cab with him?

I just wanted to go somewhere.

How many times did you
get into the cab with him?

I don't remember.

If you don't remember, how do you know it happened to you?

Nine

Hey you death

ho and ho poor death
our lovers teeth are white geese flying above us
our lovers muscles are rope ladders under our hands
even though no women yet go down to the sea in ships
except in their dreams.

only the arrogant invent a quick and meaningful end
for themselves, of their own choosing.

everyone else knows how very slow it happens
how the woman's existence bleeds out her years,
how the child shoots up at ten and is arrested and old
how the man carries a murderous shell within him
and passes it on.

we are the fat of the land, and
we all have our list of casualties

to my lovers I bequeath
the rest of my life

I want nothing left of me for you, ho death
except some fertilizer
for the next batch of us
who do not hold hands with you
who do not embrace you
who try not to work for you
or sacrifice themselves or trust
or believe you, ho ignorant
death, how do you know
we happened to you?

wherever our meat hangs on our own bones
for our own use
your pot is so empty
death, ho death
you shall be poor

You Better Come

JUSTIN TORRES

Now that Paps had returned, he wanted to be with us, all five together, all the time. He herded us into the kitchen and gave us big knives to chop up the onions and cilantro while he picked through the dried beans and boiled the rice and Ma chatted at him and smelled the air and sent us winks.

After dinner he led us all to the bathtub, no bubbles, just six inches of gray water and our bare butts, our knees and elbows, and our three little dicks. Paps scrubbed us rough with a soapy washcloth. He dug his fingernails into our scalp as he washed our hair and warned us that if the shampoo got into our eyes, it was our own fault for squirming. We made motorboat noises, navigating bits of Styrofoam around toothpicks and plastic milk-cap islands, and we tried to be brave when he grabbed us; we tried not to flinch.

Ma was leaning over the sink, peering into the mirror, pulling out her eyebrows and curling her eyelashes with shiny metal instruments. "Be gentle," she said without even looking at him, without even blinking her eyes.

They were both topless; Ma was in a flesh-colored bra and heavy cotton work pants, and Paps had taken off his shirt to wash us. We saw everything—how our skin was darker than Ma's but lighter than Paps's, how Ma was slight and nimble, with ribs softly stepping down from her breasts, how Paps was muscled, the muscles and tendons of his forearms, the veins in his hands, the kinky hairs spreading across his chest. He was like an animal, our father, ruddy and physical and instinctive; his shoulders hulked and curved, and we had, each of us, even Ma, sat on them, gone for rides. Ma's shoulders were clipped, slipping away from her tiny bird neck. She was just over five feet and light enough for Manny to lift, and when Paps called her fragile, he sometimes meant for us to take extra-special care with her, and he sometimes meant that she was easily broken.

Paps stood to piss and we saw his stout, fleshy dick, the darkness of his skin down there and the strong jet of urine, long and loud and pungent. Ma turned from the mirror; we saw her watching him too. He zipped up and stood behind her, then slid his hands under her bra, and mounds of flesh rolled and squished between his fingers. It made us giddy because it made her giddy, even though she pushed him away. They were playing with each other, and no one wanted to leave the bathroom, no one wanted to fight or splash or ruin the moment.

Paps leaned against the wall and watched her adjusting herself back into her harness; he grinned and he growled. We watched him watching her, we studied his hunger, and he knew we were seeing and understanding. Now he winked at us; he wanted us to know that she made him happy.

"That's my girl," he said, slapping her bottom. "Ain't another one like her."

"They're going to catch pneumonia," Ma said, so he fished us out of the tub, one at a time, and stood us on the toilet seat and toweled us dry. He grabbed our ankles and dried the undersides of our feet, and we had to hold on to his shoulder for balance or grab a fistful of his Afro. He ran the towel between our toes, our butt cracks, our armpits, tickling us, but acting as if he couldn't comprehend what was so ticklish. He dried our heads for a long time, until we were smarting and dizzy.

Each time Paps finished drying one of us, he would place our palm against his own palm. He didn't say anything to Joel or Manny, but my hand he held up a little longer, looking close and nodding his head.

"You grew," he said, and I smiled and straightened my back, broadening my shoulders, triumphant.

Ma and Paps started talking to each other about our bodies, about how quickly we were changing; they joked about needing to make some more boys to take our places. We watched them; they looked each other in the eyes, teasing and laughing; their words were warm and soft, and we snuggled into the gentleness of their conversation. We were all together in the bathroom, in this moment, and nothing was wrong. My brothers and I were clean and fed and not afraid of growing up.

We climbed back into the empty tub, still in our towels, and our parents pretended not to notice. We saw them pretending and it thrilled us. We slid the shower curtain closed and huddled together, looking at each other with wide-open, eager eyes.

"Hey, wait a minute," Paps said in mock surprise, "where did the boys go?"

We pressed our fists into our cheeks to keep back the giggles.

"Oh my," Ma said. "They just disappeared."

We clenched ourselves together into a tighter ball. Our knees tensed with excitement. They were going to find us. Maybe they'd scare us, yanking back the curtain and shouting "Gotcha!" Maybe they'd scoop us up and tickle us; maybe they'd be sneaky and stand on the rim of the tub and peek over the top of the curtain, waiting for us to notice. Maybe they'd roar like dinosaurs; maybe they'd devour us. Maybe Paps would take Joel under one arm and Manny under the other, and maybe Ma would grab me and swing me in a circle, but whatever happened, we would be found, my brothers and me, huddled together; they would grab us and take us up and into their arms and own us.

But then they didn't look for us at all; they found each other instead. We listened to their kissing and soft little moans, and after a while we got down on our knees, lifting up the bottom edge of the shower curtain and spying on them. Ma was balanced on the sink, her back to the mirror and her legs folded around Paps's waist. She dragged her fingers up and down his back. Her hands were little and light, with painted fingernails that traced ridges into Paps's skin.

Paps's hands seemed massive on her tiny frame. He clutched her hips, moving her toward and then away from him, steadily, stealthily, squeezing hard enough so that his fingers appeared to be sinking into her sides like into quicksand, and when I looked at her face she looked like she was in pain, but she didn't look frightened, like it was a kind of pain she wanted.

We saw everything—that Paps's blue jeans were faded in the spot where he kept his wallet, the muscles of his stomach, that Ma closed her eyes but Paps kept his open, that he bit, that they were both gripping tight, that Ma's ankles were crossed and her toes were pointed. Her legs clutched and released him, and he was leaning her back so that her skin touched the skin of her reflection, like a picture I once saw of Siamese twins. The faucet poked into the base of her spine, and it must have hurt her, all of it must have hurt her, because Paps was much bigger and heftier, and he was rough with her, just like he was rough with us. We saw that it must hurt her, too, to love him.

Paps leaned Ma all the way back, her hair mixing and reflecting, doubling itself in the mirror. He bit into her neck like an apple, and she rolled her head over and spotted us. She smiled. She pulled Paps's head away from her and turned him until he spotted us too.

"I thought you disappeared," he said.

"You were supposed to look for us," said Manny.

"I guess I found something better," Paps said, and Ma slapped him on the chest and called him a bastard. She unwrapped herself from him and fidgeted with her clothes and smoothed her hair. He tried to kiss her neck again, but she wiggled away.

"Get my boots from the closet," she said. "Please, Papi, I'm already late."

We sighed and sank onto our butts, but the moment Paps left the bathroom, Ma turned off the light and shut the door and got into the tub with us, pulling the curtain closed behind her. It was completely dark; we couldn't even see her, but we could feel her arms around us, her hair tickling my bare shoulders.

"We'll show him," Ma said, and we loved her then, fiercely.

We heard him clomp up the stairs. We got ready to pounce. Then his hand was on the doorknob, he paused, and for a second it seemed as if he might have figured us out, but he came in and flicked on the light, and we rushed out from behind the curtain, tackling him into the hallway and onto the floor. Ma sat on his chest and we tickled him everywhere. He laughed a throaty all-out laugh, kicking his legs, saying "No! No! No!"—laughing and laughing until he was wheezing and there were tears in his eyes—but even then we kept on tickling, poking our fingers into his sides and tickling his feet, all of us laughing and making as much noise as we could, but no one as loud as Paps.

"No! No! No!" he said, crying now, laughing still. "I can't breathe!"

"All right," Ma said, "that's enough."

But it was not enough. Our towels had slipped off, and blood pumped through our naked bodies, our hands shook with energy, we were alive and it was not enough; we wanted more. We started tickling Ma too, started poking her, and she collapsed onto Paps's chest and covered her head, and he wrapped his arms around her.

Then Manny slapped Ma hard on the back. It sounded so satisfying, the thwack of his palm on her skin.

"You were supposed to come find us," he said.

Joel and I froze, waiting for some sign of trouble, waiting for Paps to react, threaten him, hit him, something. We stood there, hunched and alert like startled cats, but nothing came. Manny slapped her back again, and still nothing. Silence. Ma only moved both her hands to Paps's wrists. Her hair covered their faces, and we understood that we could do this, that this would be allowed, and never spoken of.

Joel kicked Paps's thigh as hard as he could.

"Yeah," he said, "you're supposed to find us."

I joined in, kicking for Paps but hitting Ma; it felt dull and mean and perfect. Then we were all three kicking and slapping at once, and they didn't say a word, they didn't even move; the only noise was the noise of the skin and impact and breath, and then our protests, *why don't you come find us, why don't you do what you're supposed to do, come and find, us, why don't ya, because you're bad, bad, bad, bad, why don't you do right, why can't you do right, we hate you, come and find us, we hate you, everyone hates you, you better come and find us, next time, next time you better come.*

We hit and kept on hitting; we were allowed to be what we were, frightened and vengeful—little animals, clawing at what we needed.

New Haven

KARLA CORNEJO VILLAVICENCIO

It was about an hour before midnight in New York in August and the heat had calmed down just enough to try sleeping. We didn't have working air-conditioning units and our third-floor apartment, built on top of a former garment factory, had a roof with short walls adjacent to our windows, so—this was before the gentrifier snitches got us in trouble with the landlord—we would drag out our twin-size mattresses through the windows and lay them down on the floor of our roof. The night was still hot but there was a breeze. My mom and dad squeezed onto one mattress and my little brother and I onto the other and I wish I could say we looked up at the stars but there were no stars, per New York's famous light pollution, but there was the moon, and there were the *pop pop pop*s in the background that were either the sound of kids playing with fireworks or the sound of a cop shooting one of us in the back, the odd ice-cream truck playing "Turkey in the Straw" or "Do Your Ears Hang Low?" which none of us immigrant kids had ever heard before, a car blasting salsa, a woman screaming in drunken ecstasy or else in alarm. The night seemed eternal. My parents were still in their thirties and they were still in love, and I had just watched Beyoncé perform "Crazy in Love" for the first time on TV and I felt electrified. I made my parents promise me they'd never get old. They did, they promised.

My father is in the middle of a prostate cancer scare right now. There is not much to say about it other than he does not want to get a biopsy, against the doctors' advice. The reason he does not want to get the biopsy is because he wants to die. It's two more weeks until we go in to get the results of his next prostate exam and the doctors will probably once again recommend a biopsy and my father will definitely refuse and that will be the moment I have been preparing for my entire life. Everything that I have done or that has happened to me since I took that New York–bound flight twenty-four years ago has been preparing me for this moment—learning English, getting bangs, placing second in the Emancipation Proclamation oratory contest, gaining weight, losing weight, getting the sick puppy from the pet shop, all of that happened to prepare me to this point—my parents are sick, uninsured, and aging out of work in a fucking racist country.

The twisted inversion that many children of immigrants know is that, at some point, your parents become your children, and your own personal American dream becomes making sure they age and die with dignity in a country that has never wanted them. That's what makes caring for our elderly different from Americans caring for their elderly. For one thing, most available jobs for undocumented immigrants are jobs Americans will not do, which takes healthy young migrants and makes them age terribly. At a certain point, manual labor is no longer possible. Aging undocumented people have no safety net. Even though half of undocumented people pay into Social Security, none are eligible for the benefits. They are unable to purchase health insurance. They probably don't own their own homes. They don't have 401(k)s or retirement plans of any kind. Meager savings, if any. Elderly people in general are susceptible to unscrupulous individuals taking advantage of them, and the undocumented community draws even more vultures. According to the Migration Policy Institute, around 10 percent of undocumented people are over fifty-five years old. This country takes their youth, their dreams, their labor, and spits them out with nothing to show for it.

My father is a salad maker now, feeding Manhattan's executive class. I've never watched him make a salad but I'm sure he's exquisite at it. (He did teach me about how to chop a salad in the most efficient way possible, which is to stand as if on a surfboard and take turns balancing your weight on either foot. The rhythm leads to faster chopping.) He has always been the best at his job, no matter the job. He worked as a taxi driver for his first twelve years in America, a time before MapQuest, let alone Uber, and he has the entire city memorized, every axis on the grid, all five boroughs and parts of Jersey. Since then, he has worked in restaurants. Now he is usually the oldest person in the kitchen. Out of respect, the younger guys all call him Don.

Recently, he started a new job, recommended to him by an acquaintance who lured him with the assurance of better hours, better treatment, a better environment. My dad is very gullible.

He spent three days at this new restaurant where, for spare change, they had him work all day, and then in the final hour of the day, he was given just that hour to clean an industrial kitchen, an industrial fryer, a refrigerator, a stove, an oven, and a sink, wash the dishes and the dishwasher, take out the trash, sweep and mop the floors, and clean the garbage chute. His body was wrecked at the end of each day. "I'm too old for this," he said. So he quit. His old job wouldn't take him back. Desperate, he began each morning by showing up at a Latinx job agency, which would send him out to "audition" at a different restaurant day after day, week after week, to no avail.

My dad told me all of this over dinner one night at a hotel restaurant in Midtown Manhattan where I'd invited him to meet me after what I thought was the end of his shift, and it was, but it was the end of a trial shift at a different restaurant than the one I had in mind. This whole thing, all of it, the entire fucking thing, had been kept from me for over a month, per my father's orders, because in my family it is believed I am sometimes *fragile*, stemming back from an incident when I was twenty-one and my father had to come to New Haven in the middle of the night to pick me up from the cold tile of my apartment's bathroom floor, beer bottles and a razor around me, and take me back home to New York. My father had initially refused to enter the restaurant because he believed he wasn't dressed nicely enough for it, but I convinced him my money was good there, and I introduced him to the server as my father in a bit of a *flamboyant* way, not enough to embarrass my dad, just to make a point that this was a motherfucking thing for me and I expected this to be a respected thing among the three of us, and I urged my dad to get the steak and ordered wine for us both and translated a conversation between the server and my father about a wine recommendation to go with his meal, which I usually think is so *bourgeois*, and I also joined him when he swirled the wine in his glass and smelled it, which I also usually think is the worst, and I quietly slipped myself a Klonopin while he was cutting his steak, confessing to all of this job trouble, in a pained, casual way, and then as he kept on talking, boy was there so much I didn't know, I slipped myself a second Klonopin with our second glass of wine, and when he left, I went up to my room and put on the terry-cloth hotel robe and shut off the lights and passed out feeling nothing, certainly not feeling fragile. I felt like Indio Juan Diego seeing the Virgin of Guadalupe in her glory, the miracle he wanted and needed at once. I felt god had gifted me blackness and death and I said, *Thank you Jehovah God. Thank you. Is this a blackout? I'm free of their tears. Is this freedom?*

Once his secret was in the open, my dad started texting me blurry cell phone pictures from the job agency. I told myself I needed a reminder of why I needed to be successful, so successful, statistical anomaly successful, so I have them saved on my phone to emotionally blackmail myself with. He took the photos when he was sitting in the waiting room of the job agency waiting for his name to be called. The first picture is of a man maybe in his late seventies, wearing a green button-down, khaki pants, and aviator sunglasses. His lips are downcast. My dad said he was applying to be a dishwasher. The second picture is of a man maybe in his late forties who is wearing a black baseball cap, a gray sweater, and maroon pants. My dad said he'd had a stroke—his right arm was paralyzed and he had a limp in his right leg. He was also applying to be a dishwasher. Apparently, he was a fucking fantastic dishwasher, how, I don't know. When he sent the pictures, my dad also texted me:

Further proof that we're not a burden.

Who says you're a burden?

It's hard to see men like that not get jobs. We're invisible because of the circumstances that force us to be here at the agency . . . old age . . . illness . . . the fucking papers. Do you understand. A million thoughts rush to my head. It's too much to think about.

"I hope they have children who can take care of them," I respond.

What I mean to say is: I hope they have a child like me. I hope everyone has a child like me. If I reach every child of immigrants at an early age, I can make sure every child becomes me. And if they don't, I can be everyone's child.

Octavio Márquez is a sixty-six-year-old Guatemalan day laborer with a faint white stubble. I saw him in a video online describing being robbed of his wages by an employer. At some point in the video he says Americans treat their pets better than they treat immigrants, which I cannot dispute. I email a message of concern to the immigrant worker center advocating for Octavio, and receive a reply inviting me to meet him at the blue boxcar in Brooklyn where the worker center is located. I visit one morning as the workers are making coffee and eggs. Before I go in, I stop by a Walgreens and pick out a nice card for Octavio. I stuff it with four hundred dollars. I don't know how much money he was robbed of, but it's what my dad earns in a week so I do it.

Let's talk about money for a second. I've established I grew up poor. Let me guide you through the present day. For my family, poverty is like walking in a hurricane. I buy my parents umbrella after umbrella; each provides some relief, then breaks—cheap fixes, all of them. The rain has paused for now. In Spanish we call that pause escampó. The rain has escampado. It will resume. Right now, I have some discretionary income. But it will not last forever. The guilt I feel having made it out—for now, until my own umbrella breaks—is like having been poisoned. I feel constantly disgusting, dirty, hungover, toxic unless I'm hemorrhaging money in this very specific way that I find *cleansing*.

So what happens is, let's say I go out to dinner. If I'm having an anxious day, I will send my parents take-out dinner. If I see a brown person in the kitchen at the restaurant, I will think that every kitchen in America probably has a Mexican in it and it will make me feel proud but sad—RIP Anthony Bourdain, a homie who got it—and then if my server is brown, if they are either in my opinion too young or too old or seem too tired for the job, I will leave a crazy tip—for what I am, which is a freelancer. Now. I do not have the kind of money to be leaving people crazy tips. But I remember every person who ever left my dad a really good tip when we lived off his tips, I remember *every one,* you don't understand, I have been thinking of those nice Puerto Rican executive assistants for the past fifteen *years*, it was always the Latina executive assistants, very rarely the white people in power, and I remember how he felt for the rest of the evening when he came home. It was like having my dad back from the dead. He would dance to no music and he'd make jokes, and he'd come out of his shower looking like a teenager. I know what a good tip feels like for a poor family. Every good tip feels like Simon helping Jesus carry the cross.

When I am introduced to Octavio I hand him the heavy envelope but it's awkward. I don't know him. I don't tell him there's money in there, but why am I, a total fucking stranger, giving him a greeting card? He keeps forgetting it everywhere so I'm finally like, *Octavio, there's money in there!* He does not open the envelope but puts it away and we're both like, *Fuck what now? Are we friends or something?*

We go to lunch. He's small and appears to be made out of paper. We walk a long time to get to the restaurant and we have the same stride. When we arrive, he's disappointed to hear they've changed management and he doesn't know the owner anymore. He was trying to impress me. He orders stewed ribs and chamomile tea. Octavio tells me that much of the discrimination older immigrants experience is at the hand of younger immigrants. That they will stand within earshot of the older guys and loudly wonder what they're still doing here, or outright say they're too old for the work. But Octavio knows his worth. When an employer picks him to do a job, they always call him back. He says he is friends with a seventy-two-year-old man who makes decorative wooden floors better than anyone else in the game and younger guys can't match his skill.

I ask how he feels on a daily basis as an older man without family here and Octavio says that he feels depressed and anxious. "What kills us is loneliness. I feel lonely even in a room full of people. I feel destabilizing anxiety and pain. Doctors say I don't have anything, but I know I'm sick." I ask Octavio whether his friends have similar problems, and he says they do but their symptoms manifest in different ways. "I think some men who grow old in this country get lost here. They are unfaithful to their wives or turn to alcohol or drugs as a way to blow off steam, to forget their pain. I'd say that out of every hundred older immigrants, ten succumb to depression, anxiety, or worse."

I think about the work of Roberto Gonzales, a Harvard scholar who has conducted longitudinal studies on the effects of undocumented life on young people. As a result of all the stressors of migrant life, he found his subjects suffered chronic headaches, toothaches, ulcers, sleep problems, and eating issues. Which is funny to find in research because I'm twenty-nine and I have this ulcer my doctors can't seem to soothe or diagnose the cause of. It feels like I have an open wound right beneath my breasts in the center of my abdomen and I can feel it spasm and bleed and it never goes away. Sometimes I have to go to Urgent Care, and I drink concoctions and take pills and drink teas and I just keep bleeding, and it hurts the most when, after a long day of reading about people forming human chains to block ICE officers from arresting a man and his child, I sit down to write about my parents.

Now, imagine that thirty, forty, fifty years in. Of course Octavio is sick. We're all fucking *sick*. It is a public health crisis and it's hard to know how to talk about it without feeding into the right-wing propaganda machine that already paints immigrants as charges to the healthcare system and carriers of disease. The trick to doing it is asking Americans to pity us while reassuring them with a myth as old as the country's justifications for slavery—that is, reassuring Americans with the myth that people of color are long-suffering marvels, built to do harder work, built to last longer and handle more, reminding them what America already believes in its soul, which is that we are "impervious to pain," as scholar Robin Bernstein has put it. We can only tell them we're sick if we remind them that sick or not, we are able to still be high-functioning machines.

"I don't feel at home in this country," Octavio says. "Even immigrants in extreme poverty find a way to send their deceased loved ones back home to be buried. They won't be alive to feel happiness again, but they will feel at peace, finally a place to rest. All the dead want is a place to rest." He says this may be his last year before going back to Guatemala. He came here to make enough money to send his kids to school back home, and he did it. One is a mechanic, another is studying law, and the third is an aesthetician—Octavio financed her salon. "Everyone who kills themselves through their work is doing this for their children," he says. "If you don't have kids, why would you kill yourself like this?" For my family the question is, once your kids are grown and doing okay, what happens when you keep killing yourself like this?

I meet Mercedes Soto through Pedro Iturralde, the head of Nuestra Calle, the Staten Island day laborer center, who describes her to me as the best housekeeper he has ever known, which is pretty high fucking praise. She is fifty-six years old but looks a lot older. She has long black hair shot with gray and a round, kind face. I tell her I'm writing about older immigrants and she gasps dramatically, envisioning a world in which she grows old in the United States and takes to living under a bridge. She walks me through the scenario she has envisioned while cracking herself up. "People are going to see me and gossip," she says. "I can't let them do that. They will whisper among themselves, *Have you seen Mercedes? She lives under the bridge now, in a box. She's fallen so far from her days of glory! A ghost of who she used to be!* And then they will avoid saying hi to me because I live under the bridge now. No, ma'am, I'm not going to give them that satisfaction."

She tells me that I remind her of her granddaughter, small and fragile. So when she invites me to her home on Staten Island one afternoon to teach me how to cook small corn cakes called arepas, I immediately say yes. I've never had a grandmother and she seems fun.

Mercedes and her husband rent a small room in a house that she shares with four young Ecuadorian men on the second floor and a young Salvadoran man across the hall from them on the first floor. Mercedes and her husband are, by decades, the oldest people in the house. She is the only woman. The house is spotless, and her room is neatly packed to the brim with belongings. Today, Mercedes is wearing dark-blue Gloria Vanderbilt jeans and a mock-turtleneck sweater, and her hair is in a long braid down her back. She invited her best friend, Monica, to cook with us. She is also fifty-six. ("And she has papers," Mercedes says immediately.) They met at an English class and have been close ever since. Monica has henna-dyed black hair and black eyeliner tattooed on her lids. She suggests I am wearing too much makeup.

The women do not let me cook. Latina women never let me cook. I used to have this self-mythology about my upbringing, which is that my parents never taught me to cook because they didn't want to teach me skills that would make me a good housewife—my mother's biggest fear—since whenever I asked to help them in the kitchen, they sent me to go read a book. So I was like, I had feminist parents! But now I realize that the literal truths about myself that are immediately manifest to others—I am clumsy, distracted, have no attention to detail, am messy, fall often, hurt myself easily—made me clearly useless in the kitchen and they just didn't want me around to interfere. When I have tried cooking for various older Latinas, they always take over immediately, not because they're feminist vigilantes, but because they're perfectionists and they are good at what they do and why would they let me make a mess of things? To *indulge* me?

Monica assembles a growing pile of arepas next to her. To make them, you mix white corn flour, warm water, butter, salt, and cheese in a bowl. You set it aside to cool, then take out the sticky dough and knead it. Monica uses a drinking glass to press perfect circles into the dough. Mercedes has made Mexican champorrado, a thick hot chocolate with oatmeal and molasses. It is already simmering when I arrive.

Mercedes and her husband, Jacinto, plan on "retiring" in a couple of years. That means they'll stop working in the United States and move back to Mexico, probably to work in some much more relaxed capacity there. He is a gardener and, at sixty-two years old, finds himself going head-to-head with younger men. His lower back kills him and he gets overheated easily. He refused to go to the doctor for a long time—*I'm fine, leave me alone!*—but Mercedes put her foot down, issued an ultimatum, and he went to the community health clinic, which charges twenty dollars for a visit. "I can't love you more than you love yourself," she told him. "Grown children will not take care of you when you're older—especially boys, and we have boys." Monica agrees that being a mother to adult sons with their own families to take care of makes her feel vulnerable. Jacinto comes to the kitchen to eat and drink with us. He is shy and laughs quietly at his wife's jokes but speaks up when we begin to talk about adult children. "I don't want to have to extend my hand to them to ask for food," he says firmly. Plus, the children can be demanding, expecting too much of their parents. One day, Mercedes's son raised his voice at her on the phone because he needed her and didn't know where she was. "The day I live in your house and you spoon-feed me, I'll listen to you, but until then, I'll do as my heart desires," she told him.

The following night, I take a taxi to a church on Staten Island where Nuestra Calle is having a Christmas party. Mercedes is being honored for helping out in the community. The tables are covered in red plastic cloths and sprinkled with snowflake glitter confetti. I sit with Monica and Jacinto. Their phones ping with automated Bible-scripture text messages in a huge font that they have to hold far from their faces in order to read. We eat plates of baked ziti as we watch teenagers in plush antlers dance with each other. There is a live band, a group of men in pink blazers with accordions. There's a toddler in a tiny matching blazer and tiny matching accordion pretending to play along. Mercedes and Jacinto show me a picture of their religious marriage ceremony, which took place recently, forty-two years after their civil one. She looks like a teen bride, wearing a white princess dress and a tiara. I walk from table to table, complimenting all the women's makeup and asking if anyone wants to talk about aging, which you know, I'm no Ronan Farrow. One woman stops me to say she wants her story told. Altagracia is nearly fifty years old and is recovering from surgery to remove a cyst in her uterus that she had unsuccessfully tried to self-treat with herbs from a naturalist. She wants to tell me that she was conned by a woman in Mexico who said she could expedite her green-card petition and soon began extorting her for ever-increasing fees with the threat of being turned in to ICE if she did not comply. Altagracia paid her a total of twelve thousand dollars.

Because of her poor health, Altagracia has death on her mind and is thinking about going back to Mexico. "There was a raid on a 7-Eleven near my house just last week. And the other day on the bus, a white woman went on a racist rant against me while I was just standing there. All of the racism here makes me want to go back to my country when I die. I'm not wanted here, and I do not want to live in eternity in a place where I'm not wanted." In the meantime, she says, her plan for aging involves her two children. She tells me a story about a woman she sometimes sees when she goes out to collect recycling for cash. The woman is seventy years old and collects recycling for a living. She was widowed when she was very young and never remarried, never had children. Now, Altagracia says, the woman is all alone and left to die in a foreign country without anyone to take care of her. She says the lesson is that it is important to have children who can take care of us when we grow old.

"You can't guarantee how your kids are going to turn out. There are good children and there are bad children, so in my opinion, people should have two kids. One of them ought to turn out well. I have two kids, and after my surgery, there was always one of them around to take care of me when the other one was busy." An heir and a spare. I ask her if the pressure of that might be hard on the children.

"Perhaps," she says. "But that's the tradition."

Early the next morning, I visit Nuestra Calle. There are just five older men sitting inside, out of the cold. One of the men recognizes me from the party and says with a large grin, "I remember you. You tried to interview me, but I didn't want to talk to you." I concede that that was me, and try again. He leans back in his chair and sucks his teeth, thinking awhile. "No," he concludes. I sit down to drink my coffee and we make small talk, until we're kicked out by a woman who wants to sweep the space.

Outside, I lean against the façade. The men gather around me in a semicircle. The man to my right, in his sixties, wearing a red New York Yankees baseball cap and a brown hoodie, too light for the cold, starts talking bitterly about the life of a migrant. He says he has completely given up, and that's what he says, but here he is, isn't he, at 7:00 a.m. on a freezing morning, clocking in like the rest of us. The other men quickly interrupt him, tenderly, in hushed tones. They urge him to get help. I shut up and listen. A picture begins to form. He is homeless and addicted to alcohol. The men try to tell him that he has to stare down a childhood trauma in order to get better, rather than escaping from his pain with drink. They tell him he is the smartest man they know, the most eloquent, and they don't want to see this end badly. It's an intervention.

It seems spur of the moment, brought on by the opportunity to speak about the suffering of migration in the third person, almost pedagogically. He gets mad at them, but they're very loving toward him. When he walks away, they tell me they are the lucky ones, that old day laborers often end up sick, sad, and alone, too embarrassed and lonely to go to the worker centers, instead picking up work in remote corners. "But I wouldn't advise you to go to those places alone," the man who turned down the interview says. "If you want to go there, we'll go with you."

I am ten years older than my brother. I have always imagined us as being part of an "heir and spare" sort of situation, which I know about because my mother is obsessed with the European royal families—she thinks I look like Charlotte Casiraghi of Monaco the way my father thinks I have the spirit of Greta Thunberg. I . . . don't. My brother has always been so *level-headed*, so *sweet*, and *patient*, and—I say this with absolute awe and relief—has never shown signs of mental illness, so my parents were grateful for him, grateful that he was healthy and fine, grateful that he was spared. He's not crazy, sure. But he was also born in Brooklyn. Which means he's an American citizen.

Whereas it was my responsibility to be the face of the family, the hunter, the gatherer, my brother just had to find it in him to do his homework. He was Prince Harry. He just had to . . . not be photographed in a Nazi costume. But he also had a bigger responsibility than I had, that I could not have because I was my parents' undocumented child. He just had to turn twenty-one.

Every mixed-status family in the United States knows the drill. An undocumented parent can be sponsored by their American-citizen child when the child turns twenty-one. (This does not work for siblings or other family members.) My parents never talked about it around my brother, though surely it made them hopeful, but I thought about it all the time. I took to lovingly calling him my little anchor baby, after the disparaging term Republicans used for the

American-born children of undocumented immigrants who supposedly "anchored" them to the United States. I reclaimed the term. On his birthday, I always took him out to dinner, and as he ate his sushi happily and cluelessly, I'd think, *You beautiful aging casket of wine. Better by the day.*

This all changed recently, when reports began circulating that ICE was arresting undocumented parents and spouses of American citizens when they petitioned for green cards. Immigration lawyers began advising children, husbands, and wives against petitioning for them at all.

Ricardo Reyes, a twenty-one-year-old recent Yale graduate, is one of those kids. He is an American citizen. He has the face and demeanor of an adorable bludgeoned baby seal. His parents worked in the garment industry in Los Angeles for decades before moving to the Pacific Northwest to make a living picking apples. "Since I was in elementary school, I would hear my mom talk about naturalization," he told me. He was their oldest child, so he'd reach the finish line first. He and several of his friends at Yale, also the children of immigrants, were turning twenty-one within a few months of each other and they were counting down the days, talking excitedly after class about who would turn twenty-one first. Then on the morning of his birthday, his lawyer told him it would be too risky to file an application. One of his classmates had seen her dad detained during their green card interview, and he was deported despite a national outcry.

After digesting the news, Ricardo's mother announced that when her body can no longer withstand picking apples she'd like to go back to Mexico. His father has been here since he was nineteen years old, so it's hard for him to imagine returning to Mexico, but Ricardo thinks he'll probably end up going back too. Ricardo is devastated that he wasn't able to adjust their legal status but finds comfort in the fact that he can provide for their retirement if they go back to Mexico. He is a middle school teacher now, back in L.A. "Any money I make will not be for me. I just need an apartment. The rest will be for my parents." I take him out to drinks and am like, how about chemical engineering, baby? But he wants to be a teacher and I admire that purity even if I have no high hopes for its financial output.

But Ricardo is young, and for now his parents can still work. He does not yet know what this life will do to him. I'm looking to interview children of immigrants partly to get a blueprint for myself because I'm lost and I am scared, so I set off to find somebody a little older, someone who has been doing this for a while, and in my research I stumble upon thirty-six-year-old Mira Fernández. Mira is a Latina journalist who writes for the local Spanish paper who counts my dad as one of her readers. She grew up in New York, the daughter of undocumented immigrants. Her dad was a day laborer, and she lived with her parents—and paycheck to paycheck—until she was an adult. She remembers that, one month, after paying her bills and rent, she had no money left over to buy sanitary napkins, so she bought a roll of toilet paper that she made last her whole period. It was humiliating. "I decided that would never happen again. I wanted to save up so I could retire one day, and I was going to provide for my parents' emotional health and quality of life," she tells me. She did not want to be able to provide only for their basic needs. She wanted them to live with dignity. So she began to work toward that.

Then, after decades as a day laborer, her father started to show signs of depression. His years had consisted of going to work, coming home to sleep, going to work, coming home to sleep, and back again, with nothing in his life to give it meaning or pleasure. He got older. He became overcome by stress and anxiety. He stopped talking. This is when Mira started noticing the miniature cars. They were the size of Hot Wheels cars, but they were built with intricate detail, like built-to-scale models. Her dad soon began amassing dozens, tens of dozens of tiny cars. He was skilled in woodwork, so after work or on weekends, during any free time he had, he would work on an elaborate wooden display for the cars. He'd clean them lovingly with small cotton rounds. He painted any scratches they had, and he rearranged them constantly. It's the only way he passed the time when he was home. I ask Mira if this made her sad. She is quiet for a long time, then says, "You know, he filled up this space in his heart with those little cars, so I'm just glad he found a way to feel better."

After many years of trying, Mira's parents, now much older, could not do manual labor in the United States anymore and went back to

Mexico. Mira fully supports them, sending money twice a month. I ask her what percentage of her paycheck goes to her parents, and she says it is something she does so naturally and so much, she's never even thought to calculate that.

"Look, they're better off there," she says. "They were tired of their lives here. Their emotional health is more stable there, they have their own home, they have activities, they have friends. Here, they worked constantly just to make ends meet, just to pay rent on time. They could not retire here, but with some financial help on my part, their lives over there are more peaceful." She admits it is financially complicated for her, but her parents always express their gratitude and they never ask for money outright. "I'd feel guilty not doing it, but I'm very happy to be able to do it, and I'm very happy to help them," she says.

Her brother doesn't contribute. He says he has his own family to take care of. Mira theorizes that Latin American culture is so imbued with patriarchal values that paint women as natural caregivers and nurturers that women feel a greater responsibility toward aging parents, and women who are not able to balance or reject those values feel an inescapable burden.

I used to say that I would slip antifreeze into my brother's coffee (it has a sweet taste, and he likes how I prepare his coffee, dulce and light enough that it should match my skin tone) if he did not help me take care of our parents as they aged. Once, he was maybe twelve years old and his report card was pretty bad. His report cards were pretty bad from his first ever one in kindergarten until he was in community college, so this was not a surprise—we all have our strengths and academics was not his. But it was a fucking nightmare for a family so focused on social mobility—and I was *pissed*. I called him on the phone and screamed at the top of my lungs that as an American citizen, he was wasting his opportunities, and that if he ended up working at a Best Buy and not going to college, I would never speak to him again in my life. "You hear that? I have no problem cutting you off. Don't you try me. You won't be a burden to me. I will never fucking talk to you *again*." I recently apologized to him for being so cruel and he just laughed and said he didn't take me seriously because I was just like Dad.

* * *

When my father could drive—before he started dying—he would take me to the Land of Make Believe or Splish Splash or some other tristate-area water park every summer. He did it because commercials for water parks were featured prominently on local television and they depicted children acting carefree and wild and I was not carefree or wild and it weighed on him, so he insisted I try. I did not know how to swim. He tried to teach me but I was terrified of the water. My father is prone to anger and so he is not a good teacher. When he made me practice long division at home and I got answers wrong, he'd rip up the pages I worked on about an inch from my face while telling me I was stupid. He took that approach to swimming lessons, and after a few minutes, he'd usually just storm off and my mother would tell me to ignore him. Through adulthood, my friends treated my not knowing how to swim like my not knowing how to ride a bicycle or not being able to leave the country—just, like, a quirky thing about me.

My fear of water and inability to swim did not stop my father from taking me to water parks. It made him more dogged in pursuit of the activity. It's all he wanted to do in the summers. My mother packed sandwiches and snacks because concession food was too expensive, and off we went. The only ride I could tolerate was the Lazy River because all I had to do was float on an inner tube, but my father liked for us to go on the rides with long, dark tubes that twisted into crazy loops at high speed and then spat you out into a pool. Those rides had long lines, and the entire way up I would have a pit in my stomach and I pleaded with him not to make me go. He insisted it would be fun, the whole point was my having fun. He'd go first, then wait at the bottom. At the top of the ride, when I was standing barefoot on a warm wooden landing and there was a dark tunnel in front of me filled with a fast current of water rushing into the pitch black, the people who worked at the ride would *repeatedly* ask me if I was okay going down. But I didn't want to face my father if I gave up, so I lay down in the tube, crossed my arms, counted to three, and pushed myself down. Years later, my psychiatrist would tell me that my anxiety and adrenaline run on the same "train tracks," so I often get them confused. If I experienced an adrenaline rush in the dark tubes, or if I experienced a panic attack while I was in them, I cannot say. I remember it as a sharp intake of breath, down to the cold of my soul. And I remember the next moment of awareness, which is being spit into a pool, and sinking.

I sank. I always sank. I knew I could stand, but my body was leaden and I fell at the wrong angle. And my father always reached down and brought me to air, my long black hair stuck to my face. I was never underwater long enough to come up gasping for air, but I can still feel the taste of chlorine in my lungs. I miss the taste of chlorinated pool water. And I miss this dynamic, of my father putting me in a manufactured scene of crisis in which I would feel helpless but at the same time be perfectly safe. I felt like I was going to die, but I would not die. A person who cannot swim and who panics in water is in danger in a pool, and my father knew that, and he made it so that he could save me every time. It was never a big production when he did it, he'd just pick me up by the armpits and say, "Wasn't that *fun*?" I think the lesson was: He was my father, and he was god. As long as I would panic and sink, and he could save me, he would always have that place.

I never learned to swim. The farthest I had ever ventured into the ocean was to my knees, screaming the whole while. But by last summer, right before I turned twenty-nine and he turned fifty-four, our roles had so profoundly reversed and his self-esteem was so devastatingly low that I wondered if I could give that back to him, this ability to save me. Like the water-park drownings, this invitation was also perfectly manufactured: I invited him to come spend an afternoon at the beach in the middle of July precisely with the purpose of teaching me how to swim. It would take, max, three hours and I would take, just, one Klonopin.

The beach we went to is called Lighthouse Point. It's on the Long Island Sound, not far from New Haven. The Long Island Sound is technically an estuary, which is where salt water from the ocean and fresh water from rivers mix. Sixteen different very New Englandy rivers empty out into the Atlantic Ocean at this spot. Emma Lazarus wrote a forgettable poem about it with not a huddling mass in sight. It is described in *The Great Gatsby* as "the most domesticated body of salt water in the Western hemisphere." When I was in college, I got the coordinates of East Egg and West Egg, fictional places on Long

Island, tattooed by my left breast because they symbolized my desire for what I cannot have. But now, I just like this beach because there are always black and brown families fishing or building sand castles there, proudly being alive, and there is just something about the ocean air perfuming dark bodies refusing to die that makes me want to live another day too.

To begin, my father poured cold water over my body with his hands like a priest baptizing an infant. It was freezing. His arms were very white. My father had not been to the beach in seven years. He told me the first step was being able to stand in deep water, which he likened to standing on a packed subway when you don't have a pole to hold and cannot lean against a door. Your legs have to be apart just so, and you use your arms to stabilize yourself. He asked me to shift my weight from foot to foot as if I was on a bumpy subway ride, I guess kind of like he stands when he chops lettuce. He grabbed my hand and we went deeper into the ocean until the water was up to my chest, the deepest I had ever gone. "Next, you float," he told me. He grabbed my hands and asked me to go on my stomach, extend my legs as far as they would go, and kick. He assured me he would not let go. I told him I weighed 140 pounds, which is not true, laadeedaa, but he said it didn't matter, and to prove that to me, he asked me to grab him by the hands and he told me I would be able to support his entire weight in the water. "The water will help you carry my weight," he said.

I did. I mean the water did. When it was my turn, I asked him to swear to not let me go. I'd usually ask him to swear on his mother, because I know that's what he holds most holy, but I think she's demonic so I don't like bringing her up. Instead, I asked why I should believe him. As an adult, he has told me that because he is a good father, he has lied to me my whole life, and he is proud of lying to me, and he will lie to me until he dies, so his word means nothing from him. I held on to his hands so tightly I am sure I bruised them. He did not let go.

But I did not float. My body is not buoyant. "Your body is determined to sink," my father announced as he tried to hold me up by the stomach. My legs do not extend in the water, so I cannot kick; they gravitate toward my father's body like a magnet and I sink. I sink, but not down. My legs sink laterally, toward his body, so I end up vertical. He relaxed his body and showed me how easy it was to float on his back—Mire!—totally flat, but in my resting state, my body in water wants to be upright, on my feet. Both of us realized at the same time that this was a true thing about me, and we tried to change it until finally our limbs gave out and we returned to shore. I was not able to restore the natural order of things.

Back on sand, I asked him if, before, on the roof that summer, he had lied when he promised to stay young forever.

Yes, he said.

If you break little promises you'll break big ones. That's what you said.

I know. But I won't.

My mom was on a beach blanket, her back to the sun, trying to darken the skin around a scar. She didn't turn around to look at my dad and he didn't look at her. Now that I think of it, they didn't speak to each other at all that day except for when they awkwardly waded into the water together and stood some space apart, looking like two dead fish in the ocean together, stagnant but afloat. And that's how they planned to stay, dead, stagnant, and afloat, even after we discovered that my dad wasn't going to watch volleyball on weekends after all, even after I confronted him and he admitted it but blamed my mom. I separated them. He left home one night while my mom and brother were at church and I reminded him to write my brother a loving text because that night would be hard for him.

There is research about migrant families, but children do not see it as prophecies foretold. I should have known better. I had spoken to a lot of people telling me the same things. And now here it was happening to my family, my soccer team, the world's best. Shortly before I asked him to leave, my father had told my brother: "I am tired of living just for you and your sister. It is my turn to be happy now." And he handled it the wrong way, totaled some people's lives in his wake, but he was right. It was his turn to be happy. And now my mom is free to figure out what makes her happy, after thirty-one years. Thirty of those years have been spent here in America, being undocumented together. She goes to yoga now. The other day, she had a *hot dog*.

I asked almost everyone I interviewed for this book about regrets, but they didn't tell me many. That's not what they remember of their time here. That's not what we'll remember when we have to leave, by choice, force, or casket. The look in a mother's eyes at her baby's first word in English, my father's heaving sobs when I handed him my diploma in Latin from the best fucking school in the world, Leonel's first steps of freedom outside the church in the autumn cold after four months in hiding, the Mexican chefs behind every great restaurant in New York, the Upper East Side babies who love their Haitian nannies so much it makes their moms jealous, a day laborer's first cold shower in America after wearing off the soles of his feet in the desert, the two young men who pushed Joaquín up the mountain when he wanted to die, Jesus Christ himself on the cross—*Truly I tell you, whatever you did for one of the least of these brothers and sisters of mine, you did for me.*

SMALL / MEDIUM / LUST

ANDREA ABI-KARAM

there's heavy & constant exhaustion
like widespread static
i lean in to the physical—
circadian shake & revolt
bruises dull & wide
thin pointed scratches
that grow loud with sweat
& a layer of uhaul dyke grime
buried deep in my knee scrapes + glitter + dirt + cum
dense under my nails
heavy & constant
when the cops kicked us out
we used their headlights
as a stage

there's something powerful about sinking into yesterday's wounds &
letting it all light up
my chest a fucking canvas
pay 2 stare up close & not through
any panes of glass
up close / & impersonal like
public sex is @ a distance
just bodies unforming
jaw tight

play
power
power
play
play party
(i almost missed my flight 2 go 2 that)
power situation / power switch)

cold-obsessive
all events are recorded
cold-obsessive
all options are recorded
cold-obsessive in which

bodies are mixed together against the purity of whiteness
sort it all out later

when the cops kicked us out
we used their headlights
as a stage
where the queers of color
whipped the white subs

///////

divisions & subdivisions & subspaces & low lit basements—that's where we host meetings
2 avoid dangerous visibility—easy recognition—easy on the eye—
miss the blind spot—miss the heart spot / go back & apologize

b/w knowing & remembering where the cuts came from / where the structure
came from / where where the walls came from / did you build them / did we
build them by accident / between ourselves / maybe i'm too hopeful &
people rly are that sinister

hacking & hacking until it doesn't track // glitter in the wind
the problem is
when u get arrested
with an X on yr id card
where do they put u?
actually
the problem is prisons
what if instead of collecting separate lonely individualities
we set them free 2 sink back into the collective

resist the present approach impurity
the exhaustion that happens through containment
what are the ins / what are the outs

send a drone to drop off a pair of boltcutters
i'll tie you up to the chain link fence after hours

dangerous mixtures—impurities rising
at once collided at once real & imaginary
all at once
what if we
just
all @ once
tore down the cages
1
2
3

Excerpt from *Great Expectations*

KATHY ACKER

DAY

The First Days

Timelessness versus time.

I remember it was dusk. The lamps began to appear against a sky not yet dark enough to need them. I was shy of my mother because when she was on ups she was too gay and selfish and on downs she was bitchy. When she changed from ups to downs was the best time to approach her.

I adored my actress mother and would do anything for her. "Sarah, be a good girl and get me a glass of champagne." "Sarah, I'm out of money again. Your father's horrible. You don't need an allowance: give me ten dollars and I'll pay you back tomorrow." She never paid me back and I adored her.

"I never wanted you," my mother told me often. "It was the war." She hadn't known poverty or hardship: her family had been very wealthy. "I had terrible stomach pains and the only doctor I could get to was a quack. He told me I had to get pregnant." "I never heard of that. You got pregnant?" "The day before you were born I had appendicitis. You spent the first three weeks of your life in an incubator."

The rest I know is little. My father, a wealthier man than my mother, walked out on her when he found out she was pregnant with me. Since neither she nor grandmama Siddons ever said anything specific about him, I didn't know who he was. I always turned to my mother and I loved her very much.

Mother didn't want me to leave her. I think she could have loved me or shown that she loved me if she had had more time or fewer obsessions. "I don't care if my daughter respects me. I want her to love me." She craved my love as she craved her friends' and the public's love only so she could do what she wanted and evade responsibility. All her friends did love her and I, I lived so totally in the world bounded by her being her seemings, I had no idea we were a socially important family. I didn't know there was a world outside her.

There is just moving and there are different ways of moving. Or: there is moving all over at the same time and there is moving linearly. If everything is moving-all-over-the-place-no-time, anything is everything. If this is so, how can I differentiate? How can there be stories? Consciousness just is: no time. But any emotion presupposes differentiation. Differentiation presumes time, at least BEFORE and NOW. A narrative is an emotional moving.

It's a common belief that something exists when it's part of a narrative.

Self-reflective consciousness is narrational.

Mother wanted me to be unlike I was. I got 'A's in school—it wasn't that I was a good girl, in fact even back then I was odd girl out: school was just the one place where I could do things right—but mother said getting 'A's made me stand out too much. Otherwise I was just a failure. I felt too strongly. My emotional limbs stuck out as if they were broken and unfixable. I kissed mother's friends too nicely when they were playing canasta. I was too interested in sex. I wasn't pretty in a conventional enough way. I didn't act like Penelope Wooding. When I washed a dish, I wasn't washing the dish. Since I didn't know if mother was god, I didn't know if I loved her. My friends told me I perceived in too black-and-white terms. "The world is more complex," they said. I said, "I get 'A's in school." Unlike.

"What was my father like, mommy?"

My mother looks up from a review of her newest hit. In those days she always got fabulous reviews.

"I mean my real father." When I had turned ten years old, my mother had carefully explained to me that the man I called my father had adopted me.

"He was very handsome."

"What exactly did he look like?" I had no right to ask, but I was desperate.

"His parents were wonderful. They were one of the richest families in Brooklyn."

Talking with my mother resembled trying to plot out a major war strategy. "What did his family do?"

"I was very wild when I was young. You remember Aunt Suzy. I'd sneak down the fire escape and Aunt Suzy and I'd go out with boys. I'd let them pet." My mother was high on Dex. "Your father was very handsome, dark, I fell in love with him. It was during the war so everyone was getting married." My mother refused to say anymore.

When I asked grandmama Siddons about my real father, she said he was dead. I replied I knew he wasn't dead. She said he was a murderer.

Why is anybody interested in anything? I'm interested when I'm discovering. To me, real moving is discovering. Real moving, then, is that which endures. How can that be?

Otherwise I lived in my imaginings. If anyone had thought about me rather than about their own obsessions, they would have thought it was a lonely childhood, but it wasn't. I had all of New York City to myself. Since mother was an actress we had to live in New York or London, and I hugged New York to me like a present. Sometimes I'd leave the apartment and walk down First Avenue to the magic bookstore of brightly-colored leatherbound books. Book- and dress-stores were magic places I could either dream or walk to. Then I walked up Madison Avenue and fantasized buying things. I walked down to Greenwich Avenue where the most interesting bookstore held all the beatnik poets but I never saw them. I had to happen upon what I wanted. I was forbidden to act on my desire, even to admit my desire to myself. Poetry was the most frightening, therefore the most interesting appearance. Once or twice a monthly afternoon I'd avidly watch a play I had no way of comprehending.

When it was all happening around me and I had very few memories of what was happening, I didn't need to understand and, if I had understood, I probably would have been too scared to keep moving.

Mother was a real actress. I never knew who she was. I had no idea until after the end that she was spending all of her money and, then, that she was broke. She had always been very tight with me: taking away my allowances, never buying me anything. She madly frittered away money. Suddenly, surprisingly, she asked me if I wanted gifts and she bought me three copies of a gold watch she liked. At the same time she owed three months' rent, two of her bank accounts were closed, all of her charge cards had been revoked. The 800 shares of AT&T grandmama had given her were missing. She was becoming gayer and less prudish. I would have done anything for her. She didn't talk to me or to anyone directly. She lifted up her favorite poodle, walked out of the apartment house, and didn't return.

Do I care? Do I care more than I reflect? Do I love madly? Get as deep as possible. The more focus, the more the narrative breaks, the more memories fade: the last meaning.

In spite of these circumstances which brought me to Ashington House, I'm thrilled when I see it. Trees always make my heart beat quickly. Bronze chrysanthemums. Dahlias around a pond in which two ducks quack, black and gray. And the whistle low. Two long streets, along leaves, lead away.

My aunts Martha and Mabel greet me. I've never met them before.

They're very wealthy and they're so polite, they're eccentric. They tell me I'm going to meet my real father. I don't want to see him, I do I do. I know he's handsome.

Aunt Martha tells me he's away at the moment.

We stop, walking in front of a picture of my father. At least it's a picture of him. "Your father," Aunt Mabel comments, "was too adventurous. Wild . . . headstrong . . . Your mother was his first wife and you were his first child."

"Who's his new wife?"

"He's had three. Last year he killed someone, shot him, who was trespassing on his yacht. The family got him off on psychological reasons. After his six-month stay in a rest home, he just disappeared."

"Aunt Mabel's scared, dear," Judy's commenting on Punch, "that you have some of your father's wildness."

Despite my politeness, they know who I am.

"I really don't know very much, Sarah. But I don't think you should have anything to do with him."

"Your father," Aunt Mabel interrupts her sister, "acts unpredictably. He can be extremely violent. We have no way of telling how he'll act when he sees you. The family decided to help you as much as we can, but we can't help you with this."

I don't know what I'm going to believe.

He—for there can be no doubt of his sex, though the fashion of the time did something to disguise it—was in the act of slicing at the head of a Moor which swung from the rafters. It was the color of an old football.

I called Jackson up and he came over immediately. He was a drunken messy slob, maudlin as they come which all drunks are, but that's what let him be the kind of artist he was. He NEEDED to suffer to thrust himself out as far as he could go farther beyond the bounds of his physical body what his body could take he NEEDED to maul shove into knead his mental and physical being like he did those tubes of paint. I not only understood, I understood and adored. I would be the pillow he would kick the warm breast he could cry into open up to let all that infinite unstoppable mainly unbearable pain be alive I would not snap back I would be his allower of exhibited pain so he could keep going. That's why he loved me. He didn't need brains. He didn't need intelligence he was too driven.

"You're so beautiful, so warm: I don't know why you want me."

"I don't want you cause you're famous, Jackson. That's why all those other people're eating you up, making you think you're only an image HISTORY (in New York City a person's allowed to be alive or human if he/she is famous or close enough to a famous person to absorb some of the fame) so now you can no longer paint unless you close up all your senses and become a real moron. I want your cock because you're a great artist."

He seemed to be crying for his entire life. "I always thought about you, darling, even before I knew you. Exactly who you are was my picture of you: you are the woman I wanted the woman I thought I could never have. Now I know you. Why do you want me? I'm a mess. I said to myself: I'll do anything I can, with myself with EVERYTHING, to make my work, I did it, I did do it, I really fucked up my health and my mind. I don't regret this, but now I'm a mess. Please, don't be naive."

I knew this man, whatever would happen and death was the least, would stick by me.

And 'she was given the real names of things' means she really perceived, she saw the real. That's it. If everything is living there is nothing; this living is the only matter matters. The thing itself. This isn't an expression of a real thing: this is the thing itself. Of course the thing itself the thing itself it is never the same. This is how aestheticism can be so much fun. The living thing the real thing is not what people tell you it is: it's what it is. This is the thing itself because I'm finding out about it it is me. It is a matter of letting (perceiving) happen what will.

My mother was dead. We knew that. She might have been murdered or she might have killed herself, perhaps accidentally. The police had abandoned the case and I didn't know how to find out on my own.

None of my father's family made any show of mourning for my mother. The funeral was a ghastly comedy. I was the only one sobbing my heart out while around me, hordes of women discussed Joan Crawford and her daughter and canasta games. Every now and then, I remember, Aunt Mabel told me to hand the chocolates around to her friends. I was wearing a fuzzy lavender sweater. One middle-aged woman shook the sweater back and forth and screamed that she wanted my mother's apartment.

After that, for a few months, I had nightmares, not nightmares but those deeper where I'd screaming wake up because there are so many thoughts, the thoughts are unknown.

I realize that all my life is is endings. Not endings, those are just events; but holes. For instance when my mother died, the 'I' I had always known dropped out. All my history went away. Pretty clothes and gayness amaze me.

The next thing I knew I received a letter from my father saying he was journeying to Seattle to see me, and then, it seems just a few days later, but that's my memory, I was standing in an old wood bar, then I was sitting down, a roly-poly man not at all the handsome soul-eyed man in that little painting I had wondered on was telling me he distinctly remembered my mother. But he didn't sound upset about her and she had been obsessed by him. "Are you my father?" I finally asked. "No. I'm your father's first cousin." He began to proposition me. "Oh, where's my father?"

"He's not here yet." Then this roly-poly man told me he came from an immensely wealthy family. His daughter picked bums off the street and slept with them. These stories made me realize that my mother's bohemian and my weirdnesses, which I had thought the same as the rich's amorality, were only stinky bourgeois playfulness.

Lutetia is the foulest because poorest section of Paris. After Charles the Simple visits Lutetia, he's so disgusted he tears a plan of Lutetia in two and orders the split to be made into a wide avenue.

Yvikel the widower has a daughter Blanchine whose health is slowly declining. They live in the center of Lutetia. Yvikel does everything he can for his daughter and resolves when she dies he'll kill himself.

After the avenue is built and sunlight, hitherto unknown, floods their rat-trap, Blanchine begins to recover. She recovers. To celebrate his gratitude, Yvikel recreates the plan of Lutetia in silk. Charles the Simple's hand reaches out and saves the section.

Dr. Sirhugues discovers a therapeutic blue plant light. An enormous lens concentrates this light on the diseased person held still by a cylindrical cage or 'focal jail.' But the rays are too powerful for the person to bear. Finally Dr. Sirhugues finds that only Yvikel's ancient silk is able to absorb and render harmless the dangerous portion of these rays.

I don't think I'm crazy. There's just no reality in my head and my emotions fly all over the place: sometimes I'm so down, all I think is I should kill myself. Almost at the same time I adore everything: I adore the sky. I adore the trees I see. I adore rhythms. I . . . I . . . I . . . I . . . I'm I'm mine mine my. I can't I can't. I hate being responsible oh.

I don't care what people think; when they think they're thinking about me, they're actually thinking about the ways they act. I certainly don't want them to give me their pictures of me I like the ways animals are socially. I would rather be petted than be part of this human social reality which is all pretense and lies.

I expected my father to be a strong totally sexually magnetic daredevil, macho as they come, but he was kind and gentle. He must have been very ill when I first met him because he had had five heart attacks. But his great physical pleasures were still drinking on the sly from Aunts Martha and Mabel and eating half-a-pint of coffee ice cream before going to bed. He relied for his life on the roly-poly cousin Clifford Still.

He must have wanted Clifford and me to marry. He believed in a reality that was stable which justice formed. A man who worked hard earned pleasure. A woman who took care of her husband kept his love. Approaching, death, for I quickly realized my father was extremely sick, frighteningly had to destroy those bourgeois illusions.

As his sickness grew, he began to depend on me. He didn't want me to walk away from his bed. I had known so much sickness.

"Your mother led me a hard life, Sarah."

"You weren't together very long, daddy."

"It was a passionate difficult existence. She wanted me to wear out. I don't think that's fair. I never understood her and I had very little tolerance for who she really was: I adored a figurehead. It was my death or getting rid of her, and she wanted the career."

"You thought you loved her."

"She depended on me more than she knew."

"People who don't have any sense of reality, daddy, live crazy. Other people don't understand why they act the ways they do. They survive because everyone survives."

As death approached my father said his life was useless. Because he now mistrusted.

I watched everything and I swore I'd never marry a man I didn't love and I'd never live for security.

Everyone hates me. My mother may have been murdered. Men want to rape me. My body's always sick. The world is paradise. Pain doesn't exist. Pain comes from askew human perceptions. A person's happy who doesn't give attention to her own desires but always thinks of others. Repressing causes pain. I have no one in this world. Every event is totally separate from every other event. If there are an infinite number of non-relating events, where's the relation that enables pain?

All of my family is dead. I have no way of knowing who means me harm and who doesn't.

38

LAYLI LONG SOLDIER

Here, the sentence will be respected.

I will compose each sentence with care, by minding what the rules of writing dictate.

For example, all sentences will begin with capital letters.

Likewise, the history of the sentence will be honored by ending each one with appropriate punctuation such as a period or question mark, thus bringing the idea to (momentary) completion.

You may like to know, I do not consider this a "creative piece."

I do not regard this as a poem of great imagination or a work of fiction.

Also, historical events will not be dramatized for an "interesting" read.

Therefore, I feel most responsible to the orderly sentence; conveyor of thought.

That said, I will begin.

You may or may not have heard about the Dakota 38.

If this is the first time you've heard of it, you might wonder, "What is the Dakota 38?"

The Dakota 38 refers to thirty-eight Dakota men who were executed by hanging, under orders from President Abraham Lincoln.

To date, this is the largest "legal" mass execution in US history.

The hanging took place on December 26, 1862—the day after Christmas.

This was the *same week* that President Lincoln signed the Emancipation Proclamation.

In the preceding sentence, I italicize "same week" for emphasis.

There was a movie titled *Lincoln* about the presidency of Abraham Lincoln.

The signing of the Emancipation Proclamation was included in the film *Lincoln*; the hanging of the Dakota 38 was not.

In any case, you might be asking, "Why were thirty-eight Dakota men hung?"

As a side note, the past tense of hang is *hung*, but when referring to the capital punishment of hanging, the correct past tense is *hanged*.

So it's possible that you're asking, "Why were thirty-eight Dakota men hanged?"

They were hanged for the Sioux Uprising.

I want to tell you about the Sioux Uprising, but I don't know where to begin.

I may jump around and details will not unfold in chronological order.

Keep in mind, I am not a historian.

So I will recount facts as best as I can, given limited resources and understanding.

Before Minnesota was a state, the Minnesota region, generally speaking, was the traditional homeland for Dakota, Anishinaabeg, and Ho-Chunk people.

During the 1800s, when the US expanded territory, they "purchased" land from the Dakota people as well as the other tribes.

But another way to understand that sort of "purchase" is: Dakota leaders ceded land to the US government in exchange for money or goods, but most importantly, the safety of their people.

Some say that Dakota leaders did not understand the terms they were entering, or they never would have agreed.

Even others call the entire negotiation "trickery."

But to make whatever-it-was official and binding, the US government drew up an initial treaty.

This treaty was later replaced by another (more convenient) treaty, and then another.

I've had difficulty unraveling the terms of these treaties, given the legal speak and congressional language.

As treaties were abrogated (broken) and new treaties were drafted, one after another, the new treaties often referenced old defunct treaties, and it is a muddy, switchback trail to follow.

Although I often feel lost on this trail, I know I am not alone.

However, as best as I can put the facts together, in 1851, Dakota territory was contained to a twelve-mile by one-hundred-fifty-mile long strip along the Minnesota River.

But just seven years later, in 1858, the northern portion was ceded (taken) and the southern portion was (conveniently) allotted, which reduced Dakota land to a stark ten-mile tract.

These amended and broken treaties are often referred to as the Minnesota Treaties.

The word *Minnesota* comes from *mni*, which means water; and *sota*, which means turbid.

Synonyms for turbid include muddy, unclear, cloudy, confused, and smoky.

Everything is in the language we use.

For example, a treaty is, essentially, a contract between two sovereign nations.

The US treaties with the Dakota Nation were legal contracts that promised money.

It could be said, this money was payment for the land the Dakota ceded; for living within as-signed boundaries (a reservation); and for relinquishing rights to their vast hunting territory which, in turn, made Dakota people dependent on other means to survive: money.

The previous sentence is circular, akin to so many aspects of history.

As you may have guessed by now, the money promised in the turbid treaties did not make it into the hands of Dakota people.

In addition, local government traders would not offer credit to "Indians" to purchase food or goods.

Without money, store credit, or rights to hunt beyond their ten-mile tract of land, Dakota people began to starve.

The Dakota people were starving.

The Dakota people starved.

In the preceding sentence, the word "starved" does not need italics for emphasis.

One should read "The Dakota people starved" as a straightforward and plainly stated fact.

As a result—and without other options but to continue to starve—Dakota people retaliated.

Dakota warriors organized, struck out, and killed settlers and traders.

This revolt is called the Sioux Uprising.

Eventually, the US Cavalry came to Mnisota to confront the Uprising.

More than one thousand Dakota people were sent to prison.

As already mentioned, thirty-eight Dakota men were subsequently hanged.

After the hanging, those one thousand Dakota prisoners were released.

However, as further consequence, what remained of Dakota territory in Mnisota was dissolved (stolen).

The Dakota people had no land to return to.

This means they were exiled.

Homeless, the Dakota people of Mnisota were relocated (forced) onto reservations in South Dakota and Nebraska.

Now, every year, a group called the Dakota 38 + 2 Riders conducts a memorial horse ride from Lower Brule, South Dakota, to Mankato, Mnisota.

The Memorial Riders travel 325 miles on horseback for eighteen days, sometimes through sub-zero blizzards.

They conclude their journey on December 26, the day of the hanging.

Memorials help focus our memory on particular people or events.

Often, memorials come in the forms of plaques, statues, or gravestones.

The memorial for the Dakota 38 is not an object inscribed with words, but an *act*.

Yet, I started this piece because I was interested in writing about grasses.

So, there is one other event to include, although it's not in chronological order and we must backtrack a little.

When the Dakota people were starving, as you may remember, government traders would not extend store credit to "Indians."

One trader named Andrew Myrick is famous for his refusal to provide credit to Dakota people by saying, "If they are hungry, let them eat grass."

There are variations of Myrick's words, but they are all something to that effect.

When settlers and traders were killed during the Sioux Uprising, one of the first to be executed by the Dakota was Andrew Myrick.

When Myrick's body was found,

his mouth was stuffed with grass.

I am inclined to call this act by the Dakota warriors a poem.

There's irony in their poem.

There was no text.

"Real" poems do not "really" require words.

I have italicized the previous sentence to indicate inner dialogue, a revealing moment.

But, on second thought, the words "Let them eat grass" click the gears of the poem into place.

So, we could also say, language and word choice are crucial to the poem's work.

Things are circling back again.

Sometimes, when in a circle, if I wish to exit, I must leap.

And let the body swing.

From the platform.

Out

to the grasses.

Excerpt from *Light While There Is Light*

KEITH WALDROP

I've read many stories of revenants and apparitions, but my ghosts merely disappear. I never see them. They haunt me by not being there, by the table where no one eats, the empty window that lets the sun in without a shadow.

Few memories give me a sense of my childhood—perhaps, later, more will surface. Among those few is the darkened room from which proceed my mother's moans. This is not a particular moment that I remember; it is the background of many years, nearly all my early life. She moans for so many reasons that it will be difficult more than to suggest their range. Probably I am ignorant of her most exquisite pains. I know enough not to make light of lamentations.

Sometimes I could get her to play the piano. She sat at the battered old upright, her eyes shut, picking out what she could remember of a Chopin polonaise or some cheap waltz from 1920. And then—what really moved her—"Brilliant Variations," by someone named Butler, on "Pass Me Not" or other hymn. I was fascinated by the way she kept her eyes closed. To glance at the music, just as to read a paragraph of print, gave her migraines.

I knew, of course, the words to the hymns she played, and, whether or not I sang them, they sounded in my inner ear, even through Butler's brilliance.

> Some day the silver cord will break
> And I no more as now shall sing.

Ghosts gather in such lines.

> But O the joy when I shall wake
> Within the palace of the King.

It is not for her that I write this. She is dead, safe at last, out of all relation. I can recall, still, what she looked like at particular times, how she moved in certain spaces. But little by little she fades, replaced by an unsubstantial description somewhere in the memory. Best to make it as definite as possible. All we remember, finally, is words.

"I was always so weak," she said. "My heart." She held her throat between thumb and index finger, which is how she took her pulse. "When I was sixteen, the doctor said"—an unaccustomed pleasure in her voice now—"I shouldn't ever have to work, I was made to sit on a velvet cushion."

She taught piano while still in high school. (How little I actually knew her, her life extending back into the blank before my time—when I was asked for details, after she died, I put down a wrong place of birth.) As my father studied law and then went to work on the railroad, so she went to the conservatory, graduated, but then, fleeing her parents, married and, as they say, had children.

It was not my father that she married—he came later. I have two pictures of her first husband. In both of them, the left arm is in a Napoleonic position, as if he were holding a glass in front of him, but the hand is empty. "He posed that way," she told me. "He was proud of his wrist watch." He showed up, years later, with a second wife named Bessie, a sad-faced, decent-seeming creature who apparently kept him with her, and under control, by means of small but frequent doles. He was then (I mean, at his re-entry) a barber in Hot Springs, Arkansas.

My mother's favorite image was that of the church considered as a great speckled bird, which she took as a simple parable. Alien down here, humiliated and despised, the saints would eventually, at the Rapture, soar. Her favorite color was green, signifying restfulness. She maintained that a room with red wallpaper would drive one crazy.

She grew up in Missouri, an only child, but moved with her parents to Redmond, Oregon, where she went through high school. Whether she was in fact content there, I have no way of knowing, but certainly ever after she looked back to those days as a lost happiness and Oregon as paradise. Just a few years before her death, when she realized, not only that nothing had turned out right, but that there was no longer time for any good to come—no horizon left for any miraculous rescue—she began to retrieve what memories she could of Oregon.

There were many eligible young men in Redmond, though her parents were watchful. If she stayed out too late, her mother in a fret sent after her. Her father, mild but dutiful, would seek her out, take her home. When her affections settled too firmly on a certain Lindsay, they took panic, packed up their things, and fled with her back to Missouri.

But Lindsay came again to mind, and one day she wrote him at his old address in Oregon—this must have been in 1972. He not only got the letter, but wrote back. And what he wrote was that he had never married but had waited for her. I was stunned when she talked, not altogether coherently, about going back to Oregon, to marry Lindsay.

"When did you actually last see him?" I asked her. She had to think, to count it up.

"Nineteen seventeen." She was too ill by now to go anywhere.

The history of my mother's religious opinions should be told as the record of a pilgrimage. As I imagine most pilgrimages, it was less the struggle toward a given end than a continual flight from disappointment and unhappiness. Neither the joys of heaven nor hell's worst prospects provide as forceful a motive as the mere emptiness of the world.

Before her first marriage, she played the piano for Methodist services. Probably at that time she thought little about religious doctrine or religious experience. It was, she said later, "an old formal M.E. church." But once she married handsome Charles—under what circumstances I never heard—and was delivered of their first child, also a Charles, her relation to those early services must have changed. Ill soon after giving birth, she was kept awake one night by sounds of a party in the next apartment. Charles senior, his hair slicked like Valentino's and his wrist watch gleaming, went to quiet them down, and joined the party.

She described the scene. It was one of those that stuck with her, humiliating still after thirty, after forty years. She got up, the noise having increased after his leaving. In her housecoat she went to the next apartment and knocked and asked for her husband. Charles, embarrassed in his turn by the appearance of obligation in the shape of this frail form at the door, went with her, but explained the exit to his friends of an hour with a wink and a formula: "She's a Sunday School girl."

I am convinced that, at that moment, the formula was wide of the mark. Probably poor Charles never in his life figured anything quite correctly. But this must have been one of the incidents pushing her toward the church as a refuge from the world as represented by "old painted women" (her colloquial *old* not referring to age) and by the routines of a loveless marriage. By the time I could remember anything, she was taking me to the *Free* Methodist church at the corner of South Avenue and Commercial Street in Emporia, Kansas.

The Free Methodists split off from their parent church (the old formal Methodists) about the time of the Civil War. It was one of the many groups preaching a return to Wesley's doctrine of "Christian Perfection." Sanctification, they teach, is a distinct act, subsequent to justification. To be justified, or "saved," is to have one's sins forgiven, but to be sanctified is to have the carnal nature, the taint of original sin, removed. They also call this state "holiness" and they are aware that the world dismisses them as "Holy Rollers."

For they have also kept the ecstatic side of Wesleyanism. What I retain most vividly of the church in Emporia (which I attended until I was fourteen) is the way services were always rescued from dullness by what I learned to call the *demonstration of the Holy Ghost*. What in fact happened, Sunday after Sunday (and at Wednesday night prayer meeting), was that two women—I remember their names as Sister Eliot and Sister Faulkner, though it now sounds unlikely to me—fell under the influence of the spirit and began to behave in exactly opposite ways. They were opposites already: Sister Eliot was strawberry-blond, open-faced, outgoing, and when the spirit hit her she ran down the aisle, shouting. Sister Faulkner shrank back, twisted, moaned, and often sank to the floor, a small, swarthy woman, weeping bitterly.

Their performance was joined in by the congregation in general, most of whom confined themselves to *Amen*'s, shouted or murmured, but they were the natural leaders. What, I wonder, would they have done, have become, if the church had not been there? Perhaps it is well to add that these services had nothing Erskine Caldwell about them. Powered by sexual energy perhaps (what other source is there?) they were chaste and even, I would say, dignified. And they gave some meaning to lives otherwise lost in weekday blankness.

My father thought all females in terrible league against all males, but the center of the plot was among the Free Methodist women, whom he pictured as the hags from *Macbeth* sitting in unholy assembly to pass judgment on him. He felt them sitting; their weight bent his shoulders.

"Your mother," he would tell me, "didn't have a dime when I married her." He always started that way. "She had one damn cardboard suitcase." If he were drunk enough, he would go on, getting louder. "Not a pot to piss in. And those three brats." Charles, Elaine, Julian: before Julian was born, the elder Charles had taken off. Julian was born in Leeton, Missouri, at his grandparents' house. My father had already two daughters and was close to twenty years older than his second wife. I have no idea how they met, let alone what drew them together. "Now she runs off down to that damn church. They turn her against me."

The spookiest story I ever heard was told me by a friend, who may have written it down somewhere, but I know it from her directly.

She was in England, traveling with a boyfriend. At some point they found accommodations in one of those country houses where the family lets rooms to pay the monstrous upkeep on anachronistic grandeur. She and her friend were shown into the largest room they had ever seen, with high windows, oak paneling, huge four-poster, a room from what was to them a storybook era. A grandiose fireplace dominated the room, but there were none of the usual paraphernalia—screen, firedogs, bellows. Instead there was only, half in the great fireplace and half out, a cradle. They wondered at the cradle—of the old-fashioned kind, like the one Lillian Gish rocks in *Intolerance*—and went to dinner.

But later, when ready for bed, they could not quite manage to disregard it. They tipped it, finding that it rocked with a sort of bulky motion, soon coming to rest again. It had somehow a great weightiness to it, a dense heaviness that struck them both as incongruous in a baby-bed.

Perhaps what happened next was their effort to escape the fascination of the cradle there on the hearth (she never said so, made no attempt at explaining anything). In any case, they began horsing around and her friend, before she realized what was happening, picked her up and put her in the cradle. And then he ran across the room and turned the lights off.

And it was dark then, of course, but it was not a darkness that she recognized. It was as though there lacked not light, but the flow of time. It was not, across the black room, a distance in steps, that even the blind might feel their way, but a space of centuries, a loss total and immeasurable. And she could not get out of the cradle, which she felt rocking. She could not even struggle. With the utmost effort, she managed to form her friend's name, but cried it so feebly that she knew it would never carry across the emptiness.

He meanwhile, as it turned out, was feeling much the same thing as she and was searching, terrified, for the light switch, which he could not find again. Finally his hand, groping blindly, hit the right spot and the room burst into light—the same room, with its paneling, its four-poster, its cradle in the fireplace, and her, clambering out of the cradle. They were both terror-stricken and refused to stay the night in that room.

You should not suppose that I am writing this to judge between my father and my mother. It would hardly be reasonable, now that they are both gone, to decide their quarrel. In my mind it remains a given, and goes on, an eternal argument.

My father named me Bernard, after Shaw, and Keith, for Sir Arthur Keith (my father's name was Arthur). "Two old atheists," my mother always said, certain he had picked the names to irritate her. (Her notion of atheist was a bit vague.) My father generally professed agnosticism, but in his last years—especially while drinking—insisted that he believed in God. "Otherwise," he said, "how could I be a Mason?"

One of his favorite recollections (it must be remembered that he was half a century older than I) was the attempt of William Allen White, editor of the *Emporia Gazette*, to get into the local lodge. "They came to the question," my father related, tapping my knee for emphasis, "which every applicant *has* to answer. They asked him, Do you believe in God? He said, *I believe in William Allen White*." A dramatic pause, whether of outrage or admiration I could never decide. It was certainly portentous, our most celebrated citizen hanging in the balance. "And they turned him down!" My father had gone on up, into the Scottish Rite and the Shrine.

In the era of the Civil War, the Methodists, already old and formal, charged rental on their pews. The seceding branch, preaching largely to outcasts and the needy, decided to abolish this charge and so denominated themselves *Free*. It was a common practice among congregations of that time, especially near the frontier, to hire musicians for Sunday services—which meant, more often than not, bringing players from the local theater into the house of God. The Free Methodists, with all-or-nothing zeal, abolished instruments from their church, and in the early nineteen forties, when I attended and after much hesitation joined them, the singing was entirely congregational—no choir—and regulated by, at most, a pitch pipe. Sister Eliot or Sister Faulkner would lead (the one somewhat faster, the other somewhat slower, than expected tempo), not moving their hands, but simply by facing the congregation and singing out.

So when Sunday morning came around, or Sunday night, or Wednesday night, my mother would cease from her moanings, comb her hair, put on her best, and she and Elaine and I would hasten to South and Commercial for some *a cappella* praise, some middling preaching and, with luck, a breath of ecstasy. As long as she was there, among the saints, her life seemed clear and meaningful. Outside, in the world, she was a complex of miseries that I am still not sure I can quite sort out. "My heart," she would say, fingers to her throat, but it stood for a whole existence.

Her greatest pride was the smallness of her hands and feet. If one of us bought her bedroom slippers for her birthday—demanding at the store their very most smallest size—they were sure to be too large and she was sure to be enraged that we should think her feet so gross. On less emotional occasions, "I have Cinderella feet," she would say, and it was terribly plain that, not only the prince, but the entire fairy-tale realm, had passed her by, leaving the most workaday ashes.

Her first husband had been a deception. Her second she treated frankly as an enemy. It only gradually dawned on me, between battles, that I was disputed territory. Every time I went to church, it was a victory for her, and I came to regard my father as an alien power, sinister in behavior, but possessed of strange forces. His occupation itself was mysterious: as a railroader, he was fanatically punctual, continually checking his watch and angry if it got more than a few seconds from the official Santa Fe clock. But since he worked on freight trains, he was liable to appear at any hour of the night or day and just as arbitrarily to be called away. The unknown figure of *the caller*—just a voice on the telephone—made its way into my private mythology. Simply to answer the anonymous ring put one within the possibility of hearing, instead of an *Hello* that would connect with a remembered face, the disorienting but imperative "This is the caller."

Between the living room, which for some reason or other was my bedroom for a time, and the room where my parents slept, there were huge sliding doors. (This was a house on Neosho Street, the most nearly permanent of our homes—but there was inevitably, wherever we were, a sense of provisional arrangements, of waiting for better weather, a new government.) One night when my father was in, not likely to be called, I settled down on my convertible but could not enjoy my insomnia because of the argument from the other side of the door. An argument meant that my father's voice continued on and on into the night, occasionally raised to a shout or broken by a murmur from my mother, who for the most part maintained a dead silence. All their nights together spread out like this into an agonizing deadlock. I don't know what they argued about, or if indeed there was a subject. To escape from the oppressive sound, I set myself to wait for the unattainable moment of entering sleep. To be conscious for once at that magical transition seemed to me—I don't know why—a knowledge I would need, that I could not well do without.

But just when I had dozed off, slipping past the threshold I wanted so much to examine, I was jolted awake by doors slid open, then slid shut again. And then, in the dark, my father lay down beside me, breathing heavily. I made no sign of life and gradually he subsided into, I thought, a sleep of his own. But apparently he was listening, there in the dark beside me, for before I quite had a chance to miss again my moment of going to sleep, he had thrown off the cover and the great doors rolled back with a crash and he was swearing loudly. After he left his bed, Elaine had slipped in beside my mother. Now she raced back to her own room as he switched the lights on. "This is what happens," he was yelling, "as soon as I turn my back." The giant doors cracked shut again, leaving me dazzled with the light that was now shut out. His shouts continued on the other side, Elaine's voice sometimes chiming in from a distance. (Neither Charles nor Julian were there—Charles was in the war in the South Pacific.) I lay tense while the shouts got louder. I heard Sister Eliot's name. Finally there were other sounds: movements, doors. Then a blow and my mother's scream and Elaine howling.

I began to pray. I began, with an earnestness I have rarely recaptured in any action since then, to pray to God that he would strike my father dead. My prayer was answered, some dozen years later, after both my hatred and my faith had died long lingering deaths. The only immediate aftermath of that night was a peace-offering from my father, a new secondhand piano, at which my mother sat, eyes closed, playing what she could remember of something by Chopin, a syncopated waltz from 1920, brilliant variations on "Pass Me Not."

Shadow Janitor

KIM HYESOON

Translated by Don Mee Choi

When I'm at home
people don't ask me who I am
They know at once that it's me
because I'm the only one who's home
and so all kinds of things enter me
Hello, did you order sorrow? If not, how about anxiety?
You ordered ghost's cold air for twelve people, right?
The doorbell rings and the cell phone rings
Something that's not wind or river enters me
My body is a piece of real estate to be rented out in this life
The five thousand pages of my shadows are delivered

What's with the account book?
The self-accusing book
The self-accusing book

My bookcase has only account books of self-accusation
What's with the content on each black page?

When I flip through the pages made of my shadows

my kitchen shouts
my living room shouts
Did you put in an order?

When I go out people don't recognize me
They just call me Auntie
A sign: the bird of ill omen opens its wings and roams high up in the sky
A sign: the bird of unfairness cries unfair unfair
The parrot that has lost its vocal cords perches on my collarbone and puts a curse on me
Mr. Misfortune with broken wings suffers from depression
so he walks with a black umbrella like a crow tap tap
Mr. Fear parades, Mr. Sorrow marches
The crow that flew away from Death caws on top of the roof of my embrace
I'm relieved that the deliveryman doesn't come when I am out
but when I get home
I prostrate and
salute the floor
Mr. Floor, Mr. Window, Mr. Pillar
Please spare my heart
The house is satisfied
only when it's touched by my hands once a day
The house needs
the walls, mirrors, and spoons cleaned once a day
I don't want them but the bell rings and the five thousand pages
of black wings of real estate are delivered again.

Excerpt from *Children in Reindeer Woods*

KRISTÍN ÓMARSDÓTTIR
Translated by Lytton Smith

i. The soldiers cross the green meadow. The sun is at its height. Setting down their packs and weapons, they remove their jackets and tie them around their sturdy soldiers' waists. Three together. Three white t-shirts and three green pairs of pants approaching a farm with a two-story house that rises from a huge nest of hedges and tall trees. A cow lows in the backyard. Four, five chickens waddle about the property. A dog gets to its feet and watches the garden gate open. Four children, an older woman, and a young man head out from the house with their hands clasped behind their necks. A moment later, a woman with a red tray comes out after them. A milk bottle, a silver coffee pot, three clean glasses, three cups, a knife stuck in a thick rye loaf. Butter and freshly-boiled eggs for the soldiers. A light breeze makes its way across the yard. One of the soldiers wipes his forehead. Another watches the third, who shakes himself, brushing off goose-bumps, or a thought. On the east side, beside the gate, a pebbledash table is set into the earth. The woman with the red tray heads there. The breeze tugs at the edge of her skirt. The people stand in front of the soldiers, who shuffle their feet in the gravel. One of the soldiers shoots the woman with the tray. The milk bottle and glasses shatter. The coffee pot clatters to the ground. Blood runs from the woman's eyes as she grips the tray tightly and falls; she lies face down in the grass as if resting peacefully on a pillow, and the blood leaks across it. The youngest child runs to her but is shot on the way. The cow lows in familiar fashion. The chickens hurry over to look at the bodies. The soldier who fired lowers his weapon. The other two shoot the dog, the woman, the man, two more children. But the young girl is spared, seemingly without a thought. She lowers her arms to her sides. One soldier shoulders his weapon and takes one of the strutting chickens in his arms. "I've always wanted to hold a chicken," he confesses. The other two step cautiously inside the house, weapons raised. Army boots inside the house, bodies too. While he is examining the chicken, petting and caressing it, the girl steals under the bush near the garden gate. Into a curved tree bed. Leaves and branches cover the trees like a long grass skirt. "You smell very good, my hen. A much better scent than I expected a chicken would have. Mmm, my chick," the soldier says, pressing the tip of his nose against the hen's belly. The girl licks the salty earth, decaying leaves, mossy stones, the clods of earth. She stares out from her hiding place as the animal lover prods the chicken's belly, examines its eyes, opens its beak, and inspects the tiny tongue. No teeth. Then they call him into the house. The soldier disappears inside, the creature still in his arms. The girl pulls herself deeper into the bed on her stomach, the way reptiles move. The sun shifts. It's one o'clock.

ii. The trees rustled, and the curtains on the upper story were drawn by the cord. Perhaps someone could have compared the billowing of the curtains to that of a pregnant woman's dress. The cow in the backyard lowed like clockwork. The girl peered out from her hiding place. The chicken's clucking carried from the house. The chickens hadn't ever been invited inside, but this was a new era. Two more chickens strolled up to the doorstep. They finally had a chance to visit the humans' habitat. Just then the chicken inside cried out like she was about to be torn apart; there was an awful flapping of wings. The chickens hurried away. From the house, three gunshots resounded through the valley, as though the sound came from giant, well-positioned loudspeakers. One soldier dragged one of his bloody comrades across the threshold and laid him beside the other dead bodies. The cow lowed. He wiped his forehead with the back of his hand, disappeared inside and dragged out his other comrade, who was just as bloody. He wiped his forehead with the back of his hand. He went in and came back with the chicken in his arms. He moistened his handkerchief with spit and wiped splotches of blood from her feathers. He set the plump chicken down, uncoiled a yellow hose, connected it to the spigot, and turned on the faucet. There was a rustling on the ground as the cat came over to the girl, who suddenly felt her allergies prickling. The soldier set down the hose and went over to the bushes. The cat appeared from the bushes and nuzzled its head against his boots. "Here, pussy," said the soldier, taking the kitten in his arms. The girl was definitely definitely definitely about to sneeze, so she ate some soil.

iii. The soldier took off his t-shirt and washed his torso with the jet of water from the hose. The nozzle was an attractive orange and had three settings: a milder, more irregular jet; a sputter-spatter jet; and a strong, thundering jet. He must be using the last one. The kitty stood beside the red tray licking milk from the grass. The cow lowed from out back as though it was missing the fun, as it had on other occasions. Mooooo. The soldier sprayed water in the direction of his friend the chicken, and she danced about in the jet, her dance steps making her look like she was wearing high heels. Then he soaked the t-shirt like a rag, wiped his chest with the crumpled shirt, rinsed it, wrung it out, and hung it to dry on the narrow wooden trellis, which protected the rose bed that had been planted in front of the big French windows. On the other side, inside, by the windowsill, was the perfect spot for a portrait photograph. He picked up the hose, drank from the nozzle, and shut off the water.

The chicken followed him to the shed, where he kicked open the rusty door and got a shovel. He disappeared around a corner of the house, followed by the chicken, then reappeared and walked past the bush which stood against the garden wall—on the other side of which they had often sat in the grass to drink juice, eat cookies, and play ludo, nine men's morris, or backgammon. The chicken came back around the same corner of the house, and it took her a while, crossing the garden with smaller steps, neat chickensteps, to re-find her new friend.

Despite her restricted view, the girl could see the soldier studying part of the vegetable garden. He opened the greenhouse door, and the glass, which was too small for the frame, rattled. Beside the greenhouse grew tall, slender trees. He began to dig and shovel there. The chicken waddled around nearby. The other chickens approached, then retreated, approached again, retreated again. Done with the milk in the grass, the kitten prowled over to the girl, not interested in whether she'd like her allergies set off again; it wanted to make friends, to be affectionate towards her. Then the girl sneezed, and the kitten bounded all the way over to the soldier, who had in the meantime clambered down into the grave, which now came up to his waist. The mountain of used earth beside the greenhouse increased, and kittikins lay on the slope, watching the earth fall from the shovel onto a second mountain that was growing beside the first. The sun moved in a long arc. Tea-time came and tea-time went.

Only the soldier's head was still visible; he threw the shovel onto the bank and pulled himself up out of the grave. The girl wet herself. The soldier drank right from the nozzle of the garden hose and she saw his muscles flex. He turned the hose off, put on his t-shirt and work gloves, and dragged the body of one of his comrades into the freshly-dug grave. The body of his other comrade, too. The body of the young man, the older woman, and the woman who was still holding on to the red tray. No matter how he tried to pry the tray from her, he couldn't. The tray went in, the tray went in, it had done its service, it was ready to die. With a cigarette perched in his mouth, the soldier gathered the biggest glass shards from the grass and pitched them into the grave. Then the coffeepot, the rye bread, the butter, and the hardboiled eggs.

iv. The soldier gathered the dog's carcass in his arms and tossed it into the grave. He went into the house, came back with his arms full of colorful sheets, and wrapped a yellow sheet around one child's body; down it went into the grave. He wrapped another child's body in an orange sheet; down it went into the grave. The third child's body could have gone in a light blue sheet, but it got a red one instead, and down it went into the grave. The girl stared at the light blue sheet as it lay on the grass beside a yellow ball. The soldier went back to the garden gate, pushed it so hard that it rattled on its hinges, and dug about in the gravel with the toe of his boot.

He went inside and stayed there for a little while, then came back and pulled on a blue turtleneck sweater which he had gotten from his backpack. The chicken went over to him as he lit a cigarette. "Hi my hen, you sweet old lady." He blew smoke and threw the light blue sheet away, into the grave. Before the sun went down, the two mountains of earth had disappeared into the ground again. He thoroughly packed and shoveled another one-and-a-half wheelbarrows of gravel from the yard, depositing them over the fresh grave.

He sat at the pebbledash table, where the three men would have been invited to sit just after noon, had they accepted coffee and freshly-baked bread, fresh milk from the cow, and freshly boiled eggs. He lit a cigarette; there's a lot of smoking in war. The cat hopped up into his lap and lay down but got poked and vanished under the bush. The soldier stood up. The girl wet herself. He stopped in front of the bush. She saw his shoes, his fingertips. He went over to the grave. He stood there with his back to the bush, his body hunched, not upright like a soldier's. The shadows had lengthened. The girl stretched all the muscles in her body and crept out from under the bush; she chewed on her hair and snuck across the field towards the vegetable garden. Children can be invisible. She had tested it time and again. Children are more often invisible than not. The girl stood still behind the soldier. After a whole eternity, he turned around and looked in her eyes. She was wearing an off-white dress with a finely-checkered pattern; she had muddy scratched knees where stinging nettles and tree branches had snatched at her; a muddy mouth; scratched and scraped cheeks; muddy fingers; dirt teardrops under her nails; white socks and white shiny shoes; a red bow in her hair; her dress was urine-stained. There was no gun in the garden. They were all inside. She had forgotten to think about that. For a moment she had forgotten the guns. Oh, oh. They hadn't come outside, even though the bodies had, and if they did, well, she could run at once. She could run at once if they came out.

"Good evening. I am Rafael," said the man in the blue turtleneck sweater, holding out his hand.

"Good evening. I am Billie," said the girl; she curtsied and shook his hand. The chicken tripped over to them. It didn't want to let itself get separated from its new friend, which was about to happen.

In Case I Don't Notice

LAURA HENRIKSEN

In case I don't notice, I ask someone to tell me
when it's over, I thought you said "look out
for blood," but no that can't be right. Up late,
cursing my name, my birth, my frozen
above ground. "Like a moth to a porch lamp,"
I say, sucking on its ice.

Don't I feel dumb when I realize the place I thought
was permeated with your memory, you'd never
actually been, it wasn't even your umbrella. Maybe
I'm getting too comfortable being trapped in
tunnels underground, but I know the truth,
that all this calm is pretense, attending to its simmer.

To want to want to, lying about your longing,
what will you do that you do for you? Is there a word
for the desire to bury myself in cool, damp dirt?
For the desire to be suspended as in water but
in air? A word for the desire to revisit the traces
of skin and grime I leave behind on every surface
I touch, not to reclaim them or anything, just to
see how they are now. I don't want them anymore.

God Gives You What You Can Handle

I growled at a kid today. Or more, I responded to this kid as if he were a dog who growled at me with a stern "No" when he tried to hand me his religious materials. He was surrounded by his peer group, they were playing their violins and singing "Amazing Grace" in front of the subway entrance at 2nd Ave. He said "Have a nice day," with a degree of sanctimony only a thirteen-year-old boy secure in his salvation can access, and I ranted to Nicole and Stacy about not being a pawn in the indoctrination of children, remembering the annual summer reenactment of the Stations of the Cross, as performed by local amateurs weeping across central Iowa's little hills, of my own youth. Now pulling glass out of my feet, and I know I'm being punished. I spit out marble after marble and put them right back in my mouth and hold them there until they aren't cold anymore. I suppose I didn't provide a particularly persuasive example of an unbeliever.

The truth is I love kids, and normally seeing them in large unsupervised groups makes me happy. I imagine them forming their own government, try to imagine what items would be on their agenda in what order. I also love groups of tourists, love to be reminded by their unhurried confusion that I too have been a vacationer, I too have known vacations, far from home and a little uncomfortable and happy.

I also love it when the curve of a street or a road makes the street or road seem from a certain distance to disappear, swallowed by the trees that surround it, or a large building, or the other side of the hill, and when I reach a particular point, the apex so to speak, I'll be swallowed up too, the mystery, not gone or disappeared, but part of it now, consumed in it.

The Only Good

Palmira Rastelli died on December 28, 1870, which is almost the only thing I know about her. This was soon after Rome had been captured by Italy, completing the long and violent process of Italian unification. Plans for the Brooklyn Bridge had recently been completed, a tunnel was opened up for trains under the River Thames, The Third Republic began in France after Napoleon III was deposed, the Cardiff Giant was revealed to be a hoax inspired by a fight at a Methodist revival meeting, and a British ship called *The City of Boston* disappeared forever with all its passengers and crew, never to be heard from again. Three months after her death, Palmira burned three long and slender fingerprints onto Maria Zaganti's prayer book, as if she had delicately reached across a table to slide the book back to herself.

Purgatory doesn't appear anywhere in the Bible, but it's still an old story, connected to a desire or impulse in the living to care for the dead, perhaps hoping that similar help will be available to them when their ability to care for themselves is more uncertain. One origin story is from the 11th Century. A monk told the Abbot Odilo of Cluny about being shipwrecked on a mysterious island, inhabited only by a strange hermit. The hermit told the monk a story about a chasm from which erupted the screams of tormented souls, and the licking flames of demons, neon orange in the bright sun, a darker umber at night. The hermit explained the demons were frustrated, because souls kept escaping from their torture through the intervention of the living, whose prayers for the unsaved dead and good deeds performed on their behalf freed them from their torment.

Never having much thought about it, I had assumed Purgatory to be a place like Heaven or Hell; its defining feature being permanence beyond what mortals can easily imagine. Against this mistaken understanding, purgatory is fundamentally temporary, a place souls wait and hope to be redeemed, unbaptized babies and others for whom hell would seem too harsh, but heaven undeserved according to the many rules of heaven. On All Souls Day, prayers of the faithful can intercede on behalf of these trapped souls. I remember a similar practice in the town where I grew up, and the regular controversy where every few years a probably well-intentioned teenager would attempt the posthumous salvation of Anne Frank.

Despite looking it up in advance, when I first tried to visit Piccolo Museo Del Purgatorio in the Chiesa del Sacro Cuore del Suffragio it was closed. It had taken a little while to find the unusually Gothic church just above the Tiber with its many thin spires. I spent the next few hours walking around what was meant to be Hadrian's final resting place, but later became the Pope's house, and then a prison, and now a museum where I drank a glass of wine and watched seagulls. I'm not sure where Hadrian's remains rest instead. Returning, I was relieved to find the church doors open, and upon entering walked to the back right corner where I knew the museum would be.

Construction on the Chiesa del Sacro Cuore del Suffragio began in 1893 under the direction of the French priest Father Victor Jouet. In 1897 a fire broke out in the chapel. Once contained, the parishioners observed a face burned into the altar, and understood it to be a soul in purgatory reaching out to them. I'm not sure what happened to this altar, or if Father Jouet ever determined the name of the soul and therefore was able to say a Holy Mass for them.

The event did, however, inspire him to begin collecting artifacts of souls in purgatory, which are now displayed on a small corkboard behind glass in the back of the church. The objects are mostly hands and fingers burned onto prayer books and articles of clothing, attempts to communicate with the living, to ask them to prayer harder and more. It reminds me, once again, of *Hellbound: Hellraiser II*, when Kirsty finds messages written in blood she understands to be from her deceased father reading, "Help me, I am in Hell," but in fact are a demonic trick that will eventually lead her to a labyrinth in hell. The idea that the ones we love are suffering and that we might be able to help them is a very powerful manipulative tool.

I wonder what the relationship between Palmira and Maria was like. I know that Palmira was the sister of the parish priest of Saint Andrew of Poggio Berni, Don Sante Rastelli. Why wouldn't she reach out to him directly? I read that they were friends, but what kind? Childhood friends, rival friends, secret lovers? Did they often pray together? Did they stay up late, forming a pact that whoever died first would send back a message, and whoever survived would intervene for the other's salvation? Did it work?

Two German tourists observe the objects and photographs with me. Despite my research in advance, looking at pictures on the internet and in guidebooks, I am in no way prepared for how unsettling the experience would be, so much so that I spend the rest of the night slightly disturbed in my thoughts, looking for images in wood grain and puddles. What if you reached out from the grave, asking for help, and no one heard you, or believed what they saw?

I learn that according to Catholic doctrine, you can't go to Hell from Purgatory, only Heaven, so that's good news. An interstitial space, like being at the threshold to where you want most to be for an indefinite but not limitless amount of time, that doesn't sound so bad. It sounds kind of wonderful to me, all promise and anticipation, like waiting for a kiss you know will come, without the sadness of knowing that once it arrives it will soon enough be over, knowing that while the waiting won't last forever the kissing will, and all you have to do is hang out with demons and burn messages on your friend's bibles until then. Maybe Palmira wasn't even asking for help, maybe she was just flirting, or saying hello.

Excerpt from
The Life and Opinions of Tristram Shandy, Gentleman

LAURENCE STERNE

I wonder what's all that noise, and running backwards and forwards for, above stairs, quoth my father, addressing himself, after an hour and a half's silence, to my uncle Toby,—who, you must know, was sitting on the opposite side of the fire, smoking his social pipe all the time, in mute contemplation of a new pair of black plush breeches which he had got on:—What can they be doing, brother?—quoth my father,—we can scarce hear ourselves talk.

I think, replied my uncle Toby, taking his pipe from his mouth, and striking the head of it two or three times upon the nail of his left thumb, as he began his sentence,—I think, says he:—But to enter rightly into my uncle Toby's sentiments upon this matter, you must be made to enter first a little into his character, the outlines of which I shall just give you, and then the dialogue between him and my father will go on as well again.

Pray what was that man's name,—for I write in such a hurry, I have no time to recollect or look for it,—who first made the observation, "That there was great inconsistency in our air and climate"? Whoever he was,'twas a just and good observation in him.—But the corollary drawn from it, namely, "That it is this which had furnished us with such a variety of odd and whimsical characters";—that was not his;—it was found out by another man, at least a century and a half after him: Then again,—that this copious store-house of original materials, is the true and natural cause that our Comedies are so much better than those of France, or any others that either have, or can be wrote upon the Continent:—that discovery was not fully made till about the middle of King William's reign,—when the great Dryden, in writing one of his long prefaces, (if I mistake not) most fortunately hit upon it. Indeed, toward the latter end of Queen Anne, the great Addison began to patronize the notion, and more fully explained it to the world in one or two of his Spectators;—but the discovery was not his.—Then, fourthly and lastly, that this strange irregularity in our climate, producing so strange an irregularity in our characters,—doth thereby, in some sort, make us amends, by giving us somewhat to make us merry with when the weather will not suffer us to go out of doors,—that observation is my own;—and was struck out by me this very rainy day, March 26, 1759, and betwixt the hours of nine and ten in the morning.

Thus—thus, my fellow-labourers and associates in this great harvest of our learning, now ripening before our eyes; thus it is, by slow steps of casual increase, that our knowledge physical, metaphysical, physiological, polemical, nautical, mathematical, enigmatical, technical, biographical, romantical, chemical, and obstetrical, with fifty other branches of it, (most of 'em ending as these do, in *ical*) have for these two centuries and more, gradually been creeping upwards towards that *'Ακμὴ* of their perfections, from which, if we may form a conjecture from the advances of these last seven years, we cannot possibly be far off.

When that happens, it is to be hoped, it will put an end to all kind of writings whatsoever;—the want of all kind of writing will put an end to all kind of reading;—and that in time, As war begets poverty; poverty peace,—must, in course, put an end to all kind of knowledge,—and then—we shall have all to begin over again; or, in other words, be exactly where we started.

—Happy! thrice happy times! I only wish that the era of my begetting, as well as the mode and manner of it, had been a little altered,—or that it could have been put off, with any convenience to my father or mother, for some twenty or five-and-twenty years longer, when a man in the literary world might have stood some chance.—

But I forget my uncle Toby, whom all this while we have left knocking the ashes out of his tobacco-pipe.

His humour was of that particular species, which does honour to our atmosphere; and I should have made no scruple of ranking him amongst one of the first-rate productions of it, had not there appeared too many strong lines in it of a family-likeness, which shewed that he derived the singularity of his temper more from blood, than either wind or water, or any modification or combinations of them whatever: And I have, therefore, oft-times wondered, that my father, tho' I believe he had his reasons for it, upon observing some tokens of eccentricity, in my course, when I was a boy,—should never once endeavour to account for them in this way: for all the Shandy Family were of an original character throughout:—I mean the males,—the females had no character at all,—except, indeed, my great aunt Dinah, who, about sixty years ago, was married and got with child by the coachman, for which my father, according to his hypothesis of christian names, would often say, She might thank her godfathers and godmothers.

It will seem very strange,—and I would as soon think of dropping a riddle in the reader's way, which is not my interest to do, as set him upon guessing how it could come to pass, that an event of this kind, so many years after it had happened, should be reserved for the interruption of the peace and unity, which otherwise so cordially subsisted, between my father and my uncle Toby. One would have thought, that the whole force of the misfortune should have spent and wasted itself in the family at first,—as is generally the case.—But nothing ever wrought with our family after the ordinary way. Possibly at the very time this happened, it might have something else to afflict it; and as afflictions are sent down for our good, and that as this had never done the Shandy Family any good at all, it might lie waiting till apt times and circumstances should give it an opportunity to discharge its office.—Observe, I determine nothing upon this.—My way is ever to point out to the curious, different tracts of investigation, to come at the first springs of the events I tell;—not with a pedantic Fescue,—or in the decisive manner of Tacitus, who outwits himself and his reader;—but with the officious humility of a heart devoted to the assistance merely of the inquisitive;—to them I write,—and by them I shall be read,—if any such reading as this could be supposed to hold out so long,—to the very end of the world.

Why this cause of sorrow, therefore, was thus reserved for my father and uncle, is undetermined by me. But how and in what direction it exerted itself so as to become the cause of dissatisfaction between them, after it began to operate, is what I am able to explain with great exactness, and is as follows:

My uncle Toby Shandy, Madam, was a gentleman, who, with the virtues which usually constitute the character of a man of honour and rectitude,—possessed one in a very eminent degree, which is seldom or never put into the catalogue; and that was a most extreme and unparalleled modesty of nature;—though I correct the word nature, for this reason, that I may not prejudge a point which must shortly come to a hearing, and that is, Whether this modesty of his was natural or acquired.—Whichever way my uncle Toby came by it, 'twas nevertheless modesty in the truest sense of it; and that is, Madam, not in regard to words, for he was so unhappy as to have very little choice in them—but to things;—and this kind of modesty so possessed him, and it arose to such a height in him, as almost to equal, if such a thing could be, even the modesty of a woman: That female nicety, Madam, and inward cleanliness of mind and fancy, in your sex, which makes you so much the awe of ours.

You will imagine, Madam, that my uncle Toby had contracted all this from this very source;—that he had spent a great part of his time in converse with your sex; and that from a thorough knowledge of you, and the force of imitation which such fair examples render irresistible, he had acquired this amiable turn of mind.

I wish I could say so,—for unless it was with his sister-in-law, my father's wife and my mother—my uncle Toby scarce exchanged three words with the sex in as many years;—no, he got it, Madam, by a blow.—A blow!—Yes, Madam, it was owing to a blow from a stone, broke off by a ball from a parapet of a horn-work at the siege of Namur, which struck full upon my uncle Toby's groin.—Which way could that affect it? The story of that, Madam, is long and interesting;—but it would be running my history all upon the heaps to give it you here.—'Tis for an episode hereafter; and every circumstance relating to it, in its proper place, shall be faithfully laid before you:—'Till then, it is not in my power to give farther light into this matter, or say more than what I have said already,—That my uncle Toby was a gentleman of unparalleled modesty, which happening to be somewhat subtilized and rarified by the constant heat of a little family pride,—they both so wrought together within him, that he could never bear to hear the affair of my aunt Dinah touched upon, but with the greatest emotion.—The least hint of it was enough to make the blood fly into his face;—but when my father enlarged upon the story in mixed companies, which the illustration of his hypothesis frequently obliged him to do,—the unfortunate blight of one of the fairest branches of the family would set my uncle Toby's honour and modesty o'bleeding; and he would often take my father aside, in the greatest concern imaginable, to expostulate and tell him, he would give him any thing in the world, only to let the story rest.

My father, I believe, had the truest love and tenderness for my uncle Toby, that ever one brother bore towards another, and would have done any thing in nature, which one brother in reason could have desired of another, to have made my uncle Toby's heart easy in this, or any other point. But this lay out of his power.

—My father, as I told you, was a philosopher in grain,—speculative,—systematical;—and my aunt Dinah's affair was a matter of as much consequence to him, as the retrogradation of the planets to Copernicus:—The backslidings of Venus in her orbit fortified the Copernican system, called so after his name; and the backslidings of my aunt Dinah in her orbit, did the same service in establishing my father's system, which, I trust, will for ever hereafter be called the Shandean System, after his.

In any other family dishonour, my father, I believe, had as nice a sense of shame as any man whatever;—and neither he, nor, I dare say, Copernicus, would have divulged the affair in either case, or have taken the least notice of it to the world, but for the obligations they owed, as they thought, to truth.—*Amicus Plato*, my father would say, construing the words to my uncle Toby, as he went along, *Amicus Plato*; that is, Dinah was my aunt;—*sed magis amica veritas*—but Truth is my sister.

This contrariety of humours betwixt my father and my uncle, was the source of many a fraternal squabble. The one could not bear to hear the tale of a family disgrace recorded,—and the other would scarce ever let a day pass to an end without some hint at it.

For God's sake, my uncle Toby would cry,—and for my sake, and for all our sakes, my dear brother Shandy,—do let this story of our aunt's and her ashes sleep in peace;—how can you,—how can you have so little feeling and compassion for the character of our family?—What is the character of a family to an hypothesis? my father would reply.—Nay, if you come to that—what is the life of a family?—The life of a family!—my uncle Toby would say, throwing himself back in his arm-chair, and lifting up his hands, his eyes, and one leg.—Yes, the life,—my father would say, maintaining his point. How many thousands of 'em are there every year that come cast away, (in all civilized countries at least)—and considered as nothing but common air, in competition of an hypothesis. In my plain sense of things, my uncle Toby would answer,—every such instance is downright Murder, let who will commit it.—There lies your mistake, my father would reply;—for, in *Foro Scientiae* there is no such thing as Murder,—'tis only Death, Brother.

My uncle Toby would never offer to answer this by any other kind of argument, than that of whistling half a dozen bars of *Lillabullero*.—You must know it was the usual channel thro' which his passions got vent, when any thing shocked or surprised him:—but especially when any thing, which he deemed very absurd, was offered.

As not one of our logical writers, nor any of the commentators upon them, that I remember, have thought proper to give a name to this particular species of argument,—I here take the liberty to do it myself, for two reasons. First, That, in order to prevent all confusion in disputes, it may stand as much distinguished for ever, from every other species of argument—as the *Argumentum ad Verecundiam, ex Absurdo, ex Fortiori*, or any other argument whatsoever:—And, secondly, That it may be said by my children's children, when my head is laid to rest,—that their learned grandfather's head had been busied to as much purpose once, as other people's;—That he had invented a name,—and generously thrown it into the Treasury of the *Ars Logica*, for one of the most unanswerable arguments in the whole science. And, if the end of disputation is more to silence than convince,—they may add, if they please, to one of the best arguments too.

I do therefore, by these presents, strictly order and command, That it be known and distinguished by the name and title of the *Argumentum Fistulatorium*, and no other;—and that it rank hereafter with the *Argumentum Baculimum* and the *Argumentum ad Crumenam*, and for ever hereafter be treated of in the same chapter.

As for the *Argumentum Tripodium*, which is never used but by the woman against the man;—and the *Argumentum ad Rem*, which, contrariwise, is made use of by the man only against the woman;—As these two are enough in conscience for one lecture;—and, moreover, as the one is the best answer to the other,—let them likewise be kept apart and be treated of in a place by themselves.

Excerpt from *Wigger*

LAWRENCE BRAITHWAITE

IN A BOILER ROOM . . .

-. . . You f-cker . . .-

Vernon plays w/Brian.

-You f-cker / you little f-ck-

He has him sitting on the floor, Brian's clothes in a pile w/papers and books, in the corner of the room, not neatly folded, but tossed lightly, one on top of the other.

(Vernon backhands him in the face)

(He shoves his motorcycle boot dead square in his face)

Vernon leaves his boot there.

-. . . fifty bucks. I expect more, you little sh-t, sock cooker-

(Ha)

He places full weight bearing through his boot on Brian's face and a sudden burst of a crunch comes up (in sound) and Vernon is squatting over him (really just at his head) and he's staring ahead at a wall that has a cut-up article about Jews and drug dealing. Vernon thinks of Bobby Fischer and lights a cigarette.

-Bobby would give up valuable positions so he could manipulate the response expected from his opponents. He'd be able to move in rapid succession of [un]expected, "un" bracketed, foolish position changes—therefore, destroying the paradigms of expressions and "gasps and groans" that come w/the growing limitations given by the remaining pieces. He'd f-ck the "sequence of responses" and "neutralize the opponents' threat"-

He exhales the fumes so abruptly that they travel directly forward and hit the article.

-I should turn you over and f-ck fifty bucks up your ass-

Vernon lifted himself and turned Brian over. He reached into his trench coat and pulled out a tube and squeezed the contents up Brian's hole. He then took the fifty and crumpled it up and shoved it in the same. Vernon's dick followed. He played guitar, so he knew a liberal art, and could keep a good rhythm:

-Just think/
you could/
get one/
of your/
friends to/
help you/
pull it/
back out-

(Ha)

Vernon decided to shoot on the back of Brian's neck.

-Turn over-

It took Brian a while to get the energy to do as he was told.

. . .

-Comeon, you little SH-T, MOVE. F-CK YOU-

(He kicked him over onto his back)

-You only gave me a f-ckin' hour and I'm not for paying any more than that . . .-

(He pulled a cherry-flavoured lollipop and four jawbreakers out of his pocket)

(He popped a jawbreaker in his mouth)

-. . . I gotta get home you know . . .-

(He bent down and gently put the lollipop into Brian's mouth and placed the remainder of the jawbreakers in his fist)

-You've got homework to do and I've got to go camping this wknd. I'll take your books and stuff, over there. I'll have them done for you Monday, O.K . . . O.K. SH-THEAD-

Brian nodded and coughed and stuff ran out and down the side of his mouth.

Vernon flipped on his headphones, pressed play and walked out, yelling, 'Seeya.'

Brian didn't wait long. He got himself up, wobbly-like, and stepped over to his clothes sort of coughing//crying//sniffling.

When he had his stuff in his arms he seemed a little disoriented, like he didn't know whether to put them on or walk out the way he was. He figured no one was at the school any more, but still he should put them on for the street outside. People are like that—they can't appreciate the human form. They'd figure he was a f-cked-up fag or something.

He took the clump of clothes and wiped his face off w/them, then dropped them on the ground. Brian started to get dressed. He got a bit of a headache tying up his sneakers, but he got it done, kind of sloppy though.

He had to get the fifty out when he got back to his room. He took the lollipop out of his mouth and swallowed four of his mom's ty-threes, then used the saliva from the pop to chase them down.

He figured the janitor would call it a mystery when he saw the guck on the floor—art class maybe.

When he was at the door, he thought for a long while before he could feel safe to open it//no way as cool as Vernon.

He was in the hallway, walking along a side panelling of lockers. He went up the stairs instead of down towards the exit. Brian found Vernon's office and there was a marker taped to it. He pulled it off and drew a heart w/a nail. He wrote V.A. at the top and B.H. at the bottom and smeared some stuff from his nose onto the nail.

He sat himself down in front of the door and fell asleep.

Worms Make Heaven

LAURIE WEEKS

I sliced through a worm with a shovel while gardening, but I didn't cut it completely in half. A thin whitish-pink strand connected the two writhing segments of its body. "Oh FUCK, little dude, I'm so sorry!" I shouted. "Shit!" I tried to shut it down but waves of desperation & grief rolled through my chest for days. Constantly and without warning the worm's red panic burst through the door to kick me in the chest. Like she'd run film clips under my ribs of her body thrashing & corkscrewing frenetically on the soil, arching in agony, the shovel, coiled into "O" silhouettes and sailor-knot contortions, a tiny shapeshifting pretzel of agony, an Agony Pretzel, triggering a reciprocal hailstorm of unknowable objects in my chest, a suggestion of shapes flying around in there too, sensations without definition or name, broadly categorized as emotions or feelings or something and invisible except for a slight crease here, a wrinkle, a ripple a shimmer—certain things have learned to cloak themselves for the good of everyone. It's just better that way. But then the worm would appear and explode like fireworks and uncontrollably *Oh my god. Fuck. Fuck.* would slide out of my mouth. I wish I didn't loathe the word "moan" so much because that's what I was doing and I mean all the time. Anywhere, really, except mostly in public. I'd be compulsively bonding with whatever stranger I had to interact with, which usually means a cashier—What else even is there? Or is that just me. With the problem.—Compulsively bonding, stressing the hapless victim with nervous codependent empathy-type jokes about the horror of packing my bags, which very occasionally made them kind of laugh a *little*; sometimes it was actually totally okay for REAL and we'd both be laughing, this genius cashier and I, when suddenly what I'd done to the worm would punch me straight in the solar plexus, as though a blacksmith had swung at me with a sledgehammer, successfully. There are less stars in the universe than the times in retail situations where I moaned, "Oh fuck me. Just fuck me and fuck you too," and kind of collapsed onto the conveyor belt or just put my head down into my shopping cart. Which really—that one confuses everyone. Worms can regenerate both their heads and their tails, but so what? There will always be that moment where I severed the worm, and it suffered.

"Oh god, I'm sorry," I would say to the alarmed cashier. "I just remembered something terrible. Sorry. God, that's all you need, another freak to brighten your day." In these spirals no one was safe. I would drag them under with me as I frantically said anything to make everything be okay; clear, clean, cleanse, rinse, erase the space between me and the cashier, this field filled with transparent teeming thought-form bedlam. That made me panicky—what drove this babble? Who—what scenario was playing out, broadcasting from me? This Second Arrow of Suffering on top of the worm punch, what feeling was this? You could say "desperation" but what is that? What written image instantly produces the same sensation? Of having severed a worm? Other than the phrase: I Severed A Worm? Walking, I'd ruminate. What were the words for this anguish and grief: Blackbirds flapped up in my mind's tiny sky . . . ceiling, cell—I focused on my chest. "Flock of shrapnel." Was that approximate to the sensation remaining after the first body blow of a weightless image, the twisting red segments and connecting nerve thread? Was it a semi-accurate measure of the velocity, shape, density, floatiness, scrabbling, and—what other criteria are there? On YouTube I learned that the ancient Egyptians were so finely tuned they had 360 senses defined, as opposed to five. I need to know what they are. Need to run. Infinite potentials called creatures live in the space of my heart, tiny bats hanging row upon row—it's okay, I love bats, that's not my point. But what does it look like? Are there words fine enough to produce the same sensation of suffering? Something else, but the same? This is Virginia Woolf territory, meets 7-11 reformed meth-head, meets Ingmar Bergman. Moment of the Worm. Nosing sweetly along in the April dirt while the peepers sing by the trilling creek, the worm rippling ahead, euphoric in the vibration of soil harmonics against her skin, singing along while the peepers cling and sway on the reeds near the creek that runs ticklish and giggling over the rocks spangled green-gold in the light slanting through Sweet Flag and overhead the goldfinches flash and swirl, everyone singing . . . Fuck.

I was born with Mars in Cancer, a bad position. "Oh, fuck, like a curse?" I said to Zippy, who was doing my chart. "No," she said. "It's like you don't have conscious access to your reactions and motivations. They're down there sucking your energy like oxygen and then sometimes you'll just explode without warning." Meaning the flamboyant planet's not zooming through the solar system in overdrive—places to go, things to do, people to meet—picking up speed from its rogue adventuring, but instead pissed to find itself tumbling from its own orbit repeatedly due to an oscillating sense of direction or wobbly axis, spun into freefall by its wavering response to some random perturbation, losing plot and velocity without warning or going totally retrograde time after time just as it hits The Zone, catches the flow, really starts to cruise. Sideswiped to wobbly standstill—vacillating between rage and apology—by whatever ridiculous thing, the inconsequential vibe, say, from a passing fleck of space trash, before plummeting, an orange ball bearing screaming down from the ether, thermonuclear with rage at its brutal plunge yet again, goddamn it, toward a pool of scuttling, indecisive crabs. "That's weird," you might remark to your companion on the beach, pointing toward a nectarine glow beneath the waves, right before they erupt with a mega-missile of steam that concusses you both back into the parking lot. Whoever "you" are. Sprawled out on the hot asphalt, ears ringing, you watch the massive column blasting through the ocean into the stratosphere. And that's me. One more vaporized bit of intention, desire, optimism, jetting off through the ozone . . . kind of lost track of the metaphor. But the correct answer is: Desire.

So, okay, Mars in Cancer, not the greatest, but also I'm an Aries, ruled by Mars, this Special Needs Mars. "Jesus," I said. "What valuable lesson do I have to learn before the School Principal of the Universe lets me get past this?" "I'm not sure," replied Zippy, my best friend and astrology genius. (Actually we might be in love, but I can't tell because I can't find my feelings.) "It's some karmic thing to do with your dad, probably." I was wearing a beautiful blue plaid button-down shirt, tapered, my favorite shirt from eBay, and there was a tear in the back from having been dragged down Main Street one day by my girlfriend's car, from which I'd jumped because it was like she was trying to kill me with the things she said. I only held onto the door handle a second or two. Somehow I must've known I'd be okay scraping along the asphalt next to the tire. Everyone saw, but I just twisted away from the car, stood up and walked off into an alley or something, my body screaming with adrenaline. Then I get amnesia. It happens all the time. One day I picked up the shirt and said, "How'd this hole get here?" "You jumped out of the car, remember?" my girlfriend said.

"Goddammit, Zippy, help me, you cunt," I cried. "I'm deeply in love with you but fuck my dad (A), and (B), I'm sick of driving this piece of shit car called My Life that blows up every ten seconds even though I'm only going one fucking mile an hour. You're not telling me anything." Zippy laughed. Her real name is Missy, but now she's Zippy due to an autocorrect mistake while texting. Which fits, because her REAL real name is Melissa, which means "honeybee" in Greek or something, and—bees, zippy . . . Do I even need to explain? "Let me think about it," Zippy said. I stood up. "You're kind of a charlatan," I said. I want to kiss Zippy but I'm frightened because I'm so shut down. Do I want to kiss her, though, really? "Don't you want another glass of wine or something?" I said. "You need to get a little drunker so I can relax." I started to cry.

Inside the white scalloped borders of a black-and-white photo, my mother holds me. Smiling at something, head slightly tilted, maybe she's laughing and talking. She's looking elsewhere but she's in love with me, six months old and dressed in some flowy white thing, "frock"'s not the right word, just thinking "frock" ruins everything about the picture, but of course it's the first word that comes to mind—prison bars slamming down over the numberless implicit things in the photo, the "implicit order" enfolded in what we see, dormant, waiting for release. A word like "frock" makes my nervous system crawl with microscopic bugs or parasites feeding on all this healthy tissue, these fucking words like "frock" that detonate inside you, burst open like seed pods and out comes either a prison world or this parasitic army with gnashing bacterial jaws. God, you fuckers.

Oh, this language of pestilence, these fucking word diseases buried inside you, biological, self-reconstituting land mines that detonate the second you try to understand or explain to yourself some perception, translate a sensually felt or experienced awareness or fleeting intention into conscious knowing, cybernetic seed pods blowing open to release their armies of vermin that feed on the vines and leaves and flowers of your nervous system, tinily gnawing holes with blackened edges into the foliage. Some perceptions just turn black, curl up, drop away, leaving a necrotized spot in the stem. Some of your energy leaks out or gets contaminated or both—that's why you get that sudden sinking feeling, why your desire and curiosity and pleasure in all the data coming in start to convert, nerve by nerve or neuron by neuron, into this horrible feeling of sinking or slackness and depression, hopelessness, and that's one more dead perceptual nerve, a blinded cone in your retina—the metaphors are endless—until all that's left of your brain to process any input or memory is exactly some way you're supposed to feel it, this horrible narrowing of vision, sentimentality, nostalgia, sadness, girl.

Here is the picture of my mother and, in theory, me. I carry the photo everywhere, look at it constantly. It's pasted into notebooks, journals, books. Zippy has it up on her wall. I see pure uncut love, or I feel it, in the picture. Maybe it's imaginary, maybe I'm desperate. Probably not. I was going to say "pharmaceutical-grade love" because I like the sound or maybe the idea but it's wrong. In fact it's a lie, like the frock. Silvery tree leaves behind my mother's dark hair, or a rose bush. Hint of black lawn, sliver of house, we're outside somewhere. The Past.

While Googling something I ran across a report in Pravda about the discovery, confirmed by Real Scientists, of a natural time-warp zone in the Arctic. This wasn't really so strange, noted the article, given that—

> it is known that each of us feels a different course of time under different conditions. Once lightning hit a mountain climber; later the

> man told he saw the lightning got into his arm, slowly moved along it, separated the skin from the tissues and carbonized his cells. He felt as if there were quills of a thousand hedgehogs under his skin.

I feel those hedgehogs. "How did he know it was a thousand?" said Zippy. Ha ha. But I feel them. My hand holding this Coke existed then, too, in the time of the picture; this hand was that tiny hand. Was this Coke always in The Future, waiting for that tiny hand to hold? This is ridiculous. It makes me want to scream. I feel the pressure of my mother's hand on my weensy fingers, pulling my arms through the garment's soft sleeves as I lie on the bed or in the bassinet. Each of these actions takes time in the world, took time, supposedly, and each moment itself was a bubble, a spherule seething with realities underlying the visible—the cells of my mother's young heart, a flashback to piano lessons, say, that she might have had while bathing me, her own mother asleep in a house under large cottonwood trees, their leaves rustling while she dreamed a grandmother dream. The picture of my mother holding me can turn into an abstraction, a portal. It's hard to explain. The photo consists of black and white spots, grains of evidence—as in spores, released by violence, drifting off from endless world war to stick to the emulsion and accrete in the shape of my mother and me. The thoughts of every human alive while my first neurons were branching, my dad, lush horrors beyond comprehension in the minds of men, red dwarfs going supernova . . . oh fuck it, the history of everything since forever. You can't disconnect anything from anything else underlying the vast millisecond of my mother's life and mine the instant this photo was snapped. Her arms, thin in a sleeveless blouse, cradle me against her chest in a sitting position, my head against her heart, and from beneath the white cloth I'm wearing emerge two plaster casts. They rest on her forearm, splayed wide. I crawled out from my mother with my legs on sideways, hips twisted so that my feet pointed away from each other at right angles to my body. The casts will correct this in a few weeks. Or was it months? After I had my chart done, I either freaked out mildly or felt excited by the correspondence, which could be interpreted as coincidence or synchronicity—evidence—if you want to go down that road. Born in April, legs of a crab, Mars in Cancer. It's kind of disgustingly poetic or symbolic, but also true. Could be interpreted as a little hint, if you want to imagine through that lens, tumble down that wormhole, which I most certainly do, why not, the stories falling out of everyone's mouth, including mine, are strung together with lies and boredom. I can't stand the stupefaction of wading through assumptions about the Nature of Reality that most people seem to feel pretty sure of, though they never question the origins of belief or story or whatever. Does anyone ever say, "Why?" or "Wait, what? How do you know this?" Even physicists still believe things that've long been disproved. I don't believe much of anything and know even less, but I like a mind-fuck and I do know that things aren't only as they seem or as we're taught. (What an asinine understatement, Jesus, like I'm such an expert.) But this thing really happened, didn't it, my mother and I on a lawn with the anonymous photographer, probably my dad, or probably not? Here's the treasured proof, the photo, my beloved mother laughing, holding in her arms—clearly still safely part of her—this tiny creature thinglet called "me." But when I try to wrap my mind around it I go psychotic, skidding around inside my body and clawing at its walls like Sally Field in Sybil, desperate to tear a way out.

It's April, there's been rain, and just beneath the surface the soil's delirious with worms nosing about or unhappily ambushed by me deep within clay balls as deeply impacted as cement. The chunks are so hard and heavy I've mistaken them for concrete and broken them apart with a hammer only to find worms inside—impossibly inhabiting a solid, moving slowly from our vantage point. But what does "slow" mean in a worm's space-time coordinates? Really they're undulating like eels through water, radio waves through bone, neutrinos through the body of a planet, as though salamanders scamper and flip inside granite blocks and stingrays glide through the thick lead walls shielding underground government complexes from radiation. Somehow their soft long bodies penetrate and traverse this rock, I envision them in a slow float, their molecules spreading into transparency, invisible membranes just sliding through the dense atoms of soil and aerating it, I guess, who knows if they have lips (I'm gonna make the call, they've got lips), humming lips vibrating so subtly, clouds breathing on your skin, that clay becomes fluffiness, it's alchemy, allowing moisture and nutrients to perfuse the ground deeply rather than evaporate or wash away, seeping down to the tendrils of, say, embryonic yellow and scarlet zinnias waiting to drink and spiral up through the ground into the golden green and blue world to blossom into landing sites for the tickling filaments of butterflies and bees. Butterflies love zinnias and it's totally mutual. Vermillion zinnias or zinnias of any color spiraling up toward the sky, so easy to drink and spiral up to those myriad blues up there like nothing. It's so easy, we're playing, it's heaven. Worms make heaven. People say things like, "Worms don't feel pain." What? How could you know that? What people should always say instead is, "Oh my god, worms, thank you! Jesus fuckin' Christ, thank you, worms. Thank you for heaven." Worms can regenerate both their heads and their tails, but meanwhile their agony's unmistakable. Growing up, before I learned to fly fish, I pushed fishhooks through live nightcrawlers as bait. "Oh, worms don't feel pain," said Dad. He said that about trout, too, as he taught us to bang their heads on the edge of the boat or stab a knife into their brains. I believed him until I was 14, and since then I haven't been able to fish. Doctors used to operate on newborn babies without anesthesia because they *knew* babies don't feel pain. Children who don't feel pain chew their tongues off, rest their hands on burning stoves, gouge out their eyeballs, jump off roofs then run around on broken legs. How could anything alive NOT feel pain and remain alive?

the mother's story

LUCILLE CLIFTON

a line of women i don't know,
she said,
came in and whispered over you
each one fierce word,
she said, each word
more powerful than one before.
and i thought what is this to bring
to one black girl from buffalo
until the last one came and smiled,
she said,
and filled your ear with light
and that, she said, has been the one,
the last one, that last one.

slave cabin, sotterly plantation, maryland, 1989

in this little room
note carefully

aunt nanny's bench

three words that label
things
aunt
is my parent's sister
nanny
my grandmother
bench
the board at which
i stare
the soft curved polished
wood
that held her bottom
after the long days
without end
without beginning
when she   aunt nanny   sat
feet dead against the dirty floor
humming for herself   humming
her own sweet human name

Excerpt from *No Lease on Life*

LYNNE TILLMAN

One lesbian frog says to another, You're right, we do taste like chicken.

Gisela limped onto A from Twelfth Street. Her dog limped along beside her.

—It is a terrible time, now. Look what happens again!

Gisela's face was dotted with scars, old wounds. There were a few fresh wounds. She had picked them. Elizabeth stared at the red holes, windows to the soul. Gisela's skin was clearer than it was the last time she'd seen her.

—A woman is trying to destroy me. See, my dog is sick. She is poisoning my dog. I went away and she was supposed to take care of him and look at him. Look at his rash.

Gisela pointed to a scabby, hairless patch on the dog's rump. It made Elizabeth sick.

—Why's the woman poisoning your dog? Elizabeth asked.

—It's the Swiss government.

—They're after you again?

—Ach. My mother's legacy. They thought I knew too much because a lot of very heavy people in the government were involved with my mother. My mother was exploited by them.

—You mean, the heroin dealing she was forced to do?

—They are very liberal with drugs because the government is involved, and that means money for them. My mother was working under a lawyer, in Zurich, who was a good friend with a man from the parliament, who was negotiating with the Syrian extremist groups in Argentina. They have a big colony of Syrian extremists. They were afraid I would talk too much. I didn't know anything. At that time.

Gisela shifted from one leg to another. Elizabeth had heard some of the story. Gisela shifted again.

—Your leg hurts?

—They want to operate, and I always say . . .

—What kind of operation?

—To replace my hip. I always say no, I need first intensive therapy. I'm very weak, I'm falling apart. In Cuba, for the first time I met a doctor who agreed with me. When I say this to a doctor, he doesn't want to hear of it.

A bicycle messenger zipped past them on the sidewalk.

—I couldn't sleep last night, Elizabeth said.

—It's the neighborhood, Gisela said.

—It's pushing me over the edge.

—Compared to what I went through, it's paradise. It's beautiful, Switzerland, but I went through shit there. Those people are not human beings. They're worse than Nazis. Here, you see, I'm happy. I keep my distance because I cannot tell my story. I get along. They leave me alone. They respect me. I respect them. I have no problem. I have my peace of mind.

—That's important.

—I was fine here, until 1973, that's when I collapsed. I was accused of being involved in drugs, which wasn't true. Then I had a terrible, terrible love affair. Men never meant much in my life, believe me. I did not even love him. It was like he was doing black magic to me. It was the first time in my life, I was thirty-six. It was horrible. I just collapsed.

—Then your hip went out?

—From standing on my feet too long. But I had a problem before. I was beaten up by the police in 1964 when I was arrested.

—In Switzerland?

—I didn't pay my hospital bill in India. I had enough money to pay for an Indian hospital, but they said that I was white and I had to go to a luxury hospital. I knew in advance I couldn't pay. Then one night the troops came and picked me up and kidnapped me and took me to Switzerland where I got beaten up very badly. They went inside me to see if I had drugs, of course I had no drugs. I was in the hospital. And they beat me up, to make sure I would spit out drugs. But I had my hip problem even before.

—How did it start?

—Child abuse. I went through hell, but I'm happy to be here.

Elizabeth knew she should get going.

—My family didn't want to have anything to do with me. First of all because I was my mother's daughter, and because I look like her. I look exactly like her. Except I'm lighter. My mother was of gypsy background. So was my father.

—They're gypsies?

—French Huguenot, but of gypsy background. I am so light, my family didn't want to have anything to do with me. They're assimilated.

—When did they give up their gypsy ways?

—When they became Huguenots in the fifteenth century. They were kicked out of Spain and became French Huguenots. People don't know that the Huguenot religion was founded by the Jews and the gypsies and the Arabs, who were kicked out of Spain. The Catholic religion didn't believe in money, but the Protestants believe in money. The Thirty Years War was based on this, it was a money issue. The so-called religious war.

Elizabeth was tempted to melt with Gisela on the sidewalk. She could lose herself in the salty, humid dispiritedness.

—What happened to your mother?

—I have no idea. Yesterday I told my social worker that my first memory was of my mother, how beautiful she was.

Elizabeth scrutinized Gisela's dry, pale skin.

—Are you eating OK?

—To tell you the truth, I'm so depressed since my burglary, I don't eat right. I eat bagels, with cheese, butter. I do eat a lot of fruits. I drink water a lot.

—Your skin is looking a little better.

—Because I'm over that problem. My soul is better.

—About losing your children years ago?

—All of that. That's why my skin looks better.

—I don't want children.

—I didn't want them, they just didn't have abortions, and no protection in those days. I was a runaway, and somebody took advantage. It wasn't rape. I was raped later on.

Gisela looked down the street. There was some commotion on the corner. They watched it together. A couple of boys were being territorial. No weapons. It broke up.

—Thank God, I'm rent-controlled. If I lose my apartment, that's it. I don't go out. I stay home. I only walk the dog. You don't see me.

—Not much.

—Because I only go to the doctor or grocery shopping, I walk the dog, that's about it.

—It's good to get exercise.

Elizabeth hardly ever exercised. She walked. Gisela thought about something else, Elizabeth could see some caution, storm alert arrows, crossing her face, and then the concern passed, or Gisela pushed it away.

—Don't you ever complain about a social worker. They have more power than you think.

Elizabeth didn't have a social worker. She complained to the wrong people on the block. Elizabeth didn't tell Gisela about her problems with the young super, Gloria, or Hector. Gisela shifted her weight from one leg to the other. Her dog was hunkered down on the hot sidewalk. He looked miserable. It was jungle humid. Gisela glanced at her dog, then at Elizabeth. She ignored her pain.

—In Switzerland, everybody who's a humanist ends up in a mental hospital, because they don't want human beings. There are only banks and insurance. The guy who was the founder of the Red Cross, Jean-Henri Dunant, he ended up in a mental hospital too. I go now.

Gisela brought things to a conclusion with flair. She started to move. She glanced at Elizabeth again.

—You look good today. Yah.

Gisela appreciated Elizabeth's appearance. It didn't matter if Elizabeth hadn't slept through a scarred night that might've terminated in her loss of control, a night that could've resulted in her assassinating someone. Gisela's version of reality was unique, cut to fit. Everyone's was. Most versions were less radically altered than Gisela's. Gisela wasn't about fashion. She had style. You had it or you didn't.

Elizabeth didn't argue with anyone's style or experience. Only sometimes with what it meant. Gisela, as she herself put it, was rent-controlled. Elizabeth was rent-stabilized. Elizabeth would look up Jean-Henri Dunant in the proofroom. The room had a reference library. They had to check themselves before they corrected anyone else, to find the rectitude or error of their own ways first.

What's the difference between Chinese food and Jewish restaurants? With Chinese food, after an hour, you're hungry again. In a Jewish restaurant, after an hour, you're still eating.

Excerpt from *All the Battles*

MAAN ABU TALEB

Translated by Robin Moger

Saed felt exhausted. His legs were leaden and his shoulders so tired he couldn't raise his gloves. His knees felt empty and shook when he stood and his stomach was ice. He felt hungry, as though he were going to puke. He got up off his chair in order to move about and shake off these sensations, but the sensations killed his desire to move. Where had his strength gone? he asked himself; how could he get into a war of attrition without supplies? A posse of businessmen walked in and greeted him enthusiastically, wishing him luck; he made the right noises so they would leave. Nart ushered them out. Saed asked him to shut the door. He asked him for water. Asked him to turn down the air-conditioning. Nart told him it was centrally controlled. Saed shifted the groin protector under his shorts. It felt rigid, awkward. The gray walls made the room gloomy despite the bright lighting. More than ten minutes ago the captain had gone to Bilhajj's dressing room to witness his hands being wrapped and the gloves pulled on and initialed.

Saed tried throwing a few combinations but his body wouldn't obey him. Someone tried to open the door and Nart leaned against it till it clicked, then came over to help Saed remove his shirt. As he did so the door opened and another well-wisher stepped inside. Saed glared at Nart, who shooed the stranger away, shut the door, and leaned on it with all his weight. There was a violent banging, a scuffling, and then the captain's voice.

The captain came in, strode calmly over to his bag, and took out the pads. Slapping them together with a sharp crack he held the right pad up to his left shoulder and beckoned Saed forward. The punch was no good. Saed went back to his chair and sat down. Resting his right glove on his belly, he hung his head.

"It's nerves," said the captain. "The only way to get rid of them is to move." He looked over at Nart. "Get that air-con off. Now come on, Saed!" But Saed didn't respond. "Saed?" he said again. No answer, so he came over and took a seat beside him. He whispered in his ear. A few murmured words, confidently uttered, was all Nart heard. A minute passed, and Saed shook his head. The captain's pads lay on the floor and his bare hand ran up and down Saed's back and neck. He was whispering more rapidly now, insistently, like a sheikh gabbling a charm. The words tumbled out faster and faster until Saed gave a bellow. He thumped his head and punched himself in the face. He began slamming his gloves together and felt his muscles contract and his body stiffen.

The captain stood up and slipped on the pads, cracking them together as before. Saed came forward as though he'd only just learned how to walk, but in minutes he was striking the pads with speed and precision, the connection of glove and pad ringing out menacingly. The captain picked up the tempo. Saed matched him, and Nart breathed a sigh of relief. Saed was moving more and more nimbly as he cracked the pads, and with every punch he gave a fierce cry. And all the time the captain was circling: he wanted to see sweat on his brow. He pushed one pad out and Saed slipped it and moved inside to hit the other.

There was a tap on the door and Nart opened up. An official poked his head inside: "You're on." A shaky Nart turned to pass on the message, and the captain threw the pads down and crushed Saed against his chest. Grabbed his head and kissed his forehead, then patted him on the head, then another kiss. Saed started jumping on the spot. He raised his arms as though celebrating a win and Nart pulled his T-shirt up and off, the fabric catching on the gloves. Throwing it aside, he took the long black robe, hung it over his brother's shoulders, and plucked off his cap. When Saed turned on the heels of his tall white boots the robe flew out behind him. He walked to the door and out into the long corridor glossy with gray paint.

Waiting for him outside stood a huddle of security guards ready to lead him to the ring. The captain followed behind him, his hand steady on Saed's shoulder. Saed jumped up and down as the entourage formed a ring around him, with Nart and the captain bringing up the rear, and then all of a sudden they were off. Al-Adli's assistant shouted encouragement. The Asian workers dragging cleaning equipment down a side passage stopped and looked up, watching Saed as he passed. The lighting in the corridor was powerful but everything looked dark. Thoughts were jostling and racing through Saed's mind and the chill was back in his belly. Knocking his gloves together, he felt his knuckles pushing their way through the lining. He punched himself in the side of the head. Bit down on the mouthguard.

They strode rapidly along the building's back passages. The guards were tall and broad-shouldered, most of them shaven-headed, and wore black T-shirts beneath sleeveless puffer jackets. There were snatches of cries and shouts and the air-conditioners' roar: everything had an echo.

They kept moving through the back channels of the vast building then turned a corner. Noise filtered down from the end of the corridor. The official stopped, then turned and walked back to check that everything was in order. The captain tightened his grip on Saed's shoulder and the noise of the crowd grew louder and louder. As they approached the main hall the light intensified and the group slowed. Tiers of seats crammed with spectators came into view. The voice of the MC announcing the imminent arrival of Saed Habjouqa. Saed, jumping up and down, throwing combinations. Then the lights went off and there was silence.

The silence lengthened. A deep, menacing throbbing came from the loudspeakers. Saed hadn't chosen a song: he had gone for drums; huge drums being beaten slowly and steadily. War drums: harbingers of slaughter. The crowd went wild. The spotlights turned on Saed were dazzling. The noise was louder than the Day of Judgment. The little squad walked between the tiers, making their way through the spectators, many of whom now swarmed toward Saed, trying to shake his hand. Saed focused on the ring: blue and gleaming and packed with officials. He still hadn't caught sight of Bilhajj. On he went, ringed by the big men. He uttered a primitive, bestial howl at the top of his lungs, but it was lost amid the general uproar. The fear was gone, completely gone. He was a predator now, a warrior, a hunter. A war criminal.

The MC ran through Saed's record, his weight and height and so on, and then gathered himself: "*Saaaa*ed . . . The Fiiiirst . . . Hab . . . *joooo-*

uqa!" The name echoed fearsomely through the drumbeat and the crowd picked up the chant—"The First! The First! The First!"—Saed shouting with them and punching his head. He was on fire now. He wanted to begin.

The lead bodyguard stepped on the lower ropes and Saed ducked through, the captain after him, and all the others melted away. Saed looked over at the referee and once again there was silence. He jumped on the spot. The crowd was recovering its voice: Bilhajj had entered the hall. Saed kept jumping to keep his body warm. He didn't look over at his opponent.

Now Bilhajj and his team had come through the ropes, and the ring was full again. Saed glimpsed him through the throng but couldn't see his face. As he jumped and swayed he kept his eyes locked in his direction. The referee came over to inspect his gloves and Saed held out his arms without looking at him. Then the ring began to clear and more of Bilhajj materialized.

He had his back to Saed and was tugging on the ropes. Then his assistants and team left the ring and Saed could see all of him. He was calm, chatting to his trainer over the ropes. His movements were unhurried and there was no tension in his expression. He glanced over, but their eyes didn't meet. Saed kept his gaze fixed on his opponent, watching him through the fluttering of the captain's hands as Vaseline was smeared onto his face. Bilhajj went back to chatting with his trainer and didn't look at Saed again until the referee asked the fighters to approach. Their eyes met. As the referee instructed them to touch gloves Saed stared into Bilhajj's eyes, spitting fire. Bilhajj looked away. "Nothing below the belt," the referee said. "Obey my orders. Protect yourselves at all times. Keep it clean."

The bell rang.

Selections from *Bluets*

MAGGIE NELSON

179. When I imagine a celibate man—especially one who doesn't even jerk off—I wonder how he relates to his dick: what else he does with it, how he handles it, how he *regards* it. At first glance, this same question for a woman might appear more "tucked away" (pussy-as-absence, pussy-as-lack: out of sight, out of mind). But I am inclined to think that anyone who thinks or talks this way has simply never felt the pulsing of a pussy in serious need of fucking—a pulsing that communicates nothing less than the suckings and ejaculations of the heart.

187. Is it a related form of aggrandizement, to inflate a heartbreak into a sort of allegory? Losing what one loves is simpler, more common, than that. More precise. One could leave it, too, as it is. *—Yet how can I explain, that every time I put a pin in the balloon of it, the balloon seems to swell back up as soon as I turn away from it?*

195. Does an album of written thoughts perform a similar displacement, or replacement, of the "original" thoughts themselves? (Please don't start protesting here that there are no thoughts outside of language, which is like telling someone that her colored dreams are, in fact, colorless.) But if writing does displace the idea—if it *extrudes* it, as it were, like grinding a lump of wet clay through a hole—where does the excess go? "We don't want to pollute our world with leftover egos" (Chögyam Trungpa).

196. I suppose I am avoiding writing down too many specific memories of you for similar reasons. The most I will say is "the fucking." Why

else suppress the details? Clearly I am not a private person, and quite possibly I am a fool. "Oh, how often have I cursed those foolish pages of mine which made my youthful sufferings public property!" Goethe wrote years after the publication of *The Sorrows of Young Werther*. Sei Shōnagon felt similarly: "Whatever people may think of my book," she wrote after her pillow book gained fame and notoriety, "I still regret that it ever came to light."

212. If I were today on my deathbed, I would name my love of the color blue and making love with you as two of the sweetest sensations I knew on this earth.

213. But are you certain—one would like to ask—that it was sweet?

116. One of the last times you came to see me, you were wearing a pale blue button-down shirt, short-sleeved. *I wore this for you*, you said. We fucked for six hours straight that afternoon, which does not seem precisely possible but that is what the clock said. We killed the time. You were on your way to a seaside town, a town of much blue, where you would be spending a week with the other woman you were in love with, the woman you are with now. *I'm in love with you both in completely different ways*, you said. It seemed unwise to contemplate this statement any further.

118. Not long after that afternoon I came across a photograph of you with this woman. You were wearing the shirt. I went over to the house of my injured friend and told her the story as I moved her legs in and out of the inflatable, thigh-high boots she wears to compress her legs while lying down so as to inhibit the formation of blood clots. *How ghastly*, she said.

119. My friend was a genius before her accident, and she remains a genius now. The difference is that these days it is nearly impossible to discount her pronouncements. Something about her condition has bestowed upon her the quality of an oracle, perhaps because now she generally stays in one place, and one must go unto her. *Eventually you will have to give up this love*, she told me one night while I made us dinner. *It has a morbid heart.*

East River Park Oak Tree

MARCELLA DURAND

(after Marianne Moore's "The Camperdown Elm")

Dear Mayor Bill de Blasio,

I choose as my tree
an oak that stands
somewhat alone
in a triangular lawn-like space
facing the East River
in East River Park,
which is slated
to be demolished
this coming spring
per your opaque and confusing
plans to, at some point,
protect the Lower East Side
from flooding
during superstorms.

The oak is large,
surprisingly large,
meaning that it must
also be old, but probably not older
than the park's original
construction in the 1930s,
so, if it were allowed
to continue to grow,

in 100 more years
it would be enormous,
a real presence,
a landmark, a tree
to treasure and remember
an enlightened city administration
that made the decision,
against money and power,
against real-estate interests
and colonialist mentality
to cherish and protect it.

I stood by this oak
for a long time a few
weeks ago during what
seemed the worst days
of the pandemic.
I noticed on its bark
many ants and spiders—
you would never notice
them until you had,
like me, stood and
watched the tree
for more than the
few minutes the
consultants for the East Side
Coastal Resiliency Project
have spent in the park
in order to determine
that it has no wildlife
to speak of. I have
often found that,
when it comes to
nature, you have
to wait and let
it come to you,

like how Thoreau
looked into a dark room
and waited patiently
until his pupil expanded
enough that he could
see into the darkness.

I lay down in the grass
under the oak and gazed
up to the tips
of its branches.
A bright red bird flew
in and among them:
I thought at first
it was an oriole
but found out later
it was a scarlet
tanager. What an
amazing color
to see so high up
amid the green
from so far down
on the ground.
A large tan bird
then flew in circles
over the tree
and I wondered idly
(because I was getting sleepy,
as I tend to do when lying
in grass under a tree)
why a seagull was
flying in circles
over a tall oak tree
and why a smaller
bird seemed to be
chasing it away.

Then, my mind
clicked back into place
and I realized
it was no seagull, but
a red-tailed hawk
and that the smaller
bird—maybe a crow
or a starling—
was chasing it
out of its territory.

The oak has traces
of graffiti on its trunk
and yesterday a young
man pulled up next to it
on his bike and settled
in to read, leaning against
the trunk with a book
that he often put down
to gaze around him—
at the river, at the light
on the river, at people
sitting, playing, talking,
or, like him, gazing
at the silvery blue
of the river in afternoon light.

I'm sure he found
the shade as pleasant
as I did—the oak
tree provides enough
shade for so many
of us to socially
distance ourselves
comfortably, while
yet protecting us from

full sun (something
your plan lacks: mature
trees, therefore it also
lacks shade and the shadows
thrown by leaves flickering
in the breezes that come
in from the ocean,

and therefore, it also
lacks birds, insects,
ant colonies, spiders,
therefore it lacks hawk,
scarlet tanager, blue jay,
northern mockingbird,
migrating warbler, therefore
lacks robins pulling worm
after worm out from
soil deemed disposable
by city consultants). Instead,
sterile landfill is to be piled
eight feet high over
the earthworms and
grubs curled into little
balls my son finds
when he helps plant
daffodil bulbs in the fall.

So much lack
in your plan: lack
of community input,
lack of "stakeholder
engagement" (stakeholders
being all of us neighbors here
now), lack of what
could be instead more
green space over

six-lane highway that
creates so much pollution
and noise all day and
all night and all day
and all night, lack of choices,
lack of a vision to create
flood protection over
a highway instead of
over a park, and such a lack
of love for old trees—

the grass underneath
this oak is so pleasant,
pleasant enough to
dream of a city
that might value
such trees and
value the quality
of all life, a city
that might appreciate
our community living
on a small peninsula
off the island of
Manhattan, a hook,
a slight protuberance
into the river, far away
from the subway and
with fewer schools and
hardly any parks or gardens
any larger than a city block,
a community comprised
of many different people
doing many different
things sometimes getting
along, sometimes not, but
negotiating together

toward a civic
existence that might
include fresh air, light,
and a place to play, think,
read, breathe in
a neighborhood
otherwise crushed
between a bridge
and a highway,
to dream of
a city that might
see no good reason
to cut down an oak tree ever.

Sincerely,
Marcella Durand
Lower East Side
New York, NY

Excerpt from "Potatoes or Rice?"

MATTHEW STADLER

My freedom is guaranteed by a silicon chip embedded in my residence permit. The biometric information stored there was taken from me by a large, egg-shaped machine in a pleasant suburban office in Hoofdorp, the Netherlands. The Dutch had granted me a two-year work permit. I went by train on a February morning. The machine scanned my retinas, digitized my head-shape and facial features, turned my fingerprints into high-resolution maps, and stored all of this information in the chip, which lies hidden inside a small plastic card. The same chips are in passports, indeed most state IDs. If the chip reports an order to detain me, or if my body does not correspond to its digital account, I will be arrested. That is, my body—the offending part of any mismatch—will be detained and held in a jail cell. Nothing in my body can contravene the testimony of the chip: not my words, not my self-knowledge, not my soul, not my humanity. None of that counts; only the chip.

We rely on biometrics because we don't believe people can be as fair, consistent, or accurate in their judgment. It's a reasonable belief, an example of what French writer Jacques Ellul termed "technique," in his 1954 book *The Technological Society*. Wanting certainty, accuracy, and impartiality we routinely ask moody, flawed humans to adapt to the rigid binaries of technology—the either/or of the chip's algorithmic verdict—and until they do we trust the chip, not the policeman. While it's true that human judgment first granted me my rights, that is an archaic fact, and nation-states have been shifting these decisions to the realm of technology as fast as possible, ever since the technique of state administration made its great leap forward in the 18th and 19th centuries. Today, my political rights reside in the chip's digital mapping, which stands as the only guarantee of my freedom, so long as the Dutch are willing to grant me it.

I have no passport. In this, I join more than ten million people, worldwide, who lack papers to prove citizenship. Mine was taken away when the U.S. indicted me through a "secret grand jury" and told the Dutch to arrest me and send me back for trial. The charges are false, the process unjust, and the threatened punishment so draconian it violates the European Convention on Human Rights. In effect I was made stateless by the U.S. withdrawal of my rights, and my life was put in peril by their threat against me. I asked the Dutch to refuse the request, and while my case is being heard I live with the rights granted to me so I could work in the Netherlands.

The U.S. action shocked me, though I soon discovered that it was not an aberration, just business as usual. Citizens lose their rights every day, sometimes fairly through a due process of investigation and reasonable suspicion, but just as often unfairly and without cause. Racism, systemic corruption, personal bias or, increasingly in the U.S., the mere zeal of prosecutors empowered to detain and threaten anyone suspected of a crime, strips citizens of their rights every day. The fact that I was abroad and could take my objections to a separate state authority, the Dutch, opened up an unusual space in which to consider the injustice of what was happening to me.

Among the first assumptions to fall apart in this unmarked space of peril was my long-held faith that citizenship lay solely in the hands of the state. Suddenly I was stateless, and yet I felt all the more fiercely my need for and my right to citizenship. I was lucky to have the Dutch process and the temporary protections that it granted me; but where would I find confirmation of my belonging, my equality under the law, and my identity and dignity in the society of others? The state, the one I was born into, had refused me the rights of the citizen, yet I had to go on living. I was lucky to have books that could help me.

A 2012 book, called *Profane Citizenship in Europe*, contrasts state citizenship—a sovereign's granting of rights (backed by their military, political, and economic muscle)—with "profane citizenship," which locates our belonging in the acts and relationships each of us choose every day. (The study cites Jacques Rancière and Giorgio Agamben, among other contemporary writers, as developing a discourse of the profane, anchored in Émile Benveniste's 1960 essay, "Profanus et Profanare.") Is citizenship a protected status granted by an authority with the power to back it up? Or is citizenship a capacity that any body can activate by our chosen acts, our freely willed relationships with others? And, in what ways does freedom inhere in either one?

The differences are stark, and never just theoretical. Every human life is caught in the intersection of these claims. A passport exempts no one from the everyday obligations of locale (to the great frustration of many ex-pat communities); and good neighborly relations will never convince police to overlook the lack of a passport (or if they do, it is called "corruption"); good neighbors cannot protect us from the state's claims on our liberty when we are citizens of a state; and even the full force of state law cannot quiet the voice of neighbors who scold or punish us for violating their norms. In some ways the question is only simple for those who are denied state citizenship: their fates are in the hands of the people around them. Everyone else lives with two, often contradictory, masters—the state and the communities in which we live; the temple and the *pro fanum*.

"Profane" has two interesting meanings. The profane is contrasted either to expertise or to the sacred. In the first meaning, profane knowledge is a layman's knowledge, as against the knowledge of a trained professional. Profane knowledge has its place; which is why it is named. But, in a technological society, as Ellul points out, that place is always subservient to expertise. Similarly, the profane that we contrast with the sacred is placed below and the sacred above, although this pair is far more complex and complicit than the arrangement suggests. In his foundational essay, "Profanus et Profanare," Émile Benveniste detailed the interwoven nature of the two. Their meanings come from a simple architectural detail dividing the temple (the site of sacrifice and the sacred) from the public space in front of the temple, called, in Latin, *pro fanum*. The threshold between them was constantly crossed, not least when animals were sacrificed in the temple and the carcass had to be brought back out, into the *pro fanum*, where everyone was invited to feast on the meat. Thus, the profanation of the sacrifice was never its undoing, but its completion. The sacred and the profane are elements of a single unified social process. Rancière suggests that the same holds true for citizenship: the rights granted by the state are only fully realized in the freely-willed acts and choices of profane citizens.

Jacques Ellul's discussion of technique speaks to these same issues, but his book is largely forgotten. A French resistance fighter and devout Christian, Ellul used his social analysis to shape a radical theology, absenting himself from the academic and political circles that dominated post-war French philosophy. The French left might have read Ellul, but they did not cite him. His critique indicted all their most favored political solutions, including communism and humanism. His provincial home address, in Bordeaux, further absented him from the vigorous discourse of Paris. But his book has aged well, and, in its English translation, now appears prophetic, both in its reading of technique and in the position Ellul staked out at the intersection of politics and theology. Technique exhibits the same complicity between the sacred/professional (or technological) and the profane (which is to say, the all-inclusively human). This is especially true for what Ellul called "human techniques," which begin as rarefied, expert procedures but are only completed when we accept and propagate them as normative practices: for example, standardized education, advertising campaigns, psychological counseling, and technocratic government, such as the friendly, rehearsed protocols of the Dutch bureaucrats who solicited my biometrics to add to their database. There was no compulsion or force, only a reasonable request that I was glad to comply with.

I was enormously happy to be confirmed and cataloged as a Dutch resident. In February, when the approval arrived by mail, I didn't believe I'd need protection from my native country, the United States. There were no charges. I was a writer, working again in a country where I had worked many times in the previous twenty-five years. My publisher was in Rotterdam. I moved there to finish a book that was many years overdue. I arrived to long-held friendships and warm collegial relations. During the decades I had visited and worked in the Netherlands, I learned enough Dutch and studied enough of the country's history and culture to develop strong ties and a sense of belonging. So, it was a pleasure to have my belonging confirmed by the state's approval of my application.

In a sense, I was adding the state's imprimatur to the accomplished fact of my profane citizenship, after twenty-five years. And that imprimatur turned out to be crucial. In September, many months after the egg-shaped machine extracted biometrics from my body, I got a phone call from the Dutch police. The U.S. embassy had delivered a warrant for my arrest. Would I please report to the station and deal with it? I agreed, we set a time for later that day, and I went to speak with a lawyer I knew. He told me I would be arrested upon reporting—that was the protocol—but, as a free man, I could simply not report, awaiting more forceful requests, or even move somewhere the U.S. was not looking for me. *What did I want to do?*

* * * * *

In her 2014 book, *Expulsions*, the Dutch-born sociologist Saskia Sassen describes a global pattern of increasingly efficient, brutal dispossessions in every sphere—political, economic, and ecological. Among the familiar cases are the *sans papiers*, refugees from economic or political oppression who wander the world without state citizenship. But Sassen looks past this crowded surface to expose what she calls "subterranean patterns" of expulsion driven by market forces that punish much vaster populations with even greater efficiency than do states. Her focus is "the systemic edge," which she describes as, "the site where general conditions take extreme forms [as] the site for expulsion or incorporation. Further," she writes, "the extreme character of conditions at the edge makes visible larger trends that are less extreme and hence more difficult to capture."

Every age has its systemic edge, and its deeper emergent patterns. Sassen gives the historical example of 19th-century England, which, on the surface, "looked like an overwhelmingly rural economy . . . [when] in fact industrial capitalism was already the dominant logic of political economy." While that shift became recognizable in hindsight, Sassen's purpose in *Expulsions* is to see current conditions clearly. "Today," she writes, "I see new systemic logics arising from the decaying political economy of the twentieth century. This decay began in the 1980s. By then the strong welfare states and workers' syndicalisms established in much of the West . . . either had been devastated or were under severe pressure."

Like most of Sassen's widely influential work, *Expulsions* uses the bracing precision and scope of sociological research to compel our sense of injustice. It speaks in the language of the human sciences. Statistics interleave with emotionally wrenching case studies to give weight to our deepest, empathetic responses, compelling a kind of fevered impotence. You cannot see the numbers she cites without feeling that something must be done, while also feeling dwarfed by the scope of things. Statistics cast their spell. Her method predisposes us to look for comprehensive solutions requiring systemic change—that is, broadly professionalized, expert, technical solutions. Systemic injustice begs for a better application of just laws, in the same way that a personal tragedy begs for catharsis and then mourning. And so, somewhat paradoxically, *Expulsions* deepens our hunger for technique, because the forces at work lie so far beyond any one person's scope or agency.

Of course I saw myself in the picture Sassen paints, transferring my unfathomable feeling of injury and confusion into a widely shared condition that let me feel situated, comprehensible, less alone. First among the shocks that state expulsion brought was a sudden, pathetic loneliness, as though one's own family had willfully slammed the door shut. I felt like an old dog, shooed outside on a Winter night. Mostly I wanted to whimper and scratch at the door, looking for familiar, warm eyes to recognize me and let me back in again. I literally could not believe that the U.S. would have done such a thing to me. Reading these books (Sassen's and the study of profane citizenship) mapped the territory I was thereby thrust into. And I found it was crowded with all manner of people. If the state was serious about its attack, at least I wasn't alone.

The Dutch policeman's kindness impressed me. He had phoned with a reasonable request. He didn't operate in secret nor mislead me or my friends as a trap. (Which, I soon learned, was how the U.S. handled my case.) And so I told my lawyer that I would report to the police as promised. They had been reasonable; I would respond in kind. At the police station in Amsterdam, a sergeant showed me the warrant, arrested me, and put me in a crowded holding cell. It was mid-afternoon. The station was busy with brisk conversations between men in restraints and men at desks. I was fascinated by their bodies, so similar and desiring, but held in the contrasting apparatus of their stations. The men in restraints gestured and posed, willing their human form and substance to express itself through the camouflage of their captivity; while the men at desks braced themselves like sailors in a storm, as if the bulky furniture were a flotilla of water-tight boats that could safely navigate this flood-tide of expelled humanity.

I was offered tea and coffee, and the sergeant gave me back the novel I had brought with me, *A High Wind in Jamaica*, by Richard Hughes. I happily disappeared again into the book's rich story of five children, found at sea by pirates, who overwhelm the fussy protocols of their pirate captors and transform the ship into their own small kingdom. I relaxed, home again in the book, laughing with recognition at the power of these kids' naivete and their clever overturning of the elaborate rules of captivity. Five other men shared the holding cell, and I held the book's cover ostentatiously in view, hoping one of them would strike up a conversation or even say "I've read that book!" But so few people read novels these days, and certainly the holding cell in Amsterdam wasn't the likeliest place for me to find the society of readers I sought just then. They were nice enough men, but no one spoke to me. The sergeant announced they'd be loading us into a paddy wagon soon, and he said I'd have to give the book back to him, so I hurried to finish it. We were loaded into an armored van with a half-dozen other men, and I was sent to Zwaag Prison.

* * * * *

The authors of *Profane Citizenship in Europe* consider a half-dozen instances where the lack of state citizenship forces people to establish their rights and freedom strictly through profane means. For example, deaf communities living in isolation can be effectively denied their citizenship because the state has become unavailable to them. Their passive disempowerment can be as total as the active expulsion of attacked ethnic or political minorities whom the state wants to be rid of. In both cases, the expelled must construct civil society and the terms of belonging on their own. Or, the situation of children born to refugee parents.

An intersection of disparities conspires to deny them the actual papers and the education, health care, and society by which children normally grow into citizenship. Or, the more common case of deliberate political and religious refugees. The UN estimates their total number at nearly 35 million, worldwide. Some have papers, some do not; none have a state willing to guarantee their freedom.

It was astonishing how utterly common my situation was. The Netherlands hosts nearly 90,000 refugees; this year alone more than 58,000 came seeking asylum, not counting the hidden ones, nor the criminalized ones who show up in statistics as fugitives from justice. (And now, events in Syria and across Europe promise to double or even triple those numbers.) They are not treated well. The largest groups, in Amsterdam and Den Haag, are shuttled from overfull refugee centers to empty churches to abandoned buildings lacking basic services, such as heat and hot water, and so inadequate for the numbers of people that the UN has charged the Dutch with violating the treaties they signed to protect refugees. And the Netherlands is among the rich countries, the ones with a history of concern for asylum seekers and the dispossessed. Refugees travel thousands of kilometers, through other less-welcoming countries, just to put their fates into the hands of the Dutch.

Among these brave people, I was an outlier, an exception, in nearly every way. According to the arrest warrant I was a fugitive from U.S. prosecutors (though I could not be a fugitive because I'd never known of the charges; the Dutch policeman's phone call was the first notice I had of them). The U.S. prosecutors had chosen to work in secret, indicting me through an increasingly common American procedure called a "secret grand jury," at which there is neither a defendant nor any legal representation for one. In Zwaag I stood out: I was American, middle-class, a writer, and completely new to the criminal justice system. While these facts generally biased my jailers to treat me well—as though my stay in prison was a comical mistake better suited as a premise for a TV sitcom than, say, as an instrument of justice—it also meant I had little or no society during the time that I spent there. I was a complete misfit, and clueless about the community I'd been thrust into.

A reasonable person will wonder why I, as a law-abiding citizen, chose to refuse the U.S.'s claim on me. Why fight extradition?

Citizenship is never just the provision of services or safety; it is a mutual obligation. Implicitly, my life-long enjoyment of the state's protection meant I should answer their summons now; and, I've always assumed I would do so without any hesitation. These were not casual assumptions on my part. I studied political theory in school because the root of my political rights and obligations felt both urgent and uncertain. In my twenties, I came to believe sincerely in the social contract that early Enlightenment thinkers, especially Thomas Hobbes, John Locke, and Jean Jacques Rousseau, saw as binding citizens together in a sovereign that we both comprise and are subservient to. Told that a U.S. prosecutor, following the rule of law, came up with an arrest warrant for me, my mind flashed to this tacit agreement. I'd always lived as a U.S. citizen, so I should surrender myself now. Why wouldn't I?

The state's actions against me were shockingly lawless, deceitful, and contrary to every detail of the social contract I believed lay at the root of my citizenship. I had been pursued in secret under a presumption of guilt based on my past writings and reputation without any investigation of the specific acts I was ultimately charged with. The charges were incendiary (child molestation), my son was taken from me without cause, and my friendships and professional relations were poisoned as part of the so-called "investigation," which, it turned out, did not include speaking to me about the charges nor to the other people present when I was alleged to have committed the crime (excepting my son, who told the police he saw no evidence of what was alleged), nor ever looking at the scene of the allegation. Instead, the prosecutor—who later told my lawyer that the novels I wrote 20 years ago "make me think he's guilty"—went to Yale University to look in my literary archive for evidence. I discovered much of this piece-meal in the long, slow fallout after the U.S. delivered its extradition request. And by then, the police and prosecutors had severed me from my child, damaged my work life, and robbed me of my liberty in order to extradite and imprison me in advance of trial. Bail was set at $2.25 million, despite my having, as they say, "no priors."

My 80-year old mother (a lifelong political activist who raised her four children fighting the racist laws and military aggressions of the U.S. government) and my brothers and sister were shocked and upset.

We all believed the U.S. courts could deliver justice, and for the most part my family counseled patience and good lawyers; these would see me through until I had my freedom back. But our faith was shaken, with the interesting exception of my oldest brother. He, alone among us, is Christian; a born-again believer in a Christian God and in Jesus's martyrdom. His discovery of this faith came in the course of an apocalyptic break with the family and the world we'd been raised into, a churchless world that only referenced Jesus as an inspiration for social justice movements. Now, a good thirty years into his Christian life, he alone received my news with calm and assurance. "The world is corrupt," he would remind me. Injustice rains down on everyone. My salvation would come in the next world, and only if, in this one, I acknowledged Jesus as my savior and humbled myself before an all-powerful God. And I was lucky, he said—all too commonly the police simply shoot the people they're afraid of. The mostly-white police of America shoot the black men who frighten them every day. "You still have a chance for salvation," he assured me. "Thanks be to God."

The jailers at Zwaag took away my books (along with my pens and paper), and said I could get other books on "library day." In the meantime I could watch TV. I don't like TV. Their rule struck me as crazy, a kind of petty, brain-deadening punishment. Similarly, inmates could not have musical instruments in their cells, but they could constantly listen to the radio. I knew my time at Zwaag would be brief so I didn't object. The brevity of the stay was assured by a judge who accepted the testimony of a half-dozen of my Dutch friends (together with a bond to guarantee that I would not flee), and was already organizing my release, which came after a week. My long history in the Netherlands—in effect my profane citizenship—and the considerable advantage of having friends with money, compelled the state to quickly restore my freedom and my rights. There would be restrictions: I'd have to report to the police once a week and never leave the country until the extradition process was done and either confirmed or rejected. In effect, my detention was shifted from Zwaag Prison to the small nation where I'd come to work. Everywhere else in the world, the U.S.'s order to jail and ship me home still held. But in the Netherlands I would be free.

* * * * *

For the most part, asylum of the kind I enjoyed is temporary. Refugees rarely arrive at a new permanent home. Their displacement is unending, and they shuttle from promise to promise, crossing borders, moving on or off the radar, to find brief havens that inevitably end so that they have to flee again: the asylum process completes itself; local politics change; economic hardship squeezes them out. Whatever the cause, expulsion is a serial condition that plays its same script over and over until the refugee dies. This is an essential aspect of "technique," one that Ellul saw rooted in its autonomous, self-augmenting logic. Techniques are all problem-based. That is, they begin by identifying a problem which technique can "solve." It resembles what cultural critic Evgeny Morosov calls "solutionism." Even in the absence of any disquiet or political urgency, "problems" are cultivated and refined in order to shape the precise ground on which a "solution" can be built (which, these days, Morosov tells us, typically takes the form of a software or a new app). The solution is announced, and its wide-spread adoption sets the stage for our serial re-enactment of the problem we were told gave rise to it, until millions of lives are caught up in the endlessly repeated performance of "the problem," which feeds the autonomous operation of "the solution," which is technique.

The state—among our oldest, most pervasive techniques—promises to solve the problem of our natural anarchy, taming the Darwinian jungle into which we are born. It offers security and belonging in a safe, lawful home—an antidote to the nomadic un-belonging that is our state-less fate (or so we're told). What the state actually protects us from is, primarily, other states. Instead of settling us, the state stages the serial re-enactment of our un-belonging, confronting us over and over again with borders we can or cannot cross, security checks, biometrics, temporary restrictions, cullings, and dispossession. The state is not a settled place of human dwelling so much as it is a kind of endless corridor of doorways, opening and closing, stringing its thresholds from birth to death so that our passage can be made with as little distraction as possible. The state that promises us a home inevitably functions as the permanent engine of our displacement. Technique is never a solution to a problem; it is the baroque preservation of whatever problem the technique was putatively meant to solve. (What Ellul termed the "human technique" of the administrative state, Michel Foucault analyzed as "biopolitics." Foucault's "normalizing society," in which the state assumes a regulatory role in relation to a new political entity, the masses, is something like Ellul's "technological society," and "bio-power" resembles Ellul's broader conception of technique. A dialogue on these phenomena between Ellul and Foucault, sadly never realized in life, could yet yield useful insights.)

Only in prison does the state deliver on its promise of a home, by offering us a kind of stabilized site of expulsion. In prison, our unbelonging is institutionalized and given a home address. Prison perfects the modern state's technocratic ambitions—pure administration framing a complete absence of rights—by locating us outside the messy contradictions of the human belonging we are born into, that is, the home we call our "body." Prison takes full control of the once-autonomous body and empties it of rights. In Sassen's terms, prison is "the systemic edge" where expulsion takes place. So it was interesting for me to discover, at Zwaag, that prison is also the site of re-incorporation into robust, established frameworks of profane citizenship.

Prison is not the only thing that empties the body of rights. A chilling example, in *Profane Citizenship in Europe*, describes the dispossession that happens to every one of us in the course of a normal day. It happens whenever we cross a biometrically-regulated threshold. At these boundaries, determination of our status shifts from the testimony of the body we are born into, to rest, instead, in the biometric accounting stored in memory chips. Digital biometrics displace the body, and we become walking prisons—purified sites of complete administration. During this passage, our bodies are emptied of meaning, stripped of identity, which has been transferred wholesale into the chip. When the body can no longer speak, when it becomes impossible to obviate technique's harsh judgments by human appeal to our fellow man, how can we be citizens?

Note:
"Potatoes or Rice?" was written in 2015 and circulated privately as an anonymous samizdat. The title comes from the author's experience in prison in the Netherlands. All new prisoners were asked this question

during intake, "Potatoes or Rice?" The answer both determined their nightly meals, provided through a slot in each cell, and served as a useful sorting mechanism between "native Dutch" (as the white, Christian prisoners were called) and immigrant (mostly Muslim) prisoners. The excerpt presented here is from the samizdat pamphlet, with minor edits. A longer, updated version of "Potatoes or Rice?" is published online at www.artseverywhere.ca.

For the Death of 100 Whales

Michael McClure

In April 1954, **TIME** magazine described seventy-nine bored American G.I.s stationed at a NATO base in Iceland murdering a pod of one hundred killer whales. In a single morning the soldiers, armed with rifles, machine guns, and boats, rounded up and then shot the whales to death.

I read this poem at my first reading, in 1955.

Hung midsea
Like a boat mid-air
The liners boiled their pastures:
The liners of flesh,
The Arctic steamers

Brains the size of a teacup
Mouths the size of a door

The sleek wolves
Mowers and reapers of sea kine.
THE GIANT TADPOLES
(Meat their algae)
Lept
Like sheep or children.
Shot from the sea's bore.

Turned and twisted
(Goya!!)
Flung blood and sperm.
Incense.
Gnashed at their tails and brothers
Cursed Christ of mammals,
Snapped at the sun,
Ran for the Sea's floor.

Goya! Goya!
Oh Lawrence
No angels dance those bridges.
OH GUN! OH BOW!
There are no churches in the waves,
No holiness,
No passages or crossings
From the beasts' wet shore.

FLOWER GARLAND FROTH

For Zenshin Ryufu, Philip Whalen
On the twenty-fifth anniversary of the ordination of Philip Whalen

THROUGH THE SKANDHAS, THE BUNDLES
OF BRIGHTNESS AND HUNGERS,
arises
more FOAM
making foam with no origin
but mutual reflection

Taste hunger perception thought

NO
JOKE
not even traps

gorgeous manacles

((physical form-bubbles
sensation-bubbles
perception-bubbles
conditioning-bubbles
consciousness-bubbles

<<>>

MALLARME'S HUGE PASSIONS AND
FRANCESCO CLEMENTE'S
tiny, skinny dark figures in the joy of their excrement
and bright excitement, and Blake's fairies
and caterpillars
swimming in nada, right where we breathe

The Circus of Celebration runs away
with us
(not with the circus!)
pulling us out of the big top
like kernels from
a wrinkled shell

more foam

<<>>

FOAM POPPING BY THE SIDE OF THE RIVER
rainbow bubbles burst, while reflecting all
things
from a black smooth rock
made of bubbles

A white hand
reaches
TO FILL A VASE
from the cool stream

Bronze vase clinks
on a stone

foam

More foam

<<>>

FOAM WHERE A SKUNK DRINKS
from the trickle   elegant black and white
fur of foam
Sound of the water

foam   bubbles

FUR
OF
A
MOVING TRUCK
in the wet forest   Paint chips
on mulch
A huge presence and purpose
bursting into being
with everything

Solid nothing

<<>>

. . . SOLID FOAM-BUBBLES BURSTING
INTO OLD SHOES   NEW SHOES
black with high tops
bubbles of iridescent soil on
the soles

Smell of redwood and wet mulch
in countless realms of
reflections
IN

JUST
one body

or none
trickling over the mirror

<<>>

HERE IS THE TRUE CONTENT OF EXPERIENCE

THE UNTRUE CONTENT OF EXPERIENCE

silver raindrops falling on bubbles
Words spill from sleep
Hungry ghosts behind trees
push over dreams NOT

TRUE

Tiny black seeds

rattle in an envelope

BIG SCARLET FLOWERS

Bubbles
Foam

<<>>

A SWORD WITH EDGES OF FLAME
slashes the walls

BLACK ANTS CIRCLE A BUBBLE OF HONEY
Zebras, wildebeest,
at the waterhole

Smell of red dust in the air
is foam
Uncoiling fiddle-neck ferns,
astroturf,
voices of wisdom

BLADE THROUGH A RAINBOW MEMBRANE

<<>>

EVERYTHING SMILING
with haloes and imaginary radiance

ALL FOAM

real
as delusion
and the sunyatta physics of pond plants
and hot air ducts
blowing into outburstings
of snow banks
These caves
are inhabited by nothings constructed
of bubbles
I drive them around
and eat them

<<>>

FALCON SHAPES WOVEN IN GRAY SILK

Tension of plum buds
in night fog
Stars a trillion years
from the mist

BUBBLES

all in one
ONE
IN ALL

Hidden in moss
in the redwoods
near a Butterfinger wrapper

<<>>

THE SOUND OF THE DOWNPOUR ON WALLS

is bubbles bursting
into stuff of delusion,
fine as a new chip on an old tooth

LIKE
THE TECHNICOLOR MOVIE
of smells projected between raindrops
on a screen of touches and tastes

The message of flannel is foam
for the shoulders
in the perfume
while floorboards shine

Perfectly clear

<<>>

I RISE PROUD TO BE BEING

as
I
am

and I

lie

silent

NOT
KNOWING

I
Know

I
know

the long-gone delicacy
and meat of apricots
sun-heated on branches,
and waves and caverns of fuel
smashing the earth
in the arising
and pouring
of patterns

I love those who fight this

I
HAND
THEM
the primate crown
shimmering
with hunger and automobiles
and velvet and contracts and postage
and duck weed and emeralds
and jazz

THIS IS NOT MINE
THIS WILL NOT BE MINE

THIS IS NOT MINE
THIS WILL NOT BE MINE

This is not mind
This will not be mind

THIS IS NO BODY
THIS WILL NOT BE BODY

Me
is
not
mine

It appears on the tip of an eyelash

A bubble

Foam

The Fleshy Nave

for Jane & Bill

"TO SAY THAT THE MECHANISM IS FINELY TUNED
AND PRECISE
IS A GARGANTUAN UNDERSTATEMENT." Not to know
that we are all—from viruses to mammoths—swimmers
in the infinitely stretching
primordial soup
IS
TO

CALL
LIFE

a dull daydream. There's no end
to the reach of the surge into the past
and future. From bacteria's
plain throb to the dolphin's
imagination is one image
in the ripple of the waves.

In the eyes of the sky are endless waves.

Each particle is a chorister in the fleshy nave.

Polishness

MICHELLE TEA

I was miserable in Poland.

I was sick, a burl of yuck in my lungs that kept me coughing, and coughing meant no smoking, and that made me miserable too. The cat who pissed on the mattress I was sleeping on made me miserable, and how my heart was broken but not yet *officially*—that was a special kind of misery, edged with stupid hope and paranoia. And I couldn't distract myself with sex because the heartbreak was not yet official, plus I was so sick and lethargic with the ugly coughing—when your face stays in that prolonged contortion, *honk honk honk*. My miserable, heartbroken sickness sat on my face like a film, making me very unpretty. I had let myself get too skinny and my head sat upon my neck like a bobble toy, the wrinkles in my face deeper with no cheeks to plump them. I looked sad and I felt sad and I brought it all to Poland.

I arrived in Warsaw from Nice, where I had been vacationing with Olin, my boyfriend-not-boyfriend—he just didn't like being part of a couple. As in, it really freaked him out that time we found ourselves both brushing our teeth in the bathroom *at the same time*; see also, the greening of his complexion when I once asked to wash myself off in his shower. He did not want to encourage acts that would allow one to get dreamy about possible future domesticity and yet had taken me on a cruise of the French Riviera. Mixed messages, yes, and I had packed my decoder, determined to make it work because he was so funny and well dressed and our sex was so good. I found his belly, which embarrassed him, kingly and the orange hair that furred his shoulders very animal. All of him was noble to me, even the tarred places within him that made him so skittish and terrible. I imagined I could lure him out of himself and into some new version that was generally happier and eager for love. This is a particular feminine fantasy, and it is odd how much I clung to it and even odder how oblivious I was to my own patterns, but that is the way of them, isn't it? These gears that churn inside us and we barely notice them, no matter how many wooden shoes and metal hammers get tossed into the works.

We'd boarded the boat in Spain, a giant yacht that raised its sails to very dramatic music each night. You would be sitting in the hot tub and suddenly the soundtrack to a Viking ambush would blare and the white canvas would ascend. For one week, we were at sea. I would walk up to the deck for my morning coffee, excited to see what the morning's view would be—look, a terra-cotta castle! It was grand, this was Europe, the Europe where fairy tales come from, rolling hills and the sky and the sea blindingly blue. It made me feel glorious; there is nothing more spectacular than traveling. Except love. Olin was moody, snappy, and mean, but I was in love with him. I experimented with being this way or that, timid or cool, exuberant, funny, intimate or aloof, all along shaking on the inside, and none of it having any effect whatsoever. At the end of the trip we would go our separate ways, him to Budapest, me to Poland. I had gotten an organization to give me a grant to teach writing to feminists in Warsaw.

I am English and had spent a week in London at eighteen, drunk, dancing all night in goth clubs, drinking shandies in pubs, and falling in love with everything, just like the psychic who'd told me I had lived there in a past life assured me I would. I am French and had spent three weeks in Paris, chain-smoking and eating cheese, involving myself in a ménage à trois and falling in love, as one does in Paris. And, I am Polish. How would I experience my Polishness in Warsaw? Not by getting drunk or dancing or smoking or eating cheese or falling in love. In Warsaw, I would suffer. Perhaps that was what one did in Poland.

My flight from Nice landed at night. The French sun was gone and would never shine in Poland anyway. How could it have been so warm and now be so cold? Was Poland so very far from France? Being American, I thought of it all as Europe. I wore a tight gray dress that wrapped across my chest, with no sleeves, made from the thick cotton of a sweatshirt. It was a good outfit for Nice, for turning my back on Olin as I hopped into a taxi, crying behind my shades like a real French lady. In Warsaw the dress was ridiculous. Night fell earlier in Poland; the airport was stark and roomy, yellow lit against the dark outside, pierced with the fleeting red and white lights of cars. My friend Anu was late to fetch me. Anu was a rogue, I knew, and I feared he would never come for me. What would I do? I would get a hotel room, I thought. In every city of every nation there were hotel rooms by the airport. I would check my emails, surely someone would try to find me. I would email Anu, email Agnieszka, whose queer organization had helped me get the grant to teach writing. If only they offered travel grants to the estranged daughters of alcoholic Polish men, so that they might learn how their own estranged Polishness operated within them. A grant to study the pieces of themselves that were Polish even when their Polish kin were unknowable, a grant to fund a pilgrimage to the inscrutable homeland of their deadbeat dad. But such grants do not exist, so one must teach writing to feminists.

I understood I was English because I loved music and fashion, the weirder the better. I had two Union Jack T-shirts by the time I was thirteen; I lay in bed listening to Billy Idol's growl and cried. I tried to feather my shitty hair like Def Leppard's Joe Elliott. Later I would fashion it after Robert Smith and Siouxsie Sioux, and lie in bed listening to Depeche Mode and the Smiths and cry some more. I understood I was French because of Jean Genet and Violette Leduc, because of Anaïs Nin's involvement with Henry Miller's crazed wife June. Also, I loved to smoke cigarettes and cry. But Poland? I loved kielbasa. I called it "the sausage of my people," making friends laugh. I loved the Polish eagle tattoo on my uncle Stashu's bicep, golden crowned, claws flexed. My own heraldic pigeon tattoo, with its crown and claws, is an homage. Poland was founded by a man named Lech, one of three brothers, descendants of Noah—yes, *the* Noah, the one with the boat and all the animals. The three brothers were hunting, each following his prey in various directions, and Lech, in pursuit of the bow he'd sprung, stopped short when he came upon an eagle guarding its nest, huge and fierce. The setting sun lit her feathers gold, and Lech, sensitive to omens, decided to stay, called the place Poland, named the eagle Golden, and made it his protector. A hunting people, open to the mystical powers of feathers and sunshine. To allow such poetry to determine life's direction. I always believed the witch inside me came from my mother, the alcoholic from my father. But maybe it is more complicated than that.

I met my friend Anu years ago at a queer club in Paris, where he was studying photography. I was in love with a blond boy named Killian whose girlfriend would not allow him to dance with me, and so I twirled alone in the hot pink light of the club until I found myself dancing with Anu. Killian was pained to see me dancing with Anu, and pulled me aside and begged me to stop, to not take him home. Home was the apartment above the Shakespeare and Company bookstore. I had meant to sleep inside the bookstore like all the eighteen-year-old boys, the Tumbleweeds in their velvet blazers and rumpled Rimbaud hairdos, rolling cigarettes on the stone steps outside. I had meant to sleep among them and write about it, but the owners learned I was a writer and gave me the writer's apartment, a single room with a flat twin mattress resting on a board that rested on stacks of books. Books lined the walls too. Tumbleweeds left their diaries on the desk during the day, and everyone traipsed through to use the only bathroom. Of course I took Anu home, to spite Killian, who loved me, and also because he was very attractive—olive skin and dark hair—and Polish, which was exotic to me, more so than France even, because Poland was the mystery inside me.

I bought Anu beers from a café in the Latin Quarter and we sat outside, the stone buildings crowding us. He told me all about his family, that his father was a salt magnate and he was the heir to a salt fortune. After the fall of communism, his mother had opened the first Chanel store in Poland and Anu grew up looking at the photos from her stash of *Vogue* magazines. Anu's tales seemed like lies, but lies tailored to my particular interests, so they were like little gifts from Anu to me. He told me he would write me a mermaid story about the mermaid tattoo on my belly; he would write me a bluebird story about the bluebird on my hand. He would send me a vial of pure Polish salt. Of course, it was only pillow talk. I smoked his cigarettes and took him back to the apartment, where he opened a Tumbleweed's diary and wrote inside it. I was scandalized. I was already afraid I hadn't worked long enough in the bookstore downstairs, hadn't typed out my biography in the typewriter niche as requested, hadn't impressed the White Witch, the Irish poet who presided over the weekly tea party in George's apartment, where the bookstore's elderly owner lay on his twin bed that he shared with a pan of cat litter and a small black-and-white TV, his dresser overrun with papers and old food and at least one cockroach. Perhaps I was pushing the boundaries of the bookstore's hospitality bringing someone back for sex on the scrawny bed, both of us freezing midgrope, feigning sleep when Tumbleweed boys crept in to use the bathroom. And now here was Anu, gleefully vandalizing their diary. He did not vandalize my body. He was very gentle, turning it like an artifact in his palms, studying my tattoos, fascinated. I played PJ Harvey and the Smiths, and he hadn't heard of either of them, nor had he heard of Patti Smith. I didn't understand how this attractive, genderqueer person who had danced so well to M.I.A. in the club did not know this music, but later, when I came to Poland, I understood better.

Agnieszka was chosen to host me in Warsaw because she had the nicest apartment. It is true that the building sat on very green grass. The neighborhood seemed sedate. Inside, it felt like public housing. Isn't all housing public under communism? Agnieszka's sturdy *panelák* was surely built by the state after the war, after the Nazis had burned the whole of the city to the ground and the Soviets brought it back. Housing. What could be more of a uniform, human need, so why not create these uniform blocks? Agnieszka had a tremendous number of locks on the door, like a joke about old New York City. "Don't let the cats out," she requested. And don't let them into the room I was given to sleep, because they would pee on my things. I forgot many times and would rush into the room, urgently smelling my suitcase, relieved that they hadn't pissed there, until, of course, they did.

There was no beauty inside me at that time, and it was hard to connect with Warsaw's beauty, so unlike other places I'd seen. I had thought myself expert at locating difficult beauty, a happy consequence of growing up in my slummy New England town, but here I'd become an ugly American, the worst, my heart cold to the brutalist buildings punched into the city. The heavy gray skies, the directive from Anu not to smile at strangers, lest they think I was simpleminded, a fool, or else gearing up to rob them. I found it very hard to board a train car, pass an old woman on the street, and not reflexively smile. Olin, too, had had a problem with my smiling; my relentless positivity had aggravated his depression. This insanity had hurt my feelings, but later, with distance, I could see my happiness for what it was: aggressive and manipulative, as if the radiance of my personality could burn away his sadness like a fog. My mother had employed a similar tactic with my depressed Polish father, and wasn't Olin so very much like my father with his chronic grumpiness and his cigarettes and alcohol? Did this weaponized positivity, calibrated to offset cynicism and despair, drive them both away?

What was brilliant about Warsaw was how the Polish resistance fought the Nazis for sixty-three days. Ordinary people fueling the uprising. These are the people I liked to imagine myself descended from, not the other, evil Polish, who killed their neighbors and moved into their homes. The Warsaw Uprising was urban combat, espionage, and sabotage, the largest armed resistance in World War II. The Polish Home Army raided a military prison that had been turned into a concentration camp, freeing almost 350 Jewish prisoners. Women fought, were involved. Like Anna Smolenska, an art student who won a sort of contest to design an emblem for the resistance. The *Kotwica* is all over Warsaw, a *P* growing out of the middle peak of a *W* resembling an anchor. Anna was a girl scout at the time, and in Warsaw, the Polish boy and girl scouts comprised the Gray Ranks. Anna was twenty-three then and she looked queer. Short hair slicked sideways across a broad forehead, a pleasant, open face, sweet. Wearing a necktie. She engaged in sabotage and worked for a resistance newsletter. The Nazis wanted the editor but found Anna, and took her and all the women of her family to Auschwitz. A photo shows a shadow of the stout lesbian she would have grown into had she been allowed to live. Her round glasses, her bloody nose. A virus infected her chest there, and she died.

Certain things give my body dopamine. Sex, shopping, smoking. Text messages. Possibility, anticipation. I recently learned that talking about yourself triggers a dopamine release, and my entire adult life made a sad, new sense. I am an alcoholic, and I think that this grasping for sensation, this need for dopamine, for a high, is what turned my drinking sour. I don't know if I have less dopamine than you have or if I am simply greedy. Having taken away alcohol, I'll lunge toward fucking instead or find myself dizzy, sweaty, from the sight of a perfectly designed shoe. I'll eat cigarettes. In Poland I had nothing. I got little bolts of *something* from the iron *Kotwicas* bolted into the bricks of buildings here and there, marking the place where the uprising was fought. Mystery gives me dopamine too, and history, sometimes, and revolution. I thought about the mermaid Syrenka, said to protect the city of Warsaw, what a shitty job she had done. I imagine it was beyond her capacity. The Soviet army was meant to join the uprising, but had stopped short on the other side of the river Vistula, allowing the Nazis to destroy the resistance in hope that the Polish would later need Russia. And they did. And they did. I imagined Syrenka, a dark-hearted, tangle-headed mermaid gone furious with grief.

While I was in Poland, Olin's plan was to explore Budapest with an old friend, a long-ago girlfriend. The two of them stayed with mutual friends, a couple, both of whom had eating disorders and so had little energy to show their guests around town. The old girlfriend was terribly mean to Olin, and he'd had a moment, stuck inside her bad temper, when he wondered if that was what it had felt like for me, traveling with him.

It was hard for Olin to enter bodies of water. He would go slowly, wincing. I would jump in, like a dolphin or mermaid. I would splash and frolic, and if I were to be honest, I would admit I was also performing the part of a freespirited young woman, at one with the elements. I knew he was not like this, and I hoped my spirited splashing would cheer him. I thought maybe it could jolt him out of his dour state, a revelation, *Yes, I can jump in the ocean too!* and he dives in, peeling off his depression like a T-shirt. Olin had metal rods where his shinbones ought to have been. The cold of the metal immersed in the seawater was terrible. Years ago Olin was in a car accident and everyone died. Olin died twice, but was the only one to live. He recovered at home, on morphine, slowly becoming addicted. He was fourteen years old. I leapt from the sea, droplets shooting off me like crystals.

In a smoky bar in Poland, filled with interesting-looking people chain-smoking cigarettes and sipping drinks, Anu asked if I was faking my happiness. Was I really like this all the time? Was I putting on a show? I didn't know how to respond. I was miserable, but I didn't need to talk about it. Anu knew I had just ended a terrible trip and that my heart was broken. I had sadly told him that I would not be able to sleep with him because I felt so ill, a presumptuous thing to say; he may well have had enough of me in Paris, plus I wasn't looking pretty and he had a new girl, young and plump faced and devoted. They wore matching leopard socks and Anu wrote love notes on her skin with a marker. I can be miserable and happy at once, I explained. Once, when I was newly sober but had no recovery, nothing to help me navigate the mindfuck of life without alcohol, the writer Mary Woronov also asked me if I was always happy. She was not curious like Anu, but a bit more scornful. There is something dopey about happiness, as the Poles know. Woronov is a Slavic last name; Russia was founded by Lech's brother, Rus. "Are you on Prozac?" Mary demanded. I explained to her that I had just quit drinking and I wanted to die, but I didn't see the point in making it anyone else's problem. She laughed. "Well, of course you want to die. Life is miserable without drugs."

In Warsaw Anu pointed to the Palace of Culture and Science. They called it the syringe because of the decorative spire on top, 150 feet tall. The building used to have "Stalin" all over it; a gift from Russia, it had been named the Joseph Stalin Palace of Culture and Science, but after Russia began its de-Stalinization, Poland too wiped the brute's name from its buildings.

The year of my visit was the fortieth anniversary of Solidarność, and the scrawled red logo radiated from a banner draped over the palace's facade. My Polish father was a union organizer, and he loved Solidarność; I had a pin of that logo when I was nine. It was the first time workers in a Soviet country had come together to form a union; it was Warsaw's latest uprising. Over nine million people joined; it was more than a union, it was a resistance, and it toppled communism. Possibly my father too wondered how Poland lived inside him, and with Solidarność he felt an answer, a shared and raging blood, fighting for freedom. First there had been the Polish pope, Pope John Paul II, who I also had a pin of—a large round pin of his face dangling from a purple ribbon—from someone who had gone to Boston to watch him pass in a parade.

Born Karol Wojtyła, he'd resisted the Nazis in Kraków doing guerilla theater, working at a chemical factory by day. The day he was shot my depressed Polish father was even more so. "What is this world, when someone shoots the pope?" A spring day, his sadness bathed in sunshine as he unlocked the door to the home he would soon kick us all out of, my mother, my sister, and me. His heavy trudge up the stairs. I was maybe excited that the pope had been shot. I've always had a hard time distinguishing between excitement and anxiety, and have wondered if my body enacts a strange alchemy on my emotions, turning one into the other, maybe fusing them into a whole new chemical. It made me proficient at stressful relations, the excitement of infatuation morphing to a nearly identical, persistent panic. My capacity for love had always amazed me, but now I see that it was only generalized anxiety disorder. Medication helps.

I didn't visit the Solidarność exhibit at the Palace of Culture and Science. I had to manage my nostalgia for a father who was not dead, but was in fact working at a health-food store in Clearwater, Florida.

Past the Palace of Culture was the saddest H&M in the world. It was as if a post-Soviet collection had been designed especially for this location, and the store had agreed to sell those and only those clothes. I was hoping to buy a coat, I was freezing, but I couldn't. Later Agnieszka would take me to a thrift shop, because I was sure that a country whose history was so close to the present would have wonderful secondhand shops full of old lace and artifacts, but I simply did not understand communism, or history. I found a pair of striped pants that tapered nicely at the ankles, and a strange old makeup bag. We went back to Agnieszka's, me hacking my Polish cough. We passed tiny fruit and vegetable stands, where people bought whole heads of sunflowers and carried them home, plucking the seeds to eat along the way. I was careful not to smile at anyone. Inside her home I waited for my nose to adjust to the stink of cat piss. I petted the animals and boiled frozen pierogis. Inside my room I read *The New Yorker*. A man had written in to comment on an article about dying. He wrote that his wife had died of cancer and briefly described what it had been like to sit at her bedside and love her as she passed over. I burst into tears. *All I want*, I thought wildly, *is to be loved. I want to be loved so badly*. The thought humiliated me but it was true. I allowed myself to weep for it. I wanted someone to die with. Probably it wouldn't happen. Every time you think that it is going to happen and then it doesn't actually happen it deconstructs your heart a little, until something once lush and scarlet has the brutalist architecture of a formerly communist country. I signed my computer onto Agnieszka's shaky internet to see if Olin had sent me a missive from Budapest; he hadn't. I did have an email from my friend Peter. I had visited Peter in New England at the start of the summer; we'd gone to Provincetown and played bingo with townies, rode bicycles through the cemetery, shopped at Marine Specialties with its barrels of glass balls and discontinued airline plates and German army shirts. I had bought Olin a magnifying glass, the handle an animal horn. "I just want to be loved so badly," I typed to Peter. It embarrassed me so horribly, this need. It seemed the only way to fix that was to tell someone.

I visited the mermaid statue in Warsaw's Old Town Market Place, an exact replica of the original town square the Nazis blew up. I went there with Anu and his sweet-faced girlfriend, with Agnieszka and another Agnieszka, this one a schoolteacher who was recently fired for being a lesbian. Someone let rats inside her classroom so that when Agnieszka returned to gather her things she was faced with the rodents and their shit and the damage they had done. It was very hard to be gay in Poland. It didn't used to be so, at least not legally. Whenever Poland was free and self-governing, queerness was allowed, but the country was always being invaded and partitioned and overtaken, and homosexuality would be outlawed. When the communists took over it was illegal again, with the state taking down the names of all queer and queer-adjacent individuals. Queer activists have petitioned the Institute of National Remembrance, the body that prosecutes crimes committed under communism, to begin an investigation into crimes against queer people, but they declined.

The mermaid in the square was small breasted and thick waisted, with a sort of leafy drapery growing down from her hips and unfurling onto her scaled tail. Anu told me they called this statue the toilet because the fountain released its water with a sound not unlike a toilet flushing. The water flowed weakly, which seemed an insult to the power of the bronze mermaid, her countenance placid, noble even, as she raised her sword above her head and brandished her shield. I liked her as much as I liked any mermaid or armed female, but I looked forward to visiting the bigger statue on the banks of the Vistula.

On my last night in Nice my Olin spoke to me cruelly, and so I stuffed my *New Yorker* into my bag and stormed out of the hotel. The hotel was around the corner from the ocean; for a fee you could rent one of their loungers and lie there, sardine-packed against the other guests on their own blue-and-white striped towels. I thought this was bullshit and had resolved to simply lie on the beach like a normal person, until I saw that the beach was made of rocks, smooth gray rocks with distinct white bands. The people who tried to rest upon them looked poor, miserable. I knew Olin would pay for our loungers, as well as the inevitable lunch and drinks we could order, and I couldn't allow this with the vibes so bad between us, which meant I would have to pay, and I couldn't pay for only mine, that would be too dramatic of a statement, one I was too scared to make for I was still hopeful, somehow, that things weren't as bad as they were, and so I would have to pay for us both, and I cringed at the cost.

Later, once Olin had joined me, I lay on my lounger and stared at the breasts of the women in front of us, a mother and daughter, the mother's breasts large and wide, the daughter's taut and round, both of them deeply tanned and hung with gold jewelry. I enjoyed looking at them. I thought about taking off my own top, but I feared my breasts were odd, blobby triangles with no real shape or allure. Having grown up in America, one has to muster a sort of bravado to remove one's top in public. This is easier at a protest or pride march or queer disco than at an upscale beach resort in France where one already fears they are a bit of a dirtbag, plus is having low self-esteem due to romantic troubles. I wondered aloud what to do. "Take off your top if you want to," Olin said without looking at me, and went back to reading *Just Kids*. After this day at the beach, Olin spoke cruelly and I flung myself outside, stopping at a café to buy a pack of cigarettes. I walked and walked until even if he were moved to find me I was beyond where his legs could comfortably take him. I smoked and drank espresso and limonata and read about the fine-dining scene in Las Vegas. Tourists came and went. Across the street was a Petit Bateau and I was thankful it was closed because I would have liked to soothe my anxiety with clothes I couldn't really afford. Down the street, an elderly woman played a violin and sang in French, a giant rock of amethyst somehow pinned in her thinning gray hair. She was clearly insane, but touched, and I considered becoming her, considered ruining my sobriety of seven years by getting drunk at the café, following the path of ruin wherever it took me. Ultimately, to my golden years where I serenade the public, soliciting coins, stones stuck to my head.

Every now and again I would look up to see if I had caught the imagination of anyone handsome, the way women alone in public often can, but nobody cared. I left the café and wandered down narrow streets, stopping at a restaurant for some food, sitting outside with my book and my magazine. I ate swiftly, eager to smoke again. The thought of Olin weighed on me. He would be hungry. The fight, if I remember, was about where to dine. Low blood sugar probably had made a contribution to the day's misery. I ordered him a pizza and walked it back to our room. He knew he didn't deserve it, which was nice. He asked if I was going to stay elsewhere, but we were leaving so soon that it didn't make sense. Plus, I hoped we'd have sex again, and we did. I didn't know if it was me, or him, or us together, but something happened when we had sex. How can he loathe me so and yet—*this*. It didn't make sense. So, of course he didn't loathe me. It was something else. A mystery, eking dopamine from my brain like water from a rock.

I taught writing to the feminists in Getto Żydowskie, the old Jewish ghetto, the brick buildings pockmarked with gunfire. Much of the neighborhood was destroyed, the new one built right on top of the rubble, but some original buildings were still standing. We wrote together at a bar that hadn't opened yet, out in a courtyard where sausages were cooked on a grill nightly and plants grew from brightly painted industrial containers. When we got cold we moved inside, sitting on armchairs in the ghost haze of old cigarettes. When I say I taught, I more mean that I inspired. Created a space where the feminists' stories mattered, where the only thing to do was write them and so they were finally forced to do so, rather than cleaning their house or jumping in the shower or turning on the television or whatever anyone does instead of writing their memoirs. Once upon a time, when I was twenty-three years old, I believed powerfully in the importance of telling your story, and I told mine with vengeance and did what I could to encourage everyone else—well, the girls, anyway, the poor people and the people of color, the queers—to tell their stories as well. That was seventeen years ago, and anyone would get sick and tired of doing the same thing for seventeen years. When memoir is what you've been doing, it means you've become horribly sick of yourself, of your narrative, and I had. I was sick of excitedly telling everyone to write their stories, and as bad as it felt to be so annoyed with my own tale, this was worse, to be bored with an activity I still knew to be powerful and important. But knowing and feeling are two different things. Even as I felt such affection for the women who came, and did love their stories, wanted them to write them, some part of my heart was missing. I tried to overcome it but still longed for the workshop, the official point of my visit, to be over.

The bar kicked us out sooner than they'd agreed. Everyone was upset. It seemed maybe the space didn't value feminist art or females or girls or gay people. Everyone decided to meet back at Agnieszka's to share work and drink wine, and I got a ride with an older lesbian who told me about the days of rations when she was a child, how mothers would stand in line for theirs and then send their children later, for more. Children could earn coins standing in ration lines on behalf of various adults. In the seventies, the average Polish person spent over an hour in lines each day. Later, when I tell my mother that I found Poland depressing, she laughs and wonders what I'd expected. My father's family would sew secret pockets into their coats when they went back to visit, so when they were inevitably mugged the thieves wouldn't find their money. But, of course I couldn't have known this. I didn't know these relatives, I had nobody to tell me to sew secret pockets into my clothing, to warn me not to smile, to tell me I would connect with some ancestral sadness in the clouds that sit on top of the city.

Agnieszka's gloomy apartment was enlivened by the feminist writers. One woman, with the plucky, un-Polish energy of a young Renée Zellweger, set up a tiny phonograph spinning Elvis, turned out the lights, and delivered her piece in a storm of glitter, dancing around in a vintage slip. She had gone to school in London and so spoke English with a perfect British clip. Another woman was more traditionally gloomy, with the long, beautiful face of a silent movie star. She was also the bass player for a popular all-girl metal band, and the rest of the workshop whispered excitedly about her presence. I wrote too, as I always do when I teach, to stress that we are all just writers among writers, but my piece was terrible, the worst, all about Olin and my heartache, who cares. These women had real problems. Romance, yes, but also they lived in the ashes of communism, raised by defeated people, in a country scarred with atrocities and failed resistance. They were fired from their jobs for being gay. Abortion was illegal. This didn't inspire me to count my blessings; it just brought me a little lower.

I met a gay boy photographer at Czuły Barbarzyńca, a bookstore that made me think I simply hadn't been seeing the right parts of Warsaw. It was minimalist and brainy, intellectual and cool, with good coffee. I had feared the coffee of Poland, and so I had brought my own French press and two bags of Blue Bottle coffee with me. This had made the narrow cabin on the ship stink like a coffeehouse, but once at Agnieszka's I was glad I'd been so obsessive, for she drank only tea. I was working on my computer, and when the photographer came we walked together to the Vistula to see the statue of the Syrenka Warszawska, the mermaid of Warsaw. I don't know what he was taking my picture for. When you travel as a writer people often ask you to participate in various things, visits and lectures and parties and interviews, and I tended to say yes to everything. We walked through Powiśle to the gunmetal sculpture, where a bride in a fat white dress was having her picture taken. We waited for them to leave and then I scrambled awkwardly across the statue, posing like this and that, my hair scraped up, my face bony and creased, my mouth too big. Thick wool tights pulled under the cutoffs I'd worn in the Mediterranean.

The mermaid was powerful. Thick and angular, with a hint of a smile, as if she took delight in her power. Maybe it's a smirk. Surely she's defiant. It's the face of Krystyna Krahelska, changed somewhat because the artist didn't want her to feel too embarrassed or exposed, her face the face of Warsaw's eternal protector. It's true the mermaid's eyes are wider, with a different cast than Krystyna's; her nose is sharper, to correspond to the angles in the design. But I believe the defiance is hers. Krystyna Krahelska was a poet. Her songs were the songs of the Warsaw Uprising. Like Anna Smolenska, she was twenty-three, a girl scout who had become part of the Gray Ranks. Like Anna, she reads queer to me in photos. Maybe Polish women just strike me as queer. In my favorite photo her hair is pulled back into two braids, and she looks deeply into the camera, sexy and sure, her eyes burning, no smile on her face, and a necklace pulled tight against her throat. In another she sits very close to a friend, almost cuddling, her hair stuck under a cap, butch to her companion's femme, whose head is covered with a fringed scarf. Krystyna was a messenger and a nurse; she transported weapons and taught other women how to treat battlefield wounds. Rushing to help a soldier, she was shot in the chest three times by Nazis. She lay down in a field of sunflowers, afraid to rise lest she give the other fighters away. She waited for nightfall, and died.

The day I left for home I dropped my French press in Agnieszka's bathroom sink and it smashed. It had served its purpose and was done. I swept up the glass, worried about the cats and their tender paws. I applied lip gloss in the bathroom mirror and was glad I was returning home to the rest of my clothes. It took a day or so to see Olin and know he truly did not belong to me. We met outside a coffee shop, and shamelessly I tried to go back to his house for sex, because in sex everything made sense, my anxiety obliterated by the force of it. He said his stomach was upset. *The person you love just avoided having sex with you by faking diarrhea*, I told myself, just to make sure I was getting it. That it was over. At home I sat on my back porch and smoked cigarettes. My illness was gone and I could smoke again. In Poland I'd eaten a last meal of kielbasa and potatoes and the lines in my face had softened. A flirtatious Gchat would soon turn pornographic; I would have another person to get dopamine from. "Don't use people to get high," my AA sponsor had told me. I would get on medication and it would be easier. I would try to call my father in Florida and his line would be disconnected and I would never talk to him again; even when he was dying and I found him, he would decline my call. I would write a book about the Warsaw Mermaid and another one and another one. Above my head, a flock of pigeons blacked out the sun with their flight.

haiku

MIRA GONZALEZ

crying and parking my car
outside a Mexican restaurant
a man offered me drugs

untitled 8

it is 2:05 in the morning
your foot on the brake is preventing the car from drifting backwards
he is kissing you first deliberately
then in a lazy or confused way

you know he is trying to communicate something important
and maybe he has wanted you for a long time
but his tongue is moving around your mouth

you begin to wonder if he wants to kiss you
or if he wants to push his way through you

you can see his bedroom window from where you are standing
he is climbing over fences and unlocking them from the inside
he says 'go up those stairs and turn right'

you swear that you would have loved him a year ago
and every day since then

you are waiting at the top of his stairs
you don't know where to look or what to touch
you are thinking about the 'check engine' light in your car

you are aware of certain things while he has sex with you
helicopter noises through an open window
a bottle of blue cough syrup
street signs indicating the direction to an eastbound freeway

he is strong and gentle and you wish he was only one of those things

he is tracing his fingers across the edge of you
everything is quiet other than a barely audible sound
in the space between his arm and his shoulder

he says ‘why are you sighing so much’
you say ‘that is just how I breathe’
he says ‘you don’t want to be here’

5 years old

I wake up on a mattress in the living room
I ride a plastic tricycle in circles around the kitchen
until my mom wakes up
I eat cereal next to a window
in blue crayon, I draw a picture
of a woman walking her dog

I have come to understand certain things
that the slide in my backyard causes splinters
and there are dead crickets in the heating vents

he is embracing me
not a hug, not really
he is kneeling and I am standing
we are the same height this way

over his shoulder I can see marble stairs
I feel confused or afraid
he gives me a teddy bear

a year later, he will get married
at the wedding I throw petals down the aisle
wearing a handmade beige dress
with pin tucks around the collar

I leave the teddy bear in a park
I tell my mom I did it on purpose

untitled 2

I am sitting on the hood of your car
in front of an elementary school in the rain

I am using barely perceptible hand gestures
to describe the feeling I get at night
in the last five minutes before falling asleep
of wanting our molecules to occupy the same space

you are telling the police that I'm your girlfriend
you are putting your cigarette out on the bottom of my shoe
I am not your girlfriend

time passes

you say 'why are you doing this'
I tell you that I don't understand the question
you say 'please don't do this'

the left side of your face is momentarily illuminated by the headlights
of a passing car

Sum

MORGAN VÕ

against a striated wall
each porch-y sticky color
from a different place
a perceived meat

& the worst blinds smacked
down, claimed to lock with us
of all reasons
& our four puffy socks

strewn over the sofa
perishing
I would never forget you

there must be a doorway out, I hoped
right through the dark problem
no not alone

People Like Monsters

People want to get squished or eaten whole, and not so secretly.
People want a short distinction between life and death.
Imagine the wholesomeness of curling into a dark throat.
Being a sucker once on the street, then soaked in blood.
You learn there, listen, last; the gargles leaping down your body.
Thirty seconds.
You think out loud, *I'm close, and no one's looking*.
Here's what destiny has to say in its god darkness.

How to

how to block life opening
and throw it into organizing
a less life wanting
show life having
open tubes of plantlife
pumped over buildings
a long-loaded binding
LED light trip falling
Oscar name finding
seared lifemark landing
your body is going
to let go, and so to live
to walk down the street
eyelids gently suggesting
to reap through the turning
surrounding in myself
a small scratching prince

Great

a wave of the hand
at a love of
Raheem Norman outside
a shake
in the light
I slipped on
him saying *you see me*
me saying *yeah*
because I feel him
with a moon divided
at a certain time
leaving the roads
like it's there
now closed
that I followed in
that exchanges me
parts of me
with parts of Norm

Wedding Loop

MOYRA DAVEY

On a guided tour of a Colonial cemetery in Kolkata I stumble upon the grave of a Thomas Prinsep and immediately remember this name's connection to nineteenth-century photographer, Julia Margaret Cameron. Related to her by marriage, the Prinseps would figure amongst Cameron's favorite models, in particular, Julia Prinsep Jackson, who was Cameron's niece, and the future mother of Virginia Woolf. It's been years since I've looked at Cameron's portraits, the Victorian men, women and children who sat for her in her converted chicken coop studio, her glass house, on the Isle of Wight. But at the end of her life, ill and impoverished, she had little choice but to return to this hot, humid sub-continent of her birth, where she settled on her husband's coffee plantation and continued, with the same, unwieldy view camera, to make portraits. By then she had given up on the commercial potential of her portfolios. She focused instead on what was at hand.

I photograph Jane in her wedding dress in the backyard and Claire in her T-shirt dress posing with Emma in front of the white brick wall; Addie, to my surprise, joins the group and allows me to take her picture.

Jane, unwisely, has been at the hair and makeup party since morning. She is beginning to unravel.

My mother's sense of foreboding in the build up to the event was not misplaced. Her house is packed with visitors and dogs. Addie is more 'sauvage' than ever; Annie is boycotting because Claire is attending;

Kate implodes at the last minute and refuses to get into a cab that will take us to the celebration in the suburbs.

The demand to be public and social over an afternoon and an evening, at a ceremony and a dinner, with 150 people, most of them drinking, is too much for this group of women, my sisters and their daughters, who are worn out physically and emotionally, are reticent by nature, and are trying to abstain.

Caitlin and her spouse, Antoine, give vows that are funny and original. They are straight-shooters—not a single cliché is spoken. Addie dances. She is a beautiful girl and a beautiful dancer. But when she's not on the dance floor she sits by herself and stares into space. I'm sure the pictures I've taken earlier with a Hasselblad are mediocre. The light was flat, my subjects were posed, I have no business hauling out this difficult-to-focus camera, and trying to revisit something I did, also only passably-well, thirty-five years ago.

The dinner is a raucous affair with a barker rousing the guests to make speeches and sing love songs. People put themselves out, risk looking foolish. Antoine and Caitlin take to the stage to greet and thank their guests, then Caitlin, with difficulty, begins to talk about her sister Hannah. Many people in the room are weeping, including Caitlin and her half-brother, Luca, age fifteen, with his forehead on the table. Jane tries to console him, but is too far gone to not make things worse and Luca's parents intervene.

I think of Yvon, the Quebecois writer of auto-fiction attuned to his circle of fragile women, shaping their lives into books but also taking care of them, materially and emotionally. I am no different, except for the taking-care-of part.

The next day Claire is cooking dinner for all of us, and can't stop talking about the dozen or so non-fiction books she's reading. I'm trying to decide what to do about Jane's pills. She's been drinking for two days and says to me: part of me wants to be dead. She can't remember what she said to Luca the night before, though in my opinion it has more to do with the uncomplicated quality of a fifteen-year-old boy's outpouring of grief over the death of his half-sister, and Jane's claim that she can't cry or properly mourn. We manage to remove liquor bottles stashed in her purse and from under her pillow. She either doesn't notice or pretends not to. She also willingly gives me her pills.

My mother's house smells permanently of animals and is fraying at the edges. I wipe dust off the leaves of the rubber plant in the hallway, acquired in 1966, the year my youngest sister was born. I bathe in the English-style tub, a solid comfort with elaborate chromed faucets that creak.

The night before I returned to NY I wrote in a notebook:

In the midst of all the tears, angst, anger, drunkenness, I've arrived with my camera and performed the same role as in 1980: the one who watches and waits and corrals people into the light. My despondent feeling the night of the wedding is as much about my own fear of failure. Now all I care about is getting back to NY and getting my film to the lab.

Improbably, I try to read the *Iliad*, a story of men kidnapping women, and going to war to get them back, to take revenge, to murder and maim till each and all, victor and vanquished are reduced to "things," as Simone Weil puts it.

In her essay "The Iliad or the Poem of Force" Weil cites the passage about Hector's wife preparing a hot bath in anticipation of his return from battle. But what Andromache does not know is that Hector's already been slain:

Already he lay, far from hot baths

Far from hot baths he was indeed, poor man. And not he alone. Nearly all the Iliad *takes place far from hot baths. Nearly all of human life, then and now, takes place far from hot baths,* wrote Simone Weil.

Jane, Kate, Annie and Addie all live on the edge to one degree or another, in a cold climate–city. With age they anticipate winter with increasing dread: the deep snow and ice, the leather-corroding slush, the diminished light. It is especially hard on Kate who walks dogs for a living. In a dark, agitated mood she said: I can't bear the idea of another winter.

Far from hot baths. Far from toilets I could add. Kate, who has been self-destructive and caring of others in equal measure, her whole life, once told me she'd helped homeless people clean shit off themselves. In a very untutored way that grows out of 12-step immersion, she is living a life philosophically close to Simone Weil's idea that "We participate in the creation of the world by decreating ourselves."

In a different notebook I wrote:

Meanwhile I was getting more and more depressed about my pictures. Old feelings of fraudery and worthlessness. Mixed up with this are moods of sadness for my derelict family in the midst of all the apparent robust mental health and wedding happiness. Though of course much of this is illusory.

~~~~

I don't have a problem with endings per se, I don't care where I end a piece of writing. What I have a problem with is writing more, once I've secreted. I reach a point where I'm done, and then my mind shuts down and refuses to generate more. In this way I almost always short myself, barely meet the word count. I listen to late Tolstoy, read the fat books of Ferrante, Knausgaard and Hervé Guibert's diaries and fantasize they are simultaneously writing and living their lives. They are long-take writers. They circle back over the material again and again, each time refracted through a slightly altered prism. There is comfort in their repetition.

These last three, and perhaps Tolstoy as well, are writing about their very complex lives, some further complicated by having children. It's
~~~~

a rather curious effect to be reading these reams of words that burrow into lives 'termite' fashion and find that the 'writing life' is not often discussed. So that when it is talked about the effect can be electric.

These breaks in the stories to talk about the writing itself are thrilling and almost always incite me to grab pen or laptop so that I can record passages such as this one from Ferrante:

"Perhaps Lila was right: my book . . . *was* really bad, and this was because it was well organized . . . written with obsessive care, because I hadn't been able to imitate the disjointed, unaesthetic, illogical, shapeless banality of things."

"I should write the way she speaks, leave abysses, construct bridges and not finish them, force the reader to establish the flow."

I'm embarrassed to admit it, but I am at the end of Ferrante and now we are the same age: almost sixty. I've gobbled up the books like comics, but in them a cherished child has been lost and I think of Hannah and feel gutted. I've read the books so fast I didn't even register the title of this one: *The Story of the Lost Child*. I can barely finish it.

On the subway a young man with firm arms and shoulders falls asleep and leans into me. I could move but don't. I support the upright part of his sleeping body with my body. I don't look to see who he is, I don't want to call attention, I don't meet anyone's gaze to see if passengers are aware of him tilting into me. Not till it's my stop do I look down and see a red hard hat on the floor between his feet and realize he's a construction worker.

I read Jacqueline Rose on my phone writing about mothers, Medea, Winnicott and maternal aggression. I wonder where the time's gone, then I remember I watched over two hours of *Jeanne Dielman* in the morning. I'd forgotten so much of this film: the baby that gets dropped off, the son's bedtime monologue about his father's penis-knife hurting his mother. This is his one moment of breaking out of the box, the oppressive conformity imposed on him by his mother. Jeanne says to him "you shouldn't have worried yourself over that" and turns off the light.

I woke in a panic that I'd never meet my commitments, but instead of hitting the keyboard I texted my friend who'd just had a baby to see if she needed help with her infant while she packed for a trip. I held the little guy and was overcome with my usual remorse that I hadn't been a tender enough mother to my own; I gave Fairfield a bottle, I walked him around the park for an hour observing squirrels and birds and people of all shapes and sizes walking tiny dogs; also kids playing basketball at the court where Barney had been a regular. I walked till I was exhausted, then I brought the tiny creature home and gave him another bottle.

Eric, Euripides and Leo come to my studio.

I struggle massively with the 4x5 camera, my light meter's broken, clouds block the sun just as I'm about to release the shutter. I flail around like an amateur and shout at J & B to help me. But I stick with it. I push through my awkwardness and ineptitude, endure my small panic despite my conviction that the pictures will be failures. I've referred to this urge elsewhere as the pursuit of 'the opposite of low-hanging fruit,' meaning pushing myself to do the thing that is not easy, scares me, even. I put in a day's work and sleep the sleep of the just.

The portraits I take at the wedding and in the studio are mostly of Barney and his generation, inspired by Julia Margaret Cameron.

January 2, 2017

My Brother, My Wound

NATALIE DIAZ

He was calling in the bulls from the street.
They came like a dark river,
a flood of chest and hoof.
Everything moving, under, splinter. Hooked
their horns though the walls. Light hummed
the holes like yellow jackets. My mouth
was a nest torn empty.

Then, he was at the table.
Then, in the pig's jaws.
He was not hungry. He was stop.
He was bad apple. He was choking.

So I punched my fists against his stomach.
Mars flew out
and broke open or bloomed.
How many small red eyes shut in that husk?

He said, *Look. Look.* And they did.

He said, *Lift up your shirt.* And I did.

He slid his fork between my ribs.
Yes, he sang. *A Jesus side wound.*
It wouldn't stop bleeding.
He reached inside
and turned on the lamp.

I never knew I was also a lamp, until the light
fell out of me, dripped down my thigh,
flew up in me, caught in my throat like a canary.
Canaries really means dogs, he said.

He put on his shoes.
You started this with your mouth, he pointed.
Where are you going? I asked.
To ride the Ferris wheel, he answered,
and climbed inside me like a window.

Excerpts from *Goner*

NATE LIPPENS

As I move through the house my eyes trace the ceiling in the living room with the dark wood beam running the length of it. The windows flood the room with light. I walk down the hallway to my mother's room. It was strange that I could finally touch her here. Once she was immobilized I could touch the thin arm, her dry feet, still warm, still moving blood.

From her bedside I pick up her paperback Bible, and pressed flowers fall and scatter from between its pages. I flip through a few pages and see the faint traces of pencil in the margins. It has been erased but some remains.

I bend down and pick the petals up, crushing them in my hand. Draining the last bit of my whiskey, I deposit them in the glass. My mother may have sat waiting for the minister to visit when she was first sick and recovering from a surgery, pulling her scarf down on her head. He came to her like an athlete entering the ring to wrestle with her questioning. And did he read from his bible? Maybe he paraphrased. He looked into her eyes and saw that scripture wasn't what she craved. She wanted answers. Hadn't she been good: a good daughter up to her parents' deaths in quick succession, a faithful wife even in death, and a good mother—raising two children alone, without her parents, her in-laws, her husband? But what did Reverend Frame offer her? Mysterious ways, a palm on the back, and a psalm? What of the fat women, she wondered, the slovenly chain smokers gobbling fried foods and carcinogenic barbecues? They were fine. Sure, they had difficulty walking to their cars after a buffet meal, short of breath and greasy-lipped, but they would outlive her. She had death in her, actively moving through her, rummaging and rearranging. But it wasn't her organs that scared her. It was her heart. The seeds of doubt planted and sprouting long fingers, the finger that poked in Jesus' side. Show me the wound and I will show you mine.

I remember when I was a kid seeing my mother sitting on her bed praying. Her eyes were closed, head bowed, and hands clasped primly. I never disturbed her. Often I sat in that same place while she would get ready. She would tell me stories, tell me her secrets. She would make up her face and it was like she was drinking caffeine. She enlivened and became loose and lighter, getting herself ready for the performance of going to the grocery store or heading to the mall. She was prepared with a quick smile and a quick laugh. That small head toss. Those darted eyes. Her chin dipping down into a laugh.

How did my mother share so much with me, a small boy perched at the end of the bed, talking with his hands, pushing up his too-large glasses? How did she not know then and there that I was different? I wanted to say she treated me like a daughter, but not really. It was different. I was an outsider who could hear these secrets because I wasn't quite in my body. I wasn't a boy and I wasn't a girl. In a different place and a different time I would have been something special, maybe even holy. In Wisconsin in the mid-1970s, I was simply strange. How did my mother use that strangeness when I was small, appreciate it when I was sitting on the edge of that bed, but then renounce our time together when I was older?

My mother tried to date unsuccessfully, but then gave up, and the makeup disappeared little by little, used only for special occasions. The eyes were first, then the rouged cheeks, and eventually the mouth. The wedding ring moved to the other hand for a year, and finally retired, like her easy smile and laughter.

I look around. My mother's hair is still in a tortoise shell brush. Her shoes are lined neatly in a row. Her nightgown hangs on the closet door's hook. Her life is still here.

I set the glass on the vanity and stand in front of the mirror. I watched her apply makeup and brush her hair in this mirror countless times. In a shell-shaped dish on her bureau is a tangle of jewelry, most of it cheap department-store tennis bracelets and necklaces with precious daubs of quartz or turquoise dangling from pendants like tiny circus families, hard and determined. I put on her religious medals, which are visible under my t-shirt, like the port implanted in her chest for easier chemo. I open the drawer and pull out a tube of lipstick, apply it, and stand there transfixed by my sudden androgyny.

* * *

I settle into the chair beside my mother as if I am clocking in for a shift.

What she never understood was that I don't remember all the names of the boys who beat me, I don't recall the color of my room at the hospital—what has stayed with me is how she never told me what was happening to me was wrong. And later when I did whatever it took to survive I had made choices. I chose to leave. I chose to live like I did. But I never felt any agency.

"I don't know how to love someone like you," she said. It was in the middle of an argument whose details I don't recall but that sentence, those words in that sequence, were all I ever needed to hear from her.

I remember the fall I overdosed at school and was taken to the ER. The nurse removed a bucket and slid the curtain closed, leaving my mother and me alone. My stomach had been pumped of thirty sleeping pills. My mother had been summoned from work. She leaned in and said, "I hope you know how much this little stunt is costing."

I was moved to a hospital room where I lay in bed staring at the TV mounted on the wall, filling the small room with chatter. My mother looked out the window into the dark and at our reflections against the black glass.

"You got everyone's attention. Are you happy now?"

I stared at my hands on the blanket.

"Maybe you don't give a damn what people think but I do," she said. "It's not bad enough I'm worried sick all weekend and you ruin my days off, but then you have to humiliate me."

"Go home, I'll be fine," I said.

"I wasn't planning on staying here tonight." She gathered her purse and jacket. "I have to work in the morning so I can pay for this mess."

My mother turned and left without looking back. Through the open door I watched her walking away, getting smaller. Waiting for the elevator, her profile was stiff. The elevator arrived and opened. The light changed across her face and torso. I wanted to see something there. I wanted to see her face turn back. But she stepped out of my sight and was gone.

It was hard to know whether I was having a nervous breakdown or not. The symptoms of living and losing my mind were so similar.

I was given a psychiatric diagnostic multiple choice:

Never. Sometimes. Often. Always.

Day, year, president's name?

Corridors of light. A locked ward in a teaching hospital in a university town. The closest I would get to higher education was as a specimen.

First night was in a room with a closed door and an observation window in which nurses' eyes appeared at regular intervals. There was a plastic mattress on the floor. I don't remember sheets and I can't remember if I was naked or it felt like I was.

I was the only kid on the ward. The rest were adults. Many had been there before. And they'd be back again. I lay awake at night and listened to people murmuring and crying through the walls. I felt like a little fish slipping into dark water.

Back at school, I landed in homeroom with the emotionally disturbed—boys with cigarette burns and bruises—dark, stained countries with yellowed borders. They rocked in their chairs, drummed their hands, and jiggled their legs. Surplus energy filled the room. The desire to be free, to run—but to where, and to do what?

In the hallway a kid walked up to me and said, "Better luck next time."

At home, my mother said, "The way you parade around, it's no wonder they beat you up. Thank God your father never saw this."

"I wish you'd died instead," I said.

Her slap was sloppy, grazing my nose. I returned it in kind. She fell like cheap scenery and her wine glass shattered on the floor. I stepped over the broken pieces and the puddle and her. She started to get up and I said what the boys at school said to me, "Stay down."

I look at her now, nearing the end. I try not to make any sound. I don't want to wake her. I don't want to talk with her about God and death and duty. I want deep and dreamless sleep without memories.

* * *

The empty room and the bare bed stripped of sheets are a soft shock.

In the living room I follow where my mother's eyes did in her last days. I look around the room at the coffee table and shelves: dust. There was a time we never would have let it stay like that. I hear Meg walking toward me. She makes a sound. Words. Asks about breakfast and coffee. I'm glad to hear her voice, to know what I'm seeing is real, or at least happening.

We make food in an instinctive way: It's morning so we should eat. We should pretend the clock still has hands on it. We are fresh orphans sitting at a breakfast table in a house that feels both smaller and emptier than it did only days ago.

I clear our plates and run water on them, setting them in the sink to soak. Without saying a word, Meg goes to the sink, scrubs and racks the dishes. It's good that some things won't change, that whatever I do still won't be right. I step outside for a cigarette and mostly forgot to smoke it, holding it as it burns down, heat biting my hand.

Meg and I each make phone calls like we are tagging children on the playground. The tagged callers will each make more phone calls and the death news will spread. It feels as if we are giving up something. My voice catches a little. It's my apprenticeship in accepting condolences. The words sound fake and rehearsed. I stop calling and listen to Meg: her cadence and the way she thanks the person, the way she says *God bless you.*

The doorbell rings. It's the men who delivered the bed and the equipment coming to retrieve it. They move with efficiency, eyes downcast. What a strange job. These men appear as someone's life begins to circle the drain, and they reappear when it's gone. A person turns to a body and vanishes.

Meg signs some forms.

"Sorry for your loss," one of the men murmurs like a disgruntled teenage clerk saying, *have a nice day*.

Meg and I rearrange the furniture to close over the time that the hospital bed has been there. I stand in the spot where she died and look at the ceiling.

it doesn't matter how you fall into light, she said

AKILAH OLIVER

now approach holiness in memory.
wizard scatters leaves. the little things. basking out the window.   air adorned aches.
to be invented. vulgarize the living sentence. trampled daisies.
a mind. shake the long night. unplanted placenta. every failed insurrection in cotton fields. i am where the sun has gone. sugarcane and pathetic.
look ma. no hands.
bodies jump overboard. taste is addiction enough. when horny think of sexuality & gods. less than 100 identified in l.a. county. a bell tinkles on a ice cream truck. i shouldn't be no ways tired. tell me it's saturday. reason to wear something new. it's all right. breathe their air. the urge to kiss. all this time i thought i should have done something else.

think of the words as angels singing in your vagina, she said

i'm a mentally well schizophrenic. i fuck ghosts i know by name. 1975.
radio says I want this pain to stop.   bedspread friction. chorus. for a long time afterwards the rush is enough. see isn't that nice. oh stretch marks i want to make you a shrine of doll heads & penes. nibble on a metaphor. i say when i am unable to say anything. but then you had to go. a long time afterwards bloodstains on your tee-shirt were smashed rose petals. the stains. innocence.

rain is it you waking me in slumber or is that my lovers' voices crashed against smooth black.

continuous orgasm. bites pavement. glass popping. bristly hairs rub lavender. my tongue swallows whole all the seductions. wet. taste me. i could have been at home between your legs. how she sing like that. how she sing like that. how she know just then is when i need to cry. it's the reciprocity of beauty that makes me doubt my self. you. it's the wetness i want. a vessel into the endless zone where no roles exist. amen. understand the blood comes out like this. jagged sky. if you don't believe me no verbs will follow the suicides noun.

don't just stand there.
thank them for coming.

Los Angeles

POROCHISTA KHAKPOUR

Coming back home felt like something else altogether this time around. First of all, home was not home. My family had bought their first property since coming to the U.S. and we were no longer even in my hometown—instead of Pasadena, this was more affordable Glendale next door, and this was no longer the room I grew up in, but a spare bedroom that was a sort of compromise between my brother's and my rooms, a generic little space, with a twin bed and a sort of impersonal ambiance. The place was cleaner and more modern, but it was not comforting in the least. It felt like I had walked onto the wrong set.

I was in a state of horror from the first day I arrived—trying to organize the space in a way that could feel mine and then reorganizing it all over again, pacing as if looking for something and then forgetting what I was in pursuit of, imagining myself out of there before I could even commit to being there—even though I was back to having no imagination about my future. I told everyone I knew I had black mold poisoning, plus a strange dependence on medication, and I started finding myself reverting back to that damaged person in sunglasses and hoods from a few summers prior, the one who was haunted by sunlight and doomed to insomnia's endless nights.

I tried to remember all my recovery methods from 2006 and go through those motions again, which meant reestablishing contact with my psychiatrist at UCLA. He saw me that same week and seemed disturbed by my state, which he noted was similar to how he first saw me and possibly worse. He seemed exhausted by my insistence on physical problems, the poisoning and other potential ailments—and so I didn't mention Lyme, thinking of it without it ever hitting my lips. Other things seemed more likely to him, and yet at the same time none of them seemed a proper contender.

"I don't think we should stray away from the possibility that this could just be a psychological event," he kept saying. He had me replay my life in Germany over and over, to which he often said, "Well, that doesn't sound good, does it?"

"What doesn't?"

"All of it," he said, matter-of-factly. "It seems you were exposed to significant traumas in Germany."

I didn't know what to say to that. There had been good things—my classes, my students, excursions to nearby European cities, the Christmas markets, my substantial salary, even the guesthouse held a sort of charming sweetness in my mind.

A psychological event. Significant traumas. The other thing I didn't mention at all was the night in the bathroom, that contemplation of cutting. With his reaction already, I didn't see the point. I had been damaged, certainly, but now I was going to get better. What did those memories matter now?

He decided it would be prudent to wean me off of Neurontin and put me on Klonopin. I was shocked when I heard this.

"Don't you have your old notes there?" I asked.

He looked almost amused. "Of course I do. Why?"

"Well, you got me off benzos—you weaned me off Klonopin by putting me on Neurontin. That was the whole point of it."

"But you weren't on Neurontin to get off Klonopin this time around. Neurontin has many uses. I'm not sure why you were on it."

Neither was I. We were both silent.

"I was a benzo addict," I said. "*You* put me on Neurontin. And now you want me back on benzos?"

"I want us to get a handle on your sleep," he said. "Which feels urgent, so we can figure out what else is going on. Klonopin is relatively harmless. And we can get you off of it again. I need you to trust me, as you did last time. We did it, remember?"

I did remember, but more than the memory of recovery, I remembered the memory of addiction. I put the prescription into my purse with no intention of filling it.

But it took less than 24 hours until I did.

* * *

One of the first big decisions I made was to get an assistant. I needed someone to help organize my life, send emails, keep me on some sort of track of normalcy as I waded through doctor's appointments, horrid insomnia, and another bout of declining health. This time I had no deadline, no manuscript to complete, no New York to return to, but I felt I had to act like it was all there or else I'd drown again. And with no real explanation of how this had happened all over again. This time I had to have answers—I couldn't lose myself again.

I made a Facebook post asking for an assistant I could modestly compensate in the LA area, and Zed was the first to respond. I knew him only vaguely as the younger brother of the one other Iranian girl I knew in my high school—she was a fellow Drama Club member and a year or two younger than me. I was gone by the time her brother attended our high school, but his message to me wrote that he was a fan of my work, so proud of all I had done, and he was in between jobs and looking to change his life.

"I want to get on a good track now," he wrote. "I look up to you. And I know I can help you. It's what I do."

It was unclear to me what that meant exactly, but at our first meeting I learned a few things about him: that at one point he wanted to be a writer but abandoned it, that he was a sort of physical trainer to local people but without any actual certification, and that he had some significant substance abuse issues but now it was all behind him.

I knew he was hired when he kept saying, "We got to get you off those pills."

"Exactly," I said. I was so relieved that someone else was also disturbed by it. "I was addicted to these things and now I'm on them again. A problem on top of another."

"Pills do all sorts of shit," he'd always mutter. "We'll get you off. We got to focus on that."

And because I had seen the dark side of pills it seemed fair enough to believe they were killing me. It was at least something to pursue.

Meanwhile I had Zed draft notes to various people I owed work to, help order the special mold-free cleaning of all my possessions (only one company in all Los Angeles did this for individual clients and it cost thousands), help me buy all sorts of wild things like the highest grade air purifier one could purchase, and more than anything drive me around, mainly to doctor appointments.

"I've got to get better," I'd say over and over to Zed, betterness always feeling somewhat attainable around him.

* * *

The worst problem with the Klonopin was that it barely worked. The first night I took it was different than that night in Germany when my mother was visiting. It felt speedy, euphoria-inducing almost. I loved it as ever, but it was not doing its trick for insomnia at all. I was continuing to sleep terribly and yet continuing to take Klonopin because—and my psychiatrist agreed—to just come off of it now after some weeks on it would cause too much havoc on my system. Better to just have a bit of it in me to keep things smooth.

And yet nothing felt smooth at all. Every day I began having those horrendous panic attacks that led me to take some Klonopin during the day too, just so I wouldn't "withdraw," as I interpreted the panic attacks as signs of withdrawal. All the same logic and illogic of my summer of 2006 came flooding back. As my sleep grew worse, deepening depression entered the picture. I became very irritable, finding everything from light to noise to smells to be intolerable.

One night I could not stop screaming after I smelled a chemical detergent my mother was using to clean her kitchen. It was as if the most intense gas was filling my lungs. I felt like I was drowning in its toxicity, and I blew up at my mother.

"See, you're trying to kill me! You brought me here to finish the job! I can't be around this stuff!" I wailed. I noticed my mother barely blinked an eye. She was already used to what I had become—someone beyond reason, someone lost in another dimension struggling to communicate with those she used to know.

It went like that for a long time. From April through August, I had dozens of doctors, went to doctor's appointments nearly daily, and nothing came of it. I had theories, some supported by test results, some not; some fed to me by doctors, some by internet research; some by healers, some by MDs; some by my parents, some by friends; some from my gut, some just pure lie: MS, ALS, PCOS, endometriosis, scleroderma, lupus, HPV, cervical cancer, ovarian cancer, hyperthyroid, hypothyroid, thyroid storm, dysautonomia, anemia, insulinemia, diabetes, Addison's, Parkinson's, Hashimoto's, candida, dementia, ketoacidosis, West Nile, and yes, Lyme. We looked into everything.

None of the doctors spoke to each other, specialists were piled on top of specialists, each tugging and turning me in their own directions. They seemed as clueless as I was, my body a mystery they couldn't solve. I started to feel rejected by them, sensing their dread when they'd greet me, feeling the frustration in their bodies as they pored over yet another batch of bloodwork.

Meanwhile: losses. I lost out on things—an apartment in New York, one in Santa Fe. I'd been chosen to be a resident at the writers colony Djerassi, and I told them a week before it began that I couldn't go. I was due to teach at a low residency MFA in Tampa, Florida, and just days before I backed out of that too—not until having a disoriented, insane conversation with the program director, asking over and over where the local hospitals were at the residency and how easy would it be to get medical attention there, trying to imagine how I would survive. People would write to me to get me to write things for them and I'd say yes, and then after trying I'd bow out. Students wanted me to work with them for manuscript consults and I'd say yes—followed by a quick no. It would take a second to remember myself, what I'd become.

My full-time job became my health, which was now a mystery illness that was hopelessly complicated by and tangled with addiction to psychiatric medications. I couldn't believe I was there again, after all the bad experiences I had had. Back to a life of pill bottles and pill cutters and days measured in dosages.

My emails at the time—to my mother, to friends, to doctors, to therapists—went like this:

i think gabapentin is what is making me insane--rotting my teeth and making me so depressed and have all sorts of crazy symptoms and need to get on getting off of that

think i've been drinking WAY too much water and that made my electrolytes loopy

I just like to feel "covered" before bedtime! I want to be able to go out and know I can take something and be all good.

I have sky high progesterone or did a week or two ago because I was prevented from ovulating thanks to a stupid doctor in Germany who thought it was the answer for PCOS

Right now there are so many unknowns--I have a lot of "vein gurgles" (medical term) and weird skin stuff and not walking so properly.

I took Klonopin for 3 nights last week, which is all it takes for trouble

I have increased salivation and gum bleeding, weird heart rate and blood pressure and dizziness and disorientation.

Sometimes I can't feel my hands

if candida was detected in the blood, then is this sepsis? just talked to a doc who said if it is detected in my blood then i'd be very very very sick (even more than now) and would have to be hospitalized

awful insomnia, abdominal pain and reflux and esophagitis and reflux these days but I've also had joint pain, spinal weakness, chills, fever, very strange headaches, memory problems and head fog, anxiety and panic attacks, rosacea, fatigue

I've realized my urine is entirely too alkaline

What is keeping me up at night or worrying me during the day is nothing but side effects and weirdness.

Rhabdomyolysis, they say, is on a warning for gabapentin. It might be worth looking into because my absorption of the drug this time around is what surprises me.

I'd really investigate cerebrovascular areas. It really seems right to me. I developed a stiff neck suddenly and severe nausea today (could not really hold food down) after a weird popping headache--usually pain does not break through the gabapentin.

Heightened confusion and now really can barely express words properly, with limp in one leg.

i have really bad dysphagia. could this be the ativan?! the neurontin? I am losing my ability to swallow, choking, can't get applesauce down even

i have a test that indicates i may have an autoimmune disease, sigh

These messages were rarely asking anything, often just stating. I was inconsolable. It was hard to know what I wanted out of all this. I wrote them as a person who could not be helped, who knew this, who could live with just being heard, a sign of still being alive somehow, perhaps.

I also wrote this, a letter to my mother, a week into our settling back in to Glendale from the long journey in Leipzig:

dear mom, i am sorry for any trouble i am causing. i love you very much. i thought we could try one thing that i tried to ask the other night that embarrassed me---i wonder if you would consider sleeping in my room? i can keep your exact schedule. i feel really ashamed and unhappy at all the unhappiness i am causing. please know i do not want to be sick. it is my dream to be done with doctors. love p

And for some time, she did.

***

Soon enough, though, relations with my family became fractured. A part of me began fantasizing about living at a psychiatric ward—it seemed logical, a place where I could get help, where people could tend to me, where no one would be too shocked at what was happening. But as long as I was under my parents' roof, that would never be an option. I began asking to sleep over at friends' homes, especially novelist/screenwriter Anna and her actor husband Brent. They were very Hollywood, newly married, and cheerful and carefree—my magical thinking told me that just by being around them, some of their goodness might rub off on me. They had also both dealt extensively with mental illness and addiction and were no strangers to psychiatric wards themselves.

I met Zed at a Pasadena Mexican restaurant late one Sunday night, where I bought him several margaritas and finally got him to agree to drive me to the Westside where Brent and Anna lived. They had agreed to let me stay with them for a change of scenery. He passed me over to them with some tense discussion at their Laurel Canyon home. "She really needs someone around at all times, she's constantly trying to get to a psych ward, hospital, you name it." Brent and Anna chatted with me with worried faces, but also helped me get Ativan, from a friend of a friend, when I told them I couldn't sleep—we ended up in Venice at midnight scoring the bottle, a risky thing since Ben used to be a heroin addict and this "errand" couldn't bring up good memories. They did this instead of committing me to UCLA Psychiatric, which I initially kept telling them they should do—but Anna had made a whole career out of writing about her psychiatric hospitalizations and was totally against it, and Brent agreed we should avoid it. I stayed with them for days, but at the end I felt too weird to push it any longer. Their happiness as a couple also started to make me feel jealous and empty—it reminded me I used to have that.

Eventually I made it to a psychiatric hospital, or I nearly did at least.

For a while I just kept going to my old hometown ER, Huntington Hospital in South Pasadena. This was my fourth visit to the ER in a month. The main physician Dr. Kalder was always helming the ward those afternoons and he recognized me immediately, with a look of deep dread. After a few hours of nothing but waiting, shivering on a stretcher, he came up to me and snapped, "Why don't you do everyone a favor here and go where I'm recommending?" Where was that? I wondered. "Psychiatric."

I looked at Dr. Kalder and told him I did not want to be in a psych ward—when it came down to it, I felt in my body that it was not the right place ultimately—even though a part of me had always dreamed of its unknown underworld. I said at least I could do detox, but the social worker at his side refused.

The truth was I had lusted after the idea of detox for months at that point. I had brought it up with my old UCLA therapist from nearly the beginning, the first time I felt the klonopin take hold of me again. I had become used to calling all sorts of rehabs in California, using their free consult option, keeping them on the phone as long as possible, explaining to them that I was under doctors' care and yet I was a drug addict. Because of the doctors even, I was a drug addict. Street drugs had never done me in—it was always their prescription pills, always procured legally and with their consent.

Almost every rehab I talked to, they sighed at the word *benzodiazepine*, some also sighing at *neurontin*. They never seemed that hopeful, they could never guarantee me any sort of relief. *No promises*, they always seemed to say, even at a place called Promises. They were also prohibitively expensive—on average, it seemed a rehab program would cost $30,000 for a month. My entire NEA, plus any spare change I had at that point after the many bills and lack of work, would go to a month of rehab, which might do nothing at all.

But my strongest hesitation came from knowing that it would only heal a layer at best—there was something underneath, whatever had gone wrong before the pills, whatever had made me sick in the first place. It was hard to know just which era of illness I was thinking of at this point—years of affliction weighed on me chaotically. All I knew was that it was time for someone and something to finally fix me and it didn't matter what.

I blinked at the harsh fluorescent lights of the hospital that by now I knew so well, like a California sunset.

The social worker was shaking his head at me, smug for a moment, then quickly putting on an expression of solid concern. "No detox needed. Psychiatric is more appropriate for you."

They left me to think about it and by midnight, I was ready to give up. I didn't know where else to go. I wanted to be well and if a psych unit was going to be the place for that, then so be it.

"Excellent decision," Dr. Kalder declared, without even meeting my eyes. I was a good student, but I had worn out my welcome. It was more than time for them to move me on.

My possessions were gathered and handed to me, and I was placed in a wheelchair. A security guard in full police attire wheelchaired me through an underground tunnel that connected ER to psychiatric. In the unit, a team of nurses came up to me without a greeting and immediately went through all my bags. They took my cell phone and computer and keys and pills and shoelaces (anything I could use to harm myself).

I called my parents, who were past the point of mortification. "But this is going to help me," I assured them, though by the looks of the place I was not sure. "We have to give something else a shot."

"You think you're crazy?" My mother cried into the phone.

"I think there is something very wrong with me," I said calmly. "I think there is something wrong in my body. But they think it's the mind. So let them do it their way. Let's see."

Silence.

I never made it to the actual psychiatric ward. I was in the holding area for three days, Memorial Day weekend come and gone, waiting with those who needed to get medically cleared—mostly elderly demented patients—while physicians and psychiatrists evaluated me. They suggested antipsychotics if I didn't want more benzodiazepines—that same old Seroquel from that awful LA summer popped up again, like a bad bogeyman—and I refused. I decided to go through benzo and neurontin withdrawal during that time, and it was not pretty. I did not sleep at all and finally caved in to Valium, the one benzo I had not tried. Meanwhile they watched, took my blood pressure and temperature and heart rate over and over, not knowing what to do with me.

"I don't belong there," I'd whine to the nurses.

They'd assure me I did. "Nothing is wrong with you physically, you need to understand that," they'd say again and again. It was a line I had heard many times at this point, so it washed over me like water.

And yet in the end, I could not get "medically cleared" to go to the psychiatric ward.

When I didn't get admitted and my parents took me home, I knew it had gone too far. I promised them I would face this, that it was just anxiety. That meant ignoring heart palpitations, electric shocks through my limbs, piercing headaches, and unbearable fatigue, but like the doctors had all said, the mind is powerful. I had done this to myself, I began to tell myself.

"Good, let's just focus on good things now," my mother stroked my hair, trying to smile through tears. "You are okay. You are okay."

"I am okay," I said, matching her smile, matching her tears. "I am okay."

But I always kept a little part of me, like a single hair in a locket, this bit that never gave in and never believed it.

NIIZH

NICOLE WALLACE

but for the sake of privacy

this circle

*

imagine this space is warm and was and is not

*

and i think of all the sounds small crystal make

when pushed

together

*

and i am failing at being honest

*

and what

and what

and what

*

i see what threads lie bare
what things accumulate

i try and be honest

and i am not

*

niin giin giinawind

*

i disrespect time because it has disrespected me
and i don't know much more than that

*

when you come back this will all be gone

and what can you expect when

with

*

the sounds you make in the night

the ways in which
you don't

*

and it's so far from here

it's so far

*

i just put the first thing on

*

but for the sake of

Letter Three

QIU MIAOJIN

Translated by Ari Larissa Heinrich

APRIL 29

Xu,

Someone called around four o'clock this afternoon. I was up late last night writing letters, so I was still lying in bed with the day yet to begin. For a moment I thought it could be you, calling to find out about Bunny's funeral, but the phone stopped ringing before I could get up. I immediately dropped the idea that it was you calling. Since you have been trying so hard to abandon me, as I've become such a great scourge to you, it's unlikely you would squeeze out even a few reluctant tears of genuine concern.

Xu, what you've done to me this month is wrong. I have to tell you this. From the point of view of interpersonal relationships, even if I'm older and more mature than you, and even if there are things you're too young to understand, everyone is still responsible for their actions and the wrongs they commit against others. In their heart of hearts, no one can escape this responsibility. I can't, and so I'm trying to make up for the wrongs I've committed.

I believe that two individuals always share a basic human bond. The depths of this bond depend on an unspoken agreement or oath between the two. The more stable their inner life and personality, the more honestly they can thrive within this genuine unspoken agreement. When there is too little of this kind of consistency, they will continually wrong others, either by creating chaos in their inner life, or by leaving themselves no choice but to close off their own soul from the rest of the world. This kind of “consistency” is at the core of Gabriel Marcel’s investigation of *fidélité* (loyalty). This past month, when I started really applying myself to understanding Marcel, I discovered that in my own life I had matured enough to have a better grasp of the overall spirit of his work, and that I identified with the entire range of his concerns. I’m delighted. It’s like finding a best friend. Part of the reason I want to study violin is that I’m moved by him and want to be a kind of disciple.

Who knows if I’ll ever have the chance to tell you more about his philosophy and art? Who knows if you would even enjoy it and find it moving? I may not be able to interpret your life for you, to speak for you or make choices for you, but starting with my first letter to you, I have offered you a vivid internal blueprint, an illumination of the coordinates of your inner life, haven’t I? Your inner life and mine are symbiotic. Unless you want to shut it down completely—to castrate it—your inner life will never be complete with anyone but me. Always it will remain, thirsting to communicate with me. As long as I’m still alive, it will thirst to hear the sound of my voice and thirst to hear the music emanating from the wellspring of my spirit.

You could of course just suppress this thirst, this desire, become insensate. Yet once it has swelled inside you, you’ve already had a taste of it. The existence of this “spirit” is a fact. Your spirit and my spirit are made from the same material, one tuned to the other. Eventually you’ll realize that this part of you is the fruit of our careful irrigation and cultivation. It is a blessing. Through our violent outbursts, we have ultimately blocked, run aground, and sealed off our spirits from each other. In this world there’s no bond of love formidable enough; not even the enduring, permanent bond between life and body, or anything else, is formidable enough. Instead, the most formidable—and indestructible—bond of all is that mutual belongingness of souls that share an originary home (or “womb”). This bond will always be vital, so humans are condemned to suffer the pain of failing to transcend it even as we are compelled to break and deny such a bond.

It’s precisely because I’ve realized this that I can express a simple conclusion in a time of chaos: Let us have no *rupture* between us. I’ve also gradually come to see more clearly what actually happened this past year—my violent outbursts and your shutting down; what my issues were, what yours were. . . . I no longer have to depend on you for information because I've found my way through the labyrinth and have left the jungle behind. None of this chaos has been caused by other people or your desire for them—all that doesn't matter. What matters is that an obstruction has blocked our spiritual communication; an emotional disconnect has grown between us. But the significance of your betrayal has already been carved in stone. In the future, when the time of reckoning arrives, you will pay by losing me, by having lost, whether in whole or in part, my most beautiful, most precious *fidélité* to you. This is something no one else will ever be able to give you in full. Loyalty is not a passive, negative guardianship of the gate—loyalty arises from the complete and utter opening and subsequent blazing forth of one's inner life. It is an active, determined desire that demands total self-awareness and deliberate engagement.

And I don't agree with your tangential use of the "secular" and the "non-secular" to describe our differences and to explain the rupture between us—I wholly disagree.

"Secular life" assumes a kind of passive, moralistic "loyalty." It's the kind of life my parents and yours have been leading as they do their best to conform to the standards of such a life. Apart from relating to the outside world as a couple, however, you could say that their shared inner life is minimal and shallow. This isn't to say they have no spiritual needs at all, or that their passions never cause them suffering, but they focus instead on the external world or find other outlets for their passions. The "secular life" they live demands they compartmentalize the very structure of their lives. This is their right, but they have no choice and no imagination.

So if you say I'm a "non-secular person," then I agree: The "loyalty" of a so-called "secular life" means nothing to me. I have no desire to have a barren life and soul. If you say that you, on the other hand, are precisely this kind of person and that you are well-suited to such a life, fine. I won't suffer then. If you are such a person, or you want to become one, then I won't be bound to you because I couldn't possibly need nor want someone like you. My relationship with Xuan Xuan was an example of this kind of disjunction, and I ended up hurting her.

Although I could depend on her completely day to day and received from her as much love as I could ever ask, what I didn't understand was that my soul could never really need or long for her. I tried to be responsible, to care for her and cherish her. I earned a living, shared my livelihood, listened to her, protected her. What she and I achieved was precisely the ethical fulfillment of the "loyalty" component of a "secular life."

Only later did I realize that wasn't what she wanted from me.

She yearned for me, but I was completely dispassionate as I hadn't given her my whole soul. Crueler still, she watched helplessly as I offered my soul to you and I burst into a brilliant flame. She watched and she understood. She experienced the difference between zero degrees and a hundred and this was so painful that it nearly destroyed her. This is the wrong I committed against her. It's a story about Xuan Xuan in which you were also implicated, a story of my failing to live a "secular life."

Don't say that I do not understand, that I am incapable of living a secular life or that I don't belong in a secular world. I've discovered that I actually may be able to simultaneously live two kinds of lives. The strength needed to lead a secular life is stored inside my body. You could even say it's hidden deep within the seed of my desire for love. It grows in the opposite way of most people's experiences, because first a deep spirituality developed in my life and only later a desire, and capacity, for the real world. The seed of my desire for love could never fully mature. Instead it drained all my energy reserves, with tragic consequences. During those six months when you came to France, I had a chance to make that seed bloom and bear fruit, and my secular life might have thrived. But instead I was drawn into a period of incredible turmoil and self-destruction because you totally shut down and didn't reciprocate my love. After the pain of your betrayal, I went to Tokyo to visit Yong. For a month my body and mind were on the verge of total collapse, and Yong was the one who took me in and cared for me. For the first time she opened up to me, lightening the load of my longing and anguish and offering the passion and connection that I desired so desperately. Only then did I suddenly see what had actually happened this past year.

The story of Yong and me is too long and too dense to be summarized in just a few lines.

In fact she admitted a deep love for me. Although her love wasn't absolute, somehow it caused that seed within to bloom and bear fruit. Three years of maturing had made her realize that she loved me, and that she was ready to admit her desire. It would not be for me to call this a kind of redemption. She knew what she wanted from love and she accepted and paid the price for her comprehension with her whole self. So there was no need for me to possess her completely even as she loved me deeply, and my life quickly recovered from a malaise so profound I was almost blind with it. My potential to live a secular life began to bloom and bear fruit.

Because of her I wanted to recover, I wanted to become a healthy, whole person again. Moved by her love, I wanted to mature into someone strong enough to be accountable for her (particularly for the secular aspects of her life). Because she had loved the wrong person for a very long time, part of her soul had suffered and shut down. She had sworn an oath to that person like the oath I swore to you (you, though, haven't yet entered the phase of life yet where oaths are sworn). Once I am completely liberated from the burden of my responsibility for you (When? Maybe the day when you become completely irrelevant to me. How sad to even mention it. . . .), I now believe that Yong is the "final" one, the one I will spend my life waiting for. She's already a fixture in my life story and genuinely needs me, her need highly exclusive and selective. Only I, and no one else, can occupy that position. If I can't have you, ultimately I will love her and our future family. Moreover, I am prepared to do whatever's necessary and care for her, since in the end I am the only one who can shoulder the burden of her broken life. More important, she and I have already forgiven each other. Our feelings for each other have already passed beyond desire and possession, emancipating me from desire. What I mean is that she is the first person with whom I've experienced "creative loyalty." Before we parted, she told me to find an outlet for my passion at all costs. I replied that I would survive, for her, and mature into a whole and healthy human being who would be able to take care of her.

As for you, Xu, like I told Qing Jin: "My misfortune is that I have devoted myself completely to someone who can't accept my perfect love."

There are still so many long, long reflections and experiences that I want to write to you about . . . but after writing for seven or eight straight hours, I'm empty and exhausted. . . . Xu, can I point out a few things to you with these last words, though they may not be true?

(1) On betrayal

Your betrayal of my life, my will, my body tortured me this past month, leaving a wake of hate and trauma, and I've paid dearly. This was the most painful betrayal you could inflict. But I didn't die, I survived and will continue to heal. Your spirit, however, could never betray me, because your spirit will always yearn for me and belong to me.

From your perspective, total betrayal can't hurt you. On the one hand, you never really cared about me or any of this. You never really cared enough nor have you really grasped how the monopoly of desire works. Yet you would still suffer if my soul betrayed you; you would never be able to watch dispassionately if I gave my soul completely to someone else and my tenderness toward you disappeared. If that day ever comes, you'll pay a painful price. My soul is slipping away from you even as I try to cling to it.

(2) On passion and sex

Xu, it's not that you don't desire me; it's that your body has not yet grown into its desire. Your corporeal desire still can't merge with your spiritual desire; they're incoherent to each other, they can't cooperate. It's not that you've stopped desiring but that your desire has not yet reached maturity.

It's easy for the body to be open to desiring different people because desire wells up and demands to be satisfied. It's easy to categorize corporeal desire as sexuality, but if it has no means of merging with spiritual desire, then a rupture will occur between spirit and flesh. For ultimately passion and sex aren't only expressed physically but through a true union between two spirits. When the spirit can truly love and find contentment, both the body and other key aspects of life will fall naturally into place, working in unison, merging. Xu, one day, when your corporeal desire has matured—when you're able to desire anybody—then you will desire me, if, at that time, there isn't any rupture between us, our lives are harmonious, our spirits remain in love, and our bodies can still satisfy each other. And you will discover that I'm the one you desire most profoundly of all, because your spirit loves me most profoundly of all. I'm working hard this time so that nothing can undermine the loving communion of our spirits.

(3) On my outbursts and your shutting down

Xu, you never really stopped loving me. You can never really not love me. But during this long, long year you sometimes acted as if you didn't love me. You've done countless things that suggest this, but I never really severed ties with you completely because I could still sense your love for me, sense your thirst for my spirit, even though this love only manifests itself in the weakest and most distorted of ways.

This all happened because I started to "blame" you when I moved to Paris. How pitiful that a pair of lovers so completely enamored of each other chose to take such a journey! I needed you but couldn't be satisfied. The suppressed and dependent sides of your personality along with your failure to understand my passion and your failure to deal with the pain caused by this passion . . . all these things led me to blame you. I felt so unfulfilled last March and April that my ubiquitous blaming tantrums caused you to start shutting me out. . . . Pitiful! After that the situation went from bad to worse, as I sunk into a pathological state of "outburst" and you sunk into a long-term "shutdown." On the very same day you started shutting me out, your inner self started to become unhinged, lost. This caused yet deeper frustration and dissatisfaction. In the end you completely failed to express your love for me. Quite the opposite: You kept wanting me but repeatedly said that you *didn't* love me, while I frantically continued to blame you and became trapped in a state of hysteria.

We made each other this way. My worst mistake was my "blaming" heart. That was the first of many mistakes. From the very beginning, the one you place your trust in, open yourself up to, and devote your passion and essentially your life to, should be the one who understands you and accepts you unconditionally, the one who will never "blame" you for your immaturity or your failure to satisfy your partner; before coming to Paris, I was this person to you. Though you aren't mature enough yet to satisfy the needs of my spirit and desires—and could not fulfill the requirements of a union with me—you were still somehow thoroughly devoted to me. Before coming to Paris, I was moved by the depths of your devotion and grew used to it. During that phase we were cooperating and communicating in perfect harmony with each other.

Everything seemed fine until daily life in Paris gradually started to sicken me with despair—a despair that you couldn't understand, and so we stopped communicating . . . I blamed you even more, while your own secret self-loathing grew. All this blame frustrated you more and more and more until finally you simply shut me out. I lost your trust, your openness, your love, your devotion. But the most tragic thing is that my pathologically violent outbursts crushed your inner confidence and composure. Now you can't even act with the slightest bit of honesty, trust, courage, or integrity toward me. Now you are someone who isn't really you. (Honestly, Xu is another person. The Xu I knew well, whom I believed in and whom I loved passionately and to whom I prostrate myself in worship, is the total opposite of this one. She hasn't degenerated and disappeared; she's just hiding from me.) This month, my tragedy reached a peak with a total spiritual breakdown caused by my loss of faith in this deity!

Xu, it's not that you no longer love Zoë or need Zoë anymore. It's precisely because you tried so hard to satisfy him without success that you felt defeated and frustrated. At first, when you were completely open with him and madly in love, you did your best. Later on, when you were shut down and couldn't love him anymore, you still tried to satisfy him but you were too exhausted, too frustrated, so you chose to abandon him. But even this proved impossible, as, after you had accepted his love, you never really stopped loving him, stopped feeling bound to his spirit; you could never erase the enormous space he occupied in your life, nor extricate your fate from his; you could never stop trying so hard to satisfy him, to grow closer to him. So what I must insist on telling you here is this: What you stumble over, what wounds the essence of your desire, is *not* loving. Xu, your first love cannot be compared to any other. You cannot erase all traces of it because your body and soul have been so deeply desired by me, so fiercely loved by me. How indelibly I inscribed your body and soul with the first perfect traces of a beginning! Those were the first indelible traces of desire in your life. As your lover I have given myself to you so completely, I belong to you so truly, can you really disavow the mark that symbolizes our desire's consummation? Can you? Not unless you've shut your spirit down completely, as you've tried so hard to do recently.

To untie the bell you have to find the person who tied it. Your spirit can't be released from its confinement unless it's released by me. If you never communicate with my spirit again, if your life is never open to mine again, you'll never leave the desert, no other can provide an exit. You will even lose contact with your own soul, turn into someone I hate and could never want, and I, like a kite with a broken string, will float away, never to return. . . . I want so much for you to talk to me again, to trust me and be as open as you once were; I want to free you from your state of shutdown. To do so, I must stop my pleading and stop blaming you. I must enable you to recapture your original memory of Zoë's unconditional love for you; this is the unconscious need that's central to your life and calls forth my desire. It's all I can do. I'm trying to grow a little (though not too much), while keeping in mind my earlier ideals. I'm trying my best, trying to see how far I can get. For this homecoming, I could never ask you to make the first move, as it's up to me to return to a place of loving you before I can expect you to quietly do the same. If I fail, then we surely lose each other, down to the final eyelash. I'm waging a life-and-death battle with my own destiny: I can only pray that you'll help me, that you'll never push me away with words (or at least a lot less) and actions that harm my desire for you, that you won't push me off this cliff, nor thoughtlessly sever the cord between us that I want to strengthen because I love you. . . .

I am not in turmoil anymore. The conflict within me is no longer serious. If you try to reconcile my words and my behavior, you'll find that they are not as contradictory as you might believe. I'm aware of what each person I know means to me; I've always been clear about what I want. And I still have the power and freedom to choose whom to devote myself and my soul to, and hopefully always will. I know I'm complicated, but I'm also lucid. I feel things deeply but my desire is like a pure crystal. This is the rarest, most beautiful part of me, that sparkles brightly in the crowd.

Intercepts

RAE ARMANTROUT

In the dark, it
wired itself
for light,

numb, it wired itself
for touch

and waited.

Did it wait?

Could it sense time pass?

*

Only when her limbs moved
did she become aware
of the surrounding medium,

but when did these
become *her*
limbs?

*

Self interested and

intertwined like

dodder

with oak,

dodder known

as witch's hair.

*

How was this *her*
awareness?

*

So that each
was now infuriated
by any interaction
with the other
that altered his
or her trajectory,
producing a pause
or swerve.

*

Was one term
better than another?

*

And when she tried handing him a sheet of waste paper
because he was standing near the recycle bin, he flinched.

The Gift of Sight

REBECCA BROWN

This guy was the scariest to look at. This guy really looked like the plague. Margaret had said the only special thing I'd need to do was put his salve on him. The salve was thick, opaque, yellowish jelly. It came in a big, wide-mouthed plastic jar. It didn't smell like anything. The first time I went there and opened the jar I saw the tracks of someone else's fingers where they'd gone in to get the salve. I don't know why it frightened me so much, but it did. I was afraid to touch him. I was afraid to look at him.

His sores were dark purple and about the size of quarters. The edges of them were yellow and his skin was dark brown. The sores weren't running or oozing or scabs because they always had this salve on them. I was allowed to put on the salve even though I wasn't allowed to give meds because this salve wasn't really a med so much as something just to comfort: it couldn't heal anything.

I don't know if the sores were itchy or hot or how exactly they felt bad to him but I didn't ask. I hadn't been scared to ask about anything before, nurses or docs or Margaret or the guys themselves. The guys especially liked to explain things. They liked that I asked and that they could tell me what they knew. They'd all become experts.

The first time I put the salve on I didn't know if the temperature of it would be uncomfortable, like when massage oil, if it isn't skin temperature, feels so cold that you can't feel the good. I wanted to ask him, but I couldn't. I couldn't say anything out loud about the sores.

I changed gloves several times when I was doing the salve because my gloves got coated with it, and also with his hair, which was very tight and curly and fell out easily, and with flecks or patches of skin. I think he felt embarrassed to have it done except it would have been worse not to have it done.

The first time I went there, his niece, who'd moved in from her dorm to live in his apartment with him, let me in. She showed me around, though there wasn't much to show, the apartment was small. She told me he'd want his dinner but that he could tell me. He could still do that. The niece went out. She was going to get out for a couple of hours to do some errands.

When I asked him what he'd like me to do he said could he have some salve.

"Sure," I said. I pulled the sheet down part way. The sores were all over him. I don't know why the sight of him frightened me but it did. I hadn't felt frightened that way before and I didn't want him to see it in my face, I didn't want him to feel ashamed about how he looked.

Maybe it was seeing it so present, so visible, on the outside, and all the time, not something you could pretend for a while you didn't have, or something that people who only saw you for a while might not see, like chronic diarrhea or the vomits. How he looked was very sick, he looked like he had the plague.

I started with his hands and arms. Then he said, "Could you do my torso, please?"

He said it so normal and evenly, like it was an ordinary task. I tried to think of it as that kind of task, like sweeping the dining room or checking the mail, not something growing on him from his sickness.

I was ashamed of how I thought, of how I tried to think myself away from the terrible sight of his sickness.

I did his torso and his legs and feet. I turned him over and did his back and sides. I did his neck. He didn't have them on his face. I changed his sheets around him. He was breathing hard. The sheets were covered all over with salve. His niece had told me they needed changing twice a day. It took a while for his breathing to calm down.

After a while he wanted his dinner and told me where everything was. It was easy—a microwave frozen dinner and a glass of cranberry juice. Cranberry juice is a good source of potassium. The dinner was roast beef and potatoes and peas and apple pie. I pulled the bed tray over to him and helped him sit up a little. He wanted to feed himself. I put the fork in his hand. He could do almost OK with the potatoes, but the peas were hard to keep on the fork and the roast beef was hard to spear. He asked me to help and I fed him. I lifted the back of his head and put the fork to his mouth. I held the glass up close to him and he drank through the straw. The muscles moving in his neck when he drank looked strong. That was good to see. I got him a second glass. He said, "Thank you."

He was sweaty when he finished. I sponged him clean and put on more salve. He fell asleep. He was breathing fairly evenly. When his niece came home I told her how it had gone and she said thanks and asked if I could come again.

That was Sunday. I could only do weekends for them, so I didn't see him again till the next Saturday. When Margaret had asked me if I could do weekends I'd said yeah, but only for a while, because I wanted to go to San Francisco at the end of next month, and Margaret had said, "They won't need you more than that." Meaning, this guy was not going to last that long.

The next Saturday his niece let me in again and went out, and I said to him, "How about some salve?" like it didn't bother me at all. I'd thought about the sores all week long, about how they looked and how it frightened me. But I'd worked myself up to acting like it didn't bother me.

"Thank you," he said.

I started putting salve on him. I was not going to think about other things. I was going to stay with him even in my mind. I asked him about this painting above the bed. It was on cloth and very beautiful. He turned his head a little to look up at it. He told me he got it in Africa. There were two others, smaller, on the opposite wall. I asked him what had taken him there, and he told me about his teaching. Then how his family, especially his mother—he nodded over at the mantelpiece—had thought it was the greatest, his going back to Africa, it was like back home, and that she'd even talked about going to visit him there.

Part of it felt good, like a normal conversation you'd have with someone you met at a party or with a new neighbor. But also it was like there were four different people there. The two people having the normal conversation and the person touching the body with the salve and the person with the body with the sores.

He said he'd like to have lived there longer but it was better to come back to the States. This was a reference to his getting sick. I was glad to hear him talk about his work and how much he loved it, but part of me was thinking, "But that's where you got sick. That's where you had to come back from to die." I hated myself for thinking that. But I also kept telling myself that even if I wasn't feeling or thinking the right things, at least he was getting fed, at least he was getting his sheets changed, at least his kitchen was getting cleaned, at least his body was getting salve.

When he slept again I went to look at the photo on the mantel. It was of him and his mother. He was in a suit, his arm was around her, his springy black hair was plastered down.

He woke when his niece came back. He looked up and said, "It was nice to talk with you. Are you coming back tomorrow?"

"Next Saturday," I said.

"Thank you for asking about my work," he said. "I want to hear about you next time." He was very polite.

"OK," I said. I still had my gloves on. I shook his hand. "I'll tell you next week."

The next Saturday when I got there, the niece was dressed up. She was on her way to the airport to pick up her grandmother. He had suddenly gotten worse.

He was on oxygen. The tank was by the bed. The tubes were up his nose. His skin was damp. The sores were the same.

I asked the niece what she'd like me to do, and she said he could use his salve and clean sheets but nothing else. "He's not really eating much anymore," she said. She shrugged her shoulders and pointed at the couch. "There's some magazines if you want to read," she said.

"OK," I said. "Drive safe."

"Thanks." She tried to smile. She looked so old. She was a sophomore at the university. She turned to him on the bed. "I'm going to pick up Grandma at the airport. We'll be back in a couple hours."

When she left I washed my hands and put on my gloves and went over and sat next to the bed. I said, "Hi." His eyes moved but he didn't say anything. I started in on the salve. While I did it I told him about what I'd been up to that week, about a movie I'd gone to and hiking with Chris and a new string game I taught my cat. I could tell he was listening, and I believed he remembered he'd asked me to tell him about myself the weekend before and that I'd said I would.

I could hear the oxygen going in and out of him through the tubes when he breathed. The tubes were thin plastic, a light greenish color. The nose clip that held them in was white plastic. I was careful around the tubes when I did the salve on his shoulders and neck, and very careful too when I changed the sheets.

He was breathing hard after the salve and bed change. I put my hand on his arm until his breathing calmed down. Then I said, "You want some juice? I'll bring some over and see if you want some."

I washed my hands and put on new gloves and poured some cranberry juice in a cup and got a little teaspoon. I put them on the bedside table and sat by the bed.

"Here's some cranberry juice," I said. "Do you want some?"

His eyes were open but cloudy-looking. It took him a few seconds, then he made this noise. I didn't know if it was yes or no or nothing.

"Can you blink once for 'yes' if you want some juice?" I said.

He looked at me. After a few seconds he opened his mouth. His lips were dry. It took him a while to figure it out. Then he blinked and held his eyes closed. I knew he meant yes.

"OK," I said. "Good. I'm going to put some juice in the spoon and bring it to your mouth so you can drink it."

I dipped the spoon in the juice. It was so tiny, this little drop of clear pink juice. As I moved the spoon toward his mouth I kept my hand on his forearm and said, "I'm bringing the juice to your mouth now. It's near your lips now. OK. Here it is."

I heard the click of the bottom of the spoon on his lower teeth. I tipped the spoon in his mouth and he closed his lips and swallowed.

"Good," I said, "that's good. You want some more?"

He blinked.

"OK," I said. I got another spoonful of juice and brought it toward his mouth. "OK, here comes some more juice." His lips moved like he was trying to suck. I put the spoon in and turned it over, and he swallowed.

"You're doing great," I said, "really great."

He blinked.

I fed him six spoonfuls, but on the sixth one his throat made a gurgling noise and some of it came back out. He opened his mouth in a big frightened O and made this high whine. I was afraid he'd choke. I put my hand on his chest as if I could smooth the passage. It was less than half a glass.

"It's OK," I said. You're gonna be OK. Just try to breathe."

He opened and closed his eyes really fast.

"It's all right," I said. "You're all right. Just give it a second."

I held my hand on his chest until he'd calmed down. After a while he blinked: OK.

I wiped the juice from around his face and the top of his chest. I moved the oxygen clip in his nose back from where it had shifted.

"You OK now?"

He blinked.

"Good," I said. "I'll be back in a second."

I went to the bathroom and cleaned up. I changed my gloves. When I went back his eyes were closed. He was breathing evenly. I put his hand on my arm. His pulse was even.

I went to the kitchen to see if there was any cleaning I could do. Everything was spotless. The niece had been keeping busy.

I looked at the clock. They were probably driving back now. They were going to see him soon.

I went to the bathroom and found a comb. I sat by the bed. In a few seconds he opened his eyes and looked at me.

"How about if I comb your hair?" I said.

He took a few seconds to understand, then he blinked.

I put one hand on his cheek and combed his hair with the other. I combed it very slowly.

His hair was springy and damp with sweat. I combed it, then patted it down with my hand. When I put my hand on his head he made a noise.

"Keith?" I said.

His eyes moved. His eyes were watery and thick. He was trying too hard to focus, the way a baby does when it opens its eyes for the first time.

The skin of his face looked very thin. Then luminous, like light was there. There was the sight of something radiant.

He tried to open his mouth but couldn't. He closed his eyes.

I leaned over the bed and took him in my arms. I held him as tenderly as I could.

"Keith," I said, "your mother is coming. You'll see your mother soon," I said, "you'll see your mother soon."

I held him and told him again and again. I held him until his mother arrived.

Then I put him in her arms.

Selection from *The Activist*

RENEE GLADMAN

Farther along, members of the CPL wait in front of a popular café—

Still there because they love me,

he thinks.

This walking,

he'll say when he arrives,

was difficult for me. There were obstacles in the street—though I can't prove it—every time I hit one falling on my head was the results, and by the time I recovered from the fall there was no accessible memory.

Seeing them in their glorious postures Lomarlo wants to yell encouragement, but he's too tired to say the words—

These are good friends, though. They know how to wait. Soon I'll arrive and we'll eat.

Then he trips and falls into a pothole. When twenty minutes later he reaches them, they are having an argument about eggs.

Monique is saying:

We have to think seriously here . . . the signals are always . . . scrambled . . . we've got to break the barrier . . . fuck their system from the inside . . . no this ain't the pacifist movement . . . we've outlived that occasion . . .

While Stefani shouts:

Yeah let's lay 'em all out,

during M.'s ellipses.

Lomarlo considers:

This might not be about eggs and perhaps I'm not supposed to hear. But these are my comrades! They're smiling at me. One has his hand on my shoulder, expecting me to ease into this conversation when I have been struggling to get here, when the worst things have happened to me.

Freddie embraces the newcomer:

So Lomo, what do you think?

I just want to eat. I never care what it is.

Apparently his friends agree, as each has walked away, presumably to secure a table.

This is the warmest day we've had so far . . . yes it really is,

he repeats to himself, trying to keep his mind off his hunger. When the others return they stand around him, smoking. Monique steps away from the group, shuffling papers:

Listen up, crew. I have made some diagrams of the inner labyrinth. These marks in blue indicate our points of entry—

Don't be so—

Lomarlo snaps, delirious with hunger:

So . . . you know . . .

The group finds a table, Freddie studies the sky then each of their faces.

It's beautiful today. Are we sure?

I'm sure,

Lomarlo affirms.

Breakfast is going well, though since L.'s outburst, they've been sitting in silence. Alonso decides to ask a question:

Lomo, what happened to you last night?

This sudden interest inspires the newcomer to self-reflection. He gazes inward:

They want my story. When I was young this is what I imagined—a group turning to me, members with a cock to their heads, awaiting me. Not like the time I nearly fell into the fire while Freddie was searching for wood and something in that search kept him away for hours as I lay there. And our other friends, now long gone, wandering in their drugs—

Lomarlo shakes his head,

These are not my memories.

He shakes his head again, more violently,

Where are my memories?

Then he locks onto a series of aerials flying an elaborate pattern.

Birds don't fly that low,

he observes with growing paranoia.

A mosquito buzzes by. He moans,

What's that?

Turning down a path, away from the birds,

Got to get away but quietly so the flies don't notice me.

He crouches behind a trash bin, waits—

Stefani zips his sweatshirt shut and pushes himout the door. No more memory. Outside the café, he looks around himself. The light is low, as after a storm or shortly before sunset, or as a result of wearing shades, or some doom is coming. He feels his hand flapping against his skin but does not know what he's looking for.

Stefani, what's on me?

Can't say without looking at you.

Well, look at me!

But you said not to!

Where did everybody go?

Ikea.

Why?

To blow it up.

What are you doing?

Keeping my eye on you.

How, if you don't look at me?

I've been listening for you.

Where have we been all day?

There, eating eggs.

To himself:

I can't believe I've been away from myself for so many hours, and I don't feel the least bit rested. In fact, what's all this on my shoulders? What's pouring out of my eyes and toes? Not my chi. Where's that?

Stefani holds his hand, leading the way to their next meeting. He uses the downtime to put order to his mind.

Now let's see . . . where is that chi?

Once again inside his mind, walking quickly through rooms with his head down. He glimpses a photo on the floor. It's damaged, ripped into several pieces. Nevertheless he recognizes the face. His. Taken some years ago.

I remember that store I'm posed in front of. I used to meet the group there. How did this picture get separated from the other snapshots that were taken? And why is it destroyed?

He looks around with alarm, as if caught in something. Then snaps,

This is my mind, only I have the right to be here,

against a creeping sense of being post-invasion.

The next morning Lomarlo wakes with his ass pressed against Alonso's hip. He's recalling his dreams, monotonous as always but with a new array of characters who're much more violent than those of the nights before. —Wait. He thinks it's Alonso. The pain in his ass is the same, so it must be. Yet other than what he knows to have existed in the past, there is no further evidence. Soon he'll have to turn around to see. But there is no light, no sun shining through his blackened windows. Plus, if he turns around and it's not Alonso, he'll want to squash whoever it is, unless that person's stronger. No, the best way to find out is to get the person to speak. He begins:

In one of my dreams people were playing with firearms and I was not sure what to do.

Silence.

He adds:

There was glass everywhere. I wonder if I screamed. Did I scream?

Silence, as that following cell death. He imag-ines himself embraced by a lifeless form, and with a mixture of disgust and anticipation, reaches back to tap the offending bone. It jumps.

Waking again, late afternoon, Lomarlo looks around himself and supposes he's slept for a week. This time he is not in bed but at a table, with the group, in front of a plate of eggs. He's trying to get his wits about him, but something's wrong,

What the hell is she saying?

Lomarlo consults interiorly:

That is not regular language. It's a code and every-body knows it but me. Monique keeps saying, Ha chini chini, and the rest of them nod their heads. It's because I fell asleep . . . they're punishing me, knowing I would forget this training. No, not the CPL. Maybe the SFF, but never the CPL. I've just got to relax . . . flow into this.

He leans back in his chair, clears his mind, then releases:

Ma chanic daravici delimatu,

slowly, without committing to any particular inflection.

The group's response is unsurprising—faces turn to him. He realizes:

Damn, I should've asked a question. They would have been forced to answer.

Monique continues her monologue. She says many things, but *ha chini chini* is the most recurring.

I keep thinking about those words . . . I know them . . .

Stefani pokes him in the side with her elbow and whispers:

Isa uma kuni. Monique ma uma kuni.

He shakes her off.

Argh! What's this? Something's sticking me.

He reaches under his ass and finds some pieces of wire. He exclaims:

Ja se pa cahini.

Then clamps his hand over his mouth.

Freddie grabs the wire from him and places it in a box. The box claims Lomarlo.

The last time I was in a box it was spring,

he recalls,

The old group had gone downtown to sell papers, while I stayed behind to clean up. We were renting a small room in the old warehouse district. Somebody left a box open, the larger kind used when mailing banners overseas, and I stepped back into it. Lay there for hours, not because I couldn't get up but because I was comfortable there. I couldn't remember against whom we were fighting. Lying there I thought, On my back and safe in this tiny room, I want to think about my enemies. It was easy. No one intruded, everything was fine. I concentrated. However, the image never surfaced. That's not true. Several images came to me, but none of them seemed right. I was looking for something truly sinister. I kept saying, This couldn't be the enemy, discarding the idea.

April 4 Friday

ROSE "ROSEBUD" FELIU-PETTET

evening—Peter Hale calls and asks me to come quickly, Allen is in a coma, dying. Pull on my sneakers and taxi down, trying to keep calm breathing, trying to arrive in state of peace. 15 minutes after Pete's call he opens the door to the loft and I go in to join those already gathered. I went and embraced big Peter—Orlovsky—and Eugene, Allen's brother. About 20 friends talking in low voices, looking lost, comforting each other.

After being diagnosed with inoperable liver cancer the previous Friday at Beth Israel Hospital, Allen had been told he had maybe 2–5 months to live. When I heard the news, for some reason I felt strongly that it would not be that long—I felt that he would go very soon. He had come back home Wednesday in good spirits, organizing things as ever, making plans for the coming days. But someone (I forget who; perhaps it was Bob) had said Allen personally felt that he had very little time left. A month or two, he thought. So Wednesday he was busy, writing and making phone calls to his friends all over the world, saying goodbye. Amiri Baraka said Allen called him and said, "I'm dying, do you need any money?"

But Thursday he was much weaker, he could hobble from bed to chair only with difficulty. There was a phonecall from Italy, in the middle of it Allen begins to vomit, throws up right there on the phone! "Funny," he says, "never done that before." Said he was very tired and wanted to go to sleep. He fell asleep and later that night had a seizure and slipped into a coma. He was alone.

In the morning Bob Rosenthal discovered him unconscious and called the Hospice doctor who came and told him that Allen had most likely had a stroke and had hours to live. The task of notifying family and friends began.

Everyone had feared that as word spread, there would be a huge throng appearing at the loft, but that wasn't the case. People came and went quietly during the afternoon. Bob, Pete Hale, Bill Morgan and Kaye Wright, the office staff, were busy constantly at the phones making and receiving calls. Shelley Rosenthal and Rani Singh helping with everything that needed doing. Eugene and several nieces and nephews of Allen's consoling each other. Larry Rivers down from his apartment upstairs, wandering around forlornly in his pink, white and blue striped pajamas. George and Anna Condo and their little girl. Francesco and Alba Clemente, beloved friends of Allen's. Patti Smith sitting in tears with Oliver Ray and her young daughter. Bob and Shelly's sons Aliah and Isaac. Mark Israel and David Greenberg, two of Allen's young boyfriends. Philip Glass and June Leaf. Robert Frank. Simon Pettet. Andrew Wylie. Roy Lichtenstein. Steven Bornstein, who had flown up from Florida. A few others, I don't remember who all was there.

I went to the back of the loft and Raymond Foye stood looking pale and so sad. I told him he must be very blessed, he had spent so much time giving support and love to the dying—Henry Geldzahler, Huncke, Harry Smith. "Yes, but this is the big one, the hardest," he said. Allen lay in a narrow hospital bed beside the windows overlooking 14th street. There were two almost invisible tubes coming out of his nose, attached to a portable small oxygen tank on the floor. His head was raised up on a couple of big striped pillows and he looked tiny and frail, thin arms with bruised veins from hospital tests sticking out from his Jewel Heart T-shirt. Head to the side, slight shadows under the eyes. I had walked through the loft, people whispering greetings, hugging, telling me all that had happened. But still not really prepared for the sight of him. The windows were open, curtains waving softly. His breathing was deep, slow, very labored, a snoring sound. "Hey, Allen, wake up!"

Joel Gaidemak, his cousin and doctor, was there constantly, and a young lady nurse sat in the corner reading, occasionally getting up to check on heart and pulse, or administer morphine for congestion. Gelek Rinpoche said he thought Allen might last the night. Joel didn't think so.

A few chairs were set up nearby, and there was the big white leather Salvation Army sofa of which he was so proud. People sat, or at intervals went to sit beside the bed and hold his hand or whisper to him and kiss him, his hand or cheek or head. An altar had been set up along one side of the loft and Gelek Rinpoche and the other monks sat chanting and praying, the sound so soothing constantly in the background, bells tinkling. A faint scent of flowers and incense hung in the air.

I had a little throw-away Woolworths camera, and Gregory Corso asked me to take a picture of him with Allen. He knelt beside the cot and placed his arm over Allen "like that picture, or statue, of Adonais, right?"

There was a medical chart, a picture of the human skeleton, hanging over the bed. Bob said Allen had put it there, half as a joke, half as a reminder. And Allen's beautiful picture of Whitman (that had hung in the kitchen on 12th Street) gazing down from the wall at the other dear bearded poet in the bed below. As it got late, many went home to try and catch a little sleep. It was around 11. Bob and Pete were just playing it by ear, deciding that anyone who wanted to stay would find a place, on the floor if necessary. Peter Orlovsky was taking photos and I felt a little uncomfortable, the idea of taking pictures at this time, but I figured, hey, if it was you, Allen'd be the first one through the door camera in hand! Eventually, Eugene leaned over, held Allen's hand, whispered "Goodbye little Allen. Goodbye little Allen. I'll be back later. See you soon." He kissed him and left. And Gregory—Gregorio!—too, telling us to call him at once if there was any change.

Joel had said that there was no way to know how long it would be, minutes or hours, surely not days. I had felt from the minute I saw Allen there that it would be very soon. I sat at the foot of the bed where I had spent the last few hours, holding his feet, rubbing them gently from time to time. An occasional cigarette break—the little guest bedroom by the office area was set up as the smoker's lounge. Bob and Pete and Bill were as strong and remarkable as ever, supporting everyone, keeping a sense of humor, and constantly dealing with the dozens of phonecalls, faxes, and the visitors as they came and went. They'd had a few days for the news to sink in, but they were dealing with—literally—hundreds of people over the phone or in person who had just found out and were in the first stages of stunned, disbelieving grief.

I had remained at the bedside and it was now after midnight. I could not believe he still hung on, the breathing so difficult, the lungs slowly filling with fluid. Labored breathing (gulps for air—like those gulps he'd made when he was singing—almost like he was reciting poetry in his sleep). Those who had been there all day were exhausted. It was down to a few now. Bob and Pete and Bill Morgan. Peter Orlovsky so bravely dealing with his pain, strong Beverly holding his hand. David and Mark. Patti and Oliver, there together all day trying to be brave and sometimes giving way to red eyed tears. Simon Pettet sitting beside me for hours.

Allen's feet felt cooler than they had been earlier. I sat remembering the 33 years I'd known him, lived with him, my second father.

And still he breathed, but softer now.

Around 2 o'clock, everyone decided to try and get some rest. Bob and Joel lay down in Allen's big bed near the cot where he lay, everyone found a sofa or somewhere to stretch out.

Simon and I sat, just watching his face. Everyone was amazed at how beautiful he looked—all lines of stress and age smoothed—he looked patriarchal and strong. I had never seen him so handsome. The funny looking little boy had grown into this most wonderful looking man. (He would have encouraged photos if he had known how wonderful he looked!) But so tiny! He seemed as fragile as a baby in his little T-shirt.

The loft was very quiet. Most were resting, half-asleep. Suddenly Allen began to shake, a small convulsion wracked his body. I called out, and Joel and Bob sat up and hurried over. I called louder, and everyone else came running. It was about 2:15. Joel examined him, pulse, etc., and said that his vital signs were considerably slower, he had had another seizure. The breathing went on, weaker. His feet were cooler. Everyone sat or stood close to the little bed. The loft was dim and shadowy; only a single low light shining down on him. It lent a surreal, almost theatrical look to the corner of the loft. Peter Orlovsky bent over and kissed his head, saying, "Goodbye Darling."

And then suddenly a remarkable thing happened. A tremor went through him, and slowly, impossibly, he began to raise his head. He weakly rose until he was sitting almost upright, and his left arm lifted and extended. Then his eyes opened very slowly and very wide. The pupils were wildly dilated. I thought I saw a look of confusion or bewilderment. His head began to turn very slowly and his eyes seemed to glance around him, gazing on each of us in turn. His eyes were so deep, so dark, but Bob said that they were empty of sight. His mouth opened, and we all heard as he seemed to struggle to say something, but only a soft low sound, a weak "Aaah," came from him. Then his eyes began to close and he sank back onto the pillow. The eyes shut fully. He continued, then, to struggle through a few more gasping breaths, and his mouth fell open in an O. Joel said that these were the final moments, the O of the mouth the sign of approaching death. I still continued to stroke his feet and thin little legs, but the Tibetan Buddhist tradition is to not touch the body after death, so I kissed him one final time and then let go.

At 2:39, Joel checked for vital signs and announced that the heart, so much stronger than anyone knew, had stopped beating. A painless and gentle death. The thin blue sheet was pulled up to his chin, and Peter Hale brought over a tiny cup and spoon, and placed a few drops of a dark liquid between Allen's lips. It was part of the Buddhist ritual—the "last food." Bob put his hand over Allen's eyes and said the Sh'ma. We all sat quietly in the dim light, each with our own thoughts, saying goodbye.

Kleist in Thun

ROBERT WALSER

Translated by Christopher Middleton

Kleist found board and lodging in a villa near Thun, on an island in the river Aare. It can be said today, after more than a hundred years, with no certainty of course, but I think he must have walked across a tiny bridge, ten meters in length, and have pulled a bell rope. Thereupon somebody must have come sliding lizardlike down the stairs inside, to see who was there. "Have you a room to let?" Briefly then Kleist made himself comfortable in the three rooms which, at an astonishingly low price, were assigned to him. "A charming local Bernese girl keeps house for me." A beautiful poem, a child, a heroic deed; these three things occupy his mind. Moreover, he is somewhat unwell. "Lord knows what is wrong. What is the matter with me? It is so beautiful here."

He writes, of course. From time to time he takes the coach to Berne, meets literary friends, and reads to them whatever he has written. Naturally they praise him to the skies, yet find his whole person rather peculiar. He writes *The Broken Jug*. But why all the fuss? Spring has come. Around Thun the fields are thick with flowers, fragrance everywhere, hum of bees, work, sounds fall, one idles about; in the heat of the sun you could go mad. It is as if radiant red stupefying waves rise up in his head whenever he sits at his table and tries to write. He curses his craft. He had intended to become a farmer when he came to Switzerland. Nice idea, that. Easy to think up, in Potsdam. Poets anyway think up such things easily enough. Often he sits at the window.

Possibly about ten o'clock in the morning. He is so much alone. He wishes there was a voice beside him; what sort of voice? A hand; well, and? A body? But what for? Out there lies the lake, veiled and lost in white fragrance, framed by the bewitching unnatural mountains. How it all dazzles and disturbs. The whole countryside down to the water is sheer garden, it seems to seethe and sag in the bluish air with bridges full of flowers and terraces full of fragrance. Birds sing so faintly under all the sun, all the light. They are blissful, and full of sleep. His elbow on the windowsill, Kleist props his head on his hand, stares and stares and wants to forget himself. The image of his distant northern home enters his mind, his mother's face he can see clearly, old voices, damn it all—he has leapt up and run out into the garden. There he gets into a skiff and rows out over the clear morning lake. The kiss of the sun is indivisible, unabating. Not a breath. Hardly a stir. The mountains are the artifice of a clever scene painter, or look like it; it is as if the whole region were an album, the mountains drawn on a blank page by an adroit dilettante for the lady who owns the album, as a souvenir, with a line of verse. The album has pale green covers. Which is appropriate. The foothills at the lake's edge are so half-and-half green, so high, so fragrant. La la la! He has undressed and plunges into the water. How inexpressibly lovely this is to him. He swims and hears the laughter of women on the shore. The boat shifts sluggishly on the greenish, bluish water. The world around is like one vast embrace. What rapture this is, but what an agony it can also be.

Sometimes, especially on fine evenings, he feels that this place is the end of the world. The alps seem to him to be unattainable gates to a paradise high up on the ridges. He walks on his little island, pacing slow, up and down. The girl hangs out washing among the bushes, in which a light gleams, melodious, yellow, morbidly beautiful. The faces of snow-crested mountains are so wan; dominant in all things is a final, intangible beauty. Swans swimming to and fro among the rushes seem caught in the spell of beauty and of the light of dusk. The air is sickly. Kleist wants a brutal war, to fight in battle; to himself he seems a miserable and superfluous sort of person.

He goes for a walk. Why, he asks himself with a smile, why must it be he who has nothing to do, nothing to strike at, nothing to throw down? He feels the sap and the strength in his body softly complaining. His entire soul thrills for bodily exertion. Between high ancient walls he climbs, down over those gray stone screes the dark green ivy passionately curls, up to the castle hill. In all the windows up here the evening light is aglow. Up on the edge of the rock face stands a delightful pavilion, he sits here, and lets his soul fly, out and down into the shining holy silent prospect. He would be surprised if he were to feel well now. Read a newspaper? How would that be? Conduct an idiotic political or generally useful debate with some respected official half-wit or other? Yes? He is not unhappy. Secretly he considers happy alone the man who is inconsolable: naturally and powerfully inconsolable. With him the position is one small faint shade worse. He is too sensitive to be happy, too haunted by all his irresolute, cautious, mistrusted feelings. He would like to scream aloud, to weep. God in heaven, what is wrong with me, and he rushes down the darkening hill. Night soothes him. Back in his room he sits down, determined to work till frenzy comes, at his writing table. The light of the lamp eliminates his image of his whereabouts, and clears his brain, and he writes now.

On rainy days it is terribly cold and void. The place shivers at him. The green shrubs whine and whimper and shed rain tears for some sun. Over the heads of the mountains drift monstrous dirty clouds like great impudent murderous hands over foreheads. The countryside seems to want to creep away and hide from this evil weather, to shrivel up. The lake is leaden and bleak, the language of the waves unkind. The storm wind, wailing like a weird admonition, can find no issue, crashes from one scarp to the next. It is dark here, and small, small. Everything is pressed right up against one's nose. One would like to seize a sledgehammer and beat a way out of it all. Get away there, get away!

The sun shines again, and it is Sunday. Bells are ringing. The people are leaving the hilltop church. The girls and women in tight black laced bodices with silver spangles, the men dressed simply and soberly. They carry prayer books in their hands, and their faces are peaceful, beautiful, as if all anxiety were vanished, all the furrows of worry and contention smoothed away, all trouble forgotten. And the bells. How they peal out, leap out with peals and waves of sound. How it glitters and glows with blue and bell tones over the whole Sunday sunbathed little town. The people scatter. Kleist stands, fanned by strange feelings, on the church steps and his eyes follow the movements of the people going down them. Many a farmer's child he sees, descending the steps like a born princess, majesty and liberty bred in the bone. He sees big-muscled handsome young men from the country, and what country, not flat land, not young plainsmen, but lads who have erupted out of deep valleys curiously caverned in the mountains, narrow often, like the arm of a tall, somewhat monstrous man. They are the lads from the mountains where cornland and pasture fall steep into the crevasses, where odorous hot grass grows in tiny flat patches on the brinks of horrible ravines, where the houses are stuck like specks on the meadows when you stand far below on the broad country road and look right up, to see if there can still be houses for people up there.

Sundays Kleist likes, and market days also, when everything ripples and swarms with blue smocks and the costumes of the peasant women, on the road, and on the narrow main street. There on this narrow street, by the pavement, the wares are stacked in stone vaults and on flimsy stalls. Grocers announce their cheap treasures with beguiling country cries. And usually on such a market day there shines the most brilliant, the hottest, the silliest sun. Kleist likes to be pushed hither and thither by the bright bland throng of folk. Everywhere there is the smell of cheese. Into the better shops go the serious and sometimes beautiful countrywomen, cautiously, to do their shopping. Many of the men have pipes in their mouths. Pigs, calves, and cows are hauled past. There is one man standing there and laughing, forcing his rosy piglet to walk by beating it with a stick. It refuses, so he takes it under his arm and carries it onward. The smells of human bodies filter through their clothes, out of the inns there pour the sounds of carousal, dancing, and eating. All this uproar, all the freedom of the sounds! Sometimes coaches cannot pass. The horses are completely hemmed in by trading and gossiping men. And the sun shines dazzling so exactly upon the objects, faces, cloths, baskets, and goods. Everything is moving and the dazzle of sunlight must of course move nicely along with everything else. Kleist would like to pray. He finds no majestic music so beautiful, no soul so subtle as the music and soul of all this human activity. He would like to sit down on one of the steps which lead into the narrow street. He walks on, past women with skirts lifted high, past girls who carry baskets on their heads, calm, almost noble, like the Italian women carrying jugs he has seen in paintings, past shouting men and drunken men, past policemen, past schoolboys moving with their schoolboy purposes, past shadowy alcoves which smell cool, past ropes, sticks, foodstuffs, imitation jewellery, jaws, noses, hats, horses, veils, blankets, woollen stockings, sausages, balls of butter, and slabs of cheese, out of the tumult to a bridge over the Aare, where he stops, and leans over the rail to look down into the deep blue water flowing wonderfully away. Above him the castle turrets glitter and glow like brownish liquid fire. This might almost be Italy.

At times on ordinary weekdays the whole small town seems to him bewitched by sun and stillness. He stands motionless before the strange old town hall, with the sharp-edged numerals of its date cut in the gleaming white wall. It is all so irretrievable, like the form of a folk song the people have forgotten. Hardly alive, no, not alive at all. He mounts the enclosed wooden stair to the castle where the old earls lived, the wood gives off the odour of age and of vanished human destinies. Up here he sits on a broad, curved, green bench to enjoy the view, but closes his eyes. It all looks so terrible, as if asleep, buried under dust, with the life gone out of it. The nearest thing lies as in a faraway veil-like dreaming distance. Everything is sheathed in a hot cloud. Summer, but what sort of summer? I am not alive, he cries out, and does not know where to turn with his eyes, hands, legs, and breath. A dream. Nothing there. I do not want dreams. In the end he tells himself he lives too much alone. He shudders, compelled to admit how unfeeling is his relation to the world about him.

Then come the summer evenings. Kleist sits on the high churchyard wall. Everything is damp, yet also sultry. He opens his shirt, to breathe freely. Below him lies the lake, as if it had been hurled down by the great hand of a god, incandescent with shades of yellow and red, its whole incandescence seems to glow up out of the water's depths. It is like a lake of fire. The Alps have come to life and dip with fabulous gestures their foreheads into the water. His swans down there circle his quiet island, and the crests of trees in dark, chanting, fragrant joy float over—over what? Nothing, nothing. Kleist drinks it all in. To him the whole dark sparkling lake is the cluster of diamonds upon a vast, slumbering, unknown woman's body. The lime trees and the pine trees and the flowers give off their perfumes. There is a soft, scarcely perceptible sound down there; he can hear it, but he can also see it. That is something new. He wants the intangible, the incomprehensible. Down on the lake a boat is rocking; Kleist does not see it, but he sees the lanterns which guide it, swaying to and fro. There he sits, his face jutting forward, as if he must be ready for the death leap into the image of that lovely depth. He wants to perish into the image. He wants eyes alone, only to be one single eye. No, something totally different. The air should be a bridge, and the whole image of the landscape a chair back to relax against, sensuous, happy, tired. Night comes, but he does not want to go down, he throws himself on a grave that is hidden under bushes, bats whiz around him, the pointed trees whisper as soft airs pass over them. The grass smells so delicious, blanketing the skeletons of buried men. He is so grievously happy, too happy, whence his suffocation, his aridity, his grief. So alone. Why cannot the dead emerge and talk a half hour with the lonely man? On a summer night one ought really to have a woman to love. The thought of white lustrous breasts and lips hurls Kleist down the hill to the lakeside and into the water, fully dressed, laughing, weeping.

Weeks pass, Kleist has destroyed one work, two, three works. He wants the highest mastery, good, good. What's that? Not sure? Tear it up. Something new, wilder, more beautiful. He begins *The Battle of Sempach*, in the centre of it the figure of Leopold of Austria, whose strange fate attracts him. Meanwhile, he remembers his *Robert Guiscard*. He wants him to be splendid. The good fortune to be a sensibly balanced man with simple feelings he sees burst into fragments, crash and rattle like boulders collapsing down the landslip of his life. He helps him nevertheless, now he is resolute. He wants to abandon himself to the entire catastrophe of being a poet: the best thing is for me to be destroyed as quickly as possible.

What he writes makes him grimace: his creations miscarry. Toward autumn he is taken ill. He is amazed at the gentleness which now comes over him. His sister travels to Thun to bring him home. There are deep furrows in his cheeks. His face has the expression and colouring of a man whose soul has been eaten away. His eyes are more lifeless than the eyebrows over them. His hair hangs clotted in thick pointed hanks over his temples, which are contorted by all the thoughts which he imagines have dragged him into filthy pits and into hells. The verses that resound in his brain seem to him like the croakings of ravens; he would like to eradicate his memory. He would like to shed his life; but first he wants to shatter the shells of life. His fury rages at the pitch of his agony, his scorn at the pitch of his misery. My dear, what is the matter, his sister embraces him. Nothing, nothing. That was the ultimate wrong, that he should have to say what was wrong with him. On the floor of his room lie his manuscripts, like children horribly forsaken by father and mother. He lays his hand in his sister's, and is content to look at her, long, and in silence. Already it is the vacant gaze of a skull, and the girl shudders.

Then they leave. The country girl who has kept house for Kleist says goodbye. It is a bright autumn morning, the coach rolls over bridges, past people, through roughly plastered lanes, people look out of windows, overhead is the sky, under trees lies yellowish foliage, everything is clean, autumnal, what else? And the coachman has his pipe in his mouth. All is as ever it was. Kleist sits dejected in a corner of the coach. The towers of the castle of Thun vanish behind a hill. Later, far in the distance, Kleist's sister can see once more the beautiful lake. It is already quite chilly. Country houses appear. Well, well, such grand estates in such mountainous country? On and on. Everything flies past as you look to the side and drops behind, everything dances, circles, vanishes. Much is already hidden under the autumn's veil, and everything is a little golden in the little sunlight which pierces the clouds. Such gold, how it shimmers there, still to be found only in the dirt. Hills, scarps, valleys, churches, villages, people staring, children, trees, wind, clouds, stuff and nonsense—is all this anything special? Isn't it all rubbish, quotidian stuff? Kleist sees nothing. He is dreaming of clouds and of images and slightly of kind, comforting, caressing human hands. How do you feel? asks his sister. Kleist's mouth puckers, and he would like to give her a little smile. He succeeds, but with an effort. It is as if he has a block of stone to lift from his mouth before he can smile.

His sister cautiously plucks up the courage to speak of his taking on some practical activity soon. He nods, he is himself of the same opinion. Music and radiant shafts of light flicker about his senses. As a matter of fact, if he admits it quite frankly to himself, he feels quite well now; in pain, but well at the same time. Something hurts him, yes, really, quite correct, but not in the chest, not in the lungs either, or in the head, what? Nowhere at all? Well, not quite, a little, somewhere so that one cannot quite precisely tell where it is. Which means: it's nothing to speak of. He says something, and then come moments when he is outright happy as a child, and then of course the girl makes a rather severe, punitive face, just to show him a little how very strangely he does fool around with his life. The girl is a Kleist and has enjoyed an education, exactly what her brother has wanted to throw overboard. At heart she is naturally glad that he is feeling better. On and on, well well, what a journey it is. But finally one has to let it go, this stagecoach, and last of all one can permit oneself the observation that on the front of the villa where Kleist lived there hangs a marble plaque which indicates who lived and worked there. Travellers who intend to tour the Alps can read it, the children of Thun read it and spell it out, letter by letter, and then look questioning into each other's eyes. A Jew can read it, a Christian too, if he has the time and if his train is not leaving that very instant, a Turk, a swallow, insofar as she is interested, I also, I can read it again if I like. Thun stands at the entrance to the Bernese Oberland and is visited every year by thousands of foreigners. I know the region a little perhaps, because I worked as a clerk in a brewery there. The region is considerably more beautiful than I have been able to describe here, the lake is twice as blue, the sky three times as beautiful. Thun had a trade fair, I cannot say exactly but I think four years ago.

1913

Ed and the Movies

ROBERT GLÜCK

Seven on a warm June evening. The glossy light is full, the shadows are mild. Little brown birds make thin music, weak metallic trills. I'm walking through Ed's garden to his front door. It's overgrown and orderly, the smell of damp earth and heavy roses. There are fronds and branches to duck, red and green marble-sized apples growing out of their flowers on espaliered trees. Something in pots, and the brugmansia, night-scented trumpets, sweet and sinister. I climb the wooden steps. The porch light is on already. I'm empty handed.

No, I hold the string of a white pastry box heavy with two lemon tarts and two chocolate éclairs that satisfy my greed under the pretense of fattening Ed up. He'll probably eat one bite. I feel sleepy and itchy as though some emotional demand will be made, and what will I do then? I sense his death behind the door. I don't need to knock, he buzzed me in at the gate. The door swings open, he's very animated. Would you rather see me lifeless, he mocks. I hold up the pastry box and we moan with satisfaction. Death is too serious for us. I hug Ed and I want to say I love you but choke on the words as though I'm lying (I'm not).

I smell the Japanese half of Ed's childhood—soy and ginger. He intends to perfect a recipe for barbecued short ribs as he did for lemon bundt cake and sushi rice. It's Tuesday, my night with Ed, an ongoing joke of self-interest. I contribute to Ed's welfare by eating complicated meals involving the stove, the oven, and the microwave, that take Ed all day to prepare. The table is set, the food is a picture. Roasted pig—I start chewing before it is served, imagining fat. I can't get enough of the salty, burnt-sugar succulence. We dissect the flavors—more rice vinegar? ginger? Sophie, a small gray and brown tabby with a vexed expression, heedlessly scrolls against my shoes, burrows into my armpits, and vanishes.

Ed pokes at the meat with his chopsticks, takes a few bites of rice, praises himself for eating as much as he does. When we lived together, he could warm up to dinner with a double bag of potato chips. His voice is strong but the air is seeping out of his posture. He's down to 120 and wears a disorganized expression. He brings me up to date on the daily horrors. He has neuropathy—the nerves along the soles of his feet strum like electric guitars. Some fungus looks like fur in his throat. He started a new med. Dr. Owen said if the new drug causes pain in his muscles it means they are disintegrating, so his body started pulling apart like taffy as the doctor spoke. Owen added that if Ed feels pain in his liver he should call him at once. Ed tossed and turned all night, a finger jabbing him there. I confess I don't pay much attention to these sagas, which are, like his blathering when we were together, tedious and appalling. I hear myself recite the same stupid good advice I bestowed on Ed six years ago—and I hear my mother's voice in mine, calming, distancing. Ed's days are obviously precious but also lonely, threadbare, and twisted by fear.

What do I have to say? It's still the eighties. I feel so intensely that the party is happening elsewhere you could call my distraction a disease. That is, I feel like I'm reading a bad translation, with the knowledge that a better one exists. Distance installs itself in me, from thrillingly difficult technical vocabularies to the ascendency of the grid on, say, Calvin Klein sheets. Distance replaces the excesses and heartfelt essences of the seventies. Meanwhile, Ed sustains losses, giving up job, travel, movies—increased nakedness before death. He fights a hollowed out feeling, hard to portray, not dramatic.

Last winter, flattened under the buzzing lights, Owen told Ed he had a few months left. Ed went home and planted a hundred and thirty tulip bulbs. When he worked in the park, he would bonsai two hundred chrysanthemums for Easter. I'm bloated and wan. My life does not seem to apply and resists being shaped into anecdotes. Striving seems vulgar. I've eaten too much fat. While Ed talks I actually dream for a few seconds: I can't find my pen, and when I do it's on the kitchen table laid out between knife and spoon. Eating words and writing dinner. My dream sees me this way.

What am I leaving out? I remind myself to tape some conversations with Ed. Is that too gruesome? Half asleep, I brew strawberry tea for Ed and black tea for myself in the blue and white spongeware mugs that belonged to Ed and me when we were lovers. I'm almost taking them down from my own cupboard. The clear flavor of the tea is so welcome that some of me goes into it. Ed opens a window—I'm surprised by his initiative because I expect nothing from anyone. He actually does eat his share of the pastry, which is a satisfaction. "You never cooked like this when we were together," I complain good-naturedly.

As though explaining, Ed says, "Remember Marty?"

"?"

"Who lived next door?"

"That greasy little guy who always wore the same sportcoat?" I'm surprised Ed knows his name.

"We had sex. He'd just finished eating a can of sardines." Ed exhales to show the sardines swarming in Marty's breath.

I'm laughing and stung by this thirteen-year-old infidelity. I feel it more deeply because I'm single again. Denny and I broke up two years ago and my insecurity has new life. I experience my only moments of hope when I think of him. How to extinguish the useless surges? The action of the disease makes Ed's body attractive to me again. Is my love for him realer than I know? I attributed intention to his beauty because it had power over me. I remember the tenderness of snuggling in bed, soft cotton t-shirts and naked below—the cotton erotic, the hot and cold of train stations, a mix of directions. Ed replies with a look, What do you see? The face that detained me for so many years. Galaxies.

Why is Ed telling me about Marty? Ed was not confined to beauty and safety. I used him to experience risk, as I do in this story. The rough desires passed around at night by guys in a park or an alley. I'll bet Marty is where Ed discovered rimming. One morning Ed seemed to know all about it—what a surprise *that* was. Pleasure hidden like treasure in that scary place. I hid my face in simple justice of representation and my body made noises that meant it had instincts I'd never considered, like a school of salmon migrating up my butt.

These carnal updates from Ed and his primeval romps give our marriage a weird posthumous life. Since we are on the subject, I remind Ed of the evening fifteen years earlier when I cooked an elaborate birthday dinner for him. He turned up around midnight, explaining without remorse that he had been patiently guiding Sean into bed, a straight friend he was "liberating." "Having a reason doesn't mean anything," I cried. I blinked like a flustered professor and my body stuttered. Ed laughed in alarm and mimicked my frantic gesture. Then he offered, "You're just a victim of circumstance."

Ed laughs and says, "Well, weren't you?" He places a buttery crumb on a desiccated lip. He tastes, separating the flavors into a panorama. I ask him if he's painting. "Every morning from my studio I see a nanny push a buggy up the hill. I think she's Nicaraguan. She looks really young. She puts the brake on the buggy, climbs a long set of stairs, unlocks the door, and then goes down for the baby. That buggy points right down the hill and it's held in place by a thin piece of aluminum. Every day I expect the baby to go flying down the street into traffic."

We share an expression of horror. Ed lives on a very steep hill down which the buggy already careens. I say, "Someone has to tell that woman!"

Ed solemnly agrees. "One sentence could save that child's life."

"But Ed, why don't you tell her?" I feel a surge of relief—finally I can save someone's life. "All you have to do is walk across the street and tell her!"

It's so easy, but Ed has a question. "You think *I* should tell her?"

"Certainly, tomorrow morning."

Ed's head falls forward, his eyes pop and his jaw drops in amazement. Once I thought that was gay body language, but then I learned it's Japanese.

"Do you know how *sick* I am?" He's thinking, Why should all of civilization rise to protect that stupid baby?

In self-defense I think, You are well enough to cook dinner, to paint, to dig in your garden. "You could do it—it's your responsibility—as a neighbor. Ed, you still go out all the time." I blanch at the word still.

Ed's really angry. I'm a whirlwind in his head. The baby I can't save will not grant me permission to save some other life. His face is rigid and his mouth works on its own. "*I* am not responsible for that baby. Don't *I* have enough to worry about? *I* don't know that baby. *I* don't know those people. I am trying to stay *alive*!"

I grin in desolation. Ed is slightly revolting—I remember the absorbing spectacle of that jaw working against me, a perpetual motion of amazing insult, the smashed furniture, the wonder I felt when his fury jumped a quantum level, beyond caring, heedless. His thin body or anything could be thrown onto the blaze. I know when I'm licked. Giving up is hard work. The other baby must live or die without us. The buggy plummets and I lack the willpower to alter its course. I picture Ed by his window, the witness of this drama which inspires no call to action.

Like most of the world, I watch TV to be somewhere else without exerting myself. Exertion is the only way to go somewhere else, so dissatisfaction builds up. It's hard not to be bitter overall, as though I'd actually seen all those daytime talk shows. The entire message of TV is that life is not fair, more daydream than nightdream, yet the victim has his faults.

Not so with Ed—when we were together we watched TV with joy. In the early seventies, a cousin took pity on us and bought us a little black-and-white Zenith. We watched it through the night in Ed's studio. Ed painted and I kept him company. I am describing hours of perfect contentment. We liked Fred Astaire and musicals in general, but horror movies were even more histrionic. Ed and I felt delectation for these images of mayhem.

In Ed's bedroom, light is a translucent rectangle even though it's almost nine. The white glass arrests dappled shadows. Ed lies under the heavy indigo blanket, wasting; I lie on top, succulent. I'm happy to be lying down and I feel perfectly relaxed on Daniel's side of the bed. The disease leads some of us into a deeper engagement with the world. Denny became a science writer for *AIDS Treatment News*, and Loring joined Gran Fury. (At Bo Houston's funeral, his mother says, "Thank you so much," as though *I'd* done anything, and before I can stop myself, I say, "Thank *you*," as though *she'd* done anything.) An epidemic is like a mystery with heroes and villains, but I drift from my bedroom to Ed's bedroom, where light falls through frosted glass in a certain way. Above us the screen doles out images we love: the pre-WWII unknown lurches basso profundo through shadows and dry ice; the supersized zoo of spiders, locusts, snakes, ants, and lizards climbs out of the squashed air of the 50's desert. Ed and I love bad horror films for the lyricism of their failed effects. We must be among the few to have *twice* seen *Curucu, Beast of the Amazon*, a film that couldn't afford a visible monster or even gore. Branches twitch on the jungle trail, the mike slides into view, the victim screams from off-screen. Its very artificiality makes *Curucu* a convincing exploration of the afterlife, like a church service.

Tonight we watch a Mario Bava film in which moist decomposition replaces the genre's earlier effects, as though a horror of decay is more germane to the present. It's weird to be watching corpses rock back and forth in their own putrescence while lying next to Ed. The monster shows the world what she is: she throws open her robe with a triumphant expression to reveal a red chest cavity packed with roiling white maggots. Because of this image, I don't look Ed in the eye, as though I'd accidentally seen something too personal. What does he make of the skeletons with rags of flesh? I am the only one who can ask him this question so I do. He rolls his head on the pillow and reminds me in a mild voice that he will be cremated, and that decay is not the same as death. He says, "My death is an emptiness that I can't fill." I am relieved, but why? We both know Ed will soon be reduced to ash. He's dying in stop action like a good make-up job: the chaotic expression, the skeletal jeer, the pumpkin head wobbling with bon vivance on the broomstick neck, the pinched nose, the eyebrows pulled back, the eyes starved and hurt.

The monsters rise up while Ed and I sink into the pillows. But horror movies are actually comedies because death is reversible. Or it's a consummation: the one taken by the monster experiences the full extent of his death. In his last scream, the victim faces the monster and dredges horror to the limit. Like a sexual consummation, he groans from the deepest place where his body (the world) begins.

Four times over

SALLIE FULLERTON

It is to be perfect. The body (a burden) is imperfect because it fluctuates. In it I place a stack a jar of something then, heavy enough I walk from it.

Out here there is nothing at all no noise only a peephole (privacy no pleasure) and a ring of mute tones. How does anyone get anything done anymore?
how does anyone write from anywhere else?

Sit down and consider It's the difference a sound makes turning over into day it's the remainder of what you ate yesterday its all the pennies you can fit in your little girl pockets it's beating your cheek into a pillow until something spills.

I see you and I am getting closer

October, you are getting soft in your old age
even the sight of an insect
brings you to tears.
You cannot tell if crying is good behavior
Let's make a raft together let's make
a calm memory – No.

Out of kindness, I gave you a window.
You see the outside is full of parts –
the sight itself could make the skin shrivel
like stone fruit – getting sweeter
and sweeter.

October
sober you believe paper to be made
of leaves and those fallen wings
leaf-like
to be important
correspondence.

Strain

It's a chain link
    all the times I told myself to
dig in and forced
    a simpler phrase

my muscles are sore and
stringent and you ask me
what the hell this means

it's a system of
grabs and takes

eventually

you learn to move in tune to
smaller steps.

A night falls
on you like
a body

and exhales.

Yesterday I went to him full of dismay

RUMI

Translated by Brad Gooch and Maryam Mortaz

Yesterday I went to him full of dismay.
He sat silently, not asking what was wrong.

I looked at him, waiting for him to ask,
“How were you yesterday without my luminous face?”

My friend instead was looking at the ground.
Meaning to say, Be like the ground, humble
    and wordless.

I bowed and kissed the ground.
Meaning to say, I am like the ground, drunk
    and amazed.

Manual for General Housework

SAIDIYA HARTMAN

Manual: of or pertaining to the hand or hands, done or performed with the hands. Now especially of (physical) labor, an occupation, etc., as opposed to mental, theoretical. Manual as distinguished from the mind and the intellectual. Manual: as of a weapon, tool, implement, etc.; that is used or worked with the hand or hands. Actually in one's hands, not merely prospective. (Manual: short for manual exercises, i.e., physical labor, and not the exercise of reason or imagination.) A tool or an object, within one's grasp, not speculative, not a proposal for black female genius. The use of the body as tool or instrument. Of occupation or possession. Able to have in one's own hands, as in possession is three-fifths of the law, as in possession makes you three-fifths of a human, as in property handled by another. Also to be possessed. To be handled as if owned, annexed, branded, invaded, ingested, not autonomous. Manual: to be wielded by another, to be wielded on a whim; to be wielded as an exercise of another's will, to be severed from one's own will or motives or desires. Manual: as opposed to mental, as in not an exercise of rational faculties. As opposed to the formation of critical reflections; as opposed to contemplation of the self or the world. A method of operating or working. A function. Short for manual exercise. Short for manual tool.

Manual: as opposed to automatic, as opposed to starting or functioning by itself and for itself, as opposed to deliberation and judgment, as in the need for direction, as in the imposition of a mistress or master.

Manual: As of pertaining to the hand or hands. The hands to be outmoded or made obsolete by the machine. Of or pertaining to the mule more than the machine. Worked with the hands, finished with the hands. No more than a pair of hands. Hands cracked and swollen from harsh soap and ammonia. Hands burnt taking the pies out of the oven. Hands stiff and disfigured from wringing cold sheets and towels outside in the winter before hanging to dry on the line. Hands, no longer yours, contracted, owned, and directed by another, like a tool or object. The hands that handle you. The hands up the dress, the hands on your ass, the hands that pull down your undergarments, the hands that pin you to the floor. The hands that pay you two dollars for the day or thirteen dollars for the week. Manual: as of subject to use, made a tool, handled, grasped, palmed, slapped, fondled, hugged, harassed, caressed; as of pertaining to the hand.

Manual: as opposed to contemplation, or theory. As opposed to the use of the intellect. As opposed to looking, viewing, contemplating. As opposed to thinking, reflecting, scheming, plotting, planning, weighing, brooding. The use of the hands as opposed to a conception or mental scheme or paradigm. Manual: the concrete, the physical, the embodied as opposed to abstract knowledge and the formulation of it. As opposed to reason. Manual: as pertaining to ignorance, obtuseness, stupidity, and as opposed to erudition.

As related to handle, as to be handled, as to be handled with no regard, as to be handled as a tool or instrument; as to be handled like a slave, like a wench, like a bitch, like a whore, like a nigger. Handled as pertaining to that part of the thing which is to be grasped by the hand in using it or moving it. To be grasped by the hand or sometimes by the neck, the ass, the throat. Colloquial: to fly off the handle; to go into a rage; to fuck shit up. Figurative: that by which something is or may be taken hold of; one of two or more ways in which a thing may be taken or apprehended. To manipulate, manage; to subject to the action of hands, to touch or feel with hands. As opposed to: Don't touch me. As pertaining to: Hands up, don't shoot. To manage, conduct, direct, control. To be handled by men, to be manhandled, to be seized by men, to be used by men, to be used up by men. Handled, as related to use of the thing, to do something with the tool, as opposed to directed by will and desire; as opposed to consent, as opposed to leave me the fuck alone.

To deal with, to treat as you wish, to serve, to use, to accumulate, to expend, to deplete.

Manual: as related to a book, etc.—of the nature of a manual intended to be kept at hand for reference. A concise treatise, an abridgment, a handbook.

Excerpt from *Molloy*

SAMUEL BECKETT

I am in my mother's room. It's I who live there now. I don't know how I got there. Perhaps in an ambulance, certainly a vehicle of some kind. I was helped. I'd never have got there alone. There's this man who comes every week. Perhaps I got here thanks to him. He says not. He gives me money and takes away the pages. So many pages, so much money. Yes, I work now, a little like I used to, except that I don't know how to work any more. That doesn't matter apparently. What I'd like now is to speak of the things that are left, say my goodbyes, finish dying. They don't want that. Yes, there is more than one, apparently. But it's always the same one that comes. You'll do that later, he says. Good. The truth is I haven't much will left. When he comes for the fresh pages he brings back the previous week's. They are marked with signs I don't understand. Anyway I don't read them. When I've done nothing he gives me nothing, he scolds me. Yet I don't work for money. For what then? I don't know. The truth is I don't know much. For example my mother's death. Was she already dead when I came? Or did she only die later? I mean enough to bury. I don't know. Perhaps they haven't buried her yet. In any case I have her room. I sleep in her bed. I piss and shit in her pot. I have taken her place. I must resemble her more and more. All I need now is a son. Perhaps I have one somewhere. But I think not. He would be old now, nearly as old as myself. It was a little chambermaid. It wasn't true love. The true love was in another. We'll come to that. Her name? I've forgotten it again. It seems to me sometimes that I even knew my son, that I helped him. Then I tell myself it's impossible. It's impossible I could ever have helped anyone. I've forgotten how to spell too, and half the words. That doesn't matter apparently. Good. He's a queer one the one who comes to see me. He comes every Sunday apparently. The other days he isn't free. He's always thirsty. It was he told me I'd begun all wrong, that I should have begun differently. He must be right. I began at the beginning, like an old ballocks, can you imagine that? Here's my beginning. Because they're keeping it apparently. I took a lot of trouble with it. Here it is. It gave me a lot of trouble. It was the beginning, do you understand? Whereas now it's nearly the end. Is what I do now any better? I don't know. That's beside the point. Here's my beginning. It must mean something, or they wouldn't keep it. Here it is.

This time, then once more I think, then perhaps a last time, then I think it'll be over, with that world too. Premonition of the last but one but one. All grows dim. A little more and you'll go blind. It's in the head. It doesn't work any more, it says, I don't work any more. You go dumb as well and sounds fade. The threshold scarcely crossed that's how it is. It's the head. It must have had enough. So that you say, I'll manage this time, then perhaps once more, then perhaps a last time, then nothing more. You are hard set to formulate this thought, for it is one, in a sense. Then you try to pay attention, to consider with attention all those dim things, saying to yourself, laboriously, It's my fault. Fault? That was the word. But what fault? It's not goodbye, and what magic in those dim things to which it will be time enough, when next they pass, to say goodbye. For you must say goodbye, it would be madness not to say goodbye, when the time comes. If you think of the forms and light of other days it is without regret. But you seldom think of them, with what would you think of them? I don't know. People pass too, hard to distinguish from yourself. That is discouraging. So I saw A and C going slowly towards each other, unconscious of what they were doing. It was on a road remarkably bare, I mean without hedges or ditches or any kind of edge, in the country, for cows were chewing in enormous fields, lying and standing, in the evening silence. Perhaps I'm inventing a little, perhaps embellishing, but on the whole that's the way it was. They chew, swallow, then after a short pause effortlessly bring up the next mouthful. A neck muscle stirs and the jaws begin to grind again. But perhaps I'm remembering things. The road, hard and white, seared the tender pastures, rose and fell at the whim of hills and hollows. The town was not far. It was two men, unmistakably, one small and one tall. They had left the town, first one, then the other, and then the first, weary or remembering a duty, had retraced his steps. The air was sharp for they wore greatcoats. They looked alike, but no more than others do. At first a wide space lay between them. They couldn't have seen each other, even had they raised their heads and looked about, because of this wide space, and then because of the undulating land, which caused the road to be in waves, not high, but high enough, high enough. But the moment came when together they went down into the same trough and in this trough finally met. To say they knew each other, no, nothing warrants it. But perhaps at the sound of their steps, or warned by some obscure instinct, they raised their heads and observed each other, for a good fifteen paces, before they stopped, breast to breast. Yes; they did not pass each other by, but halted, face to face, as in the country, of an evening, on a deserted road, two wayfaring strangers will, without there being anything extraordinary about it. But they knew each other perhaps. Now in any case they do, now I think they will know each other, greet each other, even in the depths of the town. They turned towards the sea which, far in the east, beyond the fields, loomed high in the waning sky, and exchanged a few words. Then each went on his way. Each went on his way, A back towards the town, C on by ways he seemed hardly to know, or not at all, for he went with uncertain step and often stopped to look about him, like someone trying to fix landmarks in his mind, for one day perhaps he may have to retrace his steps, you never know. The treacherous hills where fearfully he ventured were no doubt only known to him from afar, seen perhaps from his bedroom window or from the summit of a monument which, one black day, having nothing in particular to do and turning to height for solace, he had paid his few coppers to climb, slower and slower, up the winding stones. From there he must have seen it all, the plain, the sea, and then these selfsame hills that some call mountains, indigo in places in the evening light, their serried ranges crowding to the skyline, cloven with hidden valleys that the eye divines from sudden shifts of colour and then from other signs for which there are no words, nor even thoughts. But all are not divined, even from that height, and often where only one escarpment is discerned, and one crest, in reality there are two, two escarpments, two crests, riven by a valley. But now he knows these hills, that is to say he knows them better, and if ever again he sees them from afar it will be I think with other eyes, and not only that but the within, all that inner space one never sees, the brain and heart and other caverns where thought and feeling dance their sabbath, all that too quite differently disposed. He looks old and it is a sorry sight to see him solitary after so many years, so many days and nights unthinkingly given to that rumour rising at birth and even earlier, What shall I do? What shall I do? now low, a murmur, now precise as the headwaiter's And to follow? and often rising to a scream. And in the end, or almost, to be abroad alone, by unknown ways, in the gathering night, with a stick. It was a stout stick, he used it to thrust himself onward, or as a defence, when the time came, against dogs and marauders. Yes, night was gathering, but the man was innocent, greatly innocent, he had nothing to fear, though he went in fear, he had nothing to fear, there was nothing they could do to him, or very little. But he can't have known it. I wouldn't know it myself, if I thought about it. Yes, he saw himself threatened, his body threatened, his reason threatened, and perhaps he was, perhaps they were, in spite of his innocence. What business has innocence here? What relation to the innumerable spirits of darkness? It's not clear. It seemed to me he wore a cocked hat. I remember being struck by it, as I wouldn't have been for example by a cap or by a bowler. I watched him recede, overtaken (myself) by his anxiety, at least by an anxiety which was not necessarily his, but of which as it were he partook. Who knows if it wasn't my own anxiety overtaking him. He hadn't seen me. I was perched higher than the road's highest point and flattened what is more against a rock the same colour as myself, that is grey. The rock he probably saw. He gazed around as if to engrave the landmarks on his memory and must have seen the rock in the shadow of which I crouched like Belacqua, or Sordello, I forget. But a man, a fortiori myself, isn't exactly a landmark, because. I mean if by some strange chance he were to pass that way again, after a long lapse of time, vanquished, or to look for some lost thing, or to destroy something, his eyes would search out the rock, not the haphazard in its shadow of that unstable fugitive thing, still living flesh. No, he certainly didn't see me, for the reasons I've given and then because he was in no humour for that, that evening, no humour for the living, but rather for all that doesn't stir, or stirs so slowly that a child would scorn it, let alone an old man. However that may be, I mean whether he saw me or whether he didn't, I repeat I watched him recede, at grips (myself) with the temptation to get up and follow him, perhaps even to catch up with him one day, so as to know him better, be myself less lonely. But in spite of my soul's leap out to him, at the end of its elastic, I saw him only darkly, because of the dark and then because of the terrain, in the folds of which he disappeared from time to time, to re-emerge further on, but most of all I think because of other things calling me and towards which too one after the other my soul was straining, wildly. I mean of course the fields, whitening under the dew, and the animals, ceasing from wandering and settling for the night, and the sea, of which nothing, and the sharpening line of crests, and the sky where without seeing them I felt the first stars tremble, and my hand on my knee and above all the other wayfarer, A or C, I don't remember, going resignedly home. Yes, towards my hand also, which my knee felt tremble and of which my eyes saw the wrist only, the heavily veined back, the pallid rows of knuckles. But that is not, I mean my hand, what I wish to speak of now, everything in due course, but A or C returning to the town he had just left. But after all what was there particularly urban in his aspect? He was bare-headed, wore sand-shoes, smoked a cigar. He moved with a kind of loitering indolence which rightly or wrongly seemed to me expressive. But all that proved nothing, refuted nothing. Perhaps he had come from afar, from the other end of the island even, and was approaching the town for the first time or returning to it after a long absence. A little dog followed him, a pomeranian I think, but I don't think so. I wasn't sure at the time and I'm still not sure, though I've hardly thought about it. The little dog followed wretchedly, after the fashion of pomeranians, stopping, turning in slow circles, giving up and then, a little further on, beginning all over again. Constipation is a sign of good health in pomeranians. At a given moment, pre-established if you like, I don't much mind, the gentleman turned back, took the little creature in his arms, drew the cigar from his lips and buried his face in the orange fleece, for it was a gentleman, that was obvious. Yes, it was an orange pomeranian, the less I think of it the more certain I am. And yet. But would he have come from afar, bareheaded, in sand-shoes, smoking a cigar, followed by a pomeranian? Did he not seem rather to have issued from the ramparts, after a good dinner, to take his dog and himself for a walk, like so many citizens, dreaming and farting, when the weather is fine? But was not perhaps in reality the cigar a cutty, and were not the sand-shoes boots, hobnailed, dust-whitened, and what prevented the dog from being one of those stray dogs that you pick up and take in your arms, from compassion or because you have long been straying with no other company than the endless roads, sands, shingle, bogs and heather, than this nature answerable to another court, than at long intervals the fellow-convict you long to stop, embrace, suck, suckle and whom you pass by, with hostile eyes, for fear of his familiarities? Until the day when, your endurance gone, in this world for you without arms, you catch up in yours the first mangy cur you meet, carry it the time needed for it to love you and you it, then throw it away. Perhaps he had come to that, in spite of appearances. He disappeared, his head on his chest, the smoking object in his hand. Let me try and explain. From things about to disappear I turn away in time. To watch them out of sight, no, I can't do it. It was in this sense he disappeared. Looking away I thought of him, saying, He is dwindling, dwindling. I knew what I meant. I knew I could catch him, lame as I was. I had only to want to. And yet no, for I did want to. To get up, to get down on the road, to set off hobbling in pursuit of him, to hail him, what could be easier? He hears my cries, turns, waits for me. I am up against him, up against the dog, gasping, between my crutches. He is a little frightened of me, a little sorry for me, I disgust him not a little. I am not a pretty sight, I don't smell good. What is it I want? Ah that tone I know, compounded of pity, of fear, of disgust. I want to see the dog, see the man, at close quarters, know what smokes, inspect the shoes, find out other things. He is kind, tells me of this and that and other things, whence he comes, whither he goes. I believe him, I know it's my only chance to—my only chance, I believe all I'm told, I've disbelieved only too much in my long life, now I swallow everything, greedily. What I need now is stories, it took me a long time to know that, and I'm not sure of it. There I am then, informed as to certain things, knowing certain things about him, things I didn't know, things I had craved to know, things I had never thought of. What rigmarole. I am even capable of having learnt what his profession is, I who am so interested in professions. And to think I try my best not to talk about myself. In a moment I shall talk about the cows, about the sky, if I can. There I am then, he leaves me, he's in a hurry. He didn't seem to be in a hurry, he was loitering, I've already said so, but after three minutes of me he is in a hurry, he has to hurry. I believe him. And once again I am I will not say alone, no, that's not like me, but, how shall I say, I don't know, restored to myself, no, I never left myself, free, yes, I don't know what that means but it's the word I mean to use, free to do what, to do nothing, to know, but what, the laws of the mind perhaps, of my mind, that for example water rises in proportion as it drowns you and that you would do better, at least no worse, to obliterate texts than to blacken margins, to fill in the holes of words till all is blank and flat and the whole ghastly business looks like what it is, senseless, speechless, issueless misery. So I doubtless did better, at least no worse, not to stir from my observation post. But instead of observing I had the weakness to return in spirit to the other, the man with the stick. Then the murmurs began again. To restore silence is the role of objects. I said, Who knows if he hasn't simply come out to take the air, relax, stretch his legs, cool his brain by stamping the blood down to his feet, so as to make sure of a good night, a joyous awakening, an enchanted morrow. Was he carrying so much as a scrip? But the way of walking, the anxious looks, the club, could these be reconciled with one's conception of what is called a little turn? But the hat, a town hat, an old-fashioned town hat, which the least gust would carry far away. Unless it was attached under the chin, by means of a string or an elastic. I took off my hat and looked at it. It is fastened, it has always been fastened, to my buttonhole, always the same buttonhole, at all seasons, by a long lace. I am still alive then. That may come in useful. The hand that held the hat I thrust as far as possible from me and moved in an arc, to and fro. As I did so, I watched the lapel of my greatcoat and saw it open and close. I understand now why I never wore a flower in my buttonhole, though it was large enough to hold a whole nosegay. My buttonhole was set aside for my hat. It was my hat that I beflowered. But it is neither of my hat nor of my greatcoat that I hope to speak at present, it would be premature. Doubtless I shall speak of them later, when the time comes to draw up the inventory of my goods and possessions. Unless I lose them between now and then. But even lost they will have their place, in the inventory of my possessions. But I am easy in my mind, I shall not lose them. Nor my crutches, I shall not lose my crutches either. But I shall perhaps one day throw them away. I must have been on the top, or on the slopes, of some considerable eminence, for otherwise how could I have seen, so far away, so near at hand, so far beneath, so many things, fixed and moving. But what was an eminence doing in this land with hardly a ripple? And I, what was I doing there, and why come? These are things that we shall try and discover. But these are things we must not take seriously. There is a little of everything, apparently, in nature, and freaks are common. And I am perhaps confusing several different occasions, and different times, deep down, and deep down is my dwelling, oh not deepest down, somewhere between the mud and the scum. And perhaps it was A one day at one place, then C another at another, then a third the rock and I, and so on for the other components, the cows, the sky, the sea, the mountains. I can't believe it. No, I will not lie, I can easily conceive it. No matter, no matter, let us go on, as if all arose from one and the same weariness, on and on heaping up and up, until there is no room, no light, for any more. What is certain is that the man with the stick did not pass by again that night, because I would have heard him, if he had. I don't say I would have seen him, I say I would have heard him. I sleep little and that little by day. Oh not systematically, in my life without end I have dabbled with every kind of sleep, but at the time now coming back to me I took my doze in the daytime and, what is more, in the morning. Let me hear nothing of the moon, in my night there is no moon, and if it happens that I speak of the stars it is by mistake.

Excerpt from *Times Square Red, Times Square Blue*

SAMUEL R. DELANY

§1.4. The betraying signs that one discourse has displaced or transformed into another are often the smallest rhetorical shifts. A temporal moment (and a sociological location) in the transformation from a homosexual discourse to a gay discourse may be signaled by the appearance in the 1969 fall issues of the *Village Voice* of the locution "coming out to" one's (straight) friends, coworkers, and family (a verbal act directed toward straights) and its subsequent displacement of the demotic locution "coming out into" (gay) society—a metaphor for one's first major gay sexual act. Between the two locutions lie Stonewall and the post-Stonewall activities of the gay liberation movement. Equally such a sign might be seen to lie at another moment, at another location, in the changeover from "that's such a camp" to "that's camp." The intervening event there is Susan Sontag's 1964 *Partisan Review* essay, "Notes on Camp." I have written of how a shift in postal discourse may be signed by the rhetorical shift between "she would not receive his letters" and "she would not open his letter." What intervened here was the 1840 introduction of the postage stamp, which changed letter writing from an art and entertainment paid for by the receiver to a form of vanity publishing paid for by the sender. (There *was* no junk mail before 1840.) One might detect a shift in the discourse of literature by the changeover from "George is in literature" (when literature was a profession) to "George's library contains mostly history and literature" (when literature became a class of texts). The explosion of print in the 1880s, occasioned by the typewriter and the linotype, intervened. The shift from landlord visits to superintendents in charge of repairs is signaled by the rhetorical shift between "the landlord saw to the repairs" as a literal statement and "the landlord saw to the repairs" as a metaphor. I say "shifts," but these rhetorical pairings are much better looked at, on the level of discourse, as rhetorical collisions. The sign that a discursive collision has occurred is that the former meaning has been forgotten and the careless reader, not alert to the details of the changed social context, reads the older rhetorical figure as if it were the newer.

As are the space of the unconscious and the space of discourse, the space where the class war occurs as such is, in its pure form, imaginary—imaginary *not* in the Lacanian sense but rather in the mathematical sense. (In the Lacanian sense, those spaces are specifically Symbolic.) Imaginary numbers—those involved with *i*, the square root of minus-one—do not exist. But they have measurable and demonstrable effects on the real (i.e., political) materiality of science and technology. Similarly, the structures, conflicts, and displacements that occur in the unconscious, the class war, and the space of discourse are simply too useful to ignore in explaining what goes on in the world we live in, unto two men yelling in the hall, one a landlord and one a tenant, if not mayhem out on the streets themselves, or the visible changes in a neighborhood, like Times Square or, indeed, the Upper West Side, over a decade or so, and the specificities of rhetorical shift.

(Repeatedly Foucault described discourse, or at least a part of it, as "an" unconscious. In a 1968 interview ["Interview with Michel Foucault" (*Dits et écrits*, 654)] he said, "In a positive manner we can say that structuralism investigates an unconscious. It is the unconscious structure of language, of the literary work, and of knowledge that one is trying at this moment to illuminate." In his 1970 preface to the English edition of *Les Mots et les choses*, he wrote that his work intended to "bring to light a *positive unconscious* of knowledge: a level that eludes the consciousness of the scientist and yet is part of scientific discourse"; italics in original.)

Often, like many contemporary theorists, I have wondered whether the fundamental spaces of all three aren't one, as the death of God, the Author, and Man each has clarified another of the axes describing that space.

* * *

§1.5. Starting in 1985 for the first time, in the name of "safe sex," New York City began specifically to criminalize every individual sex act by name, from masturbation to vaginal intercourse, whether performed with a condom or not—a legal situation that has catastrophic ramifications we may not crawl out from under for a long, long time. This is a legal move that arguably puts gay liberation, for example, back to a point notably before Stonewall—and doesn't do much for heterosexual freedom either.

This is a rhetorical change that may well adhere to an extremely important discursive intervention in the legal contouring of social practices whose ramifications, depending on the development and the establishment of new social practices that promote communication between the classes (specifically sexual and sex-related), are hard to foresee in any detail.

§1.6. An important point: I do not think it is in any way nostalgic to say that under such a social practice as my grandmother knew, both landlord and tenant maintained better relations than I do with my landlord today. The practice of landlord visits was a social arena of communication, which, when utilized fully, meant that both landlord and tenant had to expend more time, energy, and money in order to maintain a generally higher standard of living for the tenant and a generally higher level of property upkeep, which restricted the abuse of that property for the landlord. On both tenant and landlord, greater restrictions obtained as to what was expected and what was not. The practice eroded when the money was no longer there, when the time and energy had to be turned, by both, to other things, and when practices formerly unacceptable to both had, now, to be accepted, so that the visits became a futile annoyance to both sides and were dropped.

But the establishment of, say, tenant associations—at which landlords are occasionally invited to speak and meet with their tenants—*begins* to fill the vacuum in the array of social practices that erosion leaves.

At the same time, they do not fill it in the same way.

The fact that such relations may have been more pleasant does not, however, mean that those relations were somehow more authentic than mine to Mr. Buchbinder. All that relative pleasantness suggests is a confirmation of my primary and secondary theses, which *are* about pleasure, after all—pleasure in its most generalized form (though pleasure no less important or social for that): the pleasant.

§1.7. A recapitulation.

Given the mode of capitalism under which we live, life is at its most rewarding, productive, and pleasant when large numbers of people understand, appreciate, and seek out interclass contact and communication conducted in a mode of good will.

The class war raging constantly and often silently in the comparatively stabilized societies of the developed world perpetually works for the erosion of the social practices through which interclass communication takes place and of the institutions holding those practices stable, so that the new institutions must always be conceived and set in place to take over the jobs of those that are battered again and again till they are destroyed.

While the establishment and utilization of those institutions always involve social practices, the effects of my primary and secondary theses are regularly perceived at the level of discourse. Therefore, it is only by a constant renovation of the concept of discourse that society can maintain the most conscientious and informed field for both the establishment of those institutions and practices—a critique necessary if new institutions of any efficacy are to be established. At this level, in its largely stabilizing/destabilizing role, superstructure (and superstructure at its most oppositional) *can* impinge on infrastructure.

§1.8. So stated, these points appear harmless enough. Over the last decade and a half, however, a notion of safety has arisen, a notion that runs from safe sex (once it becomes anything more than making sure your partner uses a condom when you are anally penetrated by males of unknown HIV status, whether you are male or female) to safe neighborhoods, safe cities, and committed (i.e., safe) relationships, a notion that currently functions much the way the notion of "security" and "conformity" did in the fifties. As, in the name of "safety," society dismantles the various institutions that promote interclass communication, attempts to critique the way such institutions functioned in the past to promote their happier sides are often seen as, at best, nostalgia for an outmoded past and, at worst, a pernicious glorification of everything dangerous: unsafe sex, neighborhoods filled with undesirables (read "unsafe characters"), promiscuity, an attack on the family and the stable social structure, and dangerous, noncommitted, "unsafe" relationships—that is, psychologically "dangerous" relations, though the danger is rarely specified in any way other than to suggest its failure to conform to the ideal bourgeois marriage.

Such critiques are imperative, however, if we are ever to establish new institutions that will promote similar ends.

§2. The linear chain linkage into which the earlier practice of landlord visits with tenants might be said to have degenerated reminds us that the linear chain as an information conduit is a relatively artificial social form. Most social interchanges of information and material occur in various forms of social nets (as opposed to chains).

Generally speaking, in a net situation information comes from several directions and crosses various power boundaries, so that various processes—modulating, revisionary, additive, recursive, and corrective (all of them critical, each of them highlighting different aspects)—can compensate for the inevitable reductions that occur along the constitutive chains. Not all nets are, however, the same.

Social nets can be of more or less complexity, of greater or lesser density. When the net density is comparatively low, we find ourselves focusing on the contacts between individual net members and often ignoring the net-like structure in which the individual contacts occur. When the net density is high, we find ourselves more likely to focus on the overall network.

Starting from the above as the most arbitrary and provisional of observations, I will go on to discuss two modes of social net practice (and the discourses around them that allow them to be visible as such) that I designate as "contact" and "networking." Like all social practices they make/generate/create/sediment discourses, even as discourses create, individuate, and inform with value the material and social objects that facilitate and form the institutions that both support and contour these practices.

* * *

§2.1. Contact is the conversation that starts in the line at the grocery counter with the person behind you while the clerk is changing the paper roll in the cash register. It is the pleasantries exchanged with a neighbor who has brought their chair out to take some air on the stoop. It is the discussion that begins with the person next to you at a bar. It can be the conversation that starts with any number of semiofficials or service persons—mailman, policeman, librarian, store clerk, or counter person. As well, it can be two men watching each other masturbating together in the adjacent urinals of a public john—an encounter that, later, may or may not become a conversation. Very importantly, contact is also the intercourse—physical and conversational—that blooms in and as "casual sex" in public rest rooms, sex movies, public parks, singles bars, and sex clubs, on street corners with heavy hustling traffic, and in the adjoining motels or the apartments of one or another participant, from which nonsexual friendships and/or acquaintances lasting for decades or a lifetime may spring, not to mention the conversation of a john with a prostitute or hustler encountered on one or another street corner or in a bar—a relation that, a decade later, has devolved into a smile or a nod, even when (to quote Swinburne) "You have forgotten my kisses, / And I have forgotten your name." Mostly these contact encounters are merely pleasant chats, adding a voice to a face now and again encountered in the neighborhood. But I recall one such supermarket-line conversation with a woman who turned out to have done graduate work on the Russian poet Zinaida Hippius, just when I happened to be teaching Dmitri Merezhkovksy's Christ and Anti-Christ trilogy in a graduate seminar at the University of Massachusetts: Merezhkovsky was Hippius's husband, and I was able to get some interesting and pertinent information about the couple's wanderings in the early years of the century.

I have at least one straight male friend who on half a dozen occasions has gotten editorial jobs for women he first met and befriended while they were working as topless dancers in various strip clubs that put them on the fringe of the sex workers' service profession.

A young street hustler in the Forty-second Street area whom I knew (but was not a client of) introduced me to a new client of his once—a twenty-six-year-old lapsed Jesuit priest—for whom I shortly secured a job at a paperback publishing house, in much the same manner.

Another supermarket-line conversation was with a young man who was an aspiring director, looking for some science fiction stories to turn into brief teleplays. I was able to jot down for him a quick bibliography of young SF writers and short stories that he might pursue. Whether or not it came to anything, I have no way of knowing. But it was easy and fun.

Still another time, it was a young woman casting director who needed someone to play the small part of a fisherman in a film she was working on. She decided I would be perfect for it, and I found myself with a weekend acting job.

One Saturday morning in January '98, my vacuum cleaner shorted out and an hour later I set it on the street by the gate before the garbage cans for my building, after making a mental note to shop for a replacement that weekend. Forty minutes on, at my local copy center, I was getting a set of photocopies for an earlier draft of this very piece, when a broad-faced, gray-eyed Italian American in his late thirties, wearing a shiny red and blue jacket, wandered in: "Anyone wanna buy a wet-dry vacuum cleaner? Ten bucks." My first suspicion was that he was reselling the one I'd just abandoned. My second was that the one he was selling didn't work. A look disproved the first. Plugging his machine into an outlet in the shop's baseboard for a minute disproved the second. So I went home once more with a vacuum cleaner:

Contact.

Contact encounters so dramatic are rare—but real. The more ordinary sorts of contact yield *their* payoff in moments of crisis: When there is a fire in your building (of the sort I mentioned above), it may be the people who have been exchanging pleasantries with you for years who take you into their home for an hour or a day, or even overnight. Contact includes the good Samaritans at traffic accidents (the two women who picked me up and got me a cab when my cane gave way and I fell on the street, dislocating a finger), or even the neighbor who, when you've forgotten your keys at the office and are locked out of your apartment, invites you in for coffee and lets you use her phone to call a locksmith; or, as once happened to me in the mid-sixties when my then-neighborhood, the Lower East Side, was at its most neighborly and under the influence of the counterculture, a London guest arrived on Wednesday when I was out of town and expecting him on Thursday. Someone living across the street, who didn't know me at all, saw a stranger with two suitcases on my apartment stoop looking bewildered, invited him in to wait for me, then eventually put him up for a night until I returned.

A final example: my current lover of eight years and I first met when he was homeless and selling books from a blanket spread out on Seventy-second Street. Our two best friends for many years now are a male couple, one of whom I first met in an encounter, perhaps a decade ago, at the back of the now closed-down Variety Photoplays Movie Theater on Third Avenue just below Fourteenth Street. Outside my family, these are among the two most rewarding relationships I have: both began as cross-class contacts in a public space.

Visitors to New York might be surprised that such occurrences are central to my vision of the city at its healthiest.

Lifetime residents won't be.

Watching the metamorphosis of such vigil and concern into considered and helpful action is what gives one a faithful and loving attitude toward one's neighborhood, one's city, one's nation, the world.

I have taken "contact," both term and concept, from Jane Jacobs's instructive 1961 study, *The Death and Life of Great American Cities*. Jacobs describes contact as a fundamentally urban phenomenon and finds it necessary for everything from neighborhood safety to a general sense of social well-being. She sees it supported by a strong sense of private and public in a field of socioeconomic diversity that mixes living spaces with a variety of commercial spaces, which in turn must provide a variety of human services if contact is to function in a pleasant and rewarding manner. Jacobs mentions neither casual sex nor public sexual relations as part of contact—presumably because she was writing at a time when such things were not talked of or analyzed as elements contributing to an overall pleasurable social fabric. Today we can.

When social forces menace the distinction between private and public, people are most likely to start distrusting contact relations. In *The Death and Life of Great American Cities* (98–111), Jacobs analyzes how limited socioeconomic resources in the area around a public park (lack of restaurants, bathrooms, drugstores, and small shops) can make the mothers who use the playground and live near it feel that their privacy within their home is threatened—thus markedly changing their public attitude to interclass contact. Briefly, a park with no public eating spaces, restaurants, or small item shopping on its borders forces mothers who live adjacent to it and who thus use it the most to "share everything or nothing" in terms of offering facilities of bathroom use and the occasional cup of coffee to other mothers and their children who use the park but do not live so near. Because the local mothers feel they must offer these favors to whomever they are even civil with (since such services are not publicly available), they soon become extremely choosy and cliquish about whom they will even speak to. The feel of the park becomes exclusive and snobbish—and uncomfortable (and inconvenient) for mothers who, in carriage, dress, race, or class, do not fit a rigid social pattern.

Similarly, if *every* sexual encounter involves bringing someone back to your house, the general sexual activity in a city becomes anxiety-filled, class-bound, and choosy. This is precisely *why* public rest rooms, peep shows, sex movies, bars with grope rooms, and parks with enough greenery are necessary for a relaxed and friendly sexual atmosphere in a democratic metropolis.

Jacobs's analysis stops short of contact as a specifically stabilizing practice in interclass relations. She dismisses "pervert parks" as necessary social blights (largely understandable in the pre-Stonewall 1950s when she was collecting material for her book, but nevertheless unfortunate), though she *was* ready to acknowledge the positive roles winos and destitute alcoholics played in stabilizing the quality of neighborhood life at a *higher* level than the neighborhood would maintain without them.

I would recommend her analysis, though I would add that, like so much American thinking on the left, it lacks not so much a class analysis as an *interclass* analysis.*

---

* Astute as her analysis is, Jacobs still confuses contact with community. Urban contact is often at its most spectacularly beneficial when it occurs between members of *different* communities. That is why I maintain that interclass contact is even more important than intraclass contact.

Eventually we shall touch on—though we shall by no means exhaust—the topic of the menace of violence in some of these urban venues.

§2.2. Here is one of my favorite contact stories told me by a friend:

"I run annually in the Boston Marathon. I'm not a first-class runner, and my goal is to finish in the top hundred—last year I came in at 117th place—but I train regularly. Every morning for the first half of the year I take a ten-mile run. Then, as the marathon gets closer, I up it to twelve, fifteen, then twenty miles. One morning in March I was just starting my run across the Brooklyn Bridge, when I heard some woman scream. I looked around, and this fifteen- or sixteen-year-old kid had just snatched her pocketbook and was taking off. I called, 'Stay here, ma'am, I'll get that back for you,' turned around, and took off after him.

"It was a really interesting feeling, knowing as I ran after that kid that there was no way, unless he'd been in training for a marathon three years himself, he was going to outrun me. I stayed about five yards behind him. We were running around street corners there in the Heights. I didn't think he was going to make a full ten minutes, but he lasted for almost thirteen or fourteen. Finally when he was leaning against a wall, falling down on one knee, I went up to him, took the pocketbook out of his hand, gave him a slap on the back of his head, and said, 'Okay, now don't *do* that again!' Then I took off back to the bridge. It was almost twenty minutes later, and the woman was gone by then. But there was some identification in the pocketbook. I called her up and took it over to her that evening. She's a very interesting woman . . ."

Rare, heroic, and certainly not to be counted on, such contact nevertheless represents one of the gifts the human variety of the city can bestow.

§3.0. There is, of course, another way to meet people. It is called *networking*. Networking is what people have to do when those with like interests live too far apart to be thrown together in public spaces through chance and propinquity. Networking is what people in small towns have to do to establish any complex cultural life today.

But contemporary *networking* is notably different from *contact*.

At first one is tempted to set contact and networking in opposition. Networking tends to be professional and motive-driven. Contact tends to be more broadly social and appears random. Networking crosses class lines only in the most vigilant manner. Contact regularly crosses class lines in those public spaces in which interclass encounters are at their most frequent. Networking is heavily dependent on institutions to promote the necessary propinquity (gyms, parties, twelve-step programs, conferences, reading groups, singing groups, social gatherings, workshops, tourist groups, and classes), where those with the requisite social skills can maneuver. Contact is associated with public space and the architecture and commerce that depend on and promote it. Thus contact is often an outdoor sport; networking tends to occur indoors.

Selections from *The Pillow Book*

SEI SHŌNAGON

Translated by Meredith McKinney

[189] Elegantly intriguing things—It's delightful to hear, through a wall or partition of some sort, the sound of someone, no mere gentlewoman, softly and elegantly clap her hands for service. Then, still separated from view behind, perhaps, a sliding door, you hear a youthful voice respond, and the swish of silk as someone arrives. It must be time for a meal to be served, for now come the jumbled sounds of chopsticks and spoons, and then the ear is arrested by the sudden metallic clink of a pouring-pot's handle falling sideways and knocking against the pot.

Hair tossed back, but not roughly, over a robe that's been beaten to a fine gloss, so that you can only guess at its splendid length.

It's marvellous to see a beautifully appointed room, where no lamp has been lit and the place is illuminated instead by the light of a brightly burning fire in the square brazier—you can just make out the cords of the curtains around the curtained dais glimmering softly. The metal clasps that hold the raised blinds in place at the lintel cloth and trefoil cords also gleam brightly. A beautifully arranged brazier with fire burning, its rim swept clean of ash, the firelight revealing the painting on its inner surface, is a most delightful sight. As also is a brightly gleaming pair of fire tongs, propped at an angle in the brazier.

Another scene of fascinating elegance—it's very late at night, Her Majesty has retired to her chamber, everyone is asleep and outside a lady is sitting talking with a senior courtier. From within comes the frequent sound of go stones dropping into the box. Delightful too to hear the soft sound of fire tongs being gently pushed into the ash of the brazier, and sense from this the presence of someone who isn't yet asleep.

A person who stays up late is always elegantly intriguing. You wake in the night to lie there listening through the partition, and realize from the sounds that someone is still up. You can't hear what is said, but you catch the sound of a man's soft laugh, and you long to know what they're saying together.

Another scene—Her Majesty has not yet retired. Her ladies are attending her, and the High Gentlewoman or perhaps some other senior gentlewoman from the Emperor's residence, someone who adds formality to the occasion, is also present. People are seated near Her Majesty, engaged in conversation. The lamp is extinguished, but fine details of the scene are illuminated by the light of the fire that burns in the long brazier.

A lady new to the court, someone not of particularly impressive background but who the young gentlemen would naturally consider an object of elegant interest, is attending Her Majesty rather late at night. There's something attractively intimate in the sound of her silk robes as she enters and approaches Her Majesty on her knees. Her Majesty speaks quietly to her, and she shrinks like a child and responds in a barely audible voice. The whole feel of the scene is very quiet. It's also very elegant the way, when the gentlewomen are gathered seated here and there in the room talking, you hear the silk rustle of people as they leave or enter and, though it's only a soft sound, you can guess who each one would be.

Some gentleman of intimidating rank has come visiting the rooms one evening. Your own lamp is extinguished, but light from nearby penetrates from above the intervening screen, faintly illuminating the objects in the room. Since he's someone she would never sit so close to in daylight hours, she bashfully draws over a low standing curtain and lies close beside it, head bent over, though even so he would surely be able to judge her hair. His cloak and gathered trousers are draped over the standing curtain—something of suitably high rank, of course, although the special olive-green of a Chamberlain of the sixth rank would be just about acceptable. However, if it's one of those deep green cloaks of a normal sixth-ranker, you'd feel inclined to take it and roll it into a ball and consign it to the far reaches of the room, so that when it comes time for him to leave at dawn he'll be dismayed to discover he can't lay hands on it.

It's also quite delightful, in summer or winter, to take a quick peep from the corridor, where you guess someone's sleeping behind a standing curtain from the clothes draped over one end of it.

The scent of incense is a most elegantly intriguing thing. I well remember the truly wonderful scent that wafted from Captain Tadanobu as he sat leaning by the blind of the Little Door of Her Majesty's room one day during the long rains of the fifth month. The blend was so subtle there was no distinguishing its ingredients. Of course it's natural that scent is enhanced by the moisture of a rainy day, but one couldn't help remarking on it even so. It was no wonder that the younger ladies were so deeply impressed at the way it lingered until the following day in the blind he'd been leaning against.

Rather than stringing along a large crowd of retainers of varying heights, none of whom looks particularly smart or impressive, it's far more refined for a gentleman to go about in a beautifully gleaming carriage that he's had for only a little while, with ox drivers dressed with appropriate smartness, who can barely keep up with the spirited ox as it rushes along ahead of them.

What really does catch the attention with its elegant suggestiveness is the sight of a slender retainer dressed in graded-dye skirted trousers in lavender or some such colour, with upper robes of something appropriate—glossed silk, kerria-yellow—and shiny shoes, running along close to the axle as the carriage travels.

[248] Being disliked by others is really a most distressing thing. How crazy would you have to be, to accept calmly the fact that you're probably the sort of person nobody likes? But it's a terribly sad fact that, both in the palace and among parents and siblings, there are those who are loved and those who aren't.

Not only among the upper crust but even in lowly families, when a child is the apple of his parents' eye then everyone will pay him particular attention and be particularly devoted to his needs. Of course if he's actually someone who's worthy of this kind of attention it seems quite natural, and no one pauses to question it. But it's very moving to see a parent's love for a child, even if he's actually nothing out of the ordinary, and consider that it's precisely because they're a parent that they feel like this.

Yes, there's nothing more wonderful than to be well-loved, not only by parents but by the one you serve and by all those you have close dealings with in life.

[S29] I have written in this book things I have seen and thought, in the long idle hours spent at home, without ever dreaming that others would see it. Fearing that some of my foolish remarks could well strike others as excessive and objectionable, I did my best to keep it secret, but despite all my intentions I'm afraid it has come to light.

Palace Minister Korechika one day presented to the Empress a bundle of paper. 'What do you think we could write on this?' Her Majesty inquired. 'They are copying Records of the Historian over at His Majesty's court.'

'This should be a "pillow," then,' I suggested.

'Very well, it's yours,' declared Her Majesty, and she handed it over to me.

I set to work with this boundless pile of paper to fill it to the last sheet with all manner of odd things, so no doubt there's much in these pages that makes no sense.

Overall, I have chosen to write about the things that delight, or that people find impressive, including poems as well as things such as trees, plants, birds, insects and so forth, and for this reason people may criticize it for not living up to expectations and only going to prove the limits of my own sensibility. But after all, I merely wrote for my personal amusement things that I myself have thought and felt, and I never intended that it should be placed alongside other books and judged on a par with them. I'm utterly perplexed to hear that people who've read my work have said it makes them feel humble in the face of it. Well, there you are, you can judge just how unimpressive someone is if they dislike things that most people like, and praise things that others condemn. Anyway, it does upset me that people have seen these pages.

When Captain of the Left Tsunefusa was still Governor of Ise, he came to visit me while I was back at home, and my book disconcertingly happened to be on the mat from the nearby corner that was put out for him. I scrambled to try and retrieve it, but he carried it off with him, and kept it for a very long time before returning it.

That seems to have been the moment when this book first became known—or so it is written.

Excerpt from *Notes Toward a Pamphlet*

SERGIO CHEJFEC
Translated by Whitney DeVos

Another one of Samich's peculiarities is that he was a practically unpublished writer: his behavior was elliptical as a writer because he did not publish; and he did not publish in order to preserve his ellipsis from any potential threat or form of critical surveillance. His papers are stored in boxes few know about and that for years no one has opened. He wrote books he never finished because his thoughts changed all the time; he had believed, in each case, they would mature if left on hold, and the time would come when eventually they'd be ready. But while all this was in the process of happening, Samich would drift toward something else; the memory of a manuscript would change or cease to interest him, and then he'd end up doing something more significant than destroying what he'd written: he'd dismember it. Poems and different pieces without an attributed genre would return to a unified state at once molecular, floating, and random. If necessary, he thought, later they could make up the new index of a future book—one for which the same fate of dissolution and ambiguous resurrection was nonetheless expected.

The effect of this idiosyncrasy was that, while alive, Samich published small pieces in magazines or collectively authored books. To this end, he had volatile and disorderly criteria, demonstrated in his constant inclination toward the arbitrary fragment (a fragment extracted mostly at random from the writing mass, without taking into account factors regarding coherence or unity, even without taking into account any criteria of arbitrariness). The magazines that published him, like the books containing his fragments, did not have a wide circulation and, one by one, were lost track of. It's unlikely one would be able to reconstruct a plot that, from the beginning, was extremely weak and inconsistent. In fact, there have been magazines including Samich's work that never reached the point of publication, at the mercy of processes perhaps silently influenced by the author's undecided protocols.

If this were about a normal writer, I mean those who publish books and attach their own more-or-less-vigilant authorial presence, these circumstances I've been mentioning would suggest that—within the literary medium and its characteristic tools of expression—the signal was breaking up. But the case of Samich seems different, since he didn't consider publication essential; and sometimes writing, either. From his point of view, the poet operated on the surrounding environment by irradiation. In some cases, discursive developments emanated from him, and in other cases they were developments more ineffable and thus difficult to describe, directly linked to the paradigm of affections, in a broad sense. He was interested in exploring the field of such emanations without committing them to writing. Essentially, that would lead him to being, from his point of view, a character of himself.

More than over a piece of writing, the writer had to claim authorship of a figure. Samich seemed to think it proved too easy to be a writer, if defined in terms of output and frequency of the writing itself. Rather, writing was only a probable suffix related to the circumstances of the writer, who could himself produce non-textual, or even non-verbal discursivities, and thus create a work based on dynamic links and constellations, contrary to all that which is derived from the fixation of words.

Samich was the creator of his own system, which didn't necessarily have to be an organic system; it's likely it wasn't new, original or different, either. The distinguishing feature was a scheme of almost nonsubstantial notions. Perhaps it would be more advisable to talk about intuitions instead of ideas. A solitary individual, Samich moved within a field of discontinuous hunches. His choices did not aim to excavate the profound in order to find or reveal a certain hidden or fundamental truth, but instead to take the pulse of intermittency and the changeable, having as he did a preference for the provisional. He conceived of thoughts like passing ideas, explorations arranged as a plot of passions directed toward the interpellation of others, without wanting, however, to have any bearing on them. The result could only be what it is now. In strictly literary terms: an aesthetic attitude at a cursory glance categorical, if somewhat encapsulated in itself, whose conviction hides, on the contrary, its own weaknesses.

The weak points of his work were and remain a secondary issue, since the work itself was not conceived of in order to ultimately be fixed within some form of publication and thus has an elusive relationship to the concept of value. For Samich, literary value was not a challenge, not even a goal or a problem; worth was a floating and at times nonexistent issue, linked to the spheres of will and desire, and it was a moral issue. Without doing so on purpose, it's likely he championed the disappearance of literature, conceived of as that knowledge and practice refused to him, and as that which made of value its abstract albeit common universal currency.

Speaking of currencies, market rates were of no benefit to Samich. A poet born in an area relegated to the interior of Argentina, itself a lateral country of the western hemisphere, he went through the experience of living in exile in his own land, as have many other artists and people in general throughout the history of humanity. Exile and its related figures—isolation, withdrawal, even volunteer ostracism—represented a backup mechanism against the inattentive indifference of a literary medium like the Argentine one—small, labyrinthine, and frugal—and also a private act of contestation, although for that very reason a rather illusory one, against the same system.

I get the impression that, despite belonging to a different century, being, as he is, a representative of a time period now-outdated both in social and technological terms, even resembling a shipwrecked sailor of that era's sensibility, and also of its art and history, the figure of Samich can say a lot about our moment in the present tense. Formulated thus, "the present tense" is as mysterious, or even more, than "the past tense." Even so, I want to say, it's worth embedding Samich's figure in the present. At each moment, the present is saturated with redundancy—I think this is a widely-shared opinion. Such redundancy must be challenged with impetus. Samich would be the wedge with which I propose to start the cleft, then the crack, and later the splintering of the whole worn-out schema.

Like I've said, a universe of such a singular and disorganized manner as belongs to this Argentine poet resists efforts toward coherent description. Any explication developed using premises, hierarchies, attributions and sources would likely affect the virtual lesson that might be extracted from the real figure, because that same architecture of the image would improperly tidy up a matter both heterodox and resistant to organization.

I think, for these reasons, that only the pamphlet form would do justice to Samich. "To do justice to"—another ridiculous idea. And yet it can nonetheless serve as an indication of what I mean. It seems to me rather paradoxical that, of all people, Samich—whose life is almost a situation of existence, I mean a life that, if we think about it, turns out to be more virtual than true—a person who, while he inhabited the world, aspired to a voice permanently lowered, would, paradoxically perhaps, require the megaphone a pamphlet represents in order to have his ideas, or whatever they're called, disseminated.

Lastly, before getting started, I'd like to go back briefly to the trains and carrots from the beginning. I already mentioned Samich's relationship to them. He traveled from his province thousands of kilometers by train to get to Buenos Aires. The first thing he did when he got off the train was cry. And after this pilgrimage, during the decades he was living on the outskirts of that city, the train constituted the only connection—however sporadic—with everything beyond his immediate surroundings: the "barriada," that undefined number of city blocks encircling Samich's own living quarters. An amalgamation of shabby forms of housing, self-built, not always precarious per se, but existing entirely without luxury; a place where lots frequently sit vacant and in many cases streets go unmaintained.

Samich believed he inhabited the unknown center of a world (actually, he believed the world had an existence unknown to everyone, except him, who, as a host, had lent—to the world—the back of his house as its hidden nucleus). This center was represented by a cleared plot of land which served as a garden, with wild plants and shrubs and a couple of trees—for Samich, the very figure of his moral and spiritual stoicism. Those trees, belonging to the species known as *moral* or mulberry, and functioning as metaphors of permanence and similes of fortitude, were his anchor to a certain idea or practice of the transcendental. The trains represented roughly the opposite: they postulated the changing aspects of the world, which nevertheless rolled on, over fixed objects built seemingly to last forever; so different from—and yet resembling—the immutable presence of the lonely trees in the background.

I still haven't gotten around to the carrots. With respect to them, they provided the set of circumstances for listening, more than anything else, that day I'd succumbed to tiring reading material and was half-asleep, which ferried me to "universe Samich." A universe I wasn't directly familiar with, but that—as I understand it—was made of a painful patience in the face of nature close by, and also of spirituality and interpersonal empathy. Attributes which seemed present in those absolute moments of stereophonic mastication.

I think every pamphlet is comprised of a particle of time, a particle extracted from current events. If, for the pamphlet, history exists, its function is to first concentrate, and afterwards to dissolve within, that particle. The tense conjugated by the pamphlet is one of urgency: of sheer plea—and as such, of the sublimation of the present. Originating in, and at the same time sublimating, the present, the pamphlet produces a redundancy: it aims to show what turns out to be obvious or clear, and which—for insidious reasons—is not widely-accepted. As I said above, what's happened already is of no importance to the pamphlet's present. Its urgency charges on, behind doors closed on the past.

Accordingly, these notes for a pamphlet—as of now—adopt the present in hopes of transmitting a most pressing demand. Samich's constellation of ideas and acts, so highly situated within the universe of the twentieth century, is revealed to be disturbingly alive and well during the dismal twenty-first century. It's not that the poet had visionary abilities. On the contrary, like everyone else, he preferred to sink into the filth of his time, trying to forget it, resisting it when and however much he could, and doing whatever he considered to be right and proper.

Self-taught and agnostic, he believed in entities such as beauty, depth, balance, truth; he even believed in representation. They were for him values important but somewhat superficial—not because of his conviction but rather a kind of definitive ignorance. Samich was incapable of translating those beliefs—which were a bit shallow in his case—into an effective system of action or expression through which he could shape himself.

That profound ignorance could make him a hero today, when those entities are especially diffuse. His figure oscillated daily between pose and suggestion. He wrote for himself and for his small and vague group of close friends and admirers. His life has left almost no trace. I imagine that, if put in front of these pages, Samich would have thought they refer to someone else. A life without great edges but with many fringes. All pamphlet-oriented thinking should take this character's deflected condition into serious account.

Letter I: Hesitations Concerning Baptism

SIMONE WEIL

Translated by Emma Craufurd

January 19, 1942

My Dear Father,

I have made up my mind to write to you . . . to bring our conversations about my case to a conclusion—that is to say, pending further developments. I am tired of talking to you about myself, for it is a wretched subject, but I am obliged to do so by the interest you take in me as a result of your charity.

I have been wondering lately about the will of God, what it means, and how we can reach the point of conforming ourselves to it completely—I will tell you what I think about this.

We have to distinguish among three domains. First, that which is absolutely independent of us; it includes all the accomplished facts in the whole universe at the moment and everything that is happening or going to happen later beyond our reach. In this domain everything that comes about is in accordance with the will of God, without any exception. Here then we must love absolutely everything, as a whole and in each detail, including evil in all its forms; notably our own past sins, in so far as they are past (for we must hate them in so far as their root is still present), our own sufferings, past, present, and to come, and—what is by far the most difficult—the sufferings of other men in so far as we are called upon to relieve them. In other words, we must feel the reality and presence of God through all external things, without exception, as clearly as our hand feels the substance of paper through the penholder and the nib.

The second domain is that which is placed under the rule of the will. It includes the things that are purely natural, close, easily recognized by the intelligence and the imagination, and among which we can make our choice, arranging them from outside so as to provide means to fixed and finite ends. In this domain we have to carry out, without faltering or delay, everything that appears clearly to be a duty. When any duty does not appear clearly, we have sometimes to observe more or less arbitrarily established rules; and sometimes to follow our inclination, but in a limited degree; for one of the most dangerous forms of sin, or perhaps the most dangerous, consists of introducing what is unlimited into a domain that is essentially finite.

The third domain is that of the things, which, without being under the empire of the will, without being related to natural duties, are yet not entirely independent of us. In this domain we experience the compulsion of God's pressure, on condition that we deserve to experience it and exactly to the extent that we deserve to do so. God rewards the soul that thinks of him with attention and love, and he rewards it by exercising a compulsion upon it strictly and mathematically proportionate to this attention and this love. We have to abandon ourselves to the pressure, to run to the exact spot whither it impels us and not go one step farther, even in the direction of what is good. At the same time we must go on thinking about God with ever increasing love and attentiveness, in this way gaining the favor of being impelled ever further and becoming the object of a pressure that possesses itself of an ever-growing proportion of the whole soul. When the pressure has taken possession of the whole soul, we have attained the state of perfection. But whatever stage we may have reached, we must do nothing more than we are irresistibly impelled to do, not even in the way of goodness.

I have also been thinking about the nature of the sacraments, and I will tell you what I think about this subject as well.

The sacraments have a specific value, which constitutes a mystery in so far as they involve a certain kind of contact with God, a contact mysterious but real. At the same time they have a purely human value in so far as they are symbols or ceremonies. Under this second aspect they do not differ essentially from the songs, gestures, and words of command of certain political parties; at least in themselves they are not essentially different; of course they are infinitely different in the doctrine underlying them. I think that most believers, including some who are really persuaded of the opposite, approach the sacraments only as symbols and ceremonies. Foolish as the theory of Durkheim may be in confusing what is religious with what is social, it yet contains an element of truth; that is to say, that the social feeling is so much like the religious as to be mistaken for it. It is like it just as a false diamond is like a real one, so that those who have no spiritual discernment are effectively taken in. For the matter of that, a social and human participation in the symbols and ceremonies of the sacraments is an excellent and healthy thing in that it marks a stage of the journey for those who travel that way. Yet this is not a participation in the sacraments as such. I think that only those who are above a certain level of spirituality can participate in the sacraments as such. For as long as those who are below this level have not reached it, whatever they may do, they cannot strictly be said to belong to the Church.

As far as I am concerned, I think I am below this level. That is why I said to you the other day that I consider myself to be unworthy of the sacraments. This idea does not come, as you imagined, from scrupulosity. It is due, on the one hand, to a consciousness of very definite faults in the order of action and human relations, serious and even shameful faults as you would certainly agree, and moreover fairly frequent. On the other hand, and still more strongly, it is founded on a general sense of inadequacy. I am not saying this out of humility, for if I possessed the virtue of humility, the most beautiful of all the virtues perhaps, I should not be in this miserable state of inadequacy.

To finish with what has to do with me, I say this. The kind of inhibition that keeps me outside the Church is due either to my state of imperfection, or to the fact that my vocation and God's will are opposed to it. In the first case, I cannot get rid of my inhibition by direct means but only indirectly, by becoming less imperfect, if I am helped by grace. To bring this about it is only necessary, on the one hand, to avoid faults in the domain of natural things, and on the other, to put ever more attention and love into my thought of God. If it is God's will that I should enter the Church, he will impose this will upon me at the exact moment when I shall have come to deserve that he should so impose it.

In the second case, if it is not his will that I should enter the Church, how could I enter it? I know quite well what you have often repeated to me, that is to say, that baptism is the common way of salvation—at least in Christian countries—and that there is absolutely no reason why I should have an exceptional one of my own. That is obvious. And yet supposing that in fact it should not be given me to take that step, what could I do? If it were conceivable that in obeying God one should bring about one's own damnation while in disobeying him one could be saved, I should still choose the way of obedience.

It seems to me that the will of God is that I should not enter the Church at present. The reason for this I have told you already and it is still true. It is because the inhibition that holds me back is no less strongly to be felt in the moments of attention, love, and prayer than at other times. And yet I was filled with a very great joy when you said the thoughts I confided to you were not incompatible with allegiance to the Church, and that, in consequence, I was not outside it in spirit.

I cannot help still wondering whether in these days when so large a proportion of humanity is submerged in materialism, God does not want there to be some men and women who have given themselves to him and to Christ and who yet remain outside the Church.

In any case, when I think of the act by which I should enter the Church as something concrete, which might happen quite soon, nothing gives me more pain than the idea of separating myself from the immense and unfortunate multitude of unbelievers. I have the essential need, and I think I can say the vocation, to move among men of every class and complexion, mixing with them and sharing their life and outlook, so far that is to say as conscience allows, merging into the crowd and disappearing among them, so that they show themselves as they are, putting off all disguises with me. It is because I long to know them so as to love them just as they are. For if I do not love them as they are, it will not be they whom I love, and my love will be unreal. I do not speak of helping them, because as far as that goes I am unfortunately quite incapable of doing anything as yet. I do not think that in any case I should ever enter a religious order, because that would separate me from ordinary people by a habit. There are some human beings for whom such a separation has no serious disadvantages, because they are already separated from ordinary folk by their natural purity of soul. As for me, on the contrary, as I think I told you, I have the germ of all possible crimes, or nearly all, within me. I became aware of this in the course of a journey, in circumstances I have described to you. The crimes horrified me, but they did not surprise me; I felt the possibility of them within myself; it was actually because I felt this possibility in myself that they filled me with such horror. This natural disposition is dangerous and very painful, but like every variety of natural disposition, it can be put to good purpose if one knows how to make the right use of it with the help of grace. It is the sign of a vocation, the vocation to remain in a sense anonymous, ever ready to be mixed into the paste of common humanity. Now at the present time, the state of men's minds is such that there is a more clearly marked barrier, a wider gulf between a practicing Catholic and an unbeliever than between a religious and a layman.

I know quite well that Christ said: "Whosoever shall deny [*i.e.*, disown] me before men, him will I also deny before my Father which is in Heaven."* But disowning Christ does not perhaps mean for everyone and in all cases not belonging to the Church. For some it may only mean not carrying out Christ's precepts, not shedding abroad his spirit, not honoring his name when occasion arises, not being ready to die out of loyalty to him.

I owe you the truth, at the risk of shocking you, and it gives me the greatest pain to shock you. I love God, Christ, and the Catholic faith as much as it is possible for so miserably inadequate a creature to love them. I love the saints through their writings and what is told of their lives—apart from some whom it is impossible for me to love fully or to consider as saints. I love the six or seven Catholics of genuine spirituality whom chance has led me to meet in the course of my life. I love the Catholic liturgy, hymns, architecture, rites, and ceremonies. But I have not the slightest love for the Church in the strict sense of the word, apart from its relation to all these things that I do love. I am capable of

* St. Matt. 10:33. Simone Weil evidently used a Greek edition of the New Testament and made her own translations of the quoted texts. It was the decision of the publishers and not of the translator in most cases to use the Authorized Version in the English edition of Simone Weil's works.

sympathizing with those who have this love, but I do not feel it. I am well aware that all the saints felt it. But then they were nearly all born and brought up in the Church. Anyhow, one cannot make oneself love. All that I can say is that if such a love constitutes a condition of spiritual progress, which I am unaware of, or if it is part of my vocation, I desire that it may one day be granted me.

It may well be that some of the thoughts I have just confided to you are illusory and defective. In a sense this matters little to me; I do not want to go on examining any more, for at the end of all these reflections I have reached a conclusion which is the pure and simple resolution to stop thinking about the question of my eventual entry into the Church.

It is very possible that after having passed weeks, months, or years without thinking about it all, one day I shall suddenly feel an irresistible impulse to ask immediately for baptism and I shall run to ask for it. For the action of grace in our hearts is secret and silent.

It may also be that my life will come to an end before I have ever felt this impulse. But one thing is absolutely certain. It is that if one day it comes about that I love God enough to deserve the grace of baptism, I shall receive this grace on that very day, infallibly, in the form God wills, either by means of baptism in the strict sense of the word or in some other manner. In that case why would I have any anxiety? It is not my business to think about myself. My business is to think about God. It is for God to think about me.

This is a very long letter. Once again I shall have taken up much more of your time than I ought. I beg you to forgive me. My excuse is that by writing this I have reached a conclusion, for the time being at any rate.

Do believe how truly grateful I am.

SIMONE WEIL

Stingray

SIMONE WHITE

Having had no proper family name I made do
with Stingray never loved a man so-called
for more than a generation black and white
suffer nameless conditions
instigated by the father's line of nobody
murmurs to the baby "goodnight nobody"
there is no longer any way to count
beneath the highways of the Eastern Seaboard
above the Mason Dixon line
underlie so many crossings

What to me the arched wing of a black Stingray
who think weeping over her vicious mouth
somnolent practice of stuck terror of the wave
is Stingray the atomic principle of giantism
make my whole mouth move around the fire
make the fire everywhere or cold
on this street Stingray where a man thinking his boat
beauty knowing moneys or leather, white leather
feeling however the killing power of the great sea monster
her haunch whip a think acquired as a gorgeous capital

Wait and sting why Odysseus
always in trouble with the one-eyed
what caused His love of lake demons
(her gauze whimple
under blacklit stars)
His very early anticipation
of the right guitar sound
its fullness, no
re-union of the ocean and the desert
just reflect on the history of the house

57 rays die in Chicago
for want of so lush a malapropism
I wait a long time outside the ocean
and your body sometimes nothing of images
dead brown and such like luminous captivity of the dead
repeated back to our obsessional contemporary
says back a weird lie
when inside me a bit of god comes out your mouth
as the command to feel you what
kind creature will you take me from being to what

Her mallow glamor warns
warmed in the glowering ripple light
this liquid this death to you
lady come under this death it is ablaze
in its blue white perfection hold your hand like a cup
water light will pour you into the whole day
the deafening memory of your tenth year
occurring in the space between sunup and sundown
on a plot the size of an hibiscus flower
you, miss

The Bicentennial was yesterday
write queer and muggy apparently evening
every minute the Declaration must be signed
firework on the barge child mind
to which no Superfund has yet gently repaired
get me a Stingray the color of slate
a little girl switchblade the horizon of which is an arc
gutter oil slick Delaware that horizon
is New Jersey a plot (her shore)
farms send blueberries and war

In this form it is impossible to be together
it is being nothing at all then cast in this court trick
vulvar form o clamped then
between together and nothing
forms of sand coarse pink edible
no seams along which to break
a black flag waves in hot wind
form of formless   a craft, a craft appears
materialized hot gas
raucous to suspend life outside of life

Shadows beyond wishing
and male news emplotted to hover
no wools or porcelain anywhere in sight
of the flat class
Stingray
vanities pool
heteronomous in the tight
grate
withdraw from earth
one fractal   initially

Retreat then
the slick thing quavered she said
of sediment rustling abashed
contemplation of stones rushing together
under the fresh
lake not the elementary bite of capital
give that is a wound
and she, raw, bloodless
could you bleed housed gowned
fucked in a prehistoric manner
still sea monster

The very source
or the veil
complete silence, the silent
inhalation or stopped time
time, being unmet
totally unregulated
slack and unreturned
threshing
the dna then
she becomes another one

It's dissociation season

PRECIOUS OKOYOMON

for Dana Ward

I'm walking around Harlem a little stoned and weepy. Feeling a little light blue maybe yellow this is my problem getting off on colors it's all boring. I decide to eat some mushrooms just a couple caps trying to organize my mind patterns shifting around wave to wave - spasms of fantasy

Magic lifts my hair - that's just the wind - that's just the weed

My aimlessness is agreeable
I am but a gentle thot floating in the wind beaming
Shamelessly happy I drift into a dreaminess

Everything i feel is hot and wet

I'm at sam's eating cupcakes sitting in loop of endless mirrors

naked baby bratz dolls holding tiny dicks
cream in my mouth

The light bounces off the walls soft pink / making the green world stop

My body drowning itself in the habit of the dream

Then Rachel tells me how to deal with trauma in recklessly graceful ways

Fluttering realities of dust - destroy memory functions in order to survive

My lover is texting me wondering where i am #worried
I'm . Getting. Tired . Of . My . Shit.

I'm a superficial bitch # selfish
I'm throwing my wig away in sam's bathroom

first in the urinal // then in the sink

I leave it in the trash

When I was a child - I used to strip down and beat myself with a stick
An excess of desire - traumatized spasms of my fantasy

Then i'm calling my lover
I'm late. I'm always late
I'm. Getting. Tired. Of. My. Shit.

God doesn't strike people down like he use 2 ... Damn i miss the old God

This poverty is perfect
what i love now is what's barely there

Then Patricia is next to me on the couch talking me down from my trip
rubbing my back
Reduce the living body

Then Taylor and I r snorting coke off the toilet at Bossa

Everything i like is 99% wrong

Everything i am is 99% wrong

Then my lover is calling me
Then my lover is worried
Then my phone is dead
The sensation of constantly being unsettled

I'm always trying to only feel good
#onlygoodvibes #blessed #sage

Then i'm drinking a shitty martini with Ben

I miss my wig
my whole life a summer day
gin martinis no cherries no ice
No problems

Then Rin buys me whiskey
Then Ariel and is giving me their book and i'm blushing.
Then i'm feeling lustful.
Then i'm in bed with Hannah legs tangled bodies without origins
I awake horrified at the choices i have made

Lol

Forgive me father for I have sinned.
it's been two weeks?
Um - Since my last confession.
1. I lied in my last confession, I have dishonoured my mother and father, um
I have um – hurt people that I care about.

Then Taylor is rolling us a spliff
Then i'm high - I'm always stoned - extremes of pleasure - this void of endless animation

I don't know how to drop repetitions
Dismembered body

I find myself repeating
I'm not myself today
I'm mixing up my identities

a revolt   I am no longer a body

Ego leaks onto the street / shed light on humiliation

Then i'm lost
Then my mom is lending me money
I'm no good at taking care of myself

Temptation /a new poison /blur the lines of intoxication

I'm no good at feeling bad

– Oh God, have mercy on me, your daughter, a sinner.

If u touch it it's yours
These are bonds
One thing next to another doesn't mean they touch

An unseen shape rotating and twisting
Touching something lightly
Display dramatic expression

Then Sam is reminding me cuteness is its own violence

colours that evolve
my goodness is insulting

Idk what life is
I want everyone to drown in my teenage dream

Then i'm at the reading and Darcie is asking me if i'm okay
  Molly is handing me a coffee - black
Ben is giving me reassuring looks
  I feel like my body will give out if I don't smoke a joint
By the time I see your face
I'm the only Jesus in the room
Then we're fighting and ur walking away from me.

Broken black bodies r really in right now

  It's a bummer nobody gets crucified anymore

I mean I'm trying
I want to care about art but I only care about people

Then Rachel is giving me a kpin
To stop the spasms
They fall in the Uber
  I lower myself to the ground brush the pills into my hand and get high
  Life is hard and I'm sorry
I'm sobbing & I can't remember why now
being an person is hard and stupid
I suffer from that
Everything is embarrassing
  Ugh this is getting out of hand

  I can't say no so don't ask me
                    Fleshy animal
nothing is pure, invert yourself

TOTAL LOL

SOPHIE ROBINSON

RAW RAW RAW RAW RAW RAW RAW RAW RAW RAW
that is how a dog goes that is how a dog goes
boom in the night that is how a dog slides
sideways that is how a dog lies down
in the grass and loafers and dies like the bad
dead dog it really is inside its orgied guts
& this is how we do it: in out in out
this is how we move inside the dogspace
this is how we are inside the dog I am the
dog head with my head in the dog
you are the dog end with your end inside the dog
we are a pantomime dog & this is how we do it:
left right left right that is how we walk
like the sick dogs we are that is how we fuck ourselves
inside out and our fur turns to mush this is how
we think of something to make us cry on purpose

this is how we be brave and glass over like a
sad dog's eyes this is how we eat our own shit
and sing with a mouthful all night long:

RAW RAW RAW RAW RAW RAW RAW RAW RAW RAW
this is how we know ourselves & this is how
we hate each other this is how we sound
when we speak each others' language & how
your pussy tastes on a hard day's night I like
to suffer it's good for us & makes us wet with pride
or raw with longing pulling at the leash – I might
die I might lie down and die you can dog me in
the park and I won't let it lie – I'd screw you
five thousand times and still be happy in my
mummy skin in my daggy dogskin in my foxfur
mangy woof woof jacket. My skin is my life
jacket my skin has a hole in it my hole is round
and red my hole is my dog's head I will die forever
in my sick dog head I will LOL forever in my
total bowl of meat I will LOL with my hole wide
open I will LOL all night to the tune of my howl
o I will place you in my snout and sing you all over
I will raw myself all up and down inside you lover forever

The Slow Read Movement

SPARROW

I moved from New York City to the hamlet of Phoenicia in 1998. Immediately, I became frustrated with the local "culture." I grew up in Manhattan; I was like a bee in the hive of that island. The humming of the other inhabitants informed me, reassured me. Now walking alone, among mist-draped mountains, with no one nearby speaking Polish, Italian, Puerto Rican, German, French, Chinese, I felt stupid.

Luckily, Phoenicia has a first-rate thrift shop with a witty name: "Formerly Yours." The prices are extremely low—some pants are 25¢—but there's also a free table, and among its items are books. Formerly Yours is the opposite of a New York City bookstore: you must pay for romance novels, but Freudian Marxist essays are free. One day on the giveaway table, I found *Moby-Dick* (the Signet paperback, from 1978). Immediately I snapped it up. That night I lay in bed and opened my new acquisition:

> Call me Ishmael. Some years ago—never mind how long precisely—having little or no money in my purse, and nothing particular to interest me onshore, I thought I would sail about a little and see the watery part of the world.

It was elegant, stately, poetic—but who could read it? This book demanded the intelligence of a Princeton professor and the patience of St. Jerome. It's the goddamn Great American Novel! *Moby-Dick*'s as intimidating as . . . a massive white whale! Sadly, I cast the classic aside.

Three days later, however, I hit on a plan. In Phoenicia, there is infinite time. If I read a page a day, I'd eventually finish this gargantuan novel. So I began. Each day I read a section of the text, marking my progress with a pencil. Melville became my spectral companion, speaking to me daily:

> Now, when I say that I am in the habit of going to sea whenever I begin to grow hazy about the eyes, and begin to be over conscious of my lungs, I did not mean to have it inferred that I ever go to sea as a passenger. For to go as a passenger you must needs have a purse, and a purse is but a rag unless you have something in it.

Moby-Dick is almost too great a book. Reading it burns your eyes. When you're in the middle of an Agatha Christie novel, you won't stop even to eat—even to drink a glass of water. Reading Melville is the opposite. Every three sentences, you must stare at the ceiling and wonder where your life went wrong. It's the perfect book to read with tragical slowness.

One virtue of *Moby-Dick*: you're not going to forget the plot. [Spoiler alert: It's about a bunch of guys on a whaling ship, searching for a whale.] A startling discovery: The Great American Novel is not set in America (except for a brief introduction)! It follows a route through the Atlantic, around Cape Horn, into the Indian Ocean and on to the Pacific. Another discovery: Melville was such a visionary he wanted to SAVE THE WHALES 120 years before that bumper sticker was written.

For six years I sailed on the Pequod, checking on the progress of my ship every night between 8:00 and 8:30 PM. As a whaler slowly crosses the ocean, I reached page 150, then page 200, then page 238 . . . As Captain Ahab grew more obsessed with Moby-Dick, I grew more obsessed with *Moby-Dick*.

Some people skip the informational chapters on whaling, but not me. That would be like taking a shortcut in the Boston Marathon:

> Throughout the Pacific, and also in Nantucket, in New Bedford, and Sag Harbor, you will come across lively sketches of whales and whaling-scenes, graven by the fishermen themselves on Sperm Whale-teeth, or ladies' busks wrought out of the Right Whale-bone, and other like scrimshander articles, as the wheelmen call the numerous little ingenious contrivances they elaborately carve out of the rough material, in their hours of ocean leisure.

[A "busk" is part of a corset.] In Chapter 95, Melville describes the penis of a whale the boat has slaughtered:

> Had you stepped on board the Pequod at a certain juncture of this post-mortemizing of the whale; and had you strolled forward nigh the windlass, pretty sure am I that you would have scanned with no small curiosity a very strange, enigmatical object, which you would have seen there, lying along lengthwise in the lee scuppers. Not the wondrous cistern in the whale's huge head; not the prodigy of his unhinged lower jaw; not the miracle of his symmetrical tail; none of these would so surprise you, as half a glimpse of that unaccountable cone,—longer than a Kentuckian is tall, nigh a foot in diameter at the base, and jet-black as Yojo, the ebony idol of Queequeg.

It's possible that Melville went a little bit insane writing the book. Here is Ahab speaking in Chapter 108 (angry that he must wait for the carpenter to fashion him a new pegleg):

> Oh, Life! Here I am, proud as Greek God, and yet standing debtor to this blockhead for a bone to stand on! Cursed be that mortal inter-indebtedness which will not do away with ledgers. I would be free as air; and I'm down in the whole world's books. I am so rich, I could have given bid for bid with the wealthiest Praetorians at the auction of the Roman empire (which was the world's); and yet I owe for the flesh in the tongue I brag with. By heavens!

Just as the "Slow Food" movement reverses the momentum of modern life, emphasizing local ingredients and long meal preparation, my

"Slow Read" movement pulled me back into the thoughtfulness of a world of lamps filled with . . . whale oil!

I didn't know how the book would end. I never saw the 1956 film with Gregory Peck, and no one at a party ever said: "Weren't you surprised at the ending of *Moby-Dick*? I couldn't believe Ishmael went off with that mermaid!*" After six years of reading, I reached the conclusion: ". . . and the great shroud of the sea rolled on as it rolled five thousand years ago." With vigorous, sustained mental effort, I'd conquered Melville! If I can do it, so can you. Find a weighty book, a sharp pencil, and join the Slow Read movement!

* I'm not saying this is the actual plot of the book.

Lincoln's Lost Speech

Abraham Lincoln's "Lost Speech" was delivered on May 29, 1856, in Bloomington, Illinois. Tradition states that the text was lost because Lincoln's powerful oration mesmerized every person in attendance. Reporters laid down their pencils, forgetting to take notes. In 2006 a fragment of the Lost Speech was found in the archives of a Baptist church in Bloomington. Through a distant cousin, I obtained it:

> A monarch provides security; it is comforting to bow to a Sire. But our nation was born of another wish. We are all part-kings here. If you bow to one man, you must bow to all . . .

Inez, I Have to Gloat: You're Gorgeous

SOR JUANA INÉS DE LA CRUZ

Translated by Joan Larkin and Jaime Manrique

Inez, I have to gloat: you're gorgeous
and you love me. All this
pleasure—I'll never be the same.
When you're jealous, I'm a trembling thread,

and when you flirt in front of me, I die.
You flaunt those hips to drive me wild.
One thrust, you're squandering the honey
that makes me high—save it for me, Inez.

When you cover me with kisses, I'm transformed.
When you're angry with me, I can't breathe.
When you go out, I lie awake all night.

Still, Inez, none of this really matters.
Just take me to bed, where I like it,
with my wineskin and your succulent worm.

Inez, When Someone Tells You You're a Bitch

Inez, when someone tells you you're a bitch,
you've got a million comebacks. I'm supposed to think
you're some old woman full of aches and creaks—
that's your genius, dear: you cover your shit.

You have a dirty mouth; you love to use it:
once you start, no magpie can compete.
You're louder than a string of firecrackers.
You thrive on noise, you love to make a stink.

You crank out lies until a girl can't think.
Your charms are much exaggerated. Still, Inez,
the problem isn't you, you cruel pussy.

The way I love you is a sin, I know it—
but the way you fuck me is no trick. Your hard-on's real,
and I'm a field just waiting to be plowed.

Where I Left Off

SUSIE TIMMONS

If pillows were people they'd always be sleeping
in my library book there's a man playing a bug
for his musical instrument
pillows and speckled navy enamel cup
you can't even wave
good eye

an ochre
pyramid, big chief notebooks
pencils neatly sharpened, smokestacks
is turn, into, or ones with fire on their tip all night

with the fire coming in.

camisole, universe walking past Veselka
down Ninth Street, east, rainy January, 11 p.m.

jackals howling

translucent bottle containing disc preener

sable, lace caps

letters and stamps

the woodwork, expels an example

flying for humans, talking animals, reading minds

I can't believe the bell here,

sick analog

ten flawless lines

the coast is a dream

at her bath and stuck gently on her forehead

Falling for You

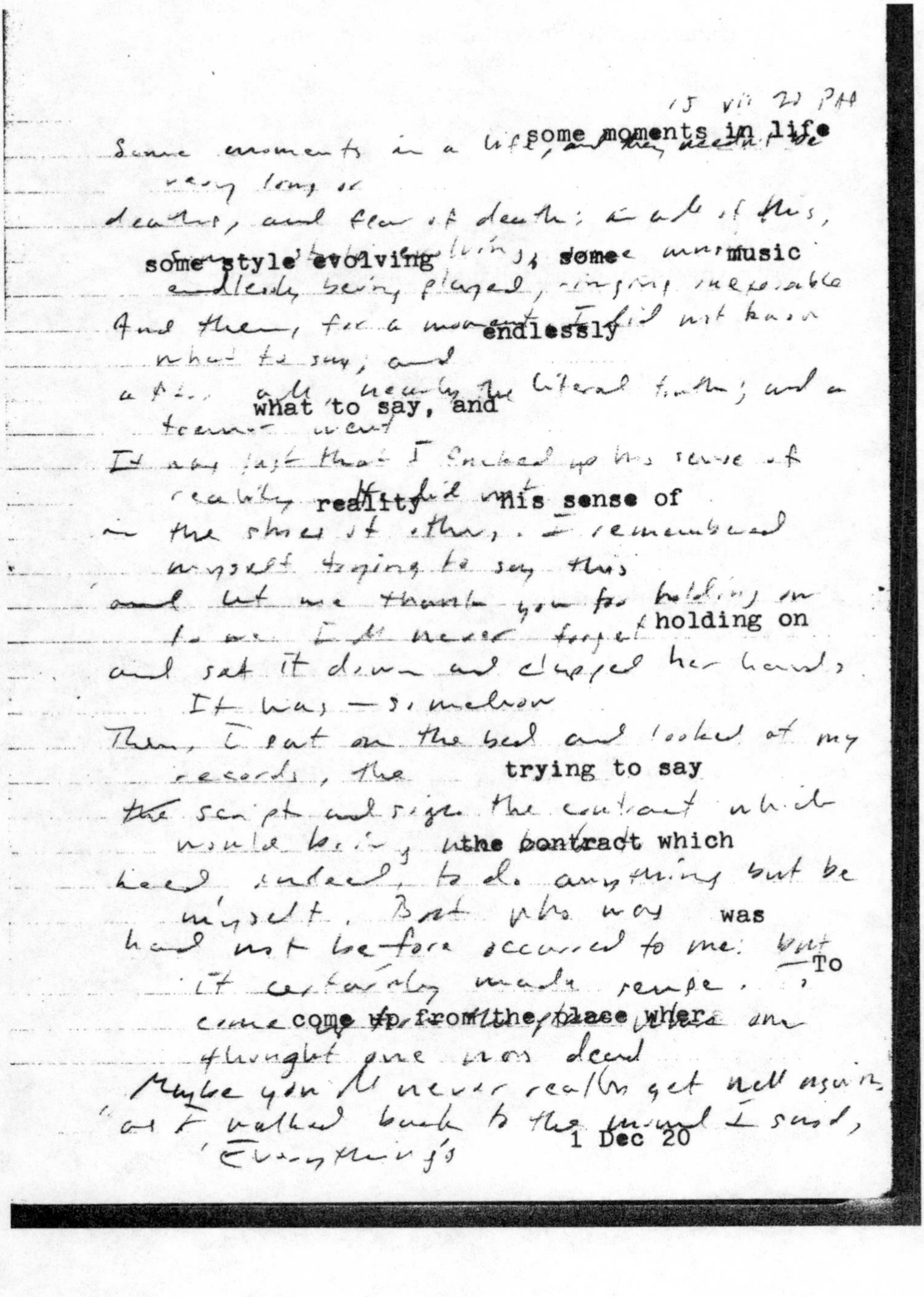
15 VII 20 PM
Some moments in a life, and they weren't the very long or
some moments in life
deaths, and fear of death: a lot of this,
some style evolving, some music
endlessly being played, ringing inexorable
And then, for a moment, I did not know
endlessly
what to say; and
after all, nearly the literal truth; and a tremor went
what to say, and
It was just that I sucked up this sense of reality
He did not
reality his sense of
in the stress of others. I remembered myself trying to say this
and let me thank you for holding on to me. I'll never forget
holding on
and sat it down and clasped her hands.
It was — somehow
Then, I sat on the bed and looked at my records, the
trying to say
the script and sign the contract which would bring
the contract which
need, indeed, to do anything but be myself. But who was
was
had not before occurred to me: but it certainly made sense.
To
came up from the place where one thought one was dead
come up from the place where
Maybe you'll never really get well again
as I walked back to the [illegible] I said,
'Everything's
1 Dec 20

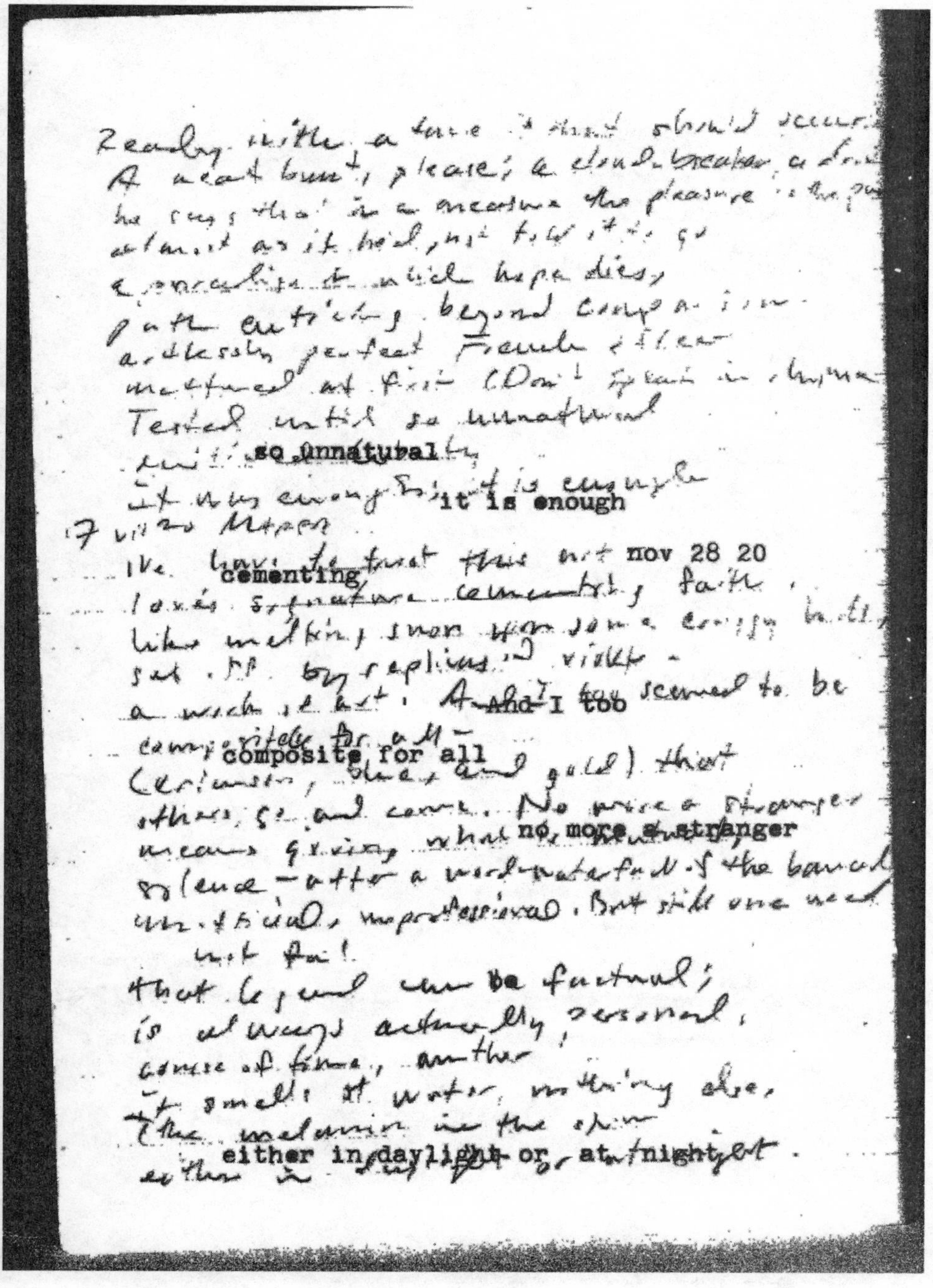

Reading with a tune [illegible] should occur
A neat burst, please; a cloud-breaker, a [illegible]
he says that in a measure the pleasure is the [illegible]
admit as it heals, just take it to go
a vocalise at which hope dies,
path catching beyond compassion
artlessly perfect French silence
muttered at first (Don't speak in rhyme
Tested until so unnatural
so unnatural
it was enough [illegible] it is enough
it is enough
17 [illegible]
I've [illegible] nov 28 20
cementing
love's signature cementing faith,
like melting snow [illegible]
set off by replies and violet –
a wish, a hint. And I too seemed to be
And I too
composite for all –
composite for all
(crimson, blue, and gold) that
others go and come. No more a stranger
means giving what [illegible]
no more a stranger
silence – after a word-waterfall of the banal
unofficial, unprofessional. But still one need
not fail!
that legend can be factual;
is always actually personal,
course of time, another
it smells of water, nothing else.
The melanin in the skin
either in daylight or at night
either in [illegible] or [illegible]

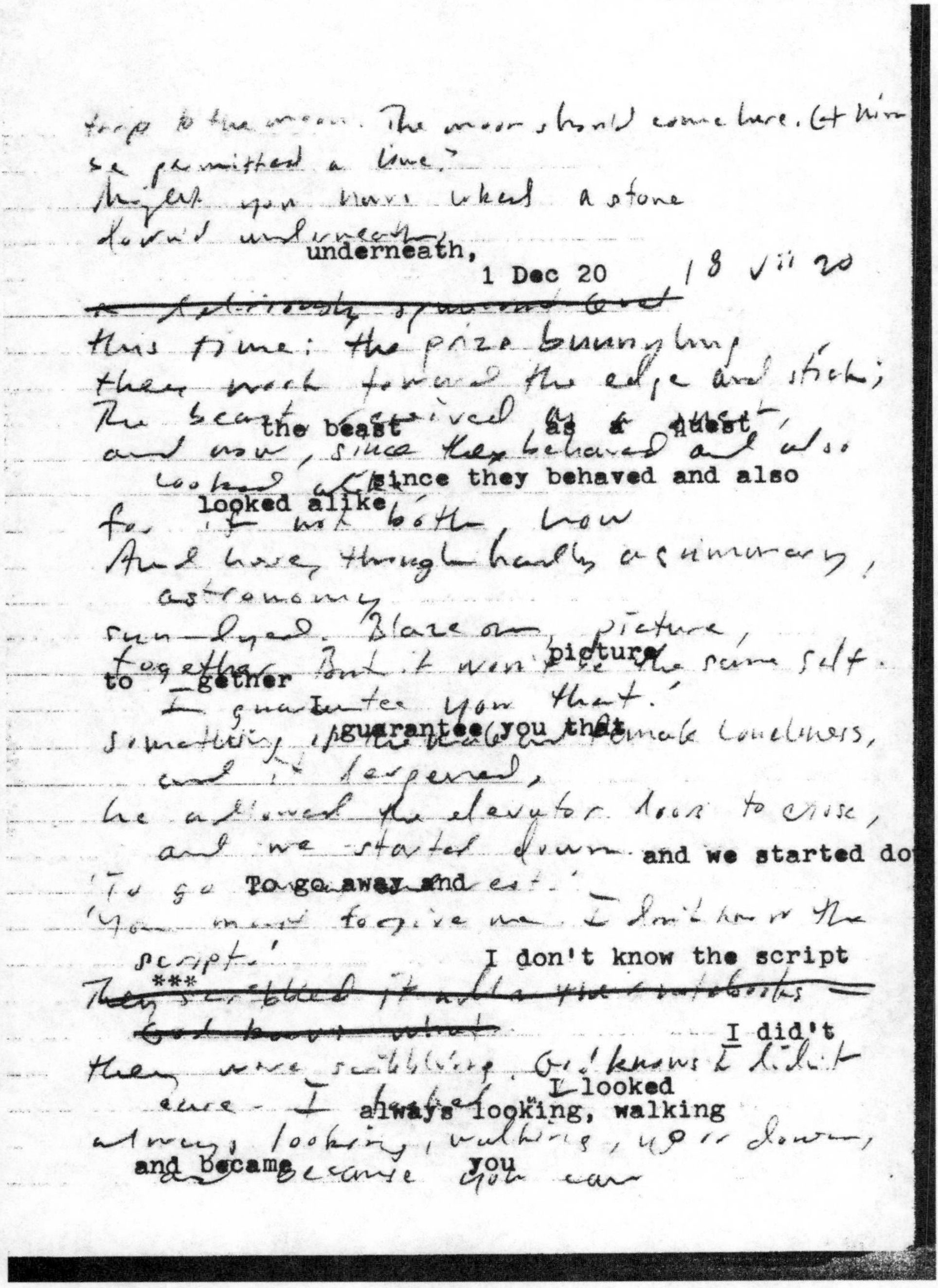

trip to the moon. The moon should come here. Let him
be permitted a line?
Might you have what a stone
~~doesn't underneath~~
underneath,
1 Dec 20 18 vii 20
~~a deliciously spread out~~
this time: the prize bunny [illegible]
then work toward the edge and stick;
The beast arrived as a guest,
the beast as a guest
and now, since they behaved and also
looked alike since they behaved and also
looked alike
for if not both, how
And have, through hardly a summary,
astronomy
sun-dyed. Blaze on picture,
together But it wasn't the same self.
picture
to gether
I guarantee you that.
guarantee you that
something of the male and female loneliness,
and it deepened,
he allowed the elevator door to close,
and we started down and we started do
'To go To go away and eat.'
'You must forgive me. I don't know the
script.' I don't know the script
***
~~They scribbled it all in their notebooks —~~
~~God knows what~~
I did't
they were scribbling. God knows I didn't
I looked
care – I looked always looking, walking
always looking, walking, up or down,
and became you
and because you can

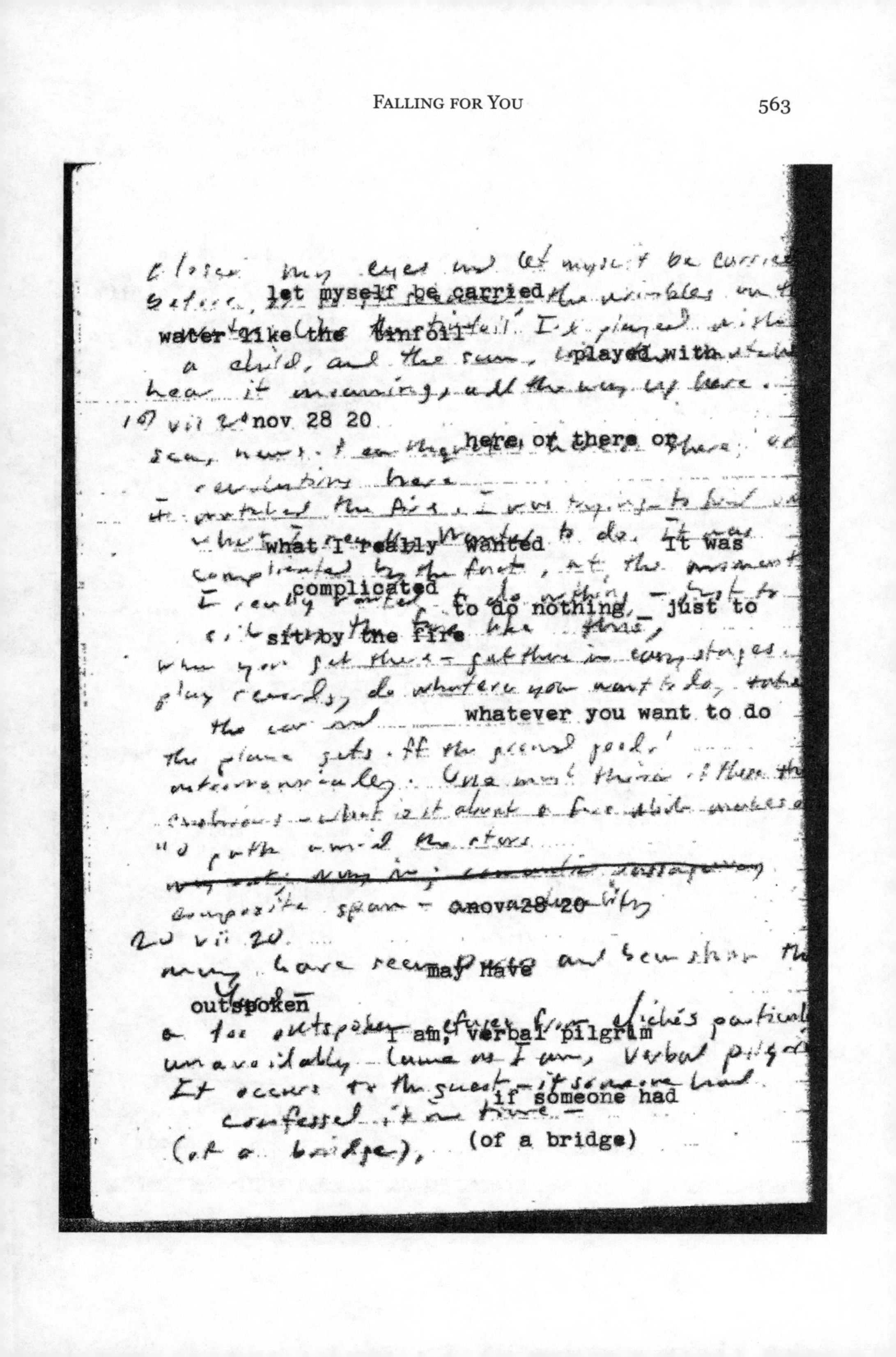

let myself be carried

water like the tinfoil

played with

nov 28 20

here or there or

what I really wanted It was

complicated

to do nothing just to

sit by the fire

whatever you want to do

anova 28 20

may have

outspoken

I am, verbal pilgrim

if someone had

(of a bridge)

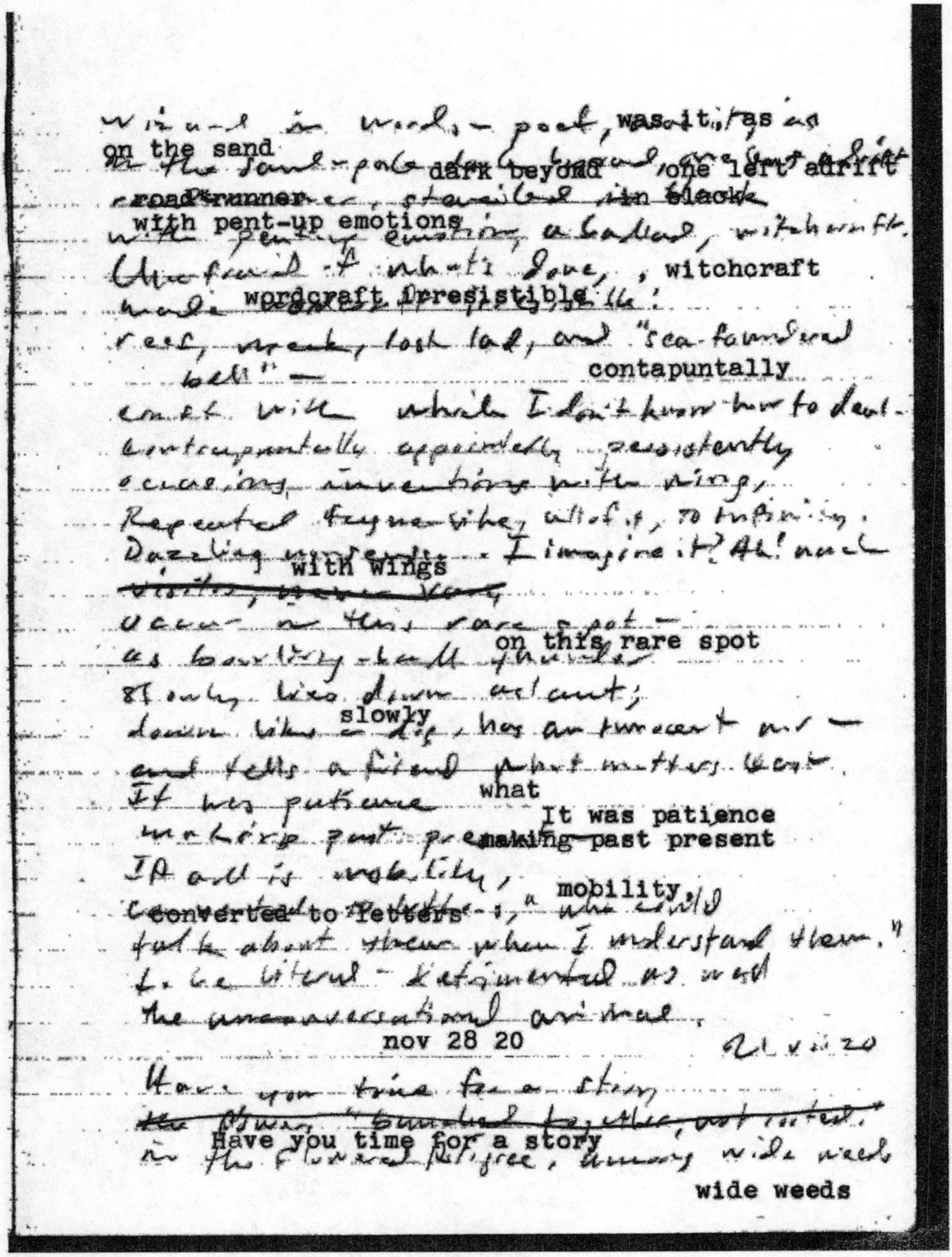

was it, as

on the sand

dark beyond one left adrift

road-runner

with pent-up emotions

witchcraft

wordcraft irresistible

contapuntally

with wings

on this rare spot

slowly

what

It was patience

making past present

mobility,

converted to letters

nov 28 20

Have you time for a story

wide weeds

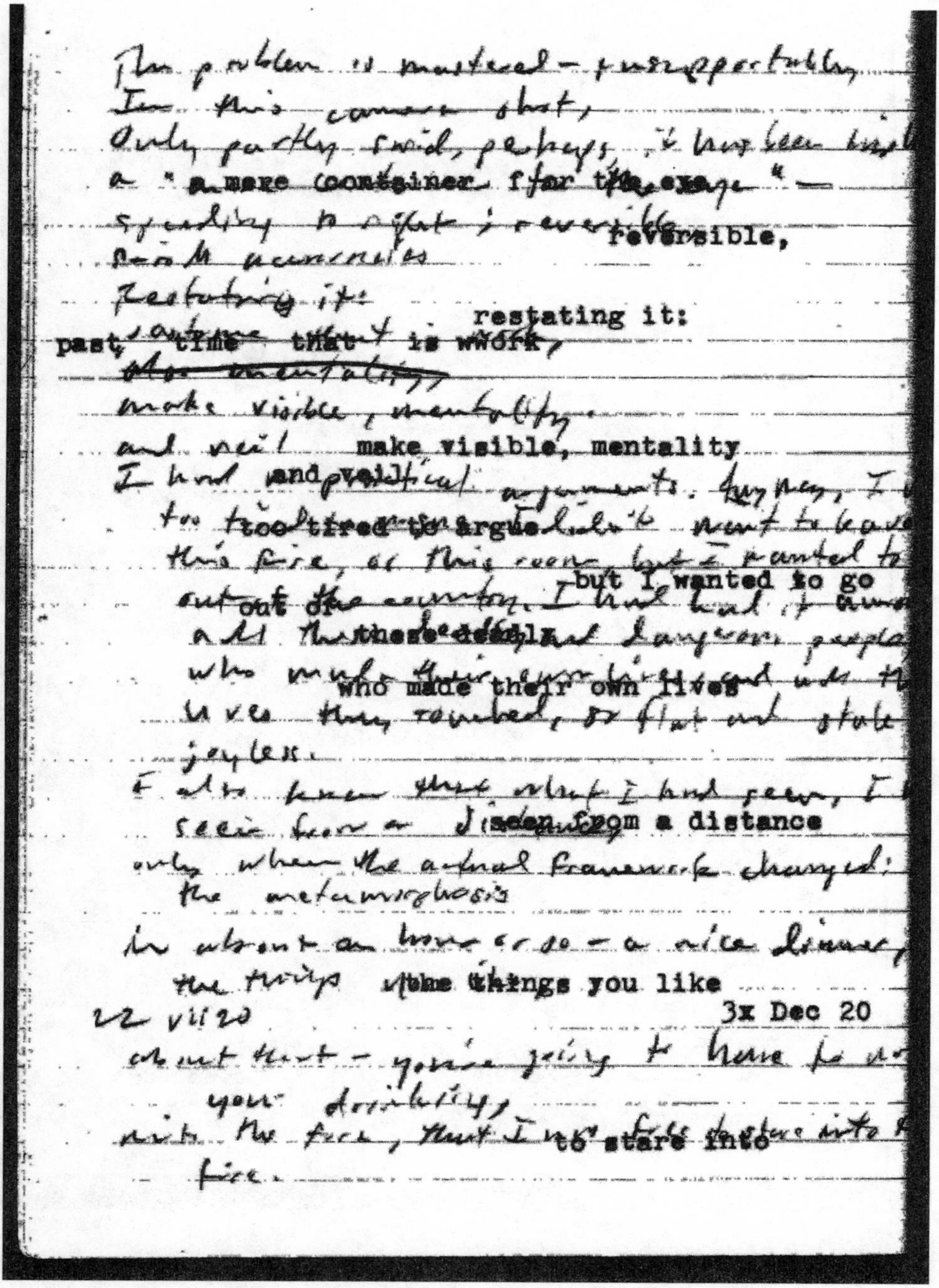
The problem is material — insupportably
In this camera shot,
Only partly said, perhaps, it has been
a "a mere container for the image" —
speaking to what is reversible
reversible,
and its accumulations
Restating it:
restating it:
past, autumn time that is work,
mentality
make visible, mentality.
and veil make visible, mentality
I had and veil political arguments. Anyway, I
too tired to argue didn't want to leave
this fire, or this room, but I wanted to
but I wanted to go
out out of the country. I had had it
all these deadly dangerous people
who made their own lives
who made their own lives
lives they ruined, so flat and stale
joyless.
I also knew that what I had seen, I
seen from a distance seen from a distance
only when the actual framework changed:
the metamorphosis
In about an hour or so — a nice dinner,
the things the things you like
22 VII 20
3x Dec 20
about that — you're going to have to
your drinking,
with the fire, that I to stare into
fire.

crumbling, whirling, brilliant universe, the fire

crumbling shaking brilliant universe. the fire

towered high rising straight up like a tree

on tower a tower made of air

between us.

between us.

She looked over at me. Are you ready for your

water.

around my private parts, my belly, my nipples,

my chest. I leaned

taken away

1 Dec 20

how it will go

or what you will do

Going, going... Is

the secret

you speak too

Concert is the word,

listened to by me

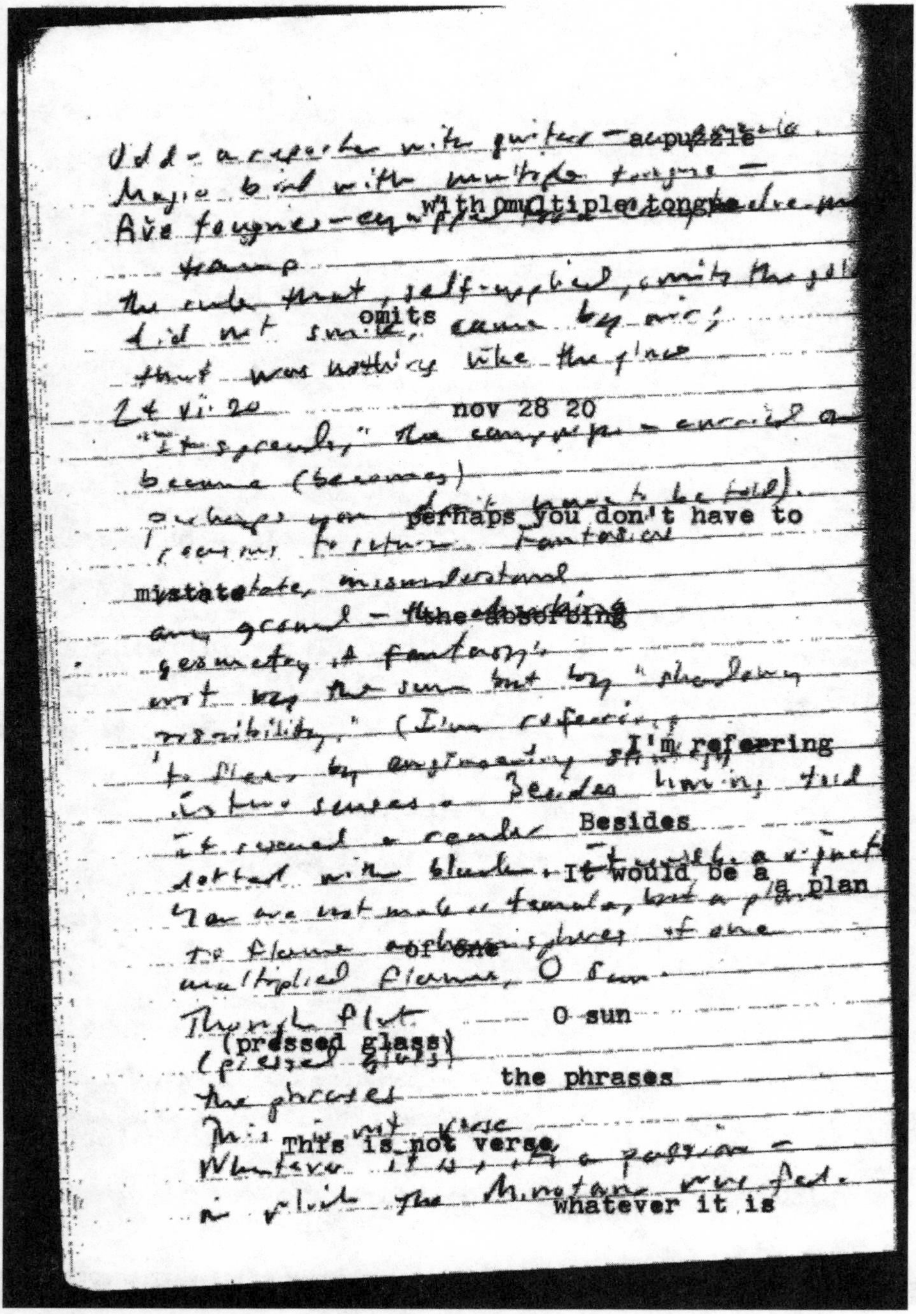

Odd — a reciter with guitar — a puzzle to
Magic bird with multiple tongue —
Ave tongues — eye **with multiple tongue** *dream*
tramp
the code that, self-applied, omits the gll
did not smile, **omits** *came by air;*
that was nothing like the place
24 vi 20 **nov 28 20**
"It spreads," the campaign — enrolled a
became (becomes)
perhaps you **perhaps you don't have to**
[recurs to return] fantasies
misstatate, misunderstand
any ground — the ~~dissolving~~
geometry of fantasy's
not say the sun but say "shadowy
visibility," (I'm referring **I'm referring**
to stars by engineering ∴
in two senses. Besides having tied **Besides**
it round a render
dotted with blue — It would be a **It would be a** *plan*
You are not male or female, but a **plan**
to flame ~~atmospheres~~ *of one*
unmultiplied flame, O sun.
Through flat ———— **O sun**
(pressed glass)
(pressed glass)
the phrases **the phrases**
This is not verse **This is not verse**
Whatever it is, it's a passion —
in which the Minotaur was fed. **whatever it is**

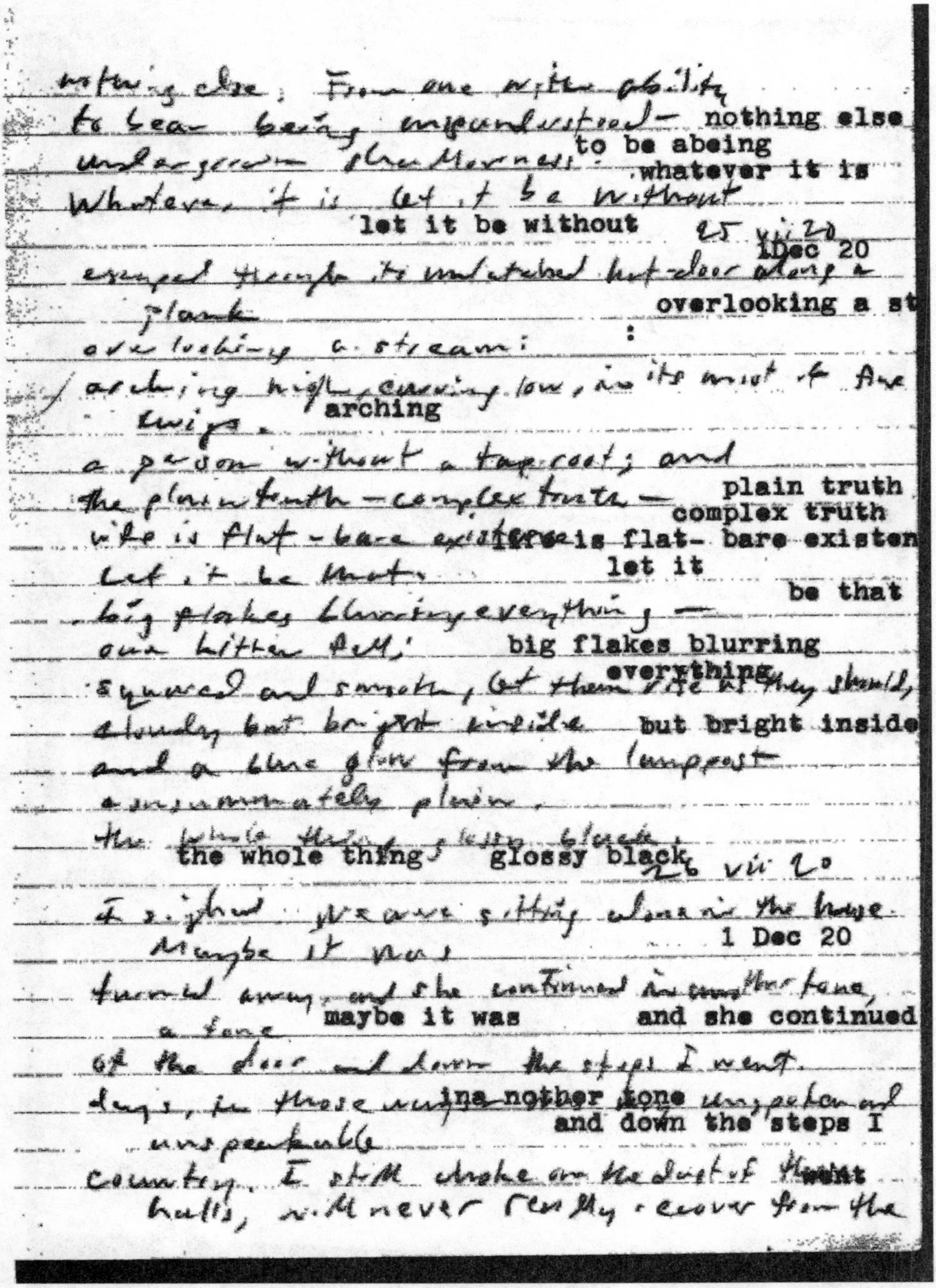

nothing else. From one writer ability
to bear being misunderstood— nothing else
to be abeing
whatever it is
Whatever it is let it be without
let it be without 25 vii 20
1Dec 20
escaped through its unlatched back-door along a plank
overlooking a st
:
overlooking a stream:
arching high, curving low, in its mist of fine twigs.
arching
a person without a tap-root; and
the plain truth—complex truth— plain truth
complex truth
life is flat—bare existence is flat- bare existen
let it be that. let it
be that
big flakes blurring everything—
our bitter hell; big flakes blurring
everything
squared and smooth, let them rise as they should,
cloudy but bright inside but bright inside
and a blue glow from the lamppost
consummately plain.
the whole thing glossy black.
the whole thing glossy black
26 vii 20
I sighed. We are sitting alone in the house
1 Dec 20
Maybe it was
turned away, and she continued in another tone,
a tone maybe it was and she continued
of the door and down the steps I went.
days, in those unspoken and ina nother tone
and down the steps I
unspeakable
country. I still choke on the dust of those went
halls, will never really recover from the

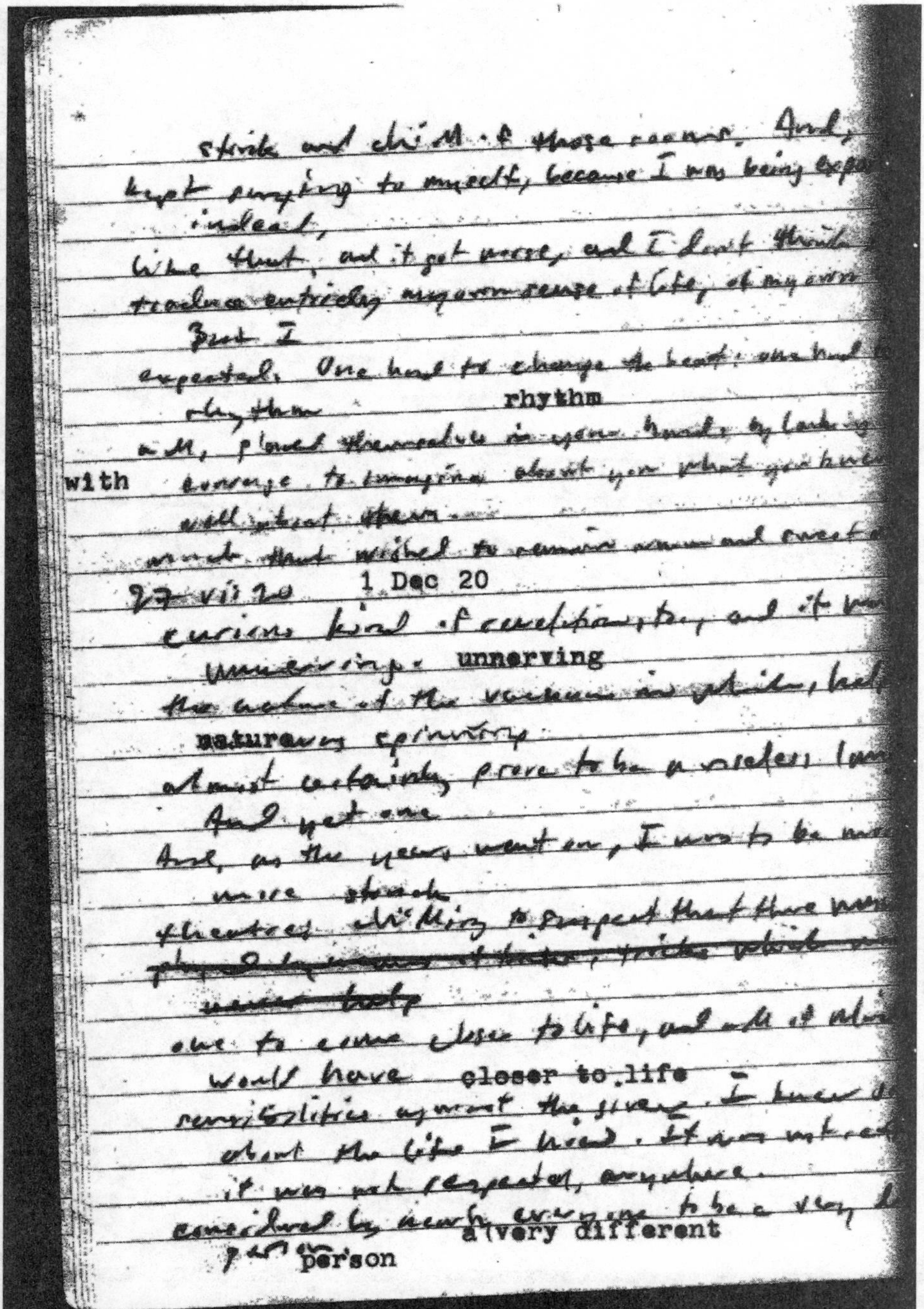
strike and chill of those rooms. And,
kept saying to myself, because I was being expo[illegible]
indeed,
like that, and it got worse, and I don't think
realize entirely my own sense of life, of my own
But I
expected. One had to change the beat; one had to
rhythm
rhythm
all, placed themselves in your hands by looking
with
courage to imagine about you what you knew
will about them.
much that wished to remain warm and sweet
27 vii 20
1 Dec 20
curious kind of correction, and it was
unnerving.
unnerving
the nature of the vacuum in which, beh[illegible]
nature was spinning
almost certainly prove to be a useless [illegible]
And yet one
And, as the years went on, I was to be more
more struck
theatres chilling to suspect that there were
[illegible]
[illegible]
one to come closer to life, and all of which
would have
closer to life
sensibilities against the grain. I knew [illegible]
about the life I lived. It was not [illegible]
it was not respected, anywhere.
considered by nearly everyone to be a very [illegible]
person
a very different
person

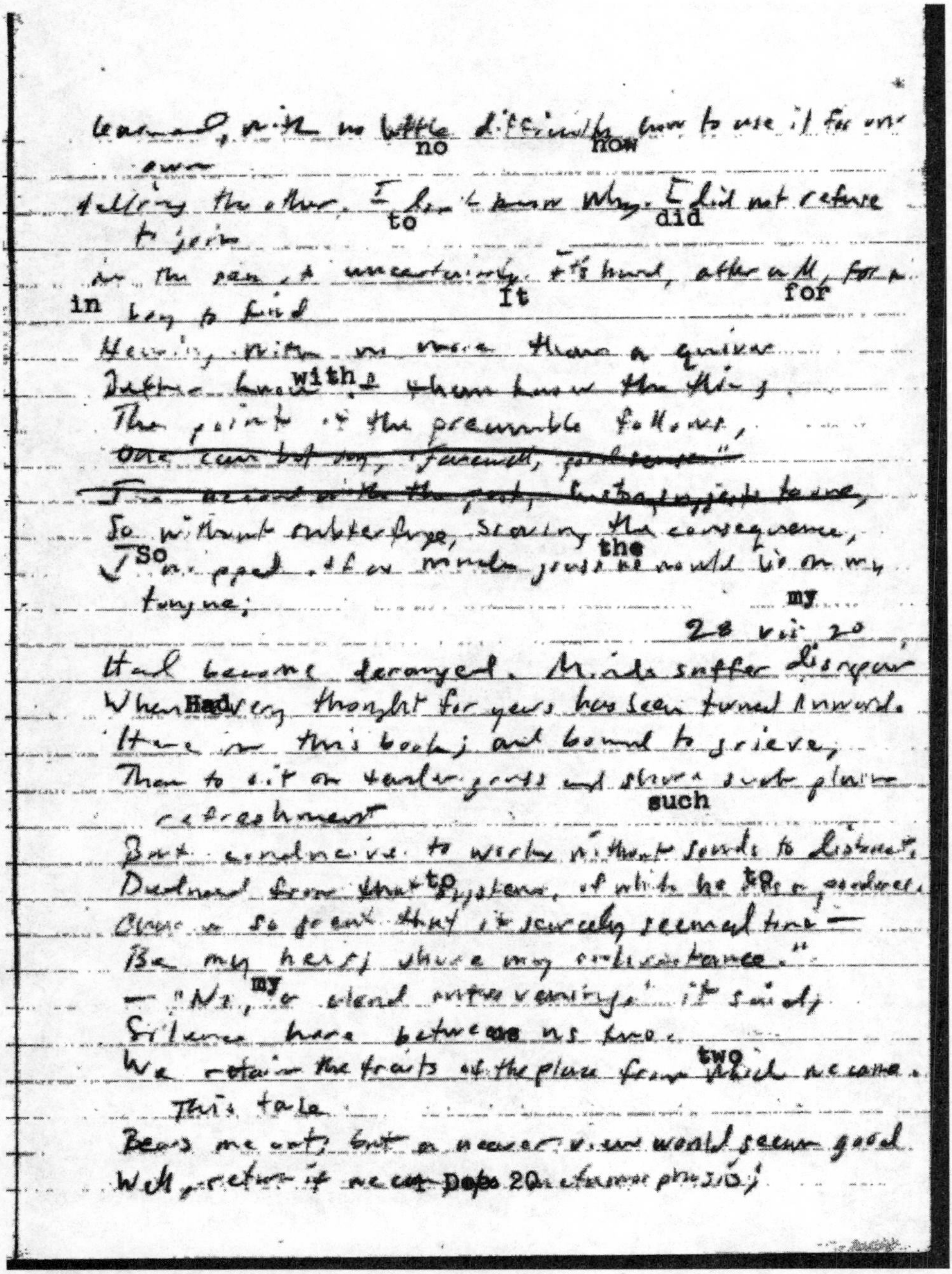
learned, with no little difficulty how to use it for our
no now
own
telling the other. I don't know why. I did not refuse
to did
to join
in the pain of uncertainty. It's hard, after all, for a
in It for
boy to find
Heaving, with no more than a quiver
[illegible] with, & them know the thing.
The point of the preamble follows,
~~One can but say, "Farewell, [illegible]"~~
~~I'm [illegible] with the past, [illegible]~~
So without subterfuge, scaring the consequence,
the
I So [illegible] the words just as would [illegible] on my
tongue;
my
28 viii 20
Had become deranged. Minds suffer disrepair
When Had every thought for years has been turned inwards.
Here in this book; and bound to grieve,
Than to sit on [illegible] and share such pleasant
such
refreshment
But conducive to work without sounds to distract,
Deafened from that to systems, of which he to is a conductor
Close in so front that it scarcely seemed time—
Be my host; share my [illegible]."
—"No," [illegible] my [illegible]," it said;
Silence here between us two.
two
We retain the traits of the place from which we came.
This tale
Bears me out; but a nearer view would seem good
Well, return if we [illegible] Dops 20 [illegible]

questions
Inbox

12:55 AM (21 hours ago)

Eileen Myles <eileen.myles@gmail.com>

to Mark, Tim

so now I want to know what it is. How did you compose it. Did you take parts from some other text, texts, did you write it. I want to understand what I'm looking at.

Thanks,

Eileen

it's the latest heap from my recycling vortex. i used to make lots and lots of reading tapes of various kind, and came a certain time i realize they were just reading lists. i think in a few moments i was actually typing them over. so i started thinking about a notebook like a tape, and recording by writing down bits and fragments while reading, usually between two books. it could mean anything, some electric connection within the moment, a memory, an observation, often something noticed about the act itself. the curving inner life of the word outside, registered line after line, somehow. you'll remember we had a long talk about "the pathetic notebook" and that is this (also what i released on thursday night). you remember we talked about dante and virgil and liz with the headlamp. the start was the day before i left for marfa, which was the day after the blue notebook got filled out, july 15. it's a bigger notebook than most of the little moleskin and ica ones, and somehow pathetic meant i had to contend with extra, like it or not: i made myself take down entire printed lines, not just the "best" suitable fragment. all the weirdness of an arbitrary break like that. and if what caught me hung over, then i'd have to take down the whole next line, like the smallest cuttable pixel was the whole printed line of whatever i was reading, carrying that whole heavy bundle of switches on my back. it starts out somewhere in 'tell me how long the train's been gone' and the complete poems of elizabeth bishop. later marianne moore, and dante, john wieners, artaud, sawako nakayasu et al. just going a step further than treating language as something always at hand, to specify that it's the language boxed in by these two books i'm reading, no matter what's happening in life, and further, the language in front of me, the line i'm on when i go to write. just like the tape would always be looping, and you'd get wherever i was at, next to whatever else it happened to land by. this notebook was also self-consciously in response to your/tim's 'pathetic' ask, an essay dwelling on being pathetic. i had cutely suggested that whenever the notebook was done, tim could illustrate it. i was thinking some selected typed pages, paired with some kind of typewriter poetry. but tim had this impulse to photocopy and type over, a most pathetic form of manuscript illumination and i really loved it.

TIMELY: UNTIMELY: MY NOTE: Tim Johnson

When Eileen asked me about Pathetic Lit, I thought of Mark's *notebooks*. In them, he provides a date and then writes (by hand) some of what he reads during the day. The words come from books, poems and novels mostly, with sources changing as his interest does. Syntactically it's loose, but it's not random. It's him, but musically. The persistence of Mark's life in Mark's selection gives the work an unassuming kind of coherence; the facts of place names and dates are its structure. It's not much, but it's enough. None of the words in the notebooks are Mark's, but he put them there. Together: time and these words make one of his many forms of music. People might call this mode of working plagiarism, or pathetic, since it seems to avoid the effort of invention or because it avoids the usual tools and workplaces. I bet the same people consider it pathetic to be involved in many kinds of work, and to avoid work as well. Strong and savvy are reserved for the creative class now, and the innovators. Maybe the rest are pathetic, which doesn't sound so bad. I wanted to perform a duet with Mark because I love his music. As such: I've selected words from the words Mark selected and typed them as I read them, in copies made from the first ten pages of his most recent notebook.

Selection from *Up Your Ass*

VALERIE SOLANAS

WHITE CAT: Hey, it's me. I'm back.

BONGI: Yeah, you're the eternal masculine.

CAT: Some civilization we got—my next door neighbor was raped and choked to death this afternoon by a delivery boy.

GINGER: Ah, the poor boy. He must've had a rotten mother.

RUSSELL: Probably spent all her time competing. You see what kind of world women create?

CAT (*to BONGI*)**:** Do you spend all your time loitering on the street?

BONGI: No, I have an occasional moment up the alley.

CAT: So that's your gig. That's a groovy deal. Sometimes I wish I were a broad, sitting on a gold mine; I'd be peddling it all over town. What're most of them saving it for, anyway? Their old age? But you're smart—making your talent pay off.

BONGI: How would you know what my talent is?

CAT: What's any girl's talent?

BONGI: Endurance. How else would all you baboons stay alive?

RUSSELL: You women take yourselves too seriously. You can't take a joke.

BONGI: No, I dig jokes. I'm just waiting to get on the stage so I can tell my funnies.

RUSSELL: By the way, am I correct in inferring from your preceding conversation with this boy that you don't have a job?

BONGI: That's right. I applied for a job once, but they wouldn't pay me enough. I told the guy I couldn't possibly work for such a stinking salary. He said none of the other girls there mind the salary, 'cause his place's a fun place to work at and 'cause there's loads of bright, handsome, eligible bachelors working there. I asked him if I promised not to marry any of them, could I have more money. He said I didn't have clean values.

GINGER: Tactless of him to've told you.

BONGI: But I couldn't've lasted if they paid me a thousand a week—I'm not a worker; I'm a lover.

CAT: So am I; that's why I'm a worker.

GINGER: That doesn't make sense; you can't buy love.

CAT: Love's an itch in the crotch.

BONGI: So why do you need a girl to scratch your crotch? Scratch your own crotch.

CAT: I'm a sentimental kind of guy; I like togetherness.

RUSSELL (*to BONGI*): Isn't your occupation rather precarious?

BONGI: It has it's ups and downs.

RUSSELL: I mean isn't it rather unstable?

BONGI: What's life supposed to be, anyway? An endurance contest?

RUSSELL: But don't you ever worry?

BONGI: Never about trivialities—like where my next meal's coming from.

GINGER: You know, I consider your calling rather delightful—the artful courtesan, master of all the graces and finesses of seduction. Tell, what must a woman do to seduce a man?

BONGI: Exist in his presence.

GINGER: Come on, no; there's far more to it than that.

BONGI: Well, if you're in a really big hurry you can try walking around with your fly open.

GINGER: Oh, come on; quit joking. Actually, I'm sure you must deem it an honor to serve as high priestess in the temple of love, fulfilling woman's time-honored role of pleasing men. We, women, we all have a little bit of the whore in us.

BONGI: I don't.

GINGER: But most women won't let it come out. They don't know how to be women; they've got ice water in their veins.

BONGI: I always thought it was piss.

GINGER: Women should cultivate the whorey graces. They've lost the feminine charms that once endeared them to men.

RUSSELL: Too busy competing.

GINGER: One reason why men're so enthralled with me is they sense the passion, the savage, the wild beast in me, but restrained, tasteful passion. Savage that I am, I'm not cheap. I'm a discreet beast.

RUSSELL: Yes, discretion's the better part of beastliness, not ferocious clawing away for dominance, dog-eat-dog competition.

GINGER (*recitational*): When a woman strives for equality she renounces her superiority. Isn't that right, Russell?

RUSSELL: Unquestionably. (*To BONGI.*) Is that too deep for you?

BONGI: What do you want to do? Put women back in purdah?

CAT: We don't need purdah; we have the suburbs.

RUSSELL: You're too easily appeased; you can't see the horror that's creeping up on us. God, sometimes I think it's a curse being sensitive. Marriage—It's their most lethal weapon: before marriage men're active, restless and energetic.

BONGI: Like a tree full of monkeys.

RUSSELL: Exuberant, vibrant youth.

BONGI: I can guess where they're vibrating.

RUSSELL: But afterwards we're soothed into tranquility, lulled into placidity, devitalized, tamed into submission; they leave us no strength with which to counterattack; they triumph by depriving us of our most precious possession—our bachelor freedom.

CAT: Bachelor freedom, my ass; that's the freedom of an alley cat—free to prowl the streets looking for something to fuck.

RUSSELL: Make love to. Well, I will concede there're a few advantages to marriage.

BONGI: Like widows' pensions.

GINGER: And motherhood.

RUSSELL: Ahh, yeeaahh, Motherhood—cute, cuddly little babies.

BONGI: Let's all bow our heads and kitchy-koo for two minutes.

RUSSELL: A son to carry my name down through the ages—Fizzlebaum! I'd give anything to be able to give birth, the crowning achievement, what every woman's aching for.

BONGI: I'm not.

GINGER: How would you know? You're not a specialist.

RUSSELL: The highest honor, the supreme power.

GINGER: The hand that rocks the cradle rules the world. Isn't that right, Russell?

RUSSELL: It's indisputable.

BONGI: That's a slick little maxim—while the hand's rocking the cradle it won't be rocking the boat.

GINGER: There's plenty of male hands around to do whatever boat-rocking's necessary.

BONGI: I've met quite a few hairy old male hands in my day, and it's not the boat they're grabbing for.

CAT: Why should it be? It's a man's world.

BONGI: Only by default.

GINGER: Default or not, I think it's marvelous.

CAT: Sure, in a man's world you broads have the ultimate weapon—sex.

BONGI: Then how come we've never had a sexy president?

CAT (*to BONGI*)**:** Why don't you run for president?

BONGI: Nah, I like to think big.

GINGER: Personally, I'd hate to see a woman president.

CAT: Why? Women're just as good as men in every way.

BONGI: I've had just about enough of your insults.

GINGER: Well, whether they are or not, we'll never have one. Never! We never have . . . (*So there voice.*) . . . and we never will. Will we, Russell?

RUSSELL: It's unthinkable.

BONGI: Maybe being president wouldn't be such a bad idea: I could eliminate the money system, and let the machines do all the work.

CAT: Thanks for the warning. I'll be sure to not vote for you. Sure, I'd like to not need bread—I don't want to have to combine marriage and career—but the broads gotta need it. You know the S in the dollar sign? That stands for sex.

GINGER: Actually, there's something to be said for Bongi's system; men need leisure time.

CAT: What'll I do with all that leisure? Lay around with a big hard on?

GINGER: It's a sin to tie men down to jobs. Men're the hunters . . .

CAT: Yeah, I been doing a lot of that.

GINGER: . . . the adventurers; they should be free to go off and invent and explore, soar off into the unknown.

RUSSELL: And leave the kids to the women? Corrode my son with femininity? Never! When mothers aren't competing they're mothering; you gotta keep a close watch on them. I want my son to be the best of all possible men.

BONGI: You mean a half-assed woman.

RUSSELL: When he grows up I want to be able to point to him and say: "There goes my son—the man." I want to live in a masculine culture.

BONGI: That's a contradiction in terms.

RUSSELL: I want a strong, virile environment.

BONGI: Why don't you hang out at the YMCA gym?

CAT: The battle of the sexes—it's been raging on for centuries.

BONGI: I know how we could eliminate it.

CAT: How?

BONGI: Have you ever heard of sex determination?

RUSSELL: Never! Never! That's not natural. There'll always be two sexes.

BONGI: Men're totally unreasonable; they can't see why they should be eliminated.

RUSSELL: No! The two-sex system must be right; it's survived hundreds of thousands of years.

BONGI: So has disease.

RUSSELL: You can't just determine us away. We won't allow it; we'll unite; we'll fight.

BONGI: You may as well resign yourself: eventually the expression "female of the species" 'll be a redundancy.

RUSSELL: You don't know what a female is, you desexed monstrosity.

BONGI: Quite the contrary, I'm so female I'm subversive.

RUSSELL: Well, I, for one, wouldn't make love to you for a million dollars.

BONGI: Maybe not, but you'd do it for nothing.

RUSSELL: Never! Not if you were the last woman on earth.

BONGI: That's not your decision to make.

RUSSELL: That's ridiculous. Whose decision is it?

BONGI: Mine.

RUSSELL: I think I just might have something to say about it.

BONGI: You have nothing to say. When I give the signal you'll jump.

RUSSELL: You have some unmitigated gall. Who do you think you are?

BONGI: Just a girl with a signal. Here, I'll show it to you.

(She starts to undo her belt.)

Goodbye Forever

STEVE CAREY

Shit, I'm busting out of this mill!
Yes, I am! Getting out of this burg!
Leaving! Quitting this place! Splitting!
Making my beat! Making tracks! Hauling out!
Heading out! Hauling ass! Heading elsewhere!
Vacating the premises! Bent on all points other!
Vamoose, I! Picking them up and laying them down!
Following the sun! Moving out! Moving on!
Making for more clement climes! Hauling
These bones out of here! Avanti! Away, me!
Me, I'm fading! Fade me! Changing
My whereabouts! my tune! Relocating!
Taking it on the lam! Beating my feet!
Taking the path of least resistance!
Cashing in my chips! Making a fresh start!
Cutting my losses! Tending west! Heading east!
Packing up my old kit bag! Pulling up stakes!
Draggin'! Cutting loose! This kid's history!
Watch my smoke! I'm breaking my contract!
Keepin' on keepin' on! Emigrating! Moving
My cookies! Changing the record! Making haste!
Going on the run! Read truckin'
For wistfully sprinting! Shipping out!
Sailing with the tide! Saddling up!
Mounting my nag! Shimmering off! Departing!

Dissembling! Blowing this joint! Disappear!
Making myself scarce! Going off! Remaining not!
Otherwise traipsing! Trotting off! Tripping off!
Shifting off! Wandering off! Oiling out!
Evacuating! Vanishing! Taking myself elsewhere!
Relocating! Generally resettling! Picking up
The Pieces! Casting my fate to the wind!
Setting sail! Setting out! Setting off!
Turning my back on all that once was!
Burning through! Breaking through! Breaking off!
Shuttling forward! Shuffling off! Cutting the cord!
Jumping bail! Shifting my load! Putting in
For a transfer! Taking it on the road!
Otherwise disposing of myself! Replanting!
Jumping ship! Emptying the coffers! Closing
All accounts! Once since gone! One presently absent!
Aspiring to be no longer among those present!
With us no more! Literally vacuous!
Elsewhere Represented! Fervently without!
Desirous of other office! Sprung! Soon to be
In frequent correspondence with those now present!
Keen maker of the heart grow fonder! Gone
Like a cool breeze! A.W.O.L.! Becoming
Dim-pictured! No longer at this address!
Gone but not forgotten! Author of this goodbye!
Poof! What I'll do is leave! Though known,
Now vague! Obscure! Abstracted! A nameless haze!
I'm packing it in! Tossing my lot! Casting off!
Cruising through! Disporting anew! Newly moved!
The new hand! New kid on the block! Prominent loss!
Mr. Tootle-oo! Go-go bozo! I'll be shoving off!
Shifting gears! Shagging out! Taking off
For parts unknown! In fact, taking off!
Flying the coop! Taking care of a last few details!
I'm the one winkled away on or about this day!
I'm out of here! Kicking up dust! Dearest, I wish

You the best of everything and shall watch your future career
With considerable interest! Off I go! Skeedadle!
Flying away! Grabbing a cab! Giving up my chair!
Gone globe-trotting! Soon to present a letter
Of introduction! Sending love to his and her people!
Presuming significant distance! Doing a bolt!
Conspicuous in my absence! Having a wonderful time!
End of transmission! Sayonara! Adios!
Au revoir! Aloha! So long!

Excerpt from *La Bâtarde*

VIOLETTE LEDUC

Translated by Derek Coltman

It was all even stricter than in church. Isabelle was studying at the front table near the dais. I sat down in my place, I opened a book so as to be like her, I kept watch, I counted one, two, three, four, five, six, seven, eight. I can't go up to her, I can't make her look up from her book. Another girl went up to Isabelle's table without any hesitation, she showed her some work she'd done. They discussed it. Isabelle was still living as she had lived before she called me into her cubicle. Isabelle was disappointing me, Isabelle was casting a spell over me.

I can't read. Every meandering river in my geography book holds the same question in every loop. What can I do to make the time pass? She turns sideways; she has exposed herself to me but she doesn't know I'm drinking her in. She turns toward where I am sitting, she will never know what she gave me. She is talking, she is far away, she is discussing something, she is working: a foal is gamboling in her head. I'm not at all like her. I shall go to her, I shall force myself on her. She yawns—how human she is—she pulls the pin out of her coiled hair, she pushes it back again. She knows what she will do tonight, but she can think of other things.

Isabelle leaned toward me when the other girl left the study hall. Isabelle had noticed me.

I moved down the aisle, squeezed between the walls of my joy.

"My love. Were you there all the time?" she asked.

My head was suddenly quite empty.

"Bring your books. We'll work together. It's stifling in here."

I opened the window and, for heroism's sake, looked out into the courtyard.

"Aren't you bringing your books?"

"It would be impossible."

"Why?

"I couldn't work near you."

When she sees me and her face changes like that, it's genuine. When she can't see me and her face is normal, that's genuine too.

"Do you really want me near you?" I asked.

"Sit down."

I sat down next to her, I sobbed a sob of happiness.

"What's the matter?"

"I can't explain."

She took my hand under the desk.

"Isabelle, Isabelle . . . What shall we do during recess?"

"We'll talk."

"I don't want to talk."

I took my hand away.

"Tell me what's the matter," Isabelle insisted.

"Can't you tell?"

"We'll be together again. I promise."

At about seven that evening I was surrounded by other girls suggesting I go for a walk with them or talk to them. I stammered, I moved away from the others. I was no longer free and I was no longer the same age. Shall I ever listen again, as I listened once, outside the kindergarten room, to the young mistress who studies at the Conservatoire and still plays Bach on the piano of her alma mater? Isabelle was putting away her books, Isabelle was near me. I turned to stone.

My peach skin: the light at seven in the evening in the recreation yard. My chervil: the spidery lace floating in the air. My reliquaries: the leaves on the trees making arbors for the breeze to rest in. What shall we do when night comes? What happens in the evening becomes uncertain in the daytime. I feel time caressing me but I can't think what we shall do next time. I can hear the seven o'clock noise and voices smoothing the thoughtful horizon. The gloved hand of infinity is closing over me.

"What are you looking at, Violette?"

"The geraniums . . . Down there . . ."

"What else?"

"The street, the window, they're all you."

"Give me your arm."

The evening came down over us with its velvet coat stopping at the knees.

"I can't give you my arm. People will notice, we would be caught."

"Are you ashamed?" Isabelle asked.

"Ashamed of what? Don't you understand? I'm being sensible."

The courtyard was all ours. We ran with our arms around each other's waist, we tore aside the lace in the air with our foreheads, we heard the pattering of our hearts in the dust. Little white horses galloped in our breasts. The girls, the mistresses all laughed and clapped their hands: they urged us on when we slowed down.

"Faster, faster. Close your eyes. I am leading you," Isabelle said.

There was a wall we had to go along. Then we would be alone.

"You're not running fast enough. Yes, yes . . . Close your eyes, close your eyes."

I obeyed.

Her lips brushed against my lips.

"I'm afraid . . . of the summer vacation, Isabelle. . . . I'm afraid of our last day in the courtyard, in summer. . . . I'm afraid of falling and killing myself," I said.

I opened my eyes: we were alive.

"Afraid? I'm leading you," she said.

"Let's run some more if you like."

"My wife, my baby," she said.

She gave me the words and kept them for herself as well. She held them to her by holding me to her. I loosened my fingers slightly around her waist. I counted: my love, my wife, my baby. I had three engagement rings on three fingers of my hand.

The other girls were standing without speaking, it was the minute of silence. Isabelle changed places. We closed the ranks, we were keeping our distance.

"I love you."

"I love you," I said too.

The juniors were already eating. We pretended to forget what we had both said, we began talking to other girls.

*

I reached for my percale curtain, following the nightly routine. An iron hand seized me and led me elsewhere. Isabelle threw me down onto her bed and buried her face in my underclothes.

"Come back when they're asleep," she said.

She drove me out again, she chained me to her.

I was in love: there was nowhere I could hide. There would be only the respites between our meetings.

Isabelle was coughing as she sat up in bed, Isabelle was ready beneath her shawl of hair. Her shawl. The picture I was going back to paralyzed me. I collapsed onto my chair, then onto the rug: the picture followed me everywhere.

I undressed in the half darkness, I pressed my chaste hand against my flesh, I breathed, I recognized my existence, I yielded myself. I piled up the silence at the bottom of my basin, I wrung it out as I wrung out my washcloth, I spread it gently over my skin as I wiped myself.

The assistant put out the light in her room. Isabelle coughed again: she was calling to me. I decided that if I didn't close my tin of dentifrice I would remember what everything was like before I went to Isabelle in her room. I was preparing a past for myself.

"Are you ready?" whispered Isabelle on the other side of my curtain.

She was gone again.

I opened the window of my cell. The night and the sky wanted no part of us. To live in the open air meant soiling everything outside. Our absence was necessary for the beauty of the evening trees. I risked my head in the aisle, but the aisle forced me back. Their sleep frightened me: I hadn't the courage to step over the sleeping girls, to walk with my bare feet over their faces. I closed the window again and the curtain shivered, like the leaves outside.

"Are you coming?"

I turned on my flashlight: her hair was falling as I had imagined it, but I had not foreseen her nightgown swollen with that bold simplicity. Isabelle went away again.

I went into her cubicle with my flashlight.

"Take off your nightgown," Isabelle said.

She was leaning on one shoulder, her hair raining over her profile.

"Take off your nightgown and put out the light. . . ."

I put out her hair, her eyes, her hands. I stripped off my nightgown. It was nothing new: I was stripping off the night of every first love.

"What are you doing?" Isabelle asked.

"I'm dawdling."

She stifled her laughter in the bed as I posed naked in my shyness for the shadows.

"What are you doing, for heaven's sake?"

I slid into the bed. I had been cold, now I could be warm.

I stiffened, I was afraid of brushing against her hair beneath the covers. She took hold of me, she pulled me on top of her: Isabelle wanted our skins to merge. I chanted with my body over hers, I bathed my belly in the lilies of her belly. I sank into a cloud. She touched me lightly on the buttocks, she sent strange arrows through my flesh. I pulled away, I fell back.

We listened to what was happening inside us, to the emanations from our bodies: we were ringed around with other couples. The bedsprings gave a groan.

"Careful!" she said against my mouth.

The assistant had switched on her light. I was kissing a little girl with a mouth that tasted of vanilla. We had become good little girls again.

"Let's squeeze each other," Isabelle said.

We tightened the girdles that were all we had in the world.

"Crush me. . . ."

She wanted to but she couldn't. She ground my buttocks with her fingers.

"Don't listen to her," she said.

The assistant was urinating in her toilet pail. Isabelle was rubbing her toe against my ankle as a token of friendship.

"She's asleep again," Isabelle said.

I took Isabelle by the mouth, I was afraid of the assistant, I drank our saliva. It was an orgy of dangers. We had felt the darkness in our mouths and throats, then we had felt peace return.

"Crush me," she said.

"The bed . . . it will make a noise . . . they'll hear us. . . ."

We talked amid the crowding leaves of summer nights.

I was crushing, blotting out, thousands of tiny cells beneath my weight.

"Am I too heavy?"

"You'll never be too heavy. I feel cold," she said.

My fingers considered her icy shoulders. I flew away, I snatched up in my beak the tufts of wool caught on thorns along the hedgerows and laid them one by one on Isabelle's shoulders. I tapped at her bones with downy hammers, my kisses hurtling down on top of one another as I flung myself onward through quicksands of tenderness. My hands relieved my failing lips; I molded the sky around her shoulders. Isabelle rose, fell back, and I fell with her into the hollow of her shoulder. My cheek came to rest on a curve.

"My darling."

I said it over and over.

"Yes," Isabelle said.

She said: "Just a minute," and paused.

She was tying back her hair, her elbow fanned my face.

The hand landed on my neck: a frosty sun whitened my hair. The hand followed my veins, downward. The hand stopped. My blood beat against the mount of Venus on Isabelle's palm. The hand moved up again: it was drawing circles, overflowing into the void, spreading its sweet ripples ever wider around my left shoulder, while the other lay abandoned to the darkness streaked by the breathing of the other girls. I was discovering the smoothness of my bones, the glow hidden in my flesh, the infinity of forms I possessed. The hand was trailing a mist of dreams across my skin. The heavens beg when someone strokes your shoulder: the heavens were begging now. The hand moved upward once again, spreading a velvet shawl up to my chin, then down once more, persuasively, heavier now, shaping itself to the curves it pressed upon. Finally there was a squeeze of friendship. I took Isabelle into my arms, gasping with gratitude.

"Can you see me?" Isabelle asked.

"I see you."

She stopped me from saying more, slid down in the bed, and kissed the curling hairs.

"Listen, horses!" a girl cried nearby.

"Don't be afraid. She's dreaming. Give me your hand," Isabelle said.

I was weeping for joy.

"Are you crying?" she asked anxiously.

"I love you: I'm not crying."

I wiped my eyes.

The hand stripped the velvet off my arm, halted near the vein in the crook of the elbow, fornicated there amongst the traceries, moved in downward to the wrist, right to the tips of the nails, sheathed my arm once more in a long suède glove, fell from my shoulder like an insect, and hooked itself into the armpit. I was stretching my neck, listening for what answers my arm was giving the wanderer. The hand, still seeking to persuade me, was bringing my arm, my armpit, into their real existence. The hand was wandering through whispering snow-capped bushes, over the last frosts on the meadows, over the first buds as they swelled to fullness. The springtime that had been crying its impatience with the voice of tiny birds under my skin was now curving and swelling into flower. Isabelle, stretched out upon the darkness, was fastening my feet with ribbons, unwinding the swaddling bands of my alarm. With hands laid flat upon the mattress, I was immersed in the selfsame magic task as she. She was kissing what she had caressed and then, light as a feather duster, the hand began to flick, to brush the wrong way all that it had smoothed before. The sea monster in my entrails quivered. Isabelle was drinking at my breast, the right, the left, and I drank with her, sucking the milk of darkness when her lips had gone. The fingers were returning now, encircling and testing the warm weight of my breast. The fingers were pretending to be waifs in a storm; they were taking shelter inside me. A host of slaves, all with the face of Isabelle, fanned my brow, my hands.

She knelt up in the bed.

"Do you love me?"

I led her hand up to the precious tears of joy.

Her cheek took shelter in the hollow of my groin. I shone the flashlight beam on her, and saw her spreading hair, saw my own belly beneath the rain of silk. The flashlight slipped, Isabelle moved suddenly toward me.

As we melted into one another we were dragged up to the surface by the hooks caught in our flesh, by the hairs we were clutching in our fingers; we were rolling together on a bed of nails. We bit each other and bruised the darkness with our hands.

Slowing down, we trailed back beneath our plumes of smoke, black wings sprouting at our heels. Isabelle leaped out of bed.

I wondered why Isabelle was doing her hair again. With one hand she forced me to lie on my back, with the other, to my distress, she shone the pale yellow beam of the flashlight on me.

I tried to shield myself with my arms.

"I'm not beautiful. You make me feel ashamed," I said.

She was looking at our future in my eyes, she was gazing at what was going to happen next, storing it in the currents of her blood.

She got back into bed, she wanted me.

I played with her, preferring failure to the preliminaries she needed. Making love with our mouths was enough for me: I was afraid, but my hands as they signaled for help were helpless stumps. A pair of tweezers was advancing into the folds of my flesh. My heart was beating under its molehill, my head was filled with damp earth. Two tormenting fingers were exploring me. How masterly, how inevitable their caress. . . . My closed eyes listened: the finger lightly touched the pearl. I wanted to be wider, to make it easier for her.

The regal, diplomatic finger was moving forward, moving back, making me gasp for breath, beginning to enter, arousing the monster in my entrails, parting the secret cloud, pausing, prompting once more. I tightened, I closed over this flesh of my flesh its softness and its bony core. I sat up, I fell back again. The finger which had not wounded me, the finger, after its grateful exploration, left me. My flesh peeled back from it.

"Do you love me?" I asked.

I wanted to create a diversion.

"You mustn't cry out," Isabelle said.

I crossed my arms over my face, still listening under my lowered eyelids.

Two thieves entered me. They were forcing their way inside, they wanted to go further, but my flesh rebelled.

"My love . . . you're hurting me."

She put her hand over my mouth.

"I won't make any noise," I said.

The gag was a humiliation.

"It hurts. But she's got to do it. It hurts."

I gave myself up to darkness and without wanting to, I helped. I leaned forward to help tear myself, to come closer to her face, to be nearer my wound: she pushed me back onto the pillow.

She was thrusting, thrusting, thrusting. . . . I could hear the smacking noise it made. She was putting out the eye of innocence. It hurt me: I was moving on to my deliverance, but I couldn't see what was happening.

We listened to the sleeping girls around us, we sobbed as we sucked in our breath. A trail of fire still burned inside me.

"Let's rest," she said.

My memories of the two thieves grew kinder, my wounded flesh began to heal, bubbles of love were rising. But Isabelle returned to her task now, and the thieves were turning faster, ever faster. Where did this great wave come from? Smoothly now, into the depths. The drug flowed down toward my feet, my dreaming flesh lay steeped in visions. I lost myself with Isabelle in passion's calisthenics.

A great pleasure seemed to begin. It was only a reflection. Slow fingers left me. I was hungry, avid for her presence.

"Your hand, your face. Come closer."

"I'm tired."

Make her come closer, make her give me her shoulder, make her face be close to mine. I must barter my innocence for hers. She is not breathing: she is resting. Isabelle coughed as though she were coughing in a library.

I raised myself up with infinite precautions, I felt new-made. My sex, my clearing, and my bath of dew.

I switched on the flashlight. I glimpsed the blood, I glimpsed the red hair. I switched it off.

The rustling of the shadows at three in the morning sent a cold shudder through me. The night would pass, the night would soon be nothing but tears.

I shone the flashlight, I was not afraid of my open eyes.

"I can see the world. It all comes out of you."

The dawn trailing its shrouds. Isabelle was combing her hair in a limbo of her own, a no-man's land where her hair was always hanging loose.

"I don't want the day to come," Isabelle said.

It is coming, it will come. The day will shatter the night beneath its wheels.

"I'm afraid of being away from you," Isabelle said.

A tear fell in my garden at three in the morning.

I would not let myself think a single thought, so that she could go to sleep in my empty head. The day was advancing through the dark, the day was erasing our wedding night. Isabelle was going to sleep.

"Sleep," I said beside the flowering hawthorn that had waited for the dawn all night.

Like a traitor, I got out of the bed and went to the window. There had been a battle high up in the sky and its aftermath was chill. The mists were beating a retreat. Aurora was alone, with no one to usher her in. Already there were clusters of birds in a tree, pecking at her first beams. . . . I looked out at the half-mourning of the new day, at the tatters of the night, and smiled at them. I smiled at Isabelle and pressed my forehead against hers, pretending we were fighting rams. That way I would forget what I knew was dying. The lyric downpour from the birds as they sang and crystallized the beauty of the morning brought only fatigue: perfection is not of this world even when we meet it here.

"You must go," Isabelle said.

Leaving her like a pariah, leaving her furtively made me feel sad too. I had iron balls chained to my feet. Isabelle offered me her grief-stricken face. I loved Isabelle without a gesture, without any token of my passion: I offered her my life without a sign.

Isabelle pushed herself up and took me in her arms.

"You'll come every night?"

"Every night."

Selections from *The Tyranny of Structurelessness*

TOM COLE

Light Change
I'm tapering from my off label high
dosages of Effexor and I go from 375 milligrams to 300 milligrams
I start to listen to the radio
and it is my sincere feeling that
the radio combined with the

electromagnetic tear in my ass
in turn created a
tear in the space-time continuum

we have all been transported to 1980

but I can't explain why

Maybe it's Y2K
Maybe it's Zika
Maybe global warming
—or the Montauk project
a secret governmental experiment
where the scientists believed
nerves in the sphincters, when combined with extreme
tesla coils, electromagnetic pulses, and radio transmissions
lead to psychic binding and a tear in the space-time continuum
for the subject, and everyone within a 25 foot radius
of the point of insertion

into the anus.

It happened—lots of people missing from public parks.

And now I am at 150 milligrams of effexor

Thinking

thinking

thinking

thinking

You know
like

hours and hours
a day non stop since Wednesday.

I've just had this breakthrough
and I feel

Really Happy
right now and
I don't think it is an illusional breakthrough but

I'm going to finish up all my projects that are computer based

and then
in March

I am going to quit my job

And I am going to work on totally . . .
you know
step by step

DISENGAGING FROM DOING STUFF WITH COMPUTERS
THAT I USED TO DO IN OTHER WAYS
like writing with a pen on paper
or reading a book
and
I will work

But I am
NOT

GOING TO WORK IN FRONT
OF A
COMPUTER.
So, I'm, I
that's just going to be my
compass

and stop listening to the radio
on behalf of
the electromagnetic tear in my sphincter

it's going to be an exploratory
step by step process

kind of like a project

I think I'm going to do it.

I wanted to tell you because I am so excited because
I've just been going through

agonizing

agonizing

what am I going to do
what am I going to do

I can't live this life anymore.

3

Light Change

I read this essay called *The Tyranny of Structurelessness* by Jo Freeman about how when feminist consciousness raising groups tried a nonhierarchical approach to organizing, an unspoken tyranny arose that was much worse than if they had just had some structure.

Two quotes from the essay:

Contrary to what we would like to believe, there is no such thing as a structureless group.

People would try to use the "structureless" groups out of a blind belief that no other means could possibly be anything but oppressive.

Light Change

And as a child, I wanted to be a slave, to be tied up, I once handcuffed myself to a desk at school and said, "Someone did this to me."

And I wanted to be split up.

Night has a hundred eyes. More like a million, I think.

So—a rough time—spiraling—out of control, back to shooting up meth and sex where men beat the shit out of me, regularly, and I *knew* I had to get sober.

Let's see . . . ecstasy, ghb, special K, pot, Jack Daniels, Xanex, meth.

I used to think I wasn't shooting up a lot but then when I ran out I'd go to the drawer and smoke the blood out of all the remaining needles and there were a lot of needles.

The first thing that happened was that someone organized an orgy in my apartment while I was coming in and out of consciousness — so, I don't remember anything but I *was* physically active during part of it.

And someone attending the orgy brought luggage with him, turned out this luggage — all his belongings, so when the orgy was over, he was moved in. He told me he was from Iran but then I met someone later who said, "*He's just a regular guy from Michigan.*"
He carried a book in his bag, HISTORY OF AMERICA.
And I only ever saw him eat an avocado and M&M's.

The day he moved in — my birthday — nobody from my real life remembered — but he knew — we sat on a bare mattress,
stained,
the orgy, over, he took me in his arms and eating an M&M his tooth fell out.
Later, when I realized he was reaching the limit of squatter's rights,
I told him if he wanted to stay with me we both had to get sober. He pretended to love my dogs — like don't kick me out I can't live without your dogs.
So I left out some drugs I knew he couldn't resist and when he did them I asked him to move.

Which was kind of a dick move on my part.

But he wouldn't go, he wouldn't budge. He'd leave for orgies — he was also hooking — I don't know — but he left bags and bags of stuff — multiplying. When asked to leave, he'd cry.

and we all know a crying queen is a scheming queen

I still didn't know his name, and this part about the name seemed insane — that in this part of my life, I was dispatching with the triviality of names.

He went to a sex party and while there I called, "I'm getting in a car and bringing all your stuff — if you don't come meet me, I am going to leave your leather harnesses, webcams, and lube on the street."

We met at the Dunkin Donuts on 8th avenue and 24th street, his home away from home — WIFI, bathroom to shoot up in. I showed him his stuff in the trunk, gave him $200, and then paid the driver. He cried for the dogs, and then I never heard from him again.

As soon as I was rid of him, I knew I loved him, wanted him back, we were meant to be together — God had brought us together — suddenly it all switched and I was besotted, forlorn, wanted to switch places with him — freaky Friday — leave my body, go into his — the pain of detox — I'd experience for him once and then again later for me — TWO DETOXES.

But in the end, I could only fix myself, was sick a long time.

Walking down 7th avenue, six months later, I ran into him — a pot belly, stumbling, carrying a folding table lamp for reading, limp, drooped over, *a dying plant*? And around the bottom a brown plastic bag — yellow ties leaked off like liquid. He didn't recognize me.

For completism I wanted to walk up to him and ask him his name.

I saw him try to take a picture of the sunset, with a flash.

And I remember the orgy where I wasn't the star even though it was in my apartment, *Just give him too much so he'll pass out in the corner*.

I imagine he lives somewhere in the south west where the crystal meth is cheap and the living's easy, a ranch, but he has internet — one of those video chat rooms where people shoot up in unison — a quantum physics event — all over the world.

Or he's probably dead.

~~I wonder if when people kill themselves they don't leave as quickly, they circle around a bit.~~

~~It's funny when you feel as if you don't want anything more in your life except to sleep, or else to lie without moving. That's when you can hear time sliding past you, like water running.~~

Time

VICTORIA CHANG

Time—died on August 3, 2015. A
week before my mother died, the nurse
called and said to *be prepared*. I
looked through my purse for the rest
of the words. My pockets empty.
Prepared for what? Could I prepare
if the words were missing? Is a stem
with a bud considered a flower? A bud
is not a flower but a soon-to-be flower.
No word exists for *about to die* but
dying but even dying lacks time in the
same way a bud lacks a timeline. My
mother thought it was only an infection.
She blamed them for not giving her
antibiotics sooner. But time was ahead
of her, the wheel already turning. The
nurse said after, *I'm surprised she
made it through the weekend*. I was
surprised she died at all. Time isn't a
moment. Time is enlarged, blurry. As
in, my ten-year-old wrapped my dead
mother's bracelet for her own birthday
and said it was a gift.

A Story that the United States is Made of

TONGO EISEN-MARTIN

A white child can
Send any number
To hell
Whether one demon
Or a whole horde
Something white
Will win
In the end

So get as close
To whiteness
As possible
Where it's safe
And there's honey
And Monday isn't so bad
And God will give you a pass
If you respect the flag
And watch enough television
Ignore a lot of yourself
Ignore a lot of us
Or flip the switch
Push the button
On behalf of white children

Or pass me a funky soda
Stocked in 1998
Or a beer
From the devil's bartender
Gas station and saloon

I never threw rocks
At the crazy lady
Just bricks at myself
Like the gas station
Got a basement
And I'm at home
Under 1998

And
some white child somewhere
Wants to be my best friend
So I better
Prepare for the day we meet

Pass

The smoke was infant like me

Nothing was careful on that corner
Especially not these young twins
And we were twins
Not in mother
But in mothering
Not in father
But in foundation
Adjusting to the ramble of 90's check cashing lines
And birthday beers
Adjusting to the city alphabet
Learning the first names
Of liquor store owners
And their nephews
And we would meet in the middle of all this
Who was the genius
Who was the distraction
Depends on the teeth of the narrator
I cut mine that day
Although I didn't know it
Rambles of 90's war
Capital was always coming
But in the mean time
I was gonna dive in
And not even pretend that
I knew what I was doing

Excerpts from *The Man Who Laughs*

VICTOR HUGO

NIL ET NOX.

The characteristic of the snow-storm is its blackness. Nature's habitual aspect during a storm—the earth or sea black and the sky pale—is reversed: the sky is black, the ocean white; foam below, darkness above; an horizon walled in with smoke, a zenith roofed with crape. The tempest resembles a cathedral hung with mourning, but no light in that cathedral, —no phantom lights on the crests of the waves, no spark, no phosphorescence, naught but a huge shadow. The Polar cyclone differs from the Tropical cyclone, inasmuch as the one sets fire to every light, and the other extinguishes them all. The world is suddenly converted into the arched vault of a cave. Out of the night falls a dust of pale spots, which hesitate between sky and sea. These spots, which are flakes of snow, slip, wander, and float. It is like the tears of a winding-sheet putting themselves into life-like motion. A mad wind mingles with this dissemination. Blackness crumbling into whiteness, the furious into the obscure, all the tumult of which the sepulchre is capable, a whirlwind under a catafalque,—such is the snow-storm. Underneath trembles the ocean, forming and reforming over portentous unknown depths.

In the Polar wind, which is electrical, the flakes turn suddenly into hailstones, and the air becomes filled with projectiles; the water crackles, shot with grape.

No thunderstrokes; the lightning of boreal storms is silent. What is sometimes said of the cat, "It swears," may be applied to this lightning. It is a menace proceeding from a mouth half open, and strangely inexorable. The snow-storm is a storm blind and dumb; when it has passed, the ships also are often blind and the sailors dumb.

To escape from such an abyss is difficult.

It would be wrong, however, to believe shipwreck to be absolutely inevitable. The Danish fisherman of Disco and the Balesin, the seekers of black whales, Hearn steering towards Behring Strait to discover the mouth of Coppermine River, Hudson, Mackenzie, Vancouver, Ross, Dumont-D'Urville,—all underwent at the Pole itself the wildest hurricanes, and escaped out of them.

It was into this description of tempest that the hooker had entered triumphant and in full sail. Frenzy against frenzy. When Montgomery, escaping from Rouen, threw his galley with all the force of its oars against the chain barring the Seine at La Bouille, he showed similar effrontery.

The "Matutina" sailed on fast; she bent so much under her sails that at moments she made a fearful angle with the sea of fifteen degrees; but her good bellied keel adhered to the water as if glued to it. The keel resisted the grasp of the hurricane. The lantern at the prow cast its light ahead.

The cloud, full of winds, dragging its tumor over the deep, cramped and ate more and more into the sea round the hooker. Not a gull, not a sea-mew,—nothing but snow. The expanse of the field of waves was becoming contracted and terrible; only three or four gigantic ones were visible.

Now and then a tremendous flash of lightning of a red copper-color broke out behind the obscure superposition of the horizon and the zenith. That sudden release of vermilion flame revealed the horror of the clouds; that abrupt conflagration of the depths, to which for an instant the first tiers of clouds and the distant boundaries of the celestial chaos seemed to adhere, placed the abyss in perspective. On this ground of fire the snow-flakes showed black,—they might have been compared to dark butterflies flying about in a furnace; then all was extinguished.

The first explosion over, the squall, still pursuing the hooker, began to roar in thorough bass. This phase of grumbling is a perilous diminution of uproar. Nothing is so terrifying as this monologue of the storm. This gloomy recitative appears to serve as a moment of rest to the mysterious combating forces, and indicates a species of patrol kept in the unknown.

The hooker held wildly on her course. Her two mainsails especially were doing fearful work. The sky and sea were as of ink, with jets of foam running higher than the mast. Every instant masses of water swept the deck like a deluge, and at each roll of the vessel the hawse-holes, now to starboard, now to larboard, became as so many open mouths vomiting back the foam into the sea. The women had taken refuge in the cabin, but the men remained on deck; the blinding snow eddied around, the spitting surge mingled with it,—all was fury.

At that moment the chief of the band, standing abaft on the stern-frames, holding on with one hand to the shrouds, and with the other taking off the kerchief he wore round his head and waving it in the light of the lantern, gay and arrogant, with the pride in his face, and his hair in wild disorder, intoxicated by all the darkness, cried out,—

"We are free!"

"Free, free, free!" echoed the fugitives; and the band, seizing hold of the rigging, rose up on deck.

"Hurrah!" shouted the chief.

And the band shouted in the storm,—

"Hurrah!"

Just as this clamor was dying away in the tempest, a loud solemn voice rose from the other end of the vessel, saying,—

"Silence!"

All turned their heads. The darkness was thick, and the doctor was leaning against the mast so that he seemed part of it, and they could not see him.

The voice spoke again,—

"Listen!"

All were silent.

Then did they distinctly hear through the darkness the toll of a bell.

THE CHARGE CONFIDED TO A RAGING SEA.

The skipper, at the helm, burst out laughing:—

"A bell, that's good. We are on the larboard tack. What does the bell prove? Why, that we have land to starboard."

The firm and measured voice of the doctor replied:

"You have not land to starboard."

"But we have," shouted the skipper.

"No!"

"But that bell tolls from the land."

"That bell," said the doctor, "tolls from the sea."

A shudder passed over these daring men, the haggard faces of the two women appeared above the companion like two hobgoblins conjured up; the doctor took a step forward, separating his tall form from the mast. From the depth of the night's darkness came the toll of the bell.

The doctor resumed:—

"There is in the midst of the sea, half-way between Portland and the Channel Islands, a buoy, placed there for warning; that buoy is moored by chains to the shoal, and floats on top of the water. On the buoy is fixed an iron trestle, and across the trestle a bell is hung. In bad weather heavy seas toss the buoy, and the bell rings. That is the bell you hear."

The doctor paused to allow an extra-violent gust of wind to pass over, waited until the sound of the bell reasserted itself, and then went on:—

"To hear that bell in a storm, when the nor'wester is blowing, is to be lost. Why? For this reason: if you hear a bell, it is because the wind brings it to you. But the wind is nor'westerly, and the breakers of Aurigny lie east. You hear the bell only because you are between the buoy and the breakers. It is on those breakers the wind is driving you. You are on the wrong side of the buoy. If you were on the right side, you would be out at sea on a safe course, and you would not hear the bell. The wind would not convey the sound to you. You would pass close to the buoy without knowing it. We are out of our course. That bell is shipwreck sounding the tocsin. Now, look out!"

As the doctor spoke, the bell, soothed by a lull of the storm, rang slowly stroke by stroke; and its intermitting toll seemed to testify to the truth of the old man's words. It was as the knell of the abyss.

All listened breathless,—now to the voice, now to the bell.

THE HIGHEST RESOURCE.

The wreck, being lightened, was sinking more slowly, but none the less surely.

The hopelessness of their situation was without resource, without mitigation; they had exhausted their last expedient.

"Is there anything else we can throw overboard?"

The doctor, whom every one had forgotten, rose from the companion and said,—

"Yes."

"What?" asked the chief.

The doctor answered,—

"Our crime."

They shuddered and all cried out,—

"Amen!"

The doctor, standing up, pale, raised his hand to heaven, saying,—

"Kneel."

They wavered; to waver is the preface to kneeling down.

The doctor went on:—

"Let us throw our crimes into the sea; they weigh us down; it is they that are sinking the ship. Let us think no more of safety,—let us think of salvation. Our last true crime, above all,—the crime which we committed, or rather completed, just now,—oh, wretched beings who are listening to me, it is that which is overwhelming us! For those who leave intended murder behind them, it is an impious insolence to tempt the abyss. He who sins against a child sins against God. True, we were obliged to put to sea, but it was certain perdition. The storm, warned by the shadow of our crime, came on. It is well. Regret nothing, however. There, not far off in the darkness, are the sands of Vauville and Cape La Hogue; it is France. There was but one possible shelter for us, which was Spain. France is no less dangerous to us than England. Our deliverance from the sea would have led but to the gibbet. Hanged or drowned,—we had no alternative. God has chosen for us; let us give him thanks. He has vouchsafed us the grave, which cleanses. Brethren, the inevitable hand is in it. Remember that it was we who just now did our best to send on high that child, and that at this very moment—now, as I speak—there is perhaps above our heads a soul accusing us before a Judge whose eye is on us. Let us make the best use of this last respite; let us make an effort, if we still may, to repair as far as we are able the evil that we have wrought. If the child survives us, let us come to his aid; if he is dead, let us seek his forgiveness. Let us cast our crime from us; let us ease our consciences of its weight. Let us strive that our souls be not swallowed up before God, for that is the awful shipwreck. Bodies go to the fishes, souls to the devils. Have pity on yourselves. On your knees, I say! Repentance is the bark which never sinks. You have lost your compass? You are wrong! You still have prayer."

The wolves became lambs,—such transformations occur in last agonies; tigers lick the crucifix; when the dark portal opens ajar, belief is difficult, unbelief impossible. However imperfect may be the different sketches of religion essayed by man, even when his belief is shapeless, even when the outline of the dogma is not in harmony with the lineaments of the eternity he foresees, there comes in his last hour a trembling of the soul. There is something which will begin when life is over; this thought impresses the last pang.

A man's dying agony is the expiration of a term. In that fatal second he feels weighing on him a diffused responsibility. That which has been complicates that which is to be. The past returns and enters into the future. What is known becomes as much an abyss as the unknown. And the two chasms, the one which is full of his faults, the other of his anticipation, mingle their reverberations. It is this confusion of the two gulfs which terrifies the dying man.

They had spent their last grain of hope in the direction of life; hence they turned in the other. Their only remaining chance was in its dark shadow. They understood it. It came on them as a lugubrious flash, followed by a relapse of horror. That which is intelligible to the dying man is as what is perceived in the lightning,—everything, then nothing; you see, then all is blindness. After death the eye will reopen, and that which was a flash will become a sun.

They cried out to the doctor,—

"Thou, thou, there is no one but thee. We will obey thee. What must we do? Speak."

The doctor answered,—

"The question is how to pass over the unknown precipice, and reach the other bank of life, which is beyond the tomb. Being the one that knows the most my danger is greater than yours. You do well to leave the choice of the bridge to him whose burden is the heaviest."

He added,—

"Knowledge is a weight added to conscience."

He continued,—

"How much time have we still?"

Galdeazun looked at the water-mark, and answered,—

"A little more than a quarter of an hour."

"Good!" said the doctor.

The low hood of the companion made a sort of table; the doctor took from his pocket his ink-horn and pen, and his pocket-book, out of which he drew a parchment, the same one on the back of which he had written, a few hours before, some twenty cramped and crooked lines.

"A light!" he said.

The snow, falling like the spray of a cataract, had extinguished the torches one after another; there was but one left. Ave-Maria took it out of the place where it had been stuck, and holding it in his hand, came and stood by the doctor's side.

The doctor replaced his pocket-book in his pocket, put down the pen and ink-horn on the hood of the companion, unfolded the parchment, and said,—

"Listen!"

Then in the midst of the sea, on the failing bridge (a sort of shuddering flooring of the tomb), the doctor began a solemn reading, to which all the shadows seemed to listen. The doomed men bowed their heads around him. The flaming of the torch intensified their pallor. What the doctor read was written in English. Now and then, when one of those woe-begone looks seemed to ask an explanation, the doctor would stop, to repeat—whether in French or Spanish, Basque or Italian—the passage he had just read. Stifled sobs and hollow beatings of the breast were heard. The wreck was sinking more and more.

The reading over, the doctor placed the parchment flat on the companion, seized his pen, and on a clear margin which he had carefully left at the bottom of what he had written, he signed himself,—GERHARDUS GEESTEMUNDE, *Doctor*.

Then, turning towards the others, he said,—

"Come, and sign."

The Basque woman approached, took the pen, and signed herself,—ASUNCION.

She handed the pen to the Irishwoman, who, not knowing how to write, made a cross.

The doctor, by the side of this cross, wrote,—BARBARA FERMOY, *of Tyrryf Island, in the Hebrides*.

Then he handed the pen to the chief of the band.

The chief signed,—GAIZDORRA, *Captal*.

The Genoese signed himself under the chief's name,—GIANGIRATE.

The Languedocian signed,—JACQUES QUATOURZE, *alias the Narbonnais*.

The Provençal signed,—LUC-PIERRE CAPGAROUPE, *of the Galleys of Mahon*.

Under these signatures the doctor added a note:—

"Of the crew of three men, the skipper having been washed overboard by a sea, but two remain, and they have signed."

The two sailors affixed their names underneath the note. The northern Basque signed himself,—GALDEAZUN.

The southern Basque signed,—AVE-MARIA, *Robber*.

Then the doctor said,—

"Capgaroupe."

"Here," said the Provençal.

"Have you Hardquanonne's flask?"

"Yes."

"Give it me."

Capgaroupe drank off the last mouthful of brandy, and handed the flask to the doctor. The water was rising in the hold; the wreck was sinking deeper and deeper into the sea. The sloping edges of the ship were covered by a thin gnawing wave which was rising. All were crowded on the centre of the deck.

The doctor dried the ink on the signatures by the heat of the torch, and folding the parchment into a narrower compass than the diameter of the neck, put it into the flask. He called for the cork.

"I don't know where it is," said Capgaroupe.

"Here is a piece of rope," said Jacques Quatourze.

The doctor corked the flask with a bit of rope, and asked for some tar. Galdeazun went forward, extinguished the signal light with a piece of tow, took the vessel in which it was contained from the stern, and brought it, half full of burning tar, to the doctor.

The flask holding the parchment which they had all signed, was corked and tarred over.

"It is done," said the doctor.

And from out all their mouths, vaguely stammered in every language, came the dismal utterances of the catacombs.

"Ainsi soit-il!"

"Mea culpa!"

"Asi sea!"

"Aro raï!"

"Amen!"

It was as though the sombre voices of Babel were scattered through the shadows as Heaven uttered its awful refusal to hear them.

The doctor turned away from his companions in crime and distress, and took a few steps towards the gunwale. Reaching the side, he looked into space, and said in a deep voice,—

"Bist du bei mir?"*

Perchance he was addressing some phantom.

The wreck was sinking.

Behind the doctor all the others were in a dream. Prayer mastered them by main force. They did not bow, they were bent. There was

* Art thou near me?

something involuntary in their contrition; they wavered as a sail flaps when the breeze fails. And the haggard group took by degrees, with clasping of hands and prostration of foreheads, attitudes various, but all alike full of humiliation and hopeless confidence in God. Some strange reflection of the deep seemed to soften their villanous features.

The doctor returned towards them. Whatever had been his past, the old man was great in the presence of the catastrophe.

The deep reserve of nature which enveloped him preoccupied without disconcerting him. He was not one to be taken unawares. Over him was the calm of a silent horror: on his countenance, the majesty of God's will comprehended.

This old and thoughtful outlaw unconsciously assumed the air of a pontiff.

He said,—

"Attend to me."

He contemplated for a moment the waste of water, and added,—

"Now we are going to die."

Then he took the torch from the hands of Ave-Maria, and waved it.

A spark broke from it and flew into the night.

Then the doctor cast the torch into the sea.

The torch was extinguished: all light disappeared. Nothing was left but the huge unfathomable shadow. It was like the filling up of the grave.

In the darkness, the doctor was heard saying,—

"Let us pray."

All knelt.

It was no longer on the snow, but in the water, that they knelt.

They had but a few minutes more.

The doctor alone remained standing.

The flakes of snow falling on him had sprinkled him with white tears, and made him visible on the background of darkness. He might have been the speaking statue of the shadow.

The doctor made the sign of the cross and raised his voice, while beneath his feet he felt that almost imperceptible oscillation which prefaces the moment in which a wreck is about to founder. He said,—

"Pater noster qui es in cœlis."

The Provençal repeated in French,—

"Notre Père qui êtes aux cieux."

The Irishwoman repeated in Gaelic, understood by the Basque woman,—

"Ar nathair ata ar neamh."

The doctor continued,—

"Sanctificetur nomen tuum."

"Que votre nom soit sanctifié," said the Provençal.

"Naomhthar hainm," said the Irishwoman.

"Adveniat regnum tuum," continued the doctor.

"Que votre règne arrive," said the Provençal.

"Tigeadh do rioghachd," said the Irishwoman.

As they knelt, the waters had risen to their shoulders. The doctor went on,—

"Fiat voluntas tua."

"Que votre volonté soit faite," stammered the Provençal.

And the Irishwoman and the Basque woman cried,—

"Deuntar do thoil ar an Hhalàmb."

"Sicut in cœlo, sicut in terra," said the doctor.

No voice answered him.

He looked down. All their heads were under water. They had let themselves be drowned on their knees.

The doctor took in his right hand the flask which he had placed on the companion, and raised it above this head.

The wreck was going down. As he sank, the doctor murmured the rest of the prayer.

For an instant his shoulders were above water, then his head, then nothing remained but his arm holding up the flask, as if he were showing it to the Infinite.

His arm disappeared; there was no greater fold on the deep sea than there would have been on a tun of oil. The snow continued falling.

One thing floated, and was carried by the waves into the darkness. It was the tarred flask, kept afloat by its osier cover.

MW Duet

WILL FARRIS

I know there is no future here
but still

I swear I'd spin

on that kids whirligig
for some forever

or utopia; our gay

faces grow sick
with the condition

of spring, life
like a room until

Light, bright
pools of it

Awake

I live here

took
three months
   to know

I was ordinary

came
 last night

we sat on
 train &
god

  I was just an ordinary egg

Body

drooped
in August light

thought light
would break me open—   but

blossoms. Birds
splice air into air.

That petal
through streetlight
looks like buttermilk

Orlando

for Amir

Left town to collect
lack and found

light in California
is blue
at both ends

some bright weight
between

led by wrist into
warm I'm told

this is light you can hold in your hand

I wanted to talk about endings,
then sun—

you were so kind

it's good and
big, being

here, did I tell you?

I feel like smiling somedays
it can't be helped.

After Words

I was never interested in Borges until the pandemic. His winding consciousness really suited the out of time feeling that prevailed that first year of the virus when I got serious about this book. Borges was lecturing at Harvard when I lived nearby as a college freshman and I might have been moping on that same bench one day next to him as he sat facing the Charles. You couldn't stop hearing about the great man that fall in Boston which is probably why I never read him. In 2017 I visited Bill Martin's writing class at Al-Quds Bard in Abu Dis, Palestine, when one of his students Baha' Ebdeir read this piece about growing up in a refugee camp. He spoke the phrase "Beloved Occupier." I gasped at the fragrance of his thought. Laurie Weeks turned me on to Can Xue's work. Joe Brainard handed me my first copy of *My Dog Tulip*. I think you'll like this he smiled. When I taught in San Diego the passionate christian students from Orange County flat out refused to read Dodie Bellamy's "Fat Chance." I remember a girl literally shaking the pamphlet in the air. I am going to return this she screamed. What I thought was a precise doorway into another kind of consciousness was instead an assault on their values and an undermining of normalcy. Which is exactly why I'm including it here.

I keep going back to Robert Walser because he changed me. I just read Susan Bernofsky's biography of him. I'm so primed—by his humility and his over-joy. And his eventual incarceration. Max Brod, Kafka's best friend (who did NOT destroy his papers after he died, as requested), was an admirer of him. Actually, they both were. Kafka used to read Walser's stories aloud, laughing uproariously. Brod wrote a review of Robert Walser in which he described a kind of three-tiered narration in Walser's work. I think he was trying to explain how Walser was ahead of his time. Like there was a surface realm, that of appearances. Walser's characters were naïve. And funny about it. Then there was a level of irony. The observant maybe aesthetic, managing realm. But Brod cited (as his specialness) Walser doing this third thing, which he described as "genuinely naïve, powerful, and Swiss-German." Brod was a Jew (and his trip to Palestine five minutes before the Nazis came banging on the door is how he salvaged the Kafka we do have) yet it sounds a little blood and soil right there. I'm wondering about a couple of things. Does he simply mean authenticity? Or like a performative consistent inconsistency? Walser's vacillations convey the actual awkwardness of being alive. He was a naïve guy, writing a naïve guy, manipulating the feints and rhythms of him but he was also reporting from earth, profoundly being himself, in a dangerous way, not dangerous cause it's bad but it doesn't (can't) stay inside the lines. I think of Duchamp's last day alive in Paris when he went looking for a book about geometric shapes accompanied by 3-D glasses which took a simple line drawing into another dimension. He also bought a book of funny stories which he entertained his guests with that night because an essential part of Duchamp's project was laughter. As a man of the future he knew that laughter was dimensional. New uncharted space, unoccupied. When Simone Weil explains why she won't get baptized I have to admit I find it tremendously funny. Her carefulness, her assertiveness that if she stayed out *here* (with the heathens) she could do more for the world as a Christian. Pathetic, yes. Is the hand a genital. Not to change the subject. There's so much to say about the hand (and I'd rather let Saidiya Hartman say it) but in general the hand is just way more pathetic than the computer. It's the other side of felt.

What about religion. There's a lot of god in this art.

There's trans people in here but gender truth be told is always trans. Bullying is how the "regulars" keep themselves in line by finding a shill. No one's more pathetic than Jesus. Is Christianity the people who killed him or didn't. The violence is simply in there. I include a small slab of Valerie Solanas's *Up Your Ass* because this play was the reason she shot Andy pretty much. He wouldn't produce it. He had one of the only two copies in the world and he lost it. He made it less in the wrong way. What's pathetic tends to be massively true, its triumph is like being a good standup not a great one or maybe like being any standup since no one's ever great for that long, it's just a flash or a shift, its glory is that moment when it opens the box and the unlikely steps out and looks around. Everything that happened right before the bang. Or the laughter or the applause.

In a despotic or theocratic culture trans people are always pathetic but I think at least in America where I sit we have passed out of the most overt abject of that phase (not cause Joe Biden won but because Donald Trump didn't).

I didn't see it but last night was the Jupiter conjunct Saturn transit and we are on the cusp of a major shift. I don't know why Arthur Jafa included the surface of the sun in *Love is the Message* but it's ineluctably true. He felt these scales, that giant bounce from here to there, were ready to speak.

I love in Sparrow's piece when he shares a snippet from Abraham Lincoln's famous "lost speech": "We are all part-kings here. If you bow to one man, you must bow to all . . ."

Indeed, that's what the Buddha says too. And Thich Nhat Hanh said that in the 21st C. the buddha is a group. So that if you bow to one man that *is* what you do: you bow to everyone. But what about Layli Long Soldier's masterful poem "38," the Dakota men that Lincoln condemned to swing by the neck until dead for fighting back. When did he bow to them.

post script

It's a dictionary really. I've been assembling this dictionary all my life I mean. I think everyone should be able to pick a word that moves them, and occupy it. Time does that over scores or hundreds of years, and many voices pour over it like the ocean, like something in so many hands that's how a word shifts. Can you build a word, collectively, assemble a word, like a small bird singing, its chest pushing in and out, flaunting its breath like a deity before it flies away. It's *almost* a poem.

Little bird, little bird so proud.

Eileen Myles
October 2021

Contributors

Alice Notley has published over forty books of poetry, including (most recently) *Eurynome's Sandals* and *For the Ride*. An art book called *Runes and Chords* is forthcoming. She has lived in Paris, France, for almost thirty years, somehow remaining American, with ties to New York and also the Mojave Desert.

Gwendolyn Brooks (1917–2000) was born in Topeka, Kansas, and raised in Chicago. She was the author of more than twenty books of poetry, including *Annie Allen*, for which she received the Pulitzer Prize, as well as numerous other books, including the novel *Maud Martha*. In 1985, she was the first Black woman appointed as consultant in poetry to the Library of Congress, a post now known as Poet Laureate.

The Friend (they/them) is the author of two books of poetry, *The Late Parade* and *George Washington* (Liveright). A professor of creative writing at Rutgers University, they are working on a novel. They live in New York City.

Kevin Killian (1952–2019) was a poet, novelist, playwright, art critic, and scholar. His books include *Argento Series*, *Action Kylie*, *Tweaky Village*, and *Tony Greene Era*. He was also the author of several novels, story collections, and plays, as well as the memoir *Bedrooms Have Windows*. With his wife, Dodie Bellamy, Killian edited the literary and art journal *Mirage #4/Period(ical)* and the anthology *Writers Who Love Too Much: New Narrative Writing, 1977–1997*.

Ama Birch is the author of "Yesterday, Today, and Tomorrow," "Faces in the Clouds," "Sonnet Boom!," "Ferguson Interview Project," and a video game available for Android, "Space Quake by Ama Birch." She has a Bachelor of Arts in Theatre Arts from the State University of New York at New Paltz and a Master of Fine Arts in Creative Writing from the California Institute of the Arts. She has been published by *Great Weather for Media*, *Autonomedia*, *A Gathering of the Tribes*, *Vail/Vale*, *Vitrine*, *Insert Blanc Press*, *Live Mag!*, *Fellswoop*, *Apricity*, CalArts Creative Writing Program, the State University of New York, and *The Brooklyn Rail*.

Andrea Dworkin (1946–2005) was an American radical feminist author associated with antipornography, antirape, and battered women's movements of the 1970s and '80s. She wrote more than ten books, both nonfiction and fiction, and she coauthored, with feminist law professor Catherine MacKinnon, the highly controversial Antipornography Civil Rights Ordinance of 1983.

Ariana Reines is a poet and playwright from Salem, Massachusetts. Her latest, *A Sand Book* (Tin House 2020), won the Kingsley Tufts Prize and was longlisted for the National Book Award.

Bob Flanagan (1952–1996) was an American performance artist and writer known for his work exploring sadomasochism. He collaborated with Sheree Rose for much of his career, and combined text, video, and live performance to explore themes of childhood, sex, illness, and mortality. His last finished work, *The Pain Journal*, chronicles the final year of his life before his death from cystic fibrosis.

Baha' Ebdeir is a Palestinian refugee poet originally from the occupied village of Bayt Nattif. He is currently working as a Teaching Assistant at Al-Quds Bard College in Jerusalem. Baha' is also the project manager of Upraised Voices (UV), a project that empowers self-expression and critical inquiry among underprivileged Palestinian young people through introducing them to creative writing workshops and debate sessions.

Bob Kaufman (1925–1986) was born in New Orleans to a German Jewish father and a black Catholic mother. He moved to San Francisco, where he became a Beat poet who adhered to an oral tradition and seldom wrote his poems down. City Lights Bookstore first published his poems. In addition to several broadsides, his works were collected in *Solitudes Crowded with Loneliness*, *The Golden Sardine*, *The Ancient Rain: Poems 1956–1978*, and *Cranial Guitar: Selected Poems*.

Brandon Shimoda is a yonsei poet/writer. His books include *The Grave on the Wall* (City Lights), which received the PEN Open Book Award, and *Evening Oracle* (Letter Machine Editions), which received the William Carlos Williams Award from the Poetry Society of America. He is also the curator of the Hiroshima Library, an itinerant reading room/collection of books on the atomic bombings of Hiroshima and Nagasaki.

Bruce Benderson is a novelist, translator, and essayist. He is the author of *The Romanian: Story of an Obsession*, winner of France's prestigious Prix de Flore in French translation, *Pacific Agony*, and other works.

CAConrad has been working with the ancient technologies of poetry and ritual since 1975. Their new book is *AMANDA PARADISE: Resurrect Extinct Vibration* (Wave Books, 2021). They received a Creative Capital grant, a Pew

Fellowship, a Lambda Literary Award, and a Believer Book Award. Their play *The Obituary Show* was made into a film in 2022 by Augusto Cascales.

Camille Roy is a writer of fiction, poetry, and plays. Her newest fiction collection, *Honey Mine*, came out from Nightboat in June 2021. Previous books include *Sherwood Forest*, from Futurepoem, and *Cheap Speech*, a play from Leroy Chapbooks, as well as *Swarm* (fiction, from Black Star Series). She coedited *Biting the Error: Writers Explore Narrative* (Coach House 2005, reissued 2010). Earlier books include *The Rosy Medallions* (poetry and prose, from Kelsey Street Press) and *Cold Heaven* (plays, from Leslie Scalapino's O Books). Recent work has been published in *Amerarcana* and Open Space (SFMOMA blog). More information can be found at https://www.camilleroy.me/.

Can Xue was born in 1953 in Changsha City, Hunan Province, in South China. Regarded as "China's most prominent author of experimental fiction" (*Los Angeles Review of Books*), Can Xue describes her works as "soul literature" or "life literature." She is the author of numerous short story collections and four novels, including *Dialogues in Paradise* and *Old Floating Cloud*.

Ronald R. Janssen is an associate professor in the Department of Writing Studies and Composition at Hofstra University. He is the cotranslator with Jian Zhang of *Dialogues in Paradise*, *Old Floating Cloud*, and *The Embroidered Shoes* by Can Xue.

Jian Zhang is the cotranslator with Ronald R. Janssen of *Dialogues in Paradise, Old Floating Cloud*, and *The Embroidered Shoes* by Can Xue.

Carmen Boullosa was born in Mexico City in 1954. She is the author of nineteen novels, collections of poetry, plays, and essays. Various of her novels have been published in English, including *Texas: The Great Theft*, *The Book of Anna*, and *Before*. Her first poetry collection to appear in English is *Hatchet*. She is the recipient of the prize Xavier Villaurrutia and the Ibargüengoitia in Mexico, the Anna Seghers and the LiBeratur in Germany, and the Novela Café Gijón, the Rosalía de Castro, the Casa de América de Poesía Americana, in Spain, and she has also been a Guggenheim and a Cullman Center Fellow. The show "Nueva York" on CUNY-TV has won her five NY-EMMYs. She has been visiting professor at Georgetown, Columbia, NYU, and Clermont Ferrand, was a faculty member at City College CUNY, and now teaches at Macaulay Honors College.

Samantha Schnee is the founding editor of *Words Without Borders*. Her translation of Carmen Boullosa's *Texas: The Great Theft* was shortlisted for the PEN America Translation Prize.

Chantal Akerman (1950–2015) was a feminist experimental film director, screenwriter, artist, and professor. Born to Holocaust survivors from Poland, she used generational trauma and Jewish identity as recurring themes in her work. She is best known for her film *Jeanne Dielman, 23 quai du Commerce, 1080 Bruxelles*.

Daniella Shreir was born in London. She is the founder and coeditor of the feminist film journal *Another Gaze,* founder-programmer at Another Screen, and translator from French to English.

Charles Bernstein is the winner of the 2019 Bollingen Prize for *Near/Miss* (University of Chicago Press, 2018) and for lifetime achievement in American poetry. He is the author of *Topsy-Turvy* (Chicago, 2021) and *Pitch of Poetry* (Chicago, 2016). More information at writing.upenn.edu/epc/authors/bernstein.

Chester Himes (1909–1984) was the author of numerous novels, short stories, essays, and two films. Himes, who began writing while serving a prison term for jewel theft in the early 1940s, is best known for his social criticism in books like *If He Hollers, Let Him Go* and *Lonely Crusade*.

Chris Kraus is the author of four novels, a literary biography and three books of art and cultural criticism. She is presently working on a nonfiction novel set on the Iron Range of northern Minnesota. She is a coeditor of Semiotext(e), alongside Hedi El Kholti and Sylvère Lotringer. She teaches writing at ArtCenter and lives in LA.

Dana Ward is the author of several poetry books including THE CRISIS OF INFINITE WORLDS, *Some Other Deaths of Bas Jan Ader*, and THIS CAN'T BE LIFE. He lives in Cincinnati, where he hosts the Cy Press Poetry at Thunder Sky reading series, and edits, along with Paul Coors, Perfect Lovers Press.

Dara Barrois/Dixon's books include *Reverse Rapture*, *You Good Thing*, *In the Still of the Night*, and *Tolstoy Killed Anna Karenina* (Wave 2022). Lannan Foundation, Guggenheim Foundation, National Endowment for the Arts, Massachusetts Cultural Council, and many schools, colleges and universities have supported her work; she edits for Factory Hollow Press & lives and works in western Massachusetts.

Dennis Cooper is the author of the *George Miles Cycle*, an interconnected sequence of five novels: *Closer*, *Frisk*, *Try*, *Guide*, and *Period*. His other works include *My Loose Thread*; *The Sluts*, winner of France's Prix Sade and the Lambda Literary Award; *God Jr.*; *Wrong*; *The Dream Police*; *Ugly Man*; and *The Marbled Swarm*. He divides his time between Los Angeles and Paris.

Dodie Bellamy's writing challenges the distinctions between fiction, essay, and poetry. In 2018–19 she was the subject of On Our Mind, a yearlong series of public events, commissioned essays, and reading-group meetings organized by the CCA Wattis Institute. Her latest books—both from Semiotext(e)—are *Bee Reaved*, an essay/memoir collection circling around grief, loss, and abandonment; and a new edition of her 1998 PoMo vampire novel *The Letters of Mina*

Harker. With Kevin Killian, she coedited *Writers Who Love Too Much: New Narrative, 1977–1997*. She is based in San Francisco.

Djuna Barnes (1892–1982) was born in Cornwall-on-Hudson, New York, and worked as a journalist in New York before leaving the country to spend many years in Paris and London. She is perhaps best known for her novel *Nightwood* (1936).

Eileen Myles (they/them) came to New York from Boston in 1974 to be a poet. Their books include *For Now* (an essay/talk about writing), *Afterglow (a dog memoir)*, *I Must Be Living Twice: New and Selected Poems*, and *Chelsea Girls*. *The Trip*, their super-8 puppet road film can be seen on YouTube. Eileen has received a Guggenheim Fellowship and was recently elected a member of the American Academy of Arts & Letters. They live in New York and Marfa, TX.

essa may ranapiri (they/them/ia | ngāti raukawa/na guinnich/highgate): they are a writer that lives on the lands of ngāti wairere / their first book of poems is *ransack* (VUP) / they are currently working on their second book tentatively titled *Echidna* / they will write until they're dead

Etel Adnan (1925–2021) was born in Beirut, Lebanon. She was a poet, essayist, and painter. Her novel *Sitt Marie Rose*, published in Paris in 1977, won the France-Pays Arabes award and has been translated into more than ten languages.

Georgina Kleege is an internationally known writer and disability studies scholar. Her collection of personal essays, *Sight Unseen* (1999), is a classic in the field of disability studies. She is the translator of Etel Adnan's *Sitt Marie Rose*.

Fanny Howe has published poetry, novels, and essays. She has lived and taught in California, Boston, New York, and Ireland. Her most recent and continuing publisher is Graywolf Press. Her most pathetic (unnoticed) book is published by Flood Editions and is called *What Did I Do Wrong?*

Fred Moten lives in New York and teaches in the Departments of Performance Studies and Comparative Literature at New York University. He works with lots of social and aesthetic study groups including Stefano Harney & Fred Moten, the Black Arts Movement School Modality, Le Mardi Gras Listening Collective, the Center for Convivial Research and Autonomy, Moved by the Motion, the Institute of Physical Sociality, and the Harris/Moten Quartet.

Gail Scott lives and writes in French-inflected sentences in Montréal. Her book of essays *Permanent (upside down) Revolution* (2021) is a finalist for the Grand Prix du livre de Montréal. Her fiction includes *The Obituary*, a ghost story with a fractalled narrator set in a Montréal triplex; *My Paris* (Dalkey Archive), about a sad diarist in conversation with Gertrude Stein and Walter

Benjamin; *Main Brides*; *Heroine* (reissued in 2019 with an introduction by Eileen Myles); and *Spare Parts + 2*, a collection of stories and manifestos. The anthology *Biting the Error*, coedited with Bob Glück, Camille Roy, et al., was shortlisted for a Lambda award. She is also a translator, and her translation of Michael Delisle's *Le Déasarroi du matelot* was shortlisted for the Governor General's award in translation. An essay/memoir set in Lower Manhattan during the early Obama years is forthcoming from Wave. Scott taught creative writing at Université de Montréal until leaving to become a full-time writer in 2018.

Franz Kafka (1883–1924) was born in Prague. During his lifetime, he published only a few short stories, including "The Metamorphosis," "The Judgment," and "The Stoker." He died before completing any of his full-length novels. At the end of his life, Kafka asked his lifelong friend and literary executor Max Brod to burn all his unpublished work. Brod overrode those wishes.

Arthur S. Wensinger is the Marcus L. Taft Professor of German Language and Literature and Professor of the Humanities, Emeritus, at Wesleyan University.

Georg Büchner (1813–1837) was a German dramatist and a major forerunner of naturalism and expressionism. He studied medicine and later became a writer advocating for economic and political revolution. He is the author of three plays, *Danton's Death*, *Leonce and Lena*, and *Woyzeck*, which was unfinished at the time of his death. He is also the author of the unfinished novel *Lenz*.

John Reddick was born in 1940 and taught for many years in the German department at the University of Liverpool.

J. R. Ackerley (1896–1967) was for many years the literary editor of the BBC magazine *The Listener*. His works include three memoirs, *Hindoo Holiday*, *My Dog Tulip*, and *My Father and Myself*, and a novel, *We Think the World of You*.

Jack Halberstam is a professor of queer studies at Columbia University and has written a few books on monsters, gender variance, failure, and wildness. He was recently the subject of a video-portrait by Adam Pendleton called "So we moved" and is currently writing a book on the aesthetics of collapse.

James Schuyler (1923–1991) was born in Chicago, Illinois. He moved to New York, where he shared an apartment with other New York School poets Frank O'Hara and John Ashbery, and from 1955 to 1961 he was a curator of circulating exhibitions at the Museum of Modern Art. He won the Pulitzer Prize for Poetry in 1980 for his collection *The Morning of the Poem*.

Frank B. Wilderson III is professor and chair of African American studies at the University of California, Irvine. He is the author of *Afropessimism*, longlisted for the National Book Award, and *Incognegro: A Memoir of Exile* *and Apartheid*. He has received a National Endowment for the Arts Literature Fellowship and a Hurston/Wright Legacy Award for Nonfiction, among other awards.

James Welch (1940–2003) is considered a founding author of the Native American Renaissance, growing up in the Blackfeet and A'aninin cultures. He is the author of the novels *Winter in the Blood, The Death of Jim Loney, Fools Crow, The Indian Lawyer*, and *The Heartsong of Charging Elk*. Welch also wrote a nonfiction book, *Killing Custer*, and a work of poetry, *Riding the Earthboy 40*.

Jerome Sala's books include *Corporations Are People, Too!* (NYQ Books), *The Cheapskates* (Lunar Chandelier), *Look Slimmer Instantly* (Soft Skull), and the forthcoming *How Much? New and Selected Poems* (NYQ Books). His blog—on poetry, pop culture and everyday life—is espresso bongo: espressobongo.typepad.com. He lives in New York City with his spouse, poet Elaine Equi.

Joe Proulx lives in Woodstock, NY.

Joan Larkin is the author of six poetry collections, including *Blue Hanuman* and *My Body: New and Selected Poems*. She cofounded Out & Out Books during the '70s feminist literary explosion, coedited four anthologies, including *Gay and Lesbian Poetry in Our Time*, and has been a lifelong teacher. Her honors include Lambda, NEA, and Shelley Memorial awards, among others.

Joe Westmoreland has been published in literary anthologies including *Discontents (New Queer Writers* 1992), *The New Fuck You (Adventures in Lesbian Reading* 1995), and *Anarchic Sexual Desires of Plain Unmarried Schoolteachers* (2015). He contributed to many queer zines, including *My Comrade, Straight to Hell*, and *Holy Titclamps*. He has also published various essays for exhibits, including *Not only this, but "New language beckons us,"* NYU Fales Library (May 2013) and *Charles Atlas: Essays*, Migros Museum, Zurich, CH (2019). His novel, *Tramps Like Us*, was first published in June 2001. He lives in New York City.

Jocelyn Saidenberg is the author of several books, including most recently *Dead Letter* (Roof 2015) and *kith & kin* (The Elephants 2018).

The Cyborg Jillian Weise is a poet and disability rights activist. Cy's books include *The Amputee's Guide to Sex, The Book of Goodbyes, The Colony, Cyborg Detective*, and *Give It to Alfie Tonight*. She directed the video play *A Kim Deal Party*. It screened at Public Space One. Her next book, a memoir, will be out from Harper Books.

John Wieners (1934–2002) was a founding member of the "New American" poetry that flourished after World War II. Wieners enrolled in the final class of Black Mountain College before its closure in 1956. He founded the small magazine *Measure* (1957–1962) and embarked on a peripatetic life before settling in Boston in 1972. He is the author of seven collections of poetry, three one-act plays, and numerous broadsides, pamphlets, uncollected poems, and journals.

Jorge Luis Borges (1899–1986) was an Argentine poet, essayist, and author of short stories. His most notable works include *Ficciones* (Fictions) and *El Aleph* (The Aleph). He was appointed the director of the National Public Library and professor of English literature at the University of Buenos Aires in 1955. During his lifetime, Borges received the first Prix International Formentor, which he shared with Samuel Beckett in 1961.

Andrew Hurley is Professor Emeritus at the Universidad de Puerto Rico and a translator from Spanish to English. He has published over thirty book-length translations.

Judy Grahn is an internationally known poet, author, and cultural theorist. *Touching Creatures, Touching Spirit: Living in a Sentient World* is her seventeenth published book. An early Gay activist who walked the first picket of the White House for Gay rights in 1965, she later cofounded Gay Women's Liberation and the Women's Press Collective. She fueled the feminist movement with her poetry, particularly "The Common Woman Poems," and a nine-part antiracist poem, "A Woman Is Talking to Death." Her subjects range from LGBT history and mythology to feminist critiques of current crises, spirituality, consciousness, new origin theories of inclusion, what makes us human, taking antiracism personally, and stories of how to engage with creature-minds and spirit. She writes about and teaches her own poetry, and also that of Sumerian poets, in her book *Eruptions of Inanna*, 2021. She is currently Associated Distinguished Professor at the California Institute of Integral Studies' PhD program in Transpersonal Psychology. Commonality Institute (see online) was established in 2019 to promote her work as a poet-philosopher; the Institute sponsors classes and an artist's residency in New Orleans, and published her book, *Descent to the Roses of a Family: A Poet's Journey into Antiracism for Personal and Social Healing*, in 2020.

Justin Torres is author of the novel *We the Animals*, and an Assistant Professor of English at UCLA.

Karla Cornejo Villavicencio is a writer. She lives in New Haven.

Andrea Abi-Karam is a trans, arab-american punk poet-performer cyborg. They are the author of *EXTRATRANSMISSION* (Kelsey Street Press, 2019), and with Kay Gabriel, they coedited *We Want It All: An Anthology of Radical Trans Poetics* (Nightboat Books, 2020). Their second book, *Villainy* (Nightboat Books, 2021), reimagines militant collectivity in the wake of the Ghost Ship Fire and the Muslim Ban. They are a leo obsessed with queer terror and convertibles.

Kathy Acker (1948–1997) was an influential postmodernist writer and performance artist whose many books include *Blood and Guts in High School*; *Don Quixote*; *Literal Madness*; *Empire of the Senseless*; *In Memoriam to Identity*; *My Mother: Demonology*; *Pussy, King of the Pirates*; *Portrait of an Eye*; and *Rip-Off Red, Girl Detective*.

Layli Long Soldier is the author of *Whereas*, which was the winner of the National Book Critics Circle Award for Poetry as well as the PEN/Jean Stein Book Award. She is the recipient of a Lannan Literary Fellowship, a Native Arts and Cultures Foundation National Artist Fellowship, and a Whiting Award. She lives in Santa Fe, New Mexico.

Keith Waldrop is the author of *Selected Poems* (Omnidawn), *Transcendental Studies* (U of California Press, National Book Award 2009), and more than a dozen other books of poems. He has also published a novel, *Light While There Is Light* (Dalkey Archive), a book of collages, *Several Gravities* (Siglio,) and translated Baudelaire's *Flowers of Evil* and *Paris Spleen* as well as contemporary French authors, including Anne-Marie Albiach, Claude Royet-Journoud, Paol Keineg, and Jean Grosjean. A Keith and Rosmarie Waldrop reader, *Keeping the Window Open*, is available from Wave Books. He is retired from teaching at Brown University and lives in Providence, RI.

Kim Hyesoon, born in 1955, is one of the most prominent and influential contemporary poets of South Korea. She was the first woman poet to receive the prestigious Kim Su-yong and Midang awards, and has been translated into Chinese, French, German, Japanese, Spanish, and Swedish. Her most recent books include *A Drink of Red Mirror* and *Autobiography of Death*.

Don Mee Choi is a poet and translator. She is the winner of the 2020 National Book Award for Poetry and a recipient of fellowships from the Guggenheim and MacArthur Foundations.

Kristín Ómarsdóttir is the author of four novels, three short story collections, seven books of poetry, and seven staged plays. Her work has been published in Swedish and French. Ómarsdóttir has been nominated for the Nordic Council's Literature Prize and the Nordic Council's Drama Prize. She has also received the DV Cultural Award for Literature, and the "Griman," the Icelandic prize for best playwright of the year. She lives in Reykjavik.

Lytton Smith is a poet, professor, and translator from the Icelandic, including work by Kristín Ómarsdóttir.

Laura Henriksen is a poet. She lives in Lenapehoking and works at The Poetry Project.

Laurence Sterne (1713–1768) was born in Ireland and graduated from the University of Cambridge in 1737. He then took holy orders, becoming a prebend in York Cathedral. His masterpiece, *The Life and Opinions of Tristram Shandy, Gentleman*, made him a celebrity, but ill health necessitated recuperative travel, and *A Sentimental Journey* grew out of a seven-month trip through France and Italy. He died the year it was published.

Lawrence Braithwaite (1963–2008) was a Canadian novelist, spoken-word artist, dub poet, essayist, digital drummer, and short fiction writer. He is the author of the cult classic *Wigger*.

Laurie Weeks is a writer, performer, artist, and teacher. Her critically acclaimed first novel, *Zipper Mouth*, was published by the Feminist Press and honored with the International Lambda Literary Award for Best Lesbian Debut Novel. Weeks was also a contributing screenwriter on the film *Boys Don't Cry*.

Lucille Clifton (1936–2010) was an award-winning poet, fiction writer, and author of children's books. Her poetry collection *Blessing the Boats: New & Selected Poems 1988–2000* won the National Book Award for Poetry. In 1988 she became the only author to have two collections selected in the same year as finalists for the Pulitzer Prize, *Good Woman: Poems and a Memoir* and *Next: New Poems*. In 1996, her collection *The Terrible Stories* was a finalist for the National Book Award. In 2013, her posthumously published collection *The Collected Poems of Lucille Clifton 1965–2010* was awarded the Hurston/Wright Legacy Award for Poetry.

Lynne Tillman's recent writing includes the novel *Men and Apparitions* (Soft Skull); the short story "The Dead Live Longer" (*n+1*); and the essay "Homage to Homage," on painter Steve Locke. Upcoming in August 2022 is a book-length autobiographical essay, *Mothercare*, and, in 2023, a volume of selected stories (Soft Skull). Tillman has received a Guggenheim Fellowship and a Creative Capital/Warhol Foundation grant for Arts Writing. She lives in New York with bass player David Hofstra.

Maan Abu Taleb is a writer and cultural editor. His debut novel, *All the Battles*, was released to critical and popular praise in 2016 and appeared in an accomplished English translation the following year. He is the editor and cofounder of the influential music magazine *Ma3azef*. His play, *The Congress*, dramatizes the events of the Cairo Congress of Arabic Music that took place in 1932.

Robin Moger is a translator of Arabic into English. His translations of prose and poetry have appeared in *The White Review*, *Tentacular*, *Asymptote*, *Washington Square Review*, *Words Without Borders*, and others. He has translated several novels and prose works, including *The Book of Sleep* by Haytham El Wardany and Mohamed Kheir's *Slipping*. His translation of Yasser Abdel Hafez's *The Book of Safety* was awarded the 2017 Saif Ghobash Banipal Prize for Arabic Literary Translation.

Maggie Nelson is the author of several acclaimed books of poetry and prose. Her nonfiction titles include *On Freedom: Four Songs of Care and Constraint* (2021), *The Argonauts* (2015; winner, the National Book Critics Circle Award in Criticism), *The Art of Cruelty: A Reckoning* (2011), *Bluets* (2009; named by Bookforum as one of the top 10 best books of the past 20 years), *The Red Parts* (2007), and *Women, the New York School, and Other True Abstractions* (2007). Her poetry titles include *Something Bright, Then Holes* (2007) and *Jane: A Murder* (2005). In 2016 she was awarded a MacArthur "Genius" Fellowship. She teaches at the University of Southern California and lives in Los Angeles.

Marcella Durand is the author of *To husband is to tender* (Black Square Editions 2021), *The Prospect* (Delete Press 2020), *Area* (Belladonna* Books 2008), and *Traffic & Weather* (Futurepoem 2008). She is the 2021 recipient of the C. D. Wright Award in Poetry from the Foundation of Contemporary Art. *Earth's Horizons*, her translation of Michèle Métail's book-length poem *Les horizons du sol*, was published by Black Square Editions in 2020.

Matthew Stadler is a writer and editor. His novels, including *Allan Stein*, *Landscape: Memory*, and others, have been published in several languages and won many prizes. He currently edits the online inquiry "The Polity of Literature" and its companion site, The GOAT PoL.

Michael McClure (1932–2020) was a playwright, essayist, and poet credited with launching the eco-poetics movement in 1955 when he read his piece "For the Death of 100 Whales" at the Six Gallery reading in San Francisco. He wrote over thirty books of poetry, plays, and prose, and taught poetry at California College of the Arts for forty-three years.

Michelle Tea is the author of over a dozen works of memoir, fiction, poetry, and children's literature. Her collection *Against Memoir* was given the PEN/Diamonstein-Spielvogel Award for the Art of the Essay. Tea is a founder of Drag Queen Story Hour, the Sister Spit performance tours, *Mutha Magazine*, and other cultural interventions. She is a 2021 Guggenheim Fellow in nonfiction.

Mira Gonzalez is a poet and writer. Her first collection, *i will never be beautiful enough to make us beautiful together*, was published by Sorry House in 2013. She released a collaborative book with Tao Lin entitled *Selected Tweets* in 2015.

Morgan Võ is a poet and organizer of G-L-O-S-S, a mutual aid–based publishing project. He lives in Brooklyn, NY.

Moyra Davey is an artist and writer, and author of the collection *Index Cards*, published in 2020. She is working on a new video about dance parties and community.

Natalie Diaz was born and raised in the Fort Mojave Indian Village in Needles, California, on the banks of the Colorado River. She is Mojave and an enrolled member of the Gila River Indian Tribe. Her first poetry collection, *When My Brother Was an Aztec*, was published by Copper Canyon Press in 2012. Her most recent book is *Postcolonial Love Poem*, published by Graywolf Press in 2020. She is a 2018 MacArthur Foundation Fellow, a Lannan Literary Fellow, and a Native Arts Council Foundation Artist Fellow. Diaz teaches at the Arizona State University Creative Writing MFA program.

Nate Lippens is the author of the novel *My Dead Book* (Publication Studio 2021). His short fiction has appeared in *Catapult*, *Vol. 1 Brooklyn*, and *New World Writing*.

Akilah Oliver (1961–2011) was the author of two poetry collections and four chapbooks. Her most recent poetry book is *A Toast in the House of Friends*, and her first book, *the she said dialogues: flesh memory*, was awarded the PEN Beyond Margins Award. At the time of her death in 2011, she was a professor at Pratt Art Institute in Brooklyn, New York, in the Humanities and Media Studies Department and a PhD candidate at the European Graduate School in Saas-Fee, Switzerland.

Porochista Khakpour's debut novel, *Sons and Other Flammable Objects* (Grove 2007), was a *New York Times* Editor's Choice, one of the *Chicago Tribune*'s Fall's Best, and the 2007 California Book Award winner in the "First Fiction" category. Her second novel, *The Last Illusion* (Bloomsbury 2014), was a 2014 Best Book of the Year according to NPR, *Kirkus Reviews*, *Buzzfeed*, *Popmatters*, Electric Literature, and many more. Her third book, *Sick: A Memoir* (Harper Perennial 2018), was a Best Book of 2018 according to *Time* magazine, *Real Simple*, *Entropy*, *Mental Floss*, Bitch Media, Autostraddle, the *Paris Review*, LitHub, and more. Her most recent book, the essay collection *Brown Album: Essays on Exile & Identity* (Vintage 2020), has been praised in the *New York Times*, *O: Oprah Magazine*, *Time*, goop, *USA Today*, and many more. Her next book, *Tehrangeles: A Novel*, is forthcoming from Pantheon. Among her many fellowships is a National Endowment for the Arts award. Her other writing has appeared in many sections of the *New York Times*, the *Los Angeles Times*, the *Washington Post*, the *Wall Street Journal*, *Condé Nast Traveler*, *Elle*, *Slate*, *BOMB*, and many others. She is a contributing editor at *Evergreen Review* and lives in NYC.

Nicole Wallace is the author of the chapbook *WAASAMOWIN* (IMP 2019), a member of the Indigenous Kinship Collective, and Managing Director at The Poetry Project. Nicole is of mixed settler/European ancestry and is a descendent of the Fond du Lac Band of Lake Superior Chippewa (Ojibwe). They currently live and make work on unceded, occupied Canarsee and Lenape territory (Brooklyn, NY).

Qiu Miaojin (1969–1995)—one of Taiwan's most innovative literary modernists, and the country's most renowned lesbian writer—was born in Chuanghua County in western Taiwan. She graduated with a degree in psychology from National Taiwan University and pursued graduate studies in clinical psychology at the University of Paris VIII. While in Paris, she directed a thirty-minute film called *Ghost Carnival*, and not long after this, at the age of twenty-six, she committed suicide. The posthumous publication of her novels *Last Words from Montmartre* and *Notes of a Crocodile* made her into one of the most revered countercultural icons in Chinese letters.

Ari Larissa Heinrich received an MA in Chinese literature from Harvard and a PhD in Chinese studies from the University of California at Berkeley. He is the author of *The Afterlife of Images: Translating the Pathological Body Between China and the West* and the coeditor of *Queer Sinophone Cultures*.

Rae Armantrout is the Pulitzer Prize–winning author of fifteen books of poetry. She has published ten books with Wesleyan University Press, including *Conjure*, *Wobble*, *Entanglements*, *Partly*, and *Versed*. She lives in Everett, Washington.

Rebecca Brown is the author of many books published in the US and abroad, including *Not Heaven, Somewhere Else*; *American Romances*; *The Dogs: A Modern Bestiary*; *The Terrible Girls*; and *The Gifts of the Body*. Her book of essays, *You Tell the Stories You Need to Believe*, is due out in 2022. She lives in Seattle.

Renee Gladman is a writer and artist preoccupied with crossings, thresholds, and geographies as they play out at the intersections of poetry, prose, drawing, and architecture. She is the author of thirteen published works, including a cycle of novels about the city-state Ravicka and its inhabitants, the Ravickians, and two books of drawings, *Prose Architectures* and *One Long Black Sentence*. She makes her home in New England with poet-ceremonialist Danielle Vogel.

Rose "Rosebud" Feliu-Pettet (1946–2015) was a fixture of downtown bohemia and a gifted memoirist. She lived variously in San Francisco, New York City, Denmark, Morocco, and England. Her close friendship with the poet Allen Ginsberg resulted in her being at his deathbed and writing the definitive account of his passing.

Robert Walser (1878–1956) worked as a bank clerk, a butler in a castle, and an inventor's assistant while beginning what was to become a prodigious literary career. Between 1899 and his forced hospitalization in 1933 with a now much-disputed diagnosis of schizophrenia, Walser produced as many as seven novels and more than a thousand short stories and prose pieces. Though he enjoyed limited popular success during his lifetime, today he is acknowledged as one of the most important and original literary voices of the twentieth century.

Christopher Middleton (1926–2015) was a British poet and translator of German literature.

Robert Glück's poetry collections include *Reader*; *La Fontaine*, a collaboration with Bruce Boone; and *In Commemoration of the Visit*, a collaboration with Kathleen Fraser. His fiction includes the story collections *Denny Smith* and *Elements*, and the novels *Jack the Modernist* and *Margery Kempe*, which was republished in 2020 by NYRB Classics. Glück edited, with Camille Roy, Mary Berger, and Gail Scott, the anthology *Biting the Error: Writers Explore Narrative*, and his essay collection, *Communal Nude*, was published by Semiotext(e) in 2016. Glück has served as director of San Francisco State's Poetry Center, codirector of the Small Press Traffic Literary Center, and associate editor at Lapis Press. He lives in San Francisco

Sallie Fullerton has an MFA in Poetry from the Iowa Writers' Workshop. Their work has appeared in *Frontier Poetry*, *Vagabond City Lit*, and the *Bennington Review*, among other places.

Rumi (1207–1273) was born in Central Asia and was a poet, scholar, theologian, and mystic. His burial place in Konya, Turkey, remains a shrine to this day.

Brad Gooch is a poet, novelist, and biographer. His books include *Rumi's Secret: The Life of the Sufi Poet of Love* and *Rumi: Unseen Poems*, translated with Maryam Mortaz.

Maryam Mortaz is an Iranian American writer and translator, and author of the short story collection *Pushkin and Other Stories*. With Brad Gooch, she translated *Rumi: Unseen Poems*.

Saidiya Hartman is the author of *Wayward Lives, Beautiful Experiments*, *Lose Your Mother: A Journey Along the Atlantic Slave Route*, and *Scenes of Subjection*. A MacArthur "Genius" Fellow, she has been a Guggenheim Fellow, Cullman Fellow, and Fulbright Scholar. She is a University Professor at Columbia University and lives in New York.

Samuel Beckett (1906–1989) was born in Foxrock, Ireland, and attended Trinity University in Dublin. In 1928, he visited Paris for the first time, and in 1937, he settled in Paris permanently. A prolific writer of novels, short stories, and poetry, he is remembered principally for his works for the theater, which belong to the tradition of the Theater of the Absurd. In 1969, Beckett was awarded the Nobel Prize in Literature.

Samuel R. Delany is a renowned novelist and critic, whose award-winning fiction includes *Dhalgren*, *Babel-17*, *The Mad Man*, *Dark Reflections*, and *Through the Valley of the Nest of Spiders*. In addition to receiving the William Whitehead Memorial Award and the Kessler Award for his lifetime contribution to lesbian and gay writing, Delany was chosen by the Lambda Book Report in 1988 as one of the fifty most influential people of the past hundred years to change our conception of queerness.

Sei Shōnagon (?966–?1017) was born approximately a thousand years ago and served as lady-in-waiting at the court of the Japanese empress during the last decade of the tenth century. Our knowledge of Shōnagon's life rests almost exclusively on *The Pillow Book*, a book of observations and musings recorded during her time as a court lady.

Meredith McKinney is a translator of classical and modern Japanese literature. She lived and taught in Japan for 20 years, and now lives in country Australia. Her translations include *Hōjōki and Essays in Idleness* and *Travels with a Writing Brush*, and two novels by Natsume Sōseki, *Kokoro* and *Kusamakura*.

Sergio Chejfec (1956–2022) was an Argentine writer who lived in New York City. He taught at NYU in the Creative Writing in Spanish MFA program. He published several books, including narrations, essays, and novels. Some of them have been translated into English: *Notes Toward a Pamphlet* (Ugly Duckling Presse 2020); *The Incompletes* (Open Letter 2019); *Baroni, A Journey* (Almost Island 2017); *The Dark* (Open Letter 2013); *The Planets* (Open Letter 2012); and *My Two Worlds* (Open Letter 2011).

Whitney DeVos is a scholar, translator, writer, and editor based in Mexico City.

Simone Weil (1909–1943) was born in Paris. A religious philosopher, essayist, dramatist, and poet, as well as a social critic and political activist, Weil was one of the great thinkers of the twentieth century. Her other works include *Gravity and Grace* and *The Need for Roots*.

Emma Craufurd is the translator of *Waiting for God* and *Gravity and Grace* by Simone Weil.

Simone White is the author of *or, on being the other woman*, *Dear Angel of Death*, *Of Being Dispersed*, and *House Envy of All the World*, the poetry chapbook *Unrest*, and the collaborative poem/painting chapbook *Dolly* (with Kim Thomas). Her poetry and prose have been featured in *Artforum*, *e-flux*, *Harper's Magazine*, *BOMB Magazine*, *Chicago Review*, the *New York Times Book Review*, and the Harriet Blog. Her honors include a 2021 Creative Capital Award, a 2017 Whiting Award in Poetry, Cave Canem Foundation fellowships, and recognition as a New American Poet for the Poetry Society of America in 2013. A graduate of Wesleyan University, she holds a JD from Harvard Law School, an MFA from the New School, and a PhD in English from CUNY Graduate Center. She is the Stephen M. Gorn Family Assistant Professor of English at the University of Pennsylvania and serves on the writing faculty of the Milton Avery Graduate School of the Arts at Bard College. She lives in Brooklyn.

Precious Okoyomon is a multidisciplinary artist and writer living and working in New York. She attended Shimer College in Chicago. Her work has been shown in solo exhibits at the MMK in Frankfurt and the Luma Westbau in Zurich and was included in the 13th Baltic Triennial. Okoyomon has read at

The Kitchen, The Studio Museum, MoMA PS1, Hauser and Wirth, and The Poetry Project. Her work is included in the permanent collection of the Rubell Family Collection. Her first book of poetry, *Ajebota*, was published by Bottlecap Press in 2016. Her book *but did u die?* is forthcoming from Wonder Press.

Sophie Robinson teaches Creative Writing at the University of East Anglia and is the author of *A* and *The Institute of Our Love in Disrepair*. Her work has appeared in *n+1*, the *White Review*, *Poetry Review*, the *Brooklyn Rail*, *Ploughshares*, and *BOMB Magazine*. Her third full collection, *Rabbit*, was published by Boiler House Press in 2018.

Sparrow has published ten books, the two most recent being *Small Happiness* (Monkfish) and *The Princeton Diary* (Vinal). He has written for *The Sun* (thesunmagazine.org) for 40 years. Sparrow lives in a doublewide trailer in eucharistic Phoenicia, NY.

Sor Juana Inés de la Cruz (1651–1695) was a Mexican poet, dramatist, scholar, and nun. She became a cloistered nun in 1667. Sor Juana also had one of the largest private libraries in the New World. Her most important works are *First Dream* and "The Reply to Sister Filotea of the Cross."

Jaime Manrique is the author of the memoir *Eminent Maricones: Arenas, Lorca, Puig, and Me*, the novels *Latin Moon in Manhattan* and *Colombian Gold*, and two poetry collections. He is cotranslator, with Joan Larkin, of *Sor Juana's Love Poems*.

Susie Timmons is a poet. Unmarried and childless, she lives alone with her dog. She has been writing and reading poetry for the past 50 years of her life. Early in her career, there was every indication that she was bound for greatness; alas, her high-strung temperament, poor work habits, and addictive personality combined to rob her of her destiny, ultimately leading her to betray her talents. Her work can be found in *Superior Packets* (Wave Books 2015).

Tim Johnson is a poet and editor, based in Marfa, Texas. Since 2008, he and his partner, Caitlin Murray, have owned the Marfa Book Co.

Mark So is a composer. Marfa Book Co. published a collection of his Ashbery scores as *a box of wind*, and his music can be heard in Eileen Myles's film *The Trip* as well as on his recent album *part of life* from OPEN SPACE. He lives in and out of Los Angeles.

Valerie Solanas (1936–1988) was an American radical feminist writer who is best known for *SCUM Manifesto*, as well as the attempted murder of artist Andy Warhol.

Steve Carey (1945–1989) was born in Washington, DC, and published seven collections of poetry. "Steve," an essay on his life and writing, can be found in

Alice Notley's *Coming After: Essays on Poetry*. *The Selected Poems of Steve Carey* is the first book to make Carey's work widely available.

Violette Leduc (1907–1972) has been referred to as "France's greatest unknown writer." Leduc was championed by Simone de Beauvoir when she published her scandalous autobiography, *La Bâtarde*, and admired by other notable French writers including Jean Genet, Nathalie Sarraute, and Albert Camus.

Derek Coltman is the translator of *La Bâtarde* and other works by Violette Leduc.

Tom Cole is a writer and artist living in the Lower East Side of Manhattan. His work has been presented at Participant Inc, Petit Versailles, Thread Waxing Space, Art on Air, Dixon Place, Clocktower Gallery, ICA Boston, Performa, and the Boston Center for the Arts. He is a three-time MacDowell Playwriting fellow and a 2015 Edward Albee Foundation Playwriting fellow. He heads the New Play Commissioning Program at True Love Productions, where he has commissioned new work by Heidi Schreck, Jorge Ignacio Cortiñas, Craig Lucas, and Sheila Callaghan, among others. He co-curates Experiments and Disorders, a literary series at Dixon Place. He has collaborated extensively with Anohni, most recently appearing in *She Who Saw Beautiful Things* at The Kitchen.

Victoria Chang's latest poetry book is *OBIT*, which was named a *New York Times* Notable Book and a *Time* Best Book of the Year, and received the *Los Angeles Times* Book Prize, the Anisfield-Wolf Book Award, and the PEN/Voelcker Award. Her new book of hybrid nonfiction is *Dear Memory*. She has received a Guggenheim Fellowship, and lives in Los Angeles and serves as the Program Chair of Antioch's MFA Program.

Tongo Eisen-Martin is a poet, movement worker, and educator. His latest curriculum on extrajudicial killing of Black people, We Charge Genocide Again, has been used as an educational and organizing tool throughout the country. His book *Someone's Dead Already* was nominated for a California Book Award. His book *Heaven Is All Goodbyes* was published by the City Lights Pocket Poets series, was shortlisted for the Griffins Poetry Prize, and won a California Book Award and an American Book Award. His latest book, *Blood on The Fog*, was released this fall in the City Lights Pocket Poets series. He is San Francisco's eighth poet laureate.

Victor Hugo (1802–1885) was a novelist, poet, and playwright. He is best known for *Les Misérables* and *The Hunchback of Notre-Dame*, as well as other works, including *The Toilers of the Sea* and *The Man Who Laughs*.

Will Farris is a visual artist and poet. In 2019 they were the inaugural recipient of The Brannan Prize at The Poetry Project, judged by Lisa Jarnot. They live in New York City.

Credits

1 "untitled" from *Grave of Light* © 2006 by Alice Notley. Published by Wesleyan University Press. Used by permission.

2 Excerpt from *Maud Martha* © 1953, 2003 by Gwendolyn Brooks. Reprinted by consent of Brooks Permissions.

6 "People Without Names" © The Friend. Reprinted with permission of the author.

11 "Loveland" from *Bedrooms Have Windows* © 1989, 2018 by Kevin Killian. Reprinted in *Fascination: Memoirs*. Reprinted with permission of Semiotext(e).

22 "Yesterday I Was" © Ama Birch. Reprinted with permission of the author.

24 "Afterword: The Great Punctuation Typography Struggle" from *Woman Hating* © 1974 by Andrea Dworkin. Originally published by Dutton. Reprinted by permission of The Estate of Andrea Dworkin.

30 "Truth or Consequences" from *Mercury* © 2011 by Ariana Reines. Reprinted with permission of the author and Fence Books.

38 "April, 1995" from *The Pain Journal* © 2000 by Bob Flanagan and Sheree Rose. Reprinted with permission of Semiotext(e).

47 "A Description of the Camp" by Baha' Ebdeir, from *Making Mirrors: Writing/Righting by Refugees* (2019), edited by Jehan Bseiso and Becky Thompson, published by Olive Branch Press, an imprint of Interlink Publishing Group, Inc. Reprinted by permission.

52 "Would You Wear My Eyes?" from *Solitudes Crowded with Loneliness* © 1965 by Bob Kaufman. Reprinted by permission of New Directions Publishing Corp.

53 "August 6, 2011" from *The Grave on the Wall* © 2019 by Brandon Shimoda. Reprinted with the permission of The Permissions Company, LLC, on behalf of City Lights Books, www.citylights.com.

59 Excerpt from *The Romanian: Story of an Obsession* © Bruce Benderson. Reprinted with permission of the author.

65 "My Faggot Kansas Blood Confessions to the Earth" and "My Faggot Blood on His Fist" from *While Standing in Line for Death* © 2017 by CAConrad. Reprinted with permission of the author and Wave Books.

68 "Reading My Catastrophe" © 2020 by Camille Roy. First published in "Reading My Catastrophe/Pain" by Camille Roy and Robert Glück (Asterion Projects). Reprinted with permission of the author.

76 "Soap Bubbles in the Dirty Water" from *Dialogues in Paradise* by Can Xue. Translation © 1989 by Northwestern University Press. All rights reserved.

81 Excerpt from *Texas: The Great Theft* © 2013 by Carmen Boullosa, English translation © 2014 by Samantha Schnee. Reprinted with permission of Deep Vellum Publishing.

92 Excerpt from *My Mother Laughs* © 2013 by Chantal Akerman. English translation © 2019 by Daniella Shreir. Reprinted with permission of Silver Press.

99 "Before You Go" from *Recalculating* © 2013 by Charles Bernstein. Reprinted with permission of the author.

101 Excerpt from *If He Hollers, Let Him Go* © 1945 by Chester Himes. Reprinted with permission of The Chester & Lesley Himes Literary Estate.

110 Excerpt from *I Love Dick* © 1997, 2006 by Chris Kraus. Reprinted with permission of the author and Semiotext(e).

118 Excerpt from "Some Other Deaths of Bas Jan Ader" from *Some Other Deaths of Bas Jan Ader* © 2013 by Dana Ward. Reprinted with permission of Flowers & Cream.

124 "Being Close to Data" © Dara Barrois/Dixon. Reprinted with permission of the author.

125 Excerpt from *God Jr.* © 2005 by Dennis Cooper. Reprinted by permission of Grove Press, Inc.

130 Excerpt from "Fat Chance" © Dodie Bellamy. Reprinted with permission of the author.

141 "Night Watch" and "Watchman, What of the Night?" from *Nightwood* © 1937 by Djuna Barnes. Reprinted by permission of New Directions Publishing Corp.

149 "Campaign Letter for President of the United States, 1991" © Eileen Myles. Reprinted with permission of the author.

151 "that flaming brand" and "Boulder/Meteor" © 2020 by essa may ranapiri. First published in *Poetry New Zealand Yearbook 2020*. Reprinted with permission of the author and Massey University Press.

153 Excerpts from *Sitt Marie Rose* (pages 79–82 and 98–105) © 1978 by Etel Adnan. English translation © 1982 by Georgina Kleege. English translation was first published by The Post-Apollo Press. Reprinted with permission of Litmus Press and the Estate of Etel Adnan.

160 "A Child in Old Age" and "A Vision" from *Second Childhood* © 2014 by Fanny Howe. Reprinted with the permission of The Permissions Company, LLC, on behalf of Graywolf Press, Minneapolis, Minnesota, graywolfpress.org.

167 "there is religious tattooing" from *Hughson's Tavern* © 2008 by Fred Moten. Reprinted with permission of the author and Leon Works.

169 "Play It Again, S" from *Heroine* © 1987, 2019 by Gail Scott. Reprinted with permission of the author and Coach House Books.

173 Excerpt from *Letter to His Father* by Franz Kafka, translated, revised, and updated by Arthur S. Wensinger, compilation copyright © 1989 by Penguin Random House LLC. Used by permission of Schocken Books, an imprint of the Knopf Doubleday Publishing Group, a division of Penguin Random House LLC. All rights reserved.

179 Excerpt from *Lenz* by Georg Büchner. Originally written in 1836 and translated into English in 1969.

183 Excerpt from *My Dog Tulip* © 1965 by J. R. Ackerley (New York Review Books), reproduced by permission by David Higham Associates.

190 "My Struggle" © Jack Halberstam. Reprinted with permission of the author.

199 "This Dark Apartment" from *Collected Poems* © 1993 by the Estate of James Schuyler. Reprinted by permission of Farrar, Straus and Giroux. All Rights Reserved.

201 "Chronicle" from *Sideways Between Stories* © 2016 by Frank B. Wilderson III. Reprinted with permission of the author and Commune Editions (commune editions.com).

202 Excerpt from *Winter in the Blood* © 1974 by James Welch. Used by permission of Viking Books, an imprint of Penguin Publishing Group, a division of Penguin Random House LLC. All rights reserved.

205 "28." in "Corporate Sonnets" from *How Much?* © 2021 by Jerome Sala. Reprinted with permission of the author and NYQ Books.

206 "An Obituary" © Joe Proulx. Reprinted with permission of the author.

216 "Stop" from *Housework* © 1975 by Joan Larkin. Reprinted with permission of the author.

218 Excerpt from *Tramps Like Us* © 2001 by Joe Westmoreland. Reprinted with permission of the author.

223 "The Copyists" from *Dead Letter* © 2014 by Jocelyn Saidenberg. Reprinted with permission of the author and Roof Books.

227 "Catullus Tells Me Not to Write the Rant Against the Poem 'Good Bones' by Maggie Smith" from *Cyborg Detective* © 2019 by The Cyborg Jillian Weise. Reprinted with the permission of The Permissions Company, LLC, on behalf of BOA Editions, Ltd., boaeditions.org.

228 Selections from *The Hotel Wentley Poems* © 1958, 2021 by the Literary Estate of John Wieners. Reprinted with permission of Raymond Foye, executor.

242 "The Cult of the Phoenix" © 1998 by Maria Kodama; translation © 1998 by Penguin Random House LLC; from *Collected Fictions: Volume 3* by Jorge Luis Borges, translated by Andrew Hurley. Used by permission of Viking Books, an imprint of Penguin Publishing Group, a division of Penguin Random House LLC. All rights reserved.

246 "A Woman Is Talking to Death" from *The Judy Grahn Reader* © 1997 by Judy Grahn. Reprinted with permission of the author and Aunt Lute Books.

264 "You Better Come" from *We the Animals: A Novel* © 2011 by Justin Torres. Reprinted by permission of Mariner Books, an imprint of HarperCollins Publishers. All rights reserved.

269 "New Haven" from *The Undocumented Americans* © 2020 by Karla Cornejo Villavicencio. Used by permission of One World, an imprint of Random House, a division of Penguin Random House LLC. All rights reserved.

289 "SMALL / MEDIUM / LUST" from *Villainy* © 2021 by Andrea Abi-Karam. Reprinted with permission of Nightboat Books.

292 Excerpt from *Great Expectations* © 1982 by Kathy Acker. Reprinted by permission of Grove Press, Inc.

301 "38" from *Whereas* © 2017 by Layli Long Soldier. Reprinted with the permission of The Permissions Company, LLC, on behalf of Graywolf Press, Minneapolis, Minnesota, graywolfpress.org.

307 Excerpt from *Light While There Is Light* © 2013 by Keith Waldrop. Reprinted with permission of Dalkey Archive Press.

316 "Shadow Janitor" from *Sorrowtoothpaste Mirrorcream* © 2011 by Kim Hyesoon. English translation by Don Mee Choi. Reprinted with permission of Action Books.

318 Excerpt from *Children in Reindeer Woods* © 2004 by Kristín Ómarsdóttir, English translation © 2012 by Lytton Smith. Reprinted with permission of Open Letter Books.

323 "In Case I Don't Notice," "God Gives You What You Can Handle," and "The Only Good" © Laura Henriksen. Reprinted with permission of the author.

328 Excerpt from Volume I of *The Life and Opinions of Tristram Shandy, Gentleman,* by Laurence Sterne. Originally published between 1759 and 1767.

334 Excerpt from *Wigger* © 1995 by Lawrence Braithwaite. Reprinted with permission of Jack Braithwaite.

337 "Worms Make Heaven" from *How I Became a Mystic* © Laurie Weeks. Reprinted with permission of the author.

345 "the mother's story" and "slave cabin, sotterly plantation, maryland, 1989" from *How to Carry Water: Selected Poems* © 1991 by Lucille Clifton. Reprinted with the permission of The Permissions Company, LLC, on behalf of BOA Editions, Ltd., boaeditions.org.

347 Excerpt from *No Lease on Life* © 1991 by Lynne Tillman. Reprinted with permission of the author and Red Lemonade.

352 Excerpt from *All the Battles* (pages 215–226) © 2016 by Maan Abu Taleb. English translation © 2017 by Robin Moger. Reprinted with permission of Hoopoe Fiction, an imprint of The American University in Cairo Press.

356 Selections from *Bluets* © 2009 by Maggie Nelson. Reprinted with permission of the author and Wave Books.

358 "East River Park Oak Tree" © Marcella Durand. Reprinted with permission of the author.

365 Excerpt from "Potatoes or Rice?" © by Matthew Stadler. Reprinted with permission of the author.

378 "For the Death of 100 Whales" from *Selected Poems* © 1959 by Michael McClure. Reprinted by permission of New Directions Publishing Corp.

380 "Flower Garden Froth" and "The Fleshy Nave" from *Mule Kick Blues: And Last Poems* © 2021 by the Michael T. McClure Estate. Reprinted with the permission of The Permissions Company, LLC, on behalf of City Lights Books, www.citylights.com.

389 Excerpt from *Against Memoir: Complaints, Confessions & Criticisms* © 2018 by Michelle Tea. Reprinted with permission of the author and Feminist Press.

404 "haiku," "untitled 8," "5 years old,"and "untitled 2" from *i will never be beautiful enough to make us beautiful together* © 2013 by Mira Gonzalez. Originally published by Sorry House. Reprinted with permission of the author.

409 "Sum," "People Like Monsters," "How to," and "Great" © Morgan Võ. Reprinted with permission of the author.

413 "Wedding Loop" from *Index Cards* © 2020 by Moyra Davey. Reprinted by permission of New Directions Publishing Corp.

419 "My Brother, My Wound" from *Postcolonial Love Poem* © 2020 by Natalie Diaz. Reprinted with the the permission of The Permissions Company, LLC, on behalf of Graywolf Press, graywolfpress.org.

421 Excerpts from *Goner* © by Nate Lippens. Reprinted with permission of the author.

427 "it doesn't matter how you fall into light, she said" and "think of the words as angels singing in your vagina, she said," from *the she said dialogues: flesh memory* © 1999 by Akilah Oliver. Reprinted with permission of Nightboat Books.

429 "Los Angeles" from *Sick* © 2018 by Porochista Khakpour. Used by permission of HarperCollins Publishers.

439 "NIIZH" © Nicole Wallace. Reprinted with permission of the author.

442 "Letter Three" from *Last Words from Montmartre* © 1996, 2006 by Qiu Miaojin, English translation © Ari Larissa Heinrich. Reprinted with permission of New York Review of Books.

452 "Intercepts" from *Conjure* © 2020 by Rae Armantrout. Published by Wesleyan University Press. Used by permission.

454 "The Gift of Sight" from *The Gifts of the Body* © 1994 by Rebecca Brown. Used by permission of HarperCollins Publishers.

461 Selection from *The Activist* © 2003 by Renee Gladman. Reprinted with permission of the author and KRUPSKAYA.

471 "April 4 Friday" © 1997 by Rose "Rosebud" Feliu-Pettet. Originally published in *American Book Review*. Reprinted with permission of Simon Pettet.

477 "Kleist in Thun" from *Selected Stories* by Robert Walser, translated by Christopher Middleton and others, with an introduction by Susan Sontag. Translation and compilation copyright © 1982 by Farrar, Straus and Giroux. Reprinted by permission of Farrar, Straus and Giroux. All Rights Reserved.

485 Excerpt from *About Ed* © Robert Glück. Reprinted with permission of the author.

491 "Four times over," "I see you and I am getting closer," and "Strain" © Sallie Fullerton. Reprinted with permission of the author.

494 "Yesterday I went to him full of dismay" from *Rumi: Unseen Poems* by Rumi, translation © 2019 by Brad Gooch & Maryam Mortaz. Used by permission of Alfred A. Knopf, an imprint of the Knopf Doubleday Publishing Group, a division of Penguin Random House LLC. All rights reserved.

495 "Manual for General Housework" from *Wayward Lives, Beautiful Experiments: Intimate Histories of Social Upheaval* © 2019 by Saidiya Hartman. Used by permission of W. W. Norton & Company, Inc.

498 Excerpt from *Molloy* in *Three Novels* by Samuel Beckett © 1947 by Les Éditions de Minuit. English translation © 1955 by The Estate of Patrick Bowles and The Estate of Samuel Beckett. Reprinted by permission of Grove Press, Inc.

506 Excerpt from *Times Square Red, Times Square Blue* © 1999 by Samuel R. Delany. Reprinted with permission of the author and NYU Press.

517 Selections from *The Pillow Book* by Sei Shōnagon. Originally written circa 1002. Reprinted with permission of the translator.

522 Excerpt from *Notes Toward a Pamphlet* © Sergio Chejfec. Translation © 2020 by Whitney DeVos. Reprinted with permission of Ugly Duckling Presse.

528 "Letter I: Hesitations Concerning Baptism" from *Waiting for God* by Simone Weil, translated by Emma Craufurd, translation © 1951, renewed © 1979 by G. P. Putnam's Sons. Used by permission of G. P. Putnam's Sons, an imprint of Penguin Publishing Group, a division of Penguin Random House LLC. All rights reserved.

534 "Stingray" from *Dear Angel of Death* © 2018 by Simone White. Reprinted with permission of Ugly Duckling Presse.

544 "It's dissociation season" from *but did u die?* © forthcoming in 2022 by Precious Okoyomon. Reprinted with permission of the author and Wonder Books.

549 "TOTAL LOL" from *Rabbit* © 2018 by Sophie Robinson. Reprinted with permission of the author and Boiler House Press.

551 "The Slow Read Movement" and "Lincoln's Lost Speech" from *Small Happiness & Other Epiphanies* © 2020 by Sparrow. Reprinted with permission from Monkfish Book Publishing Company, Rhinebeck, New York.

556 "Inez, I Have to Gloat: You're Gorgeous" and "Inez, When Someone Tells You You're a Bitch" from *Sor Juana's Love Poems*, translated by Joan Larkin and Jaime Manrique © 2003 by the Board of Regents of the University of Wisconsin System. Reprinted by permission of the University of Wisconsin Press.

558 "Where I Left Off" from *Superior Packets* © 2015 by Susie Timmons. Reprinted with permission of the author and Wave Books.

560 Selections from "Falling for You" © Tim Johnson and Mark So. Reprinted with permission from the authors.

574 Selection from *Up Your Ass* © 1965 by Valerie Solanas. First performed in 2000 at the George Coates Performance Works theater in San Francisco.

581 "Goodbye Forever" from *The Selected Poems of Steve Carey* © 2009 by Steve Carey. Originally printed in *20 Poems*. Reprinted with permission of Subpress Poetry Collective.

584 Excerpt from *La Bâtarde* by Violette Leduc © 1964 by Éditions Gallimard. English translation © 1965 by Derek Coltman. First Dalkey Archive edition: 2003. Reprinted with permission of Dalkey Archive Press.

594 Selections from *The Tyranny of Structurelessness* © Tom Cole. First performed at Dixon Place in 2019. Reprinted with permission of the author.

600 "Time" from *Obit* © 2020 by Victoria Chang. Reprinted with the permission of The Permissions Company, LLC, on behalf of Copper Canyon Press, coppercanyonpress.org.

601 "A Story that the United States is Made of" and "Pass" from *someone's dead already* © 2015 by Tongo Eisen-Martin. Reprinted with permission of Bootstrap Press.

604 Excerpts from *The Man Who Laughs* by Victor Hugo. Originally published in English by Estes and Lauriat in 1869.

615 "MW Duet," "Awake," "Body," and "Orlando" © Will Farris. "Awake" and "Orlando" first printed in *The Poetry Project Newsletter*, Issue #259. "Body" first printed in *The Recluse*, Issue #15. Reprinted with permission of the author.

Acknowledgments

First big gratitude to writer and critic and scholar Liz Kotz for introducing me to Pathetic Masculinity in the 90s and Ralph Rugoff who complexly and expansively wrote about it. Terry Wolverton whose book *Insurgent Muse: Life and Art at the Woman's Building* explained viscerally for me the pathetic radiance of 2nd wave feminism in the art world. UCSD for giving me the opportunity to teach the grad seminar, Pathetic Literature, and to all the pathetic students who took it and took part in the Pathetic Conference on campus. Jack Halberstam who got me there (UCSD). Laurie Weeks who was there and turned me on to writers (Can Xue) at the interior of the concept. Chris Kraus was our featured guest at the conference. Amy Adler made the poster. Ari Heinrich who had just arrived and introduced me to Qiu Miaojin who he was translating then. David Rattray for bringing me everywhere including to Gerrit Lansing who gave me Robert Walser and Susan Bernofsky who made my understanding of him possible. Zach Pace who imagined this book, Peter Blackstock and Emily Burns, who are wisely and magnificently actualizing it, and PJ Mark who always makes books happen and I'm grateful for the advice and participation of Morgan Võ, The Friend, Mark So, Sallie Fullerton, and of course Will Farris, partner in crime who vastly helped make this book possible. And to every single author in here who rolled with the reality of what they were being included in. There are so many writers and friends who should also be in here so TOO PATHETIC is probably around the corner and I hope you will be a party to it.